Dorothy Dunnett is the author of the Lymond series of historical novels that began in 1961 with *The Game of Kings*. Her bestselling epic novel about Macbeth, *King Hereafter*, was published in 1982. She has also written six contemporary thrillers in the *Dolly* series featuring the yachtsman Johnson Johnson, published by Penguin. With this prolific output she has earned an international reputation for brilliant historical research, sparkling wit and rich, creative imagination.

Her latest chronicle, of which this is the third volume, invites us to enter the world of trade, war and banking as it opens before Niccolò, the disarming, elusive genius who seems formed to exploit it. The first two volumes, *Niccolò Rising* and *The Spring of the Ram*, are also published by Penguin.

'Dorothy Dunnett's novels are as different from the general run of historical fiction as Renaissance paintings are from those of the Pre-Raphaelite Brotherhood. They are intensely vigorous and detailed, and without a trace of sentimentality . . . a generous feast for greedy enthusiasts' – *Daily Telegraph*

'Absorbing . . . as in all Mrs Dunnett's complex and sophisticated plots, nothing is quite what it seems to be' – *The Times*

'It is a tribute to Mrs Dunnett's ability as a novelist and researcher that she can write a historical novel which is amusing, exciting and entertaining . . . I hope it runs to at least eight volumes, which won't seem a word too long' – *Fiction Magazine*

The House of Niccolò:
Race of
Scorpions

Dorothy Dunnett

PENGUIN BOOKS

PENGUIN BOOKS

Published by the Penguin Group
27 Wrights Lane, London w8 5tz, England
Viking Penguin Inc., 40 West 23rd Street, New York, New York 10010, USA
Penguin Books Australia Ltd, Ringwood, Victoria, Australia
Penguin Books Canada Ltd, 2801 John Street, Markham, Ontario, Canada l3r 1b4
Penguin Books (NZ) Ltd, 182–190 Wairau Road, Auckland 10, New Zealand

Penguin Books Ltd, Registered Offices: Harmondsworth, Middlesex, England

First published by Michael Joseph 1989
Published in Penguin Books 1990
1 3 5 7 9 10 8 6 4 2

Made and printed in Great Britain by
Richard Clay Ltd, Bungay, Suffolk

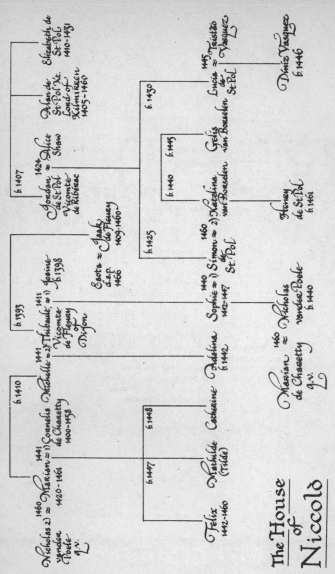

The House
of
Niccolò

Nicholas 2) ≈ Marian ≈ 1) Cornelis Michelle ≈ 2) Thibault, ≈ 1) Jeanne
vander Poele   1441   de Charetty   1441   Vicomte   1431   b.1398
g.v.   1420-1461 1400-1458   de Fleury
                b.1410   b.1410   de Dijon
                                                 b.1393

Esota ≈ Jaak
d.s.p. de Fleury
1466   1409-1460

Jordan ≈ Alice   Alan de   Elizabeth de
de St Pol Shaw   St Pol lst   St Pol
Vicomte   Lord of   1410-1431
de Ribérac   Kilmirren
b.1407   1424   1405-1460
          b.1424

b.1430

Felix   Nathilde Catherine Adelina Sophie ≈ 1) Simon ≈ 2) Katelina   Lucia ≈ Tristão de
1442-1460   (Tilde)   b.1448   b.1442   1442-1447 1440 de   1460 van Borselen   1445 Vasquez
             b.1447   St Pol
                                                     b.1425

             b.1440   b.1445

Marian ≈ Nicholas   Henry   Gelis   Diniz Vasquez
de Charetty 1460 vander Poele de St Pol van Borselen b.1446
g.v.   b.1440   b.1461

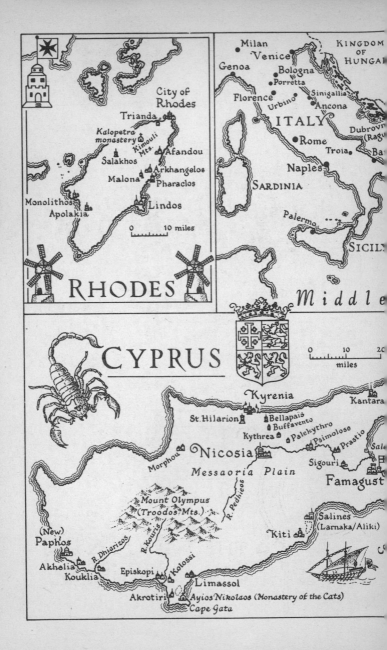

RHODES

City of
Rhodes

Trianda

Kalopetra
monastery

Kimouli Mts.

Afandou

Salakhos

Arkhangelos

Malona

Pharaclos

Monolithos

Lindos

Apolakia

0   10 miles

ITALY

Milan

Venice

KINGDOM
OF
HUNGAR

Genoa

Bologna
Porretta

Florence

Sinigallia

Urbino

Ancona

Dubrovn
(Ragu

Rome

Troia

Ba

Naples

SARDINIA

Palermo

SICILY

Middle

CYPRUS

0   10   20
miles

Kyrenia

Kantara

St. Hilarion

Bellapais
Buffavento

Kythrea

Palekythro

Psimoloso

Prastio

Morphou

Nicosia

Sigouri

Sale

Messaoria Plain

Famagust

Mount Olympus
(Troodos Mts.)

R. Pedhieos

Salines
(Larnaka/Aliki)

(New)
Paphos

R. Kouris

Kiti

R. Dhiarizos

Akhelia

Episkopi

Kolossi

Kouklia

Limassol

Akrotiri

Ayios Nikolaos (Monastery of the Cats)

Cape Gata

THE **LEVANT**

& South Eastern EUROPE

1462~4

Peter McClure 1989

Characters

November 1461–February 1464

(Those marked * are recorded in history)

Rulers
* France: Louis XI
* Scotland: James III
* England: Henry VI, House of Lancaster to 1461; Edward IV, House of York, from 1461
* Flanders: Duke Philip of Burgundy
* Pope: Pius II
* Milan: Duke Francesco Sforza
* Genoa: Doges Prosper Adorno, Louis and Paul Fregoso
* Venice: Doge Pasqual Malipiero
* Portugal: Alfonso V, nephew of Henry the Navigator
* Ottoman Empire: Sultan Mehmet II

House of Niccolò:

ABROAD:
Nicholas vander Poele (Niccolò), son of the first wife of Simon de St Pol
Tobias Beventini of Grado, physician
John le Grant, Scots engineer
Loppe (Lopez), a former Guinea slave, major domo to Nicholas

UNDER CONTRACT ABROAD:
Astorre (Syrus de Astariis), mercenary leader
Thomas, English under-captain to Astorre
Michael Crackbene, sailing-master
Umfrid, Crackbene's accountant
Andrea, Florentine under-manager of Nicosia royal dyeworks
Galiot, French steward to Nicholas in Nicosia

IN VENICE:
Gregorio of Asti, lawyer

Merchant families of France, Scotland and Portugal:

Jordan de St Pol, vicomte de Ribérac, Scots financier and merchant in France

Simon of Kilmirren his son, co-owner of St Pol & Vasquez in Portugal

Katelina van Borselen of Veere, Flanders, second wife to Simon de St Pol

Henry de St Pol (Arigho), child of Katelina

Lucia de St Pol, sister of Simon

Tristão Vasquez of St Pol & Vasquez, Portuguese husband of Lucia

Diniz Vasquez, son to Tristão and Lucia and nephew to Simon

Flanders and Burgundy:

THE CHARETTY COMPANY:

Mathilde (Tilde) de Charetty, elder daughter of Marian, late wife of Nicholas

Catherine, her sister

Julius, notary, seconded from the House of Niccolò

Father Godscalc of Cologne, chaplain, also seconded

OTHER BUSINESS FAMILIES IN BRUGES:

* Anselm Adorne
* Margriet van der Banck, his wife
* Colard Mansion, scribe and illustrator
* Jehan Metteneye, host to the Scots merchants
* Tommaso Portinari of the Medici company, Bruges
* Isabelle of Portugal, wife of Duke Philip
* Sir João Vasquez, her secretary
* Pierre Bladelin, Duke Philip's controller in Bruges
* Michael Alighieri of Florence and Trebizond, the Duke's chancellor

Fleury, Dijon:

Thibault, vicomte de Fleury, maternal grandfather of Nicholas

Enguerrand de Damparis, friend of Thibault's second wife, Marian's sister

Yvonnet, his wife

Anjou:

* René, Duke of Anjou, Count of Provence and titular King of Naples and Sicily
* Jeanne de Laval, his wife
* John, Duke of Calabria, his son
* Margaret of Anjou, his daughter, wife of King Henry VI of England
* Roland Cressant, Scottish Archer
* Odile Spinola, widow of the King's Genoese maître d'hôtel
* John Perrot, abbot of Angers, René's confessor

Savoy:
* Louis I, Duke of Savoy
* Anna de Lusignan, his wife, aunt of Carlotta of Cyprus
* Luis, Count of Geneva, his son, husband of Carlotta of Cyprus

Naples and the Abruzzi:
* Ferrante of Aragon, King of Naples
* Federigo da Montefeltro, Count of Urbino, Papal mercenary
* Paltroni, his secretary
* Sigismondo Malatesta, lord of Rimini
* George Castriot (Skanderbeg), Albanian leader and patriot
* Moses Golento, one of his captains
* Count Jacopo Piccinino, mercenary captain

Florence:
* Cosimo di Giovanni de' Medici, head of the banking house of
    Medici
* Alessandra Macinghi negli Strozzi, matriarch of the Strozzi
    merchant house
* Lorenzo di Matteo Strozzi, her son, merchant in Naples

Bologna:
* Sante Bentivoglio, lord of Bologna
* Ludovico de Severi da Bologna, Franciscan Patriarch of Antioch

Cyprus:
* Carlotta de Lusignan, daughter of King John II of Cyprus and
    Helen Paleologa
* Luis, her husband, son of Luis, Duke of Savoy and Anna de
    Lusignan of Cyprus
Primaflora, courtesan and Carlotta's attendant
Ansaldo, her lover; a knight of Carlotta's
* Sor de Naves, Sicilian defender of Kyrenia
* Thomas Pardo, Cypriot follower of Carlotta
* John de Montolif, Marshal of Cyprus
* Antony de Bon, major domo to Carlotta
* Abbot of Bellapaïs
* James de Lusignan (Zacco), bastard son of King John II of
    Cyprus
* Marietta of Patras (Comomutene or Cropnose), his mother
* Markios of Patras, Marietta's brother
* Jorgin, servant to Zacco
* William Goneme, Archbishop of Nicosia
* Sir Rizzo di Marino, Sicilian chamberlain to Zacco
* Sir Nicholas (Conella) Morabit, Sicilian vice-consul of Nicosia
* Philip Pesaro, Venetian captain of Sigouri
* Gianozzo Salviati, a commander
* Alexander Tarantin, Bailie of the Karpass

* Antony di Zucco, Bishop of Limassol
* Sir Philip Podocataro, doctor of law
* Sir Peter Podocataro, his brother
* George Bustron, commandant at Salines (Aliki/Larnaka)
* Thomas Carerio, Bailie of the King's Secrète
* David de Salmeton, agent for the Vatachino company of brokers

GENOESE CITY OF FAMAGUSTA:
* Napoleone Lomellini, captain of Famagusta
* Tomà Adorno of Chios
* Cyprien Pallaviccino
* James Doria, Bank of St George
* Babilian Gentile
* Hieronimo Verdure
* Nicolao Archerio
* Francesco de Pastino

VENETIANS IN CYPRUS:
* Paul Erizzo, Venetian Bailie in Cyprus
* Marco Corner, sugar-grower of Episkopi and ally of James
* Fiorenza of Naxos, his wife, princess and grand-daughter (with
  Valenza and Violante) of Emperor John IV of Trebizond
* Andrea Corner, his brother, serving Queen Carlotta
* Giovanni (Vanni) Loredano, deputy Bailie and Episkopi factor
* Valenza of Naxos his wife, princess of Trebizond and sister of
  Fiorenza above
* Ludovic (Luigi) Martini, sugar farmer
* Giovanni Martini, his brother
* Bartolomeo Zorzi (Giorgio), merchant refugee from Constantinople
  and younger brother of Nicholai Giorgio de' Acciajuoli
* Jacopo Zorzi, vineyard owner in Cyprus, a third brother
* Girolamo Michiel, refugee from Constantinople and ex-partner of
  Bartolomeo

VENETIANS ELSEWHERE:
* Violante of Naxos, princess of Trebizond and sister to Fiorenza
  and Valenza
* Caterino Zeno, Venetian merchant, her husband
* Giovanni Bembo, Venetian Bailie at Modon; kinsman to Piero
  Bembo and to Francesco, brother-in-law of Marco Corner

Rhodes:
KNIGHTS OF THE ORDER OF ST JOHN OF JERUSALEM:
* Grand Master Pierre-Raimond Zacosta of Castile
* Louis de Magnac, Grand Commander of Cyprus
* Brother William de Combort, lieutenant in command at Kolossi
* Brother Telli, castellan of Kyrenia
* Tobias Lomellini of Genoa, Treasurer of the Order
* Sir Imperiale Doria of Genoa, Admiral to Carlotta

* Merle de Piozasque of Savoy, Admiral, also serving Carlotta
* George de Piozasque, adherent of Carlotta
* John de Kinloch, Scots chaplain to the Knights Hospitaller
* Patrick Scougal, Scots Conventual Brother of the Hospital

OTHERS:
Limboulaki (Boulaki), a fisherman of Apolakia
Persefoni of Pharaclos, aunt of Boulaki
Yiannis of Apolakia
Lukas, his grandson

Turcoman, Ottoman and Mameluke Powers:
* Uzum Hasan, lord of the White Sheep tribe of Turcomans
* Sara Khatun of Syria, his Christian mother
* Theodora his wife, niece of David, exiled Emperor of Trebizond
* Mehmet II, Sultan of the Ottoman Empire
* David Comnenos, former Emperor of Trebizond, his prisoner
* George Amiroutzes, the Emperor's former Great Chancellor
* Khushcadam of Cairo, Sultan of Egypt and Syria
* Emir Tzani-bey al-Ablak, his Mameluke commander in Cyprus
Abul Ismail, Arab physician with the Mameluke force

Chapter 1

THAT NOVEMBER, God sent snow to north Italy, to the inconvenience of all who had to travel on horseback. The way between Porretta and Bologna became choked, and only the robust cared to use it. Among these was the friar Ludovico de Severi da Bologna who set out from Porretta one evening in a mood of ferocious good humour. The snow had brought him good luck. He had located the souls he was looking for.

The silly woman was there in Porretta, and about to ride north in the morning. The man, bless his heart, was on that identical road coming southwards, but storm-stayed in the hamlet of Silla. The two were certain to meet. The friar couldn't see how, happily, they could avoid one another. The woman (for a woman) was redoubtable. The man was a cheeky young profligate, and Carlotta would eat him for supper. Through the white gloom of dusk, Fra Ludovico plodded on mule-back to Silla, producing psalms from the caves in his chest so that clods fell from the trees and the tracks of hares melted the snowfields. He arrived late at Silla's one tavern, stabled his mule and his serving-man and was granted a mattress to sleep on. Rising early next morning, he took the squelched track to the latrines, broke the ice in the tub, and obtained punctual news of his quarry. 'He's in there,' volunteered one of the travellers. 'Big as a gallows-tree, and the age of my grandson. Niccolò, he answers to.'

'That's him,' said Ludovico da Bologna. 'Used to be an apprentice called Claes. Where's the common-room?'

Unaware of this conversation, Nicholas vander Poele idled in an inadequate seat by a window, keeping himself to himself and resenting many things, but most of all the fact that he was sober.

The storm of snow had packed the hostelry with many travellers. In the roaring hell of the common-room, he could make out five different languages. There was a group of seraphic blond courtiers from Poland, freshly blessed and addressed by Pope Pius. There were established merchants from Milan and Ferrara; Adriatic agents and runners with business in Pisa, or Florence, or Rome. Representing Bologna was a noisy south-riding squadron of its first citizen's cavalry, led by an unshaven captain who had quickly drunk himself torpid. Nicholas emptied his parsimonious jug into his niggardly cup and sat staring at it.

Being virtually alone, he could do as he pleased. The two muleteer-guides and a house-man had been hired in Venice by Thomas, his only companion. Thomas had dropped into silence some days ago. The massive cargo he, Nicholas, had brought from the East had long since been dispersed, along with the men from his voyage. He himself, delayed by affairs, was on his way to the place where his wife had died. It was the first time, since he had had news of her death, that he had had time to fill. He found he disliked the journey, and dreaded the end of it.

For this excursion, he needed no bodyguard. The brigands who preyed on rich merchants were unlikely to connect him, as yet, with the Niccolò who had emerged with a fortune from the ruins of Trebizond. Or if they knew so much about him, they would know that his wife, the head of his company, had died in his absence, leaving her business elsewhere. Leaving him, at the age of nearly twenty-one years, embarked on a pointless journey to Burgundy. And then another one, to the dyeworks in Bruges where he had married her.

There was no hurry, since the journey was pointless, to leave the tavern when the snow persisted through the night and into the following morning. He sat, the empty jug at his elbow, throwing dice against himself as the wind threw grey thrumming smuts against the yellow horn window. The young woman who had wished to get into his bed came again and then went, and two of the archers from the Bentivoglio troop invited him to join in their gaming. One of them had tried to get into his bed as well. They went away. Nicholas threw his dice steadily. Thomas came to his side and peered through his window. Thomas said, 'There's that monk again. He came late last night. The road from the south must be passable.' He waited hopefully, but was vouchsafed no comment. Thomas was tired of the inn, and of Master Nicholas vander Poele, the youngest banker in Venice.

They themselves were bound south, on a detour to the medical baths of Porretta. Sante, the ailing lord of Bologna, wished to discuss a matter of silk. He might expect to place further commissions, which Nicholas would have to refuse since, of course, he was no longer working from Trebizond. Thomas spoke, still peering out at the snow. 'There. The monk's waving. You'd think that he knows you.' He spoke in soldier's Flemish, with a gross English accent.

Nicholas said, 'Maybe it's the lord of Bologna come to hunt for his late household cavalry. I hope not. The captain's still sleeping.'

He didn't listen. That was what irked Thomas mostly. He said, 'I said a friar. A Franciscan friar built like a barn, with an old goathair cloak and his habit hitched up to his knees. He's coming in.'

Nicholas flung down the dice. The door burst open. A bulky man stood on the threshold in a pool of fresh snow and strode forward, striking his cloak from his shoulders. His bare feet, encased in wet sandals, had tufts of black pelt on each toe. He said, 'Messer Niccolò vander Poele. Remember me, boy?'

Nicholas heaved a great sigh and rose slowly. He said, 'I could never forget you. Thomas. Fra Ludovico da Bologna, the man who means to drive the Turks out of Europe. Did you collect the money you needed?'

'Have your joke,' said the monk, undisturbed. He hitched up a stool with the sole of his sandal and sat himself down with a clang of his crucifix. 'You look as if you could do with one. That the Bentivoglio cavalry?'

He gazed across the room at the soldiers. Their livery was easy enough to identify. So was their high degree of intoxication. Nicholas sat and said, 'Yes. On their way to Porretta to collect a guest of their lord. The snow and the wine delayed them.'

'And I'll wager,' said the friar, 'that you know the name of the guest of Bentivoglio. Met her in Venice, am I right? Refused what she offered you, am I right? And you're hanging about here trying not to meet her again, am I right? Of course I am. You didn't tell Thomas here, but I know your games.' A serving-girl came across and he said, 'Well, my girl. Said your prayers this morning?'

'Yes, brother,' she said, retiring circumspectly and stopping, since Brother Ludovico had retained her crucifix in his grasp like a halter.

'I doubt it,' he said. 'Kneel there, and hold that. That's what it's meant for.'

She clasped her cross obediently under her chin, then shut her eyes as he raised his voice over her. In two minutes he had ended, blessed her and given her a poke in the ribs, which made her drop her hands and open her eyes. 'That'll protect you from here to the kitchen,' said Fra Ludovico da Bologna. 'Now I'll have a jug of well-water. And tell your owner there's a humble friar here ready to call down God's grace on his house for any morsels his table can spare.' He turned. 'Well, Messer Niccolò, I have news for you. The lady from Porretta is coming here. If her escort didn't arrive, she planned to set off with her household without it. She should pass the door any time.'

'So long as she passes it,' Nicholas said. He watched the girl run away.

The friar contemplated him. His hair was so black and so plentiful that even when shaved, his crown and his jowls were as blue as fish-hide. He said, 'Well, you're giving thought, I can see, to your fellows in trouble. You would let the lady ride without extra help to Bologna, while these fellows risk the wrath of their lord, sleeping here while she went by unknowing?'

'I probably should,' Nicholas said. 'But it's going to be all right, because you'll tell the captain.'

'Well, the lieutenant,' said the friar. 'The captain is not wholly in touch with his intelligence.' He was watching the road. It struck Thomas that he was watching the road quite intently.

Nicholas said, 'Is there something wrong?'

The friar redirected his gaze. 'Wakened up, have we?' he said. 'I don't know. I thought I saw something.'

Thomas looked out of the window. He said, 'There *is* something. A man. Riding this way from the south.' He got to his feet. He said, 'A man wearing livery, wounded.'

Nicholas rose, and so did the friar, as if their interlocked gaze had been hefted. The wounded rider came nearer. He was shouting. The tavern door opened, and two of the soldiers ran out, accompanied by three of the Poles. Nicholas said, 'You knew this was going to happen.'

Fra Ludovico da Bologna would never, surely, look gratified. He said, 'Am I a necromancer? But that's the device of the lady. And thieves and cut-throats love travellers. That man has been sent here for help.'

Now there was a crowd of people in the yard, helping the man from his horse. The lieutenant passed out of the room at an uncertain run. By the hearth, the captain lay snoring. Nicholas said, 'Then isn't it lucky that there's a whole squadron of horse here to help him?'

'With no captain,' said Ludovico da Bologna.

Thomas looked from one man to the other, and out of the window, and across to the hearth. He said, 'Someone's been attacked on the road. Did you hear that? There's a mob besieging a farm with some travellers in it.'

The friar smiled, still looking at Nicholas. Nicholas said, 'So it seems.'

It puzzled Thomas. He said, 'Then shouldn't we rescue them? I don't mind.'

'There you are,' said Ludovico da Bologna. 'There speaks the professional soldier. Will you let him go? You don't appear to want to go with him.'

It seemed to Thomas that his employer was being accused of

something. He said, 'Master Nicholas can handle himself in a fight.' He paused and added, 'Nowadays.' Outside, horses were being brought and men were mounting, and running back and forth with helmets and swords. They included the Poles, and quite a number of other men who were not soldiers.

Nicholas sighed again. He said, 'I never thanked you for what you did in Florence, did I? Well, let me thank you for everything now. Thomas, get the grooms and the arms and let's go.'

The cloud disappeared from his companion's face. Thomas said, 'Well, it's the right thing. Especially if it's a lady. Who's the lady in trouble, Master Nicholas?'

'She's not a lady,' Nicholas said. 'She's a Queen called Carlotta.'

At the time of the attack, Carlotta by the grace of God Queen of Jerusalem, Cyprus and Armenia was twenty-four years of age; small, and trim, and sharp as a triple-split needle. Setting out from Porretta, she could have wished herself back in the warm baths, except that she was out of temper already, over days wasted in Rome and further days of fruitless wheedling in Florence. At Porretta, the Pope's fifty horsemen had left her, but very soon she would meet her next escort. Messer Sante had begged her to wait for them, but she was tired of old men's advice. Of any advice. If she had listened to Luis her consort she would never have won free of Cyprus. He was still besieged on the island, complaining about lack of fresh food. He should be pleased now. The Pope was sending him grain, if the ship ever arrived, and if Luis had the gumption to mill it.

In any case, she was not unescorted. With her, since she landed in Italy, were the chief of her courtiers from Cyprus, and her personal household, and enough soldiers to guard the roped boxes that contained all she had left to barter. Since they held neither ducats nor jewellery, she had not looked for trouble, but had ridden vigorously. The Greeks and the high-born, as ever, were the women who snivelled and faltered. She gave them the edge of her tongue. The others kept up, as expected. Carlotta believed in professionalism.

The attackers came from a copse. But for the snow, she would have seen them more quickly. She was riding so fast that the flying flakes made a tunnel, obscuring everything. Then she saw racing towards her a crowd of glittering shapes; the long Roman noses of horses; the studded ellipses of shields. She screamed a warning and dragged her horse round, as the others jostled behind her. The wagons halted askew. And she saw, far behind, another troop of alien horse, approaching fast and spread to encircle her.

She turned her horse round and round, alarmed and angry. The snow, lifting, showed the wall of a steading with behind it an orchard, a byre and a big, solid house with closed shutters. Through open gates, the yard showed the slush of much recent trampling: there was a child's swing in a corner, and a hobbyhorse. The Queen of Cyprus said, 'There!' and, whip-hand working, set her mare to make for the gates. Her women followed. She heard the voices of de Bon and Pardo organising the rearguard to hold off the attackers while the wagons drove through. They jolted round the side of the house and disappeared, led by a group of Ansaldo's men. Outside, arrows flew and swords clashed as Pardo and the rest began to retreat into the yard and force the gates shut. She waited to see that, before she marched up to the door of the house and struck it with the butt of her whip. 'Open!' she said. 'We are the Queen of Cyprus, and we command your assistance.'

It opened. Doors always did, for Carlotta. There was a hubbub. Then Pardo came in and said, 'We're secure. Madama, don't be distressed. I've sent someone to Silla for help: there will be men: there's a tavern. And meantime, the archers are ready.' He turned to the farmer and his servants, crowded into the end of the room. He said, 'The Queen thanks you, and will show her gratitude. The rogues outside have hackbuts, and might fire through the windows or door. Is there a secure room for the Queen and her ladies?'

They took her to a room at the back, along with the women. One of them was snuffling. The others knew better. One was missing. She knew which one that would be. She said, 'They are brigands? How many?'

De Bon had answered. 'There are fifty, madama. Mostly at the front, but some here at the back where the other gates are. They won't storm the walls: there are too few of them. You are safe. And the wagons.'

The wagons. She said, 'Ansaldo is with them?'

'In the barn,' said her major domo. 'He will protect them with his life.'

He left. The Queen stayed, biting her thumb, while the farm servants snivelled and her own ladies huddled together like hens. All but Primaflora, who would be watching the barn, not her Queen, because her lover Ansaldo was there. Court women! Imbeciles! Or if they were not, it would seem that they became so. Primaflora spoke Greek, as she must, but she was a Savoyard like Luis, and a worker. She had been thrown to Ansaldo to keep Ansaldo happy: it was her duty; she knew it perfectly; she had never given trouble before. So why act like a hen when the cock struts? The Queen marched up and down the small room, kicking her skirts, hearing the shouting outside, and the increase in noise from the front of the house. It sounded ominous. She found and slapped her page and said, 'Go! Tell me what is happening.' She pulled her dagger out of its waist-sheath, just in case, and saw the woman nearest her flinch. Idiot.

She had seen those assailants outside. They were encased in helms and plate armour, with no markings to tell who they were. Brigands wore a patchwork of armour if they could get it, but more often jacks of light leather. Knights who could afford complete harness could afford, as a rule, to be identified. So these must be mercenaries. But paid by whom? The Genoese? The Milanese? The Venetians? She grew impatient with the snivelling page and striding to the front of the house, found and grasped Thomas Pardo. Pardo the Cypriot, whose skin was so dark that he never looked frightened. He said, 'Go back, madama. Every now and then, they try to storm the gates, climb the walls. We will pick them off.'

'So long as you have arrows,' she said. 'What then? They could set fire to the buildings.'

'Then they would lose what we carry,' said Pardo.

'They could demand our goods for our lives,' said the Queen. 'If they know who we are, they may demand our person in return for your safety. Have you considered this?'

'Others have made the same offer,' said Pardo. 'I know none of your servants who has been tempted, or ever will be. Madama, they come.' She looked out of the window. The farm was ringed by blurs of fast-moving steel whose human outlines had faded under coifs and surcoats of snow. Their faces looked purple. She wanted to stay, but they persuaded her to return to her women.

The fools stood as she had left them, hugging each other. The candles guttered, and a brazier smoked. She eased back a shutter an inch and saw that new snow had already covered the wheel-ruts that led to the barn. There was a sledge, and a painted barrow, and a child's spade stuck by a well. Beside the barn, the snow had been rolled into boulders and given eyes and noses and buttons. A household of brats. In two years, she and Luis had managed no children: another failure of Luis'.

It would be remedied. She would emerge scatheless from this, as she usually did. She was afraid of dying through mishap – one had always to reckon with that. She might be robbed for a second – a third time. Her women were right to fear rape. But as Queen, she was sacrosanct, unless attacked by ignorant riff-raff, and these men were not that. So who were they? That was what was important. That and saving, with God's help, what lay in the chests on the wagons.

They brought her a chair, and time passed. She sat with her chin in her fists, hearing the whine and whicker of arrows and the explosion of hackbuts; the thud of metal and wood, and the barking voices of men. She heard fighting orders from her own men in Greek and Italian and French, and thought – but she must be mistaken – that she heard the enemy respond in much the same

languages. The snow fell. A door opened and shut and Primaflora
knelt at her side.

She had been out of doors. Her cloak was soaked, its hood fallen
back from the immaculate golden hair inside its immaculate coif. A
wisp plastered her cheek, her tinted cheek, below the pellucid eyes
and the winged nostrils and the rosebud mouth with its dimple,
above and below. It was natural that Ansaldo should have been
mesmerised. Primaflora said, 'Forgive me, madama. It is the chests
they are after. Ansaldo says they are cutting a ram for the gates. To
make an assault, they will require all their men. He says that when
they begin their attack on the front, he will try to drive the wagons
out of the barn, across the yard and out the back gate, and make his
escape to the woods. The enemy may force their way in, but you
will be safe, madama. In the field, an arrow might kill you. And if
the carts are secure, you have something. When they discover their
loss, they might give up.'

'When they discover their loss, they will follow him,' Carlotta
said. 'Where could he hide? And does he think they are deaf, even
when fighting?'

'The snow will muffle the sound,' said the girl. 'The snow will
cover his tracks. He is willing to try. And if he fails, he will have
drawn them off, and the illustrious lady can fly.' She hesitated.
'Madama, time has passed. It may be that no rescue is coming.
And we have few arrows left.'

Under the paint, the girl's face was pale. The Queen paused. She
said, 'You have said what you were told to say, but I see what it is.
He makes of himself a decoy, and allows us a chance to escape. He
is a brave man. I agree. Go and tell my lord de Bon and my lord
Pardo. Then come back to me.'

The girl did what she was told and, coming back, stationed
herself at the window, her eyes on the barn, her hand tight on the
shutter. Even in anguish, she kept her courtesan's grace. The
Queen wondered whether, impelled by true love, she had offered
to ride with Ansaldo. If so, he had not agreed. The Queen understood the advantages of what Ansaldo was doing, but it seemed
very likely that she was going to lose him, and his men, and the
boxes, and get herself taken for ransom. This was going to cost
money. Holy Bones of God, her uncle the Duke would be furious.
She promised herself, blackly, to tell the lord Sante precisely what
she thought of his absent troop of escorting cavalry. The Queen
rose, and walked through to the front room.

There was daylight here, for the windows were torn and the
shutters broken and hanging. There were also two or three fewer
than there had been; and in a corner a man lay on a cloak, groaning.
They were apportioning the last of the arrows and passing orders,
low-voiced. She didn't interrupt them. The archers were in the

room above: she could hear their footsteps. Through the window, she saw the bodies of men lying now in the yard, and beyond the gates a cluster of snow-coated helms, white as pebbles. As she watched, they moved backwards, and the noise of their voices increased. Then they began rushing forward.

Before the ram struck the gate, Primaflora called. 'Madama! The wagons are leaving!'

The ram crashed into the gate. Pardo smiled, and gave her a salute with his sword. He said, 'Courage!' and opened the door, his men round about him. The ram withdrew. A flight of arrows from over her head arched down over the wall and fell on the shields of the assailants. The ram faltered, then its bearers closed up again. Pardo dashed into the yard. Ahead, a bugle blew somewhere. Behind, a whistle shrilled. The Queen found her arm grasped by Primaflora. The girl said, 'They've seen the wagons. They left a watcher. They'll follow them.'

'Wait!' said the Queen. The trumpet flourish sounded again. Outside the gate, the ram's movement had stopped. The timber fell. The men who had carried it were running for horses. Swords flashed and men shouted commands. A banner appeared through the snow. She had seen its device in Porretta. The banner of Bentivoglio. There were also a number of fair-haired youths in green silk, with quivers of Libyan bearskin. She had seen these before, too. The Queen turned to the woman Primaflora and said, 'We are saved!'

And Primaflora said to her fiercely, 'But Ansaldo is not! Or the boxes! They are following him!'

Acute annoyance crossed the Queen's face. 'Then we must save them!' she said. 'Tell the Bentivoglio! The Queen's favour to all who assist her!'

She watched the girl run, and wondered what quality of men Sante of Bologna employed, and whether they were sober. She had no great hopes. She had long ago concluded that the world would be a more efficient place if managed by women.

Chapter 2

IT WAS QUITE a while since Nicholas had fought anybody. Leaving the inn, there hadn't been time for full armour, but he was satisfied with the weight of the jack on his shoulders, and an ordinary steel helmet without face-guards, and his Milanese shield and an extremely good sword, in a plain scabbard. His horse had no special protection, and neither had that of Thomas; but for a skirmish, they were dressed well enough. The Bentivoglio troop, encased in steel with vizors and plumes, looked fit to roll back Ghengis Khan, if you didn't know they were pickled in liquor.

They had not far to go. The royal train had been ambushed near the river; had fought off the attack and had taken refuge, as the man had said, in a farmhouse. From the tavern-keeper they knew the farmer was there, and his servants, but his wife and eight children, thank God, had gone to Bologna. 'They'll drive the wagons into the barn,' the man had said. 'Ansaldo will. It's the wagons they're after.' What was in the wagons, however, he could not be brought to disclose.

They had meant to stop short of the farm and send scouts ahead, but on nearing heard the clatter of battle. Not the sporadic noise of a siege, but the insistent clamour of hand-to-hand fighting. The lieutenant laid a hand to his trumpet and gulped. It was Thomas who removed it from his fingers and blew the good, healthy fanfare that sent the whole motley force galloping forward.

Considering the state of the Bentivoglio men, it was an excellent fight. The men assaulting the farmhouse were found to be fully armed, which was unusual. They not only fought more than competently, but had been on the verge, it was clear, of storming the gates and the building. They were, however, both surprised and outnumbered, and the Bentivoglio troop at least were properly armed. Nicholas dashed back and forth, wielding his sword and parrying with his shield until the fighting started to slacken. By then, the farm gates had opened and the Queen's men had come out to help them.

The extra numbers made all the difference. The marauding troop began to fall back. Some had fallen. Some had been forced to surrender. Quite a number had broken off and galloped away. The cavalry troop of the lord of Bentivoglio began to complete the rounding up of the rest. Nicholas noticed a woman.

It was two months since he had noticed any woman, and he felt nothing for this one, except that he saw she was handsome. She stood at the gate, her hair soaked, her cloak clutched about her and said, 'My lord Pardo! De Bon! They have gone after the wagons! Save them! Save Captain Ansaldo!'

The man beside Nicholas appeared to be Pardo. Nicholas said, 'The Queen's wagons?'

The dark-faced man said, 'We drove them out from the back as a decoy. They were seen. Some of these brigands broke away and are chasing them.' He said, panting, 'I have to stay with the Queen.'

'I don't,' said Nicholas happily. He swept a knot of Poles and traders and Bolognese with him and raced round to the back of the farmhouse. The tracks of the wagons were there, and the tracks of the pursuers. Far across the snowfields he could see the riders themselves in the distance. He hallooed, echoed by Thomas, and they hurled themselves into the hunt.

To his own surprise, Nicholas felt some excitement. For the first time in weeks, he had nothing to think of but his sword and his seat on a horse. He lifted his blade and brandished it over his head, roaring wordlessly. The fair-haired Poles, clustering about him, raised their feathered caps and screamed in chorus. The group of armoured horsemen in front, racing across the white fields to the river, turned, floundered, and then redoubled their efforts. Ahead of them was their quarry; three Cypriot carts and a group of seven or eight men with a captain. It was hard to count, through the fleece of dashed snow. Nicholas said, 'Have we an archer?'

Two of the angelic Poles had short bows. One man had a sling. They shot from the saddle, and saw two men fall, far ahead, and thought they had injured another. They went on shooting, but the snow, the uneven ground, and the distance were all against them. Nicholas bellowed, talking in snatches. 'We're not going to catch them in time. First thing, let's warn this Ansaldo. He's got to abandon the wagons and run, or he'll be killed before we can help him. If he sees us, he'll do it. Come on. Spread out, and start shouting.'

'But the wagons?' panted one of the merchants.

'We'll get them anyway. Where can the thieves go with them? They're slow; they can hardly escape us. They must know the Queen has been rescued. If they have any sense, they'll abandon the effort and save themselves. Shout. Shout.'

They spread out and shouted. Ahead, specks in the distance, they could see the wagons lumbering on. Faces turned, but the draught horses galloped. Thomas swore. Nicholas said, 'We've no banner. The captain doesn't know we are friends. He thinks the rest of the thieves have come after him.' Then paused, and wished he knew as many swear words as Thomas.

Far ahead, the little convoy was slowing. Outmatched as he thought, Ansaldo had done the brave thing. Instead of hopelessly running, he and his men had turned to confront their pursuers. Through the snow came the wink of their swords. They had set out to draw the attack from the Queen, and they were prepared to die, to help her to freedom. Nicholas whipped his horse, setting his teeth, but it had borne him from the inn, and through a fight, and was not going to turn into a bird for him. He saw the brigands arrive, and dismount, and fall upon the small group by the carts, and, distant as he was, could do nothing to help them.

The fighting was over in moments. The shouting stopped, the flash of blades suddenly ceased, and all that was to be seen was a mark on the snow far ahead, and three wagons being driven at speed, with outriders spurring beside them.

The young Poles beside Nicholas were silent. They reined in when they came to the spot, and looked down at the thick Turkish carpet of red and white snow, and the slashed bodies lying upon it. Nicholas wondered which of them was Ansaldo. Then they sprang off, in the wake of the wagons.

These were easy to follow, if not to catch sight of. The ruts, not yet filled, led through uneven country that denied a clear view, and human hands as well as snow had muffled untoward sounds. The brigands were riding in silence. Nicholas said, 'We're getting close. The ruts are clearer. I don't like it.'

'An ambush?' Thomas said.

'Wait,' said Nicholas. They stopped. Ahead were the wagons. They were motionless. Beside them were snow-covered bushes; a copse; a ridge behind which men could be hiding. It took a long and cautious approach to discover that there was no ambush here. The copse and bushes were empty of men. And the wagons, when they reached them, contained nothing.

There were footprints everywhere. One of the Poles said, 'Sir?' and pointed to a trail of them, deep as a trough. It led round a thicketed mound.

Nicholas said, 'What's over there?'

'The Reno. The river,' said one of the merchants.

Thomas swore. 'And a boat, or a barge.' He swung into the saddle. 'We'll get them.'

The river was there, round the ridge. And there were the brigands, their horses beside them. The contents of the carts stood there also, or those very few chests that were left. One by one, they were being heaved down to the water. As Nicholas and his troop came in sight the last chest was released, the last pair of men swung themselves into their saddles and the small, well-armoured force set off along the bank, wheeled, and thundered over the bridge which lay beyond it. The air they presented was one of extraordinary efficiency.

There was no time, then, to examine the fate of the Queen's possessions. But dashing over the bridge, Nicholas caught sight of the clutter of boxes below him, and conceived the impression that the barge or boat had foundered beneath them. He had the further impression that what he heard, far ahead, was the sound of men cheering. He was interested enough to be quite intent on catching them, but after fifteen minutes his horse started to founder, and two others had to drop out. After twenty minutes Thomas said, 'They've got away. Their horses were fresher. They were mercenaries.'

'Did you know them?' Nicholas said.

'No. But I know the second-hand shop their gear came from. Who paid them?'

'Let's ask the Queen,' Nicholas said. 'But first, let's go back to the bridge.'

At the bridge, they had company: a dozen of the Cypriot household had come from the farm to assist them. They stood on the bank, looking downwards. Nicholas tied his horse to the bridge and looked over it. Below lay the contents of the Queen's wagons. The exotic merchandise, to acquire which a mercenary troop had been told, it would seem, to stop at nothing. The merchandise for which Ansaldo and his brave men had perished.

The chests lay all burst open below him, some overturned, some floating and empty; one of them tranquilly sinking. He watched it. It contained a seam of grey, glistening silt which rose groggily, clouding the water. Beneath the boxes was nothing but river. There never had been a boat. The contents of the chests had not been stolen: they lay, presumably safe, on the bed of the river. So why had the men cheered?

Nicholas said, 'What was in them?'

One of the Cypriots came up, walking slowly from where the carts stood. 'What was in them? Sugar,' he said.

Diamonds, he might have said. It was nearly the same. Nicholas looked at him without speaking, and then at his companions. 'Sixteen loaves a box, and how many boxes . . .? For Bologna?'

'For the refineries at Bologna,' another of the Queen's entourage said. 'The robbers couldn't do anything with it, you see. It had to be refined. They couldn't do such a thing secretly. So they brought it to the river and ruined it. All that money lost to the Queen; the gold she needed to win back her throne.'

'Who were they?' said Nicholas.

The Cypriot shrugged. 'Venetians? Genoese? They would have taken the sugar. Only one man would have destroyed it. We know him.'

'Who?' Nicholas said.

'That is our affair,' said the man.

They took the carts back to the farm, where the Queen was, and instead of her sugar they carried her dead. Waiting outside the gate was the girl Nicholas had already noticed. She had been there a long time: her face was white with cold. He reined in his horse and dismounted. 'Demoiselle? I am sorry.'

Her eyes were on the wagon. She said, 'Would you help me up?'

Heads turned. Nicholas said, 'Yes. Take my hand.'

Running out from the house, the Queen met their tale with a torrent of questions and cries, rounding in anger on the men who had stayed with her, the major domo and the man she called Pardo. In the middle she walked sharply across to the carts and examined them. The girl Primaflora looked up.

It had stopped snowing. Her yellow hair was no longer neatly coiled in its pleatings and her paint had all gone. At her knee was a dead man in half armour. The Queen said, 'Ansaldo! But what a tragedy! I cannot bear it! What shall I do without him, after all this?'

'Find another,' said the girl. The men who had been with her in the barn were silent. She looked at them, and then about her. She said, 'Now the children can come back and finish their snowmen. Imagine how many they made!'

Reaching up, the Queen patted her cheek. 'Come, girl. They will warm you and give you dry clothes. One will help you down.'

She turned, to find whom to command, and saw Nicholas. She frowned, searching her memory. Since there was no hope of avoidance, Nicholas took off his helmet and gave a short bow. She said, 'We have met.'

'Niccolò vander Poele, madama,' he said. 'Of course, at your service.' His Greek was pure Trapezuntine. He knew she would recognise that, before anything. He saw, as her face sharpened, that she did.

She said, 'Ser Niccolò. You have my gratitude. Pray help my poor lady descend.'

He turned, obeying, and lifted the girl to the ground. She was heavy, weighed down with soaked stuff. She said, 'Let me show you the snowmen.'

The Queen shook her head, her face pitying. Nicholas said, 'Show me.'

His hand was taken. The young woman led him, as a child

might, round the side of the house, and to the yard and the barn at the back. It was as she said. The snow was littered with playthings and crude, buttoned figures with eyes and noses and hands. Nicholas stood. The girl at his elbow said nothing. One or two of the Cypriots had drifted over to join them.

The biggest and best of the figures stood just within reach. Nicholas put out a tentative thumb, rasped its cheek, and then broke off an ear-lobe and sucked it. She watched him, her face stiff but not so frozen as it had been. He lowered the fragment and considered it. 'Five ducats' worth?' he said thoughtfully. 'I'll pay you when I can afford it. What was in the boxes then?'

The girl said, 'We filled them with snow. It was Ansaldo's idea.'

'We in the barn, we all helped,' said one of the Cypriots. 'You can mould sugar with damp into anything. We planted a fortune in snowmen, knowing no one would steal it.'

'And sent us to chase a caravan full of snow?' Nicholas said.

'There were men with it,' said the Cypriot. 'Men who gave their lives as a decoy to draw the attack from their Queen.'

'I hope she is grateful,' said Nicholas.

'To those who serve her,' said Primaflora, 'she is always grateful.'

'To those who serve me,' said Carlotta, by the grace of God Queen of Jerusalem, Cyprus and Armenia, 'I show my gratitude. You may consider yourself already a knight. You may choose what fiefs in my country you wish.'

Since she was speaking in Bologna, not Cyprus, the pronouncement had its comic side, and once Nicholas would have staggered out of the meeting, repeating the words, in perfect parody, to the delight of Julius, or Tobie, or Felix. Now, it was not even an irritation but something to be endured, on the heels of an equally arid visit to Sante Bentivoglio at his mistress's house in Porretta. There, there had been a similar interest, well shrouded, in his immediate plans.

He had no plans. He had, however, respect for rank and position, and so had called on the Queen, as he'd promised. She had given him a casket of sugar and the prospect of endowments in an island she had yet to conquer.

The Queen continued to talk, with animation. He remembered listening in Venice and thinking that, as a commoner, she would have learned how to moderate her manner to men. Her physical vehemence – the beaked nose, the high complexion, the vigorous, well-jointed hands – was as alarming as the impact of her mental agility. She knew something, if Sante did not, of his history. She cupped her chin, leaning forward, and said, 'You have no objection, I take it, to a woman who runs her own business?'

'My wife did so,' he said.

'And successfully. But a man of the Muslim faith would have denied her her right to manage any such venture. In Muslim countries, the male is supreme; the illegitimate son takes precedence over the legitimate daughter. When we, Queen of Cyprus, sought help from the Sultan of Egypt, the robes of our envoy were ripped and the Mamelukes set up a cry. "What, deprive the male, and give the lordship to the female?" But perhaps you think that is just?'

'I have no vote, madonna,' said Nicholas. 'In a perfect world the fittest would rule, irrespective of sex.'

'Then you agree with me,' said the Queen. 'Yet my enemies have driven me from all but a patch of my island. Set up a puppet who has become apostate from the Christian faith, who swears the Gospel is false, that Christ is not the only one, nor Mary a virgin; who denies John the Forerunner and is already oppressing the Church of my people. Is such a blasphemer a fit person to rule?'

'What people would accept such a person?' Nicholas said.

She took down her hand. 'Accept? You have seen their valour. They fight. They die. Those who are left are here with us, or defending our lord and husband the King in his castle. We, a woman, are here to claim help. Without men and artillery, without ships and horses the infidel will rule over Cyprus, and the Middle Sea lost little by little to Christendom. You have a troop of skilled men.'

'I had. It is under contract,' said Nicholas.

'The Holy Father himself would absolve you,' she said.

'It is fighting for the Holy Father,' said Nicholas, 'in his league against Anjou in Naples.'

She pursed her lips, which were shapely. 'You need his indulgences more than rank, estates, a pension?'

He said, 'The matter is out of my hands. The force and its captain are part of my late wife's estate.'

'Indeed,' she said. 'You said nothing of this in Venice? Your captain is Astorre, is he not?'

She was clever. 'Yes, madonna,' he said.

'A famous name. A man known for choosing his employer. If he elected to leave your late wife's business in Bruges and pay his soldiers himself, or select another patron, who could stop him?'

'No one, I suppose, provided he repaid what was owing.'

'My advisers tell me that this he has done,' said Queen Carlotta. 'So he is now paid by you?'

'No. He is independent,' Nicholas said.

'But he has a respect for you? He must. After all, you made him a rich man after Trebizond. Unless it is Venice he no longer cares for? We are told you are high in favour in Venice.' She let her tone become reflective. 'In the matter of Cyprus Venice is, of course, neutral.'

'I owe nothing to Venice,' said Nicholas. 'I may not come back to Italy. It is possible that I will stay in my home town, in Bruges. You must forgive me, my lady. I do not wish another commitment, either to a cause or a country.'

'That is because you have a pilgrimage before you,' said Carlotta. 'We, a woman, understand and forgive. But you cannot mourn for ever. You must build. Build your lady a monument. Let her monument be a throne for womanhood and Christianity both. Does she not deserve this?'

He released some high-pressure breath and said, 'Perhaps. Your magnificence will allow me to consider these things after . . . after my pilgrimage.'

'Of course. Of course. We shall be in Savoy at the court of our uncle. We shall be in Lausanne. We may even visit our cousin of France. And when our ships sail, Niccolò vander Poele will be with us. May God go with you till then.'

He left, without meeting anyone he recognised, and set off with Thomas next morning. He knew, from the thunderous silence, that Thomas rather fancied the trim little Queen, and would have enjoyed sitting in Cyprus with Astorre and the rest of the boys, sucking grapes and killing Egyptians. He knew that Thomas needed a leader, and was suffering. He thought of his last encounter with the Observant Franciscan Ludovico de Severi da Bologna at a table in the tavern at Silla, after the Queen and the prisoners had left. The monk had been drinking water, but he had not. Nicholas had said, 'Brother Ludovico. Who paid them? The mercenaries?'

The Franciscan had pointed a calloused forefinger to the ceiling. 'He knows. I don't. The leaders escaped, and the sprats are never told anything. I hear the old woman is dead?'

He had asked the question quite suddenly, and got an answer as sudden. 'What old woman?' Nicholas had said.

The monk, without shifting his eyes, had put some meat in his mouth, chewed and swallowed it. He osculated a shred from an eyetooth. He said, 'I suppose that forty's the springtime of life. But don't let us argue. You didn't inherit. You're going to check that she's dead, but you know that she is. So why are you going to Bruges, if you have a fortune in Venice?'

Nicholas said, 'Who told you that? Yes, I have a fortune in Venice. Do you want it?'

The monk had a profile like a plucked fowl, and black hair in every rut of the rest of him. He said, 'Have I said so? You are alive and presumably know what shrine to thank for it. It's a pity, of course, that Christian Trebizond fell to the Turk.'

'The Christian Emperor gave it up to the Turk,' Nicholas said. 'Ask him for silver, if you should need it. He has plenty.'

The monk paused, a chicken leg in his hand. 'You're none the poorer, I notice, for serving him.' He swirled the bone. 'As for money to support a crusade, I'm an optimist. Venice will offer me something. It's more than she'll do for the little lady you rescued this morning. The Queen of Cyprus needs your men, and your silver.'

'So she has told me. Twice,' said Nicholas.

'You met her in Venice?' said the friar.

'I met everyone in Venice,' Nicholas said. 'I had five different offers. Six, now I think of it. That's why I left. The Pope made you Patriarch, then?'

The friar smiled. It was like a rat diving into a hedge. He said, 'He nearly put me in prison. It appeared I was not meant to make use of the title so early. I reassured him. I shall enter Holy Orders the moment I travel to Venice. Why are you going to Bruges?'

'To collect my belongings. To finish my business. To see my step-daughters,' said Nicholas.

'And because,' said the monk, 'you can think of nothing more original to do? You look like a fellow who likes making money but has little idea what to use it for. But what am I talking about? Queen Carlotta has seen you. You are a youth who depends on feminine patrons. You will never escape.'

'I have escaped,' Nicholas said.

He was young. He was twenty, and a widower.

Chapter 3

MARIAN DE CHARETTY, owner of a flourishing dyeworks in Bruges and not in the springtime of life, had died between Auxonne and Dole, on her way south to Italy. To make his pilgrimage, to use a recent, sickening phrase, her former apprentice and very young husband had to cross the Alps, pass through Geneva and, in foul winter weather, find his way north to Burgundy.

He made the journey in silence, with Thomas sulking beside him. For once, Nicholas made no effort to please Thomas or anyone. He knew that illness had caused Marian's death, although imprecisely the name of her malady. It had afflicted her as she travelled, but she had succumbed within reach of friends. A sister, long dead, had married in Dijon. Marian had found refuge with a family fond of her sister, and for her sake Enguerrand and Yvonnet de Damparis had given Marian shelter and nursing, and had comforted her as her illness grew mortal.

Nicholas knew of them, and supposed they knew of him. The house when he reached it was large and turreted and supported clearly by many acres of seigneurial land. Enguerrand himself was away, but his wife's greeting to Nicholas was of extraordinary warmth, tempered by something of diffidence and something even of anxiety which he took to represent the usual response to bereavement. He was glad she thought him bereaved since, not excluding Carlotta of Cyprus, most considered his loss to be monetary. He allowed Thomas the happiness of getting drunk with the steward, and sat with the lady of Damparis while she talked about Marian.

He let her talk, although he did not, in fact, want to hear. He knew the death had been natural, from other sources. An infection acquired on the journey had occasioned a crisis: she had been overtired, and burdened with anxieties. He knew that as well. He had a letter Marian had written to him: he did not wish to have repeated, however well-meant, the things she might have said about their marriage. He doubted in fact if she had said them. What lay between them had depended on privacy, and as he kept silent about it, so would she.

He had brought a gift with him: a Persian jug he had intended for Marian's office. The jewels on it were less important than the engraving. The friend of Marian's sister was touched by it; overwhelmed even, and tears came into her eyes. He rose at that point and tried to take his leave, but she insisted he eat, and asked him questions about his future, and Marian's daughters, and how they would manage the business. She had met Tilde de Charetty, the elder, to whom the dyeworks and broker's shop had been left. 'A sharp-brained girl, but still very young. And Catherine, the other, is in your charge?'

'Financially,' Nicholas said. 'I have set up a trust for her. She lives with her sister in Bruges. There are competent people to manage the business, including Marian's priest and her notary. But I shall visit them, and make sure all is well. Please don't fear for them.'

'I don't,' said Yvonnet de Damparis. 'With you as their stepfather and friend, I am sure they will never want for anything.' She hesitated. 'You are going to Dijon?'

Marian belonged to Louvain. But Louvain was far off and it was not odd, perhaps, that she had asked to be laid to rest by her sister, in the crypt of the family into which her sister had married. Nicholas knew the place well. He had been visiting it since he was seven. He said, 'Yes, to the Fleury chapel.'

She was a kind woman, his hostess: not young, for her skin was seamed and the line of hair under her headdress was grey. She said, 'You know, M. Nicholas, that your grandfather is no longer there?'

Few people knew of his relationship to the Fleury family but, of course, she would be one of them. He said, 'I know. I had no expectation of seeing him.' He had, as he remembered, partly ruined him; but he was not sure if she had discovered that.

Later he left. Thomas, rejoining him, was at least merry within himself, which was just as well, for there was nothing else to cheer an off-duty soldier. A professional from the English–French wars, Thomas was familiar with both redundancy and bereavement, and patently believed Nicholas had mismanaged both. Nicholas, having been denied the Charetty company, had lost his nerve for everything else.

Nicholas wondered if this was true, and concluded it probably was. He had left Gregorio his lawyer in Venice to set up a bank of exchange. He had neither been helpful nor sympathetic, but Gregorio had shown no sign of minding. He had allowed his notary Julius to take himself off to Bruges. But Julius had wanted to go, and he had encouraged him. Then, of course, there was the army –

the mercenary troop that had begun as a bodyguard for the Charetty money and goods, and ended as a marketable unit.

In the short term, the army was committed. It was returning to fight in the contest for Naples, this time alongside the leader Skanderbeg and his Albanians. The action would be in south Italy, and Astorre would lead his own company. The army's doctor Tobias, on the other hand, had joined the camp of the Count of Urbino, who was fighting for the same cause in the north. It made sense. Nicholas couldn't drag them all with him. He had kept Thomas, or Astorre had foisted Thomas on him. Astorre thought he was in no condition to look after himself, and had explained, speciously, that Thomas could protect his little step-daughters at Bruges. He might be right. Tilde needed a bodyguard. After Silla, Nicholas thought that he had proved he could manage quite well by himself.

On the way from the Château Damparis Thomas sang, now and then, and Nicholas wished he had got him drunk sooner. When they reached the outskirts of Dijon and began finding their way to the priest's house at Fleury, he was disconcerted to find that Thomas, too, wanted to pay his respects to his late employer. Which he had a right to do. Thomas had been a senior Charetty mercenary while her future husband was stoking the dyevats.

So Thomas was there when the priest took his keys and led them off to the family church, and then down to the crypt. He had, however, the soldier's good sense to let the first mourner enter alone. Descending into the crypt, Nicholas carried a lamp, but nothing else: in December, there were no flowers in Dijon. He went, as was right, to his usual place. After that, it was easy to see the new coffin. The light glimmered on brass, where the wreaths – old now, and dried – lay upon the shining lines of inscription. He drew them aside with scrupulous fingers. The plate said what he had expected it to say: *1420–1461: Marian, daughter of the late Berthélémieu of Louvain, and wife of Cornelis de Charetty, 1400–1458.* It continued, as he had not expected it to continue: *and of Nicholas, son of Simon de St Pol and Sophie de Fleury.*

He sank back on his heels. After a while, he brought himself to think of all the ordinary, mundane implications of that brave proclamation of his parentage. The priest would have seen it, and the engraver, and even perhaps Thibault de Fleury. They presumably accepted it as a lie. Marian had wanted it said, and to please her they had engraved it to lie here in darkness. Even so, it was as well Simon de St Pol didn't know that Nicholas was written down anywhere as his son, even ten feet underground.

Afterwards, there were papers to sign, and the priest led the way to his house. When he heard that M. vander Poele wished to endow the chapel, the priest had smiled, deprecating but amiable.

The family had made arrangements. Then, receiving the papers from Nicholas, he had scanned them and reddened. At the finish he said, '. . . but not of course on this scale. On this all too generous scale. They will wish to –'

'I would prefer that they didn't communicate. Anything to do with the fund will find me care of my own bank in Venice. From time to time, they will visit, to see if you require anything.'

The priest brought out wine at the end of the paperwork, but Nicholas made some excuse and left without tasting it. It embarrassed Thomas, as the priest was still talking, and had offered them supper. On the road, he complained. Nicholas said, 'We learned nothing new. He only wanted to gossip.'

Thomas grunted, but as time went by, his expression became somewhat more hopeful. Nicholas could read his mind. It was December, and freezing, but at least nothing stood now between him and Bruges, and warmth, and comfort, and mates of your own ordinary kind who would speak to you.

In the event, Bruges came upon Nicholas rather suddenly. He had thought he was prepared for it. The sergeant in charge at the bridge was a burgess's son who recognised him. He said an awkward word or two about the demoiselle's death, and then asked, after a pause, if Nicholas was going to Spangnaerts Street. Or the dyeyard?

Spangnaerts Street was the address of the excellent quarters – house, warehouse and stables – where he and Marian and all their clerks lived and had their offices. The yard, elsewhere in Bruges, held their work force. Answering, he saw the other's eyes flicker. But if something was wrong, Julius would have sent word, or met him. He was aware that news of his coming would have been in Bruges for days. But the sensation, surely, was over. The demoiselle de Charetty was dead, and had left her husband nothing, as everyone knew, because he needed nothing. Why should he be here, except to comfort and help his wife's daughters?

Thomas said, 'There's something up.' Simple though Thomas might be, he had an instinct.

Nicholas said, 'Yes. Never mind. Too many people. Let's go.'

As usual, he had fortified himself against the wrong catastrophe. In the crowded streets, he saw hardly any faces he knew; was stopped for no funereal outbursts. The streets were busy, of course, as they always were, and faces turned as he and Thomas rode by, but he was not called on to act. Thus, with undiluted insistence, there fell on his ears all the sounds he had missed for a year: the clack of the looms, the rumble of barrels, the creak of signs, the echo of under-bridge voices; the splash and trickle and rush of canal water. The sounds and the smells of the great Flemish town where he had grown to manhood and marriage. Marian's town.

Spangnaerts Street was not far away, and filled as usual with draught horses and oxen, boxes and barrels, servants and merchants and the chilled and shadowy scents of fruit and spices and dyes. Outside the tall, gabled house he had bought for his wife there were clusters of people who were neither neighbours nor passers-by, but who seemed to be waiting. He saw, as the faces turned, that they were waiting for him. He stopped Thomas. 'You know the *Avignon* hostelry? Go there. Find beds for us all, and wait for me.'

Thomas frowned. 'Not here? There'll be beds.'

'If I change my mind, I'll send for you,' Nicholas said. There were spikes on the high wall that enclosed the courtyard of his house. He had put them there himself. He had never had guards standing below, as they now did. He rode slowly forward to the gate and dismounted. He said, 'Will you hold my horse?' to one of the boys, and walking to the closed gates, pulled the bell. The postern opened.

It was not Julius who stood on the threshold, or Godscalc, or any of the men he and Marian had employed or trained. The stranger said, 'Yes?'

Nicholas said, 'I am the husband of Marian de Charetty, come home from Venice. Are her daughters there, or Meester Julius, or Father Godscalc perhaps?'

'They are all away,' said the man.

'Really?' Nicholas said. 'Then perhaps I might wait for them?'

'I regret,' said the man. 'I cannot admit you.'

'I understand,' Nicholas said. 'But I do intend, of course, to come in. There is nothing difficult about it. You can either bring out someone who knows me, or I will bring you a man of good faith to identify me. Which would you like?'

'Monseigneur,' said the porter. 'I regret. I have instructions not to admit the late demoiselle's husband. The guard will tell you out there.'

'Whose instructions?' said Nicholas.

The man was unlike any porter he and Marian had employed. Of middle age, weathered and scarred, he had the look of a skilled roving soldier. He said, 'My mistress is Mathilde de Charetty.'

Tilde, of course. Tilde, Marian's daughter. 'And she is not here?' Nicholas said. 'Or is here, and afraid to deal with this personally?' He pitched his voice to carry as far as the house; and stood, ostentatiously relaxed and ostentatiously alone.

Tilde's voice said, 'The porter has told you. We prefer not to receive you.' Her voice, trembling slightly, was deeper than you would expect in a girl of under fifteen. He remembered it from Venice. She had been afraid of him then: afraid that he would push her and her sister aside and take over the business; and he had played on the fear, trying to make her stand on her own feet. If her mother's workmen remained; if he released (and he had) all the senior company men who were willing to go back to Bruges, the business could prosper.

He had thought, after two or three months, that she would feel secure enough to meet him, at least. He had not expected a public rebuff, and a bodyguard. What was Julius thinking of?

He saw her now, crossing the yard and standing, her hands tightly together, at the porter's shoulder. Her hair was a duller brown than her mother's, and she lacked her mother's bright colour. Just now, she was white. The spectators around him, grown silent, moved and murmured in anticipation. He said, 'Tilde? I have something to tell you. I have come from the chapel at Fleury.'

'Is that all?' she said. 'I was there before you. If you have something to say, write it down.'

Someone clucked reprovingly, and someone gave a comic groan and a laugh. Without privacy, exchange was impossible. He said, 'Is Meester Julius there?'

'He is,' said Tilde. 'But he has been forbidden to speak to you. Father Godscalc will not come out either. This is the Charetty business, not yours.'

'And do my clothes fit you?' said Nicholas. 'If not, I should like to have them back. And the other effects in my room, unless you have sold them.'

'They will be sent to you,' said the hard voice of Tilde. 'If they have perished, you will have an accounting. There are some gifts you made to my mother.'

'Keep them. The rest can go to the *Avignon*. I shall be there for three days. Thomas wishes to call on you.'

'Why?' said Tilde.

'To serve you and Catherine. Captain Astorre wants you to have his protection.'

'I have protection,' Tilde said. 'A new bodyguard. We have no need of Thomas. Send him back to Astorre.'

'He is not under my orders,' said Nicholas. 'I dare say he will find work of some kind in Bruges. If you want him, no doubt you can find him. Is there anything else?'

'Where are you going?' said Tilde.

'To the *Avignon*,' Nicholas said. He paused, about to remount.

She said, 'No. After that. Where are you going?'

'I don't know,' Nicholas said. 'Into business of some sort. I don't want to compete with you. But we ought to talk if we're going to avoid it.'

She said, 'You want to know all our plans.'

Nicholas said, 'Tilde, I know more about your business than you do. But I'll leave you alone if you want me to. I do want to collect some things that belong to me. If you let me in, it won't take me a moment.'

'No,' said Tilde. 'Send your mistress.'

A stir of excitement. Nicholas set his teeth. 'I would if I had one,' he said.

'Your future wife, then,' said Tilde. 'She's here to petition the Duke, but the old man's too sick to appreciate her. She's been waiting for you for days. A lady from the duchy of Savoy. She calls herself Primaflora.'

When he got to the *Avignon*, Thomas was holding public court in the wet, straw-spattered yard. One or two of the listeners around him had strolled off before Nicholas reached them. Among the others were one or two he recognised as old cronies of Astorre and his friends, and one or two he recalled as well-qualified tattlers. As he came up, Thomas greeted him, his face red. 'They said you wouldn't get in. They said Spangnaerts Street's locked, barred and guarded. The girl's told Meester Julius and Father Godscalc she'll dismiss them if they speak to you. And it's the same in the yard. Henninc and Bellobras, Cristoffels and Lippin. None of them dare do anything, or she'll call in strangers and ruin the business. She says she isn't going to make the same mistake her –'

'She's off her head, the poor thing,' said a woman. 'What are you going to do, Meester Nicholas?'

Meester Nicholas. The under-manager of the Medici Bank had called him that too, just now. Had offered to lend him one or two men, indeed, to break his way into the building. Nicholas had replied, with restraint, that he had thought of starving them out. He had then added quickly that it seemed likely that the doors would be unbarred at some point, unless the company were to go out of business, but that he had no intention of forcing himself on his step-daughters. He repeated the gist of this now, and removed himself and Thomas politely into the inn. It was a good one, being sited behind the church of St Donatien, near the burgh square and within a discreet distance of Spangnaerts Street, which was why he had chosen it. There were therefore quite a lot of men of substance who heard Thomas say, as they ascended the stairs, 'You'll never guess who is here.'

'I've just been told,' Nicholas said. 'An envoy of Carlotta of Cyprus. Popular opinion has already made her my mistress. Where is she?'

'Out. But everyone knows she's been asking for you. What's she doing in Bruges?' Thomas said. He opened a door on an empty room.

Nicholas followed him in and closed the door firmly. 'At a guess, cajoling money for Cyprus out of Duke Philip,' he said. 'If the

Queen sent an accredited envoy, she would upset her dear relative
France. Hence Primaflora with, I should think, an excellent clerk,
a decent retinue and an inadequate chaperon.'

'The Duke's past it,' said Thomas.

'But I am not,' Nicholas said. 'And the Queen wants me as well.'

'I see,' Thomas said. He sat down, still in his boots. 'That
Primaflora, she's just lost her husband.'

He had picked Thomas to travel with because of all the qualities
he was now displaying. It was too late to regret it. Nicholas said,
'Ansaldo wasn't her husband. The lady Primaflora, Thomas, is a
professional courtesan.'

Thomas made a visible effort. 'You could afford one,' he said.

'No. I think,' Nicholas said, 'she would be too expensive.'

The message was slipped under his door late that night. He rose
quietly, lit a taper and read it without waking Thomas. Then he
pulled on pourpoint and hose and left, carrying his soft boots and
cloak to put on in the passage.

There was no one awake in the common-room, and he unbarred
the front door himself and stepped out into hoar frost and fog. It
was as well that he knew every bridge, every well, every street,
every house in this city. The night-lanterns were diminished by
fog, flat as sequins. As he walked, he saw the Mother of God, eyes
upturned, suspended over the city, the Child in her arms. Or
perhaps it was an image three inches high, lamplit on some near,
pious corner. His soles slid on the cobbles, and crunched on the
rime in between them. Once he heard other footsteps, belonging no
doubt to the watch. He thought, at one point, of crossing to the
warm unseen fire of the cranemen, but thought better of it. They
were good friends, who had helped him enough in his escapades.
He crossed the bridge by the Spinola quay, and felt his way quietly
through Spangnaerts Street.

The bodyguard were no longer there, although the lanterns had
been lit at the gates and all the way along the spiked wall, and there
was a rim of light round the porter's lodge shutters. He walked
round, and found the rope hanging over the wall between the
spikes, and the mattress laid conveniently over them. He tested the
rope, and then jumped, and gripped it, and hauled himself up, and
then over.

Julius met him by the stables: a familiar whisper; a grip on his
arm, and then a shadow sprinting before him to the kitchen door.
Then he was in and pausing, breathing lightly, while his notary –
his one-time teacher – climbed the stairs to see all was well. Then
he, too, was upstairs and along a passage and through a door to a
big, shuttered room where a lamp had been lit in one corner,
showing desks, and papers, and shelves of ledgers, and all the
paraphernalia of the business he had created for Marian. In the

room were the priest Godscalc, who had been their chaplain and firm friend in Trebizond; whose skill with numbers and letters was serving the Charetty company still. And Loppe, the Guinea slave he had made his quarter-master. And Julius, who closed the door behind him.

He walked first to Loppe, and embraced him; and then Godscalc. Two large men, nearly as tall as himself, and encouraging to have at your side in a battle. Julius, who had no taste for that sort of thing, slapped him on the shoulder and said, 'Well. We had to see you. This is all your doing, you know.' He had the sunburn of Trebizond still on his dark face. He looked active, vivid, successful. Factor, notary, manager now to the Charetty business, and making the best of it. Although, of them all, he had most longed for excitement, and might have made his life in the East, had their venture not come to an end.

'Let him sit down,' said Godscalc. 'And keep your voices low. The law is on the side of the girls. And Tilde owns this building, and has forbidden Nicholas to enter.' He turned, with the balanced weight of a fighting man, but his manner was priestly and calm, as it always was. 'You must believe we tried to prevent this. And, of course, it will pass.'

'Will it?' said Julius. 'Nicholas threw them a challenge, and they picked it up. They want to prove they can beat you. What are you going to do?'

'What are you going to do is more to the point,' Nicholas said. He saw Loppe smile.

Godscalc said, 'Don't worry. We're staying. Your wife's servant is with them. Anselm Adorne keeps discreet watch, and his wife has been a tower of strength. Tilde managed to throw out John le Grant, after a difference of opinion, but she knows she needs us.'

'Where did John go?' Nicholas said.

'To Venice. Gregorio is there, and Crackbene. They have begun to set up their bank. They are expecting you.'

'Is that a good idea?' Nicholas said. 'How do you see Tilde's business developing?'

'Along different lines,' Julius said. 'My God, we're not competing with you. No army, no courier work any longer. But broking, dealing, dyeing. Hides, perhaps. We have a good team, and a lot of capital and goodwill.'

'Gregorio could help you,' Nicholas said. 'And you'll have cheap alum for a while, and first quality dyes. But you must look out. The market is changing. And you don't have the army to bring in summer money.'

'The little lady wants to keep an army,' said Loppe. In the subdued light, Nicholas could make out little more than his eyes and his teeth. Loppe added, 'You have seen some of the men. She went to the armourer and got him to recruit them.'

'How many?' said Nicholas.

'Not enough to make more than a bodyguard,' Godscalc said. 'We have hopes of reducing them. They are a danger, you are right.'

'And Tilde and Catherine?' Nicholas said.

'Cat and dog,' Julius said.

'No,' said Godscalc. 'They squabble, but they are united in all that matters. In ambition. In mourning. In determination. In opposition to you. It has been, as you saw, a great strength.'

'I told you. It's all your own fault,' said Julius.

'They will mature,' Godscalc said. 'The town has been patient. As I have said, Anselm Adorne and his wife have been good. The girls have no real enemies.'

'Not even the good lord Simon?' said Nicholas. He caught the flash of Loppe's eyes. Julius frowned.

Godscalc said, 'I am told Simon de St Pol is safely in Portugal with his sister. His wife and father are staying in Anjou. And since we are speaking of Portugal, you know that the Duchess Isabelle has come out of retirement since the Duke's illness?'

He had heard as much. Demanding, brilliant, wealthy, Duke Philip of Burgundy was old, and his death, one of these days, would leave Flanders with a new ruler. And Isabelle of Portugal, long estranged, was his wife. 'So Portuguese merchants will be active,' said Nicholas. 'I shall keep clear of them.'

Godscalc was watching him. Godscalc said, 'I don't think you need be afraid of my lord Simon. He has finished with you, and bears no grudge, so far as I know, against Tilde and Catherine. It is his wife I should worry about.'

'Well, she is unlikely to harm me from Anjou,' Nicholas said. 'Nor is she likely to follow me, if I don't know myself where I am going.'

'After three months?' said Godscalc. 'That is time enough to plan a lifetime. Something must have lifted your heart.'

'That's true,' Nicholas said. 'What would you say if I went to join up with Astorre?'

They all stared at him. Julius said, 'Whose crazy idea was that? Thomas? Astorre himself?'

'The idiocy is wholly mine,' Nicholas said. 'Tilde doesn't want Thomas, so I suspect he will decide to rejoin Astorre. Why don't I take my money and join them?'

Godscalc thought. He rarely hurried to speak. He said, 'Hand-to-hand fighting? It is different from laying man-traps, and plotting. Or perhaps you mean to finance the company; to act as Astorre's wealthy patron?'

'Hand-to-hand fighting is more fun,' Nicholas said. He held the priest's eyes for a while and then said, 'I haven't decided. But while I'm here, there are some things I'd like to take with me.'

Loppe moved forward, his skin glossy black above the white of his shirt; his movements with a natural, erotic grace which, from experience, was so far unintentional. He said, 'I have some of them here. The small lady sleeps close to your room. She would wake if you went there.'

He opened a box already placed on a table. In it were the few clothes Nicholas had left when he departed for Trebizond, and some things he had always had, from the time he came, aged ten, to work for the Charetty. Among them was his first knife, and some of the playthings he had made with it. Made for the pleasure of Tilde, and of Catherine, and of Felix. Nicholas turned them over, and then lifted his head, and said, 'Thank you.'

Loppe smiled. Godscalc said, 'We'll see them sent to the tavern. Now what else?'

Julius said, 'He can't have anything else. The girl's in bed in the demoiselle's chamber.'

Nicholas stood. The room came into his mind, arranged as when he and Marian slept in it last. He said, 'It doesn't matter.'

Godscalc was watching him. Godscalc said, 'Time is passing. The mattress might have caught someone's eye. It's important you shouldn't be seen, and not only for your own sake. Without us, the company would fall into ruin. Without Julius especially. They depend on him.'

'I only thought,' Nicholas said, 'that I would like to see her office. I have nothing, you see.'

Julius was silent. Godscalc looked at Loppe. Godscalc said, 'Then I think you should go there.'

He did so, alone, after taking his leave of all three. It was better if they hid the box and extinguished the lamp and dispersed, leaving him to make his way out alone. The future of the Charetty company depended on them, not on him. There had not been much more to say. They had wished to apologise, and to explain, and to establish a channel of communication and of goodwill, all of which they had done. He knew that Loppe was waiting to be asked to come with him; but he would not invite him.

Of all the rooms in the house the office was, for him, the one Marian lived in: so close in style to the one he had known from his earliest days, when he had come to her desk to be sentenced for some escapade, or to be catechised, or, rarely, to be promised some treat. Only Marian had ever sat behind the desk in the office although, latterly, he had spread his papers on the opposite side and crouched to consider them, feet on the stool bar, knees under the chin, pen-hand dangling, while she argued and contradicted. All their relationship, all their real relationship, had been created and shaped in this office.

When he opened the door, he was reminded for a moment of the statue he had seen in the street. Fog, crimsoned by the low fire, lay like a cloud in the room and stirred as he entered. He shut the door and, crossing, fastened the half-open window and closed the shutter over it. When he turned, he saw that of course Marian's chair was empty, and his own stool replaced by a better one. By Julius, he supposed. There was a ledger laid on the table, bound in the Charetty blue. Not his colour now. He was colourless. He was a self-pitying ass. He looked around.

Everything in this room was Marian's. The high settle, copied from one lost in the fire. The chest, well-locked, in which she stored her money. The cabinet where she kept the strong wine Henninc didn't know she possessed. By the rate card were her scales. The merchant's scales, with which Vikings used to be buried. Marian had not taken hers on her journey. Instead, she had taken something of his: a silver music box, they had told him in Burgundy. It was in her hands now.

He wondered what, if she were here, she would have wanted him to have. The porcelain vase, perhaps, from her bedchamber. In season, she had filled it with roses. A cushion. A ring from her finger. But Tilde would have those; and her keys. The insignia of her profession; the essence of Marian de Charetty.

The fog suddenly stirred. He must be going. In any case, he knew what he wanted. He crossed to the desk and picked it up, and saw as he did so that the keys were lying there too. He lifted them.

Yellow light flared, from a half-open door. '*And we have you!*' someone said. A man's figure stood in the door, club upraised. Behind him, others pushed to get in. He could hear loud voices, and screaming. Someone had seen the mattress. Someone had warned Tilde. Silently, they had waited to trap him. Nicholas threw down the keys and sprang to the window. He took the first blow as he unlatched the shutter. Before he could open the window, a hand seized his arm and a stick glanced off the side of his head. He ducked, using his fists, taking blows, thinking fast.

He had no weapons, but he knew where the furniture was. He thrust one man against the hard settle, kicked the legs of another from beneath him and closed with the third, dragging him with him out into the passage. From one end, he saw another two of Tilde's bodyguards rushing towards him. He turned to the other, which led to the kitchens.

It was blocked too, but with faces he knew. Bedmakers and laundrymaids; a pair of youths from the stables; Marian's cook. Someone hissed 'Claes!' and the knot of people admitted him, and closed behind him: he could hear indignant shouts as Tilde's men tried to follow. Shouts with pain in them. He remembered the clout Marian's cook could deliver. He vaulted downstairs to the kitchen and fled to the door. It was open. It opened wider just as he got to it. Outside was Tilde, a cloak over her nightgown. And beside her was the town guard, with their swords drawn.

Chapter 4

H E SPENT THE night in prison, his bruises stiffening in the cold. It was nothing new. He had not been the most docile youngster in Bruges, and had landed up in the Steen several times, with someone's stripes on his back. What was new was the attitude of reserve among his fellow-inmates. He was no longer Cĺaes, but a rich man called Nicholas who seemed to be interfering in the lives of his step-daughters. Once, he would have worked hard at setting this right, but now it seemed easier to retire into sleep.

Before that, Thomas had appeared, gibbering, and Nicholas had calmed him, and sent him off with a message to Godscalc. *Do nothing. There is nothing to worry about. Whatever happens, Tilde must feel she can depend on you all.* But of course, they knew that already, or they would have prevented his arrest on the spot.

He did spend some time puzzling out why the town had taken Tilde seriously. They might have resented his marriage to Marian, but there had never been any doubt of his honesty. And the most bigoted would allow that a man might expect to visit his house at least once before he left it for ever. Moreover, it was no secret that he now had a great deal of money, and the emotion of jealousy had never prevented a Bruges man from scenting a profit. They ought to have welcomed him. Instead, they had made sure that he would leave.

But of course, there were quite a few people, when you thought of it, who didn't want Nicholas settled in Bruges. The friends of my lord Simon and his wife Katelina. The friends of Carlotta of Cyprus. The Genoese, who thought of him as a Venetian rival. The officials, dependants and family of Duke Philip of Flanders and Burgundy, who also knew that his funds were in Venice. The Duke was a friend of Milan, and Milan had grave suspicions of Venice. Himself, he didn't blame them. He was taken out in the morning, his hands tied, to appear before the nearest magistrate.

The magistrate, of course, was Anselm Adorne, and the place of
his hearing was Adorne's beautiful house by the Jerusalemkirk.

He had been judged by Adorne before, always fairly. Born of
Genoese stock, the family had through the generations filled the
highest offices in Bruges, and were known for their wealth and
their piety. Anselm Adorne had been a child when his father and
uncle had built the Jerusalemkirk, in celebration of their return
from the Holy Land. He was now thirty-seven and a man of great
comeliness, with a slender build which could yet carry off prizes at
shooting and jousting; a clear brain which increased his wealth and
brought him the confidence of the city, and an easy manner which
made him both a good drinking companion and the happily married
father of an increasing number of small children. He and Margriet
his wife had been among the few who had sustained Marian de
Charetty in her wish to marry her junior apprentice: the wedding
had been held here, in the Jerusalemkirk. And since, as he had
heard, they had supported Tilde and Catherine, Marian's daughters.

Of course, Anselm Adorne was still, in his heart, Genoese. It
was unlikely, from what Nicholas knew of him, that he had
connived at yesterday's experience, or would take seriously the
accusations against him. But whether he did so or not hardly
mattered. Before him lay a meeting with the persons who had
known Marian best.

He came carefully, therefore to Adorne's door, his guards behind,
and did not speak when he saw that Adorne himself was awaiting
him. Adorne looked past him and said, 'I have guards of my own.
You have no need to enter. Come back in half an hour when I have
judged the case.'

In his cabinet, which was empty, Anselm lifted a knife from his
desk and cut his bonds. 'Sit by the fire. Why not come to me in the
first place? I would have taken you to the house.'

Nicholas sat, one hand nesting the other. 'Then I wish I had,' he
said. 'Or perhaps better not. Tilde still trusts you.'

'Sometimes she listens,' Adorne said. 'You made her a gift of a
very good team, and she respects them. Only in some things she is
stubborn.' He paused. 'I find it difficult to speak of her mother. If
it was hard for Marian, it was even harder for you. To be away
when she was in need: to hear the news of her death in such a way.
To come back to Bruges and find this. I can only say that, had she
known, she would have altered nothing. Her marriage brought her
great happiness.'

'Thank you,' Nicholas said. 'I have been to Fleury. I met the
lady of Damparis who sheltered her.'

'So did Tilde and Gregorio,' Adorne said. 'She was well cared
for. Margriet has spoken to Tilde, and will tell you more.'

He didn't want to hear more. 'Tilde thought I would steal from her,' Nicholas said. 'It seems odd.'

'Does it?' said Adorne. 'Then it will seem even odder when I tell you that she is afraid for her life. All the world knows that if Tilde dies unmarried, you inherit. Behind all this agitation, of course, is something quite simple.'

'I'm glad,' Nicholas said.

'It has been shocking, I know. Especially considering the sad pilgrimage you have made. But what Tilde fears is your influence. You must know that. She was your shadow for years.'

'So whom is she going to marry?' Nicholas said.

'No one,' said Anselm Adorne. 'It is you who must marry. Then she will cease to feel threatened.'

'It doesn't seem very simple to me,' Nicholas said. 'And, by the way, I have nothing to do with a lady called Primaflora. She is by way of a bribe.'

Adorne smiled. 'We wondered,' he said. 'We had been told she was going to Brussels, but it's unlikely Duke Philip will see her. Meanwhile she is sweetening the daily existence of the Duke's Bruges Controller, and conferring frequently with the Knights of St John at the Hospital. Your friend John de Kinloch is enchanted.'

'I shall make no effort to frequent the Hospital,' Nicholas said.

'So what will you do?' said Adorne. 'I imagine the possibilities are infinite. You know your good Gregorio has set up your Bank. You have a new home in Venice, and better connections than most with the merchant centres of Europe. You have the friendship of the Medici and Milan. You have been honoured by Venice. You know all the secrets of trade from the days of your army, your couriers. You have a grasp of Levantine affairs, and a galley and a round ship with which to exploit them. You have learned in Bruges and in Trebizond how to run a business, and some of the tricks of exchange banking. What you don't know, Gregorio and others will teach you. And, of course, men will seek to employ you. You appear to have had offers already?'

And that was true. They had begun in Venice, the day after he landed from Trebizond. Queen Carlotta's had been one of the earliest. He said, 'Oh, there is no lack of choice. Rhodes or Venice, Cyprus or Albania. I could establish an agency for almost anyone in the Levant. Even the Franciscan Observatines have hopes of me. I sometimes think of rejoining my mercenaries.'

Adorne had a quality, which he shared with Father Godscalc, of sitting still when weighing news of importance. He said, 'I see. The Naples war again?'

Nicholas said, 'Yes. Astorre fought for King Ferrante before, along with the Papal forces and the Count of Urbino. This time, they'll have Skanderbeg's Albanians to help them when the season begins.'

'And you are personally interested in helping Ferrante to become undisputed monarch of Naples?' Adorne said.

Nicholas smiled. 'I could make out a case. The sooner he is, the sooner the Pope and everyone else can concentrate on other things. I don't particularly want to see John of Anjou and his French friends in Naples instead. Perhaps, like Astorre, I've begun to think of Duke John and his mercenary captain as a convenient enemy. Astorre likes fighting Piccinino.'

'I think I knew all that about Captain Astorre,' Adorne said. 'I must confess I hadn't expected the glamour of battle to enchant your mercantile soul. That is for the boy you once were. But, of course, it's not the glamour.'

'It is a simple bolt from my responsibilities,' Nicholas said. 'I thought it as well to warn you. If I do go, I shall leave my affairs in good order. Catherine is taken care of. I know I can rely on your good offices.'

'Of course. I take it you have not mentioned this,' said Adorne, 'in the hope of being dissuaded, so I shall save myself the effort of trying. I shan't pretend I am not disappointed. But it is a failure of fate, and not yours. Tell me, where is Tobias, your doctor?'

'He went to war, with Urbino,' Nicholas said. He and Tobie had quarrelled. He and Tobie had had an unforgettable quarrel.

Adorne appeared to know nothing of it. He said, 'Then Master Tobias, at least, should be pleased. He advised, I hear, against your returning to Bruges. He thought you might be tempted to retreat to the peace of the dyevats.'

Nicholas was well aware of that fact. 'I might, if I could get at them,' he said.

Anselm Adorne looked at him thoughtfully. 'There may come a time when it is possible. It is certainly barred to you now. We have wandered, I suppose, from the reason for your being here. Before we go any further, let us dispose of it. You don't wish to say that your former colleagues invited you into the building at Spangnaerts Street?'

'They didn't.'

'No. The mattress and the rope were put there by an unknown confederate. You entered the house, unwilling to disturb the girls further, because you had learned you must leave Bruges immediately, and wished some memento of their mother.'

'I was found with her keys in my hand. An odd memento,' said Nicholas.

Adorne rested an elegant hand against his cheekbone. 'You were moved to touch something of hers. Had you wanted to steal, you would have gone straight to the chest when you entered. In any case, the chest, even if full, probably contained only a fraction of what is owed you by the Charetty company for the last consignment of alum alone. Is that not so?'

'I suppose so,' Nicholas said.

'And further, although you were stripped, you were found to be carrying nothing that did not belong to you. Except, of course, this.' From a drawer, Adorne drew out a folded rectangle of cardboard and set it upright on the table before him. It was filled with columns of writing in Marian's meticulous hand. Beside each price was a tuft of fine wool, dyed in good, solid Charetty colours; dense and fadeless and reliable. 'Put it away,' Adorne said. 'There is clearly no charge to answer.'

It lay on the desk, creased now and blemished by other men's handling. Nicholas said, 'Thank you.' He did not immediately take it. Instead he said, 'Before I go, I wished to ask you something. In view of your kindness to me, and to Marian's family, I find it difficult.'

Anselm Adorne settled back, with tranquillity, in his chair. 'It has to do with business?' he said. 'Your interests are now Venetian and mine Genoese. On occasion, we shall be rivals, but honourable rivals, I hope. I don't see that our friendship should suffer.'

Nicholas said, 'I hope it won't. That's why I thought we should speak of it. You know that a Genoese tried to seize control of the Charetty company in Trebizond. You know how he chose to do it. The Doria family, which was his, are your friends, but I know you had nothing to do with it. I wanted to show, simply, that misunderstandings might occur. There is another matter.'

'The alum project,' said Adorne. His face was calm.

'Yes. An Adorno cousin of yours signed an agreement with me about alum. The monopoly that provided my profit is over, since a new mine has opened at Tolfa. It isn't a tragedy; but the new mine wasn't discovered by chance. You and I and the Venetians knew it existed, and had a pact to conceal it. Someone broke the pact. And when they came upon Tolfa, they brought in Genoese experts to sample the alum.'

Anselm Adorne placed the tips of his fingers together. He said, 'Yes. We should have this discussion. On the matter of Trebizond, I am glad you absolve me. My son Jan has a Doria for godfather, but I never knew the consul at Trebizond, and if I had known you were in danger from him, I should have told you. The alum is different.'

'Is it?' said Nicholas.

Adorne smiled. He said, 'Don't misunderstand me. Pacts should never be broken. I have to say I don't know who did so in this instance. Certainly, my kinsmen and I knew there was an unquarried mine, but only you and the Venetians knew its location. You might say that we, too, were profiting from the monopoly, although the Venetians were the chief beneficiaries. On the other hand, the Turks have overrun the old sources, and if war breaks out, will stop using Venice as agent. It would suit Venice then to have Tolfa discovered and perhaps have a stake in its management.'

'You could say the same of Genoa,' Nicholas said. 'Are you saying what I think you are saying? Pacts will not be broken by you, but erring kinsmen can count on your silence, unless they propose actually to kill me?'

'I fear,' said Anselm Adorne, 'that I am saying just that. Is it so terrible? You wouldn't expect me to denounce my friends and family any more than, I suppose, you would do. You must hope, however, that I continue to carry out my intention of never knowingly harming my friends. I expect to have your limited confidence.'

Nicholas thought. He could take it no further. It had been worth attempting. Whatever they both did in business, it oughtn't to touch Tilde and Catherine. 'You have my limited confidence,' he said, his face solemn.

'Good. Then I shall tell your brave escort they can go. Will your trust go so far as to eat with us?'

'When,' said Nicholas, 'did you know an ex-convict ever refuse a good meal?'

He watched Adorne leave, and was only aware that someone else had entered the room when a child touched his sleeve. He turned. A small girl stared at his face. 'I know you,' she said.

'And I know you,' said Nicholas. 'Your name is Lewijse, and you want to see a guessing-puzzle in cotton.'

The child's cheeks reddened and bulged. 'It is!' she said. 'It's Claes! The one that does jokes!'

Three other children pushed in, and he surveyed them all. 'Well, now,' he said. 'What first? A joke or a puzzle?'

They wanted a puzzle, but he didn't have thread.

He had wool. He lifted the crumpled rate card and, one by one, drew from their slots the soft yarns, dyed with the grains of the Orient. Then, pleating, twining and knotting, he fashioned a cord fit for Joseph. To celebrate, he tossed it into the air and made it snake and whirl like the Persian toy he had once sent home from Florence. Then he dropped it looping over his fingers and made it perform, while four intent pairs of eyes followed his movements.

He did not see Margriet Adorne come to seek him and stop, quietly drawn to one side by her husband. But he heard, when it came, the summons to dinner.

Instead of waiting three days, Adorne had hinted, he ought to leave Bruges immediately. It gave him no time to tidy the final, frayed

ends of his business life with the Charetty – but Julius, he supposed,
would be willing to act as his agent in that. Tommaso Portinari
would be annoyed, but then he had no sense of humour, or
he would hardly have offered to help Nicholas batter his way into
Spangnaerts Street. There were people he liked and hadn't seen,
like Colard Mansion the painter. Some he had caught sight of in
passing, riding last night to the inn. A good many had avoided his
eye, although he was then in a state of bereavement, not one of
disgrace. The more senior inclined their heads but didn't add to
his embarrassment – or maybe their own – by coming forward. But
some had slapped his knee and said, 'Bad luck. Come and visit us.'
John Bonkle was one of those, and Jehan Metteneye, the innkeeper,
who had cause to remember him. They probably meant it, and
would still mean it today, when all Bruges knew what had
happened.

But there wasn't time to stay, for several reasons. There wasn't
time, for one reason in particular. He said to Thomas, returned to
the yard of the inn, 'All right. I'm free. I've got a pardon. We're
leaving.'

'You can't,' Thomas said. 'The Duke's Controller is here. Pierre
Bladelin. He wants to apologise, and place an important traveller in
your care. It's the lady. It's the lady –'

Nicholas turned his horse in the opposite direction. 'Primaflora.
Tell them I've gone. Pack and meet me in Ghent.'

'You won't get out the gates,' Thomas called. 'She says the
Queen . . .'

He didn't listen. Let Thomas make what excuses he could. If he
couldn't get out, then he'd go to earth. In the end, he got rid of the
horse and doubled back to St Donatien's, where he knocked up
Colard, and he and the painter got drunk together amid the inks
and vellum and reeking tallow. He had, of course, been sober for a
very long time. It occurred to him that he hadn't managed to get
drunk, even when he wanted to, since the news of Marian's death.
Perhaps the present blessing was due to Colard's personality,
which was violently self-centred, and the fact that he was not
directly part of Marian's world. Although it was through Colard
that he had engaged the priest Godscalc. He thought he owed quite
a lot to Colard for that.

December darkness fell early, and brought a vague inclination
for food. With money from Nicholas, Colard sent a boy for a joint
and more ale – and, an afterthought, for some news from the
hostelry *Avignon*. Waiting, Colard said, 'You heard the old Duke
had a stroke? Son Charles rushed to his bedside, and the Duchess,
to boot. After all those years in a nunnery. She's been in Bruges.
Surrounded by Portuguese. Vasquez included.'

João Vasquez was the Duchess's secretary. The lord Simon,

whose name lay ten feet underground in a chapel at Fleury, had a
sister married to one of the Vasquez. Nicholas said, 'Don't try it. I
know that Simon's in Portugal.'

Colard's pouched eyes disappeared in a scowl. 'He might come
back to Bruges. Or Katelina.'

'And his wife's in Anjou. I don't want to know, Colard. I've
done with them.'

'Have they done with you? Not that Katelina. Once women get
an idea into their heads,' Colard said, 'then it's goodbye to logic.
You're thin.'

Nicholas rolled over and snatched unsuccessfully at a sketch-
pad. 'You bastard. I charge for modelling time.'

'Your face has got thinner. I could get Mabelie for you.'

'And that would make my face fatter?'

'Or Mabelie. Here's the boy,' Colard said. The room was no
more than an attic, built over the cloisters. The wood of the steps
creaked, and then creaked again. 'He's got someone with him.
There won't be enough ale.'

The door opened. 'I have brought my own,' said Primaflora of
Savoy. 'If I am welcome? By one of you, at least.'

'Christ Jesus!' said Colard Mansion.

Last seen in the snow south of Bologna, the lady who entered the
room was no longer distressed or dishevelled. She thrust back her
hood. Her hair, yellow as buttercups, fell in tendrils over her
cheeks and, rippling back from her temples, was caught in a fall of
intricate and tight-pleated loops, all threaded with ribbons. She
wore no jewels, and her dress of fine wool was high-waisted and
plain above pattens. Below her short upper lip, the curve of her
mouth made you think of soft fruit, come to ripeness. Her skin
glowed. It was impossible, in the same room, to feel nothing.

The boy, following her, laid down a basket and was given money,
for which he returned an admiring smile as he left. Nicholas rose
shakily, walked to the door, shut it and turned. Her eyes had
remained on him all this time, pale of iris and lapidary in outline. She
said, 'If you wish to leave, your friend and I will share the basket.'

Nicholas indicated his friend. 'Colard Mansion.'

Colard rose from the floor; a fairly minimal operation. 'A Venus.
I see why he fears you. Come in. I will paint you.'

'Colard Mansion, a scribe, an illuminator, a translator, a drunk.
Myself, the last only. I have only one word to say,' Nicholas said.
'I am not going to Cyprus.'

'Those are six words,' she said. 'Your floor is dirty.'

'There is a clean cushion,' said Colard. 'Nearer the light. There.
You did mention ale?'

'Ale and partridge, bread and chicken and cheese. Why is this
man called Niccolò afraid of me?'

Colard looked up, his arms in the basket. 'Don't you know him?'

Nicholas sat on the floor. 'Don't be stupid. We met for two minutes during a fight near Bologna. Carlotta of Cyprus wants me to take Astorre and some money and help her.'

'Why not? You would get away from Katelina,' said Colard. He carried the ale back to his mattress, leaving the food where it was.

The woman, kneeling, began efficiently to unpack and serve it. She said, 'Who is Katelina?'

Colard drank. Nicholas, finding chicken before him, picked up a leg. 'A woman in Anjou,' he said.

Colard wiped his mouth. 'He don't answer questions,' he said. 'But I do.'

She sat down on her cushion. She sat like Loppe, with a natural grace which, in her case, had been carefully fostered. What he had told Thomas was true. She was – in whatever guise she appeared now – a courtesan by profession. He assumed Colard knew it. He didn't know what Colard was up to, and was happy not to care. She said, 'All artists love truth. So tell me. What is Niccolò?'

'From what angle?' said Colard. 'That, for instance.' The lamp shone on the sketch-pad. 'That is the Nicholas that you see. Nicholas lost, with no mistress.' He glanced over, his face full of evil delight. 'Or that.' Another paper, pulled from a shelf. The light, shining through it, showed a drawing made long before, in this room, on another cold day in winter. Himself, with Felix, Bonkle and Anselm Sersanders. Made the year Felix died.

'Who is that?' said the woman.

'Claes,' said Colard. 'The bastard dyeworks apprentice who became servant to his employer's son Felix. Protector and servant. He went to Louvain University with him, and learned more than Felix, didn't you, Nicholas? He served under Julius, and even Julius noticed that he had a flair for numbers. Then his employer noticed that he had a flair for several things.'

'That's enough, Colard,' said Nicholas.

Colard did not even turn. 'I hear you,' he said. 'So. At nineteen, Nicholas married the widow and took her best men to set up an outpost at Trebizond. At twenty, he fought the Turks and withdrew from the Black Sea with two shiploads of refugees, treasure and alum. At twenty-one, what is he now? A happy drunk on the floor of Colard Mansion.'

She was drinking ale, pensively, from a cup she had wiped clean with her kerchief. 'And who is Katelina?' she said.

Colard glanced over again, and their eyes met. He turned back to the girl. 'I do not think,' Colard said, 'that I had better tell you. You *want* Nicholas? He has a bad left profile and those are the Devil's fingermarks in his cheeks.'

Nicholas let himself down on the floor and gazed up at the

warped and charred rafters. If he closed his eyes, they might all go away.

'No,' she said. 'I don't want him. But I have no money. And the Queen is my mistress.'

The astonished silence reached even under his eyelids. Colard said, 'I could name five nobles in Bruges who would lease twenty years of you.' Nicholas smiled.

The girl's voice, when she spoke, had the same smile within it. 'You speak your mind.'

'I know a professional when I see one,' said Colard. 'So what can the Queen do?'

'Have me killed,' said the girl. Nicholas opened his eyes.

Colard said, 'You won't lure him to Cyprus that way.'

'I don't want to lure him any way,' said the beauty called Primaflora. 'I don't want him. I don't want to go back to Cyprus. I want to get away from the Queen. I thought he might help me.'

'You've made him sit up,' Colard said. 'I didn't think he was sober enough.'

Nicholas said, 'Say that again.'

Her pale eyes met his without flinching. 'You know my instructions. To join you, and bring you to Cyprus. I need help to escape her. All the knights of St John are her spies. I want to disappear. Maybe to Italy. I would find patrons there.'

There was a silence. Nicholas said, 'How long were you with Ansaldo?'

Her face, he guessed, could not afford a change of expression. 'A year.'

'I had less,' Nicholas said. 'The Queen's plan is no more of interest to me than it can be to you. I have some money. Take it and disappear.'

'I have to leave with you,' she said.

'Then leave,' Nicholas said. 'The only possible drawback is that I haven't decided yet where I am going.'

'Yes, you have,' Colard said. 'To Italy. To the Naples campaign. To join your army and slaughter Duke John of Calabria. You can't take a courtesan there.'

'You heard him,' Nicholas said.

Primaflora smiled. Instead of dimples, she had pleats that curled round her mouth. She said, 'What kind of courtesan should I be if I hadn't found a rich sponsor long before he catches up with his army?'

'You'd go with him? You're going to take her? I must be drunk,' Colard said. 'I never heard such stupid decisions.'

'No. You never heard them,' said Primaflora, rising. 'But when you wake up in the morning, you will see the basket and account for it somehow. Messer Niccolò, when do you leave?'

'Tomorrow, by the Ghent gate, at daybreak,' Nicholas said. 'I think Colard is right. I think I shall go back to Italy and look for my army. I enjoyed –' He broke off.

She stood, holding her cloak, and looked down on him. She said, 'Thank you, at least, for remembering. I shall not encumber you for long.' The door closed.

Colard said, 'Are you asleep?'

Nicholas grunted.

Colard said, 'She's lost one man. You'll be the next caretaker, unless you are careful. I wouldn't object, but I know you. If you don't want her, turn her off in a week or two.'

'I'm asleep,' Nicholas said.

Chapter 5

SINCE HE HAD promised to do so, Nicholas left Bruges by the Ghent gate in due course, accompanied by the late Ansaldo's mistress and her servant, and protected by an adequate squad of free soldiers, picked and captained by Thomas. His mood, for various reasons, was subdued, and the girl made no effort to force herself on his attention. At dusk he chose a tavern and acquired suitable lodging for himself and the lady in ostentatiously separate chambers. He arranged for food, excused himself, and retired. As soon as his charges were sleeping, he rose, packed and left.

The following morning, the lady Primaflora was brought a letter which she read, standing very still, before dressing and summoning Thomas.

Thomas had received a missive as well. It contained a draft for a great deal of money and a letter from Master Nicholas, which he perused with the help of a finger. The letter instructed him to take the lady Primaflora and her servant safely and secretly to any destination she might select with the funds now provided. This done, Thomas was free to do as he chose. But since he was not needed in Bruges, Nicholas thought that he might wish to follow his trade, and rejoin Captain Astorre in the Abruzzi. In return, Master Nicholas could promise that Captain Astorre would be markedly liberal.

About the plans of Master Nicholas himself, there was nothing. Nor could he ask, since Master Nicholas had, of course, vanished.

Facing the lady Primaflora, Thomas saw that she was not going to scream, or cry, or otherwise embarrass him. She said, 'So he has gone. Where, do you think? Perhaps to Cyprus, after all?'

'I don't know,' said Thomas. He was counting, in his head, the money Nicholas had left him, and thinking, with slow happiness, about the Abruzzi and Astorre.

'If so,' the woman said, 'it seems a pity that he has not asked you to share his good luck there. On an island paradise, a man can live like a lord. There would be work for you in Cyprus.'

'No. I'm going to Italy,' Thomas said. 'There's a fellow called Piccinino who needs a good lesson. Astorre and me, we've fought him before. He's in the pay of Duke John of Calabria. That's King René's son.'

'I can see,' said the woman, 'that war in Italy is what you really prefer. And since that's so, I won't take you out of your way if you're going there. I only want to find somewhere to stay, where I have friends, and where the Queen can't reproach me for not bringing her your master Niccolò.'

Thomas said, 'You've got it wrong. He's not my master. He's just paid me to get you home safely. So where will it be?'

'Where? I don't know,' said the late Ansaldo's mistress. 'Not, of course, France or Savoy. Suppose you choose the route you prefer into Italy, and I shall find some secure place for myself on the journey.' She smiled again. 'Was Messer Niccolò with you when you fought against Jacopo Piccinino? I should like to have seen him.'

'You wouldn't,' Thomas said. 'It was a disaster. His first fight and all.'

'But he has learned? He fought at Silla,' the woman said.

He supposed she was hoping her next man wouldn't die like the last one, but told her the truth, anyway. 'Fight?' Thomas said. 'You want to ask what happened at Trebizond. He learned, all right. A blood bath. A blood bath. Sheer ingenuity.'

Her eyes, grey as water, looked unseeing straight at him. 'How terrible,' said Primaflora.

Nicholas, having got clean away, celebrated by taking a decision. By a route long and circuitous, he would convey himself southwards for the rest of the winter, stopping where he had never been. Cologne, for example. He had introductions to three people from Colard, and Godscalc's name would produce more. He thought he might find something of interest in Basle. If he put off enough time, the spring campaigns would get under way and, one way or another, he would find where his friends were. The main army that had once been his wife's had wintered, presumably, on the Adriatic. It was that part of the east coast called the Abruzzi that had seen much of the fighting to do with the challenge to Naples. It was there, or south of there that Astorre and his men would make for, he thought.

And Tobie? Tobias Beventini of Grado was a short-tempered physician who had preserved his life at least once, and who had expected Nicholas to buckle down to business after the death of his wife. After a stand-up quarrel in Venice, Tobie had taken himself

off to the Count of Urbino, who frequently led the Pope's armies
in the war to protect Naples from Anjou. Nicholas considered
making towards Urbino to see what news he could find. It was on
his way to the Abruzzi, and he had time and money to spare. Time
and money to lose. Time and money to throw away, since there
was nothing particular to spend them on.

Alone for the first time in his life, he let chance dictate his route.
He stayed at inns, and bought the services of a groom or a guide as
he needed them. He fell into casual talk with the people he met,
allowing the motley facts he was given to pass unexamined into his
consciousness; ignoring the slots, the niches, the network into
which he should be fitting them. If something roused his curiosity,
he pursued it without haste for its own sake and surprised himself,
sometimes, by discovering something very like a new pleasure.

The first time this happened was in Cologne, where he stayed
for six weeks. After that, he learned to foster some instinct which
told him which place, which person, which road, which new
experience was worth his attention. The journey, he began to see,
was not unlike his first taste of Louvain and its library where, with
Felix grumbling beside him, he had stepped from shelf to shelf,
looking at books or unlocking and sampling them. He was crossing
countries now, and scanning their offerings.

His anxieties grew less insistent. Sometimes he would fall into
conversation with a man and feel what he had not felt for a while,
an inclination towards understanding and friendship. Towards the
less appealing, he felt amusement, and very seldom irritation or
anger. Having dropped the frayed network of commerce he began
to see, or was reminded, that there were other worlds to be
mastered in much the same way. Observations randomly made
would arrive at a sudden coherence: from filling cells would emerge
the full honeycomb of a well-founded interest. He made room for
it all, as he had made room for his gear on his pack-mule. When
riding alone he also began, very occasionally, to sing.

He did not lack the chance of feminine comfort, but preferred to
stay free. At times, he came close to admitting that this was
unnatural. The easy love, the friendly tumbling of pretty girls had
ceased when he married, and the constraint for some reason persisted. There had been one brutal exception: the night in Venice with
Violante of Naxos. But Violante was the royal-blooded wife of a
merchant, prostituting herself for amusement. For the rest, he had
been told it was common: the impulse, after bereavement, to bury
the dead in excess. Once or twice, he thought of what Anselm
Adorne had told him. If he married, Tilde's fears would be put at
rest. He had not reached a point where Tilde's fears were of
importance. He kept out of churches.

His movements were not, of course, uncharted. His career for eighteen months had been remarkable: in the small world of merchants, a newcomer, an accumulator of bankable wealth, was perceived as an opportunity as well as a threat. Those friends of Colard and of Godscalc's who met him in Cologne were swift to convey their impressions to Bruges. The Medici couriers, cross-hatching Europe, wrote accurate dispatches, in cipher, to Italy. There were other agents, as well, who received commands and who made reports, in French of Flemish or, once, in Greek, on his journeyings. Punctually and efficiently, news of his every movement was carried to Anjou where, as it happened, Katelina van Borselen was staying.

Who is Katelina? A woman in Anjou. So, once, Nicholas had diverted a question and he had not, in fact, lied. Katelina van Borselen was, although his own age, fully a woman: she had become, if recently, both a wife and a mother. She didn't belong to Anjou, but could be found there. She came from a royally-connected dynasty in Flanders, and had divided her time since her marriage between Scotland and Portugal.

She was married to Simon de St Pol, whose loathing of Nicholas was only exceeded by her own. And she was in Anjou, much against her inclinations, with the obese and powerful father of Simon, who frequently commanded her company on his travels. Jordan de Ribérac was the King of France's adviser in financial affairs, and when he talked of business matters, she listened to him. She did not enjoy travelling with him. The alternative, however, was staying with Simon. And she was learning. If Simon's business was to prosper, she had better learn.

Katelina van Borselen had been twice now to the vast castle of Angers, fountain of all pleasures. Angers was a seat of René, King of Sicily, Count of Provence and Duke of Anjou whose son John of Calabria was in Italy, leading the new season's fighting for Naples. The court of Anjou had a magnificence about it that Burgundy, for all its wealth, could never quite match. Katelina took away impressions of paintings and tapestries, ostrich plumes and grey and white taffetas and everywhere, manuscripts. King René, a man in his fifties with a young and beautiful wife, was himself the source and arbiter of half the beauty around him, and not merely the patron.

Now, he had relinquished the struggle for Naples to John, his son by his first wife. He viewed from a distance the fortunes of his daughter Margaret, bred to battle like John, and fighting to preserve the English throne for her husband Henry against a fierce Yorkist claimant. To those who helped his children, King René opened generous doors. The Flemish Queen Mother of Scotland gave aid and shelter to Margaret. His nephew Louis of France (a race René neither liked nor admired) yet had the power to help not only Margaret but Duke John in Naples. René of Anjou was therefore willing to welcome Jordan de Ribérac and Katelina his son's comely daughter, whose provenance from that viewpoint was quite excellent. René loved handsome objects, young and old, but the love was simply that of an epicure. His Queen, half his age, was his passion.

She was with him now, in the spacious chamber he used as a workroom, and so were half the court, as well as Jordan de Ribérac and his son's wife Katelina. On the table before King René was an elaborate painting; an illustration for an allegorical romance he had just invented. His eye on his brush, the King hummed to himself occasionally, and occasionally spoke, showing that he was quite aware of his deferential audience, and not averse to teasing them. When he required observations, or broke into discourse, it was frequently Jordan's opinion he asked. He smiled kindly, now and then, at Katelina.

No one, thought Katelina, could regard the father of her husband as an object of beauty. Once, the big frame, rolled in fat, might have belonged to an athlete. Now it was simply the bolster upon which hung his silks and velvets and furs, and within which his cruel wit resided. Before kings, he sheathed it a little. It was never quite absent.

The King addressed him. 'My good lord Jordan: we see too little of your lovely kinswoman. Why not leave her with us while you attend to your business in the south? Your fleet at Marseilles must be crying out for you.'

'It is my common fate, your grace,' said the fat man Jordan de Ribérac. 'Also, as it happens, they are crying out for crew members. The Queen of Cyprus has sent her ship on to Nice, and her shipmaster is clubbing children and rivetting them into the benches.'

'So you said. It is being looked into,' said the King. He withdrew his brush and sat back, his eyes on the painting. He turned. 'But of course, when they sail, your ships will sail without you? I am not surprised. They would sink.'

'They frequently sink, whether I am on them or not,' said the vicomte de Ribérac. 'I prefer to leave adventuring to my son, Katelina's husband.'

'Then I trust he is faring better than mine,' said the King. He selected a fresh brush, and dipped it in colour. 'Your Simon has no taste for warfare? I have not heard, at any rate, that he has been persuaded to support Duke John in the war against Naples.'

Jordan de Ribérac smiled, a matter of compressing several chins. 'He has yet to master trade, monseigneur,' he remarked. 'I feel it will take a decade or two before he can successfully contemplate strategy.'

'Is that true, madame?' said the King over his shoulder. 'Defend your husband. You know no man wins praise from this cynic de Ribérac.'

In Jordan's company, Katelina was driven to feel pity, sometimes, for Simon. She treated the jibe, in any case, as a loyal wife should. 'Monseigneur, I have no need to make excuses for my lord Simon. Wherever tournaments are held, his name is recognised. He loves independence, and will follow his fortune. That is why he is in Portugal, with his married sister. Her husband needs Simon's help to market what he grows, and he has joined them in business. They have formed a new company.'

'In Portugal?' said the King.

The fat man answered before she had a chance. 'Or in its remote, safer colonies far from Flanders. Simon has a running war with a bastard of his first wife's in Flanders. He feels secure in Madeira.'

'That isn't true!' Katelina said.

René smiled. 'Pray go on. My lord Jordan?'

'About the bastard? Nicholas vander Poele, he calls himself,' said the vicomte, folding his heavy arms and contemplating the ceiling. 'An unfortunate youth with a talent for numbers. He married his employer, killed all his nearest relatives, and made a great deal of money bringing Venetians and gold back from Trebizond. It is said that the Queen of Cyprus intends to recruit him.'

Katelina sat up.

'Indeed?' said the King. 'On what grounds have you formed this expectation – Ah! The gossip from Sor de Naves' Sicilian carrick in Nice?'

'Your grace is percipient,' de Ribérac said.

'My grace has finished,' said René. He laid down his brush, wiped his hands, finger by finger, and turning, rose. So did everyone else. The widow Spinola, who cared for the royal jewels, said, 'A masterpiece, my lord king.' The man called Lomellini agreed. There were a lot of Genoese in Anjou. There were men of many nationalities. Perrot, the King's own confessor, bore a name well known among merchants in Bruges. The King employed also a Scotsman whose son was an Archer in France.

She heard King René asking about the man Roland Cressant, and the fat man replying. He was familiar with the Archer bodyguard of Louis of France. To secure the King's goods, Jordan de Ribérac was permitted on occasion to borrow their services. They were all young and stalwart and Scottish and took the place, she supposed, of his own disappointing heir. She didn't suspect him of vice. As she had reason to know, his tastes ran to women, not men. And to food and drink, she supposed. About his private life, she was glad she knew nothing.

The King's painting was exquisite, and they had returned to it. De Ribérac, straightening, exclaimed in his sonorous voice. 'Masterly. By every standard, delightful. His grace has been more generous with one wing of the angel than he has with the other.' He raised his eyes to King René, who smiled.

'I have met one man who is not a sycophant. M. le vicomte, you are right. To you, and you alone, I entrust the task of making both angelic pinions identical. Perhaps your lovely good-daughter will aid you. So I can hope for no practical help from that noble jouster, your son?'

'From Simon?' said Jordon de Ribérac. 'Whatever side he joined, it would lose. Whereas from me you will extract angelic feathers, from Simon, you could hope only for lead.'

'My lord exaggerates,' said Katelina.

'Do I?' said Jordan de Ribérac. He had bright, cold eyes, set in a face coloured and smooth as a child's. He said, 'Then perhaps you will persuade him away from his ledgers. I can offer no other hope.'

'Why, my lord Jordan!' said the King. 'Is your family sterile of warriors? What of the bastard grandson in Flanders? He at least has frightened your son.'

She wanted, this time, to shout a denial. Unshakable in his hatred, Simon was not afraid of Nicholas vander Poele. Like his father, he despised him. Jordan said, 'The youth Nicholas? Bastardy does not, fortunately, make him my grandson. If he were, I would control him. Nicholas, according to my latest information, is indeed going to Italy. Unhappily, he proposes to fight against Duke John of Calabria, not for him.'

King René appeared struck. 'Indeed,' he said. 'I thought you said he was going to Cyprus.'

'The Queen has invited him. I cannot tell if he will accept. Certainly he is on his way to take part in the Naples war first.' Jordan de Ribérac paused, and in his face Katelina thought that she saw a new mildness. He added, 'If they meet, your honoured son has my full permission to kill him.'

King René considered, the velvet drape from his hat falling gracefully upon one slender shoulder, the bows of silver and gold sparkling on the breast of his coat. He said, 'There would be a dramatic nicety about such a thing. I see that. Better still, of course, if it were to be his cuckolded father who killed him. My lady here should tempt my lord Simon from Portugal. He would listen to her. The Heart as Love's Captive. The theme of my book, my lady Katelina.'

He smiled, sweeping past her. He was, in fact, genuinely amused. René of Anjou relished these encounters with Jordan de Ribérac whose brain, of all others, he suspected to equal his own. The

vicomte came to Anjou for many reasons. This time one of them
had to do, the King suspected, with the little lady called Katelina.
It was interesting, too, that the conversation had turned so insistently on this improbable young man from Trebizond. It was clear
that the fellow incensed the dear vicomte. It was also a recognised
truth that the best way to be quit of a man was to set a woman
upon him.

Watched from every quarter, the war for Naples renewed itself,
and soon the antagonists were locked in their annual struggle. In
high summer, Nicholas rode into Urbino, and unsurprisingly found
it was empty. The Count had been south for weeks, on campaign
in the duchy of Sora. The Albanian army, with Astorre, was
further south still. Nicholas rode south. Three days later, he
approached Urbino's encampment.

Once, briefly and insignificantly, Nicholas had seen action under
the Count of Urbino. Federigo da Montefeltro was of that breed of
landed mercenaries who fought under contract for money. Then,
when each winter came, he took his fee back to Urbino to spend it
on matters truly close to his heart: on beautiful buildings, on
paintings, on manuscripts; on his people, his lands, his côterie of
poets and scholars. Nicholas could see why Tobie wished to study
this prince. He himself had, at that point, no thought of depriving
Urbino of Tobie.

The sun was still high when he picked his way down to the
Chiento valley, and making his business known, was escorted into
the encampment. A wait followed. The place, he observed, was in a
state of fevered activity. As he watched, a tent was deflated. They
were marching then; in which case Urbino might well be too
pressed to see him. He sat at ease, without especial impatience. He
was still waiting and watching when Tobie emerged from a hospital
tent.

The physician stopped. The Duke's secretary, who was walking
behind him, stopped as well, and followed his gaze. 'A dealer of
some kind, from Bruges. Do you know him? He wants to have
words with the Count.'

'Nicholas vander Poele,' Tobie said. He dragged his black cap
off his crown and then slapped it on again, as the sun struck his
bald head. 'Trebizond. The Charetty company.' He stared through
the dust at the distant figure of Nicholas, who was not looking at
him. Some tailor had cut him a light-weight doublet in dun-
coloured silk that set off his height and reduced the bulk of his
artisan's build. Or his physique had altered, as had his face. In
profile, it was firmer on its large bones, with a line or two where
there had been no room before. His skin had kept the even mid-
brown which it had acquired in the East, and which never grew

deeper. At that point, vander Poele turned his head in his direction, and the two familiar pockets appeared in his cheeks, although he neither shouted nor waved. The secretary, whose name was Paltroni, said, 'I take it the Count ought to see him?'

'I suspect so,' said Tobie. 'I suspect he might be going to get a lot of money, and maybe a useful small army. Shall I find out?'

'You do that,' said the secretary. 'I'll warn the Count.' He peered, with interest, at the distant man. 'I thought he was somewhat younger.'

'So did I,' Tobie said. He left Paltroni, and walked off to Nicholas. To vander Poele. He thought of him as vander Poele.

Nicholas said, 'You've warned him not to see me on any account. Are we still speaking to one another?'

'I'll do it in sign language if you like,' Tobie said. 'It was your company. You had a right to break it up. What do you want here?'

'To make an investment,' Nicholas said. 'I suppose the Count can do with some help.'

Tobie scowled. 'So you've had a slow look round us all, and it's Astorre you're going to amuse yourself with. Why not leave him alone? Why not go back to Venice and give Gregorio some reward for his trouble? It was Gregorio who set up the Bank for you, and got kicked in the teeth for his efforts.'

Nicholas thought, his lips in the kissing position. 'You don't think the Count of Urbino needs money and troops?'

'I'd be a fool to say that. You'll be in his tent in a trice, with your heels smoking.'

'But you don't want me to re-enrol Astorre.'

'It depends on your reasons,' said Tobie. 'Here's Paltroni to call you. I told you. You have a buyer.'

It was the Count's secretary, to call him to his tent. Nicholas half turned to the doctor. 'Shall I see you?'

Tobie opened his marble-blue eyes. 'If you stay, how shall we avoid it?'

He stood, shaken by an absent-minded volley of sneezes, and watched Nicholas go.

The interview with Urbino took place in a crowded tent, where the Count himself occupied the only stool, before a table littered with papers. The Count said, 'Ah. Niccolò the merchant. Have you come to buy or to sell?'

Nicholas looked down at the notched beak of a nose and remained thoughtful. 'To invest, my lord. I had a fancy to buy in Captain Astorre's contract, if he would let me, and develop the company to the benefit of the league against Anjou. I thought, before I went south to join him, that I might help you in passing. I have some skill with devices.'

'Trebizond,' said Federigo of Urbino. 'You're the man who got the Venetians out of Trebizond. With Astorre. And that fiend of an engineer.'

'John le Grant,' Nicholas said. 'He's in Venice. You have heard of us?'

'Well, get him out of Venice. And any other experts you have. Of course I've heard of you. I've got your doctor here, Beventini. You're not getting him back.'

'I don't imagine he wants to come back. Or John le Grant,' Nicholas said. 'I simply thought —'

'You've given up merchanting?' Urbino said. 'Or starting a new sideline in wars?'

'I simply thought,' Nicholas said, 'of turning Astorre's troops into a much larger, better-armed company with some knowledge of cannon and hand guns and some first-rate engineers. I might be able to train some of your men. Mechanics interest me.'

Urbino's single eye was positively luminous. 'And what do you want of me then?' he said.

'A little experience, before I go south. As I said, you might find a use for devices.'

'If,' Urbino said, 'you can contrive to blow up Sigismondo Malatesta at a range of thirty-five miles, you can replace me as commander. I can give you experience, but not in artillery of which I at present have none. I am about to launch an action. I am not, however, prepared to lose my best engineers to another force.'

'My lord, you are too modest,' said Nicholas. 'No one would leave you for me.'

'If I didn't believe that, I wouldn't let you stay for a day. You can stay. Don't get in the way. See my officers and get yourself a tent and provisions. We march in four hours. You needn't expect to leave until both the march and the battle are over. For all I know, you may be an enemy agent. Venice wants Malatesta to win.'

'My Bank doesn't,' said Nicholas smiling. He didn't know whether it did or not, or if he had a bank. He didn't care, he was so pleased to be here. He took his leave from the tent without even finding out where he was marching. Urbino had assumed it was immaterial.

In fact, it was back north, the way he had travelled. Tobie, whose tent was still upright, sent for him; poured him some wine in an accusing manner and then allowed him to sit, as if they were speaking to one another. Tobie said angrily, 'I suppose you know that is happening? The Pope's dearest enemy, Malatesta of Rimini, has been bribed into the war by Piccinino. He's in the north now, collecting troops with John of Calabria's money. Little condottieri from the Romagna; a large number of French-loving Genoese

bastards turfed out of their city. Rumour says they're all mustered
and about to march down to the Abruzzi.'

'And Urbino goes north to intercept them?' Nicholas said.
'You've got a better line in wine than you could ever afford in my
day.'

'I get paid more,' said Tobie. 'Malatesta is sitting outside Sinigallia, on the coast between here and Urbino. He's scared, and
pretending to negotiate. The Count's plan is to force-march north,
beginning this evening, to be within bowshot by first light on Wednesday.'

'Thirty-odd miles? The Turks could do it in half –'

'So what's the attraction?' said Tobie. 'You enjoyed fighting the
Turks, and want more of it? Or are you passing, taper in hand,
reactivating all your favourite fireworks? How is the Charetty business?'

'I thought I would buy my way into a fight,' Nicholas said. 'No
other interests. No ulterior motives. If no one else wants me, I'll
ask Piccinino.'

Tobie stared at him. Then he said, 'I almost believed you, you
bastard.'

'Never,' Nicholas said. He sat on Tobie's campaign chest and
tried not to look hungry.

Tobie swore and, getting up, sent a man for some food. He
came back and threw himself on the ground beside the box with
his cup on it. He said, 'Nothing hasty about you, at any rate.
You've taken ten months to decide this. Astorre knows, I suppose?'

'I forgot to ask him,' said Nicholas. 'What's Skanderbeg like?'

Tobie put down his cup. 'No,' he said. 'Don't get mixed up in
that.'

'In what?' said Nicholas. The food came, and he took what he
was offered, his large eyes mild.

'You know what. Albanian heroics. Father and saviour. George
Castriot, captured by Turks as a child and escaped to fight against
Turkey for his native land of Albania. The new Alexander, and
hence nicknamed Skanderbeg, since Levantines make shibboleths
of their exes. Sailed his army across the Adriatic to help the Pope
and Ferrante in the Abruzzi. You'll join him,' said Tobie grimly. 'I
know you. You'll look for a father-figure, and join him.'

There was a brief silence. Nicholas smiled. 'I have a father-
figure,' he said.

Tobie's sun-pinkened face grew ruddier. He said, 'I didn't mean
that. But since we've mentioned it, where is friend Simon?'

'In Portugal,' Nicholas said. 'And Katelina is in Anjou; unless
she has already joined John of Calabria's army. Do you think they
will guess where I'm hiding?'

Tobie was still uncomfortable. 'They know you're crazy,' he

said. 'But not so mad as to come here again. At least they won't think of looking for you in Sinigallia.'

'I thought I'd be safe in Sinigallia,' Nicholas said.

'You'd be safer there than down south,' Tobie said. 'Why go south? Your ship's in Ancona.'

Nicholas laid down his meat. Then he picked up his cup. 'Which ship?' he said.

'The round ship. The *Doria*. Crackbene got rid of the alum to a freight vessel at Porto Pisana, then got a job sailing here with some wheat. He's been refitting. You could go to Ancona after Malatesta is finished with. Or before,' Tobie said. There was a pause. He said, 'I am arranging your life again like an elderly nursemaid.'

'I oughtn't to have said that,' Nicholas said. 'But it was so true. Whereas, left to myself, I found out what I like best. The sensation of fighting.'

'The sensation of killing?' said Tobie.

Nicholas thought. 'The sensation of living through danger. Does that agree with your findings?'

'I'm not making notes on you,' Tobie said. 'I'm leaving that to the gravediggers. I have to go. We march in four hours, and I expect to be busy.'

'I assumed you would be,' said Nicholas.

Chapter 6

CONTRARY TO HIS wholly cynical expectations, Tobie saw nothing of Nicholas during the next day and a half of hard travelling. It was true that Tobie himself was much occupied: the army had been in the field for half a season, and he had some walking wounded and sick on his hands. Nicholas also had the best of excuses: his skills were those of a pioneer and a gunner, and it was among such men that he spent all his time. Occasionally the Count of Urbino would move back and take part in the intense arguments that broke out from time to time in that area of his army where the engineers were to be found. Afterwards he would ride, a frown between his uneven brows, staring at some scrawl of a diagram on a piece of paper smelling of horse.

It made Tobie suspicious. All the time he had known him, Nicholas had needed a friend. Now he had shed even Loppe. He had shed, too, the boyish camaraderie of the dyeyard, the tavern, or even the galley. Changing files; infiltrating among all the sections of Urbino's army, Nicholas kept the companionable style of his company days. But it was different: as if he had had no occasion to use it for a very long time; and as if, now, he employed it for different reasons. And not only employed it, but experimented with it.

The prohibition ended on Wednesday at dawn, when the army came within reach of Sinigallia, and crossing the lukewarm Nevola, sat down in sight of Malatesta's well-entrenched camp. Then Nicholas went and found Tobie, who was tramping back from his duties with his leather apron over his shirt. In a mask of pink dust, his small mouth was clean, as were the pads of his nostrils where he'd wiped them, and a slat on either cheek where his cap-lappets had been. He said, 'So. You've got a corn on your arse?'

'I walked some of the way,' Nicholas said. 'The rumour is that Malatesta outnumbers us by five to two, and that the town of Sinigallia has surrendered to him.'

'Then why isn't he occupying it?' Tobie said.

'Because he's getting ready to charge us, I expect,' Nicholas said. 'He's fresh and we aren't. We stand to arms, and rest by rotation.'

'Give me a girl and I'll try it,' said Tobie. 'You're really going to fight? Pull your sword out and charge, intoning *Urbino*?'

'I'm working out what to shout,' Nicholas said. '*Don't hit me, we've got a terrible doctor*? If Malatesta attacks, you'll have your sword out, none quicker. I don't think he'll attack. If he's really busy with fire-raising, slaughter, rape, adultery, incest, parricide, sacrilege, treason and heresy, he simply won't have the energy.'

'He was excommunicated last year,' Tobie said. 'Retaliated by filling a church font with ink. He's been fighting Urbino, man and boy, for twenty-three years.'

Nicholas flung down his gloves. 'I've joined an episode in the Corinthian wars. I thought this was a free-standing battle.'

'They might kill each other this time,' Tobie said, 'but I shouldn't count on it. It's all about property. And the Pope, of course, really doesn't want Malatesta marching down to join Piccinino. I wonder what Astorre's doing now. He'll wish he hadn't sent Thomas to Bruges. What happened to Thomas?'

'I wish I knew,' Nicholas said, quite as if he meant it.

They waited all day, in what shade they could find, but the enemy made no move that could be discerned. Tobie said, 'They're crazy. They should have charged as soon as we arrived.'

'They'll attack by night,' said the Count's secretary. 'We are prepared. They will regret it.'

'Five to two?' Tobie said.

Darkness fell, and no one slept. Just after midnight, the scouts came back with news. Malatesta's army had gone.

Urbino's bellow could be heard all round the camp. '*What!*'

It was true. The tents were empty. Malatesta had withdrawn his troops in the first darkness and was on his way north to the safety of the town of Fano. He had sixteen miles of country to cover. 'Then let's catch him!' roared the Count; and set his buglers to rousing the camp.

The first squadrons of cavalry were mounted and left at a speed that Nicholas thoroughly admired. He set himself to catch and keep up with them. Among the firelit uproar and glitter, he caught sight of Tobie, mounting a stocky horse with a helmet on his floss-circled head and a cuirass bulging in front of him. Then the whole army set off behind Urbino's vanguard, the foot scrambling to sort itself out as they went. They had had a day spent on watch, after a forced march at a speed better suited for winter than August. But the faces were eager. Urbino was leading, and Malatesta of Rimini was the traditional, the dishonourable, the joyfully despicable foe.

For Nicholas, it was curiously like and unlike November, when he had whooped through the snow with the Bentivoglio men after the carts which had once contained sugar. Again, he was pursuing an enemy unsuspected – or initially unlooked-for, at least. That was clear, even at night, by the circumspect pace Malatesta was setting. Believing Urbino's army exhausted, he had denied himself light and speed in his resolve not to arouse them. So, instead of a double line of bright flares, there was only moonlight to help spy out where, far ahead, he might be, over the churned fields of cabbage and wheat and beyond the ranks of bruised vines and the black mushroom shapes of the olive trees. But the moon, it soon proved, was enough. The pursuers climbed a low ridge, and looked into the darkness before them. There, in the distance, the undulating columns of Rimini twinkled like pins in a music-box. Like a dumb music-box, exercising in silence.

Urbino, too, used no flares to begin with. The bright moonlight showed him the way, and the rumble of hooves from his little company was too far off to be heard by his quarry. Soon, as his whole army moved up to follow, there could be no concealment. This, his spearhead, rode meanwhile on earth and on plants, and the scents of crushed fruit and greenery hung where they passed. The man next to Nicholas said, 'The Cesano's over there somewhere. It's only a stream, but Malatesta has got to get all his men over it. It'll slow him down.'

'What will the Count do?' Nicholas said.

'Catch them in midstream, if there's time for it. Ah. There's the order. Light the torches.'

They were still lighting them when the next order came: Blow the trumpets.

'Panic them,' said the man next to Nicholas. 'It'll be muddy, that stream. No joke for Malatesta, trying to force an army to cross and scramble up banks in the darkness.'

He spoke in jerks, riding flat out as they all were. Now, among the sloping trees and the juniper bushes they could see the dark line of the little river, and the beachhead of jostling helmets on the far bank, and the main body of enemy troops plunging over to join them. Nicholas said, 'They'll be over before we can get there. And now they can see just how few we are.'

'That's the idea, isn't it?' said his companion. 'Malatesta thinks we're a skirmishing party. Who'd expect the Count's army to be roused and marching already? So, with any luck, Malatesta doesn't ride off. He instructs his rearguard to form up and deal with us. Deal with us very thoroughly, so that no one rides back with the story. What he doesn't know is that Urbino's whole army is coming.'

'You think they're coming,' said Nicholas.

'Well, they'd better come,' said the man. 'I haven't heard an order to stop. It's my belief that the next sound you hear from that trumpet will be the order to charge.'

The trumpet sounded the charge while there were still quite a few of the enemy on the near side of the Cesano. Urbino's cavalry, yelling, rode straight at them with their swords raised, and cut them down as they leaped into the water. Malatesta's men were mostly on foot. They struck back with swords and with knives, and used their shields to parry and push. Horses slipped; others fell, slashed from below.

There came to Nicholas again the half-promise, the hint of fulfilment that had reached him in Trebizond, and again in November: the realisation that accuracy and precision could be deployed in this field as in any other. Since, if he did not kill, he would be killed, he chose his targets deftly, and dispatched them. The blows he took in return fell as weights, or vibrations: it did not even occur to him that they might matter. No man, in any case, could know whether he was drenched in water, or blood. The shouts, the clanging, the screams, the swishing of water in turmoil produced in him a sense of isolation. The most immediate sounds were his own: his breathing; the scream, with blue sparks, from his sword-edge. The spray struck his arms and sides like a harp. Then he realised there were louder sounds still, emerging from the darkness behind. The rest of the army had come.

Malatesta hadn't seen them. Half drawn up on the opposite bank was Malatesta's rearguard, clearly told off to deal with the nuisance. Behind the rearguard was Malatesta's main army, about to move off to Fano, with Malatesta himself at its head.

The moon brightened, emerging from veils, and showed to Nicholas the beaked and hideous profile of Urbino his leader before him, his sword aloft, his one eye bent on his trumpeters. The charge sounded. And with trumpets braying and every man roaring for joy, the Pope's army lunged forward through the little stream of Cesano and hurtled straight into the small, tidy squadron which had been instructed to wait and get rid of them.

The shock of the impact flung Malatesta's rearguard backwards and into the body of its own troops. Urbino's cavalry followed up. Behind the cavalry came Urbino's foot, surging out of the stream like a storm wave. The Rimini rearguard staggered, fought wildly, and broke. Urbino's force, grinding through them, came upon and engaged the central body, disordered itself by the collision. The fighting became dense, at the closest quarters, with Nicholas in the thick of it.

With the moon to go by, there was some chance of telling friend from enemy while the order of battle still held. Then the lines fractured, and it was less easy. Every man in a helm is anonymous. Only the shields, the crests, the arm bands and blazons told who they were. Nicholas fought carefully, marking and striking; using his seat in the saddle to get himself out of trouble. Well taught by

Astorre, as Astorre would be the first to agree. And by the Duke of Milan's tutors. And by the best horses in the world, from an Imperial stable. His right arm had just begun to grow heavy when he saw that the crowd round him was thinner, and that most were men of his own side. One of his engineer friends rode alongside, his sword dripping black and stuck with wads of cut hair.

'Malatesta's van has taken to flight. Orders to follow and harass, but stay within trumpet call. They'll scatter. We can't go too far.'

Nicholas slowed his horse. 'So where's Malatesta?'

'Also taken to flight, so they say. To Mondolfo, maybe, or Fano. He's got his eldest son with him.'

'The Corinthian wars,' Nicholas said. 'After all that strategy, no conclusion.'

'What do you mean, no conclusion?' said the engineer. 'Urbino won.'

In the event, the chase was short, because Malatesta's cavalry, once they put their minds to it, disappeared very fast and the foot soldiers went to earth, bounding like antelopes. The signal for Urbino's recall made itself heard when Nicholas, with the rest, was only a mile or two beyond the Cesano, and they obeyed it, if reluctantly. The towns in these parts were held by Malatesta. And towards the sea, a vague bloom told of the nearness of dawn.

The sky to the east was illumined by the time they cleared the field of their dead and their wounded, and journeyed heavily back to the camp. There, for the lucky, the camp servants waited, with food warmed and wine poured, and the pallets rolled back. The Count, unshaven, stood by his pavilion to greet and commend his victorious soldiers. They passed, and the camp began to settle to sleep. Nicholas crossed to the hospital tent.

Tobie was there, with a different pattern of dirt on his face. He straightened, looking at Nicholas across the stained ground. Nicholas said, 'Can I help?'

Tobie said, 'No. Don't drink all the wine.'

The wine was in Tobie's tent. Nicholas put his pallet there and sat for a long time, drinking in moderation as the canvas above him dried and turned taut and pink and, finally, hot and white. Tobie stopped, came in, and sat, rather suddenly, on the ground. His reddish hair looked like a shawl of wet crochet-work, and he had a ditch dug from each bloodshot eye. He said, 'If you've drunk it all, I'll open you with my gutting knife.'

Nicholas handed over a bottle. 'Many?' he said.

'For a non-battle? Nothing worth speaking of. So, you enjoyed it?'

'At the time,' Nicholas said. 'Were you hurt?'

Tobie removed his clenched lips from the orifice. 'Notches,' he said. 'The same as you, by the look of you. Did you clean them?'

'That's where the rest of the wine went,' said Nicholas. 'If you're so damned puritanical, why do you stay in this business?'

Tobie carefully straightened out both short legs, and opened his shoulders against his big box. 'So long as men like you fight, men like me have to pick up the pieces. The Count's going back to Urbino, now he's stopped Malatesta interfering. So there isn't a job for you meantime. What are you going to do?'

'Go south. That's rubbish,' said Nicholas. 'God's gift to the valiant wounded? You wanted field experience, and you've had it. The thickest student out of Pavia would have learned all he needs to by this time. You only stay on because your Skanderbeg is labelled Urbino. I don't blame you, but don't try to wave a halo at me.'

There was a silence, during which Tobie's round eyes, placed on either side of his bottle, remained trained on Nicholas. The bottle withdrew. Tobie said, 'You want me to tell you why you've resorted to fighting?'

A single dimple appeared and stayed: a sign to beware of. Nicholas said, 'If you don't dissect me, I shan't dissect you. All right. I want to meet Skanderbeg. I want to build machines. I want to . . .'

'What?' said Tobie, when the pause became noticeable.

'Make sure that Thomas got back to the Abruzzi. Why isn't Urbino marching south to help Skanderbeg and Ferrante?'

'Because the men are too tired, you fool. And also because he needs to keep some here to contain Malatesta.'

'I have a ship,' Nicholas said.

The sun burned through the cloth. The tent might have been standing alone, such was the silence now. Very far off, if one listened, a cock crew, and a horse snickered sleepily. The only voices were the muttering ones of the servants, passing quietly between canvas alleys. A man cried out somewhere. Tobie said, 'It's too late. Piccinino is marching north to confront them. The battle will be over before you can get there.'

'You weren't going to tell me. Damn you,' Nicholas said.

'You know now,' Tobie said. 'If you're collecting battlefields, don't fail to take note of this one. Astorre, seven thousand furious Albanians and darling Ferrante, claimant of Naples, against Count Jacopo Piccinino, the most successful son of the most successful condottiere in Italy. Plenty of work for the surgeons.'

'The ship might get there in time,' Nicholas said.

'Might. Given the wind. Leave it,' Tobie said. 'They'll be fighting a battle. You're in the running for worse. Simon may have lost interest, but his wife hasn't. She won't have been in Anjou for nothing. Who wouldn't John of Calabria kill to get provisions and money?'

'Money from *Katelina*?' said Nicholas.

'From Simon's father,' said Tobie. 'My God, has the hitch in your life knocked you silly? It was fat Jordan the French King's financier who gave you the scar on your face.'

Nicholas gave Simon's father some thought. Presently, by careful stages, he got to his feet and stood, neck angled under the canvas. He said, 'Well, I don't expect to meet John of Calabria in person, and I doubt very much if a paid assassin will so much as find me in the midst of pitched battle. If you like, I'll dress up in pink and pretend I'm a trumpeter. Which is Paltroni's pavilion?'

Tobie let his head drop back. 'You're going to offer?' he said. 'You're going to hire him your ship to take his army down to the Abruzzi?'

'Some of them,' Nicholas said. 'He needs the remainder against Malatesta. You'll still have some cuts and bruises to tend to.'

For some moments, neither man moved. Then Tobie said, 'I now make you free of my notes. You may be afraid of Katelina, but in your far from simple way, you are mesmerised by the results of your philandering. You would like to meet her without Simon her husband. Katelina being the mother, after all, of your son.'

Nicholas looked down at him for a long time. At length: 'Of Simon's son,' he said. 'In your far from simple way, that is all you have to remember.'

He left. Tobie, his hand resting beside the half-empty bottle remained, his eyes open, staring up at nothing at all. Then he gave a furious sigh and, rising groggily, crossed the small, uneven space to his bed.

Chapter 7

THOMAS, DESERTED in Ghent, had had a difficult winter with the exquisite courtesan Primaflora.

The trouble was, he couldn't shake the young lady off. Neither, because she was out of his class, could he enjoy himself. She wanted him to take her to Italy; she had friends there. She needed to hide from Carlotta of Cyprus, she said, till she found a new protector. As time went on, and she didn't find one, Thomas began to blame the absent Master Nicholas. If Master Nicholas had agreed to serve that little termagant of a Queen, then the lady Primaflora might well have gone with him.

She was a rotten poor traveller. A snail would have whizzed past them, the rate they made their way south; then they stayed stuck in the Tyrol because she wouldn't travel in snow. When eventually she thought the snow had shrunk enough to be safe, it was nearly spring, and he'd used half the money, and devil a friend had she found who would keep her for more than a night or two.

He got restless. He'd planned to be back with the army by spring. He picked up news, when he could, of Captain Astorre, and made sure she knew he was asking. Then, suddenly, she saw sense and got a move on, although she had no more luck in Milan, or in Florence. It was Rome and summer, finally, before he got rid of her. He didn't know who she ended up staying with, although he heard she'd been seen with a cardinal. He believed it. The Pope had been a one for the girls in his day. Thomas crossed himself, quickly, in case the thought was notched up and spoiled his next fight. He allowed himself a week of well-deserved and thorough indulgence before setting off, in high spirits, to take the long road south and east to the Adriatic, there at last to join Captain Astorre, and Skanderbeg, and the joint Neapolitan and Albanian armies.

Astorre and Skanderbeg were at Bari, where the Captain gave Thomas a good enough welcome and took him back on the strength mainly, he said, because he wanted to know how it felt to be paid to travel for weeks with a doxy. He affected to disbelieve all Thomas told him, but listened intently to what he had to say about the Queen of Cyprus, and Silla, and Bruges. He wanted to know, too, all about the chapel at Dijon. Captain Astorre had a great respect for the late demoiselle of Charetty, even after she married Master Nicholas. But for Captain Astorre, Nicholas wouldn't know how to sit on a horse. Thomas answered all the questions he was asked about Master Nicholas, but without enthusiasm.

Marching north with the rest to Orsara, Thomas was nevertheless glad to be beside the sewn eye, the belligerent beard of his old commander. After years of contract fighting for the Charetty, Captain Astorre was his own man at last and seemed to be enjoying it. He was fighting alongside Skanderbeg, the great Albanian hero. Never mind the clothes and the manners and the crowd of cousins who called themselves soldiers, the man, you had to say, was a legend.

You might not say the same of King Ferrante, whose force they were joining. The King had needed a lot of help to hold on to Naples, and keep out John of Calabria, who was the son of King René of Anjou. He still needed help. Having the Pope on his side was an asset, and the contract money was good. But Captain Astorre, like Thomas himself, was not actually waging a personal war on behalf of the Pope, or Ferrante or Skanderbeg. He just wanted a smack at Piccinino, his opposite mercenary leader, who was sitting with the combined Angevin forces just eighteen miles away, to the north-east at Lucera. And John of Calabria, it seemed, was now with them.

What lay ahead might well be the decisive battle by which Ferrante would keep or lose Naples. In public, Astorre, Ferrante and Skanderbeg were certain of victory, and hardly needed their ally, Urbino. The truth was, they had lost track of Urbino. Report claimed the Count was in the north, pursuing his feud against Malatesta. If that was so, he could never march southwards in time. Or if he did, he'd need days to recover. They had, therefore, to face Piccinino and his master without him.

Discussions of strategy didn't involve Thomas. He was with his smith at the forge when Astorre came out of the leaders' pavilion with his beard split in two with a grin. He slapped Thomas on his considerable back. 'Thomas! You said you didn't know where young Nicholas was. I know where he is.'

'Bruges?' said Thomas.

'Manfredonia,' Astorre said. 'Three days away. Two, if they hurry. Less, if they've already set out. And how's this? He's brought part of Urbino's troops with him.'

It seemed unlikely. It seemed also, in a vague way, unfair. 'They'll be too tired to fight,' said Thomas. He had spent all the money. He had got rid of the woman. Why had Master Nicholas come back into his life?

'They won't. They've just sailed in on his round ship,' said Astorre. 'Mick Crackbene brought them. That Nicholas, the cunning young devil! He'll get paid for the lease, and he'll get paid by Ferrante when he gets here. How's that for a profit? And the doctor's with him. Master Tobias. He'll get paid for him, too.'

'You're going to let him finance us,' said Thomas. 'You're going to let him take over the company?'

'I don't know,' said Astorre. 'He'll have to pay. He'll have to make a few improvements. But I have a very good rule. Never refuse money. Never refuse a man wanting to spend money, Thomas.'

If it had been money alone, Thomas wouldn't have minded. But he knew that Astorre was pleased. Astorre was delighted to have his boy back. Astorre was proud that of all the defunct branches of his defunct business, Nicholas had chosen his army to be with.

Urbino's men, foot and cavalry, arrived within hours. With them were the doctor, Tobie, and Nicholas. Nicholas had a blue hand, from which the bruises had only half faded. Tobie had a scar on his neck which disappeared down into the throat of his crumpled best shirt. Because of the heat, he had left off his gown, and his bald head was shining. He noticed Thomas and made his way over. Nicholas had been pounced upon by Astorre. 'Couldn't keep away from a good war! I knew it!'

'Is it a good war?' said Nicholas.

'I've seen worse,' said the captain. Above the beard with its random grey hairs, his lined face was rosy. 'A bit of artillery. Some handguns, and crossbow work. Plenty to play with. We're occupying that height tonight. Give Piccinino something to think about. And have you come to stay?'

Nicholas said, 'You've signed on under Ferrante and Skanderbeg?'

'For the season. For the meantime. We've only to lick this fellow, and we're just about free. If Piccinino goes, John of Calabria will have to give in.'

'Will he? He's here, then?' said Nicholas.

'He's in Lucera. They're all over there in Lucera,' Astorre said. 'What does it matter? We're going to win. You want to arrange the next contract? Can't call ourselves the Charetty company, though.'

'Nor we can,' said Tobie's voice, dipped in vinegar.

He came up. Thomas, lingering in the distance, turned suddenly and made himself scarce. Astorre gazed at the doctor. 'You've got a nice slash or two. Does you credit. Never recall you stubbing your toe in any of our battles before. So you've found out where the best army is?' He looked happy.

'I've found out where the best corpses are,' Tobie said. He was looking at Nicholas, his lip rolled, his pupils like rivets. He said, 'You got thrown out of Bruges.'

'I got thrown out of the Charetty house,' Nicholas said. 'Different matter.'

'And spent the night in the jail,' said Astorre. 'Again. I didn't believe Thomas at first, and then I thought, it's just like that little madam. And she'll fall in love with some fool, like her sister did, and send the business to ruin. You're better off here. And me. And the doctor.'

Tobie and Nicholas were still gazing at one another. Of the two, Nicholas was the calmer. Tobie said, 'You just left them to flounder?'

'The girls? They have Julius and Godscalc,' Nicholas said. 'And a good team in the yard.'

'Thomas says she's turning everyone off,' Tobie said.

'She turned off John le Grant, but I expect he invited it. Julius will see she doesn't do anything stupid. Or they'll tell me.'

'Oh?' said Tobie. 'And where will you be?'

'Here,' Nicholas said. 'You can go back to Bruges if you want to.'

'They aren't my step-daughters,' Tobie said.

'Well, thank your good fortune,' said Nicholas tartly. 'Or you might find yourself flung in jail too. Where is Thomas?'

Tobie's face relaxed just a trifle. 'Skulking,' he said. 'Over there, somewhere.'

He watched Nicholas go. Astorre said, 'He'd be embarrassed to tell you. Done down by a girlie. But at least it's shown him where his real business is.'

'Yes. And I thought it was Katelina,' Tobie said.

'Katelina? Simon's wife Katelina? No. It was some other female he'd got hold of. Or she'd got hold of him. You get the tale out of Thomas. Young Nicholas didn't tell you that either?'

'No, he didn't,' said Tobie.

'And if he had, you'd never have come to the Abruzzi,' said the old campaigner shrewdly. 'And since we've mentioned it, why did you come?'

'Because Nicholas coerces people, that's why,' said Tobie bitterly. 'I don't need to tell you? Only it's more subtle now, the way he gets people to do what he wants.'

'He wanted you with him in the Abruzzi. Well, so do I. What's wrong with that?' said the captain.

'There's nothing wrong,' Tobie said. 'Except that he didn't tell me the facts. I made up my mind knowing only half of the story.'

Astorre grunted. 'If I know him,' he said, 'what you've got is a tenth of the story, and the rest he isn't telling you, because it would make you run for your life. Well, if you're going, go. We're taking that hill tonight, and the fighting will start very soon after.'

He did not, of course, go. He rode with Astorre when the combined armies moved forward and, almost without event, took strategic position on the height called Mount Cigliano. On the way, they bypassed carefully the walls of the small town of Troia, once a Byzantine fortress; now a half-empty place where the lamps glimmered before the cathedral, where people prayed for the house of Anjou. The army which had come to destroy those same Angevins spread into position and rested, their backs to the town, staring across the twelve miles of country that lay between them and Luceria Augusta, the once-Roman town with its Duomo, castle and palace; the provincial capital which Piccinino had made his headquarters. By dawn, they knew that Piccinino had left camp with his army and was approaching. A little later, reports came of his numbers. As they thought, the Angevin troops were led by Duke John of Calabria, son of King René of Anjou.

'So,' said Tobie later, finding Nicholas near him. 'What precautions are you taking?'

'If I meet a soldier in skirts, I'll be careful. Anyway, I'm wasting my time. Piccinino's got all the heavy artillery.'

'You've time to cross over to his side,' said Tobie. 'I'm staying to enjoy the Albanians. All that cloth. And the smell. And all the time they must save by not shaving. Where are they going to fight?'

'Infantry mixed with the rest in the centre,' Nicholas said, 'and cavalry on the right wing; the Dibrians under Moses Golento, and the Macedonians under Giurize. What are you worried about? At nineteen, Skanderbeg led five thousand horse for the Sultan, and was later commander for all Lesser Asia.'

'Commanded Turks,' Tobie said. 'These are nephews and cousins. I've heard about Moses. He's been thirty years with George Castriot, barring the time he went off and fought for the opposite side. They'd cheat their grandfathers.'

'So would I, given the chance,' Nicholas said. 'Are you going to stay with us, after the fight? Stay with Astorre? Help build the company?'

'Let's have the fight first,' Tobie said. 'And there they are. Piccinino's banner. The banners of Anjou. Three lines of battle to our two. Artillery coming up to the front. Pikes, hackbutters and crossbows in the line behind that, and two rows of plain infantry to the rear of them. Boys from Naples, boys from Apulia, Genoese French . . . they should do better than us: they've a common language. They've split the cavalry too. Look at the flags. Anjou to his right, Naples to his left. Nicholas my boy, you're in the block opposite Anjou if you stay with Ferrante. Join the Albanians. That's my advice.'

'I will if you will,' said Nicholas. Together, they turned their backs on the Albanians and rode amicably over to the left of the assembling army, where the cavalry of King Ferrante was taking its stance. Astorre awaited them, his mighty crest wagging above his red, bearded face. 'Now we'll show 'em!' he said. His sewn eye was convulsed with delight. With heady determination, Ferrante's horse took their places around them, and the two lines of their foot assembled with clattering vigour.

Nicholas laughed and said, 'What do you shout when you charge?'

The wicked smile spread. 'Niccolò!' said Astorre. 'That's what I'm going to shout. Niccolò!'

Tobie opened his mouth. It stayed, wordlessly open. A blaring trumpet had sounded just behind them. In a moment, it was joined by another, and an immediate and shocking crashing of drums. A moment later, and all of it was drowned by a bellow: a moose-like roar from the ranks of the Albanians, and the combined crash of handguns fired violently into the air. The army shuddered. Astorre said, 'Attack! We aren't –'

'Go,' Nicholas said. 'Go, go. It's Skanderbeg's order. We're not ready, but neither's the enemy.'

They were on the move as he spoke. Crazily, chasing into position as it went, the army of Ferrante and Skanderbeg rolled down the slope, racing, galloping, shrieking, to crash into the totally unprepared army of Piccinino.

Nicholas, urging his horse, saw Piccinino's guns fire, grey carnations in the hot sunlight, and then saw them tossed aside as the terrified trace-horses reared at the noise. He heard the crackle and flash of hackbuts, and the soaring whine of cross-bolts, but in the packed throng about him saw hardly anyone fall. With a sense of awe at the sheer naked effrontery of it, he found himself there, his horse's shoulders blundering against Angevin horse, his sword engaged, while Piccinino's left wing, disrupted by panicking animals, took the brunt of the Albanian cavalry and fell staggering back. Nicholas wished the Albanians luck.

Here, facing his wing, were not, this time, the amateur army of Rimini. These were soldiers from Provence and from Anjou. Some of them were French, displaced by the rising in Genoa, or even Genoese, flung out with them by those who disliked friends of the French. Nicholas had time to think it ironic that his round ship that had brought Urbino's army was still called the *Doria*, that most famous of Genoese names. Then he had no time to think. He fought on the level he perceived was required of him, and within the extra dimension of fire, for the crossbow and hackbut fire did not cease. Once, he was hit, but the armour he had brought back from Trebizond allowed him to suffer no more than a blow. He saw no faces he knew among the enemy, but often the intent eyes of one of his own men, flashing him a look of recognition and welcome between one blow and the next. One of Astorre's men. His own, now.

After a time he could not count, he realised that his wing was prevailing. At first it was only a thinning of the opposing horse. Then it became, here and there, a movement away from them. Then, suddenly, the Angevins broke, and he and Astorre and the men of Ferrante were thundering after a retreating foe. They killed as they went, and only stopped when summoned by trumpet. To turn, and to engage Piccinino's troops at the rear.

At the rear was Piccinino's third line of foot, the Genoese and the Calabrians. Pushed back by Skanderbeg's attack on the two lines before them, they now received the impact of Ferrante's attack from the rear. They gave way, fighting, and broke, back to back, into the corps of the army behind them. At that point, all order in the enemy's ranks was disrupted. For moments, ally and enemy were indistinguishable. And then, suddenly, the army of Piccinino and the Angevins gave way and, running, determined to save themselves. It became a rout; then a bloody rout; then a victory. Then the aftermath of victory.

Astorre, drawing rein, said to anyone he knew within earshot, 'I told you! That was a fight to be proud of. They'll never come back. My view is they'll never come back. That's Ferrante made King of Naples at last. And we did it.'

He said it again to Tobie, as they regrouped in due course on the silent battlefield, and began to look for their dead and their wounded. Tobie said, 'A great victory. Twenty-five enemy flags. A thousand prisoners. Four thousand enemy dead.'

'A victory,' said Astorre with satisfaction. 'How many of ours?'

'Only a thousand,' said Tobie. 'A few hundred wounded, of course. They didn't capture John of Calabria?'

'Escaped,' said Astorre. 'Fled to Troia. The bastards hauled him in with a rope, and he's probably on his way to Genoa by now. Good riddance. Where's Nicholas?'

Tobie's horse stopped. He said, 'He fought in your company. Don't you know?'

Astorre stared. 'Fought very well. Lost sight of him when the Angevin wing took to flight. There's the dead. He's not among them.'

'Or the wounded,' said Tobie.

Astorre rubbed his nose. 'Well, that's all right. He'll be with Ferrante, or Skanderbeg. Without the men he brought down from the north, it might have been a different story. They owe him something.'

'You mean you think he's getting happily drunk in someone's

pavilion? It's possible,' Tobie said. 'But I'd like to know. After all, I gather he's our employer. You find out. I'm going to be busy.'

Astorre viewed him without rancour. 'That's all right,' he said. 'You go off. I'll track him down somewhere.'

'Now,' said Tobie. 'Go and find where he is now.'

In the hospital tent, as in battle, time lost all shape and importance. But once, moving from patient to patient, Tobie thought to summon a boy and send him with a question to Captain Astorre.

It was Astorre himself who came to walk through the tent, stopping where he saw a man that he knew, until he reached Tobie. Tobie straightened.

Astorre said, 'That's odd.'

'What?' said Tobie.

'He's not here,' said Astorre. 'Not in the camp. Not left on the field. Not to be found anywhere. He didn't run off. He wasn't killed.'

'He might have been captured,' said Tobie.

'By a retreating army? Who would want to capture him?' said Astorre.

'Almost anyone,' said Tobie wearily.

Chapter 8

O F HIS OWN volition, Nicholas had gone nowhere except into oblivion. When he emerged from it, he was at first conscious only that he was extremely unwell. He recognised the signs of past fever: the weakness, the thudding headache, the shirt sodden with sweat. He was lying somewhere in darkness on a sheet and mattress equally clammy – no one, then, could be tending him. This was odd, because even a tavern would offer some sort of service. He attempted to shift his position, and stopped at once. This was different. This stiffness, this burning soreness was the result of some fight. And a fight he had lost, for he was not among friends. So what had happened?

It was not at all easy to trap his thinking processes and set them to work. When they did, they were muddled. He had been in many fights, and suffered from many feverish illnesses. He began to trust his most vivid memory, in which he had been contending somewhere on horseback and had found himself cut off from his fellows. He thought he remembered being pulled from the saddle, and booted feet around him, and the beginning of the blow they had felled him with.

And that part, at least, was quite accurate. He moved one arm and brought his hand slowly up to explore. His hair was stuck with dried blood over a vicious cut which, although swollen, was already closing. Time therefore had elapsed since all this happened. As, of course, it had. Dimly he began to recall a long journey. He remembered being manhandled. He remembered wondering what had happened to his sword. He remembered no faces.

He slept, and woke, and tried to force himself to stay awake and return to that memory. Bit by bit, his recollection came back. It had been a battle, in Italy. Astorre and Tobie. Ferrante and Skanderbeg. And his side had not lost, they'd been winning. The Angevin cavalry had been beaten and started to fly. He'd turned to make for Piccinino's Genoese rearguard. He had been snared

between the soldiers of Anjou and Genoa, against whom Tobie had
so frivolously warned him. Katelina, who wished him no good, had
been in Anjou with her husband's father. Her husband did business
with Genoa. Between them, a genteel family bargain might have
been struck, which had just found its physical target. He felt a
twinge of distant amusement. He should have stayed with the
Albanians.

His closed eyes were stinging with sweat; the place where he lay
was without light or air. He felt by turns heavy and bodiless; his
head swam as the rest of him swayed. Like a child awake in the
night, he became conscious of adult voices above him, a woman's
among them. Footfalls suggested space, unlike his own stale confinement. He supposed himself to be in a cellar. He heard the voice of
the woman again.

Despite all he and Tobie had said, it was unlikely that Katelina
van Borselen had personally joined the son of King René in Italy.
An agent of hers, it might be. What was entirely probable was that
Duke John of Calabria was his final captor. The Duke had lost the
battle. He must be in hiding. To him, perhaps, Nicholas represented a possible fortune. Jordan was capable of offering a fortune,
to get rid of Nicholas.

His awakening mind prompted him to wonder what day it was.
The engagement had taken place on a Tuesday. Astorre and Tobie
must surely have missed him. Fleeing, the Angevins might have
taken him with them to Troia, which was loyal to Anjou. And then,
maybe west to the coast. From there they could take ship anywhere
northwards.

Ship. Abruptly, he pulled himself to his elbows, and banged his
head as he did so. The succession of noises, of movements explained
themselves suddenly. He was on a ship. He was on a ship as his
enemy's prisoner, and was being taken wherever the enemy wanted.
If it was an Angevin ship, he would be in Provence in a matter of
days.

He objected to that. He thought, if he could find the wits and
the energy, he could get up, find a weapon, and take someone else
prisoner instead. He began some sluggish movements. He had
already stopped when the door opened on daylight, and a man in a
rubbed leather jerkin came in. The fellow said, 'You're awake. And
about time. I've brought clothes. You're to wash. They want to
talk to you.' That was all he said. Setting to work, he paid no
attention to questions.

Nicholas submitted. His wound ached, but his senses were clearing.
Washed, dressed and fed, he was able presently to follow the man
out of his cabin, his limbs uncertain but his head swimming only a
little. In the fresh air on deck, he felt better. He began to look
about him.

He was on a round ship, sailing fast under canvas, and high in the water. Haze prevented a view of the coast, but the sun was on his right quarter, which meant it was late in the morning. If there were soldiers on board, he could not see them. He noticed seamen, but couldn't judge their nationality. Of identifying banners and pennants there were none. So near to Naples, the beaten claimant of Naples would lie exceedingly low.

His captor had, however, commandeered the best quarters. From the threshold, Nicholas saw that the master's cabin was as large as his own, but better painted. Ushered in, he found the usual settles and a large central chair, upon which was seated a middle-aged muscular man in a straw hat speared and pinned with good gems. Buttons of gold closed the thin stuff of his doublet and a chain of gold spanned his strong shoulders. The ringed hands on the knees of his hose were nevertheless soldier's hands, and under coarse brown hair, his gaze was peremptory. This could be Duke John of Calabria. It could be one of his captains. Beside the chair, to one side, sat a young man and one a good deal older. Both were also well dressed, in the Italian style. On the other side, on a bench, sat Primaflora.

Nicholas looked nowhere else. She wore a purple silk dress with its bodice lightly embroidered and her hair, threaded with laces and ribbons and pearls, was caught in intricate pleats round her head, in the way he remembered from Ghent. Her eyes on his were like aquamarines under water; her fingers moved a little, interlacing together. She spoke, looking at him all the time. 'He is unwell. You should not have brought him here.'

She spoke Italian with the accent of Savoy. The man in the chair answered in a purer version of the same language. 'Then let him be seated beside you. Messer Niccolò?'

Nicholas stayed where he was. 'I do not know,' he said, 'in whose company I should be sitting?'

The man smiled. 'Let us use French. My name does not matter, nor that of my companions. But you know the lady Primaflora, do you not? Is that not enough?'

'More than enough,' Nicholas said, 'if she planned my abduction. But I imagine you yourself had some part in it?'

'No, no,' said the man. 'Absolve the lady. She has been an unwitting conspirator.'

'You tracked me through her then?' Nicholas said. He made his anger quite plain, although he made his way to her bench and sat down. She looked at her hands.

'You might say so,' said the man. 'I apologise for your treatment. Speed was necessary, and the men who brought you here were not the kind I would have chosen. Your wounds tell that you fought a brave action at Troia.'

'There were no cowards, that I saw,' Nicholas said. He paused. 'The Angevin losses must have been heavy.'

'They deserved to be. They were led by a fool. And Piccinino, everyone knows, serves only for money. Duke John has fled to Ischia, I hear, and King Ferrante has a secure throne in Naples, and is likely to stay there.'

Nicholas became aware that silence had fallen. He drew his hand down from the back of his neck. He said, 'I seem to have lost count of time. What day are we in?'

'You have been ill. It is Saturday. Late afternoon on the twenty-second day of the month of August. You have missed four days, that is all. Where are you going?'

He had reached the door before they could stop him. He drew aside the curtain and looked. The sun had moved a little from the right quarter and was now more clearly aft. If it was the late afternoon, it could not be so. Unless they were not sailing north. Standing there, he said, 'We are sailing east.'

The voice behind him was composed. 'You are not surprised, Messer Niccolò? You knew – surely you guessed – that you are going to Cyprus?'

Cyprus. He was struck dumb before his own incompetence. He had not guessed. His mind bent on his intricate plans for his army, he had neglected the obvious. He had been curious, as Tobie had said, to see what Katelina might do. He had failed to see that the choice he had finally made might be threatened not by Katelina, but by Carlotta of Cyprus.

Nicholas turned back, smoothly closing the curtain. He spoke to Primaflora in a voice perhaps softer than usual. 'My congratulations. Colard Mansion would add his, if he knew. All the time, you were working for the Queen. You questioned Thomas, you traced me, you told Queen Carlotta where to find me. Well, you have failed. I will not work for her.'

The girl said nothing. The man in the chair plucked his lip with his hand, and the jewel in his hat winked and shivered. He said, 'The Queen is a powerful woman, and a bad enemy.'

'I can believe that, if this is her friendship. I will not serve her,' said Nicholas.

'She offers land, rank, possessions – all the wealth in the world, once she has been restored to the island,' the soldier said. 'The Pope commends her. The Duke of Savoy her uncle supports her. She is raising armies to help her. You married a woman of great worth, I believe, and found it no hardship to work with her. So why not this Queen?'

'The reason is quite immaterial. The answer is no,' Nicholas said. 'So what happens now? Am I thrown overboard, or do her servants stop short at that?'

'Not often,' said the man. 'So it is fortunate, perhaps, that I am not her servant. Do you really feel so strongly against her?'

'For her personally, I have no feeling at all,' Nicholas said. 'The matter is just as I have stated. I do not wish to go to Cyprus, and I will not be coerced into it.'

'Ah,' said the man. 'But that is a different argument. Once, I am told, you had no objection to trade in the east? You considered sugar, I'm told.'

'I considered many things, before my wife died.'

'In Cyprus,' said the man, 'we grow, as you know, the finest sugar reeds in the world. We need an able, vigorous man to revive those trades that the long war has disrupted. The manufacture of sugar is one. There are other prospects of note in the capital. If you wish to fight, a princely contract is yours. If you do not, there is ample scope for the rest of your skills. May we not tempt you?'

Nicholas said, 'What sort of offer is that? You hold Kyrenia in the north. The prime cane fields are all in the west or the south. The capital is Nicosia which is not, either, in the Queen's hands. My other skills, as you call them, could find no outlet unless I fought for you first. Until you clear Cyprus of the usurper and his Egyptian soldiers, you have no such posts to offer.'

The man sat back, and clasped his hands before him. He said, 'But, Messer Niccolò, I speak for the usurper, as you call him, and his Egyptian army. The usurper holds the sugar, the royal capital. The usurper has driven Carlotta into Kyrenia. The usurper, whose servants you fought so worthily, so disconcertingly that day south of Bologna, has been most impressed by the tales of your resistance to the blandishments of the Queen, tales which I have now seen for myself are quite true. I,' said the man, rising suddenly, 'am making no offer to you on behalf of Carlotta of Cyprus. I speak to you in the name of James, her half-brother. All she offered, he will give you and more. And much more, if you will come and work for him in Cyprus.'

Nicholas stood, ignoring the pain in his head, and let the implications of that burst like metal filings around him. His main emotion, he found, was one of exasperation. He walked to a stool, and sat down on it. He said, 'The Queen's brother approached me before. In Venice. His delegates failed with the Pope and, passing through Venice, came and spoke to me.'

'The Bishop and Sir Philip Podocataro. Their approach to you was untimely,' his captor said peaceably.

'And again at Silla? Then it was her brother's hirelings who attacked Queen Carlotta, and made off with the sugar? Of course,' Nicholas said. He understood now the words of the Cypriot. *Venetians? Genoese? They would have taken the sugar. Only one man would have destroyed it.*

And Queen Carlotta, without naming him either, had talked of the rival set up by her Egyptian enemies. *A puppet . . . apostate from the Christian faith, who swears the Gospel is false, that Christ is not the only one, nor Mary a Virgin.* Small wonder the puppet had failed to extract support from the Pope. The puppet who was James de Lusignan, her bastard brother and would-be usurper. In whose hands, at one remove, he now found himself. Nicholas said, 'I refused him in Venice and fought against him in Silla. Is it reasonable to expect me to agree to work for him now?'

'Men change their minds,' said the other. 'King James wishes to see you. He is merciful. If you insist, you need not fear he will keep you.'

The spokesman glanced for the first time at the two men on his right. The older, his black hair mixed with grey, returned the look from under his brows, grimly silent. The younger shifted position and, as if compelled by the other's taciturnity, said, 'There are opportunities such as perhaps you could not imagine. But we know the King well. You may trust him.'

Nicholas said, 'Then let us save my time and his. No argument will persuade me. When you next touch land, I wish to disembark.'

'I regret,' said the other. 'Not only my own life would be at risk. We have the lady, Carlotta's servant, to consider.'

So we had. Through his considerable headache, Nicholas considered the problem of the lady Primaflora, who had clung to Thomas for months and who had undeniably been attempting to rejoin himself. Why, he did not yet know. On the affirmation of the man in the chair, the girl had not knowingly led his captors to him. But his abductors were working for Carlotta's rival and, though she denied it, Primaflora might still be attached to the Queen.

He had a memory, suddenly, of a girl desolate in the snow with a dead man's blood staining her breast. In Bruges, he had thought he saw truth in her face and had given the help that she asked for. Help to hide from a Queen who took it for granted that she would move from Ansaldo's arms to his.

She sat, her head downbent, without looking at him, while he weighed one thing against another. Nicholas said, 'She has left Queen Carlotta. You must know that.'

'To bring you back,' said the other. Through the passable French ran a strain of amusement.

'No!' said the courtesan Primaflora. She stood.

'Then why?' said the man in the chair.

Nicholas said nothing. The girl looked at him, and then at the man in the chair. She said, 'The Queen ordered me to recruit him, but I only pretended to do so. I was escaping her.'

'By following the man she had told you she wanted?'

The girl said, 'Because he understood, and was kind, and I had nowhere else to go.'

'You have formed an attachment to him,' said the man in the chair, for whom Nicholas was forming a respect several degrees short of liking.

She did not answer at once. Then she said, 'No. My lover is dead.'

'So,' said the man, 'there is no feeling between you. On the other hand, Messer Niccolò is clearly a man of chivalrous impulses. I must tell him therefore that we intend to hold the lady as hostage for his good conduct. Any attempt to leave ship, and we kill her.'

'Kill her! She's a courtesan; a messenger; she earns her living by moving between men in high places. She has done nothing to deserve death,' Nicholas said.

'No. But there is a risk in moving between men in high places. You have incurred it yourself. She is aware of it. Nor is she in the least danger except for your actions. She looks to you for her life,' the man said. 'And now, we have spoken enough. You have suffered. You need food, fresh air, rest in a more salubrious cabin. We have one, at present occupied by the lady. She will not, I am sure, object to sharing it.'

'There is no need,' Nicholas said. 'My own room will serve.'

The man raised his brows. 'I am afraid the choice is not yours. You say Carlotta of Cyprus impelled you together. If that is your fate, then James of Cyprus will not reverse it.'

Someone took his arm from behind. Someone else came, and gave the girl a push to the door. The man in the chair spoke sharply, 'With courtesy! I will have no more unmannerly handling!'

Nicholas turned to go, and then stopped. Approaching the master's cabin, head down, was a newcomer: a fair, bulky man with a complexion of brick, against which his chin-bristles twinkled like bird-quills. Purposeful, light on his feet, he took the steps in a stride, like a man with a job he was good at. Then he looked up, and halted. He stared. From brick, his fair face turned scarlet. He said, 'Master Nicholas? Lord of Mercy, you're better!' It was his own sailing-master, Mick Crackbene.

They looked at one another. The man in the straw hat appeared suddenly at his back, speaking calmly. 'Master Crackbene has work to do. Take Messer Niccolò to his quarters.'

Crackbene said, 'Have they told you –'

'That's enough,' said the man behind Nicholas.

'No, it isn't,' Nicholas said, without turning. 'How does Master Crackbene come to be here?'

Crackbene drew breath, but once more his abductor forestalled him. He said, 'He is not here by his own choice. Don't blame him.

We found him near Manfredonia, in charge of a ship we felt would serve very well back in Cyprus. The King would also prefer that the vessel should not be sent, full of corn, to Carlotta. We were present in strength, and Master Crackbene had dispatched all his protectors to fight for Ferrante. We took the ship as she lay, and Master Crackbene and his officers with her. You will not lose by it. It will be paid for. It will be regarded, shall we say, as an indefinite charter?'

Nicholas looked slowly about. The round ship pattern, so familiar to all of them. The big cabin, so like his own, except that it was newly painted. The place he had lain which, he now realised, was a cell of the round ship he had brought back from Trebizond. The *Doria*. He was in his own ship the *Doria*, a prisoner, and sailing to Cyprus. He said, 'May I talk to the master?'

'I am afraid not,' said the man. 'Or not at present. It depends. All depends, as I have said, on your conduct. Agree, and there is nothing that is not within your grasp.'

Passing Crackbene, Nicholas contrived, he hoped, to look both resigned and reassuring and Crackbene, in return, managed a faint worried smile. Nicholas supposed he had cause to be worried. Himself, he had lost his ship, the ship by which Astorre and the rest might have followed him. On the other hand, he knew all its officers.

Later, there might be something to be done about that, when he felt less unsteady, and his head had ceased to ache. Meanwhile, he had the problem of the girl Primaflora.

In the cabin which, embarrassingly, they were to share, Nicholas found a second pallet already made up, with his horse gear and satchel beside it. The clothes he had fought in were absent, and so were his sword and his knife. The room, wide and low, was wainscotted and pleasantly furnished. It had made a bridal chamber, only last year, for Pagano Doria and his step-daughter Catherine. Forget it. Forget it.

The girl Primaflora stood by her bed until they both heard the lock turn in the door. Then she said, 'They will bring us supper. We will talk after that. You should sleep now.'

He still stood, though not easily. 'I'm sorry,' he said. 'You've lost your privacy.'

She looked as though she found him naïve. She said, 'Through me, you have lost your freedom. You owe me no apology. Lie down. I don't intend to nurse you or seduce you or slaughter you.'

Nicholas let himself drop and stretched out. He felt his eyes close. He said, 'Please yourself. Whatever you do, I'll be asleep when you do it.'

The promise on both sides was kept. She shook him awake, in the end, when the food came, and he demolished more of it than he had expected. The Lusignan family employed capable cooks. Astorre, who liked his food, would have enjoyed this. Astorre. Both he and Tobie would learn immediately of the pirating of the *Doria*. But if they did, would they connect it with his abduction? And would they link it with Cyprus, or be misled, as he had been, by the more personal danger from Anjou? Again, incoming ships would soon tell where the *Doria* was calling. Except that there were a lot of round ships at sea, and her name might have been changed. Or perhaps not. The Doria family were Genoese; and the Genoese sided with Queen Carlotta. On a ship called the *Doria*, this crew would get to Cyprus unmolested. The girl said, 'Solemn thoughts.'

He looked up. 'A sobering matter, abduction. Why do you think they brought you on board? Once they had me, there was no need.'

'I think I know,' she said. 'You heard them. They hoped by threatening me to keep you quiet, and prevent you escaping. And, too, they thought I still served the Queen, and they don't want the Queen to know what has happened. I don't know which they want more – to use you, or simply to deny you and the ship to the Queen.'

'Thank you,' said Nicholas.

She frowned. 'Well,' she said, 'you are very young, and you have wasted almost a year.'

'So have you,' he said.

She lifted one shoulder. 'What do you expect me to say? All my life is a waste? I enjoy my life. Or did. I shall enjoy it again.'

'In Cyprus?' said Nicholas. 'I thought we might do better than that.'

'We?'

'I can't jump ship without you.'

She said, 'You won't get a chance to jump ship. This is a round ship, remember. She sails, she doesn't have to rest oarsmen, and her holds will carry all the provision that's wanted. She need hardly call anywhere. They will lock that cabin door, and they will keep your friend Crackbene under guard, and all his officers. In any case, I wouldn't come with you.'

'No?' said Nicholas.

She said, 'Would you keep me with you when we had escaped? I rather think not. And what would I do on some remote Venetian island? If I am going anywhere, it might as well be to Cyprus. And you heard what he said. If the King himself cannot persuade you, then they are prepared to let you go.'

'And risk my crossing to Queen Carlotta? Of course not. If I don't agree, it will be prison, or worse.'

'Perhaps. But not for me,' said Primaflora.

'No. Not for you,' said Nicholas slowly. 'You don't mind that?

You'd rather join King James's Egyptian court than escape with me?'

'Why not?' said Primaflora. 'Perhaps, after all, you should try to escape. Did you believe their threats against me? Of course not. If you go, I expect I shall pass between those two or three Cypriot-lovers up there. Then they will take me back, a prize for the Lusignan. If you see a chance, leave. Shall I play to you?'

'What?' said Nicholas.

'You are puzzled and weak. There is wine. I have my lute. Lie down, and let me play for you. Has music a place in your life?'

Hearty folk song in Bruges, and obscene versifying in the dye-yard. Consorts, scratchily playing at some big house where merchants were tolerated. Violante, once heard to sing. And in Trebizond. . . . In Trebizond, the anthems that had come through the doors of the church of the Chrysokephalos, and the song of the nightingale, drowning them.

'No,' he said. 'No. I know nothing of music.'

The tunes she played him were French, and once or twice she sang, playfully, making the words teasingly clear. They were a courtesan's songs about dalliance, and quite specific. He thought that she didn't expect him to understand all the words. But although his working language was Flemish, he had been reared in Burgundy, and his mother tongue was the same as hers. He lay and listened, the empty wine glass beside him, his eyes shut. He heard, but gave no sign, when the sound came nearer and when, still singing and playing, she stooped and sat, gently, on the edge of his bed. He heard his own breathing, and opened his eyes.

'You have a dimple. Two,' she said.

If he smiled it had been in self-mockery. She lifted a hand from the strings and touched his cheek. 'And a scar.'

In the lamplight, she looked like a painting; a pristine confection of tint and line drawn from the ether. Her brows were fine as threads; the twisting forms of her hair echoed the curl of her lips and the little curve between nose and cheek, with its exact carmine crescent. Below each underlid, he observed a fine crease: part amusement, part exhaustion, partly the mark of something, he thought, that was inexhaustible. Queen Carlotta had been married and widowed at fourteen. No one, probably, would know when Primaflora was first wakened, or how.

Her hair was yellow as butter. Silver, with the radiance all round about it. It clasped her head like a shell. He began to wonder, and stopped himself. He said, 'I have never heard anyone play so skilfully.'

She laid the lute slowly down, and straightened again. 'And I have never seen a worse actor. So you understood all the words?'

'So you didn't mourn him long,' Nicholas said.

Her back straightened. She sat without answering, studying him. Then she said, 'Do you think I am offering love?'

There was a long pause. 'No,' he said.

'No. I am offering *this*. Release. Relief. Oblivion. You need not take it.'

'I wouldn't take it,' he said. He didn't look at her hands.

There was a pause. 'But?' she said. She swept him from head to foot with her eyes, and then returned her gaze to his face. She was not smiling. She said, 'But you need to receive it. So the blame would be mine. You betray nobody.'

'I wouldn't say that either,' he said. 'If you heard my friends: it is my lifetime's interest, plotting.'

She said, 'So, say it.' She withdrew slowly and stood, always watching him. Her fingers, slipping down her own body, parted one by one the fine fragile clasps of her gown. The garment lingered and fell.

'But I need to receive it,' he said.

She stood in her chemise. Then, raising her arms, she drew the fine voile steadily over her head. She knelt, then lay on his bed. Her breasts, suspended, were oval. Her calves and thighs were perfect, as if moulded and grown from ripe peaches. Her head came to rest on his arm. He bent his wrist, and touched the tightly-bound cap of her hair. His hand stood away. She said, 'Let me do it for you,' and lifted herself and, sitting beside him, disengaged the ribbons and cords and unfolded her long, silken hair with her fingers.

It was yellow, not chestnut; and the breasts lifted below it were perfect spheres with unused nipples, soft as bruised fruit. She said, 'Close your eyes. This is my profession, not yours.'

His hands sprang to grip her, smiting the breath from her lungs. He said, painfully smiling, 'You think so?'

Chapter 9

ESCAPING CAME naturally to Nicholas, for it required youth, strength and agility and he had all of those, as well as the kind of mind that solved puzzles. It failed to solve this one. Someone, somewhere, knew very well what kind of animal they had lured to their trap, and nothing he did, from the time he recovered his health, enabled him to take over his ship, or to land.

He was prepared, if escaping, to abduct Primaflora, if only to preserve her from the perils of her own philosophy. He was equally prepared, if he got off alone, to return in some fashion and rescue her. He was not at all sure that she would thank him for either effort. He did not, of course, have her affection. He doubted if he had even her friendship. He felt responsible for her for other reasons. Perhaps even because of a look on her face, caught sometimes unguarded.

Extraordinary precautions were taken to secure them both. In port, they were locked in separate cabins. When sailing, they were each allowed on deck closely guarded, but never together. Primaflora's servant attended her, and he was served, cheerfully enough, by the man in the rough leather jerkin. He cherished his moments under the sky, if only because he knew every quirk of the *Doria*, and could assess the wind and the sea, and judge the set of the sails, and set his hand on the sheets he had learned so swiftly to work in two dangerous voyages. He had no chance, however, to direct his ship now. He hardly glimpsed Michael Crackbene, and was never permitted to speak to him.

He could, if he wished, have dined daily in the great cabin with those three well-dressed seigneurs, his captors. They had expressed disappointment at his first refusal, but soon had ceased to send messages. He had no interest in Cyprus, and no wish to add to his prejudices. He felt, however, some slight gratitude that they had not compelled him to attend, as they might well have done. As far as the route went, they made no secret of it, and much of it doubled the way he had taken himself, last October. They rounded Greece, calling at Corfu and Modon. He knew the Venetian Bailie at Modon, and had thought that there, if nowhere else, he might slip ashore. But nothing worked: bribes, ruses, or cajolery. And Crackbene, he heard after, had been shut away bound like himself when the ship sailed into harbour. He himself was not only bound, he was gagged.

Lying helpless, he realised why, from the commotion. They had invited the Bailie on board. His name was Bembo, and Nicholas had met his cousin in Venice. Another of the same name had married a girl from the house of Corner, one of whose former palazzi had been presented to Nicholas by a grateful Republic. He still owned it, he supposed, and Gregorio his lawyer should be presiding there, conducting the Bank of Niccolò without Niccolò. The family Bembo, in other words, could begin a campaign which, with any luck, would bring the Signory of Venice to his rescue. It was unfortunate, therefore, that Nicholas was locked in the *Doria*, and the Bailie's voice, in time, receded; and there came the clank of the anchor chain coming up, and the first tug of the oars, and then all the running about to get the sails ready. And then Modon was behind them.

There was only one other chance, and it turned out to be no chance at all. After they had paid their call at Crete, another ship hailed them. Nicholas was on deck at the time, and watched its coming with attention. From its size, it was a carrier, one of the biggest he had seen, and it came from the east, which meant it was returning from Alexandria, or Cyprus, or Rhodes. Then, as it came nearer, a trumpet call came over the water, and it ran up its flag.

The emblem was the eight-pointed Cross of the Knights Hospitaller of Rhodes. It was all he saw before an angry voice spoke somewhere behind him, and he was hustled below. Later, the man who came to unlock him was smiling. 'Gave them a fright, didn't it, those bastards in the big cabin? Stands to reason, if a ship's called *Doria*, it'll attract every friend of the Genoese on the ocean. Especially if their commander's called Doria as well.'

Nicholas said, 'I thought it was a ship of the Order from Rhodes.'

'It was,' said the man. 'Knights of St John, effing bastards. Sail all the time, getting supplies for that prime bitch Carlotta. Sir Imperiale Doria it was, on that ship. Brings the Queen cattle and grain, and hocks her silver when she calls for more money. Wanted to come aboard and tell us what the Turks are doing on Lesbos. I can imagine what they're doing on Lesbos, and we're not going to help stop them, I can tell you. Your rich friend in the cabin had to tell him we were infectious before my lord of Doria would go.'

'Who is the rich man in the cabin?' said Nicholas.

The man tittered again. 'They don't tell you, do they? Well, I'm not going to risk a whipping and let on. What's it to you, with free food and drink for the asking? Whenever, that is, you've breath to spare from laying the woman.' He backed and said, 'None of that. Digi!'

By the time Digi flung open the door, Nicholas had recovered. The men left. He flung himself down on a chest, and a moment later the door was unlocked again and Primaflora rejoined him. She said, 'What was the shouting?'

'Nothing. I made a threatening gesture,' Nicholas said. 'Stupid of me.' He was still breathing quickly. And aware, in his anger, that she was here again, and the afternoon would be spent as it was always spent, in exquisite instruction.

Well, not today. When he got up and walked over, he did not even undress her. He ignored, as if he had never learned them, all the delicacies; the devices to postpone, to heighten, wonderfully to protract, and simply made straight, as if time were short, for what he wanted. And she, extinguishing self, met him with feverish greed as if she, and not he, were in extremity. Her skills were, after all, to give pleasure.

Later, he lay on his face. She said, 'I cannot go away. I could ask for another cabin. I am not sure why you suddenly think this is wrong.'

He had explained nothing. She was good at divining. He said, 'It isn't wrong. But it is a waste.'

'Waste!' she said. 'That word again? What blows have you had, that you feel unshriven unless someone is beating you? Ten months of misery were a waste. But pleasure is not.'

'Then let us say,' Nicholas said, 'that I don't deserve it. One should work, and one should take relief from one's work. That, my dear, is the Flemish way.'

She was quiet, as she always was when he held her at arm's length. His thoughts were his own, and not Primaflora's. His vision of Catherine and Pagano, locked exactly thus in this room by their voracity. Catherine his step-daughter, and Pagano Doria, whom he had caused to be killed. He turned over. 'But your way is better, and I've been ungrateful. So long as you're prepared for a parting. You know I'm going to refuse to serve this man. James the Bastard. This alternative king of the sorry island of Cyprus.'

She said, 'If you worked for him, you could have both your relief and your trade. In the Flemish way.'

Her eyes were not smiling. He said, 'You would stay with me? There must be more . . .'

She said, 'Do you expect a declaration of love? You won't get it. I made that mistake once, and fell out with my employer. Now I need another patron, and it would amuse me to stay with you.

Also, you require someone like me. You learn quickly. You conceal what you know. I had not expected –' She paused.

'What?' said Nicholas.

'To talk,' she said. 'In the evenings, when we hold conversation, it is what I enjoy most.'

He smiled at last. 'Shall we,' he said, 'write this down and post it up on the door? It might earn me the respect of the crew; but I very much doubt it.'

She said, 'Then you will keep an open mind about James?'

'No,' said Nicholas. 'If I don't serve Carlotta, then I've no wish to serve James. I will hear him and leave, if he will let me. If he does, will you stay?'

She had a robe she wore in the heat, light as a chemise. It lay crumpled about her as she reclined on one elbow, considering him. He had given her no time to undress. She had not complained, but had been generous. He added, 'I should be afraid for you.'

Her eyes opened. 'Would you?' She lifted her head from her hand and, stretching her arm, ran her fingers down his bare arm. She said, 'I said you were young. I can look after myself. What happens to me is not your affair.'

'But you wouldn't leave with me?' Nicholas said.

She smiled, and moved the track of her fingers. 'You don't want me. We share an appetite, and satisfy it as well together as any man and woman could do. But your mind is set on war, and I need a great household to live in.'

He bridged her hand with his fingertips, stilling it. He said, 'But you were willing to stay with me in Cyprus?'

She looked at the silent embargo, but made no effort to break it. 'Because you would have earned a great household,' she said. 'I won't deceive you. I tease you over your youth, but you have in you the fire of success. I should profit from that, as you would profit from – what you have just had. I shall ask you something. Why have we been made to share a chamber like this?'

'I thought we knew,' Nicholas said. 'To exhaust me into docility.'

'So once we reach Cyprus, I am not needed,' she said. 'Unless there is another reason for making us lovers.'

Of course, she was far from simple. She had wondered about this, as he had. He had not talked about it. They might have been thrown together for the sake of prurience. Even at second hand, such things could excite men's imagination. But of course, it was not only that. He said, 'Perhaps they are uncertain of both of us, and hope passion will solve all their problems. If I elect to serve King James on Cyprus, you will reject Carlotta for ever and stay with me. If I leave, you will go with me and will not remain to betray them.'

She became very still. 'I am not a spy. I am not Carlotta's agent.'

'They don't know that,' he said.

He saw her relax, bit by bit. Her lips curved, the little creases of irony deepening. She said, 'They don't fear, then, that I shall seduce you to Carlotta's side?'

'I suppose,' Nicholas said, 'that I have given proof of resistance. I left you in Ghent.'

'And paid for my freedom,' she said. 'Do you think I had forgotten that?'

He said, 'A freedom you didn't take.'

'A freedom I did not want,' she said. After a moment, 'At the time, there was nothing for me in Italy. As I told you, I have certain requirements. It is a profession, like any other.'

A freedom I did not want. He pursued it only obliquely. He said, 'Where will you go, then, when I leave Cyprus? If I am right, and they won't let you stay?'

'I shall tell you,' she said, 'when you leave Cyprus. Make your decision. Niccolò, Niccolò, I am not your concern.'

Her eyes smiled, with a small frown between them. He turned, and made her his concern with tenderness, as if they had been truly lovers. It was the last such conversation they held before they reached Cyprus.

Nicholas vander Poele had seen, in recent years, many beautiful islands and the empire of Trebizond, the gold and ivory relict of Byzantium. Byzantium had once reigned over this island too. Before that, Cyprus had been part of the Hellene kingdom of Egypt, whose coast was so near to her shores. Then Rome had come, with her shrines to Apollo and Venus, and after Byzantium, the isle had been seized by Crusaders. Rich, lovely Cyprus: a floating fortress in the Levant, so conveniently close to Asia, Africa, Europe: a strategic prize for any red-blooded soldier.

On his way to the Third Crusade, King Richard of England had stopped to marry there, and later presented the island to that grasping Crusader Guy de Lusignan, son of a French count and last Latin King of Jerusalem. The English King could hardly have foreseen how tenacious, how fertile the family Lusignan were to be, once uprooted and planted in Cyprus. Their descendants still reigned there, and still called themselves Kings of Jerusalem. But that kingdom, long since, had been in infidel hands.

For nearly three hundred years then, the Lusignan family had ruled over Cyprus, bringing Latin landowners, bishops and nobles to a place whose natives spoke Greek, not French or Italian; and whose worship used the ritual of Orthodox Greece. The Latins built themselves great mountain fortresses, and gave fortifications

and holdings to the Knights of St John, stocked from their neighbouring island of Rhodes. Nor did the people of Cyprus find it
better when the Lusignan rule became weak. Then the Genoese
jumped in, and seized the best town and harbour for trading. And
later, worse than that, the Mameluke rulers of Egypt threatened
the kings so successfully that, for a generation now, the Christian
rulers of Cyprus had been paying craven tribute to the Muslim
rulers of Egypt, and taking oath to behave as their vassals.

All this, Nicholas knew. It was as a Lusignan queen, married to
her own cousin, that Carlotta was scouring the world, begging
money and troops to drive the Muslim interests out of her island.
And it was as an ally and protégé of infidel Egypt that James, her
bastard brother, had invaded Cyprus, capturing all but the patch in
the north to which the Queen and her consort had fled. Carlotta
possessed Kyrenia, and had the use of Famagusta, the port where
the Genoese ruled. All the rest belonged to James, and the Egyptian
army. It was a beautiful land ripped asunder, and Nicholas vander
Poele wanted nothing to do with it.

He stood, as the round ship drew close, and saw with impassive
eyes the green mountains, the creaming ocean, the rosy bastions of
rock that fringed the seashores. Here was the birthplace of Venus;
the prize of royal Alexander; the love-gift of the Roman Mark
Antony to Cleopatra of Egypt.

Beside him stood Primaflora. She said, 'Have you heard of the
grapes of Cyprus? Do you know the Song of Songs? Over there are
the vineyards of Engedi.'

He said nothing aloud. His mind said, without reason, *I wish I
were dead, and had sown no seed, and had left no one to suffer*. He
thought, not of the usurping royal bastard and his Egyptian hordes,
but of a Greek with a wooden leg listening somewhere, amused.
And of his grandfather, Jordan. He didn't know why he thought of
them. He turned without speaking and went below, and stayed
there until he was called to the boat that would land him on
Cyprus.

In the event, they took their prize to the south coast of Cyprus at
night; standing off the bay called Episkopi long after the sun had
sunk to their left. Ahead in the darkness spread the land conquered
and held by James the Bastard, who had had Nicholas brought
here by force. Beyond the seas at his back lay Beirut and Damascus
and the Syrian coast. Below, on the water, the ship's boat had been
lowered for its passengers. The September night was sticky with
warmth. Nevertheless, leaving the *Doria*, Nicholas had been given
a cowled cloak to put on, and so, he saw, had Primaflora and the
woman her servant. The maid looked frightened. Primaflora descended into the skiff like a court lady entertaining the poor. He

had seen her brace herself for the rôle, withdrawing even from him. He thought she was afraid, but was too wise to console her. In the boat, he did try to speak once, but instead of answering she glanced over her shoulder to where the seigneurs from the cabin were ensconced. The boat-master said, 'You will be silent.'

He could make nothing of it and sat weaponless, his hands clasping his knees, thinking of Crackbene, who was not present and who must therefore still be on board. But Crackbene, like Astorre, was a thorough professional, and would be treated well no matter who employed him. And, unlike Astorre, he had no prior allegiance to the Charetty company. Crackbene was unlikely to do anything rash, even had he had enough men to support him. Nicholas was therefore alone, he and Primaflora, in the hold of the Bastard. Should Nicholas decline to co-operate, he had been told, the Bastard James in his mercy would free him. Nicholas had learned, with some pain, never to believe what he was told, especially by strangers.

The skiff laboured on. At first, it seemed to make for the river where he had heard the Corner jetty lay. Then it turned south and east and instead, rounded the whole squat peninsula that lay between Episkopi and the hamlet of Limassol. In Limassol was a castle, and the seat of the bishop who had been James's envoy in Rome, and perhaps even James's agent at Silla. But once more, instead of going to Limassol, the boat turned, and the journey suddenly ended. They had been brought to shore just round the cape, at a place where the beach receded to shadowy flats and a glimmering cluster of lights told of some group of low buildings far inland. He was made to exchange the boat for a firm timber jetty, and the fresh air of the sea for the miasma of land, warm and rank and smelling of citrus and brine. A sea bird cried and was answered by a low mellow sound, whispering over the sands. Across the pale rise of the beach a shadow fled, dark as a shred on the eyeball, to be followed by several others. He stopped, and somebody chuckled. 'There is nothing to fear, Messer Niccolò. You do not know the name of this cape?'

It was the voice of his interviewer from the cabin, come in a rustle of silk to his elbow. Today he wore a round hat of cut velvet, below which sweat was trickling. 'I don't know it,' said Nicholas.

'You will find out. We are taking you to a place where your name-saint has been honoured for eleven hundred years. Over there is the monastery of Ayios Nikolaos, where the abbot has spread us a feast.' His voice was encouraging. 'You have been patient. Soon you will learn what is wanted of you.'

There was a vague path of sand mixed with dust, pale in the moonlight, and chequered with the shadows of men who led the way without torches. The remaining two from the cabin walked behind him in silence – one surly as before, and the other uneasy, Nicholas thought. Behind that, Primaflora trod the soft ground in her pattens; at the rear, other men followed closely. Nicholas saw they didn't wear swords. They had no fear, now, that he could escape. It was something else that made secrecy necessary. What it was, he had to find out. Then he smelled lemons again, and a scent that could have been spices or incense, and saw a high wall appear, with a lamp in a niche. There was a basin, made from the capital of a Corinthian column. Nicholas turned to his captor. 'Am I to meet James de Lusignan here?'

A bearded man robed in black had appeared at a gate, preparing to welcome them. The man beside Nicholas replied with what seemed to be his natural briskness. 'No. The lord King is in Nicosia, his capital. You will ride there. An escort will come to this place soon to fetch you. Tonight, very likely.'

'Tonight?' Nicholas said.

The man said, 'It is two days' journey away, and better to travel in coolness. Save your questions. There will be time enough.' They stepped through the gate, and Primaflora's face glimmered like pearl in the lamplight.

It was an old monastery, and blessed, in these flat lands, with space for its orchards and gardens, its church and its cloisters, its cells and its stables and offices, all thick-walled, rounded and white, and fragrant with incense and woodsmoke. There was a smell of fruit and risen bread and cooked meat and, behind all these, the coarse odour of brine and something acid which was harder to place. In the centre of the yard was a well and a washing place, both of weathered carved marble of an age much before that of the monastery. Nicholas caught, again, a glimpse of fleeting dark shapes but said nothing of it.

His curiosity, buried by anger, had sprung to life again. He felt little fear or anxiety, but an awakening of his faculties, a clarity that always came with the prospect of competition. Perhaps what lay before him was something so overwhelming, so final, so crude that no kind of ingenuity would serve him. But he could try, and if he survived, he could learn from it. Since Troia he had been nobody: a collection of assorted reactions. He began, quite suddenly, to feel like a person again.

He saw the servants had gone. Alone with Primaflora and the three men who had abducted him, he stepped through an archway into an ancient cloister, with lamps which afforded a glimpse of bold furzy flowers, and the scarlet of hibiscus, and the shadow of vines. There stood before him a man with the veiled hat, the black robes and the beard of an Orthodox abbot, a nun at his side. The woman, smiling, advanced and took Primaflora by the hand. The man said, 'We have long awaited you. My daughter, be welcome.

Your room is prepared, and Sister Eudocia will see to your comfort.' The abbot watched her leave, then gave his attention to
Nicholas. His eyes were long-sighted and clear, like those of a
sportsman. He said, 'They tell me you are a child of my Saint. Be
welcome, be happy, be worthy of him. Come and gave thanks for
your journey.' He had spoken in Greek. He turned, as if refusal
were inconceivable, and led the way into the church.

Primaflora had gone. Beside him, his senior abductor was smiling. He said, 'I can see that you hesitate. But the good abbot
believes you have volunteered, of your kindness, to help us. It will
do no harm, surely, to thank the Almighty for your safety?'

Nicholas said, 'I thought I was sponsored by Allah.'

The seigneur seemed undisturbed. 'King James,' he said, 'makes
no demands on the conscience of those who choose to work for
him. Pray to whom you please, or to no one.'

Since the abbot was waiting, he went in. It was a small church,
dimly lit, and the brethren themselves already half filled it. The
scented haze round the lamps revived an unwanted memory: of the
moving fog in Marian's office, just before her daughters set their
men to attack him. And if he turned his back on the lamps, there
appeared something else from his past: the iconostasis: the wall of
worked gold that screened the sanctuary, throwing its light into the
deep coloured bowl of the dome, and illuminating the thick, painted
pillars like sunlight. He had seen that, too, last year, before he left
Trebizond. He had stood in the church of St Eugenios beside the
Emperor David, and Amiroutzes, the chancellor who had betrayed
him; beside Violante of Naxos who, out of the coolest expediency,
had given him the use of her body in Venice; beside the Imperial
children who now, with their parents, lived in luxury under the
Ottoman Sultan – the reward the Emperor had claimed for his surrender.

Served to Nicholas now was not the Divine Liturgy which had
preceded the anguish of Trebizond; but the plain chant of com-
pline, which echoed the same close-written, cerebral music. *Hear
us, O God; we beseech Thee to hear us.* . . . *Possessing Thee, O Christ,
a Wall that cannot be broken* . . . But despite the prayers, Constantinople had fallen, and Trebizond had fallen; and in the end he,
Nicholas had done nothing to prevent it. It would have troubled
Marian, perhaps, had she lived, and had he told her what he had
done. So it was as well she was dead.

His thoughts were far away when a touch on his arm showed
him that the service had ended. Whoever touched him had gone. A
monk, seeing him turn, said in Greek, 'It was Otto: forgive. When
the doors open, they enter, the little children of Christ.' He was
smiling, his arm crooked around something. The object, made of
some soft material, was white as ermine and seemed to be studded

with jewels. Emeralds caught the glow of the candles. Behind it, the monk's stomach rumbled. Nicholas moved, and something silken passed by his ankles, accelerating as it went. A candle-flame bent. The monk said, 'You do not dislike them? Apologise, Otto,' and held out his arms.

The emeralds were not jewels, but the eyes of a large and muscular cat which came courteously into his grasp and settled itself, its white chin on his forearm, its tail furling with graceful finality. Nicholas laughed and, to silent instruction, found and fondled a spot by one ear. Otto purred and, caressing still, Nicholas scanned the half-emptied church all about him. Between the feet of the monks, the marble floor was laid like a loom with moving skeins of fine silk in dyes he could never have dreamed of: smoke and silver and black, cream and tortoiseshell, orange and butter. But the sinuous shapes were not silk, and the hues came from God, and not man. He was looking at cats.

Cats proud and indolent, young and playful, arched against monkish robes, sat hunched between icons and lay stretched upon ledges. Kittens played with the gold fringe of carpets; boxed with ungainly paws smooth as catkins. Through the open door he could watch them in the cloisters, slipping from pillar to garden, the same dark forms he had seen on the beach. In his arms Otto stretched with politely soft paws, gathered himself, and sprang elegantly to the ground. The monk said, 'He is the leader. Watch. They go where he goes. It is called Cape Gata, this place. You had not heard of it?'

'Why?' said Nicholas. Outside, he could see his abductors waiting for him. He walked slowly, the monk at his side. The monk said, 'Because of the serpents. It is an island of vipers. Then St Helen of the Cross, when the monastery was young long ago, brought a litter of cats and said, "These will serve you." And so it has been ever since. By day the cats hunt, and by evening, they come to the bell for their food.'

'They are beautiful,' Nicholas said.

'They lead us into sin,' said the monk. 'We love them too much.'

They had almost reached the door. Nicholas said, 'I thought it was an island of scorpions. There is a legend there too, is there not? The Grand Master of Rhodes at least knows it. ". . . hac in insula Cipri scorpionelis regie domus spurcicia surrexit?"'

The monk halted. His eyes, like those of the abbot, were remarkably level and clear. He said, '. . . est enim hac pestifera Jacobus de Lusignano. I know, of course, the quotation. The enemies of James of Lusignan have only to look back to myth to find the bewitched half-serpent Melusine, wife of Raymondin de Lusignan his ancestor.'

'But, unlike the Knights Hospitaller, you are not his enemy?' Nicholas asked.

The monk smiled. 'We have our cats to defend us,' he said. 'That and Our Lord. It seems sufficient.'

Led away by his captors, Nicholas looked back once and saw the monk had remained at the church door. The white cat Otto had returned to his feet and smiling, the man swept it into his arms by one leg, addressing it softly in Greek. Then a door closed between them.

The room to which Nicholas was conducted was stone-walled and cool, with a board laid to one side with melons and plain meats, bread and a pitcher of wine. There were no servants, and none of the brethren. He counted four seats. His two silent abductors preceded him. The senior, closing the door, walked to the centre of the room and addressed Nicholas neither in French nor in Greek, but in perfect Italian. 'We begged the abbot's indulgence to dine with you privately here, since time may be short. Your escort for Nicosia may come at any moment.'

'I am to learn who you are,' Nicholas said.

'While you eat. Sit. You too, Luigi. Vanni, will you oblige me by serving?'

The youngest of the three had already moved to the board and was filling platters. Nicholas did not take the seat he was offered. He said, 'Luigi? Giovanni? Good Cypriot names.' The lean man with the grizzled hair and the grim manner gave vent to a grunt, but the younger one smiled.

The man in the velvet hat said, 'And mine is Paul. You have probably guessed which state we come from: let us proceed without quibbling over it. The elder of the signori beside you is Luigi Martini who, with his brother, has long handled the sugar crops at Kouklia and at Kolossi here in Cyprus. Vanni, who wishes to give you some food, is surnamed Loredano, and is factor to the lord Marco Corner at Episkopi, as well as being my deputy. And I am Paul Erizzo, with no post as yet, because I come to take my first appointment in Cyprus.'

'As?' said Nicholas.

'As Venetian Bailie. We are all Venetians. You have realised. You are wanted by James. You will be taken by James's men to meet James at Nicosia. We shall receive some approbation for bringing you, but James would have seized you, whether we had helped him or not. We have no power here,' said Paul Erizzo. 'We are here on sufferance, as traders and growers. Without us, James would find it hard to get the returns or the produce he needs, but if we push him too far, he could massacre us freely tomorrow. However, we are skilled at learning just how far to push him, and how to nurse all that we have developed so that we may thrive as he thrives, and even should he cease thriving. Although, of course, Queen Carlotta must never return. Or the Genoese would overrun Cyprus.'

'Of course,' said Nicholas. He thought with quiet fury of Modon. Small chance that the Bailie of Modon would have rushed to his aid, or that the Signory – the grateful Signory – would have thrown in their cohorts to rescue him. The Signory had condoned his abduction.

Paul Erizzo said, 'So sit down, and eat. Of course you dislike what has happened. If we had told you on shipboard, you might have found violent means to escape without giving the matter the thought it deserves. We are here to talk, and to answer your questions. You left Venice for some reason that seemed good to you, but a year has gone by. You are a gifted young man, clever, vigorous, with the world to win if you rouse yourself. The moment has come to take your biggest step forward. We have chosen you to work for yourself and for Venice. We are giving you a chance you would never have had. You will emerge a great man from this venture.'

'I prefer not to sit,' Nicholas said. 'Or to be in your debt, even for food. I left Venice for precisely this reason. I had been used as a tool. But not a second time.'

Paul Erizzo said, 'You don't know, as yet, what we are offering. Knowing what you do, how can you be anyone's instrument? The King desires to employ you. You will answer to him. You will be paid by him, royally. You will do what we cannot do, and secure Cyprus for James and for Venice. You and your Bank will have no cause to regret it.'

'No,' said Nicholas again. His hands had steadied, and his face had ceased to feel like pigskin. He detached a stool with his foot from the companionable circle that had been drawn, and kicking it to the wall, sat down with his arms folded and his shoulders against the plaster. He said, 'Well: let us look at the realities. The Bastard James is actually expecting me: this is not a gambit of your own? Yes. And he is sending someone to collect me – could that be the noise that we hear?'

'It could be,' said Erizzo. He glanced at the others. 'But they will wait.'

Giovanni Loredano got up. 'I'll see to it.' The door closed behind him.

'But you are not going to Nicosia? Because King James doesn't know you are here?'

'Because it is better for you to go alone. We shall come later,' said Erizzo.

'And the lady Primaflora?' Nicholas said.

'She may go with you,' said Erizzo.

'Why?' said Nicholas. 'She has no value now. Queen Carlotta can't stop me coming: I'm here. Send the girl on to Rhodes on the next ship.'

The door opened. The young man Vanni said, 'They won't wait.' He spoke in anger, with something held down behind it.

Erizzo said, 'Nonsense. Tell them.' Then he broke off and said, 'Luigi. Try.' The older man Martini rose, looking at him, and then left with Loredano. The door closed. The Venetian Bailie said, 'Yes, the lady. You don't want her in Nicosia? Well, she is a free agent. If the convent will have her, no doubt she could stay until she has the means to leave.'

He spoke with his eyes on the door, behind which an amazing noise was developing, compounded of shouting, and the crashing of timber and something that sounded like, but could not be, the clashing of steel. Nicholas said, to get it quite clear, 'The lady Primaflora may leave Cyprus?' He could not, yet, believe that Erizzo was making no use of his most powerful lever. With three-quarters of his mind, he was listening. The door opened again, and Loredano stood on the threshold.

This time the Bailie stood up. The sound of shouting came clearly now from the cloisters, and the thud of blows, and of running feet, and of screaming. Erizzo said, 'Christ Jesus. I have no sword here.'

The man in the doorway had blood on his face. He said, 'I asked for five minutes. They say the time has expired. The servants have gone. The monks are in the church. They are fetching the lady.'

'*Who?*' said Nicholas. 'Who are fetching her?' He had got to the door but Loredano held it against him, his fissured cheek welling. Loredano said, 'The Mamelukes. The King has sent the Mamelukes for you. You can't do anything now. No one can.'

'Of course they can,' Nicholas said, and wrenched open the door and came face to face with Primaflora half-naked, in the grip of a fully-armed Mameluke.

Nicholas saw he was alone in his shock. The delightful bare breasts of Primaflora were not those of a housewife. In Venice, he had heard, the courtesans looked not unlike this, with their plucked brows and their dyed golden hair and the gowns cut as nearly to cradle the breasts as to conceal them. And Primaflora herself contributed the disdain of the courtesan, her dishevelled head high, her arms hanging loose over the brown fingers grasping her ribs.

The man behind her held her thus for a moment and then, forcing down with his wrists, compelled her to sink to her knees. Grasping her long loosened hair he twisted it, to hold in his fist as a leash. He said in Arabic, 'Whose is the chattel?'

He was not, Nicholas thought, of pure blood. Broad, and of medium height, this Mameluke was still taller than an Egyptian should be. Beneath his conical helmet with its burst of short feathers his face could hardly be judged: little showed between the tongues of his face-guard but the red of his lips and the glossy

black of his untrimmed moustache. Below that, the man wore a
brigandine, covered with bright brocade studded with metal. His
curved sword, sheathed in shagreen, had a handgrip inscribed in
fine gold, and the heavy band at his waist was set thick with it.

It was the costume of an emir, and an emir of forty or even a
hundred. His use of Arabic, a language foreign to most, was quite
deliberate. He said, 'Whose is she?' and Nicholas responded immediately, in the same tongue. 'She belongs to King James. Who
are you who comes, like the ass bearing books, and dare touch her?'

He thought then he had lost his arm. The other's sword blurred
in the air, and he felt the steel bite in his shoulder. Erizzo shouted.
Primaflora lay thrust to one side. The emir spoke in a voice of
calmest contempt. 'Conduct yourself, log, or I shall bring you a
brass bowl to look upon, that will shrivel your eyes and your
arrogance. What renegade taught you the tongue of the Prophet?'

'Sultan Mehmet, lord of the Ottomans,' Nicholas said. The
sword pressed and pressed, and he felt the blood begin to run,
drenching.

'Liar,' said the emir, his lips stretching.

'Whom your lord the King James hopes will help him,' Nicholas
said. 'King James, who is expecting me.'

The blood ran, but the sword had ceased to cut. 'You are the
man Niccolò,' said the emir. 'Friend of the Sultan, I do not think.
But friend of the Genoese, I am told. You have a ship called the
Doria?'

'That is the name of its former owner. A man who I caused to be
killed,' Nicholas said. 'Are you here to debate trifles, or is there
one who gives you orders and will be displeased if you disobey
them? Your lord James expects me in Nicosia. He wishes the
woman to wait for him.'

'It is not so. I will take the woman to him,' said the emir. 'I,
Tzani-bey al-Ablak, lord of the Mamelukes of Cyprus.'

'And I say you will not,' Nicholas said. He struck up as he
spoke, deflecting the sword from his arm and dragging the girl to
her feet and behind him. At her back was the wall. The emir's
blade swept up and glittered above him.

Vanni Loredano said, 'No!' and threw his weight on the Mameluke's sword-arm. Martini and Erizzo both started forward. What
they meant to do was never known, for in a blaze of steel, the doorway
became crowded with soldiers. Loredano dropped his grasp. Nicholas
stayed where he was. The emir, withdrawing his stare from Loredano,
lifted his arm once again. Paul Erizzo spoke in clear Greek. 'This is
the man King Zacco has sent you to bring. Punish him if you will.
But if you kill him, you will answer for it to Zacco.'

The emir turned. He said, also in Greek, 'Tell him to release the
woman.'

Nicholas said, 'I will release her to the monks, not to you. Send the monks, or strike through me, and learn how King James will reward you.'

There was a silence. Behind the open door, the soldiers grinned and muttered and moved; further off came the sounds of other men moving about, mixed with low cries and sobbing and a high-pitched continuous stabbing of sound, like the shrieking of night-hunting owls. The emir laughed and said, 'On the road, I can do what I like?'

'You must not kill him,' said Erizzo. From flushed with heat, the Bailie's face was now pale with anger.

'I will not kill him. Fetch the monks,' Tzani-bey said.

The monk who came first had been crying. The abbot followed and stood in the doorway, intoning Greek in a high nasal voice until Tzani-bey, losing patience, thrust him out of the way. Then others came. As soon as he judged it safe, Nicholas said, 'My lord Bailie. You have no hope of me unless you take care for the lady.'

Erizzo said, 'She will be safe now. I am appalled. The emir has power. I can do nothing for you. I am sorry.'

'You have done enough,' Nicholas said. He thrust the girl between the robed figures and stood. The emir jerked his head. A pair of armed men came forward, both carrying sacks. They set them aside and laid hands on Nicholas. Other sacks stood outside the door, leaking blood and rammed full of objects.

Mutilation and theft. Nicholas, his wrists twisted together, wondered what the girl's chances were, or the monks', if the tyranny of King James was of this order. James, or Zacco, they called him. Zacco the Bastard. One of the monks sobbed aloud. Tzani-bey, his grasp on Nicholas, turned at the sound. He smiled, and spoke to the monk. 'Which was yours? You can have it.' He nodded, and one of the soldiers gripped and upended a sack, and began shaking it empty.

Smoke and silver and black, cream and tortoiseshell, orange and butter, the children of St Nicholas lay, a carpet of silk on the marble. On the top, still the leader, lay the powerful cat, white as ermine, called Otto. 'Skins for the winter,' the Mameluke said. 'Pets are for women, and catamites. Your saint gave you cats to divert you from mounting each other. Everyone knows this is true. There are no vipers so vicious on Cyprus. It is the Christians; it is the serpent of Melusine; it is the Lusignan's sting you must fear.'

He pulled Nicholas through the door and whipped him idly before him with the flat of his sword. Behind him in the room there was horror on the girl's face, and calculation in Erizzo's, and doubt in the look of Loredano. And tears, shamed, uncontrollable tears in the eyes of the monk.

It is the Lusignan's sting you must fear.

Chapter 10

THE ABSENCES of Zacco their King were not entirely mourned by the folk of his capital. Within the seven crumbling miles of its walls, the Greeks and Franks who lived and worked in Nicosia were reasonably pleased to be allowed to continue making shoes, beating silver, working copper, weaving linen and operating the markets which, as an inland capital, the town employed to disperse its wares. The husbandmen tended the fig and olive and mulberry trees, the oranges, the lemons, the pomegranates that grew in the thousand walled gardens, and in the flat lands round the city; and saw to the vines and the barley and the herds of heavy-rumped sheep. The irrigation wheels turned; the smiths hammered; the cooks and butchers attended to their ovens and work-blocks. Those churchmen who had not fled to the Queen continued their rounds unmolested, and under their new lords, the great households continued to demand food and service and pay for it, even if the old barons were all off to Kyrenia to huddle there with the Queen and her consort.

The new owners were the Sicilians and the Aragonese and the Catalans who had come two years ago, when Zacco conquered Nicosia and three-quarters of Cyprus. Zacco, the Venetians called him, the latter Z requiring less effort than J, and the nickname had stuck. The new lords spent as much time fighting for Zacco as the old spent at hunting, only they came back with bales of cloth and sacks of silk and boxes of iron they'd looted from the houses of Carlotta's supporters. They flattened the vines round about Famagusta, which did no harm to the grape prices everywhere else. They captured ships and brought men back in chains who were glad to pay for their freedom. Or if not, King Zacco cut off their heads and stuck them on the Bridge of the Pillory. And, of course, they hemmed in the Queen's men at Kyrenia, killing their forage parties, diverting their food and making sure that neither she nor her consort would ever get back to the capital.

Not that the people of Nicosia had anything much against Queen Carlotta who was, if you thought of it, the legitimate Lusignan heir, and spoke Greek, even if she worshipped in the Latin way. She had to, didn't she? Only the Latin church could call on Christian rulers to hold off the Turks; only the Latin church could rely on the help of the Knights of the Order in Rhodes. Zacco didn't have that advantage, even though his loving father made him Archbishop of Nicosia when he was thirteen: four years, that was, before he had his loving father's chamberlain murdered. Zacco didn't have that advantage because he called in the Mamelukes instead of the Pope, and filled Cyprus with hordes of crooked-sword Saracens. But while it was all very well to say that Carlotta and the Pope could perhaps hold off the Turks, the fact was that the Turks weren't here yet, but the Mamelukes were, and someone had to control them. Someone like Zacco.

He took the Egyptians along with him, too, when he went off on campaign, and the boys in the villages round St Demetrios all fell idle and went to the city. Zacco had most of the Mamelukes out with him now, while a few were with Tzani-bey, off south on some errand. In the event, Tzani-bey came back first, riding through the Dominican gate with a prisoner chained to his girth by the neck. The doorkeeper said he let them all go straight through to the citadel, and that Tzani-bey went and reported to Cropnose. Crop-nose, Zacco's mother, who lived in Queen Carlotta's apartments and had a way, it was said, with Zacco's prisoners. And good luck to him, whoever he was.

The woman called Cropnose was seated on a chair of state when Nicholas was brought in. Most of the things of value had been taken from the apartments either by Carlotta, or by the Dominicans when they fled; but in two years the deficiency had more than been made up by the Usurper. His mother's attendants stood against walls hung with silk and wool carpets, reversed for the summer; the carved service table was laid with tapestry and piled with objects of bronze and ivory, silver and gold as well as fine glazed ware from Syria. Chained to a stand made like a tree was a red and blue bird which nibbled its foot and turned its head quickly now and then.

The King's mother, whom the Greeks called Comomutene, looked like the parrot: spare and quick, with a brilliant cap on her hair, which was the dead russet of henna. Her eyes, which were black, were outlined with kohl beneath high shaven brows. Below her eyes, she wore a thin cerise kerchief in the manner of Saracen women, its hem heavily jewelled. The kerchief hung straight from the bridge of her nose, and blew in and out with her breathing. A burly, coarse-featured man, leaning against the back of her chair, studied the rings on his fingers. The Usurper's mother said, 'What can my son do with that? He is dead.' She spoke in whistling Greek, her words timbreless; dead as her hair.

The emir Tzani-bey, who had let the chain slacken, lifted it up so that Nicholas was pulled by the neck from the floor. 'Dead, Madame Marietta? No, there is good service to be had from him yet. Better than you would have got from him yesterday. He was insolent yesterday. Now he is merely tired; a little thirsty; a little footsore perhaps. It amused the men, to see how fast he could run.'

The woman said, 'How dare you bring him before me like that? Is he deformed? I cannot see him for blood and for filth. What use can he be to the King? Markios?'

The man behind her said, 'I would not, myself, make him Grand Bailie, it is true. What did Zacco want him for?'

The emir said, 'My lord, I was not told. The person came ashore as a prisoner of the Venetians. He had a woman with him, a courtesan employed by the lady Carlotta.'

The man called Markios said, 'So he is Carlotta's man, captured for questioning. It must be so, or Zacco would hardly have kept him alive. What has he said?'

'He speaks insolence, my lord, but withholds information so far. I have not the skills of Monseigneur the King. I can extract nothing from him.'

'But he is Carlotta's man?' said the woman in the chair noisily. 'He can hardly deny that. Are you not?' She made an impatient movement. 'What language does he speak? Pull him. Are you not?'

Hearing and speaking were two different things. Nicholas, staring at her, did not try. The bald, painted brows drew together. Tzani-bey said, 'He needs the whip again.'

The man behind the chair said, 'He needs a lesson, certainly, but I should like to hear him speak first. Unshackle his throat, and give him water. The emir has our thanks, and those of the King, for taking upon himself an unwonted commission. We should not detain him.'

The emir stood, his hand on his whip. He said, 'He is somewhat violent. I will send in two of my men to protect you.'

'Do that,' said the man by the chair. He glanced down at the woman, and drawing a ring from his hand handed it to her. She in turn held it out. 'You have our thanks. Our own men-at-arms will defend us. Go and take your ease. You will hear from Zacco when he arrives.'

'You will hear from me, now,' Nicholas said. He lifted himself to his knees, the hardest thing he had ever done; and then to his feet, the second hardest. He said, through his bruised, waterless throat, 'Tell me. Is this Muslim son of a she-pig your master, or do you have a King?'

The blow returned him to the floor. He lifted himself to his knees, and then to his feet. The woman said, 'That is most unwise. But for my clemency, the emir would have leave to kill you. Whoever commands you to speak, you will reply. What is it to you, where your orders come from?'

'What is it to you?' Nicholas said. His throat burned. 'Do you obey this man, or your son? Who had me brought here, this man, or your son? To whom do I say, I do not serve Carlotta; I will not serve her brother. To this man, or your son? Which is the servant?'

Once, Nicholas had rarely felt anger. In the leisurely journey that had now ended here, he thought he had found again, and would keep, his habit of easy toleration. He had been wrong. The Venetians had lied to him: they would regret it. So too would the man to whom the Venetians pandered. The emir, Nicholas intended to send to his death. It didn't cross his mind, at any time, that he would fail to do this.

The Egyptian was smiling. The man behind the chair said, 'Does one answer scum? No. Here, all men are your masters, including this lord and my nephew the King. To them you must look for food and shelter and life itself without expectation or complaint, or the death you will die will make what you complain of seem sweet. Are you answered?'

'Yes,' Nicholas said. 'You are afraid of the Mamelukes. You are the dupe of the Venetians. So what species of ruler is Zacco? A bully, like Tzani-bey, but a doltish bully?'

The woman called Cropnose looked beyond him to the emir. 'Before you leave, whip him,' she said. 'You are due satisfaction. Or if you prefer, my servants will see to it.'

'It would be more seemly,' said Tzani-bey al-Ablak. 'Serfs should discipline serfs. I have Madame's leave to depart?'

He dropped the chain as he left. The weight, slight as it was, was enough to bring Nicholas to his knees once more, his eyes shut, his head bent. Beatings he had had; punishment he had suffered, but never this. Never what had happened to him on the road from Cape Gata to Nicosia.

He knew, now, that he had used, temporarily, the last of his strength. He remained passive, attempting to gather it. Sounds flowed through his head like the sea. A great door closed: the emir leaving. Another opened, in a different quarter, with a click much more subdued. The soldiers of Cropnose, come to deal with him. A man's voice, speaking in his own sweet French, said, 'I cannot forgive myself. I cannot forgive myself. Water, wine, quickly. And the key to these shackles.' Nicholas opened his eyes.

Kneeling beside him was a man who could have been Anselm or Felix, John or Lorenzo, or any other of the merry, carefree, comely companions who had shared his boyhood in Bruges. This was a young man of their kind, with the bronzed skin and trim build of an athlete, dressed in a plain leather brigandine over a pourpoint and hose like his own. The man's hair, streaked with the sun, fell over his brow in long, yellow-brown waves which he pushed back, now and then, with a gesture of troubled impatience. His eyes were hazel. He said, 'Stay still.' He bent forward, a key in his hands, and unlocked and opened the neck-band. Someone came quickly and lifted the irons away. Then he said, 'Rinse your mouth and then drink. Slowly. There will be more for you later.'

It was water. Nicholas let it pass his split lips and fill the dust-filled cavity of his mouth, and spat. The third time, his bruised throat moved, and he was able to swallow. A small amount was enough. The young man sat back, and someone came for the cup. The young man turned his head and said, 'Mother? How could this happen?'

The woman Cropnose sat with her hands lightly folded. Her manner, if slightly softened, remained quite undisturbed. She said, 'Have we been misled? I was told this was a soldier of Carlotta's, sent to you by the Venetians for questioning. So the emir Tzani-bey believed. If that is not so, then who is he?'

The young man said, 'No! No! What a tragedy! Tzani-bey surely knew. He must have known. Did Messer Niccolò not try to tell him? He is not Carlotta's man. He is a merchant, a captain, a banker. It is to persuade him to help us that the Venetians brought him. Brought him against his will, which was injury enough, but unavoidable. And now –'

Nicholas listened, his lids half fallen. The Venetians had not lied. Some Cypriot baron had blundered. Tzani-bey, lacking orders, had made a mistake. No: had not made a mistake: had taken the chance to enjoy himself. Nicholas, thinking of it, was certain of that. The woman in the chair interrupted his thoughts and the flow of the young man's distress. 'The harm is not irreparable.' Her roaring voice was no different from before; her gaze merely speculative. 'Messer Niccolò is young. He is strong. He is intelligent enough, I am sure, to understand that a mistake has been made. Let him be bathed, and his wounds anointed and bound. Let the monks give him a sleeping-cup, and after rest, some good food. You will talk, you and he, by the evening.' A moment ago, she had invited the emir to whip him. Her brother, now silent, had threatened far worse.

The young man let her finish, then turned back to Nicholas. He said, 'All these things will be done. Then we shall speak.'

Nicholas stood, a thing he had not thought possible. The room blurred and wavered about him. The other rose swiftly, made to approach, then desisted. 'Who are you?' said Nicholas. How many more nephews, uncles, would he have to see?

The other man stood, his arms at his sides, like a soldier answering a charge. He said, 'I am the man you should have met at Cape Gata. It is my fault, what has happened. It is for me to make amends, if amends should be possible. My name is James de Lusignan, King of Cyprus. You will hear me called Zacco.'

For a space, he could not think. Then he said, '*Amends!*' He sent it through the room like a curse.

Above the veil, the black eyes of the noseless woman were fixed on her son. Her son, James of Lusignan, usurping ruler of Cyprus, dropped a hand to the hilt of his sword. He drew it and rested it on his arm, pommel pointing to Nicholas. He said, 'Do with it what you wish. There is my right hand.'

The woman moved, then. Behind her chair, her brother took a step forward, his heavy face flushed. The young man snapped, 'Stay where you are.' They both halted.

Nicholas stretched out his stained fingers and laid them on the grip of the sword. The goldwork on it was Arabic. He looked up. Unclouded and steady, the King's eyes were on his, and the King's right wrist was so held that one clean stroke could sever it. Behind it, unprotected, was his body. Nicholas let his eyes dwell on both, and then return to the sword and his fingers. He ran them over the gold, and lifted his hand from the weapon. He dropped his arm to his side. Nicholas said, 'The weight, I believe, would be beyond me. Perhaps tomorrow?'

Become a little pale under its tan, the other face slowly warmed to a smile of untempered delight. The young man named Zacco said, 'Tomorrow, all things will be possible.'

Later, wakening from his long, healing sleep in the monks' deserted infirmary, Nicholas thought for a long time about what had happened. Questions brought him few answers from the nursing brethren. Those he received, in time, from the boy who saw to his dressings. Jorgin was the King's own chamber servant and delighted to prattle.

'How should you know who he was? The things he's done, you'd never expect at that age. Four and twenty, he is. We call him Zacco. He might never have been born, you know. The last King and Queen, they never had more than a daughter. Carlotta. The one that's blackening his name all over Europe. When Queen Helena found the King's mistress was pregnant, you never heard such a row. That's when the Queen bit off her pretty nose, to make her miscarry. But she didn't, and when the boy was born and grew up handsome and brave, then the King couldn't do enough for him. Made him Archbishop, but then children have got made into Popes, haven't they?'

'He killed his father's chamberlain?' Nicholas said.

'For plotting against him. He wasn't the only one who tried to bring him down, but Zacco always fought to defend himself, as was no more than right. A wild lot, the Lusignans, but they needed to be. And they married wild women, too. Queen Helena was a Byzantine lady from the Morea, and the lady Marietta's another Greek from Patras. Old King Peter, now, had a harem of mistresses, and *his* Queen tried to stop one of them carrying. Held her down, fixed a big marble slab on her belly, and pounded a measure of salt on it. Next, they ground flour on her, working a handmill. But she gave the King a live child just the same. That's the stuff Zacco comes from. You were lucky to keep your left arm. What did they do to it?'

'I don't remember,' said Nicholas. 'How did the new clothes appear?'

'The Venetians,' said Jorgin. 'My lord sent to the Venetians and they brought clothes that would fit. They've got a fine house. You will like it. . . . Why is Monseigneur laughing?'

'Because there is nothing else left for Monseigneur to do,' Nicholas said.

The young Usurper of Cyprus, who had nearly not been born, received him that evening on the first floor, in an apartment which Nicholas took to be his private chamber. Apart from the large curtained bed, it was not lavishly furnished, and could have seated few guests apart from the swarthy man already ensconced there. Nicholas saw a cast of face he had found among the Sicilians of King Ferrante's army: lean and bold of feature, and alarming sometimes in its intensity of expression. This man could not be much over thirty but he was scarred like a fighter, and his dark eyes, watching Nicholas under the drapes of his chaperon, were unfriendly and searching. He looked like a mercenary, but one who had risen to hold office as well as a sword. Nicholas thought it interesting that, of all his court, the King had brought such a man to hear their first conversation. Nicholas bowed, and turned to look for his host.

The King had seated himself on a ledge by the window, which was glazed. Outside, Nicholas could see a balcony, and a glimpse of gardens that ran down to the river that formed a wide moat. James de Lusignan, changed into a pale brocade doublet, was fingering the cord of his shirt and gazing across the flat roofs and towers of the city as if deep in thought. In repose, he showed none of the volatile temperament of the Queen his half-sister. His father's height, which she had missed, was carried with the strong, disciplined grace of a hunter, and he had his father's long-boned, regular features. A tapping foot; an alertness about the eyes were all that might recall a brotherly likeness. His mother was not in the room. Nicholas said, 'You sent for me, my lord.'

The young man turned his head quickly. He rose, and stepping down from the window, stood before Nicholas and examined him seriously. Then he said, 'Good. You look better. You and I are to talk, but I have brought a knight of mine here to reassure you. The lord Rizzo di Marino leads my armies from time to time and advises me, on the field and at home. The advice I hear most often is that I must win the friendship of a genius called Niccolò, who performed miracles in Trebizond, who has made his company famous, who desires adventure and is esteemed by his friends and who suffers from the loss of a greatly-loved wife. Sit and tell me. This is so?'

Nicholas sat. 'My suffering at the moment is of a different order,' he said. 'Suppose we first talk about that.'

'It is my intention to do so,' the young man said. He resumed his seat at the window, studying one swinging foot. When he looked up, his face and voice were both sober. 'We are of an age, you and I, or near enough to make no matter. You have been brought to Cyprus without your consent. In Bologna, you refused to join Carlotta my sister – we know that; but it did not mean that you were willing to come to me, or would have listened had we tried to induce you. Indeed, you would not hear my envoys in Venice. Therefore we took the decision to bring you, and risk your rejection of us, because we thought that, once here, you would use your own judgement to form a conclusion. Will you let me tell you what I have to offer?'

'Willingly,' Nicholas said. 'When you have given me back two months of my life, and Tzani-bey's head in a pig trough.'

The young man Zacco said, 'Our mothers think we are young and careless, and we do not disabuse them. If I were the child I might seem, I could never have kept friends like Rizzo, or have conquered three-quarters of Cyprus. To do more, I needed your help. I did not want to antagonise you. If I could have had you brought in any other way, I should have done. So far as money and honours can help, those you have. There is a fief in this country which is already paying its rents to your Bank in Venice. As for Tzani-bey, I will not deny it. I sent him to bring you. But do you think, do you imagine I would have him half kill you? That was none of my doing.'

'Then he disobeyed you?' Nicholas said. The Sicilian stirred.

'What he did, he did without orders,' said the young man.

'And how do you punish him?' Nicholas said. 'For if he disobeys in the field, more than a captive, one supposes, will suffer. Your own power of authority, even, might be questioned.'

There was silence. Zacco said, 'Of course. How would you punish him?'

Nicholas drew a long breath. He said, 'Every army has its own rules. In mine, he would be publicly flogged and turned off, and his superior degraded for failing to check disobedience.'

'But you would ask his superior first if he had good reason?' said Zacco.

'If I were not the victim, I might do so,' Nicholas said.

The swinging foot in the window had stopped. The young man Zacco held the edge of his seat and considered, the Sicilian knight silently watching him. He returned his gaze to Nicholas. He said, 'You speak of army customs. But what you were offered was physical abuse and dishonour. Man to man, what does he merit?'

'From me? Death,' said Nicholas. 'In fair fight, which he did not give me.'

A profound silence fell on the room. The Sicilian said nothing, his eyes on his leader. The young man by the window did not move, but Nicholas felt the weight of his eyes, and knew he was being studied and weighed, like the most precious of merchandise. Zacco said, 'From me, too.'

Then, for the first time, the swarthy man spoke. 'My lord King. You can't do it.'

'I thought not,' said Nicholas.

A slam answered him, as Zacco stamped to his feet. 'You are wrong, and I can.'

Nicholas said, 'How many men has he?'

The man called Rizzo di Marino said, 'Here, a hundred cavalry and a hundred fantassin. In Egypt, an army that could sweep us all into the sea.'

Nicholas said, 'So why doesn't it do it?'

The Sicilian looked at the King. The King said, 'The Sultan Khushcadam is not secure on his throne among the Mamelukes. He has powerful Muslim neighbours – in Persia, the Turcoman prince Uzum Hasan; in Constantinople, the Sultan Mehmet, lord of the Ottoman Turks. Khushcadam parades his friendship for them, but in fact is afraid of them both. Cyprus serves at the moment as a place of exile for his more unruly subjects.'

Nicholas said, 'Then who would care if Tzani-bey is punished as he deserves?'

The King sat down again. He said, 'First, it would be an affront to Egypt which Egypt could not be seen at present to condone. Secondly, I need the Mamelukes. The Genoese still hold Famagusta. My sister Carlotta and her husband still have their court in Kyrenia. When Kyrenia and Famagusta both fall, the Mamelukes will get what they deserve.'

Nicholas said, 'You think Venice will send you an army? Neutral Venice?' He heard a sound, and saw the Sicilian had moved.

The King said, 'I let the Venetians bring you. They have rich holdings here which they don't want to see destroyed by the

Mamelukes, or the Turks, or the Genoese. The Venetians need you in Cyprus as much as I do. At the very least, they are at a loss for skilled managers to replace those who fled when Carlotta left. They want the Genoese driven out. They want the island strongly held against Constantinople, but held by Christians, even if those Christians have to pay tribute to keep Cairo neutral. You have the skills. You have the soldiers. Perhaps you have friends among the Genoese? I confess I do not. Eighty years ago, the Genoese invaded and ravaged this island, and hung its king, my great-grandfather, in a cage. His son had to pawn his crown jewels to pay them. They own Famagusta and rule there like lords. They chose Carlotta's husband. The Bank of St George and the Knights of St John support Carlotta in all she does. But for the Mamelukes, Genoa would own all of Cyprus: we should be a vassal like Chios.'

'Would you be worse off?' Nicholas said.

Zacco said, 'Ask me that again when I hold Famagusta and Kyrenia, and have ordered the Mamelukes from my shores. This island is rich. We need and cherish our traders. But there can only be one ruler, and that is the Lusignan.'

'I see,' Nicholas said. 'But meantime, the Mamelukes may do as they please. Tzani-bey goes free, and you talk of giving me honour?'

'This is not a court of chivalry,' Zacco said. 'This is a kingdom, fighting to live. Tzani-bey will be told that he has made a serious error. He will be asked, when next he meets you, to offer you public apology. If you fight for me, you will fight as his equal. As for the reparation: your time will come. Did the Venetians stop Tzani-bey?'

'No more than you did,' Nicholas said. 'It is not a court of chivalry, that is certain. I am supposed to fight the Genoese single-handed, for the satisfaction of murdering Tzani-bey at the end?'

The young man smiled and glanced at his Sicilian commander, who leaned forward. 'Not single-handed, Messer Niccolò. We have just received news. Your company is in Rhodes.'

'Explain,' said Nicholas. From head to foot, his body ached.

The man in the window said, 'Why be angry? They found you missing after the great victory of Troia. It was natural that they should look to the coast, and find your ship gone. Venice gave all their assistance – Messer Martelli of the Medici; your own lawyer, Messer Gregorio. A galley was found, and your man Astorre took his soldiers on board, with all your chief officers. It has landed at Rhodes.'

Nicholas didn't hurry to speak. Two hundred and forty miles to the west, Rhodes was the island home of the Knights of St John, the friends of Carlotta, of Genoa, of the Angevins. Now, it seemed, Astorre and all his army were there. Rushing off to the rescue, and sailing to the wrong place. For, of course, it was Carlotta who was known to be pursuing his services; Thomas would have told Astorre and the rest about Silla. And Carlotta, scouring Europe for money, was as likely to come back to Rhodes as to Cyprus. Likelier, Astorre must have thought. In the end, Nicholas said only, 'What will happen?'

The young man said, 'You have forged a strong bond with your officers. They fear for you. Finding no news in Rhodes, they might well sail for Kyrenia or Famagusta, expecting to find you awaiting Carlotta in Cyprus. If they do, they will be intercepted and killed.'

'By whom?' Nicholas said.

'By me,' said the young man in the window. 'Or of course, should they elude me, by Carlotta. She will know by then that you are in Nicosia with me, and that she cannot rely on them.'

'You will tell her,' said Nicholas.

'Yes,' said Zacco. The hazel eyes remained clear. He pushed his hair out of them. He said, 'These things must be done. I have been as candid with you as I can be. There is nothing you now do not know.'

Nicholas remembered something. 'The lady Primaflora?'

'She is with the nuns of the monastery where you left her. The Venetians kept their promise. They want your allegiance. You now know exactly why they want it. You may think that they, too, will not be content to be traders when the Genoese leave, and are building their strength against that day. Perhaps, by then, I shall need them less. I do not know.' He spoke to Nicholas, but the dark man in the shadows had smiled.

Nicholas rose, his wounds aching, his muscles ill-fitting and grinding. He said, 'So what price do I pay for the lives of my company?'

And received, again, the shock that reminded him that he did not know this young, comely man; that he must beware of comparing him with any of the careless, laughter-loving friends from his home. Zacco said, 'It is not a high price. We face winter: they will not sail just yet, especially as Carlotta is expected in Rhodes. They will wait for her. Therefore, you will send to Rhodes, to say where you are. When it suits you, you will go there. You will tell them all I have told you. If they wish to go home, you will send them home. I shall not stop them. If they wish to come here and fight for me and for you, then I will pay them their full worth and more. But the choice is theirs, and yours. I will tell you this, too. I hope they will come. But my real need is for one man, and that man is you.'

Nicholas said, 'And if I choose not to return?'

Zacco said, 'I have already told you. For what you have undergone, reparation in rents will be paid, so long as I rule. You will suffer no harm. I shall merely know I was mistaken.' The hazel eyes gleamed. 'Despite my friends, I make many mistakes. But still, I trust my senses. Have you heard enough to reach a decision?'

'When do you want my answer?' said Nicholas.

'When you are ready. You have heard of Marco Corner? He and Giovanni Loredano married sisters. They share a town palace here in Nicosia which other Venetians use: they offer you chambers there, while you consider your decision. It will give you peace, away from the Haute Cour. It will give you time, too, to hear the Venetian side of the dilemma. I think I am being fair?'

'It was the word that sprang to my mind,' Nicholas said.

The watching face of the knight remained stern: only the young man threw back a quirk of the mouth that changed slowly to something that was not laughter. Zacco said, 'Try and come. Try. I need you with me, not against me. I need someone to think far, far ahead. I need another scorpion.'

'I can see that you do,' Nicholas said.

Chapter 11

NICHOLAS FOUND himself with the Venetians the following morning, after a night in the infirmary which restored some of his energy and gave him time for profound thought.

A speculative temperament was not something he would be credited with. Since he left the shores of Italy, he had been surrounded by men who knew nothing about him but hearsay. But then, even friends of his boyhood would not have been surprised at what had happened. He had been removed without his consent from what he had chosen to do; had objected; had been mishandled; had objected again. He had not been meek, but he had followed from habit his childhood response. Where nothing could be helped except by submitting, he submitted. Except once, in this case, on the journey from Cape Gata to Nicosia, where he had resisted to the end of his powers. On that occasion, however, he had known what was going to happen, whether he resisted or not.

On the morning he was to leave, Marietta of Patras had come to visit him. She wore a different kerchief, but the whistling voice was the same. He realised, when he stood, that she was above medium height as red-haired Greeks often were. She waved off the seat she was offered. 'I have no time. My son says you have not immediately joined him? Because of Tzani-bey?'

'Partly,' Nicholas said. 'It was not a welcome I should care to repeat.'

She had ordered him whipped. She had shown neither dismay nor embarrassment on learning her error, and he could detect none now. She had come to say something, and could see no reason to greet him with an apology. 'If I arrange to have Tzani-bey killed,' Cropnose said, 'will you join my son? Bringing your army?'

'Most certainly not,' Nicholas said. 'If your son punishes Tzani-bey as he deserves, then I might. Or again, I might not. But if you act without leave of your son, nothing whatsoever will induce me to come.'

The kerchief, motionless, was a threat in itself. 'You think my son is more sagacious than I am?'

Nicholas said, 'Probably not. But you are not the King-claimant of Cyprus.'

The kerchief slowly sucked itself hollow, and dropped again. She said at length, 'So you will go to Carlotta? You have Genoese friends, so I hear. And Portuguese friends. The Duchess of Burgundy is Portuguese. So was Carlotta's first husband.'

Nicholas sighed. He said, 'Madame, I have your son's undertaking that he will wait for my answer. When I know what it is, I shall give it to him. But I shall tell you this. I will not join Queen Carlotta.'

The silk snapped like a whip. '*Queen* Carlotta?'

'She is still Queen of Kyrenia,' Nicholas said. 'And the Pope calls her Queen. Only Tzani-bey and the Sultan of Cairo allow your son the supreme title. Tzani-bey is worth more to you at present than I am.'

'Yes. I see that,' she said. 'And he is a man, who understands men. Go home. This is no place for children.'

She left without looking round or she would have seen, with satisfaction, that he was unsmiling. Despite this, one profile was pierced by a dimple. In the whole of Cyprus there was no one to guess, as Tobie might have guessed, what that implied.

The Venetians' house, when he got there, proved to be an old palace, built in the rich and decadent days when the Latins had come straight from Jerusalem, and brought all their luxury with them. There were warehouses adjoining, and a yard with many crates and two kneeling camels. An ornate marble-flanked gate led to a garden with orange trees and a fountain, at present not functioning. He gave some thought to the best way of leaving his mule, and this done, looked about him and won a small wager with himself. Observing him from an inner balcony was Messer Giovanni Loredano, the young vice-Bailie who had served him food at Cape Gata. Messer Loredano exclaimed, disappeared, and reappeared running from the house door. He stopped just before knocking Nicholas over. 'My God: what have they done?'

'What they should have done to you,' Nicholas said. 'I have an itemised list in my satchel.' The distress, he thought, was genuine, although several generations of artifice had perfected its expression. He thought, now he had time, that Vanni Loredano looked like nothing so much as a fully articulated model of a Venetian nobleman. He was led indoors, seated, and given excellent wine in a silver cup, quickly. He was in what appeared to be the nave of a cathedral. Loredano, sitting so near in his anxiety that their knees appeared to be touching said, 'What can I do? What can I say? The Bailie will complain to the Palace tomorrow. Has the King seen how you were treated?'

Nicholas lay back and let the wine go to his head. He said, 'Does it matter? I'm leaving.'

Loredano in turn shifted a little. 'Of course,' he said. 'Who could blame you? And you will take your men?'

'What men?' Nicholas said.

'We had word –' Loredano began. He broke off. He said, 'I'm sure they told you at the Dominicans'. Your captain and men are at Rhodes.'

'That's useful,' Nicholas said. He waited, sipping.

The other man said, 'You will be glad to hear that the lady is safe. The lady Primaflora.'

'Where?' said Nicholas.

Loredano said, 'In the south. You were right. It was safest. Since the monastery was in such distress, we lodged her with the Knights of St John at Kolossi.'

Through his abused and beaten body, a delightful, vinous glow was beginning to spread. Check. Check and check. The night's internal debate duplicated itself in his mind, with certain premises illuminated the way Colard Mansion illuminated them when he was drunk. Nicholas said, 'Well, that's useful too. Carlotta wants her.'

Check and check. The Venetian said, 'The Order does not know, it is true, that the lady has left Queen Carlotta, but her presence at Kolossi is only a temporary measure. As you know, she does not wish to return to the Queen. She feels her place is with you.'

'Then she does have a dilemma,' Nicholas said.

There followed the sort of silence into which Zacco's mother Cropnose had fallen. Loredano said, 'Because of Tzani-bey, you have decided to join Queen Carlotta?'

'My soldiers are joining her,' Nicholas said. 'Or so I was told.'

'But King James!' Loredano said. 'Did he not tell you –?' He stopped.

'That he would have them all intercepted and killed unless I stayed to fight for him? No, he didn't. If he made you that promise, he broke it. I,' Nicholas said, 'am free to join my army and leave if I please, when I please.'

They were no longer sitting knee to knee. The Venetian's broad, suntanned face, brown and flat as a chestnut, had lost its understated veneer. He pushed his cup aside and rose, stepping among the painted chests and gilt stools. He turned, his hands on a ledge. He said, 'I understand. You are entitled to do this. We deserve it. But the issues are momentous, and not only for us, the traders. Not only for Venice. But I do need to know one thing. I believe that Zacco has left you a free agent, although I can't understand why. So will you go to Carlotta?'

'Would I have come here and let you kill me if I intended it?'

Nicholas said. 'And of course, you have Primaflora. You only have to tell the Knights that she had betrayed Carlotta, and they would see that the Queen got to know of it.'

'Does that matter to you?' said Loredano. On his smooth face was real surprise.

'You thought it didn't?' Nicholas said. 'Then you sent her to Kolossi for other reasons. I'm sure the Knights, for example, have no idea that Venetians brought her. Of course not. Queen Carlotta's household has nothing to do with Venetians. So she was muffled going ashore, and I was muffled. So that, when I appear at Kolossi, I can pass for one of Queen Carlotta's men too. Unless, of course, my inconvenient army appears . . .'

Nicholas paused. The brown gaze of the Venetian appeared mesmerised. Nicholas wondered what the man had expected. From what they had seen of him on shipboard, perhaps not very much. He resumed his exposition, which was giving him some enjoyment. 'For you didn't expect Captain Astorre and his friends to follow so quickly, did you? And especially, you didn't foresee that he would guess wrong, and try to follow me to the wrong side. But still, it gave King Zacco a weapon to force me to join him. And since he chose not to use it, you will now have to fall back on your second weapon: the girl, which I have just presented you with. And if that doesn't work: if, despite all my protestations I really don't care a hoot for the lady, there is the best lure of all: the Venetian franchises. You are factor for the Episkopi sugar estates.'

'I am not offering you these,' Loredano said. His speech had changed.

'What a pity,' Nicholas said. 'Because, as everyone keeps reminding me, I do have friends among the Genoese and their Portuguese associates. In return for helping Carlotta and the Genoese, I might have done quite well out of sugar. If not here, then on Madeira, for example. Portugal's new island colony, with all those promising sugar fields. Madeira appeals to me. I have a . . . relative working in Portugal at this moment with whom I have a certain friendly rivalry.' He formed and unformed a smile, without otherwise moving.

Loredano said, 'A moment ago, you denied that you would go to Carlotta. It had occurred to you, as I remember, that you are friendless. And Carlotta is not on this island.'

'A moment ago,' Nicholas said, 'I must admit that I assumed we were talking of sugar. I also, perhaps, overstated my attachment for the lady whose chamber you were so anxious that I should share. The truth is, I'm afraid, that I am still in a position to choose. Only I, for one thing, can instruct my company not to sail to Kyrenia. And on my death, they would certainly work for Carlotta. And if Carlotta wins, the Genoese take all the sugar interests. You were saying?'

The other man released the ledge. His fingers looked cramped. He moved to a cross-legged chair a little distance from where Nicholas sat, and placed himself carefully in it without recovering his goblet of wine. The chair was covered with crimson velvet appliquéd with cloth of gold. 'I was reminding myself,' said Loredano, 'that on shipboard, the Bailie certainly mentioned that the sugar estates lacked good management. Not, of course, those in private hands, such as Episkopi. But there are others. The estates of the Knights are put out to franchise. So are the royal sugarcane fields. At present, the rights to both are held by Venetians.'

'They must be deeply concerned,' Nicholas said. 'If Carlotta prevails, they will lose them. Which Venetians hold them at present?'

The vice-Bailie looked at the pointed toes of his ankle-length boots and, receiving no help, back to Nicholas. He said, 'You met Luigi Martini on the *Doria*. He and his brother hold both of the franchises. They manage the Kolossi crop for the Knights, and the cane fields at Kouklia and Akhelia for the King.'

Nicholas kept his face solemn. It was difficult. Hence, therefore, the grim face of Luigi Martini on shipboard. It was by no wish of his that Nicholas was to be tempted with sugar. It explained why sugar had vanished so soon from the offer. Nicholas said, 'I could hardly remain to serve Zacco in war and Carlotta's allies the Knights in the sugar fields. That seems to leave only the King's farm as an option. Do you imagine both the King and the Martini would consider leasing it to me?'

Loredano said, 'If they did, would you bring your army to Cyprus for Zacco?'

'I don't know,' Nicholas said. 'But I certainly shan't if they don't.'

He watched the pale fawn frown on Loredano's smooth face. Loredano said, 'It will be difficult. I cannot speak for the King.'

'But you could try to persuade the noble Martini?' Nicholas said.

And Loredano said stiffly, 'I shall speak to them.'

'And hoping for a happy outcome, I in turn shall mention the matter to the serene King,' Nicholas said. 'I might even ask about dyeworks. I hear there is a yard in Nicosia, at present out of commission. Unless that, too, is already spoken for?'

Loredano said, 'I think, Messer Niccolò, that you would find the sugar franchise, should you obtain it, would occupy as much of your time as you would wish. The dyeworks, it is true, have not recovered since the last fighting. But their management is traditionally Venetian.'

'I wondered,' Nicholas said. 'And, of course, there is a great deal to be said for traditions. On the other hand, we should live in caves if tradition were not sometimes broken. Perhaps I should mention this, too, to the King. I must commend your wine. It is the best I have tasted.'

He felt very pleased. He allowed Loredano, murmuring something, to pour him more wine, and watched him fill his own cup and quickly empty it. For him, the crux of the visit was over. Now, he didn't mind drinking with Vanni Loredano.

Long after, just before he retired to his sumptuous chamber, Nicholas put some idle questions over the exhausted bottles of wine to a host no longer so dapper and almost equally exhausted. 'So you manage the estates for Marco Corner. I am told you and he married sisters?'

The face of Giovanni Loredano was flushed and his lids sank now and then. He made an effort and opened them. 'That is so. Marco – Marco will be sad to have missed you. He is often in Venice on business.'

'Cyprus owes much to his family, and those others, like your own, that have been long settled here.'

Loredano laid his cup heavily on the table beside him. Its cloth was made of velvet fringed with gold, and a white lapdog was half-asleep in its shadow. A lute lay unstrung by the window, and some sheets of music beside it. Like every Venetian building, this one spoke of their women. Loredano made a visible effort. 'Where would Cyprus be without Venice? We all have the East in our blood: Corner, Contarini, Duodo; Zorzi and Michiel; Bembo, Barbarigo and Loredano. We were traders in the Crusades, and we remained traders after the Mamelukes conquered the Holy Land.'

'Zorzi?' Nicholas said. 'I knew two brothers once of that name. Bartolemeo, a farmer of alum mines, now in Constantinople. And Nicholai Giorgio, a Greek of Florentine origins with a wooden leg. He used a different version of the family name.'

'Nicholai Giorgio de' Acciajuoli. I have heard of him. There is a third brother in Cyprus. Jacopo Zorzi owns vineyards. We all know one another. It is a century and a half since a forebear of mine sent the first shipment of sugar to England. Another Loredano was Bailie for Venice in Cyprus. Through us, Venice knows all that is happening in Constantinople: how the Emperor David fares in exile with his Empress and children; how his Great Chancellor Amiroutzes is amusing himself far from Trebizond. You know Trebizond. You are not still, as we are, in touch with it. Of course, we hear it all, Marco and I, through . . . through our families.' He snatched a handkerchief from his sleeve and touched his lips with it.

'Through the ladies Valenza and Fiorenza, your wives. I envy you both,' Nicholas said. 'It is not every man who marries a princess of Trebizond. You and Messer Marco never bring your ladies to Cyprus?'

'When the children are older, perhaps.' Loredano created a pause; then tucked the kerchief neatly back in his cuff. He looked up, smiling. 'I forget. Of course, you know one of their sisters.'

'In passing,' Nicholas said. 'There are so many daughters of Naxos. But if you are writing to the madonna Violante, greet her for me. In everything, she has shown herself a perfect Byzantine. I extend to her two sisters' husbands all the respect that she commanded from me at our last unforgettable meeting. Tell her that, if you please.'

He neither knew nor cared whether Loredano could interpret the message. He saw from his eyes that he did, and that he had sobered. Loredano said slowly, 'You foolish man. After all that has happened, you are treating this as a game?'

'Of course. You invite me,' Nicholas said. 'Now I examine the board and the pieces. Then we make up the rules. And lastly, I decide whether to play, and what side I want.'

Being under no illusions, it had seemed quite likely to Nicholas that he would suffer a regrettable accident before leaving the Venetians' residence. He thought that if Marco Corner had been there, he probably would not have left with his life. It was important to Venice, for a great many reasons, that he and Astorre should not enrol with Queen Carlotta. It was clearly known that he had Genoese involvements. Anselm Adorne, guide of Tilde de Charetty, was, after all, a kinsman of the Doges of Genoa. And although, at Trebizond, Pagano Doria had been his enemy, Nicholas himself had not returned to Venice in any amenable mood. If they knew that my lord Simon was working with kinsmen in Portugal, it might seem feasible, even, that Nicholas might wish to join or compete with him. Finally, Astorre had not made for King Zacco's harbours in Cyprus: he had landed on Rhodes, where the Knights were Carlotta's supporters. Which could mean that Astorre knew his master's mind better than anyone.

All that, of course, Zacco had also identified. Zacco meant what he said when he promised to attack and to kill any company belonging to Nicholas that attempted to sail to Kyrenia. It seemed to Nicholas that it would be remarkably difficult to tell whether a ship sailing southwards from Rhodes intended to put into Kyrenia or, for example, King Zacco's saltflats at St Lazarus called Salines. It might be that Zacco had reached the same conclusion and, despite his promise, was prepared to sink Astorre wherever he went unless he turned straight for Italy, ten sailing days to the west. So that, whatever happened, Astorre had to be warned not to leave Rhodes until Nicholas managed to find his way there. And the safest way to get word to Astorre was through the Order. And the representatives of the Order stayed at Kolossi Castle, where

Primaflora had been put, passing as an innocent member of Carlotta's household. Primaflora, to whom Nicholas knew he had given too little thought in the aftermath of what had happened to him – and that partly because, perhaps, of what had happened to him. Which was unfair. She was not a young girl, but she was not a man, either, and must be afraid.

Through the night, checking over all the moves he would make if he were Zacco, or Carlotta, or a Venetian, or even an unpleasant Mameluke from the Sultanate, he had been gathering himself to decide whether or not to take part in the game, since now he was free, and a player. Loredano had been shocked by his rapacity, and his seeming frivolity. Loredano did not know that he, too, was already part of a game begun in Bruges three years ago, or perhaps even before. And that the invisible players included a man with a wooden leg, and a woman who had invited Nicholas to do what the courtesan Primaflora would never have expected, or demanded, or allowed. Knowing that, you either escaped, or you let it frighten you, or you treated it as a game.

He had escaped for ten months, and had been brought back. He didn't like the way he had been brought back. He intended to do something about it, even while he knew – he knew as if the Greek had told him, or Violante – that the violence used on him, the provocation offered at every stage had been quite deliberate. He realised, without being proud of it, that he no longer preferred, in any case, to be regarded by the world at large as a precocious apprentice. He was nearly twenty-two, and grown, with a great deal of experience, now. He should be equal, at least, to demonstrating that he did not care to be meddled with. After that, he might choose his own course, if only he knew what it was.

Meanwhile, he had made known to Giovanni Loredano the concessions he wanted from Venice before he would consider staying with Zacco. Loredano would report these to his fellow-Venetians, who wouldn't be happy. He thought Erizzo the Bailie was strong enough to overrule them. Since the concessions referred to royal property, the other half of the equation depended, of course, on the King's readiness to accede. Presently Nicholas intended to ride to the Dominicans', and raise these matters with Zacco, and request the King's written permission to send a message to Rhodes and thereafter, if he wished, to join Astorre there. Then he would leave for Kolossi Castle and make his first, tentative throw in the game the Venetians thought they were playing. Whether it was his game or not, remained to be seen.

The Knights of St John at Kolossi, vowed to chastity, had no idea they were housing a courtesan. Since the days of the Crusades, the Knights had had a presence there. When Acre fell, and there was no longer a Holy Land whose pilgrims needed Hospitallers to care for them and Knights to defend them, the Order had made Cyprus its conventual centre for twenty years before moving to Rhodes. Cyprus it kept as a high military base, opposing the Turks from the third largest island of the Middle Sea, and one of the most fertile. The Commanderie of Cyprus was the richest of all the Order's possessions, pouring thousands of ducats a year into the treasurer's coffers at Rhodes from the sales of its wheat and its cotton, its oil and its wine and, above all, its sugar. And of all the Order's properties on Cyprus, the estate of Kolossi was the largest, with its sixty villages and its acres of vineyards and sugarcane fields.

There had always been a citadel, supplied with deep wells and watered by the River Kouris, with good flat ground for the stables and offices, the guest houses and gardens, and the little Byzantine church of St Eustathios which was open-minded enough to serve the knights for their worship. There had been sugar, too, for a very long time, brought by the Arabs before the days of the Knights. The crop had not always been successful and, in later years, the Knights had found it expedient to share out the costs. That is, a so-called Magnifico from some Venetian firm of growers and dealers would buy the crops for several years in advance, pay for their packing and transport to harbour, and see to all the troublesome business of shipping and selling.

So when Constantinople fell to the Turks and the Order, delving into its pocket, financed the erection of a new, strong keep at Kolossi, built foursquare of pale yellow stone and dominating the saltflats, the plains and the seashore of all the land around Limassol, they took good care as well to see to the sugar plant. They repaired the viaduct that brought river water to the fields and the stone-crushing mill. They refurbished the vast, vaulted white factory and made watertight the warehouses where the sugar cones stood in their chests. They also built new hospices, because powerful men often came to Cyprus as guests of the Order, and they had a small hospital and a good armoury and, below the new castle, vaulted cellars to hold supplies for a siege. In their time, they had suffered a siege or two in the old castle from the Genoese or the Mamelukes, but had never been taken. In their time, there had occurred only events of minor mismanagement: a few killings, an over-indulgence in wine (they made it, after all) and, of course, the occasional girl from the village. Quite often, the girl from the village. But never a courtesan imported with the knowledge of the Grand Commander (now absent) and welcomed, in his bluff innocence, by Brother William, the castle's Lieutenant.

The guest house was not palatial, though sufficient for the lady Primaflora and her maid, the nun and the two serving girls who attended her from the monastery of Ayios Nikolaos six miles away. An honoured attendant of Carlotta, by the grace of God Queen of

Jerusalem, Cyprus and Armenia did, however, deserve better. Brother William was happy, therefore, to have the lady Primaflora and Sister Eudocia join himself and his twenty brethren frequently in the painted room adjoining the kitchen; and walk in their garden when the late autumn rain sometimes allowed, and play her lute, and take wine and chat when they sat indoors nodding on chilly evenings. From time to time she took part in their devotional processions and knelt with simple piety before the altar of St Eustathios, although not quite as often as they did.

The rest of the time, the brethren tended to be in the warehouse, or the office, or shouting at somebody in the factory, because it was the busiest time of the year; the time when the sugar cones from the Order's Kolossi estates were weighed, counted, and placed into chests, each of which must be wrapped in canvas and roped, ready to deliver on shipboard. Eight hundred quintals of sugar, reserving fourteen for the use of the Commander.

Lieutenant William de Combort, a middle-aged, active man with a vigilant eye and a few worthy scars, was the youngest of all the Knights at Kolossi; which did not mean he was young. Cyprus was not far from the Convent of Rhodes with its army. Between waves of war fever, when Sultan Mehmet emerged beating drums from the Bosphorus, Kolossi tended to harbour those Knights who were best suited to crop-growing, building and desk-work. You could not say, of course, that peace reigned in Cyprus itself, what with the Mamelukes and the Genoese and the developing conflict between the unfortunate Lusignan siblings, culminating in the return two years before of the Bastard James with his conquering Egyptian army. Recently, the Hospitallers had preferred to appoint as lieutenant a man who could take a military decision if need be, and know when to send for some help.

So far, he had not had to do so. Whenever southern Cyprus changed hands, the Order's practice was the same. It made a strong representation, demanding that the leaders and officers of the Commanderie should be allowed to conduct their affairs without let or damage, in return for which it promised the same obedience it had shown to the previous ruler. It worked rather well every time. King Zacco had been delighted to agree, and so had the Sultan of Cairo. On Cyprus, the brethren came and went between Kolossi and Rhodes and, on occasion, up to Nicosia and even Kyrenia under safe conduct. In the south, King Zacco knew they were spies, and was well able to keep track of them. In the north, Queen Carlotta used them as messengers and, occasionally, to relay misleading information which her brother immediately discounted. On Rhodes, the Grand Master knew perfectly well that if he let them overstep the mark in Cyprus, he would lose all the money they sent him. The situation was not therefore ideal, but so long as the Knights made more money than trouble, no one wished to upset them.

It did result, however, in a certain ageing of the sitting tenants, and Primaflora might have found the time passing even more slowly had the young Portuguese and his father not been in the Castle as lay guests as well. She had found them there on her arrival, stranded on their way from their homeland to Rhodes, and awaiting a ship to remove them. They seemed in no haste to leave, and very willing to repay their knightly hosts by lending help in the fields and the warehouses. The boy, dark, smooth-skinned and graceful, instantly appointed himself Primaflora's protector and followed her everywhere, like a gazelle. The father, himself comely in the cool, superior mode of the aristocrat, indulged his son's infatuation with an experienced eye, and showed courtesy, but no more than courtesy to Primaflora. If the Knights did not, Senhor Tristão well knew what the lady was.

She could have wished that the two Portuguese spent less time in the vineyards and cane fields from which they returned, on occasion, with their servants behind them bearing sacks leaking with earth. When that happened, they were not anxious to stop and converse, but excused themselves until they were presentable. And presentable was an understatement for the way they were dressed when at last they came to table, the boy making at once for her side, and the father seated beyond, between the Lieutenant and the priest called Father John, who knew relatives of Senhor Tristão and conversed with him (knowing no Portuguese) in a species of terrible English.

Meanwhile, no message was delivered from Niccolò, secretly or otherwise. At first, she had set the monastery by the ears, inveighing against the Venetians for allowing Niccolò to be taken to Nicosia in such company. Indeed, she had refused to leave the monastery until word came, early one morning, that Niccolò was quite safe, and with King James. King Zacco, everyone called him. Before leaving, the Venetians told her that Niccolò would send for her, and she was to wait for him. Since the monks could no longer keep her in their wrecked cloisters, she was to be placed in Kolossi, with some tale that she was awaiting a message to help her rejoin Queen Carlotta. The Order had seen no Venetians. There was nothing to connect her or Niccolò with them. To the Knights of St John, she was still Queen Carlotta's attendant, of whom they had heard before. And Niccolò, she was to tell them, had come to Carlotta.

The monks, in their misery, took no part in the plotting. The repairs to the monastery of Ayios Nikolaos had begun before she left, after the wounded animals had been cared for, or buried. She had watched, that first dusk, when the monks lit the lamps and then, as was their custom, gently struck the bronze bell. She did not wait to see how few were the shadows that came from the beach, or between the herbs and the citrus trees, or what scars they bore from their fighting. If there were vipers, now they would multiply.

Some time went by and, instead of sending for her, Niccolò appeared at the gates with three muleloads, two servants and a limp. From the guesthouse window, she saw him escorted over the south yard, and climb the steps to where Brother William, already summoned, stood to greet him. He was tidily dressed and climbed steadily, but not as a fit man would do. Her woman said, 'They have beaten him. Look at his face.'

Even from such a distance she could see the unfamiliar patches where the broken skin had healed over. His eyes seemed very large, as they had during the fever. Primaflora said, 'Why is he here? Unless . . . unless he has crossed to the Queen's side? Go and find out. Go to the castle and listen.'

Her woman came back quite soon, a coin in her fist. She was grinning. 'Did I need to listen? He saw me and called me over to ask if my mistress was well. He is with King Zacco, truly, but claims to have sailed here with you in order to join Queen Carlotta.'

Primaflora said, 'And his appearance? How does he account for that?'

'Captured by Mamelukes. The truth, near enough, except that he hasn't said they took him to Zacco. The Venetians have never been mentioned. He claims he escaped on the way.' The woman grinned again. 'He has his wits, that one. He asks if you will go to Rhodes with him, or if you have found other patrons.'

Primaflora laughed. She took out her purse and took from it a coin, which she placed with its fellow in the woman's lined palm. She said, 'Why Rhodes? Never mind. Tell him I shall go where he goes, provided I can think of a reason. Whom has he met? I take it Father John wasn't there?'

'You've forgotten,' said the woman. 'He's gone. They sent him to Kouklia, with a message for the Martini. He'll be back in four days. I don't know whom Messer Niccolò's met. He'll see them at dinner in any case. Remember you are the one who persuaded him, they think, to serve Queen Carlotta. The Queen is going to Rhodes. That, he will say, is why he must go there.'

'And the real reason?' said Primaflora.

'One you would never guess. His army is there. He is going to join them.'

'His army!' She stared at the woman. 'The men he left at Troia? He will join them? And then what? Will he bring them back to King Zacco?'

'Of course. King Zacco has let him out on a very long chain, but it is a chain. It would take a better man than this Niccolò to escape it.'

'Then I wonder,' Primaflora said, 'why they beat him?'

Chapter 12

WHATEVER FATE watched over Nicholas it was not a benign one, or it would have warned him not to go to Kolossi. He had no premonitions. He arrived on the heels of a mild success, firstly with Vanni Loredano and then in a much more extended and vigorous interview with the King himself. He had come from that with the promise of all the concessions he wanted, provided that he returned with his army to Zacco. The intensity with which Zacco had delivered that promise still quickened his blood when he thought of it.

Nicholas entered Kolossi with that on his mind; and besides that, two matters of pressing concern. One was the wellbeing of Primaflora, about which he was reassured at the outset by her woman. The other was a probable encounter with Luigi Martini, the taciturn Venetian of the *Doria*. Martini managed the sugar crop for the Knights and, because of Nicholas, was about to cease managing the sugar crop for King Zacco. Expecting open resentment, Nicholas was not sorry to find that Martini was not at the Castle, and that nothing awaited him but a harmonious welcome from the Lieutenant and his brother Knights.

He had no trouble in playing his role, which was that of a leader of mercenaries on his way to serve Queen Carlotta. He was made to tell the tale of his capture by Mamelukes, and his injuries were both inspected and tended. He enquired politely after the lady Primaflora who had shared his journey to Cyprus. She had shown a most sweet relief, it seemed, when told that he was at liberty, and to leave for Rhodes soon — for she, too, was on her way to her mistress the Queen. They thought the lady Primaflora one of the most modest and devout of young women. Nicholas agreed. They promised he should meet her at dinner. Nicholas declared himself gratified.

That, at least was genuine. As the worst of his ordeal receded, so he had recovered the dismantled memories of what they had shared, in which coercion had played no part. He was conscious now that his anticipation ran beyond merely a willingness to think of her. He fished out, for her entertainment, his fur-edged Venetian doublet to wear at the dinner he had been promised, and presented himself in due course in the big chamber, below the vast painted Crucifixion with the coat of arms of the absent Louis de Magnac in its corner.

She was there already. Another time he would have laughed aloud, because her robe was simple and dull and without ornamentation, and her hair, drawn into its severe inflated caul, showed none of the artifice which made men long to unplait it. A demure Primaflora had been created for the Hospitallers, as a timorous Primaflora had been fashioned for Thomas, and – he supposed – a seductive Primaflora for himself. His heartbeat changed now at the sight of her and he saw her face, turned towards him, become vivid. But she said, as any well-trained maiden might, 'How pleased I am to see you, my lord! I was afraid for you.'

He said, 'There was no need, demoiselle. A little rough usage, but I won free before worse could happen. And you?'

'I am well,' she said. 'No princess of the blood could be better treated than I, and my Queen will hear of it. And you? You travel to Rhodes?'

'To join my army. We may travel together. Brother, we are guests at your board. Place us where you wish.'

He was seated beside her. She talked to her partner, and so did he. Beneath the board, her hand found his, and her foot. He smiled, all the time he was talking. Then, at last, she turned to him. She said, 'What did he do?'

'Tzani-bey? Enough to deserve a little reciprocal attention, which he will receive, one of these days. As you see, I have my life and my limbs, and freedom to rejoin my army.'

'In order to do what?' Primaflora said.

'To reach a decision,' Nicholas said. 'But perhaps we need privacy to discuss it. Why are there so few at the table?'

'Half of them are at work. The sugar ship is due soon. And a few have gone off to Kouklia, including someone you know. Do you remember a priest called John de Kinloch at Bruges? I met him there with the Hospitallers. Of course, he has no idea you are in Cyprus, and I somehow failed to tell him. He will be the most surprised of men on his return. Is that awkward?'

She knew so little about him. There was no need to tell her all he recalled about the middle-aged, narrow-faced Scotsman who had served the St Ninian's altar in Bruges. John of Kinloch knew all about the boyhood of Claes the apprentice in Bruges: how often he had been flogged for his escapades; how many girls he had tumbled; whom he had enraged to the point of unreason. It didn't matter what he knew. All that was behind him. Nicholas said, 'Not at all. I'm delighted. I might be more delighted if Master John wasn't an idiot. But as it is, all Bruges knew we were joining Carlotta, and what he has to tell will confirm our credentials. When is he due to come back?'

'In four days, he told me. You have time to improve on your story. Is your army really at Rhodes?'

'So they say. I'll know when I get there. Are we the only guests?'

'All but two Portuguese. They are eating outside, I suppose.'

He would have to check who they were. He did not, even then, experience a real sense of danger. 'I must meet them. From Bruges, or the Duchess of Burgundy's suite? Does John of Kinloch know them?'

She smiled. 'No. They are Portuguese from Portugal, going to Rhodes: nothing sinister, that I can see, about them. The son would like to take me to bed.'

'So should I,' Nicholas said. 'We must arrange it.' Her eyes responded; he smiled and turned his attention elsewhere. His mind dwelled, as it should not, on Primaflora. It was an effort, when dinner ended, to think of anything else. He took her with him, cloaked against the bleak afternoon, when he left the castle to stroll round the sugar mill and the factory. They had hardly walked to the mill race before she pointed out the two Portuguese, standing conferring by the cold, rushing water. The younger, seeing the girl, walked forward eagerly. His face, changed by adolescence, was mildly familiar. The face of the elder was one Nicholas recognised instantly. It belonged to Bruges as well as to Portugal. It belonged to the family that, of all others, abominated Nicholas vander Poele. Nicholas spoke to Primaflora. 'You didn't say the son was a child.'

He felt, without interpreting it, a fleeting surprise, followed by pleasure. Then she said, 'Sixteen, and a virgin. Shall I take him? It would be exhausting, but one must do something. You really don't look very well.'

'What is he called?' Nicholas said. He was sure. It was as well to make perfectly sure.

'Diniz. A pretty name. Senhor Tristão, Senhor Diniz, let me present a Flemish gentleman, Messer Niccolò vander Poele.'

It was too late to stop her from mentioning his name. There was little point anyway. There was a chance, a slight chance, they had never heard his full name, had never noticed a dyeworks apprentice. Nicholas waited, keeping still. The older man gave a slight bow and a smile. The younger lost his smile and held out his hand, which was dirty. Nicholas shook it while his eyes, despite himself, searched the boy's face. The father said, 'Forgive us: we Portuguese are farmers at heart, and spend all our time in the open. Niccolò is not a Flemish name?'

They didn't know who he was. The man spoke in French, the language Primaflora had used, and with no more than a native reserve. He was dark-skinned and dark-eyed, and the boy took after him. 'I am a merchant,' Nicholas said, 'and spend a great deal of time in Italian cities. You are going to Rhodes?'

'If a ship will come to take me,' said the other man.

'You would look far for a better island to live in. I hope to go there myself, for a visit.'

'Oh, mine is purely a visit,' the man Tristão said. 'I have some small company business to execute. A business colleague is waiting on Rhodes to assist me. By the spring we all expect to go home.'

'But with some connection to bring you back, or your son, or your partner? All men of spirit should have some reason for sailing east. Or will you join the family business in Portugal?' He turned to the boy, who reddened and looked at his father.

The father said, 'Diniz would prefer not to go home. What young man would not? But we shall see. And now, what can we show you? If I may usurp the privilege of the brethren, perhaps I may take you to see something of their estates?'

'I should like that,' said Nicholas. 'If the lady will excuse me. She must have seen it a thousand times. Or perhaps Diniz would keep her company?'

He caught, before he turned away, the flash of delight on the boy's face, and smiled at him. After a moment, the young man smiled back. Walking beside him, the father said, 'He is young.'

Nicholas said, 'I can vouch for the lady's good manners. He need not think of me as a rival. You have never been to Flanders, then?'

'I lived there once,' the Portuguese said. 'With the Duchess of Burgundy's household. It was where I met the lady my wife. But that was a long time ago, as you may tell from the age of my son, and I have seldom returned. And you? You have been long away?'

'Long enough,' Nicholas said. 'If there is time, why don't we walk towards Limassol?' He kept his voice free of anxiety, wishing, for several reasons, to hear if Vasquez would excuse himself. Instead the other man agreed, and made no counter-suggestions. The walk they took was not long, considering its repercussions. Nicholas was able, for example, to see what he had been curious to see. And as they went, he and the Portuguese chatted. The name of Senhor Tristão's company, he learned, was St Pol & Vasquez. It had formed an interest in Madeira, developing vineyards and sugar fields there. It was a supplier to the Duchess Isabelle of Burgundy, whose brother Dom Henry had begun the Madeira plantations. And the Scottish lord Simon, brother of Senhor Tristão's wife, was working personally with the company. 'In Portugal?' Nicholas asked. 'Or do you both stay in Madeira?'

'We have homes in both places,' said Tristão Vasquez. 'My wife prefers Portugal, as I think does the lady Katelina, the wife of her brother. It is more congenial, when we are both away, as at present.'

'You sail with your own goods?' Nicholas said. He wore his clown's face, feeling it stiffening.

'Sometimes,' the Portuguese answered. 'Sometimes, as now, we travel to test out a market for something new we plan to export. That is our purpose on this journey, although Simon has travelled ahead of me. If you are coming to Rhodes, you will meet him. You may even have heard of him. He is a famous jouster, in his own country of Scotland. Simon de St Pol, of a family estate called Kilmirren.'

'I think I have heard of him,' Nicholas said.

Re-entering the castle, he ached as if he had been abused again. He found his room, and lying down, attempted to think. Unless he did something quickly, disaster faced him both here and on Rhodes. Here, because John of Kinloch would warn the Vasquez of the vendetta between Simon and Nicholas, and advise the Knights that, pursuing it, Nicholas was unlikely to side with Carlotta. And on Rhodes, because Simon was waiting there. If Nicholas went to collect his army, he couldn't avoid him. And Simon, too, would be sure that Nicholas had arrived for no other reason than to bring down both the Queen and St Pol & Vasquez.

He must go to Rhodes. Without clear direction, Astorre could fall prey to either party without him. It seemed to Nicholas that he could deal with Simon – perhaps – when he landed on Rhodes, for he had Primaflora, whose goodwill was becoming his greatest asset. On the other hand, he must silence the chaplain. He wondered with uncharacteristic bitterness why his game should be spoiled at the outset by the hand which, always, came over his shoulder and changed the pieces. Taking up the thread of his life, he had stumbled upon an amusement, an interest, even an absorption. He had abandoned Bruges, and Geneva, and Venice. But the past had risen up once more to frighten and plague him.

That night, rival of Diniz as he was not, he spent with Primaflora; and by morning, his stiffness had gone. By then, she knew all that he needed to tell her, except for one thing. He kept that till morning. Then he said, 'The Portuguese.'

She was smoothing her own breast with his hand. 'Yes?' she said.

'Their name is Vasquez.'

'That is so. Tristão and Diniz. You know them?'

'I know who they are. They don't know me or my name, and it's important they don't find out any more about me. Unfortunately, John of Kinloch is in a position to tell them. If he does, it could spoil all our our plans.'

'How?' She closed his fingers over the tip of her breast and watched the tip rise to fill them.

'It relates to an old feud. It doesn't matter. But it could lead both Master John and the Portuguese to deduce that I wasn't interested in Carlotta or Madeira or Genoa. They might advise the Knights that I am probably working for Zacco. And the Knights might keep me from leaving.'

She said, 'I thought you hadn't decided yet who you were working for.' This time, she had arranged his hand somewhere else, making him jerk. His concentration broke, for a moment.

'After last night?' Nicholas said. 'I thought it was all too clear who I was working for. To the bone. This morning also, I notice. Christ Jesus. Unless you stop, Mass will take place without us.'

She said, 'I have my own way of praying. So what can be done about Father John?' She lay still.

'Very little,' Nicholas said, 'without more help than we have at present.' He gazed at her, lying still. He said, 'Where is the *Doria*?'

She removed and laid down his hand and sat up with a sharpness of manner she rarely showed. 'You have lost me my mood. The *Doria*? Probably in Episkopi Bay. Why? You want to kidnap poor Father John?'

He halted then, and said, 'You're right. This has nothing to do with you.' But when he moved towards her, she stopped him.

'I want all of your attention, not half of it. Go on. Go on. I am truly listening.'

So he smiled and, sitting too, said, 'I prefer the sweet after the savoury. And it's best that you know. It really would be inconvenient if Father John met me and spoke to the Vasquez. It would be an extremely gentle detention. If he doesn't see me, he will never know who was responsible.'

She said, 'The Knights might mention your name. Wouldn't they miss him?'

'He has arranged to be away for four days. Will they be concerned if he is absent for longer? I doubt,' Nicholas said, 'if Father John plays a formidable part in their routine. Or am I wrong?'

'No,' she said. 'He pleases himself. But how could you do this alone?'

'I wouldn't. Crackbene would help me, or whoever the Venetians have left on the ship. Where is this place John of Kinloch has gone to?'

'Kouklia. The royal sugarcane centre. The brothers Martini have the franchise . . .' She stopped, her hair half-wound on her head. 'No, they don't.'

'I have the franchise,' he said. 'Or the option to acquire it, if I bring my men back to Zacco. But how far off is Kouklia?'

'Not far. You should get there and back in a day. You might

even find them all at the Martini warehouses at Episkopi. It's where the Venetian sugar ship calls. The Knights send their sugar there, too.'

'I've heard. The Martini act as their agents. I'll go,' Nicholas said. 'Can you make some excuse? I'll get a horse or a mule in the village.'

'You might take me with you,' she said. 'I could show you Venus's birthplace.' She held both hands over her head, a strand of bright hair lifted between them. Her breasts were stretched cones made of satin.

However thoroughly he was engrossed, her body spoke to his, insistently, until, like this, it drew from him an answer. His mind, seduced outwards, told him what his unseeing eyes saw, and feeling returned to every surface that made him. Slowly extending an arm, Nicholas took one end of her hair and pulled it all out again. 'I feel that would distract me,' he said. 'No. You stay here and let Diniz exhaust you. Unless, of course, someone has done that already.' He took her two wrists in one hand and, holding them high, laid her back, arched and intent, on the pillows. 'I thought you said I had lost you your mood,' he said. 'And look, you were absolutely mistaken.'

In the end, he needed to go no further than Episkopi for news of John of Kinloch. It took him two miles to the west in a direction he had not yet travelled. He found the road flat and easy, and, without Primaflora to distract him, laid his plans as he rode.

What Tristão and Diniz Vasquez meant in his life was not something he felt impelled to confide in the lovely woman who was now, he supposed, his accepted mistress. She had been curious already about Katelina. He hadn't told her that Katelina van Borselen was married, or that the Portuguese she had just met was Katelina van Borselen's brother-in-law. Seventeen years before, Tristão Vasquez had come to Bruges and met and married Lucia, whose brother Simon years later took Katelina to wife. John of Kinloch knew that. He knew of Simon's past hatred of Nicholas. If Simon and Tristão Vasquez were partners in Portugal, and hence on the side of Genoa and Carlotta, John of Kinloch would be reasonably sure that, whatever he claimed, Nicholas intended working for Zacco. If that became known, Nicholas would not be allowed to join his army in Rhodes, and Carlotta would feel free to dispose of them. Then Zacco, lacking his help, could succumb to Carlotta.

Therefore Father John by some means must be silenced. And it seemed to Nicholas that he should point out to any Venetians he met that, in this instance, his aims were their own.

He knew no one at Episkopi, but walked his horse down to the jetty where the warehouse doors stood open and carts and barrows squelched over the sand and the mud. Offshore, there were several ships waiting at anchor, but he could see no sign of the *Doria*, or of the fair bulk of his Master, Mick Crackbene. The sugar ship had not yet arrived. He left his horse, and found his way to where a number of officials were working. There he found and spoke to two men from the Corner plantation and one who worked for the Bishop of Limassol. They could tell him nothing of the movements of the chaplain John of Kinloch, but were more than ready to listen to him on other, extremely pertinent matters. He had finished his conversation and was returning to the larger warehouse and his horse when the warehouse owner stepped into his path. It was Luigi Martini.

In the monastery and on the *Doria*, Luigi Martini had looked like a man with a grievance, and he had not changed. His face, sallow and lined, was remarkable for its obstinate spade of a chin. Although made of good fabric, his brimmed cap and thick pleated doublet could have done with a pressing. He had the air of a man who was married to business, and who despised every other pursuit. He said now, 'Messer Niccolò. Your beating, I hear, earned you a profit. You are to manage Kouklia for the King.'

Nicholas said, 'Perhaps. You would still have the franchise for Kolossi. But I hope the King consulted you about it.'

'I received a message,' said the Venetian. 'As the King was kind enough to remark, half my profit is still better than what I would have if Carlotta returned. You have not even made up your mind to accept the offer, I hear. How delightful to be young and carefree, and in a position to debate what to toy with, and what to throw aside as insignificant.'

Nicholas said, 'Myself, I avoid such dilemmas. This one, I must remind you, was forced on me. I feel no compulsion, I'm afraid, to apologise.'

'I didn't expect it,' said Luigi Martini. 'You are here to command a vessel for Rhodes? Your own ship, I hear, has been dispatched on some errand.'

'My own ship?' Nicholas said. 'I have no idea where my stolen vessel may be. I am not here to find her. I want to find and silence a man who could prevent me from bringing my army from Rhodes. He is connected with the Knights Hospitaller, and his name is John of Kinloch. Do you know him?'

'I know him,' said Martini. He stepped aside, calling to someone, then returned and stood, his hands on his hips. Sand swirled round them and stuck to their skins. He said, 'What do you mean? The Knights believe you will fight for Carlotta. Why should they prevent your army from leaving for Cyprus? It is Cyprus she wants you to take for her.'

'Because,' said Nicholas, 'this priest has reason to know that, whoever I fight for, it won't be Carlotta. He will warn the Knights at Kolossi. He will tell her. And she will prevent my men from leaving. Do you know where he is?'

Luigi Martini surveyed him. 'You won't fight for Carlotta?'

'As it happens, no,' Nicholas said. 'I may not fight for James of Lusignan either, but that choice is still open. Meanwhile, where is the fellow?'

The Venetian didn't immediately answer. His face, full of distrust, had turned thoughtful. Nicholas hoped he was a student of logic. If he refused to help Nicholas, he would incur Zacco's displeasure. If he agreed to help Nicholas, the plan might still fail and Nicholas be prevented from coming to Zacco, in which case, Luigi Martini would retain the Kouklia franchise. Luigi Martini said, 'You have missed the chaplain you want. He is on his way back to Kolossi. With a good horse, you might overtake him.'

Nicholas said, 'I should need more than a good horse. I don't want to be recognised. I need a man who knows John of Kinloch by sight, and who would help catch him for me, and keep him until I've got clear of Rhodes. I don't mean the priest harm, and I should accept any blame that resulted. No one need know your share except, of course, Zacco. Will you help?'

It was hard to remain calm, and talk quietly. There were only two miles to cover, and the priest had already set out. Had there been more time, he would have added another inducement. He had made sure Martini would hear of it afterwards. Then the Venetian said, 'Yes. I will help you. There is a man who knows Father John, but is not known by him. This horse is fast: he can take it. Tell him what you want as you go. You will remember that the Knights are my employers.'

'The deed is mine. You know nothing about it. Thank you,' said Nicholas. He mounted as he spoke, and waited as Martini's man trotted up, looking puzzled, and then set off up the road. Ahead somewhere was John of Kinloch. And he had to reach him before he got to Kolossi.

He might have managed it, if the priest had kept to the road. Nicholas never discovered why Father John chose to diverge. He only knew that he and his companion raced all the way to Kolossi without catching sight of him. Across the drawbridge, the first person Nicholas met was Primaflora. She stopped. 'The priest? Didn't you find him?'

'He isn't here?' Nicholas said. Then, as she shook her head, 'He set off to come back. I've overshot him. We'll have to go back and hunt.'

'No, you won't,' said Primaflora. 'Your problem is solved. A ship of the Order is coming to load the Commanderie's wine. It's sailing to Rhodes. It will take you and me and both the Portuguese Vasquez, and you will be away from Kolossi before John de Kinloch can meet you.'

Her voice, ending, sounded annoyed because he was looking over her shoulder. 'What do you wager?' said Nicholas. 'There is John of Kinloch, riding up to the drawbridge this moment. And coming in. And dismounting. He's seen me. Where are the Portuguese? Indoors? Go and talk to them. Have congress with them individually, if you like, on the floor of the Hall, but keep them indoors and happy. You, come with me.'

With Martini's man following, he began to walk over the yard. He turned. 'The ship is coming in when and where?'

Primaflora said, 'Tomorrow evening at Limassol. You can't –'

'Yes, I can,' Nicholas said. He watched her move to the steps. If the priest had seen them together at all, it must have looked the most superficial of encounters. He turned again and advanced. 'Master John! Do you remember me?' He spoke in Flemish. No one employed by the Martini brothers would know Flemish.

The chaplain stopped. The lean face and spare body were muffled against the chill weather: the cuffs of his cassock showed under those of his gown, and over all he was wrapped in a black fustian cloak that reached to the ground. On top of his hood he wore a wide-brimmed black hat with a broken cord. His mouth opened, revealing crossed teeth and a lot of gum. He said, 'Claes. It is indeed the varlet called Claes, from the dyeshop. Well, well!' He grinned, showing where the teeth ended. 'It's well seen you've come into money!'

The tongue he used was not Flemish, but the Scots spoken in Fife. Twenty-four years before, John of Kinloch had been chaplain to the Hospitallers' Master in Scotland. In more recent years, he had served the merchants' Scots altar in Bruges, and had found no reason to be fond of a high-handed Scots lord, or an upstart dyeworks apprentice. In the hateful war between Simon and Nicholas, Father John would add fuel to both sides. Without knowing, of course, the real issue.

He was not a quick-witted man. At first, the implications escaped him. Nicholas said, 'And what brings you here? Hospitallers' business?'

The crooked teeth glittered. 'Oh, you might say. The canon of Aberdeen had some annates for Rome. Young Scougal's made Knight, and needed someone to come to Rhodes with him. I took the chance. And yourself?' The frame of his face ceased to move. He said, 'By my dear Christ. The lord Simon's on Rhodes. It's his Portuguese kinsmen you're after.'

Nicholas said, 'You are mistaken. We met here by chance.' He hardly bothered to say it. No one, knowing his past, would believe it. He trapped the eye of his helper, and looked away again. He said, 'I mean Tristão Vasquez no harm: what do you suppose I could do? They needn't even be told who I am.'

The priest's face became hollow. 'They don't know? You haven't told them? What devilment are you planning? Of course, you're going to undercut what they grow in Madeira. Cyprus sugar, that's what you're investing in!'

'Perhaps,' Nicholas said. 'I haven't even decided. In any case, what could you tell Tristão Vasquez? He's never heard of Nicholas vander Poele, or of Claes for that matter. He would think you eccentric. In fact, I should have to tell him you were.'

'Tell away,' said the priest. 'I can tell them you tried to stab Simon at Sluys. I can tell them you ruined his business at Trebizond and fought him in Venice – I heard about that. If they want to know what sort of man you are, I can tell which of your mother's kinsmen you ruined or murdered, and how you just failed to get the Charetty business when your wife suddenly died, and you found she'd willed everything to her older daughter. Won't they wonder why? Won't they wonder why the daughters drove you from Bruges for very fear of their lives? That's the story going about.'

'And you believed it?' Nicholas said. 'Next time, ask Father Godscalc. Meantime, I'm sorry, I don't want to distress Tristão Vasquez for no reason.'

'You've come here to kill him. I see it,' said John of Kinloch. 'You will not do it. I forbid it.'

He had the valour, if only the silly valour, of righteousness. Nicholas said, 'All right. Come with me to the Lieutenant. Where are your saddlebags?'

They were on his horse, which somehow had found its way into the stables. Nicholas said, 'I will wait for you.' He waited until he heard the scuffle, and then slipped through the door after the chaplain. The Venetian was already kneeling, with the priest lying pinned on the straw. Nicholas said, 'Father John? I'm sorry. I can't afford to have my affairs damaged by gossip. You will come to no harm, nor will the Vasquez. You will be kept in a safe place and then allowed to go home as soon as possible. I know the offence is great, and I shall do what I can to make up for it. Do you understand me?'

'Murderer!' said John of Kinloch.

'I think,' Nicholas said, 'we should bind something into his mouth.'

'I think you should,' said the low voice of Primaflora behind him. 'What a villainous past! With whom have I been consorting?'

Nicholas finished knotting the rope-ends and turned. She waited, wrapped in her cloak, where John of Kinloch couldn't observe her.

He said, equally softly, 'With a man. What about our Portuguese friends?'

'They are safely at table,' she said. 'Are you going to kill the poor man?'

'Not immediately,' Nicholas said. 'We are taking him, in the form of a sack of flour, to a house this fellow knows of. You can ask your questions later.'

'I shall ask one now,' said Primaflora. 'Is this why you prefer James to Carlotta? Because you have a vendetta against someone on Carlotta's side? This man Simon, now waiting in Rhodes?'

The horse trampled. 'Let us say,' said Nicholas breathlessly, 'that someone with interests in Genoa and Portugal has a vendetta against me.' They were thrusting the priest, a threshing bundle, into a pannier.

She still stood in the doorway. 'Twice, in Bruges, someone mentioned a woman called Katelina.'

Damn Colard. 'Yes. Well,' Nicholas said. 'You now appear to have heard about Simon. Vasquez married his sister. Katelina is Simon's wife. His second wife.'

'And you hate them all?' said Primaflora.

'No,' said Nicholas in sudden anger. He turned, breathing heavily. 'I don't hate anyone. Well, Tzani-bey al-Ablak I do make an exception for.'

She watched them lead the horse over the drawbridge and out into the road. Then she went back and was particularly charming to Diniz.

Chapter 13

NICHOLAS EMBARKED for Rhodes at dawn the following morning, accompanied by Primaflora his mistress. The Vasquez, father and son, went on board with them, and no screaming, dishevelled priest appeared to warn them that they were sharing their trip with a murderer. Before he left, Nicholas met once again the man Martini had loaned him, and sent him back to the Venetian with both advice and information. He hoped, as a result, that John of Kinloch would be securely kept and well treated until he need no longer fear him. He not only hoped, he felt confident.

The galley, flying the Cross of the Order of the Knights Hospitaller of St John, had come straight from Rhodes. It seemed, interestingly, to be already loaded. Nicholas, who had spent some time on the roof of the seventy-foot citadel, had observed no bustle of exodus the previous day from the storehouses. The spreading fields, on the contrary, had appeared singularly peaceful, stretching to the south, and the sea. There had been a smudge of smoke above the distant monastery of Ayios Nikolaos, and a streak of rose-tinted white told of the saltflats, with the winter flamingoes on them.

It occurred to Nicholas that he had never seen Cyprus, except in autumn and winter. He had never really seen Cyprus at all. The birthplace of Venus was unknown to him; and the vineyards of Engedi. He had inclined towards coming back, if Astorre agreed, for a number of reasons. Now, because of Simon, he didn't know. Whatever happened, he had deceived the Knights, and could never return to Kolossi.

He had formed an inexact strategy, as yet, for dealing with Simon, waiting on Rhodes for Tristão his partner. Astorre should be on the island as well, with his company. He had been told to remain, by the messages the Order had undertaken to convey to him. He had been told Nicholas was arriving from Cyprus. Fishing boats carried such intelligence. Nicholas only hoped that the

warning had reached him. If, unwittingly, Astorre took his army to
Kyrenia, Zacco would intercept and destroy him.

Meanwhile, wherever Astorre and the others might be, it was
unlikely that Simon had not come across them. Rhodes was a small
island: it would fit eight times into Cyprus. It seemed to Nicholas
that, very likely, the die was already cast, and that both the Queen
and the Order would have been told he was working for Zacco.
Simon would expect him to come, to extract Astorre and his force
from the island. Simon would perceive (and tell the Order), that
Astorre was wrong in assigning Nicholas to the Queen's faction. If
Simon's company favoured the Queen, then Nicholas, surely,
would choose the opposite side. So Simon would reason. Simon,
who loathed and despised Nicholas, because Nicholas had been
born to his first wife.

Of that, Primaflora knew nothing; or Tristão Vasquez, whom he
might have called uncle; or Diniz, whom he might have called
cousin. Nicholas did not enlighten her, or them. Only he gave in to
the temptatation, now and then, to talk to the boy, who had lost
some of his jealousy, since the exchanges between Nicholas and the
lady Primaflora were so markedly formal. The lady travelled in
state, as befitted her rank as Queen's lady of honour, and spoke as
often to Diniz as she did to anyone else. It amused Nicholas,
although the locked door of her quarters did not. She knew how to
tantalise. He ended, for his own sake, by avoiding her.

The boy's company was almost as testing, since Nicholas had to
make his way with such care. He had guessed already the bond
between the high-bred, reticent father and the lad only now out of
the schoolroom. He didn't ask about the boy's mother Lucia, but
stored the fragments he learned. He knew she had been put early
to royal service and had assumed her more worldly, he saw, than
she was. Tristão Vasquez had rescued his wife from a duty she
hated, and had given her peace and a tranquil family life away from
her wild brother Simon and their domineering father, de Ribérac.
The boy would have continued, but suddenly Nicholas felt like an
eavesdropper. He said, 'Sometimes strong fathers make wild sons,
until they find what it is they want to do. What do you want for the
future? To follow your father?'

Diniz was not to be immediately diverted. He said, 'My uncle
Simon is not very wise. My father blames his father, as you do.
Also, he has a very young bride who cannot control him. My
mother says his conduct with other men's wives is nothing short of
disgraceful.'

Simon's wife Katelina was twenty-two, and some months older
than Nicholas. Poor Katelina. Poor Katelina, who wanted to ruin
Nicholas quite as much as her husband. Nicholas said, 'Do you
want to stay in the East and serve your company? Some agents do,

for experience. After a year or two, there is more to be learned at the centre.' He stopped himself talking of Bruges. They didn't know where he came from: Simon must never have mentioned him. They knew his Bank was in Venice, and about Trebizond.

It was about Trebizond that the boy was most curious. In the end, Nicholas briefly explained. 'You know Constantinople was the capital of a great Byzantine empire, and that it fell to the Turks eight or nine years ago? Trebizond was a Byzantine empire as well, with rulers sprung from the same race. When Constantinople was taken, Trebizond was left exposed to the Turks. It was very rich, because of its trade with the East, and Venice and Genoa and Florence all had an interest in keeping it safe. So had its non-Christian neighbours, like the Turcoman tribe of the White Sheep. Because of its allies, and because it was built between mountains and coast on a rock, it was thought Trebizond would be safe, and the Imperial family would come to no harm. To make sure, they asked mercenaries to come and help them, and I took my company there, and also a commission to trade, both for myself and for Florence. We arrived there the spring before last.'

He paused. The boy said, 'But the Turks attacked and took it. How did they do it, if you were there? If it was between the mountains and the sea? If all these races were anxious to help them?'

A voice said, 'What causes such solemn conversation? Diniz, you are tiring our friend.'

It was the boy's father. The boy said, 'No! He is telling of Trebizond.'

'Ah,' said Tristão Vasquez. 'I am glad not to have been there.'

The boy was disappointed. 'You would have fought!'

The nobleman hesitated. Nicholas said, 'Your father means that he was glad not to be there, and to have to discriminate. It wasn't simple, you see. The Empire was magnificent, but the blood of the line had run thin, and the barons were self-indulgent and treacherous. They had grown too weak-willed to fight, and too spoiled to face privation. The western traders hated each other, and the White Sheep, who might have become its protectors, were not quite strong enough to take the Empire away from the Turks. Even Georgia, which might have helped, didn't. There was a moment when anything might have been possible, and a decision one way or the other might have resolved its fate. For no reason except that I was there, I played some part in what happened.'

Tristão Vasquez was silent. The boy said, 'What did you do?'

Nicholas said, 'It hardly matters now. In the long run, the Emperor was recommended to surrender by his own Great Chancellor, George Amiroutzes. For money, the Emperor sold Trebizond into slavery and was allowed to go into exile on a pleasant estate at Adrianople. He is still there, with his younger children. The older members of his family were given to the harem, or the Viziers.'

He had told it as painstakingly and accurately as he could. He had not mentioned the friendship he had struck with the mother of Uzum Hasan, prince of the Turcomans, which might have saved Trebizond if the Turcoman strength had been supported. He didn't talk of the other, attempted treachery by a man paid by Simon de St Pol to follow and challenge him. The man had died, and he now possessed his vessel, the *Doria*.

What happened at Trebizond had taught Nicholas a lesson about his fellow men he had been unwilling to learn. He did not, normally, choose to resurrect it. At the end, the boy didn't speak for a while. Then he said, 'I'm glad I wasn't there. Who would have known what to do?'

Then Nicholas said, 'Someone has to do something, even if it is wrong. We did the best we could, and when it was taken out of our hands, we saved ourselves, and our goods, and as many Western lives as we could. What we did was possibly wrong. I don't know. But at the end, only the Emperor could have changed events.'

Diniz said, 'Why didn't he?'

Nicholas said, 'I suppose he thought slavery for all his people was better than death for some or even most of them. He may not have considered what his people might want. Often a ruler can't imagine the full effect of the orders he gives. He sees only his friends and his family. He doesn't see the man who makes his shoes, and kills his beef, and brings his water from the well. The soldiers he calls in see all this. They can take their money and do as he says. Or they can refuse. If I had to choose between King James and Queen Carlotta, it wouldn't be easy.'

He didn't look at Tristão, but it was to Tristão he was speaking. Diniz said, 'But she is the rightful Queen! There is no question.'

Nicholas said, 'Where a bastard is better, he governs. Haven't you noticed? You don't look at birth. You say, "Cyprus is my dear home. Who best can rule it?"'

Diniz said, 'I should say, "Who best can protect it from Sultan Mehmet?"'

'And who is that?' Nicholas said. 'The Pope has to see King Ferrante finally on the throne of Naples, and Malatesta of Rimini finally conquered before he can think of a crusade. The Duke of Burgundy is sick and failing, and fending off Louis of France. France is threatened by England, and England is torn in the war between York and Lancaster. Genoa would take over Cyprus, as a colony. So would Venice. So would Cairo. The only traditional rulers in Cyprus are the Lusignan family, and they are divided: King Zacco supported by Venice and Queen Carlotta by the

Genoese. Is it really clear who should rule? Is it really clear who can best fend off the Turks?'

'You don't agree it is Carlotta?' said the boy.

'I think Carlotta will lose,' Nicholas said. 'All I can tell you is that the people of Cyprus won't win, whatever happens.'

'Then Zacco or the Turk would be as bad as Carlotta?' said the boy.

Nicholas smiled across his head at his father. He said, 'You have a lawyer there. No, they are not equal. I meant that the island has such importance that whoever rules, the land is always a battlefield, and it is the men of the fields and the hamlets who suffer. Nor should I place Sultan Mehmet over a Christian people.'

Tristão Vasquez spoke. 'But of the other two, you think more highly of Zacco?'

Nicholas said, 'I didn't say that. I said I thought that Zacco would win. What, do you suppose, is that vessel?'

The boat was a round ship of unspecified origin which, appearing out of the rain, turned its shining guns broadside and hailed them. Tristão Vasquez, turning, said, 'I wonder. Trouble?'

'Surely not,' Nicholas said, lying flat. The explosion, following the puff of smoke, rattled the rigging. A gush of seawater beat on the deck. 'But it seems,' Nicholas said, 'they want us to do something. Are they Mamelukes?'

The boy said, 'They are talking Italian. They want to board us. The lady must be protected.'

'That is true,' 'Nicholas said. 'I shall go and protect her. Do you have valuable baggage?'

'Yes,' said Diniz.

'No,' said his father. 'Agricultural specimens, that is all. What are our officers doing? Knights of the Order, submitting?'

'Only one Knight, and he knows superior fire power when he sees it. He may lose his cargo, but he won't lose his galley at least. The round ship *is* boarding.'

'They want the wine,' Diniz said. His young mouth sneered.

'I would rather they had the wine than my blood,' Nicholas said. 'Or that of the lady Primaflora. Here they come to open the hatches. Pirates. How do they sniff out their prey?'

Flank to flank, the galley and round ship ground buffers together, held by irons for as long as it took to transfer the cargo. They took the wine, and also the chests that filled all one hold. Diniz said, 'Are these valuable?'

'Who knows?' Nicholas said. 'Gold thread, or dyed silk, or ducats. The Knights are rich. Nothing worth perishing for. No! Look out!' His cry followed Diniz, who had burst through the cordon restraining them and run to one of the hatches, exclaiming. As his father attempted to follow, one of the boarders raised a club and struck the boy down. The father shouted.

Nicholas jumped to grasp Tristão Vasquez by the arm. 'Don't provoke them. The child will recover. He was brave, but no one can stop them that way.'

The Portuguese strained against his grip, then subsided. The boy lay still. The man who had struck him bent aside and continued to hand out fresh articles from the hold. They consisted now of deep trays, filled with earth and small plants. They passed from hand to hand until they reached the ship's rail, at which point they were halted by one of the pirates. He peered, snorted, and turned his thumb down. The bearer of the first tray stepped to the side and dropped over his burden. The other trays followed.

The face of Tristão Vasquez was stony. Nicholas said, 'I'm sorry. That was where you had buried your gold. You would have done better, like me, to make a stomacher of it for some lady.'

'They respect that?' said Tristão.

'Not necessarily,' Nicholas said. 'But finding it, they might spare the lady.' He felt, for the first time for a while, and despite everything, surprisingly happy.

It was dark before the round ship pulled away, and the galley, shaken, continued its course towards Rhodes. The master, his checking done, came to rehearse the tragedy with his four guests. 'They have taken all of value. You would say they knew what we carried.'

'I can vouch that they didn't,' said the older Portuguese with disgust. 'They knew the value of nothing.'

'They took the wine,' the master said. 'And the sugar.'

'That is the least of it,' the Portuguese said.

Nicholas said, 'The sugar? What sugar?'

'The sugar for Rhodes,' said the master. 'You're from Kolossi. You ought to know. Eight hundred quintals of sugar, less fourteen for the use of the Commander. They're expecting it. It's arranged for. They'll have the skin off my back for not bringing it.'

Primaflora looked at Nicholas and Nicholas did not return the look. He said, 'I thought the sugar harvest went to Episkopi to wait for the annual Venetian galley.'

The master shrugged. 'Who knows? In normal times, maybe.'

'I thought,' Nicholas said, 'that the Venetians had paid in advance for the right to sell the Kolossi sugar? For many years in advance?'

The master looked Nicholas up and down. 'Are you saying Queen Carlotta should suffer because the Venetians are greedy? If we had done nothing, the sugar would have gone to Episkopi, and straight to the pockets of the Martini brothers. Of Venice. Of those who secretly promote James de Lusignan. This way, it goes where it belongs. To Rhodes, to be sold by the Knights. The Knights on whom Queen Carlotta relies for her ships and her funds.'

'And what will the pirates do with it?' Nicholas said.

'Who knows? Eat it,' said the master. 'Drink the wine, eat the sugar and, if God is good, die of the flux. Excuse me. I have to prepare myself. I have to prepare myself to meet the Treasurer of the Order and explain.'

Later, pushing him surprised over her threshold, Primaflora confronted Nicholas in her hitherto solitary cabin. 'What do you think the pirates will do?'

'Oh, I don't know. Sail to Crete, probably,' Nicholas said. He assumed the face of an owl. 'The other Martini brother is there.'

'So they knew the Order was going to cheat?'

'It seems likely,' Nicholas said. He allowed his face to unpucker 'Carlotta's consort cheated last year with the royal crop. Smuggled it out from Kyrenia and tried to sell it. That belonged to the Martini brothers as well. But you know that. You were with Queen Carlotta.'

'The sugar she took to Bologna?'

'The sugar she tried to take to Bologna,' he corrected musically. 'She couldn't sell it in Venice, because it belonged to the Martini. She found Bologna had started refining, and went to sell it there. But of course Zacco's men tried to stop her. Did they ever find out, I wonder, that the chests in the river held snow? And what happened to all your fine candy men?'

'She sold them to the Vatachino. Bologna refiners. They beat her down because the sugar was extremely impure. She left in the eyeballs and buttons. You went to Episkopi yesterday.'

'Of course. I had to find John of Kinloch.'

'Of course. And now we know that what John de Kinloch said was correct. You chose the opposite side from the Queen for personal reasons, not because you think she is wrong. Perhaps, too, you are nervous of capable women.'

'I was married to one,' Nicholas said.

'Yes. But she was not twenty-four.'

'I think,' Nicholas said, 'you have put your finger on it. I felt at ease with Cropnose at once. And, of course, with you; but you are incapable. On present evidence. Well, with the door open. Perhaps even now, with the door shut. Or really, it is all these garments that get in the way.'

All her grown life, she had known how to stop a conversation. She had never in all her grown life found it so hard to get one started again. And when, since he wouldn't leave otherwise, she had indulged him, he dressed at once and departed, in case his absence caused remark, or so he said. And for the rest of the voyage he moved about, helping the master with the wounded men, for they had no doctor on board, and ending in Vasquez's cabin, salving and rebinding the wound on young Diniz's head.

Discovering him there, Primaflora stood in the doorway and watched, while the boy's father said, 'You are knowledgeable. You are not a Hospitaller?'

'No,' Nicholas said. He laid back the boy's head, and received a wan smile. 'I had the benefit of watching a very good army doctor. A nephew of Ferrari da Grado.'

The father looked up. 'The Professor? King Louis, the Duke of Milan are his patients. What is his nephew doing – I beg your pardon.'

Both dimples appeared. 'With me? You would have to meet Tobie to understand. He worships Urbino and fought Malatesta on principle. He follows armies and hates war. His uncle despises him, but he is not all he seems. He has taught me not to make easy judgements. I hope sometimes that people likewise do not believe all they might hear of me.'

'But nothing but good, I am sure,' said Senhor Tristão. His voice was warmer than Primaflora had heard it, and so was his smile.

Nicholas, on the contrary, was not smiling. 'You think not?' he said. 'Well. Don't let's take a wager on it. I'll leave him. He'll do now.' And touching the boy, he turned and left the cabin, the woman following.

She said, 'You have purloined my disciple.'

'A temporary aberration,' Nicholas said. 'You'll get back his devotion tomorrow.'

He had told her what to expect. She said, 'When they learn who you are from friend Simon? They will both be distressed. You don't want to tell them yourself?'

'No,' he said.

'And you still expect to be seized and executed as a servant of Zacco's? Is your man Simon so powerful? Without proof, I don't see how the Queen or the Order can harm you.'

'What would you do,' he said, 'if you were the Queen, or the Grand Master of the Order?' *What would the other man do*. Always, always the question.

She thought. 'If I knew you were coming, but not when? I should give orders to meet all ships from Cyprus. I should still hope to win you to Carlotta, so I should treat you politely, but keep you under some sort of restraint until your loyalty could be proved beyond question. Then, if I found you were Zacco's, I should kill you.'

'That's what I thought,' Nicholas said.

'And so? How would you deal with it?'

'Oh,' said Nicholas. 'I should join Carlotta immediately. There is really no other course.'

'I suppose not,' she said. Soon she left him, and he didn't see her

again until the drums beat for landfall. Then they stood on deck,
with their coffers piled about them, and watched the blue outline
of mountains come nearer, and the two harbours with their forts
and their long lines of windmills, and behind those, the rising
ground that contained, within its thick bulwark and walls, the
houses, churches and palaces of the capital of the Rhodian isle, the
isle of Helios and Hyacynthos, the island of roses, the home of the
Knights of St John.

On their flank was the Hospitallers' war fleet, in the harbour
called Mandraki with the chain locking its entrance. South of that
was the trading harbour of Rhodes, full of shipping. On a long pier
at its end, a new fortification was being built. 'The bastion of St
Nicholas,' said Primaflora. Excitement or fear had given her skin a
glow normally concealed by her art; her eyes were alight. Today,
too, she had replaced her sombre clothes with the style of the
court. Her sleeves were ribboned under her mantle which itself
had a trimming of ermine, and her hair was concealed by a high
rounded hat that displayed the pure lines of her face. He had felt
the same impulse to make a gesture, and had dressed finely, for
once, to escort her. She appreciated it, but it also amused her. She
pursued the question of the new bastion. 'Are you proud of your
saint's work? See how the ship bows as it passes. Built with the
Duke of Burgundy's money. He vowed to launch the world's
greatest crusade, but in the end, it was easier to build a new tower
for Rhodes.' She paused. 'What is this man Simon like?'

Nicholas, too, had been watching the jetty come nearer, and was
scanning the crowds on its length. A band of Knights, naturally, to
greet the ship and its officers, and receive the report of its master.
The Brethren whose business was imports. The merchants looking
out for their cargo. The dock workers, the cranemen, the lighter-
men. The customs officers and the searchers and the harbourmaster
and his officials. And beyond, by the walls, the stalls of the scribes
and the moneychangers. The hawkers of bread and fruit and tavern
accommodation. The friends and families of the crew, looking for
presents and wages before it all got drunk. An emissary perhaps of
Luis, King-Consort of Cyprus, come to inspect the illicit goods
which had been spirited off under the noses of Zacco and the
Venetians. An emissary of the Queen or the Order, come to see
what else of Zacco's might have arrived.

And presumably, somewhere, Simon de St Pol of Kilmirren,
come to greet his wife's brother and his half-Portuguese nephew
Diniz. And, one fervently hoped, nowhere at all, Astorre or Thomas
or Tobie, to share in the moment when Simon looked up and saw,
grown to hated manhood, the child born to his wife who called
himself Nicholas vander Poele.

Meanwhile, he had been asked a question. Nicholas said, 'What

is Simon like? Look for the most beautiful man you have ever seen
except maybe for Zacco. He has your own colouring apart from his
eyes, which are blue.'

He could feel her surprise. She said, 'I imagined, from what I
heard, that he envied you.'

He laughed. 'Thank you. No, he doesn't. He is older, though.
About the same age as Tristão.'

'The boy is dark,' she said. 'But yes. Also a pretty face, and a
delectable body. It is a pity you kept us apart.'

He didn't answer. The ship, her sails down, rowed smoothly in.
The harbour was crowded with masts and banners. There were
other banners as well on the wharf. Then he saw the one that he
knew, and felt again the hurt, and the loss. Primaflora said, 'Is it
where you are looking? I see no Apollo.'

'No,' he said. Because now he saw that Simon wasn't there,
waiting in front of the liveried servants under the insignia of St
Pol. Instead of Simon, there stood a brown-haired young woman
of middle height in a cut-velvet cloak over a gown which looked
equally sumptuous. Her face, full of character, had the potential of
beauty marred, at the moment, by a harshness amounting almost to
anger. But her grooming was perfect; her hair skilfully dressed
under a two-horned headdress with a slight veil, which under no
circumstances could be described as a hennin. Her chin was up,
and her unplucked eyebrows were drawn, as she stared intently
over the water.

He looked at her for a long time. It was a long time since he had
seen her. Who is Katelina? This, my dear, is Katelina. The girl
who asked an apprentice called Claes to initiate her into the rites of
love – not once, but the length of two nights. The girl who
conceived a son as a result and, marrying Simon, allowed Simon to
think the coming infant was his. The girl who then discovered
(unfortunately) that Nicholas was born to Simon's first wife. And
that, all his life, Nicholas had been reared to believe Simon his
father. Simon hated Nicholas, as a symbol of what he thought was
his first wife's betrayal. Katelina van Borselen hated him with far,
far more reason.

She stood on the wharf, the girl called Katelina, who had come
to Rhodes, it would seem, instead of Simon, and who knew what
Simon knew to his detriment, and would use it. Unconscious of
anything else, Nicholas stood and gazed without seeing her, and
remembered two long, sweet nights, from which had come an
abomination. Nor did he see Primaflora, her eyes wide open,
watching him.

The ship moved in to its destination. The servants of St Pol
fidgeted in their livery. The girl Katelina waited while the ship
berthed, disregarding the cold wind that tugged at her cloak. She

remained, civilly smiling, while the gangplank was lowered and Tristão Vasquez walked, surprised, towards her, the boy following. She allowed Vasquez to kiss each hand in turn and, smiling again, permitted the boy to plant his lips on her cheek. From the shelter of the deck, it was possible to see her brows rise in animation as questions were asked and answered. In Portugal and Madeira, she and Simon shared a family business with Tristão Vasquez. She must be well acquainted with Simon's sister and her family. Perhaps, when staying there, they used the same fondaco. It looked as if the acquaintance were cool rather than intimate. The boy burst into speech and her face altered, politely. She was listening, no doubt, to an account of the pirate ship's interception.

It could only be a moment before she learned of the boy's hurt, and then of how it had been tended. Too far to lip-read, Nicholas could guess how her questions then sharpened and changed, as her face did. Sooner than he expected, she turned deliberately and looked up to the deck, and along it, and found him. Across all the noisy space that lay between them, he met her eyes.

Primaflora said, 'Your Simon is not there.'

'No,' Nicholas said. 'That is the lady Katelina his wife. His second wife. Come and let me present you to her.'

Chapter 14

FOR TWO YEARS, since their last meeting in Bruges, Katelina van Borselen had been in no doubt that one day, in a place of her choice, she would confront the cold, whoring servant who had used her to impose an incestuous child on her husband. For part of that time, Nicholas – Claes – had been out of her reach, first in Trebizond, and then wandering no one knew where. Once, in Venice, her husband had caught him, but nothing had come of it, and Simon had been embroiled in his own affairs since, while always expecting and planning to compete with Nicholas, and to outwit him in whatever he did. Believing the child to be his, Simon didn't know that Nicholas had already overmatched him, now and for all time to come. Simon despised Nicholas, and could be driven by temper to attack him. Simon didn't have the reason she had to pursue Nicholas, and punish him, and make him forfeit his life.

She had learned in Anjou that Nicholas – Claes – might be fighting in Italy, and hoped that the Angevins, instructed by Jordan, would kill him. They did not. She had been told that Nicholas – Claes – had been invited to join the Queen of Cyprus, and hearing that he had vanished from Italy, concluded that Cyprus was where he had gone. Then she had learned that Carlotta of Cyprus, returned from begging, was to launch her renewed bid for her kingdom from Rhodes.

The company of St Pol & Vasquez had business in the Levant. It also produced wine and sugar, and had reason to interest itself in its competitors. It was easy to suggest to Tristão, who knew nothing of Nicholas, that he should visit Rhodes, making an excuse on the way to see Cyprus. He had required a little persuading, but had agreed. When he left, taking his son, he had expected to meet Simon on Rhodes.

Once, Katelina would have let Simon go, to finish the business between himself and Nicholas, Now, she was determined to do so herself. Simon didn't know, she discovered, that Nicholas had been invited to fight for Carlotta, and she saw no reason to tell him. After Tristão had gone and Simon, without his wise guidance, had begun as usual to see more of his mistresses than his desk, Katelina had suggested that she, and not he, should travel to Rhodes to meet his partner. Knowing her dislike of heat and travel, he had been surprised, but after a very short time, had agreed. For him, it meant freedom. He felt hampered by her, and irritated by Lucia's silent censure. Katelina had left him with relief, and no sense of maternal anxiety. The spurious heir to Kilmirren and Ribérac was twenty-two months and an infant. Far off in Scotland, he was unlikely to miss her.

For all the times she had travelled by sea, the voyage always upset her, and the journey to Rhodes had been terrible. Then, arrived there, she had found Nicholas vanished again. He was not on Rhodes, and not spoken of anywhere. Only, asking at court, she found her hopes rise again. His army was here. It had arrived, expecting to meet him, and expecting to serve Queen Carlotta. So report said but, of course, report was quite wrong. Katelina had presented herself before the Knights of the Order and Queen Carlotta, and told them what Nicholas was, and why they should suspect him.

She was listened to. She was a van Borselen, of a family connected with royalty and with the counsellors of Duke Philip of Burgundy. Her husband had business in Genoa, in Scotland, in Portugal. He was also the son of Jordan de Ribérac, France's foremost financial adviser. So the Queen and the Grand Master heard her, and asked questions, and appeared much disappointed. The army of Nicholas, under its captain Astorre, was put into custody until its future should be decided. Katelina found a place for herself among the merchants of Rhodes and had no trouble in pursuing, in the interval, her legitimate business. And in the wind and the rain of a clammy Rhodes winter the court, and the Order, settled to await the arrival – for surely he must arrive – of this subtle apprentice, who had made himself a rich and dangerous trader called Nicholas.

Despite that, the manner of his coming caught Katelina unprepared. Expecting a ship from Kolossi, she joined the other merchants who walked down to the jetty to meet it. It held, as she had hoped, Tristão Vasquez and his young son. She saw the surprise on their faces: they had expected Simon. Waiting for them, she was aware of some excitement; an eddy of movement that spread from ship to shore and rebounded. Tristão, with Portuguese courtliness, would not be hurried through the niceties of his greetings and enquiries. The boy, bursting with news, interrupted. They had been boarded; there had been fighting; he had been wounded. She let him describe it until, as she listened, a dazzling suspicion was born. She spoke as soon as the boy's chatter slowed. 'So, Diniz, you had a Hospitaller on board? With a lady?'

Tristão said, 'We misled you. Our Samaritan was a lay guest, a young merchant from Flanders. Niccolò vander Poele is his name. He had heard of Simon; it may be you know of him? He is there, still on board.'

He had walked into the trap. Out of arrogance, he had walked into the trap, even believing that Simon was here, waiting for him. And Tristão Vasquez, clearly, hadn't been told who he was. She said, 'Diniz. The seigneur in the long robes over there is the Grand Commander of Cyprus. Will you make him my compliments and ask him to join us?'

The boy hesitated, exchanging a glance with his father. 'Now, if you please,' said Katelina van Borselen.

The boy left. Tristão Vasquez said, 'Forgive me. You do know the young man, Senhor Niccolò?'

'Yes,' said Katelina. 'He knew who you were, but it didn't suit him to say so. You have both been deceived.' Her gaze on the ship, she spoke with a fierceness she kept out of her manner. Nicholas thought Simon was here. Openly or not, he would be sure to be looking for him. And openly, there he was: Nicholas, Claes, immediately marked by his height and a tilt of the head that she remembered. Oh, she remembered it.

Of course, he had been studying her. As she watched, he began to walk forward and, reaching the gangplank, stepped surefooted down it. His face, foolishly agreeable, remained turned towards her, half obscured by a large furry hat with its brim tilted up at the back. There was a woman, a beautiful woman, walking behind him. Louis de Magnac, led by the boy, approached Katelina looking puzzled. 'Madame?'

Katelina said, 'The young man disembarking. That is Niccolò vander Poele. He has come on a ship of the Order, I cannot understand how.'

The Grand Commander of Cyprus turned, surveying the subject. 'Nor can I. I know nothing of this. I shall warn the Palace. Can you delay him?'

'Probably not. You will need some excuse. And some men-at-arms. Is the Treasurer free?'

The Commander was already speaking to his secretary. He turned. 'Not at the moment. I shall stay with you.'

Tristão Vasquez said, 'I don't understand. Here Messer Niccolò comes. What am I to say to him, and to the lady?' The boy was silent.

Katelina said, 'I don't think they will stop. He wouldn't dare.'

She was wrong. Instead of attempting to pass, her betrayer

walked directly towards the waiting group, his hand in the arm of the woman. He was chatting to her. Telling her what? And who was she? No one had mentioned a woman. As he came close, Katelina tried to read his expression. The round face of Claes the apprentice had gone, although it had left behind its distinguishing features: the thick lips, the arched nostrils, the eyes large and shining as lily-pads. She could just see the white seam on one cheek, the legacy he owed to Jordan de Ribérac. At close hand, his expression was still agreeable, but no longer foolish. He stopped and looked at her. Then he smiled at Tristão and said, 'I know the lady's husband. I should have told you. Demoiselle Katelina, I wish you to meet the lady Primaflora, come to rejoin the suite of the serene Queen of Cypruo. And am I right in addressing the Grand Commander?'

The Grand Commander of Cyprus considered the other man; an experienced soldier judging another. At his back, their swords sheathed, were the men-at-arms of his escort. He said, 'Louis de Magnac. We have not met?'

Nicholas said, 'I have not had the honour. I recognised your coat of arms from Kolossi. But I expect the lady Primaflora is known to you.'

'Yes,' said Louis de Magnac. 'Yes. In the suite of Queen Carlotta. I recall her clearly, of course.'

He had hesitated at the reminder, as well he might. How had Nicholas got hold of this woman? Katelina said quickly, 'The Grand Commander is arranging for the lady to be taken to the Palace immediately. Then these tiresome formalities needn't disturb her.'

The woman spoke. The timbre of her voice matched her carriage and the excellent taste of her clothes. Katelina suddenly understood. In Rome, the conduct of the ladies of Queen Carlotta's suite had been the subject of comment. The woman said, 'I have nothing against formalities. I prefer to linger, I think, with Messer Niccolò.'

Tristão Vasquez said, 'What formalities?'

Katelina displayed surprise. 'The Treasurer and the Grand Commander will know better than I. But after a ship is attacked, do the passengers not require to give evidence of what has been stolen, or what they saw, that might lead to the arrest of the pirates?'

'We have done that,' said Nicholas. 'And we are tired after our voyage and would prefer to make for an inn. Senhor Tristão has made some recommendations.'

'There is no need,' said the Grand Commander. 'Here is a footservant who will carry your luggage, and my men to escort you. I shall merely ask you to wait while I confirm that the ship's master has no more need of your testimony.'

He gave a small bow and walked off, his secretary following. The group of men-at-arms, left behind, formed a small and far from casual circle. Katelina turned to Tristão Vasquez. 'There is no need for us to wait. Here are porters. The house I have taken is near, in the Chora.'

The Portuguese said, 'I wish to know what is happening. Why is this gentleman being detained? He has brought an army to serve Queen Carlotta. His wishes should be consulted.'

How had Nicholas won over Vasquez? But of course. By paying the boy some attention. Shrewd, percipient Nicholas. But at least the Grand Commander had gone. Katelina spoke just loudly enough to convey the quality of her scorn. 'I can see you think highly of Claes. You know he was called Claes, when he was a dyeshop apprentice? He then achieved a rather short marriage, from which he has emerged with a new name and riches. He likes to regard himself as one of Simon's most consistent rivals. That is why neither you nor the Order were favoured with the truth about his relationships. That is why the Queen of Cyprus might be forgiven for wondering which side he really means to fight for – Queen Carlotta, or Zacco.' She turned to Nicholas. 'You may as well go to the Palace. There is nowhere else for you to go. Astorre and the rest have been under lock and key since they came here.'

Nicholas preserved his appearance of patience. 'How unwise,' he said, 'if you expect them to fight for Carlotta.' It was all he said. He didn't ask where they were. Tristão was still looking at her. The Grand Commander was coming back, without haste. With equal repose, Nicholas stood and watched his allotted servant load chests on a barrow. Brutally large and black as lamp oil, the man swung them up as if they were empty. The boy Diniz spoke to Nicholas. 'You didn't tell us.'

Nicholas removed his gaze. 'No. It was awkward. Your uncle Simon and I crossed swords a few times, in trade and for personal reasons. I thought the quarrel was over. Otherwise I should hardly be here.'

'And my wife?' said Tristão Vasquez. 'Does this feud extend to her?'

'Of course not,' said Nicholas. 'She has probably never heard of me. I don't intend any harm to you or your son, as perhaps I have proved. Or even, believe it or not, to my lord Simon. I should simply like to collect my men and get out.'

Louis de Magnac had arrived. He said, 'And that is all we wish for you also, Messer Niccolò. I am sure your loyalty to the Queen is unquestioned. So soon as the Queen herself is convinced, you may join them.'

'The Queen is here?' Nicholas said.

'Yes,' said the Grand Commander of Cyprus. 'And awaiting you now, at the Palace.'

'I see,' Nicholas said. 'I am honoured. I shall, of course, attend her presently. But you will forgive me none the less if I keep to my original plan. I should like first to establish the lady, our servants and our luggage in some suitable tavern. We are not dressed for court.'

Louis de Magnac could never be hearty, but his manner came close to it. 'Will the Queen complain?' he said. 'Far from it. But you are right. A tavern it shall be. We shall send your servants there, and your luggage and the lady's. If you need them, they will be sent for. But now, we must not keep the Queen waiting. Will you walk? Or does the lady wish to be carried?'

Nicholas said, 'The Queen is too amiable. As the future leader of the Queen's auxiliary army, I would not demean her by appearing less than honourably. I shall accept, with pleasure, an escort to the tavern. Your men may wait to lead us to the palace. And it might be appropriate, and quicker, to supply the lady and myself with horses of reasonable quality. As you see, I have none of my own.'

Never had Katelina van Borselen heard Claes speak to a man of birth as an equal before, far less present an ultimatum. *Overrule me, and you will have to arrest me, and lose the chance of my army.* She saw the Grand Commander decide to concede. The inn could be guarded; communication with others prevented. 'But of course,' said Louis de Magnac. 'Provided you do not try her grace's patience too far. She is a woman. She does not like to be kept overlong waiting.'

'It seems a pity, in that case,' Nicholas said, 'that you committed me before first consulting me. Now, where do we go?'

They were taken to a large inn which was not in the Chora of the Castello, the lower part of the walled city in which the merchants, the Jews, the Latins had their trading centre, and the Knights whatever private dwellings they could afford. Uphill from the Chora was the fortified town of the Knights, in which they consulted and ate in the Gothic residences of their Langues, the clubhouses of their national groupings. There also were their church and hospital of St John, and the fortress of the Grand Master. There too were the palaces built or lent for the use of the diplomats, the envoys, the guests of the Knights. The hospice to which Nicholas and Primaflora were taken was one of these. And a long and safe distance from it, as Primaflora was able to tell him, was the palace of Carlotta and Luis of Cyprus, where he was later expected.

It was the only communication he and Primaflora were allowed on the short journey through the thick turreted gates and up the straight, classical streets cluttered with Levantine, non-classical buildings. They had parted from Katelina and her kinsmen on the jetty. Nicholas carried with him the black, furious gaze of the boy

Diniz. Well: he had known that was going to happen. Tristão Vasquez had said nothing more, but he owed Vasquez something for what intervention he had made. He would make none in the future, that was certain. And Katelina? She had been nineteen when they first met; fresh from breaking out of an unwanted betrothal; at odds with her parents; at odds with the masculine world. Now she was Simon's wife and a mother, but only three years had passed. What had been abrasive, forthright, childishly vain should not have changed so quickly into a bitter, angular spirit; a face of original beauty now full of repression. Walking down the jetty, Primaflora had said, 'That is the wife of the beautiful Simon?'

And he had said, 'She has competition, as you may imagine,' and left it at that. Primaflora must realise he had no interest in Katelina. It was quite important, indeed, that she should.

At the guest house, he and the girl were placed in separate chambers with an attendant outside each door. Primaflora was allowed her own woman, but he was given only the services of the footman from the Grand Commander's own household. The attentive services: the negro followed him in with the baggage and then closed and locked the chamber door on the inside. He turned. But for themselves, the chamber was empty. Nicholas said, 'I can't believe it. You'd do anything for money.' He punched the other man's shoulder, and then stood holding him at arms' length while they grinned at each other.

The negro called Loppe said, 'You've got to beat M. de Magnac's prices. What kept you?'

Nicholas pushed him into a seat and himself dropped to the floor, stretching his arms luxuriantly over his head. 'Never mind what kept me,' he said. 'How did you get here? Where are the rest? And what's happening?'

From slave to friend to major domo of the fondaco at Trebizond, the man called Loppe had grown into the core of the Charetty company; had still been with it when Nicholas had last seen him in Tilde de Charetty's office in Bruges. From Bruges, it now seemed he had travelled to Venice. And then, keeping apart from Astorre, he had found employment with Louis de Magnac of Cyprus, to whom all news of Cyprus must come. Here, no one who mattered either knew or would remember him: even Katelina van Borselen. Nicholas said, 'You took a risk, all the same. And porter's work! You know how you drop things.' He paused. 'Did you tell them in Bruges where you were going?'

Loppe rocked his clasped thumbs. 'I didn't know where I was going. I asked Master Julius to let me join Master Gregorio's business in Venice. He didn't mind. He had enough on his hands with the two girls. Not trouble – they do very well, and Father Godscalc keeps them right, and Ser Adorne.'

'And Gregorio?' Nicholas said. Loppe always knew by instinct what he wanted to know.

'Has set up his Bank, which is going well. Your Bank. He was a trifle anxious. We all were. We didn't want to be responsible for all your debts.'

'Then you shouldn't have taken shares,' said Nicholas absently. The misfortunes of his arrival had already receded, to be replaced by a twinge of excitement. He said, 'What you are saying is that I ought to be improving the balance. Well, I shan't deny I've been giving some thought to it. I'll need some help, unless you're proposing to porter for life. What do you call yourself?'

The other smiled. 'Lopez. If you remember, I had Portuguese owners. I don't expect to serve very long. I may give you orders, later.'

'Try it,' said Nicholas. He stretched his legs on the floor. 'All right. Tell me. About Astorre, Katelina, and the company.'

Loppe said, 'You did expect her.'

'I expected Simon,' he said. 'But we don't always get what we want. How did Astorre get into trouble?'

'Through the lady,' Loppe said. 'Captain Astorre was adroit. He came here to seek you, while apparently touting for business. You were not here; he waited; he stayed too long. By the time the demoiselle Katelina arrived, it was known that you had left Italy before Astorre did. So the demoiselle warned the Queen that you may never have intended to join her. And that if you came to Astorre, it might be to lead him to Zacco.'

He waited. Nicholas smiled, but said nothing. Loppe resumed, with some patience. 'That was when the army was put under restraint. The excuse was reasonable. Mercenaries lacking employment are a danger in any society. Either Astorre signed a contract, or submitted. The captain has maintained his position: they are awaiting your arrival; they intend to fight for the Knights or the Queen. They are in the old Hospital, and locked in at night, although the Order allows them to work for their keep in the daytime. Le Grant has transformed the defences.'

'Le Grant?' Nicholas said. Once, John le Grant and he had blown up half Trebizond. But then the Scot had gone back to Bruges, and had been thrown out, as he had, by Marian's daughters.

Loppe said, 'Your former engineer. He came from Venice at the same time as I did. He said life was getting too easy without you.'

Astorre and Le Grant. Thomas, Tobie and Loppe. From being alone, he was part of a community. One which would push, and pull, and demand, if he let them. One which would do what he wanted, now that – with blinding precision – he knew what he wanted. He was not part of a community. He was in charge of an arsenal in the opening moves of a perfect war game. He said, 'What is Carlotta's attitude?'

'The Queen? The Knights curse her, but give her what she wants. She is a fighter: she might attract help for Rhodes as well as for Cyprus. She is threatened by Constantinople as well as by Zacco her brother. She needs Astorre and his men, just as the Knights do. But rather than have them go to her brother, she'd kill them.'

Nicholas said, 'And the lady I brought with me? Does she speak of her?'

Loppe's face barely changed. He said, 'The lady Primaflora was sent to make sure you would join the Queen's party. Her absence, like your own, caused some comment. That is all I was told.'

Nicholas said, 'I have met Zacco. He has invited me to join him, with Astorre or without him. The lady Primaflora will go where I go.'

Loppe spoke slowly. 'He invited you, but did not keep you?'

Nicholas said, 'He is a man of my age, or yours, and full of confidence. A woman would have learned caution.'

There was a silence. Loppe said, 'And your lady is prepared to support the Bastard's side, too, if you choose it?'

Nicholas said, 'She is not my lady, any more than he is my lord. Primaflora had no wish to return to the Queen. If she does so now, it is only for form's sake. She will leave as soon as she can.'

'She is your strongest card with the Queen,' Loppe remarked.

He sounded like Tilde. Nicholas laughed. He said, 'Oh, don't worry. She is enough of my lady to give the Queen all the reassurance she needs. Primaflora was sent to bring me back, and used every weapon, if for the opposite reason.'

Loppe said, 'I am glad,' and went on quickly, 'I hear horses. What more can I tell you?'

'Nothing more,' Nicholas said. He got up and started to strip, while Loppe unfastened a box and began pulling out clothes.

Loppe straightened, a pourpoint in his hands. He said, 'So?'

Nicholas clawed on a fresh shirt and took the pourpoint. 'So what?'

Loppe gave a snort. 'The Queen, the Genoese, the Order? The Bastard Zacco? Or home?'

Nicholas dragged on hose and tied knots. 'You want to go back to Guinea?'

Loppe said, 'I want to know what I've been waiting for. So does Astorre.'

Nicholas buttoned his doublet, took a brush, and reduced his hair to a bumpy brown mound which immediately crimped round his nape and his temples. He slapped on the fur hat. He said, 'I thought you were waiting for me? I'll tell you when I've seen Queen Carlotta.'

Loppe said, 'You may not get the chance.'

Nicholas was ready. He smiled. 'Oh, no,' he said. 'I'll lay you a small wager I'll be allowed back to the hospice for several days. I'll see you. I'll see Astorre. I may not be allowed to see the lady Primaflora, but I shall have to put up with that. Meantime, there are two things you can do for me. One is to carry a packet. The other is to find out what you can about what the demoiselle Katelina may do, and also her nephew Diniz and his father. You saw them on the pier.'

'I know them,' said Loppe. 'You wish to cause them some trouble?'

'On the contrary,' Nicholas said. 'I have a great respect for them all. I just want to know, all the time, where they are. Can you do that?'

'They have servants,' said Loppe. 'I can do that. What are you expecting to happen?'

'What I'm expecting to happen doesn't worry me,' Nicholas said. 'It's what I'm not expecting that's the devil. And don't think, if you let me down, that you and John le Grant can do the whole thing yourselves because you most certainly can't.'

'Do what?' said Loppe, his eyes whitely innocent.

'What do you think? John's an engineer. In your Portuguese days, you didn't waste your time, did you? I'm only surprised Lorenzo Strozzi didn't come with you.'

'We asked him,' said Loppe. 'But he was leaving for Naples.' He weighed the pack in his hand in a conjecturing way. 'But of course, his mother's in Florence, with your horses.' He paused. 'It's another game. I am right? You are not going home?'

'Of course I'm not going home,' Nicholas said. 'Any more than you are. As for the game, wait and see. After I've had my audience with Queen Carlotta.'

Astorre was next to hear of his owner's arrival. It propelled him on a tour of his officers. John le Grant, about his business on the heights of the half-built St Nicholas tower, was annoyed to be summoned by shouts from below. When he heard Astorre actually climbing the stonework he exclaimed, 'Oh Christ,' and thrust his lever at someone to hold for him. From there, he leaned out from the scaffold and shouted, 'If you come one step nearer, I'll mince you.'

Astorre glared back at him, but remained where he was. It was raining. The air vibrated with the clack of the windmills. Astorre looked up at the fortress and sneered. 'That's supposed to make a Turk stop? They'll blow it down through the gaps in their teeth. I just thought you might be interested in your future. The young fellow's turned up.'

John le Grant gripped the uprights on either side of him and swung down to the plank just below. Without touching it with his feet, he performed a couple of somersaults and then let himself swing back and forth, his legs in their muddy boots held straight out in front of him. He said, 'Catch me,' and dropped. Astorre, nearly overturned into the sea, staggered, caught him, and slammed him down on the paving before him. He said, 'If they've got any sense, they'll brick you up in that thing. Did you hear what I said? Nicholas has come in from Kolossi. With a woman.'

'I didn't hear you say that,' John le Grant said. 'Well, good for Nicholas. Where is he?'

'With Carlotta. That bitch Simon's wife was waiting for him with Louis de Magnac. Suave and sweet to his face, but he's under guard.'

'You don't look worried,' said the engineer. He took off his felt cap and wrung it out.

'He came. There's nothing to worry about,' said Astorre. His puckered eye gleamed through the scar, and his beard broadened its base. 'The woman's the one Thomas trailed all over Italy. Thomas got all upset when Loppe told him.'

'Lopez,' said John le Grant. 'He's with Nicholas?'

'That's who told me,' said Captain Astorre. 'And I've news. Loppe thinks it's Cyprus we're going for.'

John le Grant put on his cap. He said, 'That's all I needed: a death sentence. Come on. If I'm not going to build it, I don't see why I need to get wet.'

Captain Astorre looked up at the tower and the scaffolding. He said, 'What did you say to that fellow? To hold something?'

The engineer followed his eye, swore, and yelled up an instruction. The man, scowling, dropped what he had been holding. It slithered down, bringing a course of stone with it. A block dropped at his feet. 'Wall you up, if you're not careful. I told you. I thought you'd be interested,' said Astorre. He climbed down to ground level. 'Not that I got much from Loppe.'

'Lopez,' said le Grant.

'Lopez. He had to go down to the harbour.'

'Why?' said the engineer. He wiped his hands on his hide coat and opened the door of the hut where his flask was.

'I don't know,' said Astorre. 'But I saw him down by the Florentine ship. The one from Constantinople. It had some alum on board.'

'I didn't know we'd left any,' John le Grant said. He wiped his mouth and passed the wine to the other.

'We didn't leave much,' Astorre said. 'But it's good, heh? He came. Now we'll see something.'

Chapter 15

I N A SNOWY farmyard south of Bologna, the Queen of Cyprus had recommended her cause to Nicholas, and had sent Primaflora to persuade him. That had been a year ago. Now, her plight was more serious, and the Queen's recommendations were about to become rather more forceful. This Nicholas saw, the moment he stepped from the hospice in Rhodes and witnessed the size and degree of his escort. Beneath the curled plumes of their helmets the soldiers' manner was nothing but courteous. His negro servant on foot at his stirrup, he found himself drawn at great speed through narrow ways lined by white Levantine houses, their walls overlooked by dripping palm trees. His cavalcade trotted through markets crowded with mules and camels and people, passing between stalls of hung game, of copper, of medicines; and beside carpets of herbs and grain and trussed fowl.

It wound among forges and bread ovens, and up streets thick with the sawdust of woodcarvers, or lined with the trestles and kiln-fires of potters. It passed innumerable shrines, and many small churches. It rode through gusts of heat, and air heavy with yeast and goat dung, mutton and incense, lemons and carobs and blood. It traversed streets sloping upwards, downwards and sideways and the only streets it never climbed and never crossed were the streets of the Knights, built of marble, which, he had been told, lined the height to the Grand Master's Castle. He wondered why.

They stopped only twice. Once, a line of horsemen in black appeared at a far-distant junction, and the Queen's cavalcade paused until they had vanished. The second time, their way was impeded by a stationary mule at a junction. Low in its saddle, sandalled feet semaphored, rode a bulky man in a cloak. Below it, he wore the white-girdled gown of a Franciscan.

Nicholas recognised him, with a groan, as belonging to the same snowy battle at Silla. He remembered a curt conversation, during which he claimed to have escaped from Carlotta. He remembered the derision in the monk's ferocious eyes. It was there again now. The man looked up, and the rain beat upon his blue bristled tonsure and jowls.

'Brother Ludovico da Bologna,' Nicholas said with resignation.

The friar turned from the captain, approached Nicholas and, as the cavalcade moved, put the mule to a trot at his instep. 'Not precisely. You may say *Father*,' he said. 'Or Monseigneur, of course.' His voice was earthy, and rumbled. 'The Venetians made me a priest. You're not surprised?'

'That the Venetians made you a priest?'

The Franciscan hawked and spat, conveying amusement. 'To see me here. You are addressing the Patriarch of the Latins in Antioch, and that's Antioch over your shoulder, give or take a sea passage and a few hundred miles. The Levant is my parish. I thought you would try for the sugar. You did well by the Queen in Bologna. You won't be sorry.'

'You're with Carlotta?' Nicholas said. 'Still? Again?'

'I don't discriminate,' the Franciscan said. 'Black or white, man or woman, dolt or traitor or zealot. I'm with anybody who'll stop that foul dog the Sultan from snapping at Christians. But don't let that bother you. I've seen boys like you, mad for land and money and titles.'

'And women,' said Nicholas.

'And women. You'll get them all. They won't cool you in hell.'

'That's all right. I was going to refuse them,' said Nicholas. 'Anything else?'

Ludovico da Bologna examined him. He said, 'And what makes you such a cheeky young bastard? The Grand Master got hold of you? Or the Genoese? Or this charming young boy-taster Zacco? You were in the brothels of Trebizond. There's nothing about the Emperor David that's novel to me.'

'I'm sorry to hear it,' Nicholas said. 'I thought his tastes ran to something younger. Is it worth going on, or should I just turn and go home?'

They had stopped before a set of high gates. The monk's face, like a misshapen tuber, remained close to him. Then da Bologna said, 'You don't suspect you might be going to get a surprise? You're a sharp fellow; but you don't know Carlotta. Enjoy yourself.'

He turned. Nicholas said, 'You're not coming in?'

The friar laughed. 'I'll hear what happens,' he said. 'I'm sailing for home in a few days. My business is starting wars, my boy, not playing the peacemaker.'

'So I've noticed,' Nicholas said. The monk left. Loppe, who had vanished, reappeared at his side, saying nothing. The gates opened upon a courtyard planted with palms and hung with ceremonial cloths of wet silk. As he rode through, trumpets sounded, and a man in a French hat and a heavy furred gown walked forward and held out his hand. 'Ser Niccolò? Descend, and be welcome.'

At the *Ser*, Loppe's chin trembled and Nicholas scowled at him as he dismounted. The trumpets sounded again, bouncing off the walls of an adequate mansion which must, in its time, have been owned by a nobleman of some taste and wealth. Now, dressed with painted devices, it was the temporary home of the monarchs of Cyprus, who appeared (considered Nicholas) to be taking a great deal for granted.

Nicholas walked through double doors, preceded by the personage in the French hat who held a wand. In the vestibule the personage turned and snapped his fingers. A page appeared, bearing a bale of blue cloth. The bale, unfolded, proved to be an extremely good indigo mantle with embroidery all over one side in Cyprus gold thread. The personage, who turned out to be Montolif, Marshal of Cyprus, addressed him. 'The rain has damaged your cloak. Their graces wish you to replace it with this.'

Nicholas bowed; was divested of one cloak and invested with another and bowed again. He began to feel strongly like one of his own mechanical toys. He avoided Loppe's eye, walked through a door and climbed a stair at the top of which another trumpeter was stationed. His ears ringing, he walked into a hall.

Although not of the grandest dimensions, the timbered chamber with its arched roof and handsome windows was not a mean setting for the Queen of Jerusalem, Cyprus and Armenia and her consort and cousin, King Luis. Below a baldachin at the end of the room they sat side by side upon a low dais, with their personal household grouped standing beside them. On either side of the room, there stood ranked against the long walls some fifty men of obvious standing. Those against the windows wore, uniformly, the same blue mantle which had been given to Nicholas himself. Those on the opposite side were dressed in styles which derived from France or Savoy more than Cyprus. Surprisingly, two or three wore the black and white cloak of the Order. But then, of course, the Order owned land in Savoy, and had allowed its Savoyard brethren to come to the aid of King Luis.

There were no women present but for the Queen and her ladies of honour. They were set on her right, and among them he saw Primaflora. She stood, eyes downcast, in her heavy court gown as if she had never planned to thwart or escape from her mistress. Of Katelina there was no sign whatever. Then the Marshal declaimed. 'Serenissima; serene lord King: the lord Niccolò vander Poele, commander, banker and merchant of Venice.'

One did not approach on the belly as at Trebizond, or kiss the ground, or the shoe, or even the hand. But Carlotta was Byzantine,

as that court had been, and was due the high style of the ceremonial.
He took his time, pacing the ground from the door to the foot of
the dais, and thought it another irony that the person who had
trained him should have been Violante of Naxos, whose sisters'
husbands worked for King Zacco.

He had seen Carlotta in Bologna and Venice, and thought she
looked little changed, though now encased in narrow, high-waisted
brocade with a fringed diadem on her hairline. Perhaps the vivid
face was more worn; the painted eyes more ready to frown. She
looked like a fierce, withering flower about to spit its thorns into
the wind. Daughter of a Lusignan father and a Paleologa mother,
she seemed wholly Greek.

And Luis, consort and cousin, son of the Duke of Savoy and of
another violent Lusignan mother? At thirty-two, seven years his
wife's elder, Luis was broadshouldered and tall with an air of
uneasy petulance. On the dais, his foot tapped. In the sandy face
the lips and chin had a small life of their own, as if munching
words in some remote, disagreeable dialogue. His clothes, rich
enough, were not perfectly ordered and his nose was swollen with
rheum. Once, Luis of Savoy had been betrothed to a Scottish
princess, and Savoy was still paying for breaking the contract. You
would guess that Katelina, who had married a Scot, would have
something in common with Luis. But Katelina, worryingly, was
not here.

The Queen said, 'My lord Niccolò. Cyprus called you, and you
have come. It is not, we know, a decision easily reached, and we
honour you for it. We honour you for the brave band of men you
have sent here, whose reputation has preceded them: who have
already fought the Turk in the East. We honour you for the
gallantry of your behaviour in Italy, when you saved our precious
cargo at the risk of your life. You saw then what a base-born
blasphemer will do, when he sets men to attack his own sister. You
have rejected the unholy union of Zacco and Muslim. You have
paid court, as was due, to the brave Knights of Kolossi, but have
decided that their war is not yours. You might have sailed to
Famagusta and sold your sword to those stalwarts, the Genoese.
You did none of these things. You sailed to Rhodes, and appear
before us. In doing this, you do more than the great kings of the
West have done. In vain have we begged for an army. None would
listen. None can see, as we can, the dripping fangs of the Turk at
our door; hear the screams of the Mamelukes devouring our subjects
in Cyprus. You and your force have come to do what they would
not do, and this we wish to mark by our special favour. Land and
wealth you will have: that we have promised you. A contract you
will have: we are not without friends; money will be found for you and
your captain. But first, we have something else to offer you. Kneel.'

Someone brought a stool. He knelt on one knee, rearranging from habit the sword that was no longer there. The Queen was standing and so, after a moment, was Luis her consort. An abbot, of Bellapaïs he assumed, came forward and handed a long object to the king. There was a baldric attached, which trailed on the floor. An equerry darted forward and looped the thing up. The object was a sword.

Luis said, 'Well, take it.'

Nicholas looked at the Queen. The Queen said, 'Let us give it him together,' and put out her hand, and led her husband down the steps to stand before Nicholas. She said, 'When the Holy Land fell, many knights vowed to recover it, and many orders of chivalry were created. Ours is more than one hundred years old. It was founded by Peter our ancestor to honour those who gave their swords to the cause: it is called the Order of the Sword, and this is its emblem.' She turned, and drawing the blade, touched Nicholas with it once on each shoulder. She said, 'And thus, you are made one of its Knights. Take this sword and wear it. Take this collar, which the lord King will place on your shoulders. Take this badge, and abide by its motto: *C'est pour loïauté maintenir*. Then by this kiss, seal the affirmation of your service.'

The bitch. The clever bitch. Someone came for the stool, and he rose. She stood before him, her scented cheek turned. Her eyes, delicately painted, were averted. Nicholas stood for a moment, the swordbelt tight over his chest, the collar of links pressing his shoulders, the silver badge glittering over his heart. Then he leaned forward and gave the Queen, with firm precision, the kiss of fealty she asked for.

Then her eyes turned, sparkling, and she said, 'Luis, my husband. Give him your hand, and let us lead him to the feast. He is our newest Knight, who is about to save Cyprus. And here is Primaflora our lady, to whom we will bind him in fruitful and sanctified matrimony.'

Loppe (Lopez) brought the news to the house on the corner of St Sebastian Square which belonged once to the Queen's cousin Eleanor, and then to the Grand Commander of Cyprus, and now, by the Queen's special desire (and to M. de Magnac's distress), to the leaders of Niccolò's army.

In this house, there were no locks on the doors, and an abundance of service, of food, of amenities. Astorre was satisfied, having expected no less from the coming of Nicholas. What pleased Astorre, Thomas was unlikely to query. Only the engineer accepted the change with guarded enthusiasm and the doctor, Tobie, looked grim. 'I don't like it.'

'You don't need to like it,' said John le Grant. 'Look on it as a wee holiday. We'll be back in the prison tomorrow.'

It was four months since the battle of Troia, from which Nicholas had been so suddenly spirited away. It was more than a year since John le Grant had parted from him in Venice before setting out for his own trip to Bruges. Since he arrived in Rhodes, only Loppe had seen Nicholas.

Of them all, only Astorre and Loppe might, of their own volition, have waited so long for him on Rhodes. Astorre, with the confidence of the sought-after, knew that, whatever had happened to Nicholas, he could pick up a job here at any time. He did not, in fact, believe that anything untoward could happen to Nicholas, and he was sure that, when he could, Nicholas would set out and find them. When his credentials were undermined by Katelina, Astorre was annoyed, but philosophical. He was reasonably well housed and fed at no expense to himself, barring a little reciprocal work. The interval would not exactly enhance his career or his savings, but with Nicholas, it was going to be worth it.

The doctor, and perhaps John le Grant were less sure. The hard words in Venice still rankled with Tobie, and he regretted quite often the impetuosity of his decision to leave Urbino and Ferrante for an uncertain career with this meteor. Mixed with that was an angry anxiety which would have led him, were he free, to track Nicholas to whatever sybaritic lair he was occupying in order to walk out on him all over again.

John rarely talked about Nicholas, and made his own decisions on grounds he never discussed with anybody. Astorre thought, perhaps rightly, that the engineer, sure of work, would remain like himself to seek the first interesting and lucrative contract. Tobie was inclined to think the same, for other reasons. It seemed to Tobie that John disliked being tied to anyone as unpredictable as Nicholas, or perhaps even to anyone who drew people close to him as Nicholas did. Thomas, who had never been close to anyone except Astorre, simply wished he were somewhere fighting, or somewhere where he could spend the proceeds of fighting. He liked the money, but was aware, heavily, that Nicholas complicated his life.

So, translated to their new surroundings, the four awaited news from Loppe, and wondered if they still had a leader, and when they would see him. At least, he had come and had found them. There was some grounds for optimism in that. Pleasure, even. Perhaps even an unconfessed exhilaration. Then Loppe arrived, with a ludicrous story.

He interrupted himself, giggling, while he told it. Tobie sat up. Astorre stared, then broke down into hiccoughing laughter. 'They made the knave into a knight! Oh! Oh! Urbino'll kill himself laughing.'

'Well, Urbino's a count,' said John le Grant. His skin was as red as his hair, although his freckled face merely looked pained. 'Other people have got to start somewhere. So that's what our Nicholas wanted? Who'd have guessed it?'

'I should,' said Tobie briefly. 'But I didn't. I'm going back to Urbino.'

The engineer turned his gaudy cropped head. John le Grant was neat and quick as an acrobat. 'Oh, now. He could get you made a knight too, very likely.'

Loppe, or Lopez, poked up the brazier and, arranging some cushions, lay down in its warmth. His ears had caught a sound. He said, 'And he's getting married. To the lady Primaflora, Master Thomas.'

'No, I'm not,' Nicholas said, coming in. He unbuckled and dropped his sword upon Loppe, who lifted an indolent hand and received it. Nicholas unshackled his chain, and bestowed it and his badge upon Tobie. Tobie picked up the badge and read the lettering.

'*To stay loyal,*' he said. 'I always thought you ought to have it written down somewhere. And is there one for the wife?'

Nicholas looked down his nose, and then pushed back the brim of his beaver. 'You're jealous,' he said. 'Some of us are lucky, and some are just born to grind ointment. You *came* here, for God's sake, because you thought I'd come to Queen Carlotta.'

'No,' said John le Grant. 'We thought she'd been clever and kidnapped you. So what kept you then?'

'That's what King Luis was asking,' Nicholas said. He unfastened his cloak and his doublet and, pulling a cushion from Loppe, spread himself with a sigh on the floor. 'All through the banquet. I'm sorry you all missed the banquet. All through the banquet, he kept saying, "So why sail to Kolossi? Why not Kyrenia? And why not come to the Queen right away?"'

'And you said?' asked le Grant.

'Ask a silly question,' Nicholas said. 'Have you *seen* Primaflora? We got to Rhodes a month before we were ready, never mind Kyrenia.'

'And King Luis believed you,' said Tobie.

'Well, I hope someone did,' Nicholas said. 'I went to the Palace to join the Queen's party. I'm not going to complain if they make me King of the Bean as an extra.'

Tobie said, 'I'm sure you aren't. But you chose your side without consulting us. I don't happen to be greatly interested in Carlotta of Cyprus.'

'Well, that's a relief,' Nicholas said. 'Anyone else?'

John le Grant said, 'Have you chosen sides?'

Tobie looked at him. 'According to Loppe, he swore fealty to the Queen and her consort.' He turned slowly and stared at Nicholas. 'Or were you playing again? An oath doesn't matter?'

'I've chosen sides,' Nicholas said. 'But I needn't commit you. You can go home. You can stay with the Order. If it matters, you'll be paid for all the time you have spent. I didn't expect you to follow me. I'm glad that you did. But now the choice has to be yours.'

They all gazed at him. Tobie said, 'In Bruges, you spoke to Anselm Adorne. He's watching the Charetty girls. You want to befriend the Genoese for some purpose?'

Nicholas said, 'That would be difficult. I was abducted by Venice. I've reached an agreement with Venice. Anyone who wants to be a rich villain will have to fight with me on the same side as the Venetian interests. Anyone who wants to be chivalrous, of course, ought to choose either the Queen or the Hospitallers. As a knight, I could explain all the finer points.'

Tobie laid down the chain and the badge and folded his pale, furry arms over his doublet. 'May I summarise? You've accepted a knighthood and sworn to be loyal to Carlotta. You propose to serve not the Queen but her opponents the Venetians. Last year, you declined to work with the Venetians. The Venetians abducted you and now you've let them untie your buskins and marry you. What has changed? How and why are you going to serve them?'

'I don't propose to serve them at all,' Nicholas said. 'I propose to abstract their sugar trade and their dyeworks and anything else they leave lying about when they have to go off and make war on Turkey. The person I propose to be paid by is Carlotta's bastard brother, King Zacco.'

The brazier whispered, and the voices of servants could be heard through the thick walls. Tobie said, 'You've met him.'

'Yes,' said Nicholas.

'And he gave you a knighthood?'

'A fief, and a house in Nicosia. Also control of the royal dye-works, and the sugar franchise of Kouklia and Akhelia.'

John le Grant said, 'You'd lose the Queen's money, your knight-hood, your wife. You sealed a contract today.'

'King of the Bean,' Nicholas repeated helpfully. 'Incantations, cauldrons and mirrors. It was all an illusion.'

'Luis thought it was genuine,' said Loppe softly. 'And the Order will think so. She stole you from them.'

One of Astorre's ears had been torn off long ago at the lobe. When concentrating, he proceeded, as now, to finger it. He said, 'I'd prefer the Order to Zacco. I wouldn't fight under Mamelukes.'

'I've arranged that,' Nicholas said. 'You would fight under me, and I should answer directly to Zacco, as does the Mameluke leader Tzani-bey al-Ablak. That way, you won't get the blame when I kill him.'

Astorre's good eye narrowed as much as his sewn one. John le Grant said, 'Really? So what has this Tzani-bey done?'

'Killed some cats,' Nicholas said. 'You were willing to fight under Uzum Hasan. The Mamelukes are not very different. They'll leave the island when Zacco possesses it. And he will. With or without us, Carlotta can't keep it.'

Thomas looked at Astorre. He said, 'Captain?'

Astorre grunted. 'I don't greatly fancy Hospitallers, and the Genoese make me sick. All things being equal, I'd sooner work to a man. That is, the late demoiselle was exceptional.'

'I know. John? You've worked to a Genoese officer.'

'And I had a grandfather who took fees from the Order in Scotland. Forbye, my mother's a woman,' said the engineer. 'Maybe I ought to branch out and try this lad Zacco. I've a question. What about yon lord Simon's family? The Vasquez pair? His lady wife Katelina? She got us shut up. So why did she let Queen Carlotta enrol us? And an order of chivalry, to my mind, is not what she'd like to hang round your neck.'

'She wasn't there,' Nicholas said. 'After all, the Queen badly wants us, and she isn't likely to let the lady Katelina stand in her way. I don't know where Katelina may be, but at least the Vasquez pair are going home. I discussed it with the Queen. She thinks they can sail with Ludovico da Bologna.'

The red herring failed to work. Naturally, it failed to work because Tobie, alone of all the men there, knew exactly what he had done to Katelina. Tobie said, 'If you're getting rid of people, why not Katelina? She's going to spoil your plans if she can; I can't imagine why. Don't you think she and that God-awful friar would be good for one another? Is he really here?'

'There are six of him,' Nicholas said. 'That's why we keep meeting him everywhere. I'll be lucky to get rid of the Vasquez, never mind their good-sister and aunt Katelina. The lady won't go while we're here.'

'So what's she plotting?' said John le Grant.

'Nothing that can't be dealt with,' said Nicholas comfortably. He avoided Tobie's eye, and tried not to feel anger with Tobie. 'I'll tell you my guess, if you like. Then you tell me if you want to join Zacco and his Egyptian hordes. Then we plan something jolly to fill in the few days before the Queen has second thoughts. And then I want your advice about my impending marriage.'

Tobie's face was pink as a cochineal mouse. He said, 'I'm always ready with tips. So now you want Primaflora? Astorre says she's a courtesan.'

Nicholas said, 'I've got her, haven't I? But the Queen is insisting on marriage.'

'I don't suppose,' Tobie said, 'that the Sword is a celibate order? You could join the Hospitallers.'

'Think again,' Nicholas said.

'I have thought,' Tobie said. 'I have the perfect solution. Introduce her to Katelina van Borselen. She'll see you dead before she lets you remarry.'

'I'll think about it,' Nicholas said. 'It's drastic. It might end up with a massacre, like the cats and the emir. Perhaps I ought to woo the Fairy Melusine instead and be done with it.'

'The Fairy Melusine? Who's she?' said Tobie.

'Oho,' said Nicholas mildly. 'Ask Ludovico da Bologna, next time you see him.'

Chapter 16

IN HER STUFFY, leased house in the Chora, Katelina van Borselen impatiently fulfilled her duties to Tristão Vasquez, her husband's kinsman and partner. The boy, who was moody, she left to stay in or go out as he pleased. She felt no enthusiasm for either of them. Her mind was occupied with what was happening now at the Palace between the Queen of Cyprus and Nicholas vander Poele, who used to be Claes.

Of course, Nicholas should be in the hands of the Order and not at the Palace at all. She had made a mistake on the jetty that morning. She had invoked the help of Louis de Magnac, who was a devotee of Cyprus more than he was a Knight of the Order. As a result, he had taken Nicholas straight to the Queen instead of locking him up with his company. The Order had believed Katelina when she warned them to distrust Nicholas and the destination of his army. The Queen, too, had appeared to agree. But the Queen needed Nicholas more than the Hospitallers did. She was vain; Nicholas was plausible; she would deceive herself. Katelina was afraid that the warning she had brought was not enough. To be sure to bring Nicholas down, she needed evidence.

She and Tristão were in her small office discussing some futile matter of business when the news she wanted arrived from the Palace. Bearing it, her man was so breathless his voice was unsteady as he reported. 'Her grace the Queen received the Fleming, demoiselle. The man has not been denounced. He and his officers go wholly free, and have been given the house of the Grand Commander de Magnac. The man has sworn to serve Queen Carlotta. And the Queen has made him a Knight of the Order.'

'*A Knight of the Order?*' said Katelina.

He amplified quickly. 'Of the Order of the Sword. An honour given to foreigners, implying good service and zeal against heathens. The title is empty, demoiselle.'

Katelina sat down. She said, 'Is it known where he is to serve?'

'In Kyrenia, my lady,' the man said. 'Within the month, so they say, he will set sail with his army, to make Cyprus safe from the Turks and clear out the imposter Zacco.'

He waited, and after a moment she dismissed him. Tristão Vasquez said, 'You mistrust Senhor Niccolò's motives. But perhaps you are mistaken? The young man spoke no ill word of Simon. He claimed the vendetta was finished.'

He was a kindly man, beneath the formality. If she had been less wracked with anger, Katelina would have felt sorry for him. She said, 'You give him a gentleman's title. This is a labourer who has threatened my family. Whether he gives up or not, the score between us has to be settled. Simon is in Portugal, and cannot do it. But I am here, and I can.'

The Portuguese hesitated. Then he said, 'It would not be fitting to tell me in what way this man has offended?'

'You found him agreeable company?' said Katelina. 'Most people do. He finds it easy to make himself liked. He is devious. Those who cross him are ruined, or killed. If he can, he will harm you and Diniz. I can say no more than that.'

The other had sobered. He said, 'I can hardly believe it, but of course, I must. I shall warn Diniz. He is already much attached to the lady. It is a trouble to me. Ah, here he is.'

He sounded surprised. His son, though unruly, at least observed the rules of good conduct in company. But now he burst into the room as if it were a stadium. He said, 'Father!' and stopped.

'Come in, Diniz,' said Katelina politely.

The boy flushed and gripped the door. Then he said, 'I saw your messenger. The one who went to the Palace, senhora.'

'Yes?' said Katelina.

The boy looked at his father. 'He was telling his friends about how the Queen had made a great lord of this nobody Niccolò. And how a lady of the Queen's suite had been told to take him in marriage.' He turned. 'Father! The man Niccolò is a scoundrel! My aunt here says he is a scoundrel; and he is to marry her!'

'He is to marry the lady Primaflora?' said Tristão gently.

The boy nodded. The father turned to Katelina. She said quickly, 'It should be prevented. She is a – a –'

'I know what she is,' said Tristão. He didn't look at his son.

Katelina flushed. She said, 'Vander Poele would be lucky to win her. I was thinking of the lady's welfare. Whatever she wants, or deserves, it couldn't be this. This man marries only from expediency. His last wife made him a rich man, and died a year later.' She had run out of breath. She drew another and added, 'She should be told.'

'Would you tell her? Would you? And warn her?' said the boy. But the father shook his head at her, frowning.

She ignored him. Her mind was on Primaflora, who had spent days, perhaps weeks, perhaps months in the company – in the bed, she knew it – of Nicholas. From that, a woman would emerge believing anything that he told her. Nicholas, she was sure, had been convincing, in bed and in throne room. But it would be Primaflora, her own trusted attendant, who persuaded the Queen that Nicholas was truly the loyal knight that he seemed. Katelina looked at Diniz. She said, 'We are traders. We cannot interfere with the affairs of a royal household. A lady-in-waiting must obey her Queen. But perhaps, away from the Palace, one might do something. I shall send the lady a message. This is an evil man, and no woman deserves to be tied to him.'

When the message arrived from Katelina, Primaflora took it at once, smiling, to Carlotta her mistress.

Since she returned to Rhodes, Primaflora had taken care to prove herself once again the most elegant, the most amenable, the most useful of all the Queen's servants, and never again had she given the Queen reason to doubt that her mistress was the object of all her solicitude. She had betrayed her private feelings once, with Ansaldo, and knew now what a mistake it had been. She had also absented herself for an extremely long time, although she had taken care, while in Italy, to send reassuring messages to keep Carlotta from interfering.

The result, naturally, had been a loss of trust between herself and the Queen, and she couldn't guess how long it might take to restore it; or to restore it to the same degree as before. Carlotta never truly placed her trust in anyone. Since their reunion, the Queen had seldom let her former attendant, graceful, complaisant Primaflora, out of her sight.

With Luis there, on the other hand, the task of making herself indispensable was made easier for the same attendant. The Consort and his courtiers crowded the Palace, filling it with witless clamour. To his royal wife, the understanding presence of Primaflora was both soothing and a source of mild stimulation. The Queen enjoyed testing the girl, and Primaflora tolerated the malicious fencing. Of the two, she thought she was the better swordsman.

So, presenting herself in the Queen's chamber, she disregarded its disorder, and the high colour in the Queen's sharp young face. The kingdom needed an heir, and after courting the princes of Europe, Carlotta's severest trial, her servants thought, must be the duty of courting her own cousin and husband. So Primaflora entered, curtseyed, and standing before the royal chair said, 'You foresaw correctly, Serenissima. The Flemish lady is disturbed by the favour shown to Messer Niccolò. She wishes a meeting with me. After the marriage contract is signed, the serene Queen might permit me to agree to this?'

The Queen stretched out her little ringed claw. 'Show me. No, translate it into Greek.' Primaflora drew up a stool and sitting, read smoothly aloud, while the Queen's nails dug into her shoulder. Then, finishing, she was silent as the Queen considered.

The room was crowded with ikons. By the shrine in the corner, a relic encased in silver stood below the jewelled cross. Everyone fleeing from infidels bought their way into a pension and grace by purveying holy bones of some sort. Cathedrals all over the west were filling up with apostolic skulls, and Carlotta was never one to bypass a marketable commodity. She was also devout. But she was less devout than she was shrewd.

Waiting, Primaflora thought of her last audience, when the knighthood for Niccolò had first been mentioned, followed immediately by the news that the Queen intended to marry her to the young man.

The proposal had disturbed Primaflora. It was true that Niccolò was a lover she liked. She was, of course, accustomed to making the best of things. But, occasionally, in her profession, one found a partner equal in imagination and finesse, if not in experience. Such a discovery was a matter for delight, and one to be explored and savoured over the years. But marriage had no place in a courtesan's life, and no man of standing would dream of accepting her. Only because he was young, and base-born and presumably ignorant did the Queen feel able to impose such a marriage as a condition of Niccolò's service, or even as a reward which would keep him loyal. The Queen never underrated Primaflora's powers to enchant.

The scheme had, of course, other benefits. As his wife, Primaflora could spy for Carlotta. And as his wife Primaflora, too, was deprived of an independent career and would be well advised to see that her husband chose the right path, and flourished. It was perfectly obvious to Primaflora that the Queen would judge her by her willingness to go through with the marriage, and that she might have to comply. And if that were so, she might as well make the most of it. For example, a loving couple should not be forbidden to meet.

So, offered marriage with Niccolò, Primaflora had hesitated only a moment. 'As the Serenissima wishes.'

'As the Serenissima wishes?' the Queen had said. 'Do you not wish it? He has, I take it, proved himself vigorous?'

'There is no difficulty,' Primaflora had said. 'But he may try to talk his way out of marriage. On the other hand, he is young and vain: he would respond to fatherhood. That is why I do not think he and I should be separated.'

The Queen lifted her fingers and, caressing a wisp of the other's blonde hair, tugged it briefly. 'I know you,' she said. 'Really, we must observe the proprieties until the contract is signed. On the other hand . . . He has not heard you are barren?'

She shook her head. That she had no children and could have none was, in many ways, her greatest asset.

'Then you had better contrive to see him,' said the Queen. 'But discreetly. It is most important. I command you.' As she had always believed, Primaflora found herself proved the better swordsman.

Now, she waited for the Queen's decision on the Flemish woman's communication. At length, it came. 'You will meet her. This cannot wait for the contract. See the woman van Borselen. She has friends in authority, and we must not offend her. Tell her the truth: that we are fully aware of the risks we are running with this mercenary troop, and that we shall take steps to see that the man does not cheat us. Satisfy her.'

'I suspect,' said Primaflora, 'that she will not be satisfied.'

'No,' said the Queen thoughtfully. 'Then let us find out what she wants and harness it.'

'It may be his death,' said Primaflora.

'Or yours. Be careful,' said the Queen. 'She must understand that your marriage with the man Niccolò is an arranged one. She must not conceive that you want him. My advisers say no, but I think this is a spurned woman. She could be useful. If this young scoundrel does cheat us, we can help her to punish him. Unless you object?'

Primaflora showed amusement. 'The world is full of young men.'

The Queen's expression remained thoughtful. 'Yes. I know your weakness, Primaflora. But remember. At this moment, you are my protégée, and your conduct must be impeccable.'

Leaving the room, Primaflora forced herself to walk slowly. She had won a meeting with Niccolò – perhaps several. The Queen knew her, that was true. Envied her, even; for the Queen's own conduct, however impeccable, was wringing no heir from the limp flesh of her poor cousin Luis. Even so, she was unlikely to imagine quite how much Niccolò differed from other men. In a way, Primaflora was sorry.

And Katelina, the lady she was going to meet? The Queen was wrong. The young apprentice of Bruges would hardly have spurned the kind of girl Katelina must have been several years ago. Or if he had, his singular abstinence could scarcely have caused the notorious rift between himself and Simon, the lady's good-looking husband. So had Niccolò made Simon a cuckold? It seemed unlikely. The feud predated the lady's marriage, and since the marriage, according to Niccolò, he had met her once only in public. Of course, this might not be true. To discover the truth was one reason why Primaflora was calling on this high-born demoiselle from the Low Countries. For in one thing the Queen was quite right. Where Niccolò was concerned, Primaflora was not objective.

*

The Basilica Mercatorum was the trading hub of the City, where merchants met to do business, and the Bailie settled disputes. Built inside the harbour wall, it was not far − not at all far − from the Square of St Sebastian, and the house of Louis de Magnac. Naturally, Primaflora was escorted to the Basilica; but was permitted to leave her protectors ouside the galleried entrance, taking only her woman as chaperone. The men, she knew, were paid by the royal household. As Zacco was doing with Niccolò, the Queen had let her out on a chain. Having lost sight of her once, Carlotta was taking no chances.

Inside, the rooms were busy, for ships came and went all through winter, exchanging the products of Greece and Italy, Asia and Africa. There was always money to change, and bills of payment to sign. The brokers, the notaries, the moneychangers all had their tables, and the merchants congregated, as the Knights did, according to tongue. Except, that is, for the Jews, who were familiar with every language. Modestly dressed, Primaflora passed among the dealers from Venice and Genoa, Marseilles and Ancona, Damascus and Chios, Crete and Sicily, overturning the tilth of their attention like the lightest of harrows. There were one or two Portuguese, but none from the family Vasquez, who had presumably completed their business. Nor did she see merchants from Florence. The ship from Constantinople had sailed, and their transactions were over. Eventually, a boy in the livery of St Pol appeared and led her upstairs to a gallery. In one of its many small rooms, she was again introduced to Katelina van Borselen.

The Flemish woman had been dictating, and a clerk was just leaving with papers. He stood aside for Primaflora, his eyes flickering. Primaflora smiled, and smiled again at the page, who closed the door on himself and her attendant. The room held a side table, a desk, a book box and two chairs, and no one else but herself and the woman called Katelina. Katelina van Borselen said, 'It was kind of you to come. Please sit. I have some Candian wine. You see in me an envoy of my young Portuguese nephew. You have a disciple in Diniz for life.'

Primaflora sat, and pushed back her cloak. She had expected passion, but instead the young lady seemed remarkably calm. Then she saw the wine spurt from the flask, and realised that, like herself, the girl had been much about courts and was used to dissembling. And that in fact, she was angered, and even somehow afraid.

Primaflora said, 'I thought your nephew had changed his mind. My young friend Niccolò said that he would. The child fancied himself in love with me, and no doubt thinks I have given my heart to someone else.' She shrugged and smiled. 'How difficult if marriages were truly thus! Or − Of course, demoiselle, your own is certainly of that order. I was thinking of my young fiancé, whose second matrimonial venture this is. And perhaps of my friends, who like myself, cannot afford the luxury of marriage except for reasons of policy.'

The wine flask clattered as Katelina put it back. She raised her cup, and they each drank. Katelina said, 'We know Nicholas well in Flanders. I wondered if you had heard of his first marriage. It was successful, until his wife died.'

Primaflora, though polite, was less than serious. 'There was nothing ominous, surely, about that? He was absent, I supposed, at the time.'

The younger woman reddened, but persisted in a level voice. 'He was absent, with his step-daughter. He owes all his fortune to the help of his wife although, by merest accident, he failed to gain control of her original company. The step-daughters now have it, or one of them, and are determined to have nothing to do with him. He did well in Italy, after his uncle's business was ruined. He succeeded in Trebizond, after his Genoese rival had died.' She paused. She said, 'He has nothing to gain from your death, that I know of. But of course, he will secure the goodwill of your Queen through your marriage. I have only to say to you that, in view of what I have told her, the Queen's goodwill may not last. And neither may this marriage.'

Primaflora allowed her face to become sober. She put down her cup. 'You are saying that Niccolò is capable of violence to gain his own ends? And that the violence may be used against me?'

The Flemish woman looked down. She was attractive enough, with a slim neck and bold features and an excellent complexion, abandoned to Nature. With some attention to that, and her brows, she could have found lovers anywhere. She said, 'I have already warned Queen Carlotta that he is dangerous. Men discount him because of his upbringing. But even in Bruges, he was clever enough to get the better of anyone he took a dislike to. It doesn't spring from ambition. It is his idea of . . . of sport.'

Primaflora sipped her wine thoughtfully. She said, 'He has sworn loyalty, accepted a knighthood. Why should he do that, unless he means to stay with her? And if he does, I am surely in no danger.'

Katelina van Borselen said, 'Of course he swore loyalty! He has to get his men off the island, and he can hardly do that by declaring for the Venetians and Zacco. Give him a ship, and he'll sail straight for Salines and Queen Carlotta's brother. And you will be with him, and no longer needed.'

Primaflora smiled. 'You underrate me,' she said. 'What if I might reform him? Why, anyway, should he make for King Zacco? Perhaps the Queen's party could offer him more.'

The girl's face had changed from red to pale. She said, 'I am sure you would be persuasive. Perhaps you think you have his friendship. But Nicholas has no close friends, men or women; only people he uses. He tolerated Marian de Charetty, but his manhood will demand a master this time, not Queen Carlotta or another wife he must please. And I know – I have spoken to those who sailed from Kolossi with you, and I will soon have proof – that he is still working for the Venetians, ànd that his feud with my husband is as violent as ever. He will join whatever party supports the Venetians and opposes my family. He will join Zacco. I have told the Queen. You must tell her as well. It is true.'

Primaflora said, 'If that is his plan, he won't stop because I refuse to marry him. And meanwhile, perhaps I can find out his intentions.'

The Flemish woman said, 'You don't know him. You will never learn his real aims. And if you put off your marriage, at least you won't end up in Nicosia, in the hands of a Mameluke emir.'

She was breathing quickly. Primaflora said, 'You hate him a great deal. You must be very fond of your husband, to come so far to outface his enemy.'

There was the briefest pause. Then the girl said, 'Simon has risked his life many times, fighting Nicholas. Perhaps I can achieve without a sword what he has tried to do with one. With your help and the Queen's, we might defeat him.'

Primaflora watched her. She said, 'If Niccolò tries to go to King Zacco, the Queen will kill him and all his men. This is what you would like?'

'He would deserve it,' said Katelina.

'Then,' said Primaflora, 'why not let matters take their course? Let me go to the Queen and repeat all your warnings. Bring me, when you have it, all the proof you can find of his duplicity. If he is what you say, the Queen will not have him, or the Order. They will allow me to postpone the marriage. And you may be sure they will make quite certain he does not go to Zacco.'

There was a long silence. Then the Flemish woman said, 'Very well. I will bring you proof. And when I have brought it, marry him. You will be a very rich widow.'

Primaflora said, 'You don't think that is dangerous advice? He might seduce me from my purpose.'

Katelina stood. 'He has probably done that already,' she said. 'But whatever proof I get, I shall give to the Queen as well. If he goes to Zacco, you would die with him.'

'And if he doesn't?' said Primaflora. 'If I marry him, and he stays with Queen Carlotta?'

'Then you would still be a rich widow,' said Katelina. 'Because I should make you one.'

Slowly, in her turn, Primaflora rose, her eyes on the other. She said, 'What has he done to you?'

Katelina made a short, dismissive gesture. 'There was something. It was done to injure my husband, not me. No one else knows of it, because it was designed by Nicholas to be savoured by Nicholas only. You think of Nicholas as an adventurer. He is a man who maims, I have told you, for sport.'

Primaflora listened. The Queen was right. The woman was dangerous; in some way obsessed. But now was not the moment to find out the root of it. She rested her manicured fingers on the other's silk sleeve. 'Leave it to me. But meantime, let him feel safe. Keep out of his way for your own sake. He must know you and Tristão Vasquez are his enemies. He is at liberty, and you say he is cruel. If that is so, then you must be in danger.'

'Perhaps,' said Katelina van Borselen. 'It doesn't make any difference. He is a traitor. I will prove it. And nothing will stop me.'

From the door, Primaflora stood and considered her. Then she took a decision, and spoke. 'You are still unsure of me, so I will tell you. This Niccolò is a lover I like, but that means very little. I am the Queen's lady, but I am also a courtesan. The Queen uses me to attract and hold knights to her cause. I was with such a man in Bologna when he was killed, and the Queen told me to attach myself to vander Poele if I could.'

Another pause. 'Was it difficult?' the Flemish girl said. Despite an obvious effort, the contempt showed.

'No,' said Primaflora. 'He will go to bed with anybody. On the night they told him his wife was dead, he found consolation until dawn in the arms of a Greek married lady of means.'

'He told you?'

'I heard from one of his men. Is that your page, or my woman?'

Katelina answered the scratch on the door. 'Your woman, madonna. Someone expects you.'

For once, her woman had chosen correctly. It was time to interrupt: the right moment to go, leaving that news behind her. The leave-taking on both sides was smooth. Followed by her chaperone, Primaflora moved to the stairs, and was almost pushed aside by the young St Pol page dashing past her. In the hall below, she could see a stir, and hear men's voices upraised. Her woman said, 'Not down the stairs, madonna. My lord is in one of the rooms in this very gallery.'

Primaflora stopped. She said, 'Who is in one of the rooms?'

The woman stopped also, looking surprised. 'My lord Niccolò, your betrothed. I gave him your message, and he is waiting for you. You are blessed. He is ardent, madonna.'

'But he was not to meet me here until later! He is too early! The maniac!' she said.

The room she had just left was behind her. As Primaflora spoke, she heard the page open its door. She heard the boy's voice within, and that of Katelina, responding. The Flemish girl's voice sounded nearer: she was on the verge of stepping out to the gallery. Primaflora, distracted, looked about her. An unwilling bride should not, on the face of it, be making assignations with her despised future husband. Another door began to open ahead of her. It led to the room her woman had indicated: she didn't wait to see who would come out.

She had fled halfway down the stairs when a man's hand took her comfortably under the arm and a man's voice said, 'My dear future bride! Are you running to me, or from me?'

She turned. It was, of course, Niccolò. The dimples were there, and the large eyes with their purses of mischief and the austere, contradictory nose with its drawn nostrils. Framing his face were two flaxen plaits with a veil on them, and his boots emerged from a long-waisted gown of white lawn. 'Guinevere,' he said. 'I was just off to a joust with the Knights, but I'd rather have one with you. Why are you frowning?' He looked round. 'Something is happening?'

In the rest of the building, certainly, something seemed to be happening. In the agitation below, hardly a face had turned towards Niccolò. She had no idea what had caused the upset, and didn't care. She said, 'Something is going to happen. Your friend Katelina is behind you. I've told her I'll help her against you.'

'Oh, good,' Niccolò said. Between the gold plaits, his gaze was still on the hall below him. 'Something *is* happening.'

'Nicholas!' said the voice of the Flemish woman. She had run from her room to the stairs, and was now descending them rather slowly.

Niccolò turned. 'Guinevere,' he said again, helpfully. 'I was just off to a joust . . .'

Katelina said, 'Was it you? You who killed them?'

Under the veil, the ridiculous eyes opened. 'Them? Who?' Niccolò said.

'Tristão and Diniz,' said Katelina. 'They were taken hunting this morning. Someone led them astray. They have disappeared.'

'Who brought word?' Niccolò said. He sounded as he had at Kolossi, when preparing to get rid of the priest.

Katelina said, 'Did you do it?' She was white.

Niccolò said, 'No, I didn't. *Who brought word?*'

'One of the party. He's gone up to the Castle. They need men to search before it gets dark. I must get a horse.'

'Take mine,' Niccolò said. 'It's outside, with Lancelot and Yvain and the squires. I have a spare. Who else wants to come?'

He had raised his voice, beginning to jump down the stairs.

Beneath the levity, as at Kolossi, was something quite different. Someone said, 'On a horse? Let the Knights go.'

Niccolò said, 'They'll go, but we might get there first. Come on; the Vasquez are Portuguese traders. They must owe somebody money.'

They came forward then, five or six of them, picking up their cloaks brusquely and sending their lads running for horses. Katelina, her face still bleak, was staring at Niccolò. Primaflora said quickly, 'Have you a spare horse for me?'

Niccolo turned to her. She couldn't tell if he read what she was thinking. She was prepared for impatient surprise. He only said, 'I dare say. In fact, I'll take you on mine. If anything will bring Diniz back from the dead, it will be you with your hair down.'

She held his eyes, still transmitting her warning. She said, 'Who are Lancelot and Yvain?'

'My captain Astorre, and your old friend Thomas,' Niccolò said. 'My engineer is the Lion, and the Loathly Damsel is a doctor called Tobie. King Arthur refused to be present. Can we run? Or are we both too God-damned ladylike?'

Primaflora halted. Beside her, Katelina also paused. Then, their hands gripping their skirts they began, from quite different motives, to race after Nicholas.

Chapter 17

THE COURT OF King Arthur, asked to interrupt its journey on the way to a joust, waited outside the merchants' basilica with some impatience for the return of its Guinevere. The Loathly Damsel in particular was fretful. 'It's wearing off,' said Tobie. 'I tell you, I am not doing this sober. If he doesn't come soon, I'm going back.'

'Spoilsport,' said the Lion. 'Forbye, you are rejecting a significant re-creation of history. In 1223 –'

'The crazy Lord of Beirut held a tournament in Arthurian dress on the island of Cyprus. This isn't Cyprus; the Saracens are in Beirut, and the only similarity – and I do grant you that – is that the man who arranged it is crazy. What's he doing?'

'Rumour has it,' said the Lion, 'that he had the chance to make an assignation with his lady. I doubt it will be successful in that get-up.'

'Which lady?' said Captain Astorre. He chortled.

'The one Thomas escorted all over Europe,' said Tobie. 'Go on, Thomas. You enjoyed it.'

Thomas, in a normal suit of armour with a fancy helmet, looked sulky. Le Grant tipped his muzzle back and let it lie with his mane on his shoulders. He said, 'But for Thomas, Primaflora might be running the House of Niccolò at this moment. I heard she was trying to get hold of Katelina van Borselen.'

Tobie stared at him, breathing heavily, and stopped scratching under his wig. He said, 'That's a frightening idea.'

'Is it?' said John le Grant.

'Of course it is,' said Lancelot, his stitched eye glittering. 'Two women, one man. Pick each other's eyes out, or turn on him together. God's little finger.'

From the basilica emerged Nicholas, running, with a girl on each side. One was fair and one was brown-haired, and both were delightful. Other men came out without girls, and scattered. There was some shouting. Nicholas said, 'The joust's off. The Vasquez, father and son, are in trouble.' He bent, and gave a foothold to the golden-haired woman to mount, and then turned to do the same for the other one. Two armed men ran forward and caught the reins of the yellow-haired woman who had turned to speak, smiling, to Thomas. Nicholas stopped what he was doing and went back to her. He said, 'Your escort? We can't mount them, Primaflora.'

She looked down at the two men. 'Then they will have to stay,' she said.

One of the men took her reins, and then her elbow. 'We have our orders,' he said. The girl looked at Nicholas.

Nicholas said, 'You still want to come? All right. They can take the free horse and ride with us. Tobie, take the lady Katelina behind you.'

The lady Katelina stepped back and looked where Nicholas pointed. Tobie, recoiling, saw that she was recoiling as well. He peeled off his nose and threw it away. 'The Loathly Damsel,' said Nicholas. 'Go on. He's a doctor, but he won't rape you in public. Who knows where we're going?'

'I do,' said Katelina van Borselen. 'We go to Mount Phileremos. The Knights at Trianda will direct us. Why do you want to come?'

'Because if I don't,' Nicholas said, 'and there's been a catastrophe, you will certainly say I arranged it. In fact, you'll say it in any case. I just want to be there to deny it.' He looked from Katelina to Tobie. He said, 'If you both ride side-saddle, that horse will fall over.'

Tobias Beventini, physician, hurled his wig from him, dragged up a double layer of taffeta skirts and bestrode his horse, swearing. His wimple, which had not disappeared with his wig, threatened to cut his throat with its wire. He saw that Nicholas, mounted, was being embraced becomingly round the fitted waist by the exquisite blonde Primaflora. Behind Tobie himself, the other young woman sat sideways, looking for something to grasp. She settled at length for his girdle: he could feel her knuckles. Katelina van Borselen, whom he had last glimpsed in Bruges, newly married to Simon and heavily pregnant. Pregnant, as he now knew, with the son of Nicholas. He had never spoken to the girl Nicholas had wronged, and had hoped never to have to. He could see, well enough, that she could make a man lose his head.

But, barring the principals, no one else here knew what he did. Lancelot, turning round, said to her, 'Well, demoiselle, I hope you notice the good turn we do you, considering that you saw to it that we had a poor welcome on Rhodes.' His beard jutted, an exclamation under his silver helmet.

The demoiselle showed no sign of intimidation. 'Blame your leader, not me,' she said curtly. The last word ended in a jerk, because Tobie dug in his spurs, and they all began moving at speed towards the gates of the City.

After the weeks of confinement, it was a relief to leave the City behind: to exchange the massive walls, the stately buildings, the burnished court etiquette of chivalric Europe for the open country of a Levantine island, with its fields and its hamlets, its fishing villages and its broken pillars, residue of ancient cities at least as great.

From end to end, Rhodes was less than fifty miles long. Setting out from its northernmost tip, a group of people might expect very soon to find two men who had lost their way, but who were not unintelligent, and had arms, and the ability to call for help. But riding along the sandy shore towards the plain and the wooded hill that was called Mount Phileremos, Tobie recalled that the island was also mountainous. The long spine of afforested hills provided in summer a rough, dusty traverse from one side of the island to the other. Now, in winter, the way was treacherous with swollen streams and slippery inclines and mud.

He supposed that accidents were not uncommon, and that it was usual for the Hospitallers to offer aid to noble guests in distress. He knew Katelina believed that these particular visitors were victims of malice. It was possible. On the other hand, her theory might owe a lot to her suspicions of Nicholas. Notwithstanding his own suspicions of Nicholas, Tobie observed that Guinevere had, on the whole, responded as any innocent man might to a mild emergency which had not yet turned into a serious one.

Riding beside the white beach, with the low sun on his right, Tobie found himself watching Nicholas and the girl racing in front, her gilt hair flown aloft like a pennant. The flogging pigtails of Guinevere raised dust from his shoulders, and his earrings jangled like buckets. Primaflora, holding him fast, was speaking into his ear. Over Tobie's shoulder, Katelina was speaking as well. She said, 'Can't you ride faster? I'm supposed to help find the way.' If she wanted to eavesdrop on Nicholas, Tobie had no objection. He moved up to ride beside Guinevere's fluttering girdle and sleeves. Primaflora smiled at him sweetly, and stopped speaking immediately. She was an amazingly beautiful woman.

They left the sea, and the ride became much more unpleasant. There was a blustering wind from the north, and splattered mud dashed in their faces. Other men joined them, and before they had gone very far, one or two of the Knights came up quickly. One of them, Scougal, was a Scottish Hospitaller whom Tobie knew. Tobie said, as they rode, 'What do you think has happened?'

The Knight heard him, but threw an uneasy glance at Katelina. She said, 'You might as well tell us. I've heard the party's dogs came back, injured, but the horses haven't been found?'

The Knight said, 'The gentleman and his son seem to have been deliberately sent where riding is difficult. They had with them two guides who have disappeared too. And if they found their way to the shore from the mountains, they might have run into a raiding party. Without guides, it is a dangerous island.'

'A raiding party. Of Turks?' Tobie asked. He was taken aback.

The Knight said, 'You haven't seen the burned houses and ruined fields by the shore? The coast of Asia Minor is only seven miles away. The pirates make a quick landing, and pillage and destroy what they can. If someone wished the demoiselle's family ill, it wouldn't be hard to snatch them and hold them to ransom. I hear Tristão Vasquez is highly valued. And Muslims esteem handsome boys.'

Tobie said, 'That's enough. They're more than likely just wandering lost on the hills.'

But it was Astorre, not far away, who shook his head. 'Rhodes is a small place. The first search party must have used dogs. If they didn't find them, they're either hurt, or concealed, or off the island.'

Guinevere removed a hank of hair from his teeth. 'If I were a Turk, I doubt if I'd have heard of the Vasquez. If they were deliberately cut off, it wasn't the work of a chance raiding party. Demoiselle? Who had a grudge against the Senhor and his son?'

'You,' she said. 'And your men.'

'But we were kept inside the City. So, business rivals? Who else?'

'No one else,' she said. Her knuckles bruised Tobie's back.

'That you know of. How were the dogs injured? Did the page say?'

'He didn't. They'll be at Trianda: the stronghold; the monastery. The Knights are sending a servant to guide us. You could have paid someone to do it,' said Katelina.

'I could have paid someone to do it on shipboard, but I didn't,' Nicholas said. He didn't sound frivolous, and the earrings looked less a conceit than an irrelevance. Ahead, Tobie saw the wooded height which must be Mount Phileremos with the fortress, the ruins, the monastery on its crown. A group of men, emerging from trees, was running towards them. Among them, leading them, was a hulking black figure he recognised. Tobie slackened his knees, and felt the weight shift behind as Simon's wife peered round his shoulder.

Katelina van Borselen turned towards Nicholas. 'I know that black man. He's your servant.'

Tobie opened his mouth and then shut it. Astorre, still riding, said nothing, nor did le Grant or Thomas. Nicholas, spitting out hair, said, 'You mean he's the spy planted on me by the Grand Commander Louis de Magnac. I don't mind. He's good with a razor.'

'Maybe too good with a razor,' said John the Lion.

'No. He's called Lopez. He's Portuguese, like the Vasquez,' Nicholas said. 'He wouldn't harm thèm. Unless you think he's got orders from Louis de Magnac? But the Knights at Kolossi were friendly.'

Loppe came up. Loppe, who – Tobie knew, Astorre knew – was indeed the servant of Nicholas, and would do whatever Nicholas wanted. Loppe went straight to Scougal with his black mantle and said, 'Senhor, do you lead for the Knights? The horses have been found, and two of the four men. They are dead. I have to take you to where they lie. There are tracks, but they are confused. We need many men to follow them before it gets dark.'

It was not a mild emergency any more. The Knight said, 'Sit behind me. Which men have died?'

'I will run,' said Loppe. 'Not the foreigners. The men who died seem to be grooms. They were killed with arrows, like the dogs. You are all armed?' He turned, scanning the rest of the party, and let his eyes widen.

Nicholas said, 'You nicked my knees, but I forgive you. We're all armed. We were on our way to a joust. Let's go. There isn't much daylight.'

Tobie stayed where he was. More, he grabbed Guinevere's reins. He said, 'That's far enough for the women. It'll be dark soon; it's dangerous, and they'll slow us.'

Primaflora said, 'I don't mind staying behind, if –'

'I'm not stopping,' said Katelina. 'Get me a horse for myself.'

The courtesan smiled. 'Then neither am I. Two horses.'

Tobie waited, expecting Nicholas to turn off the woman and leave her. Instead Nicholas pushed up the coils of his sleeves. 'There's no time. Half a horse each, as at present. Let's go.' He dug in his spurs. His burdened horse leaped and broke into a canter. Tobie hesitated. Behind him, his co-rider lifted both feet and kicked the flank of their mount which shied, collected itself, and began racing after the other. Astorre gave a short bark of appreciation and set off at speed, with the rest.

There was nothing to be done about Katelina. Of all people, Tobie couldn't blame her for her aversion to Nicholas. None the less, it made him uncomfortable, or more uncomfortable than he already was. The Loathly Damsel's dress was coated with mud, and it had begun to rain on his scalp. Tobie let his horse open up to a gallop, and cursed Nicholas and all his women.

It wasn't far to the place where the dead servants lay. The negro, running ahead, stopped and waved. There were dark shapes among the thickets of broom, and a smearing of brown. Tobie drew rein, but the woman behind him neither spoke nor dismounted. Men were on the turf, bending over. He saw Loppe straighten, his eyes meeting those of Nicholas, although nothing was said. Tobie said, 'Hell and damnation, what are they doing?'

Astorre answered him, mounted again. 'Two dead men: the servants. They were killed by arrows, shot from a distance. They still had their swords at their sides. We've tracks from the two Vasquez horses, and a lot of footmarks, and a place over there where other horses were waiting.'

'So someone's got hold of the Portuguese?' Tobie said.

Primaflora walked over. She had tied up the skirts of her gown, showing fine linen stockings full of holes and whiskered embroidery. Her hood had dropped back, and her hair fell treacle-gold in the wet. She said, 'Messer Niccolò and the negro think not. They think they escaped on foot from the struggle, and the attackers set off to pursue them. The early searchers found horses' tracks near Kalamonas, but most of the marks have been lost in the rain. It means casting wide in small groups, with only a short time before dark to do it. The Knights will give orders.'

'Are you going on, madonna?' said Tobie.

'Why not?' she said. She was not smiling. 'It is quicker than going back.' She said to Katelina, 'Demoiselle, your kinsmen may have escaped. They may hear us, and come out of hiding.'

'They may see us, and go into hiding,' said Nicholas. 'If you're coming, get up.'

As she swung into the saddle, Tobie received a view of one arching limb, clean from ankle to garter to thigh. To white and gold glimmering thigh. He dropped a rein and, fumbling for it, cursed Nicholas all over again.

There were only seven now in their group. On horseback, Astorre and Tobie, Nicholas and one of Primaflora's protectors, with the two women still riding pillion. On foot Loppe, known to all but his colleagues as Lopez. As the light left the sky, the party grew silent. Loppe, striding ahead, spoke or called in a low voice, and sometimes one of the men spoke to him, or to each other. Sometimes they stood still, the salty wind tugging their clothing, while two or three cast about on foot. Far off, others were doing the same. Above the blustering noise of the elements could be heard distant voices; but never the sound of the trumpet that would announce the end of the search.

It was an intolerant country in winter, when the sun no longer smiled on its children, and the oleanders were dead, and the cots round the shores were in ashes. The windmills creaked. The fortresses stood on their hills; the crumbled temples of the Greeks, the staunch keeps of the Genoese, the stout castles of the Knights; and round them the cottages huddled, with the pigs indoors, and the goats safely penned, and the geese and hens secure from the fox, or the Turks.

They saw few such houses, for their task was to search the marshy areas, where men on foot might try to escape men on horseback. On rising land, they passed patches of ploughed ground, and put up hares, and smelled a plantation of carob trees. There were olives, some long stripped; some with their January windfalls half gathered. Twice, Loppe found deer slots. Then he found something else: the clear print of a spurred boot in the mud.

Its owner must have slipped sideways, and recovered himself. Further on, there was an impress of the same sole, overlaid this time by another. Nicholas dismounted, peered, and straightening, whipped off his wig by the plait and sent it whirling into the gloom like a pelican. Elation? No. Satisfaction, the doctor diagnosed. The satisfaction of an engineer, when the engine performs. The Lion said nothing but Captain Astorre said, 'See? See, demoiselle? We'll find them!'

The sky to the east had grown dark, and the sugarloaf mountain ahead was now dim. The Knights had provided pitch torches. Lighting their own, they saw where others jumped in the distance like woodsparks. Astorre said, 'Will we call them?'

Nicholas said, 'Numbers won't make any difference. We'll call when we've found something. Look. The prints lead to that dip.'

Primaflora's protector said, 'They hoped to get to the monastery, perhaps. They were making for Kalopetra, and were headed off. The dip is a ravine: half a mile of it, with hiding places in plenty. But the first search party passed this way earlier, and no one answered their call.'

Loppe said, 'Here. They have come down the bank and followed the water to escape from the horses. One is hurt.'

He was speaking ostensibly to the soldier but always, Tobie felt, indirectly to Nicholas. They spread out, and the men dismounted. Here and there, in the light that was half flame and half twilight, Tobie could see the uneven track that Loppe had deciphered. One of the men was indeed injured. Tristão, who had married the sister of the hated Simon? Or Tristão's son Diniz who – perhaps – Nicholas thought his first cousin?

That was why Loppe was speaking to Nicholas. Because of that, or because everything he said confirmed something Nicholas expected to hear. Death tended to come very often to kinsmen of Nicholas.

The ravine wound on, sometimes broadening to enclose trees and bushes and patches of meadow, sometimes narrowing to the extent of a footpath skirting a deep, tumbling pond. The rush of water shot back from the cliffs on either side and the groves of oak and pine masked the darkening sky with their tight-ravelled branches. There were other trees, smooth and leafless and eight times a man's height, which Tobie had never seen before. A hail of objects dashed over his head. Katelina screamed in his ear. Her fists gripped Tobie's sides, cloth and skin wrung together. The horse plunged, and Tobie whipped his sword from its scabbard. 'Birds,' said Nicholas.

Primaflora laid her cheek on his back, laughing breathlessly. Then she caught herself, and turned to Katelina. 'It could have been dangerous. They looked like bolts, or arrows, or stones.'

There was a pause. Then Katelina said, 'I thought they were insects.'

Astorre, plodding beside her, grunted without looking up. 'Insects won't kill you.'

'No,' said Katelina.

Tobie felt her heavy as lead at his back. She had been afraid, and Primaflora had reassured her. Indeed, they might have been sisters, so carefully had Primaflora been watching the other girl. Katelina, of course, was intent on Nicholas. But if she didn't cultivate Primaflora, neither did she seem to avoid her. In the wet and the dark, Tobie thought about it. Then Nicholas suddenly spoke. 'That's Lopez. Listen. He's shouting.' He gave an answering call, and started forward. Leading Katelina's horse by the reins, Tobie splashed after.

The noise of the swollen river increased. A roaring made itself heard. Turning a corner, Tobie saw before him another pool, white with foam, into which tumbled a cataract. The cliffs, high on either side, enclosed a dim sky streamered with cloud. Below it, Loppe's torch burned steadily at the brink of the water.

On the ground at Loppe's feet lay a still figure, half in and half out of the stream. Astorre joined Nicholas. Tobie dropped the reins and strode forward into the mud, leaving the soldier to tie up the horses. Primaflora stayed in the saddle, and Tobie took time to hope that she would stop Katelina dismounting. But as he knelt by the fallen man, he heard her footsteps stumbling towards him.

Before he touched him, he knew he was dead. The arrow that killed him lay broken beneath him and blood, already half washed away, lay black on the grass and mould by his body. His hunting cap had fallen aside, showing the thick dark hair, and the olive skin, and the calm, elegant profile. Tobie rose slowly to his feet as Katelina came up, her face marked by fear and by mud. He said plainly, in Flemish, 'I am sorry, demoiselle. It is Ser Tristão, and he is dead.'

Chapter 18

THE RAIN BEAT into the ravine, and hissed into the water, and pattered unnoticed on the group of men and women and the dark-haired man at their feet. Nicholas, who had seemed to move, was now standing quite still. Astorre swore. The soldier stepped up as if to come to the support of Katelina, but she stood rigid, warning him off. Tobie said, 'The arrow went clean through the heart. It would be quick.'

The soft, organ-voice of the negro said, 'They killed him from a distance and then came to make sure. There are their footprints. Three men, if not four. He had his sword drawn.'

'The boy?' said Nicholas. His voice was so quiet, Tobie hardly heard it.

'I have found a boot mark. Wait,' the negro said. His torch moved off. The others remained, looking down. Watching the young woman, Tobie saw her eyes were dry, though her face was very pale. The dead man had been her husband's new partner as well as his brother-in-law. Katelina must have come to know Tristão Vasquez a little; must sometimes have shared the same trading quarters, although perhaps no more than that. His death was clearly a shock rather than a matter of intimate bereavement. And a shock made no less by the fact that she had feared it. This would leave Simon's sister a widow, and the boy fatherless, if he lived still. And what did it make Nicholas? Pleased, perhaps? Tobie cast about him aggressively.

Nicholas sat on his heels, gazing at the dead face. He had met the man at Kolossi, it appeared, and sailed with him from Cyprus. A short acquaintance, based on deception. His face at the moment was grave, his earrings motionless. There was mud to the knees of his white lawn, which had begun to smell strongly of horse sweat. The woman Katelina said, 'Then the boy must also be dead.'

Nicholas rose slowly, and spoke as if thinking aloud. 'He had drawn his sword. He may have been defending the boy. When he died, the boy may have fled.' He turned his head suddenly.

Primaflora said, 'I heard it, too.' She urged her horse forward, and the smoke from her torch veiled her hair. 'The killers may be still here, under the cliff, in the bushes.'

The soldier said, 'Then that's easily dealt with,' and drew back his arm with the torch in it.

Nicholas grasped his shoulder. His face, streaked with mud and speckled with soot, seemed merely watchful. 'I shouldn't do that. The negro's gone over there, and he doesn't show up in the dark. Tobie?'

But Tobie had already started to run to the cliff, feeling for his sword hilt with slippery hands. He could hear Nicholas following. Nicholas said, 'Lopez? Are you listening? Be careful. Tobie, don't draw your sword. Astorre, stay with the women, and you, sir. *Lopez!*' His voice on the one word was raucous.

Echoing, the negro's voice answered him. 'There's a cave, senhor. There's someone in it. Ah! I have got you!'

Someone screamed inside the cave. Nicholas said something wildly and shouldered past Tobie, whose torch lit only glistening cliff face and boulders. Then he saw the dark entrance and Nicholas disappearing into it, so that the mud of its ceiling turned rosy. He dashed to follow.

It was not a large cavity, but formed a passage of reasonable length, scoured by flood water and ejected boulders. At the far end a light silhouetted the curled head and broad shoulders of Loppe, crouched over something. He said in Portuguese, 'Senhor, we are friends. The Knights have been looking for you. Your aunt the lady Katelina is outside. Are you hurt?'

The boy. Not his killer, but the boy himself. His neck bent, Tobie scrambled further in. His hair sizzled, and he laid down his torch. Nicholas, ahead of him, had come to a halt and was not advancing. Beyond him, he could see nothing for Loppe's bulk, although he could hear the murmur of voices. He said, 'Let me past. Is he hurt?'

'No,' said Nicholas. 'A sprained ankle. They shot at them both from above, and thought he'd run off when they came down to check. Four, he says.'

The boy's voice, raised, said, 'That is Senhor Niccolò.'

Loppe turned, giving Tobie a view. Diniz lay rigid on the rock floor, his mask of mud streaked by his tears. Loppe said, 'He led the party that came to find you. And here is Master Tobie, his doctor, to help you.'

Tobie pushed forward. The boy did not move. He said, 'My father is dead.' His eyes were on Nicholas.

Nicholas said, 'A nobleman's death. I want to find who killed him.'

'Why?' said Diniz.

'Why should they live?' Nicholas said.

The boy was in shock. Tobie passed his hands over the swollen ankle and then leaned back. The boy said, 'They are still close at hand. Two of them. Two others took fright and fled.' He gulped and said, 'There are snakes here. In the cave, and outside. My father trod on one. He cried out. The men heard him, and killed him.'

Nicholas said, 'They are still looking for you? What do they –'

He didn't finish, because of the scream outside the cave. The boy sobbed. Loppe turned round. Nicholas said, 'Stay there,' and without his torch edged round and flung himself towards the cave entrance. Disobeying instantly, Tobie followed.

Katelina lay collapsed on the ground by the dead man. Rising beside her was Captain Astorre, a blur of silver and white. The torches had been extinguished. Primaflora said, 'They shot her. From above the waterfall.' Her voice was quite out of its normal pitch. A horse trampled and Tobie caught sight of the soldier from the Palace, one foot in his stirrup.

Nicholas said to him, 'No. Stay.' He was bending over Katelina. Astorre said, 'She's all right. I pushed her. The arrow went through her cloak. What do you mean, stay? They're up there, the murdering villains.'

'I meant, our friend should stay with Lopez and the women. You and I will go and catch them.'

'*No!*' said Primaflora. Already mounted, Nicholas looked at her and she said, 'If something goes wrong, you will be blamed.'

'Astorre will be with me,' Nicholas said. He looked amazed.

'And me,' said Tobie. He rose from beside Katelina, who was stirring, and made at a run for his horse. 'Why is nobody blowing a horn?' He got into the saddle at the same time as Astorre and they both followed Nicholas, already setting his horse towards the quickest way out of the ravine. Behind them all, the soldier's horn blared. That would bring help. And now, away from the water, Tobie's ears picked up the sound of horses not far away, galloping. Only two of them. The sound was receding. He set himself to catch up with Nicholas, who was following it.

It was now almost dark. They carried their torches unlit: the danger of unknown ground was less than the risk of a bowshot. The men ahead, invisible against rising ground, had the advantage of knowing the territory. It was odd that Nicholas had left behind the only man familiar with the whole island. It was not odd, if Nicholas didn't want Primaflora's soldier to meet the murderers of Tristão Vasquez and learn who had paid them.

But in that case, why not let the killers escape? Why ride like this, crazily crashing through vineyards, between dimly-seen olives, into streams and through trenched plantations? Once, Nicholas hadn't even known how to ride, until Astorre taught him. Astorre, galloping now at his side, would raise no objection no matter what Nicholas did: his fool boy, his villainous boy; his successful boy. On the other hand, the same boy had let Tobie come, and Loppe stay. Loppe, now stationed behind with Katelina and Diniz. But then, the soldier was there also, with Primaflora. Nothing could happen, surely.

A tree loomed, and Tobie swerved. He could hear Astorre cursing, with an undernote in it of pleasure. They seemed to be gaining. And there were only two horses ahead, and three of themselves. Nicholas was still in front. Tobie had no idea what the man was going to do. Just now, Nicholas had seen Tristão dead, and Katelina supposedly dead, and had given away nothing, unless you counted a certain coarsening of his voice. In the cave, calling to Loppe, he had betrayed something real. It had sounded like fear. Was it fear? Was it fear that was driving him on, not some knightly compulsion to punish? For of course, one must not forget that Nicholas was now a member of an order of chivalry, sworn to uphold Christianity, honour, and the Queen of Cyprus. Nicholas was a Knight and, dressed as Guinevere, was riding across the island of Rhodes preparing to kill somebody.

They were getting very close now, and their quarry's cover was patchy. Occasionally, against a patch of pale rock or stubble, Tobie could see the two horses flying ahead, and the dull glint of helmets. They must know, now, that they couldn't escape. Black on indigo, a stand of pines loomed ahead, and beyond that, the broken outline of what might have been primitive buildings. The killers' horses disappeared into the trees, and the beat of their hooves became muffled and irregular. Then, sharp and clear, the beat resumed again on the far side. Bursting through the trees after, they glimpsed the horses ahead. Astorre said sharply, 'Slow!'

Nicholas had already reined in. Clear and light, they all heard the patter of receding hooves. Clear and very light. Astorre said, 'That's an old trick. They used the trees to dismount, and let the horses lead us on without them. They're here somewhere. We'll catch them. They can't get far without horses.'

'They could always seize ours,' Nicholas said. 'They have bows. So what do you think we should do?' With Astorre, Nicholas was always meticulous.

'Right,' said the captain. 'They need cover, and they want us out in the open. They're either still in the wood, or over there in those buildings. I need a volunteer.'

'I knew you would,' Nicholas said. 'Stay with Tobie, then. If I don't report back, you can keep my dress.' He had dismounted. Crossing his arms, he pulled up Guinevere's gown and dropped it in a heap. The next moment he had vanished, and Astorre and

Tobie, dismounted also, were standing under the trees, gripping
their horses. Tobie, his wimple dragged down, unhooked his shield
and stood listening.

The rain had stopped. The trees rustled. Where Nicholas had
gone, he could see nothing but flat ground interrupted by in-
determinate objects and, in the distance, a huddle of shapes which
seemed to include a low oblong edifice like a shed. Astorre, a stout
pine trunk at his back, had his sword in one hand and his shield
and reins in the other. Outside the grove, the wind whirred through
the heath and thornbushes and whined among the buildings before
them.

The whine was fast and high, and ended in a thud. It was not the
wind, but an arrow arriving. A flock of them followed. They came
from the rectangular shadow, and sprayed the ground between the
watchers and the buildings. No one called out, and there was no
sign of Nicholas. Tobie said, 'Are the bowmen inside the shed?'

'If they're stupid enough. Fools!' said Astorre. 'They might as
well surrender.'

Tobie said, 'They've spotted Nicholas, then.'

Astorre's head swivelled round. 'Heh? That's why he's there, to
be spotted. Tie the horses, and let's go and find him.'

Nicholas found them first, reappearing to crouch bare-armed
and bare-headed in the dark beside Astorre. He was breathing
quickly but, like Astorre, merely critical. 'They're in the byre.
Mud bricks, reed thatch, double doors and one window they're
using to shoot through. It's the only intact building. The farmhouse
is a ruin. There's a well, a broken waterwheel, and a crushing
trough. Someone's still using the place for the olive harvest. Captain?'

Astorre said, 'Exhaust their arrows. They'll have to surrender.'

Tobie said, 'Why don't we wait for the Knights?'

No one appeared to hear him. 'All right,' Nicholas said to
Astorre. 'But even then, they won't want to come out.'

'There are ways of dealing with that,' Astorre said.

'So there are,' said Nicholas. They both sounded happy. Nicholas
said, 'Tobie? Do you want to stay, or do you want to ride back for
the Knights?'

Tobie said, 'I should prefer to stay.' His wimple, rising, interfered with his chin. He saw Nicholas was looking at him, but couldn't
decipher his expression. Nicholas said, 'All right. All the better.
We are three to their two: seeing that, they won't be likely to rush
out until they've had a shot at picking off at least one of us. We'll
draw their fire. All you have to do is show yourself now and then
so that they know you're still there. But be careful. These bows
have a long range, and you're bound to be within it.'

'I'll be careful,' said Tobie.

He saw a brief gleam from Astorre's decayed teeth. 'That's my boy,' said Astorre. It annoyed Tobie to be Astorre's boy as well.

Nicholas said, 'And, Captain?'

They were moving away. 'Yes?' said Astorre.

Nicholas said, 'I want them alive. Alive. Alive. Do you hear me?'

'Of course,' said Astorre's voice. Its tone was professionally reassuring.

Tobie was now alone. Wherever Nicholas and Astorre had gone, he couldn't see them. From the byre and its surroundings no sound emerged: the arrows had stopped. It became again very quiet. Somewhere in the muddy darkness, a channel of water was trickling, and even further off, a donkey brayed and went on mournfully hooting. A gust of wind shook the trees, and Tobie shivered. The Loathly Damsel's tunic hampered his movements. He tied it up and, picking up his shield and his sword, moved from bush to bush, his shield-arm protective. He almost missed the hiss of the arrow when it came. It tipped his shield and bounced harmlessly off. Before it reached the ground he was running, throwing himself into the shelter of something solid and cold, that gave off a strong reek of olives. The crusher. He lay there, getting his breath back, and immediately heard the whicker and thud of arrows beginning again. He stiffened. This time, it came from some distance away. Astorre, or Nicholas, had diverted the archers' attention.

He realised he was lying in a mess of pulped olives. It would ruin his gown. He found he was smiling, and stopped. He was a doctor. A man lay dead behind at this moment. To want to hunt down his killers was natural. One should not, however, start to enjoy it. Tobie frowned, shifted, and prepared to make another contributory dash in the darkness. Then he stayed where he was.

A horse was approaching from the pine grove at a gallop. With it streamed light from a pitch torch. The rider, veiled, wore the flying white muslin of Guinevere. The horse fled across the flat ground to the byre. Trough, well, farm buildings stood illuminated in flickering gold. For an instant Tobie saw the byre window, with the archer standing, bow bent, aiming from it. Tobie rolled, flat on the ground, into shadow. While he was moving, he saw the first barbs pierce the rider. They struck without cease: veil, gown, the horse itself. Transfixed, the animal whinnied and reared. The torch, no doubt meant for the thatch, dropped to the ground and was extinguished. In the sudden darkness, little could be seen but the threshing bulk of the dying mount, and the shreds of white cloth lying under it. Tobie began to rise to run forward, and stopped, as his wits returned. Whatever had been on that horse, it wasn't Nicholas. But seen for a single menacing second by the men in the byre, it was good enough to look real. The bowmen would assume one of their pursuers was dead. And they were the poorer for a great many arrows. He watched, entranced, as the drumming of hooves heralded a second horse.

This time, the rider wore Astorre's glittering helmet but carried no brand. The unseen archer shot again, and the figure rode for a while, and then toppled. Its helmet rolled off. The horse swerved, hesitated, and cantered away. The sound of its hooves receded, leaving silence behind. Tobie rose and, forsaking the trough, crept to a position nearer the byre. He was close enough, now, to see the horseblanket stuffed into Guinevere's dress. He was aware, too, of the glutinous smell of olive oil from the pulp stuck to his boots and his clothes. It made him feel hungry. He remained where he was, awaiting whatever Nicholas and Astorre were going to try next. While he waited, he received another whiff of the oil, this time from his right. The trough was not on his right. Someone else, therefore, had stepped on the olives.

The thought had just struck him when he heard a creak from the direction of the byre. One of the doors must have opened. A man's voice, speaking in Greek, said, 'Takis? There is only one left. We will take him between us.'

His voice broke off in a scream. Astorre must have been standing beside him. Tobie heard the sounds of a struggle, and saw the two figures, entwined, stamping backwards and forwards. Tobie began to run, peering through darkness for Nicholas or the mysterious Takis. Now he could see the heads of the struggling pair at the byre door, the bowman's helmeted and Astorre's grizzled and bare. He caught the glint of a dagger in the hand that had been holding the bow. It rose, and remained rigid as the man's wrist was held by Astorre. Tobie saw Astorre's right fist swinging back, with his sword in it.

If the captain remembered what Nicholas had demanded, there was no sign of it now, any more than there was a whisper of protest from Nicholas. Astorre's sword came down with a whistle and took the other man clean in the neck. He fell, killed on the instant. Astorre looked round. Tobie, hesitating, began to move forward again, straining to see through the darkness. He experienced, once again, a whiff of oil that did not come from his own person. Then someone took hold of his arms, and wrenching them hard behind him, held something tight at his throat that both glinted and cut. A voice at his back shouted in dreadful Italian. 'Gentlemen! Lukas is a fool, who doesn't know a man from a dummy. I am one man against three, and I am not afraid. I have a knife at the throat of a bald man. Do as I say, or he dies.'

Tobie stopped struggling. The man behind him was big. Tobie could feel the thick leather jack he wore, and winced at the strength of his grip. Astorre's voice said, with admiration, 'There was one of you outside all the time! A nice trick.'

'Mine,' said the man. 'I have the brains. Lay down your sword and get me the last horse. Where is the third man?'

'Behind you,' said the calm voice of Nicholas. 'You cut the throat of the bald man, and I'll take your head off with my sword. We can do it at the same time, if you like. If you don't like, drop your knife.'

He dropped it. He thrust Tobie sprawling in the same movement and, whirling round, drew sword on Nicholas as if he were not outnumbered three to one. For a moment, Astorre was too far away to help him, and Tobie immobilised. Nicholas said, 'Don't be a fool!' and parried a wild sword-thrust, frowning. The blades clattered. Nicholas parried again, and again. Astorre said peacefully, 'That's enough,' and stepped forward.

It distracted Nicholas for a moment. He turned his head, still frowning, and said, 'No!' The killer's sword flashed towards his exposed body. Tobie exclaimed. And Astorre, with the speed of a veteran, sprang forward, sent the man spinning, and before he could be stopped, plunged his blade in his throat. Nicholas looked at him, gasping, and swore.

Astorre withdrew his sword, wrenched some grass up, and wiped it. 'He would have killed you,' he remarked. 'What did you want him for? A long, nasty trial and a hanging?'

'Yes,' said Nicholas.

'I could have saved the other fellow for you, then, if you'd reminded me,' said the captain reproachfully. 'I just got carried away.'

'He didn't want to remind you,' said Tobie.

Nicholas was staring at him. Nicholas said, 'I was tracking olive oil all over the yard, and had just found this fellow about to cut your God-damned wimple. How could I yell without giving away where I was?'

'I don't believe you,' said Tobie. 'I think you got what you wanted.'

'Well, you know best,' Nicholas said. 'Three positive kills and two blunders: I missed Katelina and Diniz. Never mind. By now, Loppe will have finished them off.' His voice was bitter.

Tobie stood motionless. Astorre gave a cackle, bending to pick up his helmet. 'Lost your sense of humour, Master Tobie? The boy saved your life for you, there. Not but what you did a good job. Quite a good job. It did us a bit of good, having you with us.'

'I suppose it did,' said Nicholas, relenting suddenly. 'Oh, come on, Tobie. Danger stirs everyone up, you know that. Let's get back to the others, and you can prescribe something to sweeten our tempers.'

They brought the bowmen back on the last horse and met, on the way, a detachment of cavalry sent to help them. Remounted, they turned and rode back to the valley together. By then, the Knights had already found the ravine, and brought victims and bereaved to high ground. Laid on shields, the body of Tristão Vasquez was set to make its last journey on horseback. Beside him his son, his swollen foot bound, dumbly shared a horse with his uncle's wife Katelina. Around them, torches blazing, the rest of the searchers were assembling for the journey back to their fort and the City. Primaflora watched Nicholas come, her eyes and her face speaking for her. Katelina, her face bleak, addressed him. 'You didn't find the men who murdered Tristão? Or you found them, and they were dead?'

'We killed them,' said Nicholas. 'Before they could tell us who had paid them, or where the other two are.'

'I thought you might,' Katelina said. 'Are you satisfied?' The boy, sitting before her, turned his head.

Nicholas mounted. Without his dress, he had nothing to wear but hose and boots and a light sleeveless jerkin. He looked dirty and cold. He paused for a moment, his hands holding the reins and the pommel, before he lowered himself in the saddle. He turned his face to the boy. He said, 'Diniz? None of us harmed your father, or tried to harm you. You will be told otherwise. You must take what precautions you wish, but that is the truth.'

The boy stared back at him. Was there a likeness between Nicholas and the youngster? Black and brown; dark-skinned and fair: surely not. Katelina put her hand on her nephew's shoulder. It was a defensive gesture, not a maternal one. She said, 'You will never get near him again.'

'As you like,' Nicholas said. He and the boy were still looking at one another. It came to Tobie that Nicholas, alone of them all, knew what he was doing. The boy, in his heart, was not afraid of him. If Nicholas took him in his arms, the boy would break down and weep, as he must.

But that was the last thing Katelina would allow. The boy stayed in her grasp, an object of pity, but not of understanding. And, clenching his teeth, he didn't break down. Then they were moving, and Primaflora brought her horse close and spoke to Nicholas. 'They should thank you. Without you and Lopez, the boy might not have been found. You risked your life to follow the murderers. Are you hurt?'

Nicholas rode without answering. Then he said, 'We all took scratches. You, too.'

She said, 'I wouldn't have missed it. I didn't know you, before. When can we meet? Niccolò?'

It was softly spoken, and Tobie supposed none but himself had overheard it. Nicholas said, 'When the Queen lets you come. She will. We are affianced.'

Primaflora said, 'I want a bond stronger than that.'

Through the dirt, one indentation appeared. 'Soon,' he said. She looked at him and then, with discretion, drew a little apart. Nicholas spoke again, without raising his voice. 'Tobie: the boy would be better with you.'

Tobie said, 'I thought of that. The demoiselle wouldn't allow it. What is it – fourteen miles, fifteen? He should manage.'

Silence fell. On his other side, Astorre frequently talked, addressing his neighbours; rehearsing some recent or long-ago fight. Sometimes he drew Tobie into the conversation, until Tobie's monosyllables annoyed him too much. Nicholas said nothing at all until they were past Phileremos and could see, very distantly, the glow in the sky that spoke of the City of Rhodes.

Now, the cavalcade was much smaller, reduced by the Knights who formed the garrison on the Mount. For the first time in a long while, Nicholas spoke. 'Where are le Grant and Thomas?'

Tobie looked round. In the uncertain light, he saw several of the Knights who had set out with their party, but the two men of their own were not visible. He said, 'They'll have gone back on their own.'

'Without reporting?' Nicholas said. 'Look again.'

Tobie looked. The cavalcade still stretched before and behind, obscured by the smoke and the darkness. Closer at hand, its nature had changed. Where Katelina and the boy had been, there were now well-armed horsemen quite strange to him. Captain Astorre trotted still at his shoulder. But beyond him were two other well-accoutred Knights of the Order, and behind him, Primaflora's protectors. Primaflora herself had been drawn out of sight. There was no sign of Loppe, or of any other faces he knew.

Tobie said, 'What was it you said? Incantations, cauldrons and mirrors?'

Nicholas turned. With whatever effort, the weariness had been banished, to be replaced by a view of one dimple. He said, 'You remembered. If you hadn't, I'd have made a small wager. Our standing has changed, as I said it would.'

'We are about to go back to prison?' said Tobie.

'Or worse,' Nicholas said. 'We foiled someone's plans; so probably worse. Tell Astorre. We make no resistance. We make no excuses. I do all the talking. We shall probably be met at the gate. There you are. We are being met at the gate. Do you see anyone you know?'

Tobie was abruptly put in touch with his last meal. Only Nicholas did that to him. Only Nicholas could orchestrate this kind of disaster. Ahead, flushed with light, stood the great drum towers of the entrance. There was a squadron of soldiers beneath, their spears flashing. He could see the Grand Commander of Cyprus, and the Treasurer of the Order, and a man in black, wearing a broad-brimmed black hat over the cowl of his cloak. The man in black had crossed teeth and was smiling. So was Nicholas. Tobie didn't like either smile.

'John de Kinloch,' Nicholas said. 'A Scottish chaplain from Bruges. He knows the demoiselle Katelina.'

He looks happy to see you,' said Tobie.

'He is,' Nicholas said. 'I kidnapped him in Cyprus to stop him telling the Vasquez who I was. To stop him telling the Knights who I was, for that matter. If Katelina doesn't have me hanged for killing Tristão, then that fellow will.'

Chapter 19

To receive the judgement of the great prince Pierre-Raimond Zacosta, Grand Master of the Order of the Knights Hospitaller of St John of Jerusalem, it was necessary to march through the gates of the Castello, the inner town of the Religion, and by climbing between the tall Inns of the Knights with their pointed doorframes and marble-grid windows to attain the austere Gothic arch at the top. There, beside the loggia and the church, stood the fortified Palace of the Grand Master, in whose courtyard the Court of King Arthur ought to have displayed its martial prowess two days before.

Nicholas walked to his appointment between two files of armed men, and with him were all four officers who had set out on that abortive joust; for John le Grant and Thomas had been put under restraint like themselves immediately on their return from Kalopetra. In the two days of their confinement, Nicholas had spent most of his time with Astorre's men. Barring a few new recruits, they all knew him – either as the wild Charetty apprentice, or as the husband of Marian de Charetty who employed them, or as the man who took them to Trebizond and brought them back again, richer than they had ever been before. And since then, of course, as the future patron who had fought with them in Italy, before he turned up in Rhodes.

They knew him, and they trusted Astorre, so that they believed that there was nothing, in the long run, to be anxious about. For two days he worked to impress himself on them, and also to get to know them again in his turn. With some it was easy to revive the old camaraderie. With others he brought out the whole battery of bawdy talk and good-natured roughhousing, of reminiscent exchanges, of gossip and long, deep talking late into the night. He could never go back to the techniques of his boyhood – they had to respect him, as well as enjoy his company. Judging men was an art at which he excelled, and he enjoyed practising it. He could have done with more than two days, but it was enough to carry them with him, when eventually he talked of the immediate future.

Not that he told them the whole story, any more than he had told it to Tobie or Astorre or the rest. He did, however, place before men and officers the greater part of his plans, because he could see that Tobie, at least, would not follow him further in ignorance. And they needed to know, or they could spoil it all.

But for the mistakes beside Kalopetra, he would have been elated. Stage by delightful stage, his process was activating itself. He knew how dangerous it was, and that all his future hung on this confrontation with the Grand Master, and what was bound to follow. If he made another miscalculation, he could lose everything. But of course, that was the attraction. And the responsibility was entirely his. He had chosen the game, and others had elected to join him, or to oppose him. Playing was not compulsory.

The Palace of Rhodes was magnificent. No one spoke entering the portal between the drum towers and passing into the noise of the vast inner courtyard, full of people and animals, banners and armour. They carried no arms, he and his four companions, and appeared only in sober pourpoint, doublet and cloak, their hats little adorned, their hose plain, their buttons and belts less than flamboyant. He wore, since he had not yet been deprived of it, the blue and silver badge of his Cypriot Order. As they crossed the yard, men stopped and looked, and he could hear the tramp of their feet repeated from the hollow arcading, and see men looking down from the open galleries above. In the far corner, on its uneven arches rose the ceremonial flight of steps leading to the great chambers of the second floor of the north range. From here, the highest point of the Castello, the Knights kept ward on the City, the harbours, the inimical sea to the east and the north. Approaching as miscreants, as suspects, the broker Niccolò and his officers were led up to the pillared door at the head of the steps, where they were halted. Then, in silence, they were marched to the hall of the Knights, where the Grand Master awaited them.

The walls were chequered, and so high that the blocks of cream and sienna, white and umber and russet responded to darkness and light as if patterned in damask. The size of the hall, from the timbered roof to the marble floor, dwarfed the stalls of the Knights, and the band of painted escutcheons which ran above them. Beside the black and white of the Knights were the priests, and men in ordinary clothes who might be civilians, or merchants, or witnesses. At the end of the room, the Grand Master sat on his dais, bearded, yellow, dressed in black, with a monstrous veiled hat, its brim turned up all round like a pilgrim's.

This prince Zacosta was Spanish, and newly appointed. A Catalan, he had lingered long in Barcelona before leaving to take up his duties. He had been reluctant, it was said, to give up the income he was already drawing. He had refused, it was said, the kindly offer of Carlotta of Cyprus to sail home in the Queen's ship to Rhodes. And naturally, being a Catalan, he had no time at all for Ferrante of Aragon, King of Naples, on whose behalf Captain Astorre and his company had just been successfully fighting. Despite this, the Grand Master had not rejected Astorre when he first arrived; had not, despite Katelina, thrust them from the island. With Sultan Mehmet's conquering fleets moving out from Constantinople, the need for soldiers to protect the Religion was desperate and, given a chance, he would have overlooked much. He had not, however, been given a chance.

They were to be ranged in front of the dais. Moving forward, Nicholas scanned the men on either side of the room. Of course, John de Kinloch, with Louis de Magnac beside him and another knight whom he recognised from Kolossi. Scougal, the well-born Scot from East Lothian who had ridden with them two days ago, and who had been John de Kinloch's companion. A man he had heard identified on the pier – Tobias Lomellini, the Genoese Treasurer of the Order. And beside him, several others who looked vaguely Genoese and one who certainly was. Tomà Adorno of Chios, who, long ago in Milan, had helped seal an alum contract. Tomà Adorno who was, of course, a kinsman of Anselm Adorne.

Nicholas found that disconcerting. He was standing in line before the dais before he remembered to look for the Queen's party, and saw, when he found it, that it was exceptionally strong. The faces of Guichard, Piozasque, de Bon, de Montolif, Pardo and Sor de Naves, her naval commander, had all turned to examine him. Some of these courtiers he had met with Carlotta in the Italian snows; there were others he had seen with her husband.

John le Grant, who had been looking in the same direction, turned his sandy lashes up to the ceiling-beams and hissed, almost inaudibly, between his front teeth. Astorre stood, his chest and buttocks cocked like a sparrow, his beard jutting straight out before him. Tobie, his bald head encased, showed a face which reflected the robe of his calling. Nicholas lifted to the Grand Master the same serene look he had employed in the court of the last Byzantine Empire, and laid his fate in the lap of the sun God, whose island (in summer) this was.

The Grand Master spoke in Latin. The Duchy of Burgundy had sent twelve thousand gold écus to the Isles of Religion. It had seemed a gift of God when, from the same region, a band of experienced soldiers had arrived to await their leader. One did not have to take knightly vows in order to fight for the Church: the Christian world, in its extremity, accepted with humility whatever help it was offered. It was therefore with sorrow, with horror, that he had been told that these were men of straw; evil men who had harmed the Order and those it protected.

It was, however, said the Grand Master, not the custom of the Knights to condemn men unheard. One of them, moreover, bore the badge of another order of chivalry, and had pledged his service as soldier and pilgrim. For these reasons, he had summoned Niccolò vander Poele to answer to the accusations, and his chief officers to stand with him. Did the Knight Niccolò vander Poele wish to make a statement?

It was intended to belittle, and indeed, only the doctor could be supposed to have the learning to understand such a pronouncement. In fact, John le Grant had good Latin, and Nicholas himself had had Felix's entire course at Louvain, with a considerable amount of subsequent practice. Before the translator could speak Nicholas replied, in the same ordinary, serviceable Latin that all the Knights used. 'My lord prince. We appreciate the opportunity to hear our accusers, and to speak for ourselves. If it pleases you, we ask that the hearing be conducted in the Order's second language of French.'

The Grand Master looked at him, and then at his Chancellor. He said, 'If you wish. Proceed.' Which made things faster, and meant that Astorre and Thomas had less time to get angry.

It was just as well that he had briefed everyone about his misdemeanours, because they began with John de Kinloch, and that sounded crazy enough. The priest himself spoke, and the man from Kolossi corroborated. The man Niccolò had arrived in Cyprus, representing to the Knights of Kolossi that he intended to serve Queen Carlotta with his company. He had duped the Queen's demoiselle into believing the same. He had disguised from the Portuguese merchant Tristão Vasquez that there existed a long-standing feud between the man Niccolò and Senhor Tristão's partner and relative Simon. His reason for concealing this feud was assuredly that the man Simon was deeply involved in Genoese and Portuguese trade and therefore, implicitly, a supporter of Queen Carlotta and not of her illegitimate brother, the self-styled King Zacco. When this deception was threatened by the appearance of Father John de Kinloch, who knew of it, the man Niccolò had disposed of Father John by having him tied up and imprisoned with the help of an accomplice. The man Niccolò had then left for Rhodes, revealing nothing of this to Tristão Vasquez. Fortunately, the lord Simon's wife was in Rhodes, and able to enlighten him. Since then, as was known, the Portuguese gentleman had been killed, and his son and the lord Simon's wife had been fortunate to escape.

At that point, Nicholas intervened. 'My lord, my men and I helped them escape.'

The Chancellor, whom he did not know, wore no expression. 'I am told that Senhor Tristão was dead when you arrived, and that the assassins were waiting to dispatch his son and the demoiselle Katelina, whom you did nothing to protect. I am told you killed both assassins, without witnesses. We cannot tell, therefore, who paid them.'

'You have no proof, therefore, that I paid them,' Nicholas said.

'None,' said the Chancellor. 'But you had a motive. Or why go to such lengths to conceal your relations with the lord Simon? Father John is a priest, a chaplain of the Order and a man respected in Scotland, in Bruges and in Rhodes. He was attacked and humiliated in the Order's own castle of Kolossi. Why? And who were your accomplices?'

'Men I came across in Episkopi,' Nicholas said. 'I removed him because Tristão Vasquez, a stranger, might well have reached the same conclusion as yourselves, and have caused my company to incur the distrust of the most serene Queen Carlotta. Once acquainted with Senhor Tristão, once proved loyal servants of the Queen, there would be no need for deceit. Was Father John injured?'

'My knee,' said John of Kinloch. He looked livelier, brisker and more sure of himself than he had in Cyprus. 'My knee was skinned. And my elbow. I could have had a tooth out.'

'He was not severely injured,' Nicholas said, his manner earnest. 'He was treated, I hope he will agree, with courtesy, and well looked after and fed. He would have been released in due course. Above all, I hope it will be noticed, he was not murdered.'

'The scoundrel!' said John of Kinloch.

'It is a point,' said the Chancellor, 'if a small one. So you intended to join the serene and excellent lady?'

'As her lady-in-waiting will confirm,' Nicholas said. Primaflora was not there.

'As you certainly persuaded her lady-in-waiting,' the Chancellor corrected. 'But you did not sail to Kyrenia, or to Famagusta? You sailed to Episkopi, the Venetian bay?'

'I landed at Cape Gata. So did the Queen's lady,' Nicholas said. 'The ship had cargo. We hoped for the Knights' hospitality. We believed it possible to travel north with the Knights' protection. It was only later that we learned that Queen Carlotta was in Rhodes.'

The Chancellor looked at him. 'You are saying that you did not know the Queen was not in Cyprus when you left the lady in the south and made your way towards Nicosia?'

Nicholas said, 'I didn't know, either way. I thought it best to present myself to her Marshal at Kyrenia and ask for orders.'

'You did not know that your company was waiting at Rhodes?' said the Chancellor.

'We had lost touch. They knew, as I did not, that the Queen was coming to Rhodes.'

'So you say. You had lost touch? How?'

So they knew that. But of course they did. Nicholas said, 'My company is a professional one. They had undertaken a contract in Italy, and there was some confusion after the battle. We became separated.'

'You were fighting,' said the Chancellor, 'as I understand it, for Ferrante of Aragon. As you did in an earlier battle, and again some years ago, in the Abruzzi. This self-styled King of Naples has found your Captain Astorre loyal, I see, and effective. I wonder, therefore, what attracted you to the Queen of Cyprus and the Order of St John, to whom King Ferrante has shown himself no friend?'

Astorre had begun breathing heavily. Nicholas maintained his serious voice. 'I had met the most serene Queen. I had met the Knights at Kolossi. I had had time to reflect. I had also, as you may know, had an opportunity to measure King Zacco's forebearance. The Knights of Kolossi will tell you.'

'I am told,' said the chancellor, 'that the Bastard Zacco sent the emir of his Mamelukes to waylay and capture you, and that you only escaped after severe mishandling. I note however, as has been pointed out in a similar context, that you were not murdered.'

'If I had met the Bastard, and refused to serve him, I hardly think I should be alive,' Nicholas said. 'As it was, before I escaped, more than my knees and elbows had suffered. I intend to take payment for that.'

'I see,' said the Chancellor. 'And for that, you would abandon your feud with the lord Simon?'

Nicholas spread his hands. 'It is on his part, rather than mine. He is in business in Portugal. If there is to be any rivalry between us, I can pursue it as well if not better when supplied with information from the same side. Trade is my business,' Nicholas said. 'If my lord Simon causes trouble, I can find a way of retaliating without dragging nations into the quarrel.'

'Trade,' said the Grand Master. It was the first word he had spoken since his opening speech. One wrinkled finger beat, like a ponderous hammer, on the arm of his chair. 'You profess to favour the Queen and the Order. Your actions in the matter of trading signally fail to support this hypothesis.'

And now it came. Beside Nicholas, he could feel the gloom weighing like soot on the other four. Of all the things he had done, they had regarded this as most irresponsible when he had told them. Only John le Grant, who also lived by devices, had eyed him in silence. Nicholas, beginning with the easiest part, said, 'My lord: I saved Queen Carlotta's sugar two years ago. There was a fight south of Bologna. She will confirm it.'

The Chancellor looked round, but the finger was still tapping.

'She has,' said the Grand Master. 'But I understand that, while professing to save it, you allowed the entire cargo to land in the river. But for her servants who had contrived a substitution, it would have been lost.'

'You could put it that way,' Nicholas said. 'On the other hand, we alarmed the thieves and made them abandon it. I didn't know it was sugar, and soluble. And the Queen was alive. I trust the Grand Master considers that of some importance.'

'You think her life was under threat?' said the Grand Master. 'I conceived it was simply a matter of money. The Queen was raising funds to free Cyprus, and the Bastard Zacco wished to impede her. With your help, he might have succeeded.'

'My lord,' Nicholas said. 'I am quite willing to concede that I may not have saved her from murder. I do affirm, however, that it was my intention to salvage her fortune.' Incarcerated, he had not had his meeting with Primaflora. He knew how much she had wanted it, for he had wanted it for the same reason. So they had not talked. So he could not be sure of what she had said. So he had to invent. He continued, in the same reasonable voice, 'The incident doesn't seem to have shaken the faith of the lady who devised the subterfuge to save the sugar. It was she who travelled with me to Cyprus; and she who, as the Chancellor said, remained convinced I meant to join the Queen, and not Zacco.'

The Grand Master's fingers disappeared inside his palm. The Chancellor spoke for him, drily. 'The lady's powers of judgement, we feel, may have been subject to some impairment. Without prejudice, you seem to have acted against the Queen's interests.'

'Without prejudice, the Queen herself did not think so,' said Nicholas. 'She subsequently asked me, on the most lavish terms, to join her faction. So did her brother in Venice. I refused both times. I was not ready.'

'But,' said the Chancellor, 'You were ready when you sailed to Cyprus? You had made up your mind? You were going to offer yourself and your men to the Queen, or if not to the Queen, to the Order?'

'That is so,' Nicholas said.

'Then why,' said the Chancellor, 'did you, sailing for Rhodes on a ship of the Order, bearing a cargo of sugar grown and milled by the Knights of the Order, pay a ship to intercept yours, to attack it, to board it and, having caused death and injury, to carry off all the goods of the Knights, to the damage of all who serve the Cross in the east?'

There was a rustle round the hall, under the chequers. They had not heard of that, most of them. Nicholas remembered the burgomaster of Bruges, replying to the latest accusation of Duke Philip's Controller. His voice expressed hurt, as well as surprise. 'I did?

My lord, why should I waste money on such a thing? I remember the fighting, of course. I tried to protect the young Vasquez boy.'

'You deny it?' said the Grand Master.

'Show me proof, my lord,' Nicholas said. 'Did the master of the attacking ship tell you? Where is the draft on my bankers that paid for it? What became of the sugar?' Beside him, he could smell Tobie.

'You want proof?' said the Chancellor. 'We did not trace the ship, but we traced the sugar. The Vatachino have many refineries: one in north Cyprus and one in Crete. The stolen sugar to the exact amount was sent to the Cretan refinery, and the man who sent it was Luigi Martini of Venice. Venice, the republic which, supposedly neutral, will do all it can to place the illegitimate Zacco on the Cypriot throne. You stole the sugar, and Zacco is your master.'

Nicholas waited. Then he said, 'You are saying that, when this sugar was sold, the gold went to Zacco instead of the Order?'

The Grand Master, about to speak, was interrupted by his own Chancellor. The Chancellor said, 'All we say is that the Order was deprived.'

'But the money went to Zacco,' said Nicholas.

This time, the Grand Master did not try to reply. The Chancellor said, 'No. Not directly.'

'Not directly?' Nicholas said. He could hear the stir. He knew he did not need to ask the next question himself.

The Grand Master said, 'Where did it go? Let us have it clear.'

The Chancellor said, 'It went into the account of the Martini brothers in Venice.'

'It did not go to the Bastard James de Lusignan?'

'My lord, no.'

'It did not go into the Bank of Messer Niccolò himself?'

'My lord, no.'

'And was there any withdrawal from Messer Niccolò's Bank that might account for the hiring, which he denies, of this piratical ship?'

'My lord, no,' said the Chancellor meekly. He turned and looked at Nicholas, and Nicholas knew what he was going to say. 'But,' said the Chancellor, 'there is, and has been since the autumn, a record of a considerable and generous payment being made at stated intervals into Messer Niccolò's own Bank in Venice. The payments are to his personal account, and they come from the agents of James de Lusignan in respect of a fief outside the town of Nicosia. This fief, it seems, belongs to the Knight standing before you. To Niccolò vander Poele who says he does not know, and has not met, the Bastard Zacco.'

It was a perfect small coup. Even dispersed by the high timbered ceiling, the comber of comment and exclamation was louder than was respectful in this, the inner court of the Knights. Nicholas saw that beside him, le Grant and Tobie were displaying adequate alarm and surprise. Astorre had to be kicked. Nicholas said, 'I was afraid of that. I was offered some such bribe by the Bastard's envoys in Venice. Queen Carlotta proposed a fee equally generous, I gave both a refusal. Only the Bastard, it seems, began transmitting the money as a form of coercion. Did you discover that any of it had been withdrawn and sent to me?'

'Such a thing would be hard to prove,' the Chancellor said, 'You have certainly drawn on your account.'

Nicholas said, 'Did you discover that my agents had notified me of this?'

'No. But your agents are singularly discreet, Messer Niccolò,' said the Chancellor. He had begun, in the last little while, to address him formally. Nicholas enjoyed the sensation.

Nicholas said, 'Then it is simply my word against your interpretation in this instance. I have told you that I did not hire the ship that intercepted yours. I don't know who did. But surely, the hirer had much in his favour? Some might think he was performing an act of justice.'

'Justice?' said the Grand Master. The Chancellor looked at his slippers.

'After all,' Nicholas said, 'the sugar belonged to the Martini brothers in the first place. They bought the crop in advance. They paid the Knights twenty-five ducats a quintal to have eight hundred quintals of crystal sugar cased and ready for shipping each year. They were waiting at that very moment for the arrival of the Venetian sugar ship to take on the cargo. And instead, the Knights, in error of course, freighted a ship of their own and seemed to wish to take the sugar to Rhodes and even sell it again. So,' said Nicholas diffidently, 'despite the unfortunate means, you might say that the Martini brothers only obtained their rights, and the Knights their deserts.' He paused. 'I believe the Queen performed the same trick . . . made the same error two years ago, when she took the Martini brothers' sugar to Bologna. Of course, I may be mistaken.'

This time, no one spoke. The Grand Master, rather slowly, shifted his gaze from that of Nicholas to the face of his Chancellor. The Chancellor said, 'My lord, I shall look into it.'

'Do that,' said the Grand Master, even more slowly. One hand left the arm of his chair and rose to sink into the beard under his chin. He said, 'We have still to learn, of course, how the robbers – whoever they were – knew the sailing time of the ship of the Order, and what it was carrying.'

'How could they know, my lord?' Nicholas said. 'No doubt, as has been said, they were merest pirates, and simply took whatever of value they found. The Martini would happily take it off their hands, for a price that would still leave them a profit. My lord, I have heard these accusations, and I have replied to them as well as I might. But if this is all the substance of the complaints against me, it seems that you are depriving your cause of my soldiers for reasons that are as doubtful as they are slight.'

He waited. With the old Grand Master, he would have had no chance: that he knew. He had been lucky. No. Luck didn't enter into it, or should not. The pause stretched on, while the Grand Master, crooking his finger, brought the Chancellor to his side for an exchange. They muttered. Thomas, whose soldier's French had a different vocabulary, suddenly appeared to come out of a dream, and belched concisely. Tobie made a sound which could have been anything. The Chancellor straightened and moved away, and the Grand Master sat up. He said, 'Messer Niccolò. You have heard the complaints. The integrity of both yourself and your company has been impugned. Proof is lacking on many counts, but on some the indictment is clear. You did seize and detain against his will a chaplain of this Order. You are and have been for many months a recipient of a fee from James, the bastard claimant of Cyprus. Your acts to date have been to the detriment of the Queen and the Order, rather than the reverse.

'You say, and rightly, that our cause is in need of men, and you claim to wish to serve it. I cannot think that, great though our need is, we on this island can afford to maintain a company of such equivocal loyalty. You will therefore leave Rhodes. You will leave on a ship of the Order, which will ensure that wherever you go, it will not be to James of Lusignan, or to the infidels of Constantinople or Cairo. You will pay for your passage by work. And ahead of you, by means of the Order, we shall let it be known that this company, whatever its value as mercenaries, has shown itself suspect in other ways. This is our judgement. I will hear no appeal.'

He had lost. Had he lost? Someone was getting up; was coming forward from the stalls, his eyes on the Grand Master. 'My lord.'

A tall, bluff man, with gold stuff all over his doublet, glinting under his robe. One of the Genoese. Who?

'My lord,' said the man. 'Her excellence my mistress asks you to hear me.'

'Sir Imperiale,' said the Chancellor. The Grand Master looked irritated at the reminder, as well he might. Imperiale Doria, commander and seaman, was a luminary of both the Queen and the Order. Last autumn, his ship had encountered and hailed the *Doria* as she brought Nicholas on his enforced trip to Cyprus. Another Doria, but one whom he had never met.

The Grand Master said, 'Yes?'

Nicholas stood still. No matter what you did, no matter what you planned, the unexpected happened. The gamester he didn't know and wouldn't acknowledge suddenly leaned over and picked up a card, or a lever, and everything changed, and had to be newly thought of, and accounted for. Sir Imperiale Doria, Genoese, said, 'My lady the serene Queen of Cyprus has some pity for this young man. She believes that in the past he has indeed endeavoured to help her. She believes that he has been importuned, but has in the main resisted the advances of the Bastard Zacco. She believes him brilliant, but also unstable, so that his company cannot reach their full potential unless the young man himself is placed under restraint.'

He stopped, and turning looked closely at Nicholas, and then at the other men at his side. He said, 'Rather than throw this gift back into the furnace, the Queen asks me to say that she is prepared, if your lordship agrees, to take it for a short term to Cyprus, under the most stringent safeguards, extending to the imprisonment of the young man himself. He is held in high regard by his company and they will not desert, she believes, while he is so held. At the first sign of defection, naturally, she would retaliate. Any who rebelled could expect a dishonoured death.'

The Grand Master prodded his chin through his beard. 'Is the lady serious? She invites a Trojan horse, it may be.'

'She is confident,' said the commander.

The Grand Master thought. Beside him, the Chancellor caught his attention and nodded. The prince's gaze sought that of Lomellini, and after a pause, the Treasurer nodded too. The Grand Master said, 'Ser Niccolò. I have a choice. I can send you away, or I can release you into the custody of the Queen of Cyprus, with leave to do with you as she wishes. You have heard what the admiral has suggested. On my terms, you would be out of this country and free, although with your reputation diminished. On hers, you would have a chance to prove that what you have said is true. But if you fail her, the punishment must be death, for you, for your officers, and for your men, as if you were captured in war.'

He stopped. Nicholas slackened his hands, and hoped Thomas had lost the French again, and that Astorre could keep his temper for a moment – just a few moments longer. The Grand Master said, 'You have been bold in your assertions: some might say too bold for a young man new to command, facing such an assembly. I have decided therefore that you shall be held to what you proclaim was to be your bond. You will be handed to Queen Carlotta of Cyprus, to send to Kyrenia or wherever on Cyprus she may choose, there to be held in constraint while your men fight for her cause, until such time as you have proved yourself loyal. In time, you may show yourself worthy of the Order you bear. Until then, it is for the head of that Order to decide whether or not you tarnish it by naming yourself one of its Knights. You may leave.'

The rumble of comment again ran round the hall. You could see, from faces mocking or puzzled, disappointed or thoughtful, the three factions whose unseen interests had moulded the outcome of what had just happened. Of course the Hospitallers were angry: they had had their lordly dismissal revoked by the Queen, and might have to watch this equivocal group of mercenaries rising to power and wealth by whatever means in Cyprus. The Genoese, warned by Katelina, must have been inclined to the Order's belief that dismissal was the safest course, and were not wholly reconciled. Only the Queen's officers, Nicholas saw, looked content.

Beside Nicholas, John le Grant eased his shoulders, but Astorre still stood like a poker. Thomas said, 'Is it all right?'

'Yes,' said Tobie. 'Of course it's all right. We're under a woman again, and she's going to eat us for supper.'

They had to bow, retire and, turning, march between guards from the room. It would never do to look happy. Nicholas couldn't feel entirely happy, in any case, until he knew the last piece of his plan was in place. He produced an expression which he hoped combined simplicity, dignity and reliability with a hint, maybe of penitence. He caught, by accident, the eye of Tomà Adorno and thought again about the Genoese. He had expected them to support the Order's own view and reject him. He had thought Imperiale Doria, coming forward, had been about to do exactly that. Instead he, a Genoese, had put forward Queen Carlotta's proposal, and had saved all his schemes from disaster.

He thought that curious, and forgot, for a moment, to look reliable.

Chapter 20

THE SHIP THAT was to deposit on Cyprus the mercenary broker Niccolò vander Poele and his company tossed with the rest in Mandraki Harbour, while the winds that had begun on the night of the killings howled themselves into a storm. In the trading haven, the cog carrying the embalmed body of Tristão Vasquez managed to leave before the gale reached its height, due no doubt to the supplications of the Patriarch of Antioch, who was keen to get back to Italy. From there the boy Diniz could take ship for Portugal, to find and comfort his mother.

From their latest place of confinement the four immediate colleagues of Nicholas could, if sufficiently curious, obtain a view of the ships in the harbour. Watching the sea blooming white along the rocks of the half-built new tower Tobias Beventini observed from his single barred window the fluttering procession of Knights and of monks which attended the casque to the mole and saw, sombre among them, the boy Diniz in black, walking with his aunt Katelina. Later, he watched the ship slowly move out of shelter to rock on the steaming, grape-coloured water. Goodbye, poor lad. Goodbye, also, Ludovico da Bologna.

Later still, the procession came back, wet and hurrying. The demoiselle and her maid returned with it. Beside the demoiselle, against all probabilities, walked again the slight, black-clad person of Diniz Vasquez.

The boy's face was swollen with tears. With his medical eye, Tobie studied the young Portuguese, and was troubled. This gave way to an emotion less worthy. Tobie said, 'And *that* wasn't part of the plan.'

'What?' said Astorre. Surrounded by bits of a handgun, he was discussing something with John le Grant. Their hands were black, and so was the engineer's nose, which he tended to pinch when expounding.

'The boy didn't sail. He was supposed to,' Tobie said. 'Nicholas expected the Borselen woman to stay. She'd want to see us disposed of. But the boy was to sail with the coffin.' Tobie's pink lips curled unkindly. 'Nicholas *is* going to be cross.'

'Wherever he is,' said John le Grant.

They didn't know where Nicholas was. He had been parted from them unexpectedly, at the gates of the Grand Master's Palace, and immediately after their audience. Since Nicholas had been committed to the custody of Queen Carlotta it was reasonable, on reflection, that he should be given a guard of his own and marched straight from the audience to her residence, leaving his officers behind in the courtyard. They watched him go. He made no effort at resistance, and indeed, threw them a grimace in passing that implied complaisance, if not absolute joy. A moment later, an angry crowd had run upon him, and stones were being hurled.

It happened outside the gates and, surrounded by soldiers, Astorre and the other three officers could only shout, and try ineffectually to beat their way through to help him. From the language they could hear, the attackers appeared to be of Portuguese nationality. For a worrying interval, Nicholas seemed to disappear in the crowd, while the Grand Master's soldiers stood back and did nothing. Then the noise came to an abrupt end, and before they could find out the reason, the escort arrived for Astorre and the rest, and tried to march them out in their turn. It was Astorre who planted his booted feet firmly in the Grand Master's courtyard and refused to move until told what had happened.

The captain of the escort had been dismissive. 'The Portuguese gentleman Tristão Vasquez was killed, and your friend is thought to be somehow responsible. It is untrue, no doubt. But the Portuguese are an excitable nation.'

'I can't say I'm surprised,' had said Captain Astorre, 'if this is all the restraint they are ever put under. Who stopped them? Not any men of the Order, that I could see.'

'I hardly know,' had said the soldier. 'May we move, sir? I believe a beneficial intervention may have been made by some passing Genoese gentlemen. Your friend, I am sure, is quite safe.'

'Is he?' Astorre had said. 'I would feel better, none the less, if you would be so kind as to make certain.'

They had received an assurance of sorts, and had been forced to leave it at that. From there, they had been marched to join the rest of their men at the Arsenal, where the padlocks were bigger, as John le Grant said, and where there existed the anvils, the workshops, the furnaces with which (under supervision, and with no grant of powder or shot) they could adjust and refurbish their weapons. For after all, they had not had a good fight since Troia, and they wanted to start off in Cyprus with their swords sharp.

Thomas, even when harangued in English, remained mystified

about their Cyprus commitment. Working outdoors with the men, he kept his doubts to himself. On the day the cog left, he sat with Astorre and the rest round the dismantled handgun and doggedly returned to his worries. 'All those things they complained about. Nicholas did them, not us.'

John le Grant possessed the most patience. He tweaked his nose again, blackening it further. 'That's right. Katelina van Borselen told the Queen what she knew about Nicholas. Katelina van Borselen, knowing Nicholas, smelled a rat over that pirated cargo. She reckoned there was a lot more to be found out, and presumably set someone to doing it. The missing sugar was tracked down to Crete. That busybody of a chaplain escaped, and was rushed to Rhodes with his accusations. The report got to the Queen, and the Queen used it to persuade the Order they didn't want to keep Nicholas and filched him herself, this time with his hands officially tied.'

Thomas said, 'But the Queen had him before. He swore an oath to her.'

Tobie descended from the window. 'She gave him the knighthood to keep him quiet until she had the means to lay him over a barrel.'

'He's over a barrel?' said the red-haired engineer.

'I've found out who the Fairy Melusine was. He's over a barrel,' said Tobie. 'And we are with him, since we agreed to the plan. You too, Thomas. Sink or swim or get sawn in half by black men in turbans. Talking of which, do you suppose Loppe killed Vasquez?'

Captain Astorre frowned. 'In self-defence?'

'On the orders of Nicholas. I asked Loppe on the ride back. He wouldn't admit to the killing. He did admit Nicholas had got him to watch the two Vasquez and Katelina. The two dead servants had been in Loppe's pay.' Tobie saw the engineer's expression, and felt himself flushing with anger. He said, 'Don't tell me Nicholas couldn't have stopped the Borselen woman from coming that night if he'd wanted to. Vasquez got killed, despite all the so-called precautions. And Nicholas made sure we couldn't question the murderers.'

'He was annoyed when I killed him,' said Astorre. He sounded surprised, but tolerant as ever of his unprofessional colleagues. Astorre had never worried about the frequent deaths that occurred among the kinsmen of Nicholas.

'He seemed annoyed,' said the doctor shortly.

'And now Diniz is still on the island,' said the engineer, who knew little more than Astorre, but whose mind moved in more devious patterns. He embraced the knees of his working-hose. 'But you think Nicholas wanted the boy to go home? And his aunt Katelina?'

'Well, he couldn't harm Diniz now, or Katelina,' Tobie said

with some satisfaction. 'Not if he's in Queen Carlotta's prisons, surrounded by soldiers.'

'But equally, Katelina can't damage him. How annoying for her,' the engineer said. 'All that trouble, and she's no better off than when she started. Do you think she got the Portuguese to stone him?'

'Do you think she got the Genoese to rescue him?' Tobie said. 'I'll wager the Genoese worried him more than the stones. They might do him a service in public, but round the next corner, what? Maybe a Doria dagger again with his name on it.'

Astorre grunted. 'Talk! We heard he was safe.'

'Well,' said Tobie. 'I suppose we should have heard if they'd killed him. But if you ask my opinion, the sooner we sail, the better for that contentious young bastard.'

'The better for all of us, provided his calculations are right. Do you think his calculations are right?' said John le Grant.

'They'd better be,' said Tobie. 'We agreed to stay with him. It's too late to change now.'

In a strong room of the Palace of Cyprus, Nicholas had no view of the sea, but could imagine perfectly well what Astorre and the others were talking about. The hail of stones that had greeted him as he stepped from the Grand Master's audience had startled him as much as it must have alarmed his officers. Caught unarmed in the open, he could do nothing to protect himself. His escort, who obviously agreed with the stone-throwers, fell back and made no effort to stop them. For a moment, indeed, it seemed that this might be a feint preceding some sort of ill-advised rescue. Then Nicholas saw there were women among the gauntlet of men, and heard the threats they were shouting. They were Portuguese, and friends of Tristão Vasquez. Word had got about quickly. Then he had a chance to think of very little else, because they began to close in, and the attack began to be determined.

It occurred to him that if he ran, his escort would have an excellent excuse to dispatch him. If he didn't run, the Portuguese would do the job for them. He retreated quickly with the idea of re-entering the castle, or at least of snatching a shield from some soldier. He was confronted with swords. Katelina, or someone, had spread the idea that he was a killer who deserved very short shrift.

If he wanted to run, his choice was limited. Below him was the Street of the Knights. To the right, stood the church and the way to the Palace of Cyprus. There were men and women, in groups, on both streets. He chose the way to Queen Carlotta, and took to his heels. The missiles thickened, and the men on either side of him closed in. Then it all stopped. Suddenly, in place of the stone-throwers, he found himself surrounded by a cordon of officious, protective Genoese.

His first reaction, which no one else, perhaps, could have predicted, was one of cold rage at their presumption. For a silly moment, he actually considered fleeing them too, rather than have his finely-tuned programme upset.

Well, it had been upset. The Genoese had surrounded him and marched him, chipped and bruised, to their Langue. Correctly, of course, they had sent to tell Queen Carlotta. But either they took a long time to send, or Queen Carlotta took a long time to collect him, because he was held in the Langue for fully an hour while the Genoese made sure he had something to think about.

They held him in a small conference chamber adequate to contain himself, a dozen Genoese, and one or two silent squires. They used the utmost courtesy. His contusions were bathed; the cuts swabbed and patched. He knew three of the Genoese personages; Imperiale Doria, the Treasurer Lomellini and Tomà Adorno. He recognised a Spinola, a Pallaviccino. Half of them were interrelated. All of them had familiar connections – with alum, with vines or with cork. With the Genoese Bank of St George and with Chios. With Madeira and Scotland, with Bruges and even with Anjou. Small wonder the Genoese had protected him. The Republic of Genoa in the Levant operated a smooth-running machine, in which he could be quite a large wheel, or a wrecking-bar.

It was Imperiale Doria who drew his chair into the circle of his companions and began, with quiet geniality. 'The chance to speak to you in private, Messer Niccolò, was one we thought we had lost. I can only say that I am glad it has come, but regret the circumstances that have made it possible. We do not have much time, so forgive me if I come to the point. Soon you will be fighting for Queen Carlotta in Cyprus. Zacco the Bastard holds two-thirds of that island. Naturally, the Queen fears to lose her castle and town of Kyrenia. It is, however, Famagusta, the trading harbour, the Genoese city, to which her enemy will turn his main strength and that, as you may imagine, is of concern to us.' He paused and smiled. 'You will forgive me a remark. You are fond, Messer Niccolò, of Venetian women?'

'Who is not?' Nicholas said. 'Why do you ask?'

The commander had a heavy brown beard, and a long naked nose, cleft like a pig's trotter. He had no look of Pagano Doria, whom Nicholas had caused to be killed. The commander said, 'It is relevant, Messer Niccolò. You have an association with Violante of Naxos. Caterino Zeno her Venetian husband signed a short-lived alum monopoly of yours: Adorno has told me. Her two sisters are married to Venetian merchants in Cyprus. Over the alum, over your doings in Trebizond, in the matter of women it seems, Messer Niccolò, that you signally favour Venetians.'

'I am willing,' Nicholas said, 'to give up Venetian women.' He summoned a ravishing smile, and extinguished it.

'A formidable concession,' agreed Imperiale Doria. 'But it is your dealings with their husbands which concern me. Dealings sweetened, no doubt, by the deep regard in which their wives hold you. As well as your army, you continue your interest in trade.'

'Of necessity,' Nicholas said. 'My army has earned nothing for six months. In Italy, it would have been under contract. That, however, is my fault, not theirs.'

'You were delayed. We heard. In fact, their expenses were met by the Treasurer and, now they are under contract, the Treasurer has orders to be more than generous. The Queen has offered you land. Once the island is conquered, you will have all the trading opportunities you wish. Meanwhile the greater part of the vines, of the sugar fields lie, as you know, in the south, in the grip of the Bastard Zacco, aided by the Venetians. You will understand therefore that you cannot trade. You will not trade. You will bend all your energies and those of your army to fighting to free Famagusta, and once Zacco is beaten, you will be recompensed as you deserve.'

Nicholas said, 'The Venetians grow and sell these crops, under licence, for themselves. They buy the harvest from the Knights at Kolossi. They used to work under licence from Queen Carlotta. Marco Corner works in the south, in the Bastard's land, while his brother works in the north for Queen Carlotta. It seems to me,' said Nicholas modestly, 'that in that island, trade knows few barriers.'

The Treasurer said, 'That is hardly the point. The Venetians have no army in Cyprus. You will have. If you fight for one party, you cannot trade with the other. If trade is your business, your business will be best served by the flourishing of Famagusta when the Venetians have gone, as they will, to fight the Sultan of Turkey.'

'You expect the Venetians to leave? They will need Cyprus,' Nicholas said.

Imperiale Doria spoke in the same tolerant voice. 'Why does Marco Corner spend so much time in Venice? Venice knows war must come if she is to stop the Ottoman Turks from seizing all her trading posts and spreading west, as they might, to threaten Venice herself. By prolonging the resistance of Trebizond you yourself gave Venice time to prepare against Sultan Mehmet. When the fighting season opens this year, Venice will need all her strength, even if it weakens her interests in Cyprus.'

'And you think the Ottoman Turks under Sultan Mehmet will leave Cyprus alone? Certainly, the Sultan of Cairo regards Mehmet as an ally. Perhaps the Ottomans might prove less an ally than a predator. By taking Cyprus out of Egyptian hands, the Sultan Mehmet would gain an income from tribute and trade. And if he were to throw out the Mamelukes and rule, he might prefer to keep the Venetians to deal with. He did when he took Constantinople.'

Doria looked at the Treasurer. The Treasurer said, 'Whatever the Ottoman sultan wants, he will be too busy to attack us this summer. We have this summer to free Cyprus of Zacco and his Egyptians. And if the alliance between Cairo and Constantinople should break, what can it bring us but good? In that event, the Ottoman sultan won't interfere when we drive out the Cairo sultan's Egyptian forces. At best, a Christian fleet may then set out from the west to defeat Sultan Mehmet before he can attack us. At worst, Sultan Mehmet in Cyprus might well be an overlord – a temporary overlord – whose exigencies are tempered by distance. Cairo is near, but Constantinople is not. The Queen has given thought to these things. The Queen has already sent an envoy to Constantinople offering tribute and land in return for Sultan Mehmet's forbearance.'

Nicholas said, 'The Count of Jaffa. I heard.' He added apologetically, 'I thought the Sultan sawed him in half.'

Tomà Adorno looked away, not quite in time. Imperiale Doria remained impassive. The Treasurer said, 'A killing because of some private feud. It doesn't weaken our hopes of the Ottoman Turks. When matters settle, the fortunes of Famagusta will be the fortunes of Cyprus.'

'But,' said Nicholas, 'I am bound to go to Kyrenia. Literally, I understand.'

'Your army is so bound,' said Imperiale Doria. 'You yourself will be held not in Kyrenia, but in the Genoese city of Famagusta, which we here believe will be the Bastard's prime target.'

Nicholas was silent. Then he said, 'You must realise that my army won't fight unless they know I'm alive. Famagusta is under strict siege, and starving.'

The man from the Bank of St George remarked, 'Rubbish. The town is well supplied by Sir Imperiale and the ships of the Order. The siege is a farce, interrupted as often as it continues. There is no danger of starving. In any case, the choice is not yours.'

Nicholas said, 'The choice, I supposed, was the Queen's.'

'Indeed. But the men who will be travelling with you are servants of King Luis,' said Doria. 'And the King owes his position to Genoa.'

'So I have heard. But the King,' Nicholas said, 'does not control my army. You may kill them, of course, but you need them. As a hostage in Kyrenia, I might direct them from prison. As a hostage in Famagusta I am worth nothing to you, unless they fight in

Famagusta as well. They are skilled men. They would join the
garrison in Famagusta, if I required it. But to submit myself and
them to the extra danger without the compensation of an income
from trade? The Queen would not ask it.'

'The Queen,' said Imperiale Doria, 'does not control the sugar
trade of Madeira.'

Nicholas had always been a good actor, a good mimic, but it took
all his skill to disguise his amusement at that. Far away, off the
African coast, the island of Madeira was a Portuguese colony in
which Genoa had many interests. Barred from trade with Venice
and Zacco, he was being offered business instead with the island
home of St Pol & Vasquez. Nicholas wondered, with part of his
mind, what the stone-throwing Portuguese would have made of
this offer. He remembered it had crossed his mind, once, that the
stone-throwing had been a feint. He said, 'I should be interested.
You offer me property on Madeira?'

Imperiale Doria said, 'It is not in my power. But you see here
several men who have influence on the island, and who are willing
to find you some sort of concession once, that is, your period of
probation, shall we say, has been served. Once you have shown
yourself loyal to . . .'

'King Luis,' Nicholas supplied helpfully. 'And in Cyprus: the
sugar fields in the south, once the Bastard has left?'

'Naturally,' said Imperiale Doria, 'all previous contracts would
be null, and the King and Queen would be free to allot them
differently. You may expect to be among those so favoured. The
extent of the franchise will be in direct proportion to the speed
with which you help free Famagusta. Do you understand me?'

'I am honoured,' Nicholas said. 'We understand one another. I
shall do what I can. I take it we sail when we have weather?'

Doria rose. 'Ah, here are the Queen's men to fetch you. You are
impatient to leave? The wind has set in a bad quarter. I give it a
week. Yes, a week.'

The others rose, but only the Treasurer spoke. 'Time for leisure,'
he said. 'Time to reflect. Time to eat, if that is your pleasure.' He
smiled, for the first time. It was not an improvement.

By contrast, the Queen of Cyprus received him formally immediately on his arrival at the Palace. As before, her consort was with
her, and they were again in their chamber of audience. This time,
of course, Nicholas was her prisoner as well as her employee. No
one presented him with a gold-embroidered blue mantle to take
the place of his own abused cloak, and he was introduced into the
chamber by an official less exalted than the Marshal of Cyprus. His
bruised face attracted neither comment nor sympathy and did
nothing, he supposed, to enhance his present diminished standing.

Outside the room there were soldiers, but no trumpeter. Inside, there were more men-at-arms, but few others except for pages and counsellors. Primaflora was not to be seen.

Since the ride back from the ravine he had been locked up, and she had had no chance, it seemed, to send him a message, so the meeting they had both wanted had not been possible. Meantime, she was free to take what pleasure she chose, and he supposed she would do so. He had no such freedom. The boy in Bruges had never gone hungry, but took girls for joy when he needed them. During the weeks with Primaflora, he had lived like that again, and was being made to regret it. As he should. There was a difference between satisfaction and gluttony.

He was not here to think about Primaflora. He was here to remove his army safely from Rhodes. Before him sat the Queen and her consort, subtly changed from the time of his previous audience. The gaze of Luis this time was belligerent. The Queen's manner was brisk, but also in some way uneasy. She did not want, at the start, to hear excuses about his supposed crimes (he did not make any) or to recall that last time they met she had been investing him with the honours of knighthood. She merely wished to confirm (she said) that his company was to fight for her in Kyrenia. They would be under Captain Astorre, and so long as they fought well and remained loyal, they would receive their fee and all else they could wish. Until they had proved themselves, and Messer Niccolò had shown himself faithful, Messer Niccolò would be in the care of Napoleone Lomellini, captain of Famagusta.

Famagusta, again. He must pick his way carefully. Above all, he had to contrive that he was not landed in a different place from his army. Nicholas thought of Madeira, and further thought that it would do no special harm to give Imperiale Doria a present. He said, 'Madonna, my company will fight as I tell them. If they do not see me, or hear from me, or know how I am being treated, there is no incentive for them to be loyal. If you place me in Famagusta, you must put my men in Famagusta as well. If they are to be in Kyrenia, then give me to the Marshal there as hostage.'

Queen Carlotta opened her mouth. Then she shut it and looked at her consort. The sandy jaws moved. The King said, 'You claim to have loyal followers. It is for them to fight all the harder, so that Zacco is driven to lift both his sieges and abandon his efforts. If your men are not moved to strive and Famagusta falls while you are there, it will be, of course, your misfortune.'

So Luis was hedging. The Queen broke in, speaking faster than usual. 'And you will tell them, your men. If they defect, they are dead. I will see to it. I have given orders. You know this man James? The Bastard de Lusignan? Zacco?'

'I have heard of him,' Nicholas said.

'And the noseless bawd, his unmarried mother. You will hear,' said Carlotta, 'that Zacco has charm. He knows the sinful longings of men; he encourages avarice. There have been men who have been tempted, and joined him. He thought Sor de Naves was one. Sor de Naves of Sicily.'

'He brought you from your visit to Savoy,' said Nicholas.

The Queen sat still, her hands loose on her lap, her bright eyes on Nicholas. 'James de Lusignan thought to seduce him. He persuaded Sor de Naves to leave us; to cross to Syria and bring back troops and munitions. Signor de Naves did indeed bring back troops. He also brought arms, and gunpowder, and bombards. He sailed with them to Cyprus. But he gave the bombards to the Genoese instead of to Zacco, and sailed with the rest to us at Kyrenia.'

Nicholas bowed his head in an edified way. He knew the story. The brother of Sor de Naves had long since deserted the Queen and now served, a rich man, under Zacco. But Sor had kept faith with Carlotta, even though his brother with Zacco might pay for it. Perhaps the brothers were rivals. But no, that was naïve. Many families halved the risk by supporting different sides: Marco and Andrea Corner, for example. As a policy, it was not always successful; but the more skilled the operator, the more likely he was to be cherished. By Zacco, who charmed, or by Carlotta, who did not recognise charm. Nicholas kept his gaze lowered, and tried to look useful.

The Queen said, 'We made you a member of an Order of Chivalry, and we have not rescinded it. We promised you land, and a title. The land we do not yet have: it has to be fought for. But we keep our word. We offer no blandishments. We rely on our rightful claim, and the princes of Christendom who support us. We know the day will come when you will take your place, as our Knight, in Nicosia. We hold your pledge. You have only to prove yourself.'

'In Famagusta,' said Nicholas.

She looked coldly upon him. 'You are a Knight, and this is your trial.'

'And my marriage?' said Nicholas tentatively.

The Queen looked impatient. She said, 'That, of course, cannot take place. Primaflora is required here on Rhodes to attend us. Ask for her hand, if you wish, when Zacco is dead or vanquished.'

Nicholas said, 'I see. So your serene excellencies are staying on Rhodes?'

She had come to the end of all she intended to tell him. She said, 'How else can we reach the free world, and capture its conscience? You will go as soon as the weather allows. You have an oath to keep.'

He had forgotten that. He had forgotten his bruised face for the moment as well. He was thinking that he had recently received a number of very good offers although, of course, they were no more than he expected. You didn't go into the game without having worked out, at least, what the prizes were.

Before the storm had blown itself out, the company of Niccolò the banker left Rhodes on a round ship commanded by Louis de Magnac, the Grand Commander of Cyprus, with the best seamen of the Order serving under him. Marching down to Mandraki Harbour, the hundred picked soldiers tramped in a dazzle of cuirass and helmet. In front, Astorre and Thomas were shaken by wind-battered plumes, and even John le Grant, walking with scarlet-clad Tobie, glistened in his suit of tooled German armour that Thomas, privately, had tried to buy from him twice. Behind came their clerks, their grooms and their servants, and behind that, the well-packed wagons with their arms and their baggage.

Nicholas was missing still. It was presumed that the head of the Bank of Niccolò had spent the week locked in the Palace of Cyprus. The mercenaries who fought for him tended to believe, on the other hand, that the lucky bastard was in bed with the blonde, and would be found spent on board when they got there. Astorre had done nothing to destroy this conviction, which might even be sound. It surprised him, the regard in which the young fellow was held by his army. It was natural enough, he supposed. The boy had a brain. He was friendly. He made money. He'd come a long way since Bruges, that was certain.

On board, there was still no sign of Nicholas, nor any news of him that they could gather. The ship, they found, was heavily loaded, although the only other passengers in evidence were some three dozen soldiers, armed as they were not. Their own weapons, armour and harness were locked away as soon as they arrived, and the hundred men of their company equally bestowed under lock and key in a different part of the hold. The four officers of the House of Niccolò were given a cabin. Travelling with them, they gathered, were officials bound for the royal garrison at Kyrenia, some merchants, and a Genoese called Tomà Adorno, at whose name Tobie brightened. Attending this assortment of voyagers was a full complement of servants and some women, who might or might not have been wives. These shared the space below deck with a full cargo of arms and gunpowder and food, destined for the Queen's remaining strongholds on Cyprus. Also aboard, but presently confined with his shipmaster, was Louis de Magnac, who was to command the voyage. With him, they fervently hoped, was his useful black servant called Lopez.

They had proceeded so far with the inventory when a sequence of thuds from above indicated that the time of departure was now close. It was John le Grant who asked for, and received, permission for the four to take the air on deck until sailing-time, a privilege no one else begged since the rain at the time was horizontal. They stood by the deck-rail and gazed all about them. Rhodes, for four months their prison, was about to relinquish them at last. They should have been joyful. The wind screamed and the sea surged, slate and white to the misty horizon. There was a sequence of celestial mutters, and a white vertical crack appeared between heavens and sea, followed by a thorough-going crash. Astorre's eyelashes shook in the downpour like groundsel. Astorre said, 'So where is the madman?'

It was the urgent question in all their minds. If Nicholas was already on board, no one would admit to it. If he was not on board, then something was seriously wrong, and no one except Astorre wanted to think of it. In silence, therefore, they watched the wharf, the pier, and all the distant traffic out of the city. In rigid silence they observed, through the rain, a detachment of soldiers progressing smartly out of the gates and marching the length of the jetty. They arrived at the foot of the gangplank and two of them came aboard, with a man in a heavy cloak following.

Beside the man in the mantle was Nicholas, hatless, cloakless and wearing an untidy doublet. From the frizz of his hair, the rain hopped down the lines of his brow and sluiced the familiar face, which was fawn and bland and marked with occasional scabs. He saw them, and caused his tied hands to rise in a shrug. He looked cheerful. Turning, Tobie saw why he looked cheerful. Advancing towards him was the Grand Commander of Cyprus, Louis de Magnac. And behind him, eyes downcast, was Loppe. Astorre said, 'Hah!' and John le Grant trod on his foot. Nicholas said nothing at all, but smiled vacuously.

The newcomer conferred with de Magnac. The stranger was broad rather than tall, and the fur inside his cloak made him thicker. His wrists looked powerful, and his hands were heavily ringed. The conversation lasted rather longer than might have been thought necessary: at the end of it, the two shore soldiers were replaced by two from the ship who, assuming control of the captive, marched him towards the rear castle. Passing, Nicholas turned his head and shrugged again, grinning. It seemed to have become his habitual posture. Above the grin, it could be seen, he was looking about him intently.

The man of the mantle had left the Grand Commander and was coming over. 'Messer Niccolò's officers? I am Napoleone Lomellini. I have the duty of escorting your young master to my city of Famagusta. I regret the bonds, but you may speak to him later. It would not do, as you may imagine, for the company of Niccolò to seize the ship and take it anywhere but the island of Cyprus.' He smiled and turned. His brows were thick and dark, and so was his hair. 'You may sail, master.'

The shipmaster hesitated, his eyes on de Magnac. The Grand Commander gave a nod, and the master, turning, began to give orders. Astorre said, 'See that? Commands from a Genoese? The rest didn't like that, did they? Well, we're going. It's all working out as the lad said.'

John le Grant said, 'Is it? He didn't say anything about going to Famagusta.'

'Does it matter?' said Tobie.

'Yes, it matters,' said le Grant. 'It matters if they land him in one place and us in another.'

'He wouldn't let them do that,' said Astorre.

'He mightn't be able to stop them,' said John le Grant. 'I don't like it when he looks cheerful.' The ship had begun to cast off, the oars poised, the anchormen working. Nicholas, about to disappear into a cabin, had prevailed on his escort to let him turn and stand, gazing landwards.

'That's all right, then,' said Tobie. 'He's stopped looking cheerful.' He was staring at Nicholas. 'He's regretting something. I wonder what it is, apart of course from being about to land on Famagusta. What other disasters have befallen him recently? Failing to kill John of Kinloch? Achieving poor results with the Vasquez family? Getting stoned by the Portuguese? Or not getting to keep Primaflora? Mind you, maybe he did. Maybe she's aboard. Maybe they're married.'

'She isn't. I asked,' said Thomas surprisingly. He flushed.

Tobie said, 'You asked?'

Thomas said, 'I wondered. The Queen might have forced her to marry him. But they said not. She's to stay in Rhodes with the others.'

John le Grant said, 'Thomas. I thought you had had enough of the lady?'

Thomas flushed deeper. Tobie said, 'He had; and he didn't fancy her running the company. That it, Thomas? So why is our Nicholas looking like that, unless he's found she isn't on board?'

They all looked at what they could see of Nicholas. Certainly, his face was no longer cheerful. He was staring at the long mole behind them. The ship rocked, the oars dug in, and the space between the ship and the jetty started to widen. Tobie said, 'It's the tower John was building. Look at it. Crooked as Pisa.'

'He's missing the Queen,' Astorre ventured. He guffawed. 'Knight of the Order!'

Tobie said, 'Well, Christ, he's happy again. Whatever he was missing, he seems to have seen it. What's he looking at now?'

'A boat,' said John le Grant. 'Coming across from that galley. Hailing us.'

Nicholas had thrown back his head. His face was the face of a child at a carnival. The shipmaster walked to the rail. A man in the advancing sloop called again, and continued to flourish his arms. The shipmaster signed to his trumpeter, and the oars back-pedalled and held. The sloop came nearer. 'Hell and damnation,' said John le Grant under his breath. Tobie said nothing.

In the sloop was the courtesan Primaflora. Her hood fallen back, she let the rain beat on her face as she gazed up at the deck of the cog. Nicholas raised his bound arms in a gesture of unassumed and explicit delight and, seeing him, her face opened in a smile to make every man envious. He stood, prevented from moving, and watched her. There was an interval, during which the sea lifted the sloop and the girl and her woman clung, struggling to board. Boxes were transferred. Then Primaflora was on deck, and greeting the shipmaster, the Grand Commander, Lomellini.

They looked mystified, Tobie thought. He said, 'They didn't expect her. Do you suppose . . .'

'She's here against the Queen's wishes? I was supposing just that thing,' said John le Grant. 'And look at Nicholas, man. He's got her again, and no marriage. I grant you. That laddie can plan.'

'I should think the planning was hers,' Tobie said. 'And either a convincing lie, or a fair greasing of palms, or they would never have agreed to her boarding. She's coming over.'

They hadn't seen her since the miserable night when the Court of King Arthur attended the death of Tristão Vasquez. Then, she had been the Queen's attendant but not, perhaps, enjoying the Queen's fullest confidence. There had been soldiers with her, Tobie remembered, clearly told to stay with her wherever she went.

There was no one with her now but her woman. She left the Commander, the Genoese and the shipmaster and came across to them all. She said, 'The Queen was so reluctant to allow me to come, I feared to miss the ship altogether. I have held up your sailing. I am sorry.' She walked as she spoke, taking them out of earshot of the ship's officers. She said, 'They won't let me talk to Niccolò, or at least, not yet. Will you give him a message?'

'Of course,' said John le Grant. Tobie looked at him suspiciously.

She smiled. She said, 'I trust you not to give me away. I have no leave to come. I have left the Queen, but they mustn't know until I have landed. Will you tell Niccolò?'

'Won't they send you back?' Tobie said.

'They would find it hard,' she said. The Commander had come to her side. She smiled to them and, turning, to Nicholas, and then left the deck.

Tobie said. 'Do you believe that? What are we talking about? We can't give a message to Nicholas.'

'Loppe can,' said John le Grant. 'Didn't you see? Nicholas is to share the Grand Commander's own cabin. They don't trust him anywhere else. So all the trip, Loppe can run between us.'

'And between Nicholas and Primaflora,' Tobie said. 'That makes me feel a lot better. No, it doesn't.'

'Don't worry,' said Captain Astorre. Crossing the harbour bar, the ship lurched again, and gave every sign of continuing to do so. 'Don't worry. Remember which is the lee rail, and don't think of Nicholas. You'll get back your sea legs in no time.'

Very soon after that, the willing black servant Lopez had cause to unlock his master's cabin in search of a boat cloak. Nicholas, lying on one of the seats, said, 'Well, well. Tobie been sick yet?'

Loppe looked at him in the way Tobie sometimes looked, which reminded Nicholas of a collector searching for chips, scratches and signs of dubious craftsmanship. The African said, ignoring the question, 'The lady Primaflora wishes you to know that she is here without leave of the Queen, although she has told the Grand Commander otherwise. She expects to join you on Cyprus.'

'I counted on it,' said Nicholas. 'You can tell her that, if you like.'

'It was obvious,' the negro said. 'I wonder, though, if she will be allowed to stay. Whoever employs you, they will want your undivided attention.'

'They won't get it if they don't do as I ask. Primaflora will stay. Loppe, I must talk to her.'

The rich, musical voice never gave anything away. Loppe said, 'I shall try to arrange it. She shares a cabin, but the other lady, I hear, does not travel well. You know, of course, the demoiselle is also on board?'

'Who?' said Nicholas. He saw by the look in Loppe's eyes that he had spoken too quickly.

'Katelina van Borselen,' said Loppe. 'At her own request, she goes to Kyrenia. And the boy.' He paused and said, 'I see I have given you some very bad news. I am sorry.' Presently he said, 'Messer Niccolò? I must go.'

Nicholas said, 'Yes, of course. The boy?'

'Diniz Vasquez. He did not sail for home with Ludovico da Bologna. He stayed on Rhodes with his aunt. I imagine,' said Loppe's gentle voice, 'that he wished to protect her in the course of vengeance on which she is set. She blames you for the death of his father.'

'I'm a fool,' Nicholas said. 'And it's too late. She is here.'

He spoke to himself. But he saw, from Loppe's eyes, that he understood him.

Loppe said, 'It can be dealt with. There is only one thing that matters now. There are many lives in your hands. It would be wise to forget these family concerns until you are safely in Cyprus.'

'Of course,' said Nicholas. Loppe hesitated, and then took his leave, locking the door of the cabin behind him. Nicholas remained in the rocking chamber, gazing at the place where he had been, and seeing nothing. Katelina, Diniz, Primaflora. Obscuring his concise and elegant plans, the promise of misery.

Chapter 21

THE PROSPECT of being locked up in the cabin of Louis de Magnac for four or even five days and nights was one which Nicholas might have found depressing, had there not been worse things to dwell on.

Wealthy, grey-haired, distinguished, the Grand Commander of Cyprus had held the fief of Kolossi for twelve years, and his was the hand that had built the present great keep of the Knights there. It was de Magnac's special domain that Nicholas had polluted by his attack on John de Kinloch, and by his abstraction – far more serious – of the diverted Kolossi sugar. Decked with the Order of the Sword, Nicholas had been allowed to house his men in Louis de Magnac's own palace in Rhodes. Even his condemnation and banishment by the Grand Master had been transmuted by Queen Carlotta, whom Louis de Magnac revered, and whose very loyal servant he was. The Queen needed the services of this man Niccolò's army, and the Grand Commander therefore was prepared to deliver him, as undertaken. He was not likely, however, to allow the fellow to enjoy the voyage.

So Nicholas read the mind of his unwilling host, and from the silent contempt with which he was treated, he gathered that he had read it correctly. They shared no meals together, and by day de Magnac was mostly on deck. At night, they slept on their own mattresses along with the Grand Commander's personal servants. Whenever Nicholas was left alone, the door was kept locked. For the first day of the voyage and half of the next, he saw no one else.

He had asked Loppe to work a miracle and persuade Louis de Magnac to let him see Primaflora. He should not therefore have been as amazed as he was when informed curtly on the second afternoon that the Queen's lady attendant wished to question him, and that the Grand Commander had given permission. She arrived flanked by two soldiers who took their stance, with difficulty, on the heaving floor of the cabin. The Grand Commander, as was usual, was absent.

The seas had remained very high. During her few steps on deck, his mistress's hair had tugged itself from its caul and her cheeks were whipped into colour behind the light creams. Her eyes sparkled. He smiled back, taking her hands as she tried to keep her balance. Helping her to a seat, he took one beside her and addressed her in Greek, 'It's like old times. Whom have you beguiled this time?'

The soldiers were frowning. She withdrew her hands and replied gravely in the same language. 'The Grand Commander thinks I am a servant of the Queen, and obey the Queen's wishes. I am to remind you of your duties to Carlotta, and make sure you have no seditious thoughts.'

'Seditious is not the word I should apply to them,' he said. It sounded jocular, which was not the way he felt. He said, 'I thought we had lost each other. But what have you done? Are you sure you want to come with me?'

'I am here,' she said, and the small pleats had formed, again, at the corners of her ripe, dimpled mouth. 'Do you question what the gods send?'

'Not when they go mad and send me a goddess,' Nicholas said. 'But the cost? And it must be difficult. They've put you to share with Katelina?'

'It isn't difficult. She's unwell, and I can help her. Sometimes she comes near to accepting that the Queen has changed her mind and sent me to watch you. Sometimes she thinks you have lured me without the Queen's knowledge. I'm sorry, though, that she's here. She means to cause you harm. She is here only for that. She and the boy.'

Nicholas said, 'I could forgive her anything but keeping the boy from his home. He's too young for all this.'

Her pale, clear eyes considered him. 'He is fully grown, and knows his mind. It was his decision to stay. Since his aunt won't abandon the feud, he has made himself her protector. He did not, perhaps, expect her to follow you to Cyprus but he'll stay so long as he thinks she's in danger from you.' She paused. She said, 'You are very tolerant, are you not, of all these people who have set out to injure you? You once said, I remember, that there was only one person you hated. Is that why you are letting the Queen send you to Cyprus?'

'Because of Tzani-bey al-Ablak?' said Nicholas. 'If you are asking whether I've forgotten what he did to you as well as to me, I can assure you I haven't. You would like me to do something about it?'

She smiled. 'Some day, I should like you to tell me your plan. I don't need to ask if you have one.'

'Oh, I have one,' Nicholas said. 'Only the details change from time to time, according to circumstance. I can promise you, however, that he'll have time to be sorry. Primaflora, there is something else. They are sending me to Famagusta. That isn't for you. Until I can join you, we shall be separated for a while.'

She had become very still. 'They are under siege at Famagusta. Who is sending you there?'

'The Genoese,' he said. 'And King Luis. The Queen was forced to agree. Napoleone Lomellini is captain of Famagusta: that's why he's here. After they land me there, you must go with Astorre and the rest to Kyrenia. There is food in Famagusta. I'll come to no harm, and shall join you as soon as I can. It's only a way of compelling Astorre to fight hard.'

'Then he must,' she said. After a moment she said, 'If that's how they want to test your allegiance, then accept it. You would prosper under the Genoese if they win. They must have made promises.'

'They have,' Nicholas said.

'Then stay in Famagusta,' she said. 'If you don't, the Genoese or the Queen's men will slaughter you all. And Katelina will encourage them.'

'I've said I shall,' Nicholas said. 'Until Kyrenia is taken, at any rate. Then, surely, they'll free me to join you.'

There was a look she had, that he had learned to know. She wore a scent he knew also, as he knew every fold in her body. She said, 'But I shall be with you already. If you go to Famagusta, so do I.'

'No,' said Nicholas.

'Why not?' she said. 'If there's no hardship?'

Above the smile, her eyes searched his face. Nicholas said, 'Where is the large house you wanted to run, and the fine clothes to choose from?'

'They will come,' she said. 'But not if you flout everyone by trying to reach me. I will come with you to Famagusta. That is a promise.'

The ship rose into the waves and crashed, shuddering before rising and rolling again. One of the soldiers suddenly opened the door and went out. The other grinned. Primaflora, her eyes intent, showed no distress at all. Indeed, perhaps reading some change in his face, she seemed heartened. He said, 'I shall now make an admission. I want you in Famagusta. And here.'

'The soldier would complain,' said Primaflora. Her colour had risen again.

'Would he? He could report that you were testing my loyalty. Primaflora, what will the Queen do about this? She's bound to make it known you've defected. Would they let you stay with me then?'

'I shall be in Famagusta by then,' she said. 'If they want you to fight well, then they must, surely, allow you suitable solace? I don't think they would send me away. Is that your last objection?'

'I think so. I give in very easily,' Nicholas said.

'I have noticed. I should go, then. Niccolino, you will have a care? Katelina is resolved to bring you down somehow.'

'I know. Katelina thinks I seduce women,' Nicholas said. 'She doesn't know it's the other way round.'

She turned then, and spoke in French to the soldier, and soon she was ushered out, and he was alone, and aware for the first time of the hideous motion of the ship. He hadn't asked after his men and his officers, although she might have been able to bring him news of them. On his side, there were several things he had spared her.

There was no need for her to know, as his company knew, that he and they might never be allowed to set foot on Kyrenia, or to see Famagusta alive. James de Lusignan had brought him a captive to Cyprus, and had set him free on the starkest of conditions: Nicholas must either take his force home, or return to help Zacco drive out his sister. *Your officers might well sail for Kyrenia or Famagusta*, the King had suggested. *If they do, they will be intercepted and killed.*

Nicholas had been well warned not to do what he was doing.

The third day passed. Once, he was allowed briefly on deck, and glimpsed Astorre and Tobie, exercising likewise. They waved without speaking. Against the wind, it would have been necessary to scream. He knew, without being told, that they must be as much on edge as he was. Two days to go, or maybe three, to his arrival in Famagusta, a prisoner. But perhaps before that, the masts of a ship would appear above the horizon, and the guns of James de Lusignan would bear down on them, and on him. He had taken one precaution. He didn't know if it was sufficient.

Later, returning with his guard to the cabin he had caught sight of another face he knew. Half-concealed by the mast, Diniz Vasquez stood watching him. The boy looked tired. Nicholas stopped, and resisted when the soldier tried to pull him on. He said, 'Diniz? Is the demoiselle better?'

The young Portuguese looked taken aback. After a moment he said, 'She is sick. But for you, she wouldn't be here.'

The soldier tugged again, and Nicholas laid a hand on his arm while he spoke quickly to Tristão's son. 'Listen a moment. I want you to remember this, and try to believe it. I had nothing to do with your father's death. If I can, I will help you find out who killed him. But if you don't trust me, speak to the doctor. You remember him. Talk to him. Ask him what you want. And if you need help, go to him.'

'I have spoken to him,' said the boy. 'He doesn't know whether you had him murdered or not. He has offered help, and I've accepted it.'

'He is a good man,' Nicholas brought himself to answer. The

soldier put pressure on his arm and he let himself be escorted away.
The boy looked after him, circles under his eyes. Nicholas
wondered how often he had had cause to damn Tobie, and also to
be in his debt. Tobie's doubts had led Diniz to trust him. Katelina,
of course, trusted nobody. Katelina would take his life if he let her;
and if it hadn't been accomplished already by the rather more
powerful parties who were now, all of them, ranged up against him.

He went to bed that night half dressed under his blanket as
always, and slept as soundly as he usually did, waking early to find
that the crash and heave of the vessel had moderated. The ship
they had been given was old, and of clumsy design; and this was
the first night that de Magnac had not risen at least once to check
with the shipmaster. The Grand Commander was fast asleep now,
although the grey light showed it was dawn. Nicholas lay where he
was, judging the weather from what he could hear and feel. As on
the voyage from Italy, he found he longed to lay his hands, too, on
the sheets, on the helm. He had discovered some time ago a
passion for sailing; for navigation; for the arithmetic of the sky.

He had been afraid, once or twice, of being trapped by his own
fascination, as he was afraid of being trapped by progressions of
sound. One should school such emotions. He had discovered as
much in Byzantine Trebizond. Primaflora, although not Byzantine,
had with her courtesan's detachment reminded him again of the
virtues of self-restraint – which was not the same, thank God, as
celibacy. With the mind in control, there was no need to be at the
mercy of anything. He noticed, with slight irritation, that with or
without the mind in control he was thinking again of Primaflora.
There came, at that exact moment, an imperative knocking on the
cabin door. The voice of Napoleone Lomellini said, 'My lord?'

The servants jumped up. De Magnac's white-capped head
moved, and he lifted himself on one elbow and nodded. The door
was opened. Since he had come aboard, Nicholas had seen nothing
more of the captain of Famagusta, or of Tomà Adorno, the other
Genoese. His segregation, he had begun to think, was not acci-
dental. Now, Lomellini's sharp eyes under the thick brows went
first to himself, before they rested on Louis de Magnac. Instead of
an expensive furred mantle, the Genoese captain was wearing a
cuirass. He said, 'I am sorry to wake you. The shipmaster says
there are two galleys approaching.'

'Of what kind?' said the Grand Commander. He swung his feet
to the floor and laid his hand on the jerkin that went under his
armour. A servant, tumbling, knelt with his boots.

'Saracen,' said Napoleone Lomellini. He glanced at Nicholas
again, while speaking to de Magnac. 'We have fifty sailors, two
dozen soldiers – it won't be enough if they board us. Perhaps we
should free Messer Niccolò and his men?'

'Not yet,' said the Grand Commander. 'Board a round ship? Let them try. Come with me.' He looked back from the door, his servants already jacketed and beside him. 'Lock him up,' he said; and the door shut, leaving Nicholas alone and staring at it.

Saracens. Who? Not Sultan Mehmet; his crescent flags would proclaim him. So, Egyptian marauders? Corsairs from a Syrian or Turcoman port? It barely mattered. All that mattered was that it was not James de Lusignan, come to accost a young man he thought he had befriended. Nicholas found and put on the sword-less belt, the boots and the leather tunic that was all he had to wear over his shirt and hose. His cuirass and weapons were packed below, along with those of his army. He thought of them, and of the merchants, and the Kyrenia high officials, and the women. Especially the women: Katelina sick, and Primaflora immured with her. And, of course the boy, whom Muslims found so appealing.

The ship lurched. He heard the thud of feet on timbers, and the sound of orders, then drumming and trumpets. Nicholas sat erect on his mattress and listened. More orders. The thud of many feet, heavily shod this time. And soon, the jingle and clash of metal harness, and men's voices raised in command. The ship's soldiers were on deck, and armed. Well, thank God for that. How close were the enemy? Two ships, they said. And galleys, so they would be low, and manoeuvrable. He knew what he would do in their place.

The door opened again. It was Louis de Magnac, and someone else whom he glimpsed, and who then stepped out of sight. Loppe. De Magnac said, 'We are being attacked by Mameluke ships. Do what you like. The door is unlocked. I have freed your officers also.'

Nicholas said, 'Release my men. A hundred will make all the difference.'

'You are right,' said the Grand Commander. 'If they panic; if they surrender. If we sink, I shall free them. Not before.' He made to leave.

Nicholas grasped his arm in supplication, half turning him round. 'They are Christians. They run the same risks as you. Let them save you.'

The Grand Commander lifted his elbow to thrust him aside. He said, 'Not now.' He stood, looking at Nicholas, surprise on his face. As he fell forward, Nicholas caught him.

Loppe, entering, closed the door while Nicholas lowered the Knight to the floor. Loppe said, 'He has the key. Here it is.' He knelt by the side of the unconscious man. 'I tried not to hit him hard. Do you want him tied up?' He looked up as Nicholas hesitated. 'He'll put you in chains.'

'Not once the fighting has started. No. We'll lock the door on him for the moment, and let him out presently. He's an experienced man. We all need him.' In the doorway he stopped. 'The ships have Mameluke crews?'

Loppe said, 'Yes. They're not corsairs. They could be from Egypt, or Cyprus.' His voice was quite steady. He said, 'I saw the message was taken aboard. There is no way of telling whether it arrived or not.'

Nicholas said, 'You did all you could. It either works or it doesn't. Anyway, if those galleys come from Egypt or Syria, they're out to destroy a Christian ship, and it's nothing to do with James de Lusignan. If they're from Cyprus, Zacco sent them. So I can't tell you what to do, except to prepare for the worst. Can we get at the hackbuts?'

'Not with a key; the master has it,' said Loppe. 'I might break in: there's no one with time to watch now.' The ship lurched, and spray fell with a clatter. He said, 'They are aiming better.'

Nicholas said, 'Yes. Free the men. If it's Zacco, bent on destroying us, at least they can put up a fight for themselves. Get them armed if you can, but keep them below. I'll send Astorre and talk some sense into somebody.' He staggered, and so did Loppe.

Loppe said, 'The cog's guns are mounted too high. Master John has gone to see what he can do. Captain Astorre is waiting outside the door. I'm going.'

He opened the door and disappeared. After a few moments, Nicholas followed, locking the door behind him. The wind buffeted him, its twanging voice part of a cacophony. The sails were down and the oars were out and dipping, keeping the ship in its place, its guns trained. The deck shook as another gun fired. Astorre rose up before him and said something. After a moment his ears cleared, and he heard what it was.

'Mameluke ships, there and there. Fired five times into the sea. Bigger oar power. Lower freeboard, hard to hit. Blocking the only way we could sail.'

Nicholas said, 'Where's Diniz?'

'Who?' said Astorre. 'Oh, him. He's with John le Grant in the bows.' His face had turned ruddy with battle-elation. He began to laugh. 'That woman!'

'I've sent Loppe to unlock the men and break open the weapon store. Bring them up when they're ready. I'll see that Lomellini and the shipmaster are prepared for them. What woman?'

'That Primaflora,' said Astorre. 'Got all the women into one cabin and locked it. She was the one who told Loppe where the key was.'

'Good. Go,' said Nicholas. He saw the two war galleys now. The seas were so big that sometimes one or other would be lost to sight for a moment, but mostly they were in view, as the cog was so high. They glittered with helmets and chain mail, shields and the crooked swords of the East, and their oarsmen worked like the slaves they certainly were. The ship to the north of them had its bows elaborately picked out in leaf gold. It was the nearer of the two. On his way to Lomellini, Nicholas swung himself up to a better vantage point and looked at it, screwing his eyes against the spray and the wind, his shirt sleeves snapping.

Lomellini's voice said, 'Do you want a spear in your chest? What are you doing here?' More than ever, he looked like a soldier, about soldier's business.

Nicholas slid down and steadied himself. He said, 'The Grand Commander changed his mind. He freed me, and sent for my men. We need their handguns, or the galleys will come up too close.'

The Genoese gazed, his black brows lowered. His armour was dented, and not very bright, as if it had seen long and hard service. He said, 'Where is the Grand Commander?'

He had guessed. Nicholas said, 'He is unhurt.'

Lomellini still stared at him. He said, 'In five minutes, I shall send a servant to look for him. Make yourself scarce.'

'No need,' Nicholas said. 'In a few minutes, there will be only one thing to think of. Or – no – *Get down!*'

They were hardly in time. As they rolled on the deck, a ball from the enemy ship smashed into the rail of the forecastle, leaving a prodigious hole, and sending timber and iron flying. One of the bombards had gone. Among the dust and smoke, suddenly, there was a flicker of fire. As Nicholas scrambled upright, he heard John le Grant's voice, swearing, and he began to breathe again. Before he could run, a dozen men were already there, and the fire was out. The men were his own, armed and efficient. Nicholas turned and found Lomellini, flushed, on his feet. Nicholas said, 'We could beat them.'

Lomellini said, 'We shall certainly try. But even your hundred men won't help save us if they get in under our guns and board us. There are at least four hundred men in those galleys, and this is an old single-mast cog. It takes fifty men to swing that yard round every time she goes about. *And* her guns aren't on swivels.'

'So we keep them at a distance. We can't manoeuvre against two of them anyway, not with this wind and the way they've placed themselves. Can we fix the guns? My engineer and the Order's gunner might do it. Then we look to hackbuts – we've plenty, and we're good – and some sort of shield against arrows. What about co-ordination between helm and gunners and handguns? Would you let me do that? If the shipmaster agrees? Where is the shipmaster?'

'I heard you,' said the man. He was a Rhodian, and a professional. He said, 'Ser Napoleone? This makes sense. I'll take this man back to the tiller, if you and the Grand Master get the soldiers where you want them. I don't want a prow ram through my beam while we're talking.'

'And whatever extra oarsmen you've got,' Nicholas said. 'It'll help the gunners if the storm sail comes down.' An explosion shook the boat and they staggered, recovered, and looked to the bows. John had fired one of their bombards. As they stood, another spoke. Two fountains of seawater arose, one in front of each galley. They saw, in the distance, turbanned men throw themselves low.

The shipmaster was saying, 'She'll run south on her mast. But it'll help. Come. Let's get on with it.' He ran, shouting orders, and Nicholas followed, to an outburst of drums and some trumpeting. Before they got to the poop, the yard was rattling down and men were running. He gave a slap on the back to one of his own squad as he passed, and the man looked round, grinning. Even when the odds were against them like this, no one minded once the fighting got started. Nicholas was so glad to be free, and in action, that he released a whoop, running forward. Faces turned, some of them irritated.

Then he was at the stern castle, where the steersman was listening to orders, while the trumpeter made brazen notes of them. The poop flag, undeviatingly, blew from the north and the current kicked. Below, running men formed a line along either gunwale, the long shafts of their guns in their hands, their helmets bowed over powder-satchels and matches. The galleys on either side began to change position. The cog's helmsman swung the tiller, using the current, and her few oarsmen bent to their task. The round ship ceased to point into the seas and came broadside on to each galley. As she paused, rocking wildly, the hackbuts along her flanks fired, first on one side, then on the other, raking along the low, distant galleys. With the naked eye, some confusion on both the enemy ships could be seen, and then, all too quickly, there came the uplifting of Mameluke bows, and the arrival over the water of a double shower of fast, lethal arrows.

They arrived on the deck of the cog, and men screamed and fell, despite their armour. Some of them would be his, Nicholas knew, but so far he couldn't identify them. But already the yard was again travelling up the mast, was secure, was filling with wind, and the round ship began to veer to present, again, its prow and poop to the galleys. And by then, there were working cannon on both.

Nicholas ran down among the men, and assessed the few injured, and spoke hastily to the officers he found, and began to make his way to the fighting platform at the prow. On the way, he met Loppe, who thrust a cuirass at him. It was his own, and so was the helmet that came with it. He slung both on, without fastening the buckles, and bounded upwards on his way. John le Grant met him beside the broken timber. Nicholas said, 'Well?' Despite everything, he felt better than he had since the battle of Troia.

John le Grant said, 'Calm down, and listen.' The engineer looked as he always did, tool in hand; white-lashed gaze speculative in a freckled face smeared with unspecified oils. His voice was not as it always was. He said, 'The two galleys you are looking at are from Salines de St Lazare. They're James de Lusignan's.'

Nicholas turned and, springing, handed himself fast up the rigging. Then, stopping, he gazed narrowly over the water. He saw the flank of the gilded enemy galley, packed with Muslims. Next to the pumpkin-turbans and scimitars hung the velvet cloth of the canopy, sewn with the owner's devices. The wintry light traced the cross and crosslets of Jerusalem and the three crimson lions of Christendom: one for Cyprus; one for Armenia, and the last for the royal Frankish race of the Lusignan. The coat of arms – John was right – of James, King of Cyprus, whom he had hoped was his friend.

For a moment, Nicholas stayed without moving. Then, taking slow breath, he set himself to scan the enemy vessel. The ship rose and fell. Fraction by deliberate fraction, he examined the waist of the galley: noted the thickets of bows and the bright turbanned helmets above them; moved his gaze past the waist to the prow, and lifting it at length to the foredeck, found at last the figure standing alone there, his golden belt glinting, his heavy cloak flying behind him. Nicholas considered it, shading his eyes; seeking the tall, huntsman's body, the powerful neck, the beautiful face set in some purpose he would recognise instantly. Nicholas, too, had chosen to stand in isolation so that he could be seen, and so that, whatever there was to come, there should be no doubt about it.

The figure he viewed was not tall, though it was above the usual height for its race. The shield it carried was inlaid with gold, and the helmet was shaped like a cone, with ostrich feathers that tugged in the wind. Between the cheek-tongues of the helm, the black moustache and the dark, vicious face were unmistakable.

Nicholas lowered his hand, although he kept his eyes still on that remote, triumphant figure. Before him was the war fleet of James de Lusignan, Bastard of Cyprus, sent for no other reason but to intercept Nicholas and his company. Only James had not come with it. Instead, in cold anger – in forgivable anger – he had committed the charge to the emir Tzani-bey al-Ablak.

So there was no longer much to hope for, unless he could escape. The precaution had not been enough, and the message from Zacco was clear. *I gave you your life, and you have failed me. Here, then, is your fate, at the hands of the man from whom you would most hate to receive it.* He remembered that Primaflora was on board. And

Katelina. And Diniz. He called, 'We have to beat them. John, we have to fight our way out.'

And John le Grant said, 'Look again.'

He had been searching before for a man. Belatedly now he saw the glitter of parallel tubes on the deck of the galley. Copper tubes, long and slender, with their mouths levelled at the flank of the cog. John said, 'You see them? The other galley has them as well.'

Lomellini had come to the deck. As Nicholas sprang down to his side, the Genoese examined the enemy ship in his turn. He took down his bracketting hands. 'I see,' he said.

'Tubes for wildfire,' Nicholas said. 'They were playing with us.'

'It seems very likely,' said John le Grant. 'A few shots to make us panic. All they have to do now is fire off one of those, and they've got us.'

Astorre came up. He said, 'It's Zacco's Mamelukes.'

'We know,' said Nicholas. 'We can't fight. He's got wildfire. Diniz . . . Where's Diniz Vasquez?'

'Behind you,' said the boy's voice. It sounded low, in all the hubbub.

Nicholas turned. 'Your aunt and the other ladies are locked in one cabin. Go below, free them, and stay with them. The lady Primaflora will have the key. Thomas, go to the Grand Commander's cabin and release M. de Magnac with my apologies. Messer Napoleone –' He broke off. 'Listen.'

A man from the nearest galley was hailing them. The face above the mouth-trumpet was not Egyptian, and the message coming in gusts over the water was in excellent French. 'This is the spokesman of the emir Tzani-bey al-Ablak, commander of the Mameluke forces of James, King of Cyprus, hailing a ship of the Order of Hospitallers. Who is in charge?'

Lomellini hesitated. The Rhodian shipmaster, horn in hand, was running towards him. The Genoese took the horn from him, and raised it to his mouth. 'This is a vessel of the Order of Knights Hospitaller of St John, sailing from Rhodes. We have on board the Grand Commander of Cyprus, the Knight Louis de Magnac. The Order is not at war with the Sultan of Cairo. The Order demands to proceed without let or hindrance.'

The wind thrummed and wailed. The ship creaked, rising to the crest of each wave and falling into the trough. On board, there was no sound from the seamen or the soldiers or the merchants as they stood, keeping their balance. The enemy spokesman said, 'The King, for whom the emir speaks, has no quarrel with the Order. But it has come to the King's attention that you carry grain and gunpowder and arms to those who persist in holding the lands of his sister Carlotta against him. Moreover, you carry soldiers, a troop of mercenaries under the Flemish broker Niccolò of Venice

and Bruges. His serene grace wishes no ill to the Knights of the
Order, but he holds to his right to prevent the Order from interfering in a war which is not their concern.

'Accordingly, I have to tell you that you and your ship are the
King's captives. Facing you is a battery which will send you to
Heaven before you have time to pray. You will allow the lord emir
to board you, and to place a man of his own at the helm. You will
then be escorted to the King's harbour of Salines. Those of you
who are innocent of malice may expect to be landed unharmed and
put on your way. Your cargo will, of course, be confiscated. Those
soldiers of fortune who, for gold, have come to take up arms
against King James deserve no mercy and will be shown none. You
have no hope of escape. At the first sign of insurrection, the King's
galleys have orders to burn you down to the water, no matter who
or what may be on board. Do you understand?'

Louis de Magnac, looking pale, had arrived. He stared at Nicholas, then, seizing the trumpet, replied. 'This is the Grand Commander of Cyprus. You are entirely mistaken. We carry nothing
for the garrison of Kyrenia. We come to supply the Knights at
Kolossi. We demand to pass.'

The voice on the other ship took its time replying, and when it
did, the results of a consultation were apparent. 'You do not carry
on board Niccolò vander Poele and a hundred of his men?'

Answering the glare of the Grand Commander, Nicholas spoke
low and quickly. 'We are on our way home.'

The Grand Commander raised the trumpet again. 'We do. They
are on their way to the west. They offer no threat.'

On the other ship, the spokesman again turned aside to the emir.
Then he lifted his trumpet once more. 'You are far from the
shipping lanes to the west, Grand Commander. You will forgive
the lord emir if he does not believe you. You will come to Salines
with your broker of mercenaries. Once on land, he and his fellow-
adventurers will receive their deserts.'

The Grand Commander, his eyes on Nicholas still, allowed his
face to relax. He said, 'I can say no more. It is for Messer Niccolò
to make his own case. We go to Salines under protest, and on the
understanding that, once there, all the others on board will be
freely released. There are ladies among them.'

'We shall treat them with honour,' said the voice from the galley.
It translated, no doubt, the exact words of the emir. It didn't
translate, Nicholas observed, the mockery behind the pronouncement. For Zacco's reprimands, for his subsequent restraint towards
Nicholas, Tzani-bey was now about to claim restitution.

It was the end of the dialogue. On the other ship, the emir
walked to the rail, where the galley's boat was swung out and
lowered. On the round ship of the Order, Louis de Magnac turned

to Nicholas. 'I could have you hanged from the yardarm, and no officer of the Order would blame me. The death you now face is, I fear, not undeserved. I cannot say I regret that the Queen will not have to trust her interests to one such as you.'

'I am sorry, too,' Nicholas said. He spoke formally, and controlled his own anger. 'I hoped to have your understanding. As soldiers going to fight for Queen Carlotta, my company was at greater risk than anyone else here on board, and it was their right to be free to defend themselves. If we alone are now to die because of our allegiance, I cannot see our end as either deserved or dishonourable. But that is for others to judge. Now the ship is yours, as we are. I will do whatever you wish.'

'What can prisoners do, pray?' said the Grand Commander. 'Except display the courage of soldiers placed under duress. Mine will stand on deck, and wait for the heathen. If you wish, you may place yours beside them. The ladies and the lay passengers should remain below, where they are.'

'You don't mean to offer defiance?' said Nicholas.

Beneath the silver hair, the handsome face paled, then flushed. The Grand Commander said, 'It would provide a quicker death, I have no doubt, for you and your men, but a piteous one for innocent passengers. They will not burn to save you from torture.'

Nicholas said, 'My thought was different. The emir, too, might think that burning was too easy a death. If you turned your guns on him, he might prevaricate. But of course, it is a risk.'

'It would be the act of a madman,' said Louis de Magnac. And, Nicholas supposed, he was right.

In silence, they took their positions. The seamen stood in their ranks, and the ship's soldiers behind them, and his own behind those. In front waited the Grand Commander, and the captain of Famagusta, and the Rhodian shipmaster, his face impassive. Beside them stood Nicholas and the four officers of his troop. The enemy skiff laboured over the water and they could see the emir plainly, his cloak wrapped about him in the prow. He was looking upwards, at Nicholas. Nicholas, unmoving, stared back. The boat arrived, and the emir started up the companionway. Diniz Vasquez said, 'Is that the man who whipped you before you came to Kolossi?'

Nicholas turned. 'Go below! What are you doing here?'

'Is it?' said the boy.

'Yes. Go below. Diniz, stay with the others.'

There was colour in the boy's face. He said, 'But you are to be punished for not joining Zacco. So you are the Queen's man. They all doubted you.'

'The Grand Commander still doubts me,' said Nicholas. 'Diniz, you are not safe up here.'

'Why?' said a voice, speaking in Arabic. 'A spent catamite of yours would hardly excite me. Although he is pretty. Has he African ways?'

The emir had climbed the steps and stood on deck before them all. His smile was broad, the black moustache spreading, the dark eyes liquid. Nicholas said, 'Excuse him. He has only two legs.'

The emir's face hardly changed. It was the man behind him who stepped forward and swung his powerful mace. Although Nicholas flung his arm up, it brought him down to one knee. He rose, and replaced his innocuous smile. His hand, at his side, gripped Astorre's arm. Thomas growled. The emir stood, his head on one side. Then he said, 'Perhaps that is sufficient, for the moment. For serious intercourse, I prefer a wider audience, and land underfoot. Which is the fool who commands? This dotard? Ah, I remember him.' And switching to accented French, he began to list his demands.

He was obeyed. Officers and men unbuckled their armour and laid down their weapons. John le Grant in silence watched the guns deprived one by one of their ammunition and saw all their defences taken away. At the end, Tzani-bey came again and stood before the Grand Commander. 'And now I wish to see your cargo, and your passengers. The Genoese will come with me. You, my lord Napoleone. And our sorry young Fleming. The mace has opened your head. Does it pain you? Soon, I will cause you to forget it.'

'I am to come with you?' said Nicholas. He kept to Arabic.

Tzani-bey looked surprised. 'Of course. Don't you have women on board? I should like to see them.'

It was Primaflora, of course, whom he wanted to see. Katelina, on her sickbed, he hardly looked at. The merchants' women screamed when he entered the cabin: he took one by her bodice, pulled her close to examine her, and then flung her away. Primaflora he saw last of all, because she was seated behind all the rest, and hadn't stirred. The emir pushed the others aside and stood before her.

She looked up. Nicholas saw her eyes turn to himself, and then move and rest, with supreme boredom, on the emir. She was exquisitely gowned, and had a little pillow of lace on her lap. She said, 'Ah, the Mameluke who fingers women. May I undress for you? I should prefer not to have my gown torn.'

The smile left his face. The mace-holder stirred. Tzani-bey said, 'No. I do not require it. I have seen the goods.' And he passed on.

Napoleone Lomellini, pulled in his wake, dragged himself free and bowed, deeply and deliberately, to all the women. Nicholas, walking as slowly as he could, found Primaflora at his side. She said hastily, using Italian, 'What will they do?'

'Nothing to you, or the other passengers, or the ship. They'll take the cargo, and me and my company,' Nicholas said. 'From their point of view, I was on my way to fight for the Queen.'

'But you had no choice; you were under compulsion!' she said. 'Tell them! Tell them! The Usurper needs you more than the Queen does.'

'I don't think,' Nicholas said, 'that I could bring Tzani-bey to believe it. And if I did, the Order and the Genoese would never, I'm afraid, see that I stepped off this ship. You are here because of me, and I am so sorry. Go back to the Queen. She will forgive you. There will be someone courteous and wealthy waiting somewhere to be made happy.'

He smiled at her, even as they were roughly separated and he was hustled back to his place by the emir. Looking round once, he saw her standing still in the doorway to the women's chamber. Her face looked austere, and even frightened.

No one else urged him to save himself by crossing to Zacco. If they thought it likely he could, neither the Order nor the Genoese would let him or his company get to Salines alive, as he had told Primaflora. On the other hand, their execution would be quick, compared with anything Tzani-bey had in mind. He began to think as he walked. Salines. How could he extricate himself and the others at Salines? Or would the emir keep them at Salines? An audience, he had said. A public audience for what was to happen. Well, they would see.

The tour ended. Lomellini was removed, and Nicholas had time to wonder why the Genoese had been forced to be present and not, for example, the Grand Commander. But Zacco and the Order at Kolossi had some kind of working association, while the Genoese at Famagusta were Zacco's implacable enemies. The emir would enjoy displaying his power to Lomellini. Perhaps he would allow himself to go further. Lomellini doubtless suspected as much. He showed no fear, however, on parting from Nicholas but, again, gave his punctilious bow. 'Famagusta would have been the better for your assistance. I regret what has happened. I shall report, in my turn, how you bore yourself.'

'I hope you have a chance to do so, Ser Napoleone,' Nicholas said. Then he, in his turn, was taken off.

And now, at least he was among friends, for they threw him into the windowless apartment in the hold where they had already imprisoned Astorre and all the rest of his company. He had to guess as much from the voices, for lamps and candles were missing, and the only light came from the cracks round the locked door. 'Well, well,' said Tobie. 'They took away all the lights in case we burned the ship down, otherwise you'd be able to see how happy we are. What was all that about taking precautions?'

'This is just a test,' Nicholas said. 'They give us two days to learn the Koran, Loppe gets made a muezzin and they set us up with a harem apiece. Is there anything to eat?' It was not bravado. Danger made him feel hungry.

'Not yet,' said Astorre. 'Well, let's put our heads together. You told Zacco you'd serve him or nobody. Zacco said if you brought us to fight for the Queen, he would make sure that he stopped you and killed us. You thought that he mightn't. It seems that he will.'

'I suppose so,' said Nicholas.

'You suppose, man? He's intercepted us and the Queen's men all right. He's sent the Mamelukes to fire their damned guns at us. He's sent this emir, who's not your greatest admirer. And we've had threats and abuse and manhandling in private as well as in public. So all in all, we have to reach one conclusion. King Zacco is out for our blood. Yours and everybody's. Am I right?'

'I think you are,' Tobie said. 'I'm not complaining. Or not more than usual. We knew the risks, and it was the only way to leave Rhodes. So what now? How long do we have here at sea?'

He was speaking quite loudly, against the thud and creak of the vessel, because this was something that all their men ought to hear. When about to wring Tobie's neck, Nicholas always had to remember what a good doctor he was. Now Nicholas said, 'A day. Not more than two. The harbour's down in the south. After that, it depends whether the emir or Zacco wants to finish us off. The emir, as you see, is longing to indulge himself.'

'A nasty piece. I've fought against plenty like him,' said Captain Astorre. 'You too, eh, Master John? Now, why don't we break out and take the Mamelukes hostage? Or if we can't, the Commander might think of it.'

'I hope he doesn't,' Nicholas said. 'The emir will have gone back to his own ship by now, and I'm sure he meant what he said. If we make a false move, the men in those two galleys will burn us down to the water, no matter who is on board. The emir's soldiers go straight to Paradise, and the Celestial Court will also receive the captain of Famagusta and a number of Carlotta's favourite officers, to King Zacco's great sorrow.'

'So we just walk ashore to our fate?' Tobie said. 'And the rest? The boy? They think he's yours. That won't save him.'

'It depends,' Nicholas said, 'what you want to save him from. I wonder what Simon would say? Death before dishonour?'

'I suppose he would,' Tobie said, 'if he got the chance. Myself, I'm considerably drawn to dishonour.'

'You're thirty-two years old,' Nicholas said. 'Senile, bald, and you talk too much. You're past dishonour. Consider survival as an alternative. We land at Salines, and three possible things will then happen. Let's discuss them.'

He could feel the rustle of hope. He tried to feel hopeful himself.

It was only a game. It was only a case of thinking out the next move. Of thinking what you might do if you hated anyone as much as Tzani-bey hated Niccolò vander Poele. And, of course, vice versa.

Chapter 22

TWENTY-FOUR hours later the company of Nicholas arrived, still with their skins whole, at the harbour of Salines in Cyprus. On the way, they had been given food but no light, and had spent the latter part of the journey for the most part in sleep. The Mamelukes who herded them up into the stormy, dazzling daylight carried maces, and would answer no questions. There was no sign of the women, or the merchants. On the other hand, there was no sign either of distress or confusion. The Rhodian shipmaster, still under guard at the poop, looked relieved at the sight of Nicholas, and made a slight sign which seemed to convey that so far, nothing worse had occurred. Then Nicholas with Astorre, the men and his officers were ranged by the deck-rail, and shivering, could see what they had come to.

The salt lake which gave Salines its name was not in view from this, the only south-eastern port left to Zacco. Below a line of unremarkable hills rose an abrupt, minor height with the remains of an acropolis on it. Beneath the hill stood the triple domes of the church, next to the low roofs of a primitive hospice and the ruined stones of a tower. A two-storey building some distance off could have been a tavern, or an office, or both. Beside it was a scatter of huts of the kind used by porters, or boatmen or fishermen. A track crossed the flat land patched with palms to the shore, where had been erected a couple of warehouses and a short timber jetty. A number of boats lay on coarse sand.

Since the Genoese had taken Famagusta, the bastard King had no real harbours but Salines and Limassol, and none at all where a ship could lie up in all winds. You would think, none the less, that he would have tried to improve what he had. John le Grant said, 'The Saracens burned all these shores forty years ago, and they've seen plenty of landings since then. All the good houses and the market are over that hill at Aliki. Safer, you see, from marauders.'

He spoke, as he always did, in factual terms, and with an

engineer's eye. John le Grant was familiar with Cyprus: the others knew less about it than Nicholas did. Yet they had volunteered, aware of the risk. The risk embodied in the two powerful galleys now at anchor beside them, from one of which a skiff had already put off for the shore. In the chill, clear air, Nicholas could see the brilliant clothes of the emir in the stern of the boat; and on shore, a cavalcade of armed men trotting forward to dismount and greet him. Astorre, of the single, far-sighted eye, said, 'See that troop? That's the Lusignan banner. A lean, swarthy fellow in front. Would that be the King?'

'No,' said Nicholas. He remembered the Sicilian Rizzo di Marino, and the King's quiet bedchamber in Nicosia, and receiving news of his army in Rhodes. He had thought, then, that di Marino distrusted him. He said, 'It might be a lord, bringing orders.'

'Such as whether to tear our livers out here, or wait till suppertime?' said Tobie.

'Something like that,' Nicholas said. He was listening to a flourish of trumpets from the shore. It had been a signal. Men ran. Almost immediately, their own ship's boat was lowered and Nicholas and his officers were thrust down the boarding-steps into it. As their skiff set off for the land, a second boat in its turn took its place at the foot of the gangway, and Astorre's soldiers could be seen preparing to file down and board it. Tobie said, 'Well. He keeps his word, this bold robber king. He said he'd make us sorry if we fought for the Queen, and he didn't mean just you and me. Where's his lair? Nicosia?'

They were near the shore. On the jetty stood the emir Tzani-bey with a line of horses and metal-clad men; the knight Rizzo di Marino, if it had been he, was no longer present. John le Grant said, 'They'll take us somewhere nearer, to start with. Maybe to finish with. The Lusignan have a house at Aradippou. There's the monastery of St George. Or there's a half-ruined castle at Kiti which the Bastard filched from one of his sister's supporters. We could spend the night there.'

'I'd rather not,' Tobie said. 'And if this is Salines. I don't want it on my next egg, I can tell you. What's the church?'

'It's called after St Lazarus. He settled here when he rose from the dead.'

'Good,' said Tobie. 'Did he leave any notes?'

Nicholas had never been to Salines before. He had never been anywhere on Cyprus except the Cape of the Cats, to which the Venetians had brought him, and the adjacent land and estates of Kolossi Castle. And, of course, Nicosia, where he had promised a young man called Zacco his service or his neutrality. Nicholas avoided John le Grant's blue, naked stare. He suspected that John le Grant, of them all, knew what Zacco was like.

Then the skiff jounced at the jetty, and Nicholas met the different stare, equally appraising, of the emir. The Mameluke's cloak boomed, and his helmet-brush panted like bellows. The emir said, 'Did you think to meet death here? I am not greedy. One should savour a banquet. You ride with me to Kiti.'

'And the men?' Nicholas said. The jetty, when he gained it, seemed to sway like the sea.

'They will march there,' said the emir. 'There is no haste for them. They will be taken care of quite simply.' Below his cloak, he wore an Islamic coat over his brigandine. Beneath the playful threat of his manner there lay something both foreign and chilling.

Nicholas said, 'I prefer to stay with my soldiers.'

The emir surveyed him. 'We are stating preferences? It is a march of four miles to the castle. Your captain will make it on foot, with your one hundred men. We have mounts for you and your comrades. Your doctor. Your engineer. Your charming mistress. Your delectable catamite.' Between the tongues of his helm, he was sneering.

Nicholas said, 'Have I mistaken you? The merchants and ladies were to go free?'

'Oh, they will,' said Tzani-bey. 'The merchants and their cattle will stay on board and disembark later. Only the chosen are invited to Kiti. You and your company, for reasons you know. And the rest as spectators. Every execution requires witnesses, does it not?'

'To be carried out by you, my lord emir?' said Nicholas. At his back, another skiff was arriving.

'By me?' said the Mameluke. 'Of course, I should have no objection, but it is usual, when injury has been done, for the injured party to take his own satisfaction. No, I am not your executioner. I have been ordered to take you to Kiti. King James waits for you there. For you, and your men, and your fellow-travellers.'

His eyes, full of malice, held those of Nicholas and then moved behind, to the boat just arrived at the jetty. Nicholas turned. In it, stiff-backed and stern, was the Grand Commander of Cyprus with Napoleone Lomellini seated beside him. In the forepart of the skiff lay Katelina van Borselen, her eyes closed, her face drawn with exhaustion. Primaflora knelt at her side, half supporting her. Behind, their faces pallid and anxious, were her serving-woman and her young nephew Diniz.

Nicholas turned back to the emir. He said in Arabic, 'You exceed your orders. The King your *ustadh* has no concern with these ladies. And one is ill.'

'You can read my lord's mind from Salines?' said the emir. 'He has heard of the painted lady Primaflora. Have I not heard you claim that the lady belongs to him? And the other, as you see, requires to be taken to shore. The journey below deck has discommoded her.'

'But when she has recovered?' Nicholas said. 'Katelina van Borselen is a merchant, and related to princes. The King would be unwise to abuse her.'

'As to that,' the emir said, 'no doubt the King will make up his own mind. If so valuable, she would seem a good hostage. Meanwhile the St Lazarus hospice may care for her. The boy and your other woman are summoned to Kiti. Do you presume, a dead man, to argue?'

Nicholas was silent. His bonds cut, he was pushed with Tobie and John to the horses, and saw Lomellini and de Magnac also mounted. While the cortège assembled, Katelina was lifted ashore. She was carried past Nicholas on a litter, her woman trotting beside. As the sick girl came abreast, her eyes opened. Nicholas said, 'Get better quickly. We are not far away.'

Her lips were white. She said, hardly breathing. 'You threaten me?'

Before he could reply, the litter had gone. Primaflora's voice said, 'Let her go. The nuns will care for her. Will you look at that fool of a boy?' She stood, preparing to mount, and gazing behind at a tumult. At its core could be seen the hatless head and flailing arms of Diniz Vasquez, attempting to force his way after the litter. Before Nicholas could speak, a mailed fist was raised and the boy subsided, unconscious. 'I have to say,' said Primaflora, 'that I have sometimes thought that force works better than words in that family. Now they will have to tie him on a horse. Where are they taking us?'

'Not far. To a Lusignan castle at Kiti. The King is there. Don't be afraid,' Nicholas said. He tried to make his voice light and comforting.

She flushed. She said, 'Afraid! The King won't trouble a courtesan. At worst, he'll use me as a means of taunting his sister. But you! What will you do? Whatever you say, Lomellini and de Magnac will swear you meant to fight for Carlotta. They will give you no chance to change to Zacco's side. You must escape.'

'And my men?' Nicholas said. They had begun moving. He could see the emir turn his head and begin to ride over.

She said, 'It is you I am thinking of.' Then, after a moment, 'Would they kill them? You think they would. And of course, you wouldn't leave them.'

Nicholas said, 'None of us can leave. Whoever escapes, the rest would be punished.'

'And so?' she said. The emir had arrived, and had taken her reins.

'I don't know,' Nicholas said. He had no chance to console her, even if he could have thought of something to say. The emir led her away, and he rode in silence to his meeting with Zacco.

By the second hour of their incarceration, Tobie had been five times to the latrine and even Astorre, most doughty of captives, had taken to pacing their prison; a room small enough for six persons.

Their arrival at the palace of Kiti had taken place after dark. Even Nicholas, Tobie and John, the first to dismount, had seen little more than a plank bridge, a small courtyard, and a dark building of several storeys. The ground was deep in mud, leading Tobie to observe that Noah's great-grandson, after whom the place had been named, might have been advised to bring the Ark with him. Diniz Vasquez, the fourth to arrive, had seen nothing at all, being still bound to his horse, and half-conscious. Diniz shared their small prison. Where Primaflora had been taken, or the Grand Commander or the Genoese, they had no means of knowing.

By the time their hundred soldiers arrived, the moon had risen behind racing clouds. The news that the men were here, housed and settled was brought by Astorre and Thomas when they in turn were marched into their chamber. By then, Diniz was awake, pale and frowning, but restored enough to put up a fight when armed men burst through the door and herded them off, without speech, to a bath-house.

It seemed curious, as Tobie said, that the Bastard required them to meet their God purified. Being men of war, they made nothing, as Diniz did, of being stripped and thrown into hot water. When they emerged, they were given clean drawers, nothing else. Then they were returned to their prison, which had once been a place to house valuables, possessing barred windows and doors, but nothing of comfort except a brazier. John le Grant said, 'Of course, if Nicholas could talk, he could tell us what to expect of this Zacco.'

Nicholas, whose normal high spirits could elate a platoon marching over a cliff-top, had been perplexingly dumb since Salines. On the journey, speech had been discouraged. Since, he had sat, hugging his knees and keeping his own rigid counsel. The situation failed to please Diniz, the ache in whose head was compounded by feelings of fear and inadequacy. He stopped pacing the floor and went to stand, his arms folded, over Nicholas. He said, 'She was sick, and you did nothing to save her! You took your own woman and left her!'

Nicholas said, 'You did all you could. Your aunt couldn't have travelled. They have no use for her, Diniz. They'll let her go. The monks will see to that.'

'Who feeds the monks and defends them?' the young Portuguese said.

'The Lord God of St Lazarus,' Nicholas said. 'Or so I should like to think. For the rest, you will have to rely on me. As well as I can, I shall protect her.'

'As you protected my father,' said Diniz.

'With you, I succeeded,' said Nicholas. 'Let me say one thing only. I have met the King before. When he summons us, let me speak. When I finish, say whatever you please, if you're not satisfied.'

Diniz said, 'Why should he listen to me, when he's heard what you have to say?'

'Why?' said Nicholas. 'Because he has eyes, like the Mameluke.'

No one spoke. The boy, flinching, lowered his eyes. Astorre coughed. You bastard, thought Tobie. How do you know? How do you know how to get your own way? In the corner, Thomas scowled, as he usually did when matters went beyond his understanding. Only John le Grant remained looking at Nicholas and Nicholas, feeling his gaze, lifted his head and returned it. The engineer said, in his ordinary voice. 'Someone is coming to fetch us.'

The professionals jumped to their feet: Astorre with his puckered scars and teak belly and muscular calves; Thomas with his carpet of hair, throat to belly-button. Pink as marzipan, Tobie was slower, his fuzz of hair dispensing slow teardrops. Le Grant waited until Nicholas stirred, and then rose at the same time. With them both rose Diniz, perforce, with the grasp of Nicholas under his elbow.

The door opened on a glitter of arms, but all that entered were clothes. Conveyed on a succession of legs there arrived shirts and pourpoints and doublets, hose and slippers, hats and robes. Last to promenade was a man in the robes of a chamberlain. He said, 'The High Court requires that all who attend be fittingly dressed. Prepare yourselves for the summons.'

A suitable remark rose in Tobie's throat and evaporated at a look from Nicholas. No. If the King wanted puppets, he should have them. But at least, he would get puppets with voices.

They dressed, with dry jokes, prosaically exchanging what fitted less well for better. Nicholas, the largest of all, was best suited with a mantle that might have been made for him. But then, the King had met Nicholas. That was why they were here. Tobie said, 'I need –'

'You haven't time,' Astorre said. 'They're coming for us.'

On this occasion, the doors opened only on soldiers: a double file lining a passage, and established on the stairs beyond that, where sconces flickered on feathers and steel. At their head was the Mameluke emir. He smiled. He said, 'Now is the appointed time. The King waits. You will follow.'

They had not far to go. The castle had once been more extensive,

and the repairs had been inexpensive and hasty. They passed
blackened walls, where the wind moaned and wailed through distant fissures, and the torch-flames caught their breath and burned
yellow, rippling. Once a breach opened black at their feet, the
broken flags marked by a guard rail. But the hall doors, when they
reached them, were intact, although the timbers were cracked, and
the coat of arms bruised, as by a mallet. Tzani-bey struck the doors
and they opened. Blinding light fell upon Nicholas and, dazzled,
he paused.

'You falter?' said the emir. 'You hear the sound of the saw, of
the pincers heating? Take your courage. Think of your men. Step
to meet your fate bravely.' He had spoken in Arabic. Smiling still,
he pushed past Nicholas over the threshold and, advancing, took
his stance upon a square of Turkey carpet. He bowed. 'My lord
King. Niccolò vander Poele, Knight of the Sword of Carlotta, and
his mercenaries.'

It was too late to be affected by malice. It was too late for
anything he could count on, and certainly too late to remember the
moment when he had promised himself that he was no longer a
member of a community. When he had told himself he had taken
charge of an arsenal in – what was it? – *the opening moves of a
perfect war game.*

He walked into a small hall which had lost its timbers, but whose
brilliant lights fell on costly wall-hangings, and on the deep-dyed
velvets and silks of the courtiers who stood on either side. He knew
some of their names. There was Rizzo di Marino, ridden ahead as
his harbinger, still carrying the cloak he had worn at Salines. Beside
him stood a man in Archbishop's robes: William Goneme, the
King's wily Cypriot counsellor. Here surely was Conella Morabit,
the other Sicilian knight. And men the Venetians had told him of:
Zaplana and Galimberto; Salviati and Costanzo. And even, at the
foot of the throne, the page Jorgin, who had helped tend his hurts
from the last time he had found himself in Mameluke hands, by
Zacco's orders. Without raising his eyes, Nicholas stepped the
required number of paces and stopped short of the throne, as his
friends halted behind him. He heard someone – le Grant or Tobie –
draw a short breath. In Astorre's shadow, the boy Diniz was silent.

Nicholas looked up at the King, and the remembered eyes
looked into his.

He had prepared none of his companions for the beauty they
would see on the carved seat on its dais. They looked up as he did
to a golden king in the flower of his youth, the splendid line of his
body wrapped in sable and velvet and gold. Above the robes, the
brown, careless hair was now schooled under a hat bound about
the brows with fine velvet. Next to its ruby-pinned fall, the fine
skin kept the glow of high summer, and the glow of the autumn

showed in the clear hazel eyes. Showed, then died. James de Lusignan said, 'Kneel.'

He was not looking at Nicholas. After a moment, the emir Tzani-bey, at his side, sank to one knee. His face was blank.

The King's eyes turned to Nicholas. The King said, 'You have been ill-treated?'

Nicholas looked at Tzani-bey. 'No, my lord,' he said. He heard Diniz move sharply behind him and felt, rather than saw, Astorre grip the boy's arm.

The sunburned face of the King remained perfectly still. The King said, 'But your eyes say, *Not yet.*'

Nicholas waited. Then he said, 'And my intelligence also, my lord. We have set out to serve you, and have been told to expect torture and death. I will not beg my life from a Mameluke. I would lay it, with my explanation, at the feet of the King.'

No one spoke. Slowly, the King turned his head, his brows rising. The kneeling emir lifted his voice. 'My lord. While on the ship they were bound. You desired it. Once on land, they were freed. You required it. They have been housed, bathed and clothed, as you requested. More than that you did not ask.'

'Why,' said the King. 'Do you not know our mind, even from so far as Salines? You carried out my instructions, you say. Did we instruct you to warn them of my anger?'

The dark face of the emir conveyed humility. 'The man Niccolò, my lord, leads a considerable army. Unless chastened, he might have attacked us. Further, had I been mild, the Queen's men on the ship would have turned on him. You asked especially, my lord, that he should appear in good health.'

The King lifted his gaze and ran it over Nicholas. 'We see,' he said, 'that he has a self-inflicted wound to the head. Shall we seek corroboration? We understand Messer Napoleone Lomellini is in the castle. Have him brought.'

A servant left. The room remained in absolute silence. The King allowed his eyes to travel over the faces of the strangers before him. He did not give the emir leave to rise, or look again at Nicholas. There was a pause. Then the broad figure of the Genoese entered, wearing again the rich clothes and rings of his land costume. He held himself stiffly, and bowed.

'Messer Napoleone,' said the King, his voice sweet. 'We have met. You have heard, perhaps, that we are not always lenient, but we try to be just. You are captain of Famagusta, a city which is in arms against us. Were you not in our grasp, we have no doubt that you would return to that city, and would immediately continue your campaign of resistance against us. Are we right?'

'I am a citizen of Genoa,' said Lomellini. 'And Famagusta belongs to the Republic. Yes, I should return to my duty if freed.'

'We expected no less. It is not a post we should choose, these coming months. We are doing you no great service in telling you that, upon certain considerations, you will be allowed to return to it. You are a prisoner, Messer Napoleone, and the convention is that prisoners should pay for their freedom. We require to receive from you or your Republic a sum equal to twice the purchase price of a fit, well-trained Mameluke. The lord emir will be able to tell us the current rate. On payment of that, you will be free to go where you please, including the city of Famagusta. Is this agreeable?'

The captain of Famagusta had flushed. He said, 'The lord king is generous. I accept, with gratitude.'

'Are we generous?' said the King. 'We think you will come to doubt it. Now, another matter. You see here Messer Niccolò and his men?'

'I do,' said Lomellini. He frowned.

The young man on the throne settled himself, as if in enjoyment. 'Messer Niccolò and his army have been in Rhodes. When found, they were on their way to Kyrenia to fight for our sister. This is true?'

'It is true,' said Lomellini.

'You murmur,' said the King. 'Is it true?'

'Yes, it is so,' said Lomellini. He kept his eyes on the King.

'And,' said the King, 'they entered the service of the lady Carlotta of their own accord, and without outside compulsion?'

Lomellini's face was still flushed, but his square jaw was firm. He said, 'The man Niccolò received a knighthood and swore an oath of loyalty to Queen Carlotta. There was no compulsion. Ask your emir. He was in no doubt which side this army would fight on.'

'We are asking our emir,' said James de Lusignan. 'My lord Tzani-bey, you may stand.'

The Mameluke rose, not quite hiding his stiffness, and divided his black stare between the King and the Genoese. He said, 'I made pretence of dealing harshly with the Fleming, my lord King. I admit to causing some injury. It was necessary. As you see, any suspicion of leniency would have been dangerous.'

The eyes of the Genoese switched from the King to the emir, and then rested on Nicholas. He said, 'This man is the Queen's. I have told you. If you think anything else, you are mistaken.'

Zacco smiled. 'We are so often mistaken. We are fortunate in having men around us to tell us the truth. At times, even a half-truth may content us for the moment. My lord emir, we think we have detained you long enough. We have heard what you have to say. We suggest that on another occasion, you heed our instructions more carefully. You may leave us.'

The Mameluke bowed, stepping backwards; and again; and again; before he turned and left the hall. But as he passed Nicholas, he sought his eyes and, for a moment, held them boldly with something in them not far short of derision. The door closed at his back, and men stirred.

On the throne, the King had also moved. With the robe discarded behind him, he stood on the dais for a moment, and then ran down the steps like an athlete. Before he reached the carpet, Nicholas knelt. The King stopped and touched his shoulder, keeping him there. Then he turned his head to Lomellini. 'Ser Napoleone, you serve your Republic as best you can, and we do not blame you for the lies you have told. But it happens that we know of the oath sworn to our sister, and the circumstances which forced Ser Niccolò and his army to leave Rhodes to sail to Kyrenia. We know because a message was sent us by Ser Niccolò himself assuring us of his loyalty and asking our help to bring him to us.

'This we have done.' He looked down, and spoke directly to Nicholas. 'We made a mistake, sending the emir. He was officious. He was afraid, for your own sake, to appear as your friend. So you were not told that the Florentine ship had arrived with your letter; or that Rizzo here has been haunting the Rhodes seas awaiting you. If you cannot forgive the lord emir, I trust you will accept our apologies.'

Nicholas smiled, his eyes on the ground. He said, 'With all my heart, my lord King. It was, at the same time, an unforgettable journey.'

'A fearful one, we can see. For, of course,' the King said, 'had you truly set out for Kyrenia, we should have sent to kill you all. As it is, you may stand.'

Nicholas stood. Of the two, he was slightly taller. He felt he had no advantage. 'As it is,' Zacco repeated, 'you have presented us with a ship full of merchandise, which we shall certainly take. Of arms, which we shall be glad of. There are merchants, we believe, with their ladies, and officers of my sister's whom we have a mind to free and have taken, under suitable escort, to enter the gates of Kyrenia or of Famagusta, as they may wish. And, since we respect the Order, and the guard it keeps on the seas, we shall send their ship back to Rhodes, with its master, its soldiers, its seamen. Do these provisions seem fair?'

'They seem generous, lord,' Nicholas said. 'And the ladies?'

The clear eyes did not alter. 'The lady Primaflora is behind you,' James de Lusignan said. 'We have spoken to her. We have sent word also to the sick woman, Katelina van Borselen, who lies at St Lazarus. We have decreed that the lady Primaflora be returned to join her mistress our sister at Rhodes. The demoiselle from Flanders will stay.'

Zacco, the unreadable, the chameleon. Nicholas stood, every muscle relaxed, every sense as alert as if hunting a boar. Behind him, moving slowly, as in regal procession, Primaflora came to stand at his side: he smelled her scent and saw her face, paler than ever, with a line between her brows. She said in a low voice, 'You have deceived me. You let me agonise over your fate, and you knew Zacco would stand your friend, for you had warned him. I cannot forgive you.'

'The lady berates you,' said the King. He looked amused. 'Indeed, she deserved your confidence if, as she says, she had given up all to leave our sister and join her fate to yours. Fortunately, our sister does not know of her true defection, and will welcome her back.'

'My lord, the lady Primaflora has my confidence,' Nicholas said. 'I believed that my dispatch to the King had been lost. The behaviour of the emir confirmed it. I saw no point in raising false hopes. We have had a voyage of despair, in which the lady has suffered greatly. I hope to obtain her forgiveness. If I have been less than well treated, I could imagine no better recompense than to have the lady stay with me, as she intended.'

The intelligent eyes almost smiled. 'What is this we hear? You beg that both of your gentle conquests may stay? We think that would be greed.'

Nicholas said, 'The lady here has long been my companion, but the other belongs to the west, to her husband. Perhaps the lord King would think it a kindness to send Katelina van Borselen home, along with her nephew.'

'Perhaps. Eventually,' James de Lusignan said. 'We see a time may come when we may refuse you little. In this instance, however, we have decided to dismiss the lady Primaflora, and she will sail immediately for Rhodes. As for the boy and the lady, we have it in mind to hold them for ransom. Until it comes, the matron Katelina van Borselen will remain in Cyprus, well protected and honoured, you may be sure. As for the boy, he shall be our page. Or yours, if you wish it. He is charming.'

'I am no one's page,' said Diniz Vasquez.

The King looked at him. He lifted a finger and the boy was pushed forward and stood. Zacco tilted his head. At length, 'No,' he said. 'You are no one's page. You are a prisoner. That being so, you bear yourself as a gentleman should, and expect and receive, I trust, courtesy in return. Do not be afraid. I do not shame those in my charge.' He turned his head. 'And now, I think we should see the Grand Commander.'

The boy, flushed, was pulled back. Primaflora, making to speak, suddenly made a small gesture and gave way to the attendant who, gently but firmly, took her arm to remove her. Nicholas took a step after and felt, light and warm, the King's touch on one of his shoulders. It hardened. 'You will wait,' Zacco said. A moment later a grey-haired man, robed and hatted in black, was being ushered in, with a shadow behind him.

The King turned, dropping his arm. Nicholas remained where he was, in the full view of the newcomer whose eyes narrowed in angry suspicion. Primaflora had gone. The King said, 'My lord Commander of Cyprus. You thought to bring an army to the lady our sister. Instead, as you see, a brave and able man has tricked you into fetching us the soldiers we need. You have nothing with which to reproach yourself. Your vessel and all of your company are to be taken unharmed where they wish. We brought you here to say more. It is not our intention to make war on the Order, or on the brethren of the Order who live and work here in Cyprus. If you wish to pass to Kolossi, you are free to do so; and we ourselves shall give you an escort of honour. Tonight, you will feast as our guest. Tomorrow, you have only to make your wishes known. Does this please you?'

'My lord is generous,' said Louis de Magnac. He spoke the words to the King, but Nicholas felt the heat of his gaze. De Magnac muttered, 'Knave and mountebank! Murderer!'

'I am a mercenary,' Nicholas said. 'You gave me, once, a good servant.'

De Magnac bared his teeth. 'He told me your every move, boy,' he said.

'I know just what he told you,' said Nicholas. 'And I think it is time he came back.'

The Grand Commander, consumed with serious anger, detected some impertinence, but brushed it aside with a snort. His African servant said, 'Sir?'

The fellow had stepped out from behind the Commander. A magnificent negro, the best he'd ever had, and wearing a doublet from the Queen's tailor. The Grand Commander barked 'Lopez?'

'Sir?' said the negro again. He had walked in front of de Magnac. And the question was directed at Nicholas.

Nicholas smiled. He said to Zacco, 'Our private spy with the Order. His own idea. It was he who lodged my message to you with the Florentine ship calling at Rhodes. May I present the major domo of my household? And the rest of my officers are unknown to you. And one hundred more, waiting outside.'

'We shall meet them all,' Zacco said. 'But we have not told you yet what we think of you. Come.'

He put out both hands. His fingers round those of Nicholas were warm and hard and threateningly strong. He leaned forward and Nicholas felt the press of his lips on either cheek and then, deep and hot, on his brow. The King tightened his clasp at arm's length.

'Sweet Niccolò, welcome,' he said. 'You have brought us your mind, and your loyalty. Accept in return the heart and soul of a friend.'

Five pairs of eyes watched that, with choler. Six, if you counted those of Diniz, the boy. Restraint had to be observed among the shareholders and partners of the House of Niccolò until, after a supper that did indeed deserve the title of feast, they were relinquished unprotected, unguarded, unwatched in the palatial room which was their new sleeping apartment.

Nicholas was not present.

'Is anyone astonished?' commented Tobie. He rounded on le Grant. 'You knew about Zacco, you snake. You never said he was young. Nor did Nicholas. I'm company doctor to Cupid.'

'I knew,' said Astorre. He had taken his clothes off, and was admiring them. 'Stood to reason. Our boy doesn't want another woman to answer to. Our boy wants some fun.'

'Well, he's lost the woman he had,' said John le Grant. 'Primaflora's on her way back to Carlotta. He has his own way, has Zacco, with the competition.'

'Good riddance,' said Thomas.

'Well, that depends,' Tobie said. 'Have I got it right? Following some artful footwork between the eighth and ninth courses, it's been agreed that the dazzling Diniz is no longer to be anyone's page, but will be found an occupation, until ransomed, in Nicosia. Likewise the gentle Katelina, whom the King will confide to his very own mother. Meanwhile, you and I and the rest of us start earning our keep as the saviours of Cyprus. What I want to know is, shall we be accompanied by Zacco and Nicholas?'

'In spirit, I'm sure,' said the engineer. 'I'd rather know, to tell the truth, where Tzani-bey al-Ablak will be. That dressing-down our emir got from the King? I don't believe it. You look at what happened. No one told us Loppe's message got through, and the Mamelukes treated us as if it hadn't. Damn them, they wanted us scared.'

'What?' said Astorre.

Tobie said, 'I recognised the quotation. The King had an informer at Salines.'

'At Salines?' said le Grant with some grimness. 'I'll give you a wager that, from the moment our ship was waylaid, that same King was behind all that happened. That bullying wasn't planned by the Mamelukes. It's your bonny Zacco's trick. Fear as a weapon.'

'And love,' Tobie said. 'An arsenal to beware of. Do you think Nicholas has seen through it? Or is bewitched? Or isn't bewitched, and will yearn after Primaflora and arrange, with ingenious traps, to bring about the deaths of Diniz and his much-hated aunt Kate-lina?'

'Nonsense,' said Astorre. He was under his blanket. 'We're here to fight. He likes fighting.'

'I think,' said John le Grant, 'that that is what Tobie is saying. And we ought none of us to forget. He likes meddling in business as well. Whatever is selling in Cyprus, you can expect Nicholas to corner it soon.'

Tobie grunted, and rolled into bed. 'It looks to me,' said the doctor, 'as if Nicholas has been offered it free. But I'm damned sure it's not a monopoly.'

Chapter 23

TO BE ALONE and sick among enemies wouldn't trouble a man: it should not trouble, therefore, a woman of twenty-two years with a bastard son and a profligate husband. Nevertheless Katelina van Borselen came to consciousness to lie, her eyes closed, struggling with a remembrance of fear. Fear, and an enemy's voice saying, 'We are not far away.' The voice of Nicholas. Claes.

Where had she heard it? On board ship, she supposed. Even here, in her cabin, since she had never left it. She recalled the storm on leaving Rhodes, and some of the subsequent misery. She remembered the small shock of finding herself in the care of the courtesan Primaflora whose attentions, unhesitating and detached, might (conceivably) have been those of a humane-minded mistress of Nicholas, or (if Fortune were kind) those of a spy of the Queen, concerned for the health of an ally. Katelina knew that Nicholas was being sent, heavily monitored, to fight for Carlotta. She understood, but at the time hardly cared, that there had been a sea battle. She didn't know what had resulted. But she was presently awake, and in bed, and unmolested. So, whatever the outcome, the ship was proceeding calmly enough on its way, and—she was recovering. And if Nicholas was near, she would, somehow, protect herself. She dozed. Her hearing brought her the slight, rumpled beat of a moth, and the kindred fizzings of sound that suggested that it was night, and that candles were burning. Or lamps. On a ship, as a rule, there were lamps.

She was not on a ship. The bed beneath her was still. Moreover, in winter the light drew no moths. Not yet alarmed, Katelina opened her eyes. She was in a firelit room, well proportioned and furnished, whose casement transmitted the paleness of a cool and overcast day. The chamber was warm, quiet and clean, and apparently empty. A convent. A hospice. The home of Genoese well-wishers, perhaps. A haven far away, she could hope, from the

threatening presence of Nicholas. She closed her lids and lay thinking.

Always she had hated the sea, whether sailing to Scotland or
south with her husband to Portugal. At sea, she lost Simon's
attention. On land, she had worn him down with her passionate
desire for a second child. At first, he had partnered her avidly.
Then, bit by bit, he had resumed the old ways of debauchery
which came so easily to a man of his looks. A system of barren
debauchery, she had discovered, which had never been known to
bear harvest.

Of course, women had ways to check pregnancy. But Katelina
came to understand, too, that the women Simon patronised were
not unwilling to bear to her beautiful husband, and that it was a
surprise and a disappointment that they did not. Observing his
persistent philandering, she slowly realised that her husband's
virility was the point at issue; that their common infertility must be
in origin his; and that the blight, whatever it was, must have struck
him since his first fruitful marriage. They never discussed it. For
him, such a flaw was inconceivable, and she gave thanks, every
day, for his vanity. But for that, he might ask himself, and then
her, who had fathered the heir she had given him. At the thought,
her lips parted and, abruptly, she stirred in bed and tried to change
her position.

'She is not cured, sister,' a man's voice announced crossly. It
was thick, and used adequate Greek-flavoured French. 'We do not
want her corpse here. Send her to Famagusta to die.' Hastily,
Katelina re-opened her eyes.

Against the light, the speaker looked bulky: a grizzled man in
golden-badged velvet, his jowls infilled by untidy whiskers which
he scratched with one nail, looking down at her. Beyond him in a
painted panel-back chair was the person he spoke to: an auburn-
haired girl, who moved a fan like a wing between her jewels and
the flash of the firelight.

The fan whickered and stopped; the buzzing breath produced
bolts of invective. 'She moves?' The young woman rose to her feet.
'She is awake? Depart, idiot. She will speak to me. Seasickness
kills no one. Especially not herring-fed Flemings.'

The man's form disappeared and was replaced by that of the
speaker who bestowed herself, with some briskness, at her bedside.
She leaned forward. Seen close at hand, the woman's face no
longer seemed young. The hair beneath the stiff headdress was
dyed, the lips and eyelids skilfully coloured, the skin of the straight
nose and high cheekbones more pink than in nature. The woman
said, 'You are Katelina van Borselen, whose husband Simon loves
Genoese, and co-trades with the Vasquez in Portugal. Do you
know where you are?'

The voice, the words, the manner told her she was in no friendly palace or hospice. 'With his enemies,' Katelina said. Her head ached. She lifted herself, as best she could, on her pillows.

'You are weak, but good food will cure you. After all,' said the woman, 'we cannot ransom you if you are dead.'

Ransom! She heard the word, and could make nothing of it. In desperation, she had to prevaricate. 'We are not landed people.'

Where the eyebrows were drawn, the skin hoisted. 'According to Markios my brother, the van Borselen are married to royalty. And your husband's father, I hear, is a magnate. Between them, they might afford to redeem you and your nephew?'

Katelina said, 'I am on the island of Cyprus?'

'It is better,' said the woman, 'than being in Cairo. Yes. Your ship fell into Cypriot hands. You were landed at Salines. You have been brought from Salines to the capital. You, demoiselle, are in Nicosia, in the hands of James, a Christian monarch. You will remain until your ransom is settled. You will not find us harsh jailers. Here are ladies of culture, who serve us and tend the royal nursery. The King's children are well-reared and biddable. When he takes a wife, they will never disgrace him. You have given your husband many fine progeny, I imagine?'

'I have a son,' said Katelina. The woman knew that already: she sensed it. Knew her to be twenty-two, and productive of a single accouchement, and ageing.

'My commiserations,' said the woman. 'But your husband, perhaps, will have others. He will wish, no doubt, to reclaim you. Until he responds you are welcome to stay, as I have said, with the ladies. Or I can offer a cell with the Clares?'

A cloister, or the suite of the royal mistresses and their bastards. Katelina felt herself flushing. She said coldly, 'A convent would be to my taste. Where, may I ask, are those who were with me on shipboard?'

'The Genoese, the merchants, the Athletes of Christ? All dispersed without harm, and their ship sent back to Rhodes. As I said, our King is Christian and merciful. The trader Niccolò and his mischievous warband faced, of course, a different destiny.'

Katelina sat up. The fire glowed red and hot. Her skin was damp; a trickle of sweat divided her breasts. She drew her nightrobe closed and smoothed its edges. She said, 'So I should suppose. He sold himself to the Queen for a knighthood.'

'Foolish knave,' the woman said. 'But it was, of course, the simplest way to leave safely. Now he is here, as he planned. King James has reinvested him in the same Order, and gifted him rights and acres which more than exceed Carlotta's dream charters. Madame suffers?'

Katelina felt suddenly dizzy. The sweat on her skin had turned chill, and her tormentor's face blurred like a junket. She said, 'Nicholas and his men are alive?'

'Of course,' emitted the shimmering features. 'The young man sent a message from Rhodes. It promised his service. It let the King meet his ship; seize its cargo. You admire Carlotta, it seems. That young scoundrel does not.'

She felt as sick as she had done at sea. *We are not far away*. It was true. He had threatened her. She said, 'My nephew Diniz. Where is he?'

The pink, liquid face made a tolerant smile. 'Where he can be useful. In the fields, it may be, digging and burying.'

'*Burying?*'

'Digging pits and burying hoppers. The young and eggs of the locust. Unless they die, the crops will be ruined.' She made a pause, and perhaps an assessment, and perhaps a decision. She said, 'You have never seen this? The eggs are gathered in handfuls. They swell and crackle, madame. They fight to fabricate legs and wings and fly in the face of their handler. Peasants fear to collect them. We save the task for our captives. You. Your nephew. Your servants. You wish to ask me anything else?'

In the voice was deliberate malice. Who had told this woman her weakness? Her maidservant? Katelina felt the blood drain from her skin, and a shivering fit overcame her. She said, 'I don't understand what has happened.'

'To the locusts?' said the woman, amused, 'Or no. The Ascension of Niccolò? Of course, he was treated harshly on board. Had he not been, neither he nor his men would have escaped the Genoese swords, or the Order. A brave schemer, that Niccolò. Indeed, your nephew might do worse than cultivate him. He is well placed to do so.'

'Where?' said Katelina. She returned, like an automaton, to the one question it was her duty to ask. 'Where is Diniz?'

'Here. In Nicosia. In Messer Niccolò's villa, much admired and well guarded. Nor will he spend all his time among locusts. The city boasts a royal dyeworks, much damaged. Messer Niccolò is setting your nephew to work there. So what next have I said? I have made you ill. The thought of Messer Niccolò makes you ill. I find him a witty young man.'

Katelina quelled the pulse in her throat. She said, 'He knelt. He gave Carlotta his sworn oath of fealty.'

The woman looked at her. 'So did you,' the woman said. 'And you meant it. What then should I do to you? Skin you as the Mamelukes do, and make hawsers out of the peelings?'

Her voice had warped into something outlandish. The firelight glistened. The fan whirred and the shutters thudded and creaked as if belaboured by flocks of live locusts. The woman's face sagged and yawned in the heat, and her nose crawled like a tongue through her lip-paint.

The woman put up one hand and grasping a mess of pink blubbered skin dragged it all from her face. Behind it was the snout of a pig: a twisted hull of dead flesh with two holes in it. A double bore of spiced wind struck the pillow. 'Carlotta?' remarked the wheezing, snuffling voice. 'Carlotta's dam bit the nose from my face. I did not retch then or now. I did not whine then or now. I may offer you charity, my weak-stomached Fleming, but sympathy is not in my cure.'

The door closed with immaculate quietness behind her, leaving the storm, the vertiginous storm, inside the chamber.

A few days later, the demoiselle Katelina van Borselen entered the gracious closed-house of the Clares, where she had her own rooms and where, from time to time, she was allowed to receive the stained and unkempt youth, coldly purposeful, who had been the susceptible and civilised Diniz.

The noseless woman had spoken the truth. Diniz was in their enemy's grasp. Diniz had been set to work, as once Nicholas had been set to work, as a dyers' apprentice. Soaked and weary, he toiled in the pitted yard and shabby buildings of the royal dyeworks in Nicosia. He didn't resist when forced to drag their cloth through the vats or weigh their alum or shiver over their badly-kept ledgers. He used his limited freedom. He talked to the slaves and the Cypriots, the house-women, the menials, the half-trained lazy men who were all that were left in the business. Thereby he learned of events and prayed to be able, one day, to turn the knowledge to his advantage. What information he got, he brought to Katelina, his uncle's stern wife. For Diniz wished only three things. To free himself and his aunt, and kill Nicholas.

Nicholas himself was in the north, and for a month was out of reach of his victims. Instead, he passed these first weeks undergoing a series of trials which Diniz Vasquez would have been hard put to it to equal. The trials were perpetrated by Zacco, and their aim was to kill or to captivate.

All winter, Zacco's tents had occupied those plains in the north that spread from Nicosia towards the enemy forts on the coastline. Before the turn of the year the King, or so Nicholas suspected, had spent much of his time at the Palace, leaving to his Mameluke army a half-hearted blockade of the shore towns. Now, sweeping Nicholas with him, a reinvigorated Zacco led out Astorre and his men to the encampment; gave them horses, provisions and tents, and made them acquainted with the land and their fellows.

To such sensible practices, the King added, on whim, his own wayward pleasures. Having called for a council, he would cast his papers brusquely aside, demand his leopards, and sweep his companions for days to the mountains, flying hawks on the pinnacles and hunting the powerful wild sheep called moufflon among the snow-laden pines of the valleys. The leopards, packed snarling and blindfold in ox carts, were subject to the same whims as their master, who alternately struck their gold-harnessed muzzles and kissed them. Nicholas, quick as any to learn, was still novice enough to begin with, and brought back an upper arm rutted with claw marks. It was deadly play, if not without logic in moments of leisure. At such times, some of the Lusignan's soldiers would die, or be maimed: there would be rivalries. But from such escapades men emerged hardened; exposed to rough weather; experienced in seeking food and adopting crude quarters. Those who failed were discarded. Those who survived were given other tests, more severe and more sudden, until they triumphed, or died, or were moved to rebellion.

Nicholas chose to rebel. Roused nightly to service some exploit – to capture a mule-train, set fire to a renegade's house; judge a fierce, drunken horse race by torchlight – Nicholas didn't return from the last to his tent but, without gown or armour, stood bareheaded in his plain pourpoint outside that of Zacco and requested admission.

He didn't need the gleam of men's eyes in the firelight to know who had seen, who was watching. His own corps would, to be sure, be among them. Chosen companion for weeks of this young and dazzling King, Nicholas had shared his sport, his forays, his pleasures, but he had not shared his bed. James de Lusignan gave himself to those lovers he had, of both sexes, and issued no new invitations. Nicholas, who also knew how to wait, had been glad of it, although his air of willing neutrality was misleading. Primaflora had gone, sent to Rhodes despite all he could do. Her physical loss had unsettled him to a degree he had not enjoyed or expected, but since then, he had taken no partners. Celibacy was a test, a reminder, a punishment, and he kept his bargain quite well with himself, with the aid now and then of the wine cask. Astorre liked it when he was in a carousing mood; Loppe did not.

Now, tonight he was sober as he entered the royal campaign tent, its brocade alcoves disfigured with overturned stools and spilled food and wry candles. The horse race had sprung from an argument here, so they said. Now there was no one within but the King, his long-lidded stare curtained by tangled, waving brown hair, his young-boned wrist poised on the arm of his seat with a painted map hung from its fingers. Zacco looked: the servant who had brought Nicholas vanished. Zacco said, 'Well, Niccolò. You have come to resign?'

He had not been asked to sit, so Nicholas stood. 'Do they all do that?' he said. 'My lord Zacco?'

The King's eyes were like a Cathay's, half open. He said, 'Sometimes they shout, and throw down their shields. They are seen to talk in corners with priests, or the lords of my army. The lords, of course, listen and tell me. I am lenient in the death I give little men. Their error is simple, as yours is. They forget who is King of this country.'

'It is to be regretted,' Nicholas said. 'It is my duty and perhaps even yours to make sure that they cannot forget it.'

There was a silence he did not like. Then, 'Go on. If you think it wise,' Zacco said.

Nicholas spoke carefully. 'If I want an engine, my lord, first I design it, and then I fashion the tools for its making. You are training men without knowing what you will need them for. You don't need to bind them first. They will follow you anyway, and if you give them a goal, they will stay with you.'

'For what I can give them?' said Zacco.

'For what you are,' Nicholas said. 'Why doubt it now?'

'You tell me,' said Zacco.

Nicholas made a small pause. 'My lord, kingdoms can be lost by men vying for favour. It is better to make the goal plain. Those who achieve it deserve the best following.'

Zacco made a slow movement. The hand holding the vellum rose and released the map flat on his knee. Where he had gripped it were imprints like claw-marks. He said, 'Do we speak of the King, or of some woman with suitors?'

Nicholas said, 'We speak, my lord, of brave men who are inspired, and how best to use them.' He watched, and then said, 'If my lord would allow. I was brought here for a purpose, and I would fulfil it. Now is the time to make plans. A single meeting would do, provided your men come prepared. I have a list of questions for each of your officers. I should like them to bring you their answers. With what that will tell us, the campaign could be designed now for the spring. By next year, my lord could be King of all Cyprus.'

There was another silence. Then Zacco said, 'Where are the questions?'

They were in the satchel he wore. Condensed, the text still ran to several pages, spaced for clarity and penned in the model hand he had taken from Colard. He gave them to Zacco who, looking down, half raised a finger. It gave him leave to sit, which he did. He relaxed, with some trouble. Zacco read them.

It had taken two weeks to guess some of the reasons for Zacco's delay. Vanity, lust, instability – a Lusignan who was Cropnose's son would have defects of that order, and had. But Zacco often channelled his impulses. There was a legitimate need to bind men of uncertain allegiance. Zacco must pander as well to his faction –

the Egyptian army, which preferred looting to fighting; the native Cypriots who called themselves White Venetians and didn't want their lands ruined. And the Venetian merchants themselves, who represented the future wealth of the island, and wished to prosecute their daily business without inconvenience. If he wanted the Grand Turk kept from Cyprus, Zacco had to please and placate the Venetians.

In a military sense, the problems were clear, and even straightforward. Zacco held all but two centres. He had to dislodge the Queen's men from Kyrenia, built between the sea and the mountains, and attained by a single pass barred by a fortress. And he had to drive the Genoese from Famagusta, the viscounty and port on which Kyrenia drew. In each enclave was an enemy castle, strongly protected by sea and defended by land.

These two castles might fall to a great fleet, a great army, to ruse or to cannon. Failing these, a blockade might reduce them. Now, beginning the season, it was a matter of weighing the chances, and choosing. In such things, one made no assumptions. One calculated. One dwelled, most particularly, on the heavily guarded pass that led to Kyrenia, and the fort of St Hilarion that defended it. And in the end one looked not to Kyrenia at all, but to the key of the land, which was Famagusta.

The King, he already knew, preferred action to scholarship. To read the papers cost time, during which Nicholas waited. At the end, Zacco looked up. He said, 'You think you know the answers. You have made up your mind.'

Nicholas said, 'No. I know what has gone wrong before. I don't know what can be done to correct it.'

'How do you know?' Zacco said.

'From the Genoese,' Nicholas said. 'They talked about it on Rhodes. They thought, you see, that I was going to fight for Carlotta.' He didn't mention the name of Lomellini, who had dispensed a number of crisp and positive tales of past invasions and Genoese genius. Nor did he name Tomà Adorno, who – knowing Nicholas from the past – had told him more than anyone else and who, perhaps, had been less sure than anyone else that he was going to fight for Carlotta. From him he knew the depth of the sea moat at Famagusta, the excellence of the walls of the capacious castle which could hold seven hundred troops, and deploy from its towers enough fire power to shatter ships. Once, said Tomà Adorno, six thousand men and thirteen Catalan galleys had tried to take Famagusta and failed. Tomà Adorno was concerned, it was clear, to demonstrate to any foe of Famagusta that their task was hopeless, and the city impregnable. His information had interested Nicholas, as had also the fact that he offered it.

Now, speaking to Zacco, Nicholas developed the subject. 'To

take Famagusta, you would need a fleet and army from Cairo, or from the Grand Turk at Constantinople. You must know if that is likely.'

'To invite the Grand Turk would be suicide. Otherwise, everything is possible,' Zacco said. 'Even help from the West. You know a friar called Ludovico da Bologna? He does not mind using Muslims in a Christian cause.'

'I rather think,' Nicholas said, 'that the Pope is not on his side. Will Cairo help?'

'No,' said Zacco. 'I have the Mamelukes they have already supplied, whom I must not slight. You know this.'

'I understand,' Nicholas said. 'Then Kyrenia, too, cannot be stormed with the forces you have. You need what you don't yet possess, such as cannon.'

'We had artillery once,' remarked Zacco. 'Venice sold guns in secret to both sides. They did no damage worth speaking of, before they were captured.'

'I have a gunfounder,' Nicholas said. 'In sixty years, skills have improved. If we are to consider a siege, guns would shorten it.'

'We have a siege. Two,' Zacco said. 'You haven't noticed. You think we are here to hunt and play games. We have cut the lines between the two cities. We have penned each of them in. We track down their foraging parties. We flatten the country around, so that there are no stores they can raid. They are starving.'

'Not while Imperiale Doria supplies them by ship,' Nicholas said. 'Carlotta's consort has only now moved from Kyrenia. Merchants still use Famagusta. Traders don't like the short commons, but they are not starving yet. Unless they are gripped round the neck, both cities may hold out for years.'

'You wish to give me advice,' the King said.

'No,' said Nicholas. 'After the meeting, you will make up your mind. It is your country.'

'I thought,' said Zacco, 'you had forgotten. It has slipped my mind. Do you wrestle?'

'No,' said Nicholas. He was flung to the floor as he spoke. He had half expected it, and saved his spine by a twist and a jab before he recalled he was supposed to be ignorant. His arm was seized and twisted and he prevented it breaking in time, and got a leg where it would hurt. Zacco swore and changed grip. His muscles were young and elastic and, in exertion, solid as boxwood. He said, between breaths, 'A Milan teacher?'

'Primaflora,' said Nicholas, croaking. They both laughed, and he yelped as the breath thudded out of him. A pair of thumbs stuck in his neck and his head cracked on a pole, then a carpet. He kicked the King in a place fractionally clear of the genitals and hurled himself to one side. A mace-head buried its spikes where he'd been. The King, grasping the club, stood astride him. He was pale, with red on his cheekbones. Nicholas said, 'I've got another three pages with the answers on. If I don't come back, Astorre will burn them.' Without much effort, he kept his face drawn.

For a moment, the young man looked down at him. His hair, tossed in the struggle, clung in coils to his skin, and his breath hissed in his throat from exertion. He said, 'You have the kick of a traitor.'

Nicholas lay looking up. He said, 'I could do it again.' It didn't go down well. He said, 'I hit what I aim for.'

'So do I,' said James of Lusignan slowly. 'So do I. So tell me why you attack me. You resent that I sent the woman away? She was a spy.' The club hung from his grasp, and he was frowning.

Nicholas said, 'I doubt that. But spy or not, she was under my eye and yours, and in my bed, damn it all. What good is the Borselen woman?'

The young man above him slowly stepped to one side. He said, 'None. Do what you like with her.' He sat down, equally slowly, on the floor, with the mace across his knees, and examined Nicholas. Their eyes locked. After a long time, the King said, as a boy would, 'Have you ever attended a siege? It is tedious.'

'For the men. Once it's in place,' Nicholas said, 'it needs only regular supervision. Astorre doesn't mind being bored. I could get the structures in place. John le Grant could arrange the munitions and sapping before he goes south.'

'South?' said the young man. He drew a hand down his own cheek, following the flounce of his hair, and lifting the swathe at his neck with one finger. The finger rested, the heavy hair turning beneath it.

'To Kouklia and Akhelia to join me. You did say,' Nicholas said, 'that I should have the sugar franchise? I hear the second crop is next month, and May is the time for the crushing. By then the siege will be in position, and there will be nothing to do but supervise it. Tzani-bey surely won't find that too tedious.'

Zacco stared at him, thumb and finger caressing an elflock. He had opened the delicate band, worked in black, that collared his shirt, and the shirt itself was partly unbuttoned, the fine pleated fabric stained and torn from their struggle. In the right calf of his hose, a pale fissure was also apparent. The silence grew. Nicholas did nothing to break it. Zacco lowered his hand. He picked up the mace in two palms and sat, weighing it. He said, 'I don't mind greedy men. They fight well. I do, however, insist that they fight first. I did not buy a one-eyed man with a beard. I bought you.'

Nicholas met his stare, without moving. He said, 'My lord shall have value for money. First the meeting. Then the preparations for the campaign. Then the opening moves. I shall be here for all that.'

'And if I say,' Zacco said, 'that you do not go south until the summer fighting is over?'

'My lord, you are King. You may say anything. You will be obeyed. Only,' Nicholas said, 'how will my lord King fund his war if the royal sugar crop fails?'

'Why should it?' said Zacco.

'I have a premonition,' Nicholas said. 'War has already caused damage. Men who have worked for Venetians might prefer to move to Venetian estates. The previous holders might not take kindly to a stranger owning the franchise. Even the Knights at Kolossi have a grudge to pay off. I should be there.'

Zacco said, 'If a war needs no leader, why not appoint an Astorre to grind sugar?'

'But I shall,' Nicholas said. 'In due time. When I can promise you profit.'

Zacco smiled. He said, 'You speak as if it were for you to say. Shall I overlook it?'

'You have bought my mind. It pursues its labours for you, and brings you its conclusions. You have no need to accept them if, when equally primed, you are of a different opinion.' He did not return the smile, which was not genuine.

Zacco lifted the club, hefted it and, his eyes on Nicholas, hurled it hard through the door of the tent. There was a scream and a crash. Zacco said, 'You plan to take St Hilarion. I could read it in your mind.'

'It should be taken,' Nicholas said.

'An inaccessible peak, on a pass held by the enemy? Well, take it,' said Zacco. 'When I have it, you can go to your sugar crop.' And to the Saracen who came in, his cheek torn and bleeding, the King said, 'And did you hear all you wished? Bring meat, and sweetmeats and wine, and wake the boy with the flute. I am hungry.'

Chapter 24

A MONTH LATER, in the full explosion of spring, Nicholas attacked the precipice fort of St Hilarion. Through meadows of orange and scarlet and yellow, between the shrieking greens of fresh leaves and among drifts of dizzying scent, the coffer-camels paced with their parcels of gunpowder; mules and oxen dragged wainloads of flour and wine-casks and arrows, tents and iron, balls and forges, scaling-ladders and springals across the plain to the foothills of the Kyrenia mountains. And beside them trotted the Egyptian and Christian army with the young King at its head, and Nicholas riding a Lusignan warhorse beside him.

In Italy, a common soldier under Urbino, Nicholas had plunged into war as a catharsis; an escape into physical combat. The excitement of battle drew him still, as it also burned, he saw, in the Bastard. But this time, Nicholas had a share of Urbino's role. When the counsellors met, his voice was heard: the plans they made owed more than they knew to his strategy. Nevertheless, in the weeks of preparation that followed he sometimes lost sight of this divine detachment. He became entranced, as so often before, by the beauty of pattern-making: of computing, of fitting pieces together to form a whole as perfect as forethought could manage, while still aware – oh, always aware – that the heavens were garnished with giants, and this mortal kingdom with traps for the cocksure.

Most of the pieces he dealt with were human. The common soldiers he reached through their officers. To the Cypriots, the Catalans, the Aragonese who led the King's forces, his manner was courteous and plain, neither deferential nor brash. He had their envy already, as the King's special favourite. He had at least to command their respect. The antagonism of Tzani-bey was of longer standing and deadly, but in public or private, the Egyptian's manner was unremittingly suave, and his opinions delivered with honey. Nicholas minded less the captains who shouted: Markios, the Lusignan's uncle, who snarled and bullied and was revered by the Mamelukes; or Astorre who, although his employee, was always first to pounce, cackling, on an error. Most of all, Nicholas was mesmerised by Zacco himself who, seen at last at his business, revealed what the glitter had hidden.

Here, it would seem, was a just prince; a man who understood discipline; a leader who could win a man's esteem as well as his heart, and keep them both. In years James the Bastard of Lusignan was of course immature, with the zest of youth and sometimes its rages, its silliness, its cruelty. But only an able man could have come to overrun Cyprus and hold it; keep his two armies together; win victories and men from his sister. As James and Nicholas argued late into the night, the King's voice interrupting, overriding, applauding, and once breaking into peals of surprised laughter, Nicholas understood that whatever happened, he had been right to come and discover this man; as he felt that Zacco, who had wanted him, was not in every way disappointed. But still, he slept apart.

It was hardly remarked, so occupied were his own men in those weeks. The sailing-master Mick Crackbene was tracked down and sent to join them by Loppe, who had returned to the south armed with letters of credit, and shopping lists directed to agents in Venice and Florence, Milan and Palermo and Ancona. Crackbene, a self-contained man, seemed quite pleased to be restored to the company. King James, it seemed, he had encountered already. Since the *Doria*'s compulsory voyage to Episkopi, the ship had spent half the winter afloat, shuttling cargoes and indulging in brigandage. Her instructions reached her from Zacco, and it was Zacco, not the Venetians, who employed her. Crackbene and his men received wages, and the Bank of Niccolò, as was right, was paid lease-money. For a little time, Mick Crackbene remained in the King's camp, and lent his impartial voice to their councils. Then, following a long silence from Loppe, there arrived a much-delayed packet for Nicholas. It contained a dozen pages close-written in Flemish. It had come from Loppe's hands, and bore signs of discreet if, one hoped, fruitless tampering. Crackbene received his new orders and left for his ship at long last, rather thoughtfully.

Captain Astorre, his inventory over, set his smith to refurbishing weapons, checked the horse gear, and dispatched Thomas to bring in draught beasts and wagons. He spent a great deal of time with the captains of other companies, some of whom he already knew, and the practices of the camp and its exercises began to improve. He received an invitation from Zacco, which resulted in a number of exchanges in which the Captain aired his opinion of Skanderbeg, Piccinino, Urbino. These were followed by gifts for his table. He examined sacks of lead shot, his cheeks stuffed with almonds and dates and green walnuts, and pored over plans whose edges were weighted with oranges.

Tobie also spent time with Zacco, whom he found attractively bold as well as receptive. On his first visit, he was given mulled wine, and became eloquent on the topic of dysentery. The name of Tobie's uncle, physician to kings, was not mentioned. On his second visit, Tobie found that the King had asked to his table an Arab mediciner from the Mamelukes. The conversation proved highly agreeable. Afterwards, back in his tent, Tobie continued drinking until Nicholas came to investigate. Immediately, Tobie made a pronouncement. 'If you don't want Zacco, I'll have him. I know how to take St Hilarion.' After which the evening ended quite well, for Nicholas, entranced, helped him finish the wine-cask.

Thomas, brought in to carouse with the other lieutenants, heard their tales of their lord, and felt a different awe. 'This man who cheated at cards,' Thomas related that night, back in the company tent, 'Zacco knocked him down, and ground his spurred boot in his face.'

'Makes an example. Sharp boy,' said Astorre.

'And the merchants he let go from Salines. Remember? You know why he released them?'

'To add to the mouths that would starve in a siege. Even I thought of that,' said John le Grant. 'He's got a bonny body and brain, has the Bastard, but don't let it fool you. You don't inherit three hundred years of scorpion blood and end up a buttercup.'

Alone of the group, John le Grant resisted the temptation to enjoy the King's easy confidence. He answered the Bastard's legitimate questions, of which there were many; but his private life remained his own, as did his philosophy. Or so perhaps he thought, since work with cannon, with tunnels, with bombards appeared to him as normal as breathing, and he thought nothing of what a man might observe as he chalked out the plan of a project, or sat by a forge, silent, watching a new tool take shape. James de Lusignan was a good observer. Nicholas, never quizzed, had cause to know it.

Only the negro escaped, and on purpose. When Zacco was near, Loppe melted into the shadows. Before he went south, it was Loppe who watched the Lusignan, not the other way round.

Meanwhile the garrison at St Hilarion, of course, knew all that was happening. Separated by twenty miles, the protagonists could hear one another turning in bed. Nicosia knew when the fortress sent out its last foraging parties, got in its supplies, and closed its gates with reluctance. St Hilarion knew when the Bastard Lusignan's army moved north to cross the eleven or twelve miles from Trakhona to the hamlet of Agridi. From there, the Pass of St Catherine led through the hills to Kyrenia. And on the height to the left of the Pass stood the enchanted palace and fort of St Hilarion, Byzantine watchtower, Frankish ward and Lusignan bower, built for pleasure and killing.

By the middle hours of the day he set out, Zacco's tents and camp fires surrounded Agridi; the scouts and sentries were placed, and the Bastard's banner hung over a settling host. Over their heads sprawled the mountains: the long jagged range that lay between them and the flat coastal selvedge. From the camp they could see the start of the Pass, the way that led to Kyrenia, three miles from its end. Kyrenia could not be taken by any means they now had. What they needed was unchallenged domination of the road through the Pass. Tobie said, 'How high is it? The castle?'

He and Nicholas were waiting for food; seated not far from the ovens with the afternoon sun warming Tobie's bald head. There was a smell of fresh bread and camels and ordure. 'Two and a half thousand feet above sea level. You can't see it from here. You're not worried?' said Nicholas. 'And you the great doctor's nephew?'

There was also a smell of calendula. Remembering, Tobie put up his hand and removed the field marigold he had tucked over his ear. When he twirled it, his cuirass gleamed orange. He said, 'According to the good lord, you plan to leave for Kouklia if you manage to take St Hilarion.'

'That's right,' said Nicholas. 'I'm going to be seventy-five miles away. News will take decades to travel between us.'

'He said he hired us to fight, but if you're longing to trade, he won't stop you. I'm not complaining,' said Tobie.

'But you're not coming with me,' said Nicholas. The tone was one of confirmation. He added, 'I suppose Thomas wants to stay, too. I don't know how I'll manage.'

Tobie's face became heated. He said, 'Will the sugarcane bite you? I'm needed by soldiers.'

'I suppose you are,' Nicholas said. 'And if not, who am I to compete with the Arabs? Anyway, you've got it both ways, haven't you? If we fail, I stay on. If we succeed, you can stay and rewrite the pharmacopoeia with whatsisname. Abul Ismail. I'd go and eat with Astorre, except that I can't manage more than eight courses. Am I being unreasonable?'

'Yes,' said Tobie, relieved.

'I'm sorry,' Nicholas said. 'The truth is, I need to get away soon.'

'Why?' said Tobie. He then flushed.

'My God,' said Nicholas, with dawning amazement. He took the marigold from Tobie's fingers. 'Do I have to tell you? I do. I have to call on our mutual friend Katelina. And if you want to know why, it's remedial. When I get all excited like this, I need a furious woman. Who were you intending this for?'

'I haven't decided yet,' said Tobie thoughtfully. He took the marigold back. 'Where are Katelina and the boy? I thought the ransom money had come?'

'So did I,' Nicholas said. 'She ought to be on her way back to her husband. She isn't. Someone is stopping her.'

'Maybe she insists on remaining,' said Tobie, squinting carefully at his flower. 'But they ought to send the boy home, wherever he is.'

'I thought everyone knew,' Nicholas said. 'He's an apprentice in the dyeyard. And working hard, too. He doesn't get out till I say so.'

'You're joking,' said Tobie.

'I expect so,' Nicholas said. 'There was another rumour today. The Sultan is preparing for war against Venice.'

Tobie said, 'I heard that last week. If it's true, you'll get all the supplies that you've sent for. But I suppose you were counting on that.'

'I trust,' Nicholas said, 'that I'll get everything that I sent for. I think I shall. I feel lucky. I feel you may even change your mind in the long run, and join me in Kouklia. We have, of course, to capture St Hilarion first, in which event you will be sent a pint of nut oil and a cake. If we don't take it, you've nothing to worry about. Zacco won't let me go; and Astorre and I will have wrung your neck anyway. I feel better.'

'Good,' said Tobie in resigned tones. They hid a low satisfaction. One of the things he liked best about Nicholas were his cowardly moments.

That afternoon, the trumpets blew for assembly, the camp proclamation was read, and after a segregated and somewhat uncomfortable blessing the army of James of Lusignan moved to the mouth of the Pass of St Catherine and turned into the steep and stony gut of the hills that were commanded by the fort of St Hilarion. They entered it like a river of quicksilver. The air was barred with their lances, and the spired and visored helms of the cavalry made a tumbling pattern, fore and aft. They beat drums as they went, and the banners flew in shivering streams, while shreds of orchid and iris, scabious, anchusa, cyclamen sprang from their feet, so that the company smelled like a whorehouse. Then the landscape of abrupt hills adjusted itself and ahead on their right stood the crag they were making for, with St Hilarion crowning its summit.

Once, this place, named after a hermit, had been sacred to God, and a monastery had stood on these stones. Now, the cloisters had gone. Instead, suspended in mist, rose the halls which Tobie perceived momentarily, chilled, to be lair of the Lusignans: a palace of half-serpent Melusine with vaults and pillars of gold, a belvedere mantled in green, a hint of gardens, of loggias; the

effulgent dome of a church. The impression was fleeting. As the
cavalcade trotted nearer, he saw that the buildings were not of leaf
gold, but of Byzantine thin brickwork and freestone, with tiled or
thatched roofs and tall windows. Set high on the hill, the castle
rose to the top by degrees: the wide lower ward for grazing, for
tourneys, for pageants; the middle for hall and barracks and kitchens.

The uppermost, high among the cool airs from the north, held
the royal suite of the Queen, and was empty. There, Tobie knew,
the traceried windows looked to the sea and would have a view,
however small, of Kyrenia Castle. Being placed on the edge of a
chasm, the northern range of St Hilarion required no defences.
Around the rest of the castle a wall had been built, and fortified
with nine towers. A quarter-mile long, it straddled the southern
slope of the hill and stalked up the height to the summit. This
rampart towered before them, firm and well-kept, and bearing
along all its length the vicious sparkle of steel. They were to be
given a welcome.

James of Lusignan held up his hand. Just out of bowshot, his
troops halted. A bugle sounded a call. The King's herald rode out,
his plumes nodding, his golden tabard sewn with the crosses and
lions of Lusignan, and, halting far below the main entrance, blew
his trumpet and shouted. After some delay, the castle gates opened
and an armed horseman emerged and rode slowly down. They
spoke, the measured sound of their voices echoing in the still air.
Then they parted and returned. James received his herald, and
turned to his captains and army. He raised his voice. 'The garrison
has refused honourable surrender. Brave men, you are to be given
your wish. You will make this castle yours, and all that is in it.'

'And that won't be much,' Nicholas said in an undertone, reappearing suddenly.

Inside his armour, Tobie was sweating. He said, 'You've placed
your men?'

'I haven't placed anybody,' Nicholas said. 'God Almighty,
there's a spy on every knoll up there, watching us. You've forgotten
the programme.'

'I haven't. Now we turn and go back to camp, leaving them to
stand to arms half the night. Then we come back tonight in relays,
and tomorrow. Then when they're worn out, we take them. Perhaps.
Maybe we'll be worn out before they are. Who's that?' Behind
Nicholas, a huddled man in half-armour hung in the grasp of a guard.

'One of the men I found watching us. The King wanted to
question him. Now he's sent him to you.'

'To me?' Tobie said. An idea puffed into his chest.

'Yes. He has a terrible pain in the belly. So have half the
Queen's troops, so he says.'

'It worked!' Tobie said. He flung back his head and shrieked in awful falsetto. 'It worked! It worked!'

Nicholas was grinning, and so was everyone round him. 'Well, they weren't going to let a wagon of new beef pass them by, were they? What did you put in the carcasses?'

'Ask Abul Ismail,' said Tobie. 'Buckthorn, heliotrope, bryony berries. Mayweed and clover, sand lilies and cyclamen tubers. Lovely blooms. Poetic inspiration. *Ilm-l'krusha*, the learning of the bowels, is the Arab name for poetic inspiration. I tell you. If the garrison touches the meat, they'll abort and shit till their eyes stream.'

'A rotten, unethical trick,' Nicholas said. 'They'll never let Abul into my Order, and Pavia will take your degree back. What d'you think of the weather?'

Tobie stared at him. 'What are you worried about? It's not going to rain. They say a sea wind gets up after dark, but you're not having my blanket. Have you seen what John le Grant's got to wear? Ten layers of thick cloth, three layers of wax cloth, and a lining of rabbit fur. He'll be so hot he'll be luminous.'

'Well. We all have our burdens,' said Nicholas, and turned sideways to talk to Astorre.

The first detachment left after midnight and, retracing their steps of the day, moved silently back to St Hilarion. Tobie, to his anger, was not with it; but he saw Nicholas ride out clad in full armour as were all of the captains. The King was with him. So were John le Grant and the pioneers, all garbed in leather or cloth, shadowy devils on shadowy mounts. He thought he saw camels. The sound of their feet died away and the camp settled again, perhaps to sleep. An hour passed, and another. The wind, rising, rattled the tents. Tobie, swearing, got up and, wrapped in his mantle, went off to check through the hospital tent. Two of his dressers were there, asleep on a pallet, and a man of the King's, whose physician had gone with his master. Awake with a book by a candle was Abul Ismail, the Egyptian. He looked up and smiled, his bearded face folded in vertical lines. Tobie said, 'The wind woke me.'

Abul Ismail laid down his book. 'Your young friend will have to be careful. And your fine engineer.'

They had long since congratulated each other on the doctored beef. Tobie said, 'The wind won't affect hackbuts. All they want is to make noise and some smoke, while John has a close look at the walls.'

'So I believe. But my ancestors, when beset, could defend themselves. Within the garrison may be slaves of my race, and the wind is in their favour. Wax cloth and squirrel, my friend, are convenient for silence. They do not promise a shield against naphtha.'

He had used the Arab word *naft*, and for a moment Tobie thought he meant firearms. Then he understood. 'Greek fire? They may throw Greek fire?'

'It was how the Crusaders were beaten. It is kindled and thrown in clay pots. Or shot from crossbows. The hillside would burn. Your pioneers would have little chance. Your knights, attempting to rescue, would boil like crabs in their armour. It is an unforgiving weapon.'

Tobie got up, took a step to the door, and turned back. 'Ointments,' he said.

'They are here. The young man and the King have discussed this. The pioneers know of the danger. Your friend has taken what precautions he can. He is a versatile youth, but like the King somewhat heedless when hunting.'

'He is there,' Tobie said.

'He wishes his plan to succeed. It is not in his nature to step aside from what he is creating. Once it is done, he will listen to reason.'

Tobie looked at him in silence, thinking of Trebizond. The Arab nodded once. He said, 'I see you agree with me. While he is in thrall, he is mad. Perhaps a God-given madness; perhaps something quite other. I do not think you can cure it, but he requires some containment. A leash for the hawk, a halter for the colt, and the horse, and the young. Here they come.'

Tobie sprang to his feet. Then, rewrapping his cloak, he walked heavily to the tent door to watch the squadron arrive. The first person he saw was the King; the next Nicholas. They were shouting. He saw they were shouting with pleasure. Behind them, dismounting, were the pioneers. He saw John, his squirrel-vest open, his felt cap wringing wet in his fist. He was shouting as well. Roused by the noise and the orders, men tumbled out in their tunics and began to buckle on armour: the second squadron preparing to leave. A man limped up, holding his arm and complaining, and two others eased a third off his horse and carried him into the tent. He was cursing.

Nicholas, his helmet under his arm, came in raking his hair and dropped his hand, staring at Tobie. 'That's all we've got. Two wounded,' he said. 'You look disappointed.'

Tobie cleared his throat. He said, 'I was getting ready to deal with your blisters. No naphtha?'

'It was a total failure,' Nicholas said. He dumped his helm and his gloves on an orderly, and unbuckled his sword for good measure. 'I'm starving. Do you want to go on this foray? There isn't much point. No one hits anybody.'

'In that case, I'll stay,' Tobie said. 'So what happened?'

No one answered directly. Presently he found himself in the

firelight in a lolling company of chewing, boisterous men, which included the King, and Astorre, and Thomas, and John le Grant, his red hair sprung like a brush and his blotched nose translucent. John said, 'Covering fire? They nearly shot me three times. Then the smoke came so far up the hill that I couldn't give orders for coughing.'

'They couldn't see you,' Zacco said. 'The garrison couldn't see you. And what did you do? You dug no tunnels, embedded no gunpowder . . .' He mimed a comic disgust, his eyes smiling.

'As you well knew, my lord King,' said the engineer. 'Whoever built those walls knew a thing or two. There's a place up the side . . . *perhaps* there's a place up the side. But it's not worth the time without cannon. And when we get cannon, we shan't need to use them on St Hilarion.'

'So what happened?' said Tobie with patience.

'He planted crackers with fuses,' said Nicholas. 'The castle stood to arms all evening after the challenge, heard us arrive in the night, made to resist what they thought was a full-scale attack; saw us ride off defeated. They'll start sleeping in shifts. An hour after we've gone, they'll hear volleys under the walls from John's crackers, rouse the fort and shoot into the smoke. Then they'll stand down again.'

'And the second squadron will arrive,' Tobie said. 'Mind you, they may not be so scared of you next time. They'll put a third of their men on the walls, and give the others some rest.'

'That's what he said,' said Captain Astorre, referring to Nicholas. He jerked his head, carrying with it a spit jammed with kidneys. 'But they won't rest very long now. Night attack from the front *and* the rear.'

'What?' said Tobie. Zacco was laughing.

'Goats,' said Captain Astorre. 'A small detail with a wagon of goats. They'll drive the beasts up the back cliff, let off a handgun or two, and watch the rest of the garrison rush to the back walls. If they haven't got the skitters already, they'll have them by then. The camels were grand.'

'Don't tell me,' said Tobie. 'They carried the goats up the hill.'

'My good doctor,' said Zacco. 'You are not taking this seriously. The camels were trained. They have no objection to noise. Your ingenious friend Nicholas placed his hackbutters on the camels, one behind every hump, and they raced past and shot at the castle.'

'Did you hit anything?' Tobie said.

'Not yet,' said Nicholas. 'That's for tomorrow. Tomorrow, they open the gates for us. I'm going to bed.'

'When tomorrow?' said Tobie. 'You don't mean tomorrow, in daylight?' But it was a rhetorical question, because he knew that was what Nicholas meant, and also King James, who had caught this crazy apprentice's infection which was not, to be truthful, so crazy. By mid-morning tomorrow, the garrison of St Hilarion would be kitten-weak and exhausted and ready for capture.

Tobias Beventini of Grado rose therefore next morning and attached himself to the army when it moved out of camp, although he had had no more sleep than they had; and rode his good horse which had got used to camels and hackbut fire and the whistle of arrows arching over the battlements. The journey to the castle seemed short, and there was less talk than before. They assembled, foot and horse, at the base of the hill of St Hilarion. The trumpets blew, and Tobie felt a pang in his stomach.

This time, under cover of smoke, the troops under King James did not keep their distance but mounted the hill, firing steadily. Their fire was returned; but the bolts and arrows that appeared through the smoke were sparse and ill-aimed, and fell to the grass, or against shields, or sprang into the hide screens the foot-men were carrying. Through the haze, you could see the relief run through Zacco's army. This was the work of sick men. If they were too ill to bend bows, they would hardly prevail in hand-to-hand fighting. Tobie watched Zacco's hand, upraised as he looked for the ladders arriving.

Advancing steadily, his hearing dulled by the clash and thud of metal and firearms, by the pounding of hooves and the continuous din of threatening voices, Tobie was not at first aware of a change inside the castle. Behind the walls, a burst of screaming made itself heard, and then travelling, broke out elsewhere. A subdued roar began to emerge, like that of an avalanche. Tobie reined and looked up.

The hackbut smoke was beginning to clear. It showed that the wall-walks above were half-empty, and the upper stretch of the tiltground full of men running backwards and forwards. Beyond and higher was smoke. Beyond that, at the top of the castle, was a coronet of clear, transparent flame. As he watched, the flames spread, with men running downhill before them, their clothing alight.

Nicholas was nowhere to be seen. Zacco said, 'Advance to the wall. Mount, and open the gates.'

Before he ended, the scaling-ladders were there, and men were up them and over. No one opposed them. When the gates were dragged open, the first to fall out were members of Carlotta's garrison – voiceless, naked, their faces raw meat flecked with carbon. One was a living torch of a woman with a child in her arms. They dropped as Tobie touched them and lay, a heap of sticks and black paper. He got up and ran into the castle, his orderlies following. The King said, 'Stand to take prisoners. Doctors, set up your hospital. Captain, put out those fires. Do we want to inhabit a ruin?'

There was a stable with straw where the burned and dying were brought, and Tobie and Abul set up their trestles. In time some wounded arrived, but none of consequence. What resistance Zacco had found on the heights had clearly been small. As the doctors worked, the noise outside dwindled to sobbing, with the occasional command, the thud of lumber, and the sharp voices of men working in crisis. The cisterns were brought into use. There came the sound of water trickling, and the random hiss of flames being doused in the thatched roofs and storehouses; the vats of grain and powder and oil. The hiss of a goffering iron, turned in gnarled hands in the laundry of his mother's home in Pavia. Above the stench of singed hair and hide and charred wood rose the scent of roast flesh. The hiss of a basket of scorpions. After a long time, Tobie walked to the door of the stable and stood, looking dully about him.

The fires were out. Around him, the lower ward was singed but intact, and part of the sector above. Above that were soot-blackened buildings and a haze of dark smoke, pierced by plumes of dazzling steam. Here and there, against the grey sky, an object glowed crimson: a shank of wood; a roll of felt heaped with red spangles. The dome of the church was half gold and half black. Outside it stood Nicholas, small in the distance. Transfixed, Tobie drew breath and shouted.

Nicholas turned, but made no audible answer. Tobie shouted again, rising to shrillness. Abul, unexpectedly near, said, 'They are counting the dead. Go up, if you wish him to hear you. Go. There is little more to be done.'

The wind had risen. The sea wind, that had forced the flames down from the north. Tobie climbed to the church. Nicholas stood where he had first seen him, his face expressionless. He smelled of singeing, and was covered with soot and abrasions, but was neither wounded nor burned. Tobie cleared his throat, an official and orderly sound, as at the opening of a tribunal. He said, 'Your men made an assault up the back cliff?'

It was not, certainly, what Nicholas had expected. He paused, then replied with equal formality. 'It was the plan. The goats were sent up last night, to disarm them. Today the climbers were men. We sent them up the back wall while Zacco drew their fire from the front.' In the black and red face, his eyes were large, bright and clean.

Tobie said, 'The climbers were Mamelukes. What were their orders precisely?'

Nicholas said, 'To get in at any cost. Some of them fell. Some of them got in and died. We have taken the castle.'

'I am sure you have,' Tobie said. 'You must show me your dead. Then I will take and show you my dying.' He paused and then said, 'How could you do this? Even you?'

Nicholas said slowly, 'I didn't order the naphtha.'

'No. But you knew Arabs used it. You must have known the Mamelukes had the ingredients. You took no steps to forbid it. You let Saracen dogs burn women and children to death. How many?'

Nicholas turned his head, again slowly. He said, 'They are all in there. You can't help them. Later, talk to me.'

'Now,' said Tobie. He walked past Nicholas and entered the church.

Already five hundred years old, the Byzantine church of St Hilarion had long outlived the monks it once served but, under Carlotta's favouring rule, the worked gold of an iconostastis sparkled still in front of its altar. Above, Christ Pantocrator looked down with the hosts of his angels, and the Prophets guarded the drum of the dome. Saints walked round the walls, done in ochre, madder and gold, and there were angels booted in scarlet, and dressed in the style of the Ushers in Trebizond. In the style of the Imperial Ushers who had abandoned the Empire of Trebizond, with the Emperor.

There were eight pillars, painted with partridges, between which stretched a mosaic floor covered with pallets. On each, lying in death, was a body. There were six children among them, and many women. None of them was burned. Tobie stood, his lips shut. Then he moved from pallet to pallet and bent, stiffly, to examine what lay there. Eventually, he reached the altar. It was very quiet, for Nicholas had remained at the door, and the church contained no one else living. Once, he heard footsteps passing the church, and once, a brief exchange between Nicholas and someone else, who did not remain. After a time, Tobie turned and came back.

Nicholas was leaning, head bent, where he had left him, slowly scrubbing his face with a towel. The fabric was black: becoming aware of it, he let it drop and looked up at Tobie's footsteps. His face was still grimy. Tobie walked past him and stopped. Nicholas said, 'My dying; your dead. Don't blame Abul. It is in the nature of Arabs.'

Buckthorn, heliotrope, cyclamen tubers. Not a griping dose, as he'd thought, but a killing dose, which had killed. After a space, Tobie said, 'Did Zacco know?'

'I expect so,' Nicholas said. 'And Tzani-bey. They don't have much patience with games. They thought it safer to poison the garrison, or as many as chance would allow. They are waiting for us. When they see us walk down, they will look for weakness, and use it.'

Tobie spoke without turning his head. 'We condone this? In front of John, Astorre, our own men?'

'We are heroes,' said Nicholas. 'That is war. You chose to heal soldiers. I elected to fight one campaign in order to leave war behind. I ask you again to come with me to Kouklia. I have won my franchise. I have taken St Hilarion. Sing ye to the Lord, for He hath triumphed gloriously.'

'You don't want to leave war behind,' Tobie said. 'You want both. Adventure of body and mind.'

'So do you,' Nicholas said. 'I don't want you to fall out with Abul. I want you to ask him a question. Why does sugar kill?'

'*Sugar?*' said Tobie. He moved out, into the acrid air that was sweet after what was inside. His stomach churned.

'Yes. Loppe has been reporting to me from the cane fields. I sent for six experts from Sicily. One of them sleeps half the day, and one acts as if drunk. Loppe experienced this in Granada. He says they die.'

It should have been no surprise. Courting Zacco, preparing for battle, Nicholas had long since taken the reins of his business in secret. And Loppe, the Guinea slave with Portuguese owners, had been his factor. Tobie said, 'I suppose you have the dyeworks running as well?'

'Not as well,' Nicholas said. 'Until now, we've been without management. But now I have hopes of a solution. I have someone to see.'

'When?' Tobie said. He stopped at the door of the stable.

'Tomorrow,' Nicholas said. 'I'm going back to Nicosia tomorrow with Zacco. We control the Pass; they can start the blockade now without me. When they have the ships and the cannon, they can break Kyrenia down.'

'Or burn it out,' Tobie said. He halted, painfully. He said, 'I have work to do.'

'I know that,' said Nicholas. 'But when it's done, think of what I have said. I'll go straight from my house to Kouklia. Unless, that is, something grisly turns up.'

'Because of Zacco?' said Tobie.

'Because of Katelina van Borselen,' Nicholas said, 'whose hands are two equal swords, and who should be in Portugal.'

Chapter 25

IT WAS NOT, however, the two equal swords of Katelina van Borselen that Nicholas found waiting for him on his return, at long last, to the capital.

Before night fell on the cooling ashes of St Hilarion, victory bells began to clang in Nicosia, and news of the triumph reached Diniz Vasquez, toiling in the mud and stink of the Lusignan dyeworks.

A prisoner of war has nothing to celebrate, and is wise to display no emotion when, from isolation, he hears his friends have been beaten. They said the Bastard would come back tomorrow, and before nightfall would proceed to give public thanks at the Cathedral. If the Bastard returned, he would bring Niccolò vander Poele with him. And vander Poele, surely, would come to his house, which was also the prison of Diniz.

As a place of confinement, it was not wholly unpleasant. Diniz was allowed in the kitchen and garden. He had even explored the master apartments, with the notion of returning one night with a hammer. It would give the bastard a well-merited shock to find his marble wall panels cracked, his flooring smashed, his inlaid Syrian couches all splintered, with their embroidered silk cushions in tatters. On mature reflection, however, he decided the dyeworks first deserved his attention. With the discreet advice of the under-manager, who resented his new employer but, being inefficient, stayed with him, Diniz had learned very quickly the vulnerable parts of the dyeing process and how to attack them: how to pollute a boiling, or lower the temperature of a vat, or crack a pipe or a cooling vessel. Then, without warning, the under-manager had been removed, and the two or three habitual troublemakers who had been happy to help him, and a new man was brought in, a Florentine with an interest in gold thread who knew little enough about dyeing, but could tell well enough when trouble was threatening, and stop it. Then Diniz realised that if he went to extremes, he risked being shut up altogether, or removed from the house to a place of much less advantage. So, although from time to time he wandered through his enemy's rooms, and opened his chests, and turned over, with contempt, his fine clothing, Diniz applied his excellent brain to studying the work in the yard, learning what the old slaves and workmen could tell him, and lifting himself thereby from the menial tending of tubs to the preparing of dyes, the timing of fine operations, the mastery, finally, of the ledgers where, in time, the damage he could inflict promised to be invisible, and wholly satisfactory.

Now the days passed, he found, much more quickly. He learned the patois of the trade, and the mixture of terms, part Arab, part Italian, part Greek, that made up common intercourse, on top of the tongues he already had – the French, the Flemish, the Scots of Lucia his mother, and the Portuguese of his father, who would never again teach him or take him travelling.

His father had made several countries his home, and had been respected and made welcome everywhere. Once, he had stayed briefly in Scotland and, of course, had found there his bride. He no doubt had hoped, as any man would, for many sons from his golden Lucia, but only Diniz the first-born had lived. Some years later, his father had made occasion to take him back to the land of his mother. Of the King, Diniz had no recollection; but he had brought back from Scotland a child's dazzled impression of his mother's brother, fair and slim in the tiltyard. He had, as a boy, worshipped Simon his uncle. It was the duel between his uncle Simon and the scheming brute vander Poele that had caused the death of Tristão Vasquez, for which Niccolò vander Poele was to pay. Payment was due, also, for other acts of inhumanity. For the betrayal of Carlotta, to whom the Fleming had pretended to give his allegiance. And for the seduction of the lady Primaflora, whose fate, in other hands, might have been very different. Diniz dreamed, very often, about Primaflora.

Since being brought to Nicosia, Diniz had seldom set eyes on his adversary, either in the house or the yard. The swine's movements were well enough known, as were the Bastard's. With the Bastard to cling to, vander Poele was unlikely to bother himself over a house, a business, a prisoner. Once or twice people talked about seeing a man wandering about in the yards late or early, in darkness, and lamps had been found warm in the sheds. The slaves who slept there even claimed to have talked to him. But it was hardly likely to be vander Poele himself, who would come, if he came at all, with a club, in daylight, and bullying.

In any case, it was not easy to enter or leave Nicosia at night. Once, Diniz himself had escaped over the walls of the villa and tried to leave with the throng through the western gate, but the

guard had stopped him immediately, for his clothes had given him
away, and the stains on his hands. His yellow clothes, and his blue
hands. After that, they escorted him everywhere, but he had
already realised how slim was his chance of escaping. Thirty-four
open miles, ringed with troops, lay between him and Famagusta.
He had no money, and the nuns had none either, although his aunt
Katelina had begged them to help.

He was sorry for his aunt Katelina, but also annoyed with her
over the fuss she made about the girl in the kitchens and the other
one who came with ash to the yard. As it turned out, he caught
nothing and Andrea the new under-manager, less bigoted than he
thought, got him a clean little whore to the house. Once he took
her through to Niccolò's chamber and engaged her several times
just as she liked until her pretty skin was pink, front and back. The
quilt was white silk brocade. Afterwards, he went back and
smoothed it, ashamed. The stolen knife in his room was a worthy
instrument of his vengeance, not this.

On the morning after the bells, no one worked as they should
except himself, for the man they liked to call King James had
arrived, so they said, and was to ride to the Cathedral with his
captains that afternoon. Already those who could afford carpets
had hung them out of their windows, and picked spring flowers to
throw. Diniz saw them as he helped carry ladders out to the street,
to hoist the strings of dyed cloth higher than normal, as the law
demanded during processions. He wondered if he might try to get
away then, but Andrea's man had a grip on his elbow. At noon
they parted for dinner, and he was escorted back, as usual, to the
villa.

He saw, as soon as he got near, that the gates were open, and
there were sumpter-mules in the yard, and several horses, one of
them with the brand of the Lusignan stud. They seemed restive.
Then he heard a shiver of bells and saw that against a far wall
another animal stood, moving delicately into its tether. He saw a
flank like spun silk, and four spindle-fine legs and a neck like the
arch of a longbow. A racing-camel. A dream of a racing-camel. It
looked at him in disdain, lashes lowered.

So he had come. Only one man could own that.

Diniz walked into the house, his face white. The house was
empty. Dust on the terrazzo showed where spurred feet had trod,
and in the inner court lay some saddlebags. From the private
apartments there came a faint odour of horseflesh, and burned
wool, and sweat. Prompted by distant noise, and wavering lines of
spilled water and the sound of hurrying feet, Diniz turned and
made for the kitchens.

The household staff were all there, and the tables were heaped
with raw food. He stepped back from the heat into the arms of the

new steward, the man who had come after the negro freeman had
left. The new steward, who answered to the French name of
Galiot, remarked, 'You'll eat well tonight. As you see, Messer
Niccolò has returned.'

'I don't see him,' said Diniz.

'He's in the cooking-pot,' cried one of the women, without
stopping work.

The man Galiot said, 'He's with the King. He'll be back. Find
yourself something. There's bread, and a cheese.'

'There's no hurry,' Diniz said. He knew that, from pale, he had
flushed. He said, 'The yard is closed. I can stay.'

The steward paused. Then he said, 'If they told you that, they
were wrong. My lord has left orders. You are to return to the yard
after dinner and work there.'

'*My lord?*' said Diniz. 'Who is this? I know a Flemish base-born
apprentice called Niccolò.'

The steward stiffened. The woman who had spoken before
scooped up the bread and the cheese and, turning to Diniz, thrust
them into his arms. She said, 'Go and eat, son, and do as you're
told. Lord or 'prentice, I wouldn't cross that Flemish brute after
what he's done in St Hilarion.'

'And that's good advice,' Galiot said. 'Over there. Find a place
to eat over there. Here, they're busy.'

Diniz moved, but not very quickly. He said, 'I thought the castle
surrendered.'

'Over there,' said the steward again. 'Yes, it surrendered.' The
Frenchman pushed him out of the door, a jug of watered wine in
one hand. The woman followed him with a cup. She said, 'Aye,
you would surrender if your women and children were poisoned,
and your men burned to cinders with naphtha. He made sure, that
young heathen, that those poor mites would never fight for Carlotta.' She gave him the cup. She said, 'If he says go back to the
dyeyard, go back. And if he comes, say please and thank you and
lick the salt from his toes if he asks you.'

Diniz found she had gone, and he was still standing. The
steward said, 'They're frightened. I've met him. He's no worse
than anyone else. Eat your food. You'd better get to the yard
before the procession starts.'

'The victory procession,' Diniz said.

It needed two of them to push a way for him back to the yard, the
press was so great. There they closed and locked the yard gates
behind him. It was a big enclosure, with sheds and an office and
scaffolded shelters over the winches and dyevats. He had never
seen it deserted before: an oasis of quiet, while the crowd roared
like the sea outside all the walls. The King . . . the Bastard must

have ridden out with his train from the Palace. If he stood on a ladder, he might see the tops of his officers' heads as they went down the road to St Sofia.

The biggest space in the yard was occupied by the well with its wheel, and the cistern. The ground was always swilling. He went to the shelf where the clogs were and strapped them under his shoes. Before the Venetians came, the cold steeping had been done in clay-lined pits just sunk in the ground, and every winter flood water diluted them. Now they had copper vats. This morning, they had let the under-fires die, since they needed long tending if the colour was not to spoil.

He remembered his first days in the yard, and the havoc he had created. If there was a part of him that had enjoyed it, as the young louts who helped him enjoyed it, he had grown out of that now. He was seventeen, and a man who stood, now, for his aunt and his father. He wondered what Niccolò vander Poele – *my lord* – might be wearing. Cloth of gold, no doubt, and silver armour, and harness and plumes set with diamonds. They would throw roses to him, and comfits. The clergy would wait, in their robes, at the Cathedral and the cheering would stop, and the chanting, the prayers begin. He would know by the silence when they entered the church.

Because of the noise, he didn't hear when behind him the yard gates unlocked. It was the sound of their closing that turned him.

Across the mud of the yard, two men stood at ease, looking about them. One, black-bearded and short, was a stranger. The other he knew, although the man didn't wear cloth of gold but a travel-stained shirt and serge pourpoint, and his sword was sheathed in unjewelled shagreen. Under the cuff of his soft-crowned felt hat his hair looked brittle and frizzed; and the fine scar on his cheek stood among a curious mottling of pink. Diniz said, 'You did use naphtha.' Halfway through the words, his windpipe blocked for a second.

Niccolò vander Poele said, 'Let us leave that for later. Bartolomeo, this is the boy I was speaking of.'

Diniz frowned. The man Bartolomeo, in whom he had no interest, wore velvet which, though dusty, was certainly jewelled, as was the drape of his headgear. Diniz observed, without fully looking, that the cut of his doublet was almost Venetian. Below a thick trunk, the calves of his legs jutted like oak galls. The man said, 'Introduce me.'

'Are you not in the procession?' said Diniz. 'Has the Bastard disowned you?'

The stranger said again, 'Introduce me.'

'If I can,' vander Poele said. 'This is Bartolomeo Zorzi, a Venetian merchant from Constantinople. He has agreed to manage the dyeworks. You will show us around.' He waited. Then he said, in the same agreeable voice, 'You can do nothing from the Palace prison.'

Diniz felt his eyes swim from pure anger. Then he pulled himself up and addressed the bearded man Zorzi. 'Messer Bartolomeo managed a dyeworks in Constantinople? He must have been thankful to escape.'

Above their furzy black rim, the man's jowls and cheeks were healthily brown; his nose was snubbed and broad, between widely spaced eyes. He said, 'A shrewd fellow, this. Yes. It's a good time for Venetians to get out of those parts. I was in the alum business myself. Alum and silks. But I looked after the interests of a dyeshop your master here knows of. Owned by one Giovanni da Castro, godson of Pope Pius and rival to Messer Niccolò.' His eyes, polished and black as obsidian, moved from Diniz to his companion. He said to the Fleming, 'Took your trade, Niccolò, didn't he, the inquisitive Messer da Castro? Found the alum at Tolfa that broke your clever monopoly.'

'Not unexpectedly,' vander Poele said. His voice was softer than Diniz remembered, and his manner repressed, as if what he were doing were unimportant, or disagreeable in some special way. He added, 'As you have lost the Turkish concessions, I suppose. Unless your partner is staying in Constantinople?'

The bearded man, also smiling, turned to Diniz. 'Girolamo? He also plans to depart. It is sad, but not so sad as it might have been. He has a brother, Antonio, who is greatly favoured by one of the Viziers.'

'And, no doubt,' vander Poele said, 'you made sure to collect any money outstanding.'

The bearded man's smile grew wider. 'You have heard.'

'That you left owing the Sultan thousands of ducats? It does you credit,' said the Fleming, 'to trust so strongly in the power of Venice. What if the Sultan defeats them?'

'Then he will very likely overrun Cyprus,' Zorzi said. 'And I shall again have to move on, to the detriment of your dyeworks. But I am one of three fond and competent brothers. Nicholai – you remember one-legged Nicholai? – has of course connections in Bruges. Jacopo has vineyards in Cyprus which will support me very well in the meantime; added to the lavish wage you have promised to pay me. Indeed, I have only one problem. Am I to see over the dyeshop or not? I have to arrange my dress before attending the banquet. So, I take it, have you.'

'Yes,' said vander Poele. He turned to Diniz. 'Show us what you can. Then you and I will return to the villa and talk. I have asked the Clares to bring your aunt there.'

Diniz stood where he was. He said, 'The ransom has come?'

The Fleming had begun to walk over the mud. He said, 'There are difficulties. Bartolomeo, this is the well. When the river dries up, we can keep working all summer. But the drainage channels are bad, and the paving must be done soon.'

'What difficulties?' Diniz said. He passed the merchant from Constantinople and caught the man Niccolò by the arm. 'What difficulties?' He remembered, for the first time, the knife in his boot.

As the thought came into his mind, the Fleming disengaged and repositioned himself, smoothly, on the other side of the wheel. Vander Poele said, 'That is what I want to speak about later.'

'*What?*' insisted Diniz. He felt himself flush.

Bartolomeo Zorzi turned from the vat he was examining and walked to the door of a shed. He said, 'Young man, you heard Messer Niccolò. Time is short. Is this where your dry stocks are held?'

'Answer,' Diniz said, standing still.

Vander Poele joined the man Zorzi and, unlocking the door, opened it so that the other could enter and look. He himself remained, as if in thought, considering Diniz. He said, 'Your grandfather has refused to pay your ransom. He says it must wait until the end of the season.'

Diniz stared at him. Jordan de Ribérac was the richest man in France, as near as maybe. He said, 'I don't believe it. Then what of Simon, my uncle? He is paying nothing to set free his wife?'

The man Zorzi had reappeared, talking, and vander Poele let him out and locked the door behind him. He turned aside. 'Diniz, all these things will be discussed later. Meanwhile Messer Bartolomeo is your master. Under him, your life can be easy or hard. He is not concerned with your troubles. He wants your co-operation.'

Diniz remained where he was. He said, 'The ransom has come, and you've seized it. Simon my uncle would never abandon his wife.'

The man from Constantinople sighed heavily and looked at the Fleming. Vander Poele said, 'Diniz. No ransoms have come. Your grandfather won't pay, or not yet, and your uncle cannot be reached for some reason. In fact, far from enriching myself at your expense, I've offered to settle both ransoms myself.'

There was a short silence. 'Then why are we still here?' said Diniz. The bearded man, looking resigned, crossed his arms.

'Because,' said vander Poele, 'the King intervened. He won't allow the demoiselle home unless her own people redeem her.'

Diniz looked at him, and kept his shoulders stiff. He said, 'Then I couldn't go either. In any case, I wouldn't take freedom from you. If you've paid for me, then get back your money.'

'I've paid your ransom, but I haven't offered you freedom,' said vander Poele. 'I need you to work in the dyeshop this summer. Until this autumn, you will make dyeing your business. You say you don't want your freedom. We have therefore nothing to argue about. Shall we proceed, then?'

Diniz stretched out his hands. Dense blue dye stained the palms and the fingertips, and each nail was marked with a different test-colour. The boy said, 'You try to reduce us. Don't you see? We can never sink to your level.'

The Venetian smirked, and turned aside with extravagant tact. Vander Poele stood alone, his head bent, a sudden, unlooked-for target. Diniz bent and, snatching his dagger, hurled it hard at the figure before him.

Faster than he thought possible, vander Poele swerved. The knife thudded into a barrel, from which a stream of thick liquid issued. The man Zorzi turned quickly, exclaiming. Before he could move, Diniz flung himself on the Fleming and carried him to the ground. In the next moments, flailing, punching and being punched, Diniz thought of nothing but his fury. Then he felt Zorzi's grip and, sobbing with rage, knew that, of course, he had no chance against both of them. There was a moment, before vander Poele broke his grasp and before Zorzi dragged him away when the scorched face of the Fleming was close to his.

Then Diniz Vasquez sent his tongue rolling and spat. He said, 'A Knight of the Order fights man to man. A coward fights two to one, like a hog. You killed my father and sold me and my aunt into captivity. I demand restitution. That is a challenge, if someone has taught you to recognise one.'

He was on his feet by then, staggering back in the grasp of the Venetian. The Fleming rose from the mud, and finding a kerchief, put it slowly to use at his lips. He said, 'All right. You've tried to pay me back, however foolishly. That's enough for the moment.'

The Venetian was laughing, although his grip was painfully hard. He said, 'My dear, he challenged you! Did you kill his father? You must reply, knight to gentleman, or face unimaginable penalties.'

'I can imagine them,' vander Poele said. He got up, noticed the mud on his pourpoint and began without hurry to untie and peel off the garment. His shirt beneath was heavily creased, and mud and dust mired his hose. He said, 'I need to talk with him, that is all. Let it drop. Let's get on with the business.'

Zorzi said, 'Let it drop! The child spat in your face! What sort of talk do you expect after that? You'll never get this puppy to rest until you satisfy him. Why not fight now, and get it over and done with? He can have my sword.' His fingers still gripped Diniz's shoulder. He said, shaking him, 'Is that what you want?'

'Yes,' said Diniz. He felt stunned. It had seemed certain that the man Zorzi would take the Fleming's part. But he was exhorting him – almost shaming him into a duel. Diniz said, 'My father was Tristão Vasquez. He was assassinated in Rhodes, because of a feud between this man and my mother's brother. Queen Carlotta didn't know that when she knighted him.'

The Venetian released him. He exuded pleasure. He said, 'My dear Niccolò! Queen Carlotta made you a Knight of the Sword! I thought it was Zacco!'

'There was a queue,' vander Poele said. 'I can't fight him.'

'Why not?' said Zorzi. He had his sword unsheathed in his hand. 'Show me yours.'

'They're not matched,' said the Fleming. Against the scorch-marks his face was pale with what seemed to be anger. He moved, too late to prevent Zorzi from drawing his sword from the scabbard and holding it next to the other.

Zorzi said, 'You are right. Then why not give the youth the advantage? Give him yours, and you take the shorter.' And as he spoke, he held out to Diniz the pommel of the Fleming's sword.

Diniz seized it. He turned, his breath coming short, and heaved the blade upright in his two hands, staring at vander Poele across the space that divided them. He said, at the second attempt, 'Messer Niccolò. I have challenged you, on grounds that you know of. Take the sword and respond, or I will strike, and the law will absolve me.'

He waited only a moment. But at the first lift of his arm, the other man stepped quickly forward and grasped the weapon the Venetian offered him. He said conversationally, 'Damn you, Bartolomeo. But I doubt, even then, if you could expect to be handed the franchise. Of course, you could try.' Then, turning to Diniz, he saluted briefly and flicked his blade to invite the first blow.

Swordplay in a gymnasium or a paved exercise yard was different from the same thing in a yard deep in mud and littered with irregular obstacles, but Diniz had all the advantages he could have hoped for: of youth and energy and familiarity with the terrain. He also had the better weapon, not only in length, but in the sheer cutting strength of the steel. The work under his hand was Byzantine, but on the blade, the inscription was Arabic.

He remembered what he had heard, with such awe, from this man's lips on the sail from Kolossi, and understood it as he had not understood it then. Vander Poele had fought in Trebizond, that was true. But vander Poele, the pandering servant of Zacco, had also learned in Trebizond the many ways of pleasing a master. It was what you would expect – his aunt Katelina had impressed it on him. The man was simply a base-born apprentice who had risen by wedding his widowed employer. And bastard upstarts didn't learn duelling, whereas Portuguese noblemen did.

For that very reason, it would seem, the man was remarkably hard to pin down. He backed, and swerved and tapped, and swerved again without ever engaging. Diniz pursued him with angry pleasure. Feet trampling, sucking, dancing in the mud, he swung his sword with joy, changing angles, direction. He knew the yard. He knew where the cauldrons were, their fires barely out, their contents still between warm and hot. He avoided the grindstone, the buckets of paste, the baskets with tongs and bellows and ladles – but his opponent was clever enough, he could see, to read his movements and avoid them as well.

He wished it were dark. Once, misreading the other man's intentions, he found himself wrong-footed and brought his blade down on the edge of a vat, half-cutting the rods with their skeins. Once the other man slipped, and Diniz, following through, leaned his weight on a wheelbarrow and found himself rolling away. He recovered in seconds, but vander Poele was upright again, with his sword in both hands. They had, by then, traversed the full length of the yard.

Realising it, for the first time Diniz hesitated. As if in some mirror-reflection, vander Poele's sword halted, suspended. The slash, the thrust that he had invited did not come. But when, drawing breath, Diniz sprang and brought down his blade, the other parried it with a clang, following with a swing to the left and the right which had nothing subtle about them, and which Diniz blocked, in his turn, with great care.

Both his elation and anger were dying. He saw that despite all the activity, vander Poele's breathing was hardly disturbed. His hands were firm on the sword, his eyes unexcited. If there was a shadow there somewhere, it owed nothing to present anxiety. Niccolò vander Poele fought with the ease of a highly-trained man of arms who had been further groomed by a master. The man was contemptible. He was also, none the less, a good swordsman who was biding his time. Bartolomeo Zorzi had known that, or suspected it, and was waiting with interest. If Diniz died, Zorzi would lose nothing more than a trainee. If vander Poele, it was different. Then the King would have a new lease to bestow for his dyeworks.

Diniz Vasquez applied his wits to the task. The problem was space, of which there was too much, and which vander Poele was using to exhaust him. Therefore he would confine him. Speed of arm and of eye were greater at seventeen than at twenty-one or twenty-two. Diniz was familiar with the dyeyard, and the Fleming was not. And, as he now had come to realise, there was another, very special advantage. For Bartolomeo Zorzi, either way, would not interfere. For all practical purposes, including killing, he and his uncle Simon's enemy were alone. Diniz kept his face blank and continued to swing, but now it was in one direction, and now it was with a purpose.

It was not easy to coax the other man between buildings, even though they were here on firmer ground, and their blows connected more often. His wrists and back and shoulders were beginning to ache, but Diniz paid no attention. If the other man noticed, it would merely make him more eager. It seemed unlikely that vander Poele meant to kill him, or he would have done so already. It would be enough, Diniz supposed, to beat him into some sort of weakly surrender by simply protracting the fight. Youth and resilience were unlikely to outlast, he now recognised, this tireless, cynical parrying.

The end of the buildings was in sight, and behind, that part of the yard which had been hidden. Diniz sucked in a breath, tightened his grip and, changing position, began to drive vander Poele backwards, round the building and into that space and all that was in it. For this was where the Venetian renovations had ceased; where the wood-lined tubs remained sunk in the ground with their cargo of dye, fermented fat water, and urine. And beyond was the copper furnace which had been boiling all morning and whose fire, he knew, was not wholly dead. He swung the sword, again and again, and vander Poele moved backwards, swerving, bending, swinging in turn, until the first of the pits stood behind him. Then for the first time, his adversary spoke.

Vander Poele said, 'No, Diniz. I know the yard too.' Diniz, frowning, lifted his sword. The Fleming repeated, 'No,' in the same unemotional voice and, with a sudden, swift movement, engaged Diniz's sword, ran one blade down the other in a shuddering scream, and with a wrench that set fire to his shoulders, pulled the sword entirely out of his hands. For a moment vander Poele held them, locked together, and then with a violent gesture, he cast them both away. He said, 'Enough. You have shown you are a swordsman.'

Diniz took in deep breaths. He said, 'That is not why I am here.'

The Fleming stood on the edge of a tub. He said, 'You are here because of your aunt and your father. So why don't we talk of your aunt and your father?'

Diniz had no weapons left, but there was a wringing-hook on the wall at his shoulder. He snatched and swung it at vander Poele's ankles. Instead of tripping, the other man sprang to one side, slipping his foot in the hook as he did so. He tugged, and Diniz fell sideways into the tub. Liquid closed over his head; he swallowed and sat up spewing. It was full of urine. Then he made to rise and could not, for the wringing-hook was fast in his belt, and the Fleming stood holding it. Vander Poele said, 'What did you intend? To trip and then kill me?'

Diniz sat in the stink, coughing and choking. He said, 'To kill you.'

Vander Poele said, 'Or did you mean the copper to do your work for you? It's there, above you, still warm. I have only to pull out the plug, and let it flood into the gutter. The liquid would scald, and then drown you.'

'Do it, then,' Diniz said. He saw, in the depths of the tub, a glint of metal and remembered what it was, and how it came to be there. A piece of carelessness, the previous day, followed by a childish unresolved brawl between coopers. *You climb down and get it. It's your fault.* The article they had dropped was an axe.

The Fleming, he heard, was still talking. 'Why should I kill you? You haven't harmed me. You couldn't harm me. I have no reason for wanting you dead. I have bought you: I told you, because I prefer to see you here, in the salubrious air of the dyeshop.'

Someone was laughing – the Venetian, strolling up. He said, 'My dear, I said fight, not dip the poor child like a sheep. I think you should tie him until he becomes a little less angry.' There was a hank of blue wool in his hands, still attached at one end to its winch. Zorzi said, 'You drop it over his shoulders, and I'll wind him up like a moufflon. Christ God, he stinks.'

Diniz gave one choking sob. The hook dragged his belt and his body began to leave the filthy water. The heavy wool dropped over his shoulders and then gripped round his waist, trapping one arm and leaving one free. Vander Poele thrust the stuff into place and held it firm with one hand, while the other assisted the pull with the wringing-hook. The Fleming talked over his arm to his winch-man. His attention was fully engaged and so was that of Zorzi, who was laughing harder than ever. Diniz began to rise free of the bath.

He had already taken hold of the axe. As he came waist-high to his tormentor, he whirled his arm round with the implement. He let it go just short of its target, which was the vein in vander Poele's neck. The flash of silver was all the warning the other man had. He began to move, but there was of course no way he could avoid it. Diniz heard the thud, and the other man's gasp. The Fleming half staggered. The stick fell to the ground, and the wool ran through his fingers. The axe, jarred by the movement, detached itself and fell beside Diniz. He felt the handle under his hip as he dropped back to the vat edge and sprawled, half in and half out of the bath, blinded by the dash of the liquid, and by the crimson spray of Niccolò's blood. He saw, through the blur, that the other man had fallen quite slowly and was lying, his head turned away, in pools of bright blood and urine garnished with wool twists of Imperial purple. He couldn't see the extent of the wound. He said, without getting up, 'Is he dead?' He started to shiver.

The Venetian Zorzi looked up from where he was kneeling. He was perhaps pale, but his expression was not one of horrified anger. He said, 'Well. Neither of us expected you to do that. No, he is not dead. But he could be.'

Diniz stared at him. Zorzi said, 'If you wanted him dead, you have only to leave him. He will bleed his life away in ten minutes, and you would be perfectly safe. It was a fair fight, and the cut of an axe or a sword can look much the same in a corpse.'

Diniz lifted himself until he was sitting. He said, 'You would do that? Support me?'

Zorzi knelt back, one hand comfortably on his knee. He said, 'I don't see why not. I've no axe to grind – ha! – over the rights and wrongs of your case, but you seem a good trainee, and vander Poele himself recommended you. This was a fair fight, or an accident.'

'And you don't mind if he dies,' Diniz said.

'No,' said Zorzi thoughtfully. 'Unfortunately, I am not a free agent. I have an elder brother, and orders to follow. I think perhaps I should make some little effort. Of course, I might try very hard, but in the end nature could defeat me?' He looked down. The scarlet pool widened, and thickened. Far across the yard, a banging noise made itself heard from the other side of the buildings. Bartolomeo Zorzi lifted his head. The banging stopped, to be followed by the jangling of spurs, and men's voices. Zorzi said, 'Who? The King's men, at a guess, come to look for the fugitive favourite. Who has had an accident, practising swordplay, and whom we are doing our best to revive. Hide the axe. Come here. I need a stick and a rag. I apply my fingers here, and you bind as fast as you can. What is wrong with you?'

'Nothing,' said Diniz through chattering teeth.

'Why deny you are weeping? It is right to show anguish. Through no fault of yours, the King nearly lost his good comrade.'

Men appeared at the end of the shed. Diniz said, his hands smothered with blood, 'He will tell them. When he wakes, he will tell them what happened.'

'Will he?' Zorzi said. 'Remember, he could have killed you and didn't. He could have freed you, and didn't. He wanted you in his power. And he has his wish now, hasn't he, to a degree he hardly expected? You are at vander Poele's mercy. And at mine, of course, also.'

Chapter 26

'SO YOU FELL on your axe?' Tobie said.

From this, Nicholas deduced that he was now expected to live; since it was the first direct, normal remark anyone had made to him during several hours of extreme pain and confusion. He had little recollection of being carried, by soldiers apparently, back to his own room in the villa. The doctor's face had immediately materialised, and the variety of sensations which ensued had been punctuated by Tobie's voice emitting phrases of bitter anger, impatience, anxiety, and at times a form of bracing reassurance which Nicholas, unable to respond, had felt nevertheless to be deeply disturbing.

He was aware that he was now fully awake after what felt like a profound sleep and that he was in his own bed, from which rose a distinct odour of latrines. The upper left side of his body was encased in wrappings, beginning at his neck and continuing down over his shoulder and chest. The seat of the screaming alarm lay somewhere at the point of his shoulder and neck. Indeed, he remembered explaining to someone that he had been struck and felled by a boulder, and asking them to go and get tackle to lift it. That had been, no doubt, one of his less sensible conversations with Tobie. His head thudded and he had no wish to move, or conviction indeed that he could. It felt, now he came to think of it, as if he had lost a lot, quite a dangerous volume of blood. Now he came to think of it, he remembered how.

Tobie's face, which had acquired a frown, was beginning to clear again. Nicholas said, 'Well, I didn't fall on my sword.' He added, 'Is the smell coming from you or from me?' He further added, 'I thought you stayed at St Hilarion?'

Tobie scowled, while looking paradoxically cheered. Ignoring this last, he said at once, 'Are you serious? We had to wrap you in rags, or the bed would be as disgusting as you were. Even after we washed what we could reach of you, and scrubbed the floor, and burned your clothes, you could tell, by God, that you came from a dyeyard. Mind you, for smell, the stupid brat was the winner. Flowers died as he passed them.' Tobie paused. 'The Portuguese. The spoiled baby who did his best to kill you.'

Nicholas wished the conversation would halt. Against strong advice from his internal organs he said, 'Who told you that?'

'Bartolomeo,' said Tobie. 'The Palace, of course, has been treated to quite a different story. But Bartolomeo made sure, naturally, that we heard the truth. I didn't like him when he came on board off Constantinople, and I don't like him now. I don't know why his damned peg-legged brother took the trouble all that time ago to ransom him. And I don't know, either, why you've brought him into the yard.' He stopped, and into his face came the critical look Nicholas recognised of old. Tobie said, 'You're not much of an audience. Sore shoulder? Sore head? A drink, maybe?'

'Not that kind of drink,' Nicholas said. 'But something wet would be nice. There's a new inlet pipe in my head.'

'Let's try the usual way.' Supporting him, Tobie said, 'It was your lucky day, whatever you feel like. You moved just a little too far, and the axe was at the end of its range. I'd like to try it again with the brat at the other end, this time.'

'Diniz?' Nicholas said. The cup withdrew. 'He wasn't hurt?'

'They didn't call me to him,' said Tobie. 'Which is as well, because I wouldn't have gone. He's here, in a cell with a stool, a bucket and a small supply of congealed food. I don't think he's been offered a bath yet, but maybe his nose has got used to it. What did you expect, an ovation when you walked into that yard?'

'I was going to talk to him,' Nicholas said. 'But I had to take Zorzi there first. I was going to talk to him along with . . .' He stopped. With the pillow behind, he could now see a small amount of the room, including the window. There was someone sitting beside it. He saw who it was.

Tobie followed his gaze. 'Katelina van Borselen. You asked her to come here to meet you, and she's been here ever since. She won't leave till she knows what will happen to Diniz.'

'Nothing. Tell her.'

'I have told her. She doesn't believe me. I don't, perhaps, sound convincing,' Tobie said. He was wearing his cap, as he always did when exercising his profession. The curl of his lips matched the neat little scroll of his nostrils; all of which, in their ways, provided a regular index to Tobie's intimate feelings. Once, in Trebizond, Tobie had attended another illness of his, with consequences Nicholas preferred not to remember. Then, Katelina had not been present: only spoken of.

Nicholas said, 'Bring her over.' She came, not very quickly, and stood by his bed.

Sick or well, you couldn't look at this face without seeing, under the strain, the handsome, high-bred young woman of three years before. You couldn't look at the slender gown, the long sleeves, the severe coif, without remembering the generous body, twice offered and many times visited. Her gaze was large and brown and impelling. She said, 'The cause in this quarrel was mine. Diniz was an innocent, acting on impulse. Punish me, but not him.'

Since St Hilarion, he had grown very tired of some sorts of exchanges. He said, 'How would you like to be punished?'

Her eyes widened. So, he saw with perverse satisfaction, did those of Tobie. Then she said, her voice steady, 'Do with me as you would do with him.'

'All right,' said Nicholas. 'He goes home, and you start in the dyeyard on Monday.' He closed his eyes without meaning to, and found it an improvement.

She said, 'You are playing with me.'

Tobie said, in an exasperated way, 'He's not playing with anybody. He's tired of talking, and he's just told you the truth. Diniz is under no threat but that. He has to work with the dyes for a season. And even that was already decided.'

Katelina's voice said, 'Is that true?'

Nicholas opened his eyes. He said, 'You know how ashamed I was of my upbringing. Now the Vasquez are getting a taste of it.'

Her relief was so great that it displaced, he saw, even her scorn. She said, her voice strengthening, 'But he is in a cell.'

'That was Tobie's doing,' he said. 'A surcharge for unsolicited work conducted under unpleasant conditions. I shall give orders to have Diniz released. He will be, as before, a prisoner of war with restricted freedom of movement. Unless, of course, he tries the same thing again.'

'I shall stop him,' she said.

Nicholas looked up at her. 'He might stop himself, if he thought about it. You could tell him –' He hesitated.

'Yes?' said Katelina. 'I don't mind being your mouthpiece. I shall not, perhaps, be very persuasive.'

There was a silence. Tobie said, 'Go on.'

Nicholas lay, feeling foolish. Because he also felt rather ill, he eventually spoke. 'Tell him that his father was not killed by my agency. Tell him that, when I found my company in Rhodes, I had already promised King James that we should serve him, or nobody. If I'd told the Queen that, my men would never have left Rhodes alive. And there is one last thing. I had no idea that you and Diniz would be on board that ship for Cyprus. This was never intended.'

She said, 'So why are you keeping us?' He couldn't tell whether she believed any of it or not.

He said, 'I am keeping Diniz, since he is here, for his own good.

I am not keeping you. That is the fault, I gather, of my – of Jordan de Ribérac.'

It was not a slip he would ever have normally made, and she struck immediately, with such speed that he saw her stance had not changed by a fraction. 'Of your grandfather, you nearly said. You still pretend to believe he's your grandfather?'

'It doesn't matter,' he said. His eyes were worn out with the ache in his head.

'But you do. That is what I can't forgive,' she said with sudden vehemence. 'You knew what you were doing. It wasn't by chance. You truly thought and think Simon is your father, and devised the foulest revenge, using me.' Her voice rose. 'Using me. Using me.'

'That's enough!' Tobie said briskly. To reduce emotion was, after all, part of his job; and he was good at it. Nicholas heard him through a light haze, which made it remarkably difficult to assemble his own thoughts. He suspected that, after all, Tobie had doctored that drink. Up to the very last moment, his wits failed to warn him what was going to happen.

The girl said, 'Using me!' in a scream, and Tobie took charge. He said, 'That's enough. Stop! Forget what he did. However dreadful it was, no one is suffering. Simon doesn't know Henry isn't his son. The boy will be reared as a nobleman. Nicholas is making no claims on the child or on you. Why pursue such a feud? Look what it's doing to Diniz!'

Nicholas heard that, all right. He said, '*Jesus Christ!*' It came out muffled; rather like a short sneeze. Katelina said nothing at all.

Then she said, 'You know. Who else has – has vander Poele told?'

A sense of disaster, clearly, had come too late to Tobie. He said, 'Nicholas –' in an uncertain way. Then, slowly, he pulled himself together. He said, 'I'm a fool. I'm a fool. Demoiselle, I should never have mentioned it. Nicholas didn't tell anyone. He wouldn't. We found out by accident. He had a fever, and rambled. We guessed, and we were – distressed, and he swore us to silence.'

'He told you and who else?' Katelina van Borselen said. Her voice, descended in pitch and in volume, was now unnaturally steady.

'Myself and a priest called Father Godscalc. We gathered – I had better tell you what we gathered. That Nicholas got you with child, and then married Marian de Charetty, as you married Simon. And that Simon believes this son of yours to be his own.' He paused. He said, 'Your secret will be kept by us and by Nicholas. You must know he doesn't take this thing lightly.'

Nicholas said, 'She knows nothing. We've been apart since it happened.' His head swam, and his heart knocked his breath about. The speech he always ought to have made; the meeting they should have had long ago – both were upon him now; and, half-drugged and in public, he must find the right words now or never. He tried to speak clearly and simply. 'Given the chance, I should have said to her that I had no idea she was with child. She didn't tell me. She could not, after all, bear the child of an apprentice. Later, I understood that.'

To Katelina, it must have seemed nearly as difficult. She looked at Tobie, then straight at the bed. It was the first time Nicholas had seen her look at him properly. Katelina said, 'I was in Brittany.' Her voice had altered again. 'You knew I couldn't reach you in time. You knew Simon wanted to marry me. You knew that, to save myself, I would marry Simon. And you knew I didn't know the connection between Simon and you.'

He said, 'Katelina. How could I know you were pregnant?' He didn't speak of the assurances she had given on the night she offered herself to him in Bruges. He had been the one to speak of the risk. She had been the one to dismiss it. But there had never been any doubt that the child was the product of their next night together, and his.

Perhaps she remembered. There was a long silence. Then she said, 'I think you did. There was a woman in Brittany who suspected it. Antoinette de Maignélais, she was called. Is the name familiar? She was not unconnected, I think, with what happened to Jordan de Ribérac under the last King of France. His disgrace and exile, which seemed to suit you so well at the time. I am not surprised – I'm not wholly surprised that the seigneur de Ribérac has refused me a ransom. This family bears long-standing grudges. But anyway, what does it matter? Whether you knew you had succeeded or not, you married while I was in Brittany.'

Nothing would make him speak of Marian de Charetty. His eyes closed, and he made them re-open. He said, 'I didn't know of the child. It is all I can say to you.'

He saw her staring back. It seemed, for a moment, that something he said might have touched her. Then she sighed, and said, 'Who else have you told?'

She had removed her gaze, turning a little; conveying the close of the matter between them. With a glance at Nicholas, Tobie took over the answering. He said, 'No one. What he says is the truth. We learned of it, Godscalc and myself, by pure accident.'

She said, 'But when will there be another accident? He is prone to fever. What future will Henry have then?'

Tobie said, 'What do you want him to do? Drop dead for something that isn't his fault? It takes two to make a son, demoiselle.' He sounded angry, which was unfair on Katelina.

Nicholas, who realised his head was about to explode, nevertheless saw the humour in this, and thought he ought to explain it. He said, 'Tobie! Don't be silly. You've always believed to the depths of your soul that I plotted it all. Of course I did. A bastard for Simon. Luxurious exile for David of Trebizond. St Hilarion at all costs for Zacco. And the events of today for us all, loving scions of a fortunate family. Who says I can't plan?' His heart ran like a wheel out of gear, and his senses screwed themselves to a pitch that made his breath falter. It seemed to him, from limited experience, that there was a certain finality about the situation. He said, 'I think the future may be safe from me after all.'

An angry voice spoke from the doorway. It said, 'Is this the talk of a man, or shall I take your doctors away? A man values his life, and thinks it worth fighting for.'

Zacco, straight from the banquet. In gold and jewels, ermine and satin he stood on the threshold, tall and glaring. Through darkening eyes, Nicholas witnessed a new and complex situation appear, over which he could have no control. With infinite weariness, he watched it develop. Katelina turned, her exhausted face pale with astonishment. Tobie flushed. He said, 'My lord King, he has no wish to die. And, God willing, we shall prevent it.' Zacco stared at him and then, glittering, swept past and knelt at the bed.

His jewels flamed, but no one ever looked at them. Instead, like Tobie, like Katelina, like himself, those in Zacco's presence were mesmerised by the enchanting, remarkable face. Today, its vitality was repressed; the brows drawn under the swathe of hair that had fallen, again, from the cap of state he still wore. His warm hands closed about the cold fingers of Nicholas and he held them, gazing in silence.

Nicholas did not speak, but kept his eyes open. Across Zacco's face passed the shadows of many thoughts, bringing him, presently, to some resolve. He released one of his hands and leaned forward. The light dimmed. There was a smell of soaps, and furs, and a warm, clean humanity. Zacco's lifted hand touched his lips, his temple, his hair; then closing, calmly descended. Nicholas felt his palm smooth his lids, closing them. Blessed darkness returned. The palm lay, flat and weightless, prohibiting movement. The King's voice said, 'You need peace more than a friend. My purse is yours and your physician's, and all that my kingdom can offer. I shall come every day.'

It was the kind of thing he did say. He might even mean it. The hands withdrew. Nicholas lay, his eyes closed. He heard the King leave, and Katelina's steps apparently following. Tobie said, 'I'm still here.'

Something had to be done. Nicholas twitched his lips, without opening his eyes. He said, 'I hope Abul Ismail can take the piss out of ermine.' With the last of his consciousness, he registered Tobie's grunt of approval.

*

Outside, waiting as bidden, Katelina van Borselen raised weary eyes to the man gowned as a King who, it seemed, was young and comely and hardly older than Nicholas, for love of whom he had come here. The antechamber they stood in was private, and he did not ask her to sit. Instead he walked frowning to the window, and turned.

'We have a few moments only. We were curious to see you. We are told there is some relationship, some estrangement, between your family and the lord Niccolò?'

The lord Niccolò. But he was, officially, a Knight of the Order. To him, Zacco had spoken as to a familiar. Now he used the royal plural, which should have seemed childish, but did not. She said, 'That is so. But my nephew and I are here, my lord, through no fault of our own. We are anxious to leave.'

'For Kyrenia?' he said.

'I have abandoned that plan. For home. For Portugal,' she replied.

'Indeed,' he said. There was a jewelled chain round his neck, and his big-boned fingers played with the pendant. He said, 'Our lady mother says she has seen you.'

'Your lady mother, my lord?' she said.

'In the Palace, with the lord Markios, her brother. You were ill in your chamber,' said Zacco.

She had only been visited once at the Palace. What had happened then she had thrust to the back of her mind hoping, perhaps, that it had been a delusion. The auburn-haired girl who had turned into a cynical, acid-tongued harridan. The melting face, speaking of locusts. *What then should I do to you? Skin you as the Mamelukes do, and makes hawsers out of the peelings?*

It had been a real person. Her brain told her as much. But – this man's *mother*?

'She frightened you,' Zacco said. 'We are afraid that, in her zeal, she sometimes goes too far to protect us. But she is not harsh to those who are reasonable. She says we should be lenient, and should prepare to release you even without recompense for your lodging. We have agreed. We have said that if by autumn the gold has not come we shall send you away. Meantime, you will be lodged in the south, where you will have no temptation to incite your nephew, or communicate with Kyrenia or Famagusta. There are several families of good blood near Episkopi. You will take your woman, and stay with one of these. You will suffer no hardship.'

Her limbs were trembling, but she tried to keep her voice steady. 'And my nephew, my lord?'

'That is settled. He remains here, and works in the dyeshop. Messer Bartolomeo, we are sure, will be a good master. That is all.'

She said quickly, 'I should prefer to stay with the Clares. Or at some –'

His eyes, full on her face, were brilliant hazel and colder than metal. 'We have spoken,' he said; and walked out.

For love of Nicholas, he had come. Katelina thought of what she had heard, and the caress she had seen. She had always assumed that one kind of love precluded the other. She had held herself firmly apart from the plebeian tangle of this apprentice's conquests – from the serving-wenches of Bruges to his elderly wife; and from there of course, to Primaflora. There had been a rumour from Venice. There had been another, which she discounted, from Trebizond. But now, slowly, she began to consider whether or not there were reasons for this strange inconstancy which had nothing to do with simple lust or base blood or ambition.

She went back to the Clares, and could neither pray nor go to a friend, for she had no friend to turn to, here or anywhere.

Chapter 27

WHAT HE SAID and did when ill, Nicholas had learned, often ran counter to his own diligent planning and was capable, sometimes, of messing it up quite considerably. While recovering, therefore, he obeyed Tobie to the letter, and received no calls until he was sure of himself. The exception was, of course, Zacco, who came, as he had promised, every day. Each time a servant preceded him, bringing fruit, or pastries, or little birds pickled in vinegar.

Once the King brought his own gift: an offer to fetch Primaflora. Since she was in Rhodes with Carlotta, the gift would have been as expensive, in cost and in lives, as any he could have devised. On those grounds, but not only on those grounds, Nicholas declined with due deference. The day after that, to Tobie's outrage, Zacco sent a charming girl-child to the sickroom, explaining in an oddly spelled message that, to satisfy Flemish chivalry, he had had her used first. 'But,' reported Nicholas, 'he said he was willing, if wrong, to replace her.'

'Barbarians!' exclaimed Tobie, whose imagination in respect of Zacco was fortunately not of the strongest. He added, 'It's too soon, anyway.'

Lying alone, Nicholas exercised himself on affairs of the mind, such as an evaluation of profit and loss. Recognising what he was doing he would pull a face, remembering Tommaso Portinari, with his rings and his ledgers; or Metteneye's wife and her books. Or, without smiling, would think of Anselm Adorne. Or Jaak de Fleury. Or Julius and Marian, who had taught him all they knew. All they knew, not all he knew.

His profit and loss he weighed on scales slightly different from theirs. Profit, that he had impressed Queen Carlotta sufficiently for her to send Primaflora after him. Profit, that he had mercenaries again under his hand. Profit that, after he had chosen to fight in the right place at the right time, the Venetians working for Zacco (whom he had also impressed) had used his own ship to bring him to Cyprus. Profit that, in return for himself and his army, he had land, money, a title and the franchise of the Nicosia royal dyeworks. Profit that he had bought the skills of Bartolomeo Zorzi, who knew all about non-Papal alum . . . and who of course, had brought him back Chennaa, his camel. And finally in the balance of profit – the lure, the prize, the object of all he was doing – the right to earn whatever money he could from the richest franchise in Cyprus: the royal sugarcane fields of Kouklia and Akhelia, bestowed on him by Zacco.

There had, of course, been losses, of which the most distressing was time. But if he could not immediately travel, he could conduct operations very soon from his bed. He had, after all, been exploiting both franchises from the day he landed at Salines. In any game, application was of the essence.

Soon, he was able to call a war meeting for sugar, as he had induced the King to do for St Hilarion. For that the key figure was Loppe, who arrived in Nicosia almost before he was sent for, bringing with him Michael Crackbene and Umfrid, his excellent round-ship accountant. By then, Nicholas could sit for spells at his board with his boxes, which contained variously the receipts, the bills and the lists for his war, his dyeworks and his sugar business. Joined to them recently were the reports now reaching him often from Venice. Quite soon, Tobie had noticed one. 'That's from Gregorio!'

Tobie, with his pink inquisitive face, was the one person he couldn't keep out of his chamber. Nicholas said, 'I'm quite glad to hear from him too, considering he's sitting on top of our money. He seems to be lending it out at exorbitant rates. I must ask which army he's backing.'

'He's well?' Tobie said. He appreciated Gregorio for himself, and for what he had done as the company's lawyer. Nicholas, who owed Gregorio rather more, considered again, and dismissed again, the thought that he would like him in Cyprus. He would like him in Cyprus, but he depended still more on his link between Venice and Bruges.

Nicholas said, 'He must be. He's operating from the Corner mansion down from the Rialto. The House of Niccolò now. He's got quite a staff. They'll soon be almost as big as the Charetty company.'

He and Tobie and Astorre and Gregorio and Godscalc had once all belonged to the Charetty company, before his wife died, and his step-daughter inherited it. If Tilde died unmarried, he would own the Charetty company. Tobie said, as Nicholas expected, 'You're not competing with them?'

'No, I'm not,' Nicholas said. 'Gregorio keeps to his orders. But

he has had a clash or two in the marketplace with St Pol &
Vasquez, Simon's firm. He says they're heavily committed, without
much free money to spend. It explains the absence of ransom for
Katelina.'

It didn't, but that was his worry, not Tobie's. While he was still
fairly weak he had broken his rule and had Diniz brought to his
room, where he talked to him mildly, remembering that the guilty
always felt most vindictive. Diniz had been silent, resentful and
frightened, and he had got nowhere with him at all. Katelina, on
the other hand, had never been seen since her visit, and the
Clares were silent as only Clares afraid of Marietta could be. He
was sure of this, that Cropnose had something to do with it.

The day after that, Loppe's party arrived, and at the same time,
John le Grant rode down from St Hilarion. He broke his rule
again, and had them into his room. They all exclaimed at his
appearance, made a number of jokes, and got fairly drunk, which
sent Nicholas's temperature up and restarted the bleeding. Then
Tobie returned him to prison conditions, and no one came near
him for days. He spent the time making lists, and sending them out
to be studied. They had to do with men and buildings and plant,
raw materials, packing and transport. He also had Loppe's reports,
even though he wouldn't admit Loppe as yet. For Loppe was the
key, and needed meticulous handling. In fact, all of them did.
Nicholas was no longer a boy being indulged, or a young man still
proving himself. They had accepted him as someone to follow, and
he had to show he was right most of the time, if not quite all of it.
Or the game wouldn't come out as he wanted.

He thought he had a team. Twice, he thought he had lost Tobie;
once at St Hilarion and again over the business with Katelina. But
for no very pleasant reason, Tobie had been unable to cast stones
over St Hilarion, and whatever had emerged from that raw, dis-
jointed wrangle with Katelina seemed to have earned him a reprieve.
Or perhaps he had to thank his own condition and Tobie's overriding professional instincts. Or, far more likely, the matter of bryony
berries. At any rate Tobie did not, he said, intend to return to St
Hilarion. If anyone fell sick, that bastard Abul Ismail could deal
with it.

And John le Grant? Up till recently he had been like Crackbene,
a man who would peddle his ingenuity anywhere for the sheer
personal pleasure of exercising it. John was a red-headed German-
speaking Aberdonian who had joined him in Florence and shown a
backbone of iron through the Trebizond war, as he had through
the fall of Constantinople. Mick Crackbene, with the Scandinavian
name and the Scandinavian bulk and fair hair, had come to Nicholas
from Pagano Doria his enemy, and in the course of a career that
contained, Nicholas suspected, its fair share of piracy. But he was

a brilliant seaman and had shown himself, so far, a reticent but
perfectly satisfactory employee. It had not been his fault that he
had been forced to sail for Cyprus, and he had performed his
duties well and sensibly since. There existed, of course, a way to
gain his friendship and understanding, but so far Nicholas had not
been able to find it. He knew, from Loppe, that Crackbene's
accountant was in the same mould.

And so he was reminded of Loppe, and the quality of his
intellect, and the barrier of his colour. It seemed a long time since
they had first met: he an apprentice of eighteen, Loppe a slave on a
Venetian ship, and far from his home in West Africa. The Olym-
pian frame with its play of black muscles came no doubt from the
forebears he had lost, but owed its development to the various
masters in Spain and in Portugal who had christened him Lopez.
Loppe had given them physical service, and he had taken from
them their tongues and their knowledge. Loppe was polyglot, and
an expert in many things. Among them was the nurture of the
sugarcane plant.

When the day came that Nicholas was his own man, he gathered
them all in the garden: Tobie, John, Loppe and Crackbene, with
Umfrid. The cooks had brought food. The women knew him by
now, and their manner was cheerful and easy, although they never
stepped out of bounds, and he fancied that was not because they
were afraid of the steward. Galiot, chosen by Loppe, managed the
household remarkably well and dealt, too, with the food for the
dyeworks. Under Zorzi, the dyeworks were busy.

Today, the House of Niccolò in Cyprus met under an awning,
although the sun was mild, and the air still had the freshness of
spring. For a moment, oddly, it seemed that some vital component
was missing; and then Nicholas saw that he had been thinking of
his garden in Trebizond, and the persons missing were Godscalc
and Julius.

He said, 'I want you to hear me, so that we all know what we are
doing, and also to have your advice. At present, John can't stay with
us. Once his cannon are cast, we shall launch an attack on Kyrenia
and I shall come north to join him. The rest of the time I'll be in the
south, and you will be with me. By the time the war has moved to
Famagusta, the sugar crop should be dealt with, or at least capable
of continuing without us. We have to make this business self-
sufficient, secure and well-managed. Whether we personally stay in
Cyprus or not, the sugar franchise can support us for years; give us
capital for other ventures, and cushion us against losses.'

'So long as Zacco is King,' said John le Grant.

'So long as the Turks don't defeat Venice,' said Tobie.

'So long as the Venetians don't steal it from us,' said Nicholas.
Loppe smiled. There was a silence.

'What?' said Tobie. 'They brought you here.'

Nicholas licked smoked pork from his fingers, and let the jellied brawn he was supposed to be eating melt slowly into its dish. He said, 'They brought me here to get rid of Carlotta. They'll keep us here as long as there's danger. But they don't want a strong, permanent business competing with theirs.'

'How competing?' said Tobie. 'They could sell a hundred times what they grow.'

Nicholas said, 'They can't plant much more than they've got. They're short of trained men and slaves. Any ship calling anywhere is in danger of being requisitioned for war. And foreign imports are hard to come by – I know that from the dyeworks. There's also a shortage of craftsmen – the family links with potters and weavers have gone. Remember, Zacco's war to seize Cyprus caused a lot of damage in his part of the island. A lot of people fled with Carlotta. What happened changed the sugar industry. Loppe has looked at sugar estates all over the island. Most are small, some are spoiled, some have lost practical access. The only three worth anything are in the south, and we have one of them. The other two are Venetian-connected or -owned. One is the cane of the Knights at Kolossi, marketed through a Venetian company. One is the private estate of Marco Corner, the Venetian merchant.'

'And they are situated together,' said Loppe mildly. He had chosen to sit on the grass. His cap and sleeveless jacket were red; his shirt white, as was the wand-like lily upright on his fingertips. He inclined its stem to the map on the table. 'The Knights near Limassol, with the Martini brothers selling their goods for them. The Corner lands at Episkopi, managed by the Corner and their factor, who do their own marketing. And furthest west, the royal estates for which we have the franchise.' He tapped and lifted the flower, leaving a dust of gold pollen on Kouklia.

John le Grant said, 'Don't go on. I want to ask something. Nicholas, didn't the Knights cheat the Martini last year?'

'They tried to,' Nicholas said. 'I stopped them. Nevertheless, they're repeating the contract. The Martini have bought the Knights' crop, and will make their profit from how well they sell it.'

'So the Knights think we're dirt,' said le Grant. 'Upset their schemes, mishandled their wee man Kinloch, flouted Carlotta for Zacco, got their ship waylaid and gave Zacco its cargo. And now you're competing with them in the sugar business. That being so, why are the Knights using the Martini brothers again? You saved the Martini sugar. The Martini must be the best friends you've got.'

'Not exactly,' said Nicholas. 'Until now, the Martini held the royal franchise. The Martini had to go back to the Knights, because there wasn't another job for them. They don't like me at all.'

'Can they harm you?' said Tobie. 'The Knights? The Martini brothers?'

'Openly, no,' Nicholas said. 'We have the royal fief.'

'But?' said John le Grant.

Nicholas said, 'But, of course. Imagine what you would do if you were an outpost of Rhodes, and wanted to make an impression on the Grand Master, or on Carlotta. Fortunately, there are the Corner. Venetians also, and lying between us and Kolossi.'

'But competing also for men and equipment. Here's another thing,' said John le Grant. His hat clashed with his hair, and his skin shone under his freckles. 'Corner are privately owned. They manage their business, top to bottom. But aren't we in the same situation as the Martini? The royal estates turn out the sugar, and it's our job simply to sail off and sell it? I'm supposing that that's why Crackbene is sitting there. So why should we bother ourselves with all these lists I've been seeing? That's the estate manager's job, reporting to Zacco.'

'It should be,' Nicholas said. 'But because of the war, the estate is in a mess. What men there were left when the Martini left. If I hadn't done something as soon as we arrived, we should have acquired a most expensive franchise to nothing. As it is, there's a lot to do still. You see that. But we've got the replacement cuttings we need, and the experts, and the buildings and vats are being repaired. And Loppe has installed a new manager.'

'How?' said Tobie.

'He came from Syria,' Nicholas said, to save Loppe replying. 'All the sugar in Cyprus came from the Crusader factories at Acre and Tyre and Beirut. The country's under Mamelukes now, but they'll trade equipment and management skills from time to time, provided you use the right intermediary. We employed an Observatine friar to take the offer. The Patriarch of Antioch at times has his uses.'

'Ludovico da Bologna!' Tobie said. He paused. 'He's at Ferrara in Italy.'

Nicholas said, 'You'd be amazed, but ships do sail from time to time between Cyprus and Italy. Ask where we got the manager's new highly-trained sugar staff from.'

'Ferrara,' said Tobie, who never did puzzles.

'Consider,' said Nicholas. 'Ferrara is not far from Florence, and in Florence is a powerful lady whose two sons work in Naples. One of them trained in Spain and was a friend of mine in Bruges. The other trained in Palermo. And the name of the family is —'

'Strozzi,' said John le Grant. 'You got Lorenzo and Filippo Strozzi to send you men from Sicily. You cunning bastard.'

'And more than men,' Nicholas said. He threw a paper over and le Grant caught it and spread it on the table. Tobie craned. Crackbene, who had not so far opened his mouth, said, 'That is good. It is a diagram of a sugar mill.'

John said, 'It's more than that. It's a three-roller mill, and I've never seen one before. I've heard of it, though.' He snorted. 'In Sicily. Of course. The University. You want me to make you one?'

'Yes, please,' said Nicholas happily.

After that, it was exactly the kind of discussion he liked, with ideas and arguments flowing and fists pounding the table or knee. Halfway through, Umfrid spoke. He was quite as blond as Mick Crackbene, but short and neat, like a family mascot. He said, 'You expect a yield of 11.2 in the hundred on your cane? If the acreage is as you say, you will need a new refinery. You cannot afford both that and the plant you are building.'

'We refine once only, and subcontract,' Nicholas said.

'Then you will have to book capacity and be sure of your rates,' Umfrid said. A look of shock crossed his face and he sat back on his stool, diminishing. Nicholas said, 'No. Go on. You say that, in time, we should build our own refineries. Get me figures, and we'll have a look at it. But I still think it would be cheaper to contract out. Carlotta was using Bologna.'

'Only because she wasn't allowed to use Venice,' Mick Crackbene said. 'There is a refinery here, and in Rhodes. And one in Crete. As I sail, I ask questions, and report to you.' At the time, Nicholas was pleased with the intervention.

Later, a breeze came to flap the awning and they went indoors and scattered to their various purposes. Tomorrow, John le Grant would return to the army, and Crackbene would travel west to see timber merchants before returning for orders. The royal fleet was not large, and much extended in the cause of supplies and defence and, of course, the double blockade. Meticulously, as Nicholas knew, the fee for its requisition was paid into his business in Venice. He hoped Gregorio was happy.

Tomorrow he, too, would take the road at last for the south, Loppe and Tobie riding with him. He had been to the dyeworks already, and satisfied himself that it was beginning to run well and effectively, and that Zorzi had no cause to complain. He had seen Diniz once, in the distance, but the boy had turned his back, and he had not persisted.

Now he had one final task, which he contemplated with a mixture of amusement and revulsion. He changed his shirt for another, and put on a light taffeta robe which hid what was left of the bandaging. He knew he still held himself stiffly, but Tobie had been reassuring, and, slowly, he was permitted to move and exercise the injured muscles. It hurt, but not when he was thinking of something else. He had his hat brought by one of his entourage, and Tobie said, 'This meeting. Shall I postpone it for you?'

Nicholas looked at him. He said, 'Tobie, it's a contract for millions. How can I fail to appear?'

Tobie pulled off his bonnet, so that his bald head and face shone together. He said, 'Well, you fool. Don't drink. You're tired.'

Fair enough. Where he was going, he was unlikely to be offered hospitality.

The lady Marietta of Patras had several noses: some of wax and some, of various shapes, in painted wood. Today, receiving Nicholas, she appeared as at their first meeting, with a cloth of silk fastened under her eyes and below the mantle of gauze that covered her hair and her robe. She was in a plain room containing a table and chair and several boxes, as well as a velvet-topped stool, to which he was bidden. She herself sat at the table. She said, 'And has my son taken you yet?'

He did not blink, or move a hand or a foot. He said, 'Greetings, Highness. No, Highness.'

The veil skipped, and a snuffle emerged. The King's mother said, 'It is the art of the fisherman. You engage your prey. The pleasure lies in the dalliance, in the uncertainty. Once it is trapped, it is trapped. I commend you.'

'Madam. I thought you were commending your son,' Nicholas said.

The veil blew, but not unduly. The eyes watching him over it were almost lazy. She said, 'You have a penchant for dangerous conversations. I remember. But Tzani-bey had no trouble teaching you manners. Is he still somewhat crude? Is this why you escape to the south?'

'Certainly,' Nicholas said, 'I found he had no more to teach me. But he has my lord King for company, while I serve the same King in the south. For that reason, I asked for an audience.'

She laid her clasped hands on the table and opened her eyes. She said, 'You are directing this interview?'

Nicholas produced a face contorted with thought. He said, 'Highness. All the topics so far chosen are yours.'

'And you wish to escape them?' she said.

'Both of them?' Nicholas said. He reduced, politely, the surprise in his voice. He said, 'Highness. I have tried to explain. I am going south only on business.'

He did not know why he was treading this knife-edge, except that he sensed she liked a challenge, and was bored and wanted, too, a mirror through which to watch her son. He had not misjudged her. She said, 'Why do you think I will tolerate this sort of talk?'

'Because you can end it whenever you wish, Highness,' he said.

'Well?' said the woman called Cropnose.

And Nicholas smiled suddenly, so that both dimples showed, and said, 'You have forbidden me to choose a topic. Do we return to fishing, or not?'

'We do not return to insolence,' she said. She did not look disturbed. She said, 'You ask permission to buy some supplies from me.'

'From the villages your Highness owns. I am told there is a surplus. Your factor has agreed a price he thinks is generous. I have to receive your Highness's imprimatur.'

'And you require these for my son's business?' she said.

Nicholas lowered his lids, in lieu of inclining his head. He said, 'Without them, it cannot be successful.'

'I see,' she said. 'Well, Messer Niccolò, I have decided to take advice. I have asked the opinion of your neighbour in Episkopi.' She rang a bell. The door opened. She said, 'Messer Loredano and Messer Erizzo may enter.'

Without stirring, Nicholas heaved a great sigh. Then he got to his feet. The one prudent step denied him by Diniz's axe was the renewal of his commerce with the Venetians. By now, he had assumed they were all in the south but for the Bailie. He had planned to call on Erizzo tomorrow. But here he was, the representative of the Serenissima here in Cyprus: the bluff man who had kept him prisoner on the *Doria*, and whom he had last seen among the cats of Ayios Nikolaos, on the night that Tzani-bey called.

With the Bailie was Vanni Loredano, who had, of course, been on the ship and in the monastery and even in the Venetian house in Nicosia, where he and Nicholas had talked about sugar. That had been after Tzani-bey's small intervention. Nicholas recalled Loredano's dismay. Loredano thought, very likely, that he spent all his time being beaten. Nicholas bowed from the waist and Erizzo said, 'You are better. We were distressed: an unfortunate accident. It will leave no ill effects?'

'None, I am told. You sent the kindest of messages. They reached me. I am most grateful,' Nicholas said. They both looked affable. Stools were brought, and they sat. A number of the Queen's household entered and took their usual positions, and wine began to come round. Nicholas scratched his ear, and then took what was offered.

They were talking about the climate, a topic introduced by their hostess. Wives and children were mentioned, whose company was so delightful before the weather turned hot. The Bailie, Paul Erizzo, had a daughter called Anna. Marco Corner's daughter Catherine was with her dear parents at Episkopi. Vanni Loredano (who was Marco's factor as well as Erizzo's deputy) had been joined on the same estate by his wife and their little son Matthew. Nicholas listened, not lifting his wine-cup. He remembered, with a tremendous suddenness, who the mothers of Catherine and Matthew must be.

The King's mother said, 'But we are not here to waste time. Messer Niccolò has brought a proposition. He wishes to buy up all the surplus eggs from my farms, and transport them to the royal cane fields in Kouklia. He also wishes a number of good laying hens and some cockerels. The request is not out of order. It is our practice, however, when a commodity is in short supply, to make sure that the Republic, our good friend, does not suffer. You, Messer Loredano, manage the neighbouring cane fields for the Corner. Would the Corner find this transaction disadvantageous?'

An involuntary smile crossed Erizzo's face, and vanished. To Vanni Loredano, life was more serious. He looked at Nicholas, at the Bailie, and at the floor. Then he said, 'Highness, to my recollection we have enough hens, and they are laying. We should not deprive the lord King of what is necessary.'

The woman's veil blew in and out with quiet regularity. She looked speculatively at him, and then remarked 'Good! And Messer Erizzo?'

The Bailie coughed. He said, 'I believe the present number of birds to be quite sufficient for those already in business, Highness. It is true, however, that the flocks in Kouklia have been ... depleted. We shall be delighted to help, of course, with anything that will assist the lord King's estate to become profitable.'

'Excellent!' said the woman. 'Now, Messer Niccolò, I am able to give you your answer. My secretary will draw up and sign the papers required, and the birds will be delivered as and when you desire them. You dislike my wine?'

'Highness . . .' Nicholas said.

'Then pray drink it. We propose a salute to your new venture. Your new venture, and your new neighbours. You have heard that Messer Marco and his wife are already in residence?'

'In Episkopi. Yes, Highness,' said Nicholas.

'And with them, of course, Messer Vanni here and his family also. And, of course, their charming guest, your compatriot.'

'Guest?' said Nicholas. He held the cup to his lips and gave a good imitation of sipping.

'The demoiselle Katelina van Borselen,' the King's mother said. 'She does not go home until autumn, and Nicosia is trying in summer. She will enjoy Episkopi, the garden of Cyprus; the home of Apollo and sacred to foam-born Aphrodite. You can supply her with eggs.'

'I told you not to,' said Tobie. 'If one glass does that, thank God they didn't give you a refill.'

'It wasn't only the wine,' Nicholas said, while maintaining the ceiling in focus. 'It was the wine and the news.'

'You didn't get the hens,' Tobie said, wringing cloths.

'I got the hens,' Nicholas said. 'I also got Katelina van Borselen in the next house all summer, in company with two of the Naxos princesses. Diniz knew what he was doing. I tell you, Diniz had the right idea from the beginning.'

Chapter 28

NICHOLAS MOVED to the sea, and was glad to trade the oppression of Nicosia for the bewitching attractions of business. Katelina van Borselen, forced to abandon the Clares and enter a high Venetian household at Episkopi, exchanged a cell for a honeycomb, and found herself drowning in sweetness.

The villa of Marco Corner was white-painted, airy and full of delicious apartments of which Katelina and her servant had one, the Imperial sisters another. In a twitter of crystalline Greek, or Greek-French, or Greek-Italian, the wife of Marco Corner and the wife of Vanni Loredano fled across the cool inlaid floors and between the delicate furniture and out among the blossoming lemon trees, bearing their Flemish guest with them.

By day, their oval Byzantine faces glowing beneath enchanting straw hats, the ladies Fiorenza and Valenza would take her fowling: cantering through clouds of wild lavender to the saltflats. Or they would press through meadows of poppies to the white-pillared groves where Apollo (admirer of Ganymede) was himself anciently worshipped; or climb through anemones to scented forests of pine and fine cedar. Or they would stroll by the shore, and eat curds and sesame bread by the red rocks where Venus was born (without embarrassment, effort or afterbirth) out of the sea that foamed over the sand, with no more than an antiseptic odour of brine to taint the scent of crushed myrtle and narcissus. Lucky Venus. Lucky Venus's mother.

Towards evening, when the swifts darted and screamed, they took her indoors and played checkers or dice or backgammon, or made music, or read poetry or talked among their Venetian or Saracen friends. Sometimes their husbands were present; but not always. In the afternoons, when even the children were sleeping, other footsteps were heard, and at night also. The husbands, if they knew of them, made no remark. Like the fine clothes, the exquisite furnishings, the corps of servants who accompanied them everywhere, such things were accepted in the household, part Syrian, part Greek, part Byzantine, in which she was an unwilling visitor.

They were at pains to put Katelina at ease: they had exquisite manners. It was only at night, when the frogs pulsed, and the lizards hung on the walls and obscure flying creatures prodded the bed-veils, that Katelina, freed from the silvery feminine speech, heard breathing about her the ancient voice of the island. Beneath the prettiness, the chivalry, the conceits and scratchings of minia-ture war, the older gods were still there, threads in the earth, still brooding, still to be pacified.

The shrine of Venus was here. The Byzantine voices, quoting, laughing, singing, spoke of it every evening. Here Paphian Aphro-ditc was born – not sweetly from the foam, said the voices, but from the gouting member of her sky-father Ouranos, scythed off and cast in the sea by his own monstrous son. Here, on the hill above her birthplace, was the great Sanctuary where the rites of the goddess were performed; to which her wreathed adorers made their way from the strand in torchlit, chanting procession. Here she was worshipped as Aphrodite, as Paphia, as Wanassa the Mistress; as Kypris, or the Lady of Copper; as goddess of Love, Beauty, Fertility; as, further back still, the divine Phoenician As-tarte. Here, washed clean of its blood, stood the altar, and here, obedient to the goddess, maidens came once a year and settled like doves on the marble, crowned with hemp, bound to give themselves to whatever stranger brought his gold and his manhood to the myriad courts of her shrine.

Here were set the bubbling cauldrons to which were fetched aromatic herbs from the gardens of Erythrea, mingled with oils and Assyrian flowers. '*And there the Graces bathed her with heavenly oil such as blooms upon the bodies of gods. And laughter-loving Aphrodite put on all her rich clothes, and leaving sweet-smelling Cyprus, went in haste towards Troy* – where, of course,' had said the voice of Valenza that evening, 'she was the cause of the Trojan war. How beautiful the poems are! She passes over the land in her golden chariot; she rides the waves between Naxos and Cyprus. She takes as lover perfect Adonis, whose father Cinyras was richer than Midas or Croesus. And Cinyras, Ovid says, was the son of the founder of Paphos, born of Pygmalion and his warm-blooded statue. To the west – I shall take you there – was her fountain, where she bathed after giving herself to the crippled god Hephaistos . . . But we must stop! How tedious we are, talking of love! When would you like to see over the sugar mills?' had said Valenza. The twittering voices of Valenza and Fiorenza, children of Naxos, granddaughters of John, Emperor of Trebizond, saying what they did not mean.

When, next day, Valenza repeated, warmly, her invitation to traverse the sugar estates of Episkopi, Katelina accepted. Somewhere in Cyprus, in a sugar-growing manor called Kouklia, Nicholas vander Poele was pursuing his desire to become rich as Croesus, rich as Cinyras who begot his fine son Adonis on his own daughter. What was his business was also hers.

She was taken, on foot and on horse, by Marco Corner himself, gross in build, domineering in manner except, she noted, when in the presence of the princess Fiorenza his wife. The great-grandfather of Marco Corner had been Doge of Venice, and for three generations the gilt star and red horn of the family had been attached to their palaces on the Rialto and here. Four hundred souls, black, white and brown, worked in Corner's Cypriot fields, and he was their unquestioned master. She remembered her father, in Bruges, talking wryly about Marco Corner.

The sun, now, was losing its mildness. After the welcome green shade of the reeds, the yards shimmered with heat from the boiling-hearths. Shadow-streamers of steam wandered over the dust, crossed by the capering shadows of workers. In caps and drawers, tunics and aprons, men and children loaded and carried and dragged. Bent over the long wooden tables, the fish-muscled backs of the cutters gathered and flowed as if buttered. The staccato flash of·their blades made her think of war-fleets and armies. Slit and chopped, the cane was carried from there to the presses. She followed, with Marco.

The hot air vibrated with noise: of shouting, hammering, grinding; the thunder of wheels and of barrels; the dashing of water; the hissing of steam. From the rollers exuded the smell, dense and herbal, that enveloped the villa some evenings, along with wafts of sugar and sweat and fogs of sweet orange blossom. Here, the juice spat and shuddered in dented wood-handled vats. Sunlight flashed from the copper as men leaned on the tilt-blocks to pour, their hide aprons stiff, their arms rose-coloured with perennial scorching. Clusters of flies stuck to their skin and hovered over the cauldrons: the veil Katelina wore over her hat was taut with the grasp of her hands. A child with a switch walked at her back, beating the wasps that sizzled about them.

There were bees and wasps, flies and gnats in the houses of pouring as well, where the boiled juice sagged and settled in conical moulds, steaming up from long benches like mangers. The place smelled of rank wood and straw, of the molasses filling the under-pots and the flat odour of clay, from the stacks of red funnels and vases. Marco Corner opened the door of a warehouse and let Katelina see the precious white cones of crystal sugar, the wealth of Cyprus, the costly indulgence of kings. Katelina praised them, as she had praised everything. She said, 'Who can equal the Corner in the making of sugar? Yet the royal estates are in other hands. That surprises me.'

Marco Corner took her arm as they moved to the stables. 'You speak of Messer vander Poele? Of course, he knows nothing of sugar. But then, he fights for King James, and should be rewarded. I have no objection to that. You might even say, to be cynical, that Kouklia and Akhelia are sadly in disrepair, and unlikely to offer much revenue. On the other hand, there are some who find Zacco's choice of beneficiary distasteful. You saw the burning last night?'

The sky had flickered red in the west. Her woman had told her. So near? She said, stiffening, 'That was Kouklia?'

'It was quickly put out. Vander Poele has installed some system which draws on the aqueduct. But there have been other mishaps. The servants of God, demoiselle, offer their produce to God, and would prefer no competition.'

Katelina moved from shadow to sunlight. She said, 'The Knights of Kolossi would harm a royal fief?'

The lord Marco Corner smiled. 'The Grand Commander Louis de Magnac would be shocked if you said so. But their crop is owned by the Martini, who mourn the loss of their franchise in Kouklia. Other accidents may occur. Young Messer Niccolò would be wise to guard his new property. Now, it is late and you are pale: I have tired you. Let me find Vanni to escort you back to the house.'

She answered with gratitude, and only realised, received in the coolness of the villa, how exhausted she was. The princesses exclaimed, seating her, bringing her sherbet. 'The heat! We should never have sent you. And what you have missed! An elegant deputation from Kouklia, on black-muzzled horses that cost someone, my dear, a great deal of money. We are bidden to visit the royal manor tomorrow. You will come? You do not mind meeting Niccolò vander Poele?' Valenza said.

Katelina sat, feeling cold. Cured, then – if he had ever been as sick as he seemed – and well enough to take the initiative. She recalled the protestations he had made, threadbare now in her mind. He had said what anyone in his position would say. And for proof, he had kept Diniz captive, and had let the King's mother send her here. Here to the Naxos princesses, whose sister had been with him in Trebizond and who were watching her, their narrow eyes smiling.

Katelina said, 'I have no objection to meeting him. I hear there has been trouble at Kouklia.'

Fiorenza rose and lifted a flask. 'He sent to warn us to look to our safety. It was kind. But privately Marco, of course, thinks we are in little danger. The Martini, after all, are from Venice. My dear, give me your glass.'

Katelina said, 'The young man must be concerned on his own account. It is a royal fief, and his duty to manage it. And he cannot be here all the time.'

'Because of the war?' Valenza said. 'That is true but, of course, Zacco will be the first to forgive him. And Kyrenia will fall to them soon enough. The guns are in place, and the harbour cut off, I am told.' She glanced at Katelina and made a small sound of apology. 'But you cannot be an admirer of Zacco, who has immured you here. Forgive me. We do what we can, but of course you wish for your freedom.'

Katelina said, 'I don't blame the King. My fate, for some reason, seems to be in the hands of his mother.'

It was Valenza this time who smiled. She said, 'My dear, it is the same thing. If the lady Marietta has sent you here, it is because the King wants it.' She paused, considering. 'Zacco is not, of course, such a man as you would meet in the West – a step-mother called after Medea, Cleopatra the name of a sister? He knows himself to be unique. He is proud of his heritage, and his beauty.'

Was she meant to understand some connection with Nicholas? The modulated voice held no discernible malice. 'I have heard tales of all kinds,' said Katelina. 'Though King, he has no consort?'

Fiorenza answered. 'He has a daughter, Charlotte. Others also, I think. The tales you hear are probably true, but James of Lusignan can inspire an army of Muslims and Christians, which I doubt if Carlotta could do. And one day, of course, he will marry.'

Her tone was reflective. It came to Katelina that, of course, the perfect bride for the King should have been one of the Naxos princesses, had Fate's timing been better. Now, wed too soon and not yet entered on widowhood, none would ever be princess and Queen. Of course, marriages could be set aside. But Valenza worshipped her son. And Fiorenza could hardly dismiss her lord Marco: not with small Violante, Cornelie, Regina, Catherine, Blanche and the others about her. Catherine, nine, was plump and pale and underfoot at the moment, as always. Fiorenza sighed, and ran a fingertip over her daughter's straight hair. Katelina said, 'It seems the King trusts his good chevalier Niccolò.'

The sisters looked at her, their heads tilted. They might have been made out of seashells. Valenza said, 'Unwisely, you think? I suppose those who fight risk their lives. He appears to have shown himself faithful.'

'He is faithful, at least, to himself,' said Katelina. She couldn't say more. She couldn't yet, openly oppose the man who could kill Diniz by speaking one word in the ear of the King. She had already, in her pain and despair, said more than she should.

'But you would like him more if he freed Diniz, your nephew? How well we understand!' the lady Fiorenza said. 'And it may be possible. You will speak to him tomorrow. We shall plead with Messer Niccolò also. We shall solicit the support of his other guests. He has invited Jacopo Zorzi our neighbour, whose brother now governs his dyeworks. How pleasant if we succeed in freeing this Diniz. A charming boy to join this sad household of women.'

The words made her shiver. And not only the words. She couldn't ask a favour of Nicholas, to whose silence she owed Diniz's safety. Who, by his silence, thought he had bought her complaisance. But the princesses were not to know that. She could read nothing but tranquil pleasure in the two ivorine faces. They had never met Nicholas vander Poele. She couldn't tell if they were indifferent to the reports they had of him; or envied their sister Violante, or despised her. She didn't know whether they were prepared to love him or hate him. Or if they had learned, as she had, to fear him.

They rode to Kouklia in the coolness of morning, a fine company of noble Venetians, men and women, with their servants attending them. On the way they were joined by Messer Jacopo Zorzi, owner of vineyards. Katelina did not know his brother Bartolomeo, but surveyed with misgiving the blue-jowled sardonic face and straddle-legged stance. The princesses thought this man could influence the release of Diniz. Once, Katelina would have welcomed the prospect with joy.

Their way took them west, through the cornfields that bordered the sea, past the gleaming stadium of Apollo and above the foaming, rock-scattered shores where Aphrodite was born. In the sunlight, stone was stone, and no voices spoke that were not Italian, and hearty. Katelina smiled, but was silent, turning her will and her mind to the encounter before her. Shortly after, the road left the sea and attained the base of a low limestone hill at the top of which spread a long, irregular building, massively formed. Pennants fluttered over the sky, and a twinkle from the flat roofs hinted at distant observers. From there, sea and country and approaching cavalcade would be wholly in view.

It seemed that Marco Corner and his party were familiar with the route and the building. Without a glance they followed the road, which continued upwards and inland and, curving round, met a wall that seemed to be that of a monastery, and then another wall, and a gate within which a group of people awaited them.

In the front was Claes, her Flemish workman, motionless on a high-bred racing-camel streaming with gilded leather and tassels and silks. The animal swayed forward and stopped, to allow its rider to convey his welcome. Nicholas vander Poele, behaving like a Byzantine mountebank.

She watched his gaze number the company and thought him a little pale still, although he sat at ease, with one gloved hand on the reins and no sign of the stiffness of Nicosia. He was dressed in the Venetian manner, from his high-collared white shirt to his doublet, which was cut from thin double damask in a deceptive grey-blue, quite unlike the strident shade of the Charetty company. As he introduced them, she saw that all his servants and officers wore the same colour. It went well with the badge of his Order. Below his cylindrical cap, his hair was shorn to a spider-brown frieze. He said, 'Be welcome and enter. First, to the house for refreshment. Then, if you wish, we shall ride through the lord King's estates before supper. You honour us with your visit. My lord Marco. My lady Fiorenza. My lord Giovanni. My lady Valenza. My lord Jacopo. The demoiselle Katelina.'

He seemed to know both Corner and Loredano. His demeanour was free and a little amused; theirs was guarded. He had never before met Jacopo Zorzi or the two princesses. The sisters greeted him with the fragile delight of two fawns. Fiorenza said, 'We have heard of you from our sister.'

His dimples deep, his hingeless eyes fully open, Nicholas said, 'Yes? But she exaggerates.'

To Katelina he bowed, no more or less than courtesy demanded. Then his animal turned, and they entered the way to his manor.

At first, it agreed with what she had learned to expect. She caught glimpses of the same sunny copper she had seen on the Corner estate, and the same long sheds, and the same tables and barrows, although different in arrangement. His head turned, Marco Corner said as he passed, 'Here are changes.'

And Nicholas, leading them down the long avenue towards the deep fortified arch of his manor answered with perfect composure. 'It is a benefit, sadly, of vandalism. It allows one to replan a little. Later, you will see better designing down the hill there at Stavros. Meanwhile please come into the shade, and be welcome.'

Only then, passing between branches of myrtle and under arches of orange and almond, did Katelina catch sight of the flower-strewn quadrangle that lay beyond on her left, tenanted by dazzling, half-broken terraces, by Corinthian colonnades and fragmented chambers, by worn flights of great steps and fallen cylinders, gartered in bindweed. Paint-red oleanders leaned through crumbling marble and, near an arcade, a naked girl waited, grass in her breast, her white shoulder and flank dappled under the fig trees. In the centre, the marble flags beaten glassy about it, stood a single conical stone, black as sugar was white. There was a scent of sweet oils, and of earth, and a deep silence, tempered by the murmur of bees. On the horizon, the sea stood, still and blue.

Katelina said, 'Where is this?'

Nicholas manufactured a small, glottal sound. The camel turned and stood, dipping. He said, 'Demoiselle? This is Kouklia.'

'*This?*' repeated Katelina in anger. She flung out her crop, point-ing.

'It is Kouklia,' Nicholas said. His face was seamlessly vacant. 'The ancients knew it as Paphos. The royal sugar estate, built on top of the Sanctuary sacred to Venus.' His eyes remained on her. 'The cone is the goddess. You can see the libations, perhaps, and the flowers laid freshly before her. We don't stop women coming, although it is inconvenient. Would you like to see it more closely?'

'No!' said Katelina. 'No. It will be pleasanter in the shade.' She didn't turn her eyes either, although she knew the pearly shell-faces were watching.

Kouklia was ancient Paphos. Kouklia was the island's name for the shrine and temple of Paphian Aphrodite, the goddess of spring and gardens and love. The roots of the island were here, where Nicholas was; and of course, the princesses had known it.

Part castle, part fortress, part palace, the manor of Kouklia had been built over many periods, by many hands. On the east, the yellow masonwork blocks belonged to the great Frankish castle, two hundred years old, with its great gothic hall and its airy upper quarters. The north held the guardrooms and deep chambered archway, by which they had entered. To the west and the south were the kitchen offices and also the private quarters, recently rebuilt, Katelina could see, with open windows and long wooden balconies to invite the sea airs of the plateau. Presently, when they had eaten and talked in the coolness of the hall, they took their ease, as they wished, in these chambers. Then, as the sun lost its heat, their horses were brought and Nicholas conducted them through his domain. No one had yet spoken of Diniz.

Katelina watched not Nicholas but Corner and Loredano as they passed through the well-ordered fields in the shade of the eight-foot solid viaduct, whose high limestone troughs fed into the fields and the factories from distant springs in the Oridhes forest. Soon, they began to ask questions and without effort, Nicholas answered them. He showed them devices: deterrent mouse-walls of clay and chopped straw; tar-doctored water to guard against caterpillars. He willingly entered discussions. The lady Fiorenza said, 'But, Messer Niccolò, you show us all your secrets.'

And he, smiling, replied, 'But, lady, you would discover them anyway.'

'Of course, you are lucky,' said Zorzi. 'The aqueduct. Also, the river Dhiarizos is yours, and in flow through the summer. Whereas the Kouris –'

'We have different problems,' said Marco Corner heartily. 'Now. This development you speak of at Stavros. It was a farm. I remember little but a small farm.' And Nicholas smiled and led on,

and in a short time, the ground levelled and distant sounds, now
familiar from yesterday, became loud and compelling. Soon, a high
wall appeared, and a well-trained gatekeeper, and they were within
a big compound where everything looked new.

'The mill is Syrian,' Nicholas said, 'with Sicilian refinements.
John could tell you more about it than I, but he's had to go back to
Kyrenia. The aqueduct leads into here – if you will come down the
slope – and becomes a covered channel narrowing into the mill-
house. The jet from that, as you see, operates the horizontal wheel
turning the millstones. The floor is braced over a vault, and the
tailstream comes out there. You see the mash being dealt with. The
canal – over there – passes under the grinding hall, where the cane
gets its first pounding. I'm building a second mill for next season.
Do the ladies want to come into the hall? It is not very salubrious.'

'I should like to see it,' said Katelina.

The building was vast, with a flat roof supported on arches,
beneath which oxen plodded. They were forcing a stone to revolve
on a millbase the length of two men. It was poundingly noisy, and
malodorous. Nicholas clapped a man on the shoulder, and the
fellow stopped working and grinned as Nicholas, raising his voice,
began to explain.

Katelina left the party. She went and stood on the edge of the
juice-pit, and watched the greenish-black liquid rushing and swirling below. There was more juice in cisterns outside, and clean
water, and places where men and women were washing vessels and
jars. They talked as they worked, turning their heads and watching
the visitors. Nicholas called something as he came out and most
of them laughed. If you looked at all the faces in the mills and
the yard, they seemed engrossed, and not dissatisfied. Spoken to,
they quite often smiled, and the women gave a small curtsey. To
Nicholas.

There were sheds full of new moulds and jars, far more than at
Episkopi. 'I've set up our own pottery,' Nicholas said. 'They're
not bad either at tableware. You'll see some of it at supper. And
now, of course, the boiling-vats and the refining houses. Nothing
changes much there. We reckon, with all our various kettles, to
boil two tons of juice daily, but we'd like to speed all that up. Fuel,
as you know, is the problem. And here we use mostly the tall
moulds, as you do.'

The familiarity of the refinery process soothed the Episkopi
men: Marco's colour, quite heightened, settled a little. He said,
'And how are your hens laying?'

'Hens?' said Jacopo Zorzi. 'I thought the Martini lost all their
birds to the raiders.'

'Messer Niccolò obtained more. He had his sources,' said Marco
Corner. He caught the look on his wife's face. 'If you came oftener

into the yard, you would know that eggs clarify the cane juice. I wish to ask, Messer Niccolò, before you go further. You have laid wooden rails from the yard?'

The wooden rails, it appeared, enabled one horse to draw three wagons bearing thirty hundredweight of cut cane apiece. 'Or, of course, chests of sugar,' Nicholas said. 'A packhorse could take only two hundredweight. And the rails can run all the way to the jetty.'

Katelina stood dumb: it seemed kinder. Marco Corner had flushed again. He said, 'Ah. I see. Well devised. Well devised. And the working areas, so well fitted for continuous movement. With labour so short, it was worth planning.'

'Labour can always be imported,' said Nicholas. 'I allow my sugar-masters, incidentally, unlimited cheese, wheat and wine plus a sum of one hundred and fifty gold ducats paid after the season, and a percentage dependent on improved production. If you want to steal them, you will have to offer them something quite un-economic. I think the ladies are tiring. But perhaps you would like to see more?'

'No,' said Marco Corner. 'You have been too good, taking this trouble. I have to congratulate you. And the King. We believed we had brought him a warband.'

'Oh, I don't know,' Nicholas said. 'Organising a sugar business and organising a war – as I supposed you've already noticed, there isn't much difference between them.'

They had reached the gates, where their horses were waiting. Marco Corner said, 'And when will Zacco be King of all Cyprus?'

'Before next summer's harvest,' said Nicholas.

'And,' said Marco Corner, 'do you rely on King Zacco to let you keep the proceeds of an estate returning so fast to profitability? The Lusignan are notorious spendthrifts. They once pledged the whole village of Kouklia with the sugar they'd leased out as lien.'

'Just like the Knights,' Nicholas said. 'Whom can one trust? Except, I suppose, that even though Zacco is King of Cyprus, the threat of the Turk still lies over us. He may feel he still needs to sweeten his warband. I'm thirsty. Let's go.'

Because she was close, she saw Corner halt, and cause Nicholas also to fall back. The Venetian spoke. 'Why do you show me all this?'

For once, Nicholas returned the look soberly. 'Because I think we should work together,' he said. 'I would rather have you with me than against me.'

'But not to the extent of having me steal your sugar-masters?' the Venetian said. His expression had eased.

Nicholas laughed. 'Anything but that. But I have a ship, and good provisions. We can help one another. I bear you no grudges.'

'I hear you bear one,' Corner said.

'But not for a Venetian,' Nicholas said.

There were Moorish dancers to entertain them at supper, and a juggler, and acrobats who walked on their hands. The meal was taken at dusk under awnings, with torches burning all round the courtyard, and lamps set on the two oblong tables with their silver cups and white napery and big, childish bowls glazed and blurred with blue and brown patterns. Fiorenza, who missed nothing, had long ago given Katelina a small fan with which to protect herself. But someone, she saw, had lit pastilles, and the scent, not unpleasant, seemed to keep the air free of mosquitoes. It was mildly warm.

She was seated nowhere near Nicholas, who was properly in the centre, between the princesses. He was wearing an unusual expression which seemed to change with undue rapidity. Catching the sound of his voice, she realised he was relating some sort of tale involving mimicry. A cry broke from Fiorenza. It seemed to be of laughter.

'He has set to work,' said Jacopo Zorzi on her right. 'You were surprised today? You were not so surprised as our Venetian friends were on shipboard. That unlikely young man attracts women.'

'On shipboard?' Katelina said. On her other side, a man in physician's dress turned, and she saw it was the doctor whose saddle she had shared during a desperate evening in Rhodes. The man who had betrayed, in Nicosia, that he knew her secret.

Zorzi's face, darkened with stubble, smiled at her and continued to talk about Nicholas. 'Vanni and Paul Erizzo met our host for the first time on shipboard,' he said. 'Travelling with a lady they call Primaflora. You know the lady Primaflora?'

'We do,' said the doctor, speaking across her. 'The lady Primaflora, happily, has gone back to Rhodes. You mean you thought she'd have Nicholas begging, and instead it was the other way round?'

Zorzi's smile grew broader. He said, 'It's a crude way of putting it.'

'I'm a crude man,' said the doctor. 'I don't agree with you. I think she was a spy for Carlotta. Zacco got rid of her.'

Jacopo Zorzi observed a short silence, then said, 'Yes. Well, of course. Gossip, demoiselle Katelina. In the Levant we all thrive on it. I wish I could be concealed in the chamber, for instance, when you and the ladies Valenza and Fiorenza dissect us. But you are acquainted with the princesses, Master Tobias? You met their sister in Trebizond.'

The doctor had curious, curled nostrils which he now inflated, and pale eyes like an innocent cat. He said, 'Before that, in Bruges with her husband and later, on shipboard with her priest. I assure you, we all observed the niceties.'

'And of course, in Trebizond, there was another King Zacco. How sad,' said Jacopo Zorzi, 'to hear the news from Adrianople. Is your Niccolò deeply distressed?'

'What news?' said the doctor. Katelina, in the middle, turned her head from one to the other.

Zorzi looked surprised. 'You haven't heard? David of Trebizond has been thrown in prison with all his young children. You recall, of course, that he surrendered the Empire in return for safe exile under the Sultan. Now, it seems, the Sultan has accused him of treason on the word of his false friend and former chancellor Amiroutzes.'

'*George Amiroutzes!*' hissed the doctor. Katelina gazed at him. He pulled off his cap, an unseemly gesture in company, and revealed a bald head congested with pink. He compressed lips equally pink and declaimed, 'The bastard!'

From the place occupied by Nicholas, an amused voice said, 'Tobie!'

The doctor made no effort to replace his cap. He said, loudly, 'That turd Amiroutzes has got the Emperor David flung into prison. And his family.'

'I hear, six children,' said Zorzi helpfully. 'And their cousin, Alexios. His daughter Anna, of course, went as a concubine to the governor of Macedonia. The sons were all put in chains except for the three-year-old, George. Wasn't it Amiroutzes who engineered the Emperor's surrender?'

Across the table, Katelina saw the eyes of the negro, Loppe, meet those of the doctor who, in turn, engaged the apparently resistant attention of Nicholas. The doctor said, with the same pointed belligerence, 'We were all in Trebizond when Amiroutzes was Chancellor. How, Messer Jacopo, did you hear of all this?'

Jacopo Zorzi betrayed, and indeed rather overdid, an air of surprise. He said, 'Of course, from my cousin Bartolomeo who came straight from Constantinople. Messer Niccolò knows. It was Messer Niccolò here who invited him to manage the dyeworks.' He turned and beamed at Katelina, who responded with half her attention.

The doctor said, 'Of course.' The lamplight on his flushed face turned his eyes bright as crystals. Perhaps he remembered, as she did, the voice of Nicholas rambling in Nicosia. *You've always believed I plotted it all. Of course I did. Luxurious exile for David of Trebizond* . . . Nicholas had known about this. Nicholas who, carefully enjoying his wine, was saying nothing. He was saved, in any case, from an unusual quarter.

'How kind you are,' said Fiorenza of Naxos. 'We respect your reticence: we have felt your unspoken sympathy for our great-uncle the Emperor and his family. Messer Jacopo, these sad affairs should not intrude on our host's hospitality. Messer Niccolò: I hear flutes. Are we to be given some music?'

Nicholas then emptied his cup and turned, saying something, and in a moment the performers arrived and began. They were reasonable enough; they were indeed the players the princesses invited when they wished to entertain: there were not so many artists on the island. But what they played was appropriate, and their manner of presentation was correct, and the behaviour of Nicholas equally so. He was talking, now, in a civilised way to Valenza, and she was leaning at ease, replying coolly with a bantering undertone. Jacopo Zorzi said, 'He knows proper conduct. He trained at their court and has read the same books.' The doctor beside her suddenly rose and went out. Zorzi said, 'About Diniz.'

Katelina turned. The Venetian looked earnest and a little sorrowful. She said quickly, 'The princesses told me. Your brother employs him. On the other hand, there are special difficulties in asking for his release. I should not trouble you.'

His eyes shone in the lamplight. 'I was not sure if you had been told. My brother is discreet, but it is important, of course, that the truth of the incident does not reach the ears of King James. The fact, that is, that Messer Niccolò was not injured by accident. Naturally, Messer Niccolò himself is the last person to ask to free your nephew. On the other hand, my brother is sympathetic.'

Katelina said, 'That is the best news I could have. But no one can help. If Diniz escapes and is caught, everyone will suffer, for Zacco is bound to find out the truth from Messer Niccolò.'

Zorzi said, 'You have not thought of persuading Messer Niccolò yourself? Forgive me.'

Her outrage turned to acid amusement. She said, 'He would hardly believe, I'm afraid, an attempted seduction by me. In any case, as you have said, I might find myself the victim, like Primaflora.'

'Of that young man?' Zorzi said. 'Surely not. He is an amalgam of replicas: a composite of dubious models. You are your own person. If you ever do fear for yourself, it is not hard to get off the island. The Alexandria galleys pass and call, at Episkopi, at Akhelia, at Salines. There are always responsible men such as Luigi Martini who would help you. On the other hand, you have been promised freedom at the end of the summer.'

She said, 'Do you think I should wait?'

And Zorzi said, 'I think you should do what you say is impossible. I think you should speak to friend Niccolò. You underrate your charm, demoiselle; but it was not a persuasion of that kind I was thinking of. Our generous host did not mean to lose that

delightful lady Primaflora when he did. He might be prepared to
do a great deal to get her back.'

'In the face of the King and his mother?' said Katelina.

He looked at her thoughtfully. Then he said, 'Perhaps even then.
He is in a position of strength, and is young, and greedy for
women.' He smiled and, relaxing, passed her a dish. 'In which
case, he has made his home in a singularly appropriate place. Look.
People are rising. We leave in an hour. Will you allow me to
arrange a meeting –'

'With me?' said the voice of Nicholas behind him. Zorzi, half
risen, stood and turned. Katelina subsided. A moth, substantial as
brown rotted fruit, advanced through dying smoke and opened and
closed its wings on the table. Nicholas, his doublet caught on one
shoulder, was a blur of white, below shadowy features. He said,
'Young as I am, and greedy for women? If she wants to exchange
her services for her murdering nephew, she should come back to
Kouklia tomorrow. Today and tonight, I am suited.' She saw the
heaviness of his eyes, turned towards her, and heard the one
clumsy word in that speech. He said, 'Did he persuade you to
escape?'

'No,' she said. The moth shifted, and she stood up quickly. She
said, 'While Diniz is here, I am here. I won't beg.'

'It wouldn't matter if you did,' Nicholas said. 'Do you know
who he is?'

'She knows,' said the Venetian patiently. He had recovered himself.

'She knows,' Nicholas said, 'that Bartolomeo of the dyeworks is
your brother. She doesn't associate you as yet with your other
brother. Nicholai Giorgio de' Acciajuoli, who once shared your
journey from Scotland, demoiselle, and whose good advice sent me
to Trebizond. The Greek with the wooden leg. I broke it at Sluys.
You must remember that, Katelina.'

She remembered. She remembered the crazy, joyous apprentice
whose name was not yet Nicholas. She remembered a tall, elegant
Greek of Florentine descent whose affairs she had always known,
vaguely, to be involved with those of the Charetty company; with
its great new ventures; with the marriage, even, of Nicholas and
Marian, his employer and wife. She said, 'Do you mean to destroy
his brothers as well?'

The thing on the table moved. Following her eyes, Nicholas
picked up a napkin and, leaning forward, placed it over the live
moth and pressed on it. He said, 'I don't destroy everyone who
hurts me. You know that better than most. I don't even know
whether the Zorzi wish me well or the opposite.' He lifted his
hand, leaving the crumpled cloth on the table. Nothing moved. He
said, 'What do you think?' to the Venetian.

'I think it's dead,' said Jacopo Zorzi, 'whether it harmed you or not. And the Zorzi family? You blame us, I cannot think why, for the loss of your alum monopoly. Because I am a friend of Giovanni da Castro, does it mean he finds mines with my help? And today, I know of no insidious plot against you, nor will you think it likely once you're sober. Bartolomeo is making a gold mine for you out of the dyeworks. Nicholai, cripple that he is, can hardly be an opponent. And I – I merely live in Cyprus and work honestly in my vineyards. You must come and visit them some time.'

'Are they near?' Katelina said. She tried and failed to capture Zorzi's eyes. He had offered help of a kind against Nicholas. She had had no idea then that some real quarrel existed between them.

Zorzi said, smiling not at her, but at Nicholas, 'Not too far. In the hills, at a place called Engedi. You have heard it sung of, in the sweetest words in the world.' He stopped, and waited. Distantly, someone plucked a stringed instrument and voices spoke, idly, over the courtyard. The supper tables were empty and, for a moment, around them was silence.

Nicholas said, 'I shall send . . .' and stopped.

'Go on,' said Zorzi softly. She moved, and without speaking, the dark man reached and restrained her.

Nicholas said, 'I shall send gems of lapis lazuli: I shall make her fields into vineyards, and the field of her love into orchards. My beloved . . .' He stopped again. It was, Katelina thought, as if he were remembering something from long ago, or listening to someone telling him something he had not known. Nicholas said, 'My beloved is unto me as a cluster of camphire in the vineyards of Engedi . . .' He stopped again, and said, 'My beloved is dead.'

Zorzi lifted the lamp. By its flame she saw the face of Nicholas vander Poele, and it had no identity. Then he said, 'I must see to my guests,' and walked away.

Katelina found she was standing, looking after him. Zorzi's hand dropped and, turning, he laid the lamp slowly back on the table. Then he drew breath and looked at her, his unprepossessing, half-shaven face full of thought. He said, 'My beloved is dead? Who?'

Katelina said, 'No one. I know of no one.' She thought, disjointedly, of the life of Claes, and the life of Nicholas. *He is young, and greedy for women.* Perhaps. But none of his lovers was dead.

Jacopo Zorzi said, 'But surely. He has lost his wife?'

The Song of Songs, and Marian de Charetty. She found tears had filled her eyes – of fear, of pain, of disbelief. Zorzi saw them and said, 'Demoiselle. I'm sorry. We frightened you. One forgets. Wine acts quickly after an illness. He was not himself.' He was smiling; his face blotted and crawling with shadows from the insects that covered the lamp. Katelina said something and, stumbling, fled.

The other guests spent their final hour in the gardens. Pleading weariness, Katelina passed it indoors, in darkness. *I shall make her fields into vineyards, and the field of her love into orchards. Here, washed clean of blood stood the altar and here, obedient to the goddess, maidens came once a year . . . How tedious we are, talking of love!*

Katelina van Borselen had taught herself not to talk or think of love. She had thought so much of it, once, that she had refused the man her parents had chosen as husband. Because it had not come to her as she wanted – noble, adoring, irresistible – she had, from a kind of fear, a kind of defiance, bought herself the experience. That is, she had – twice – laid a small part of her pride in the blue-stained hands of a decent, trustworthy workman. But the workman had betrayed her, and she had resorted to the least of all the choices she now knew she had had. She had married a sulky Adonis who had dragged her into a land of mean landscapes, not the high peaks of delight and adventure.

She lay breathing quickly in the hot, infested darkness, but what she wanted was not Simon, or the careless traffic of a Cypriot night.

She sat up when someone knocked on her door, and after waiting a man came in bearing a torch. The doctor. The doctor who had been moved to stride from the table in anger. Who was not the dupe of Nicholas, as the others were. The man said, 'Nicholas. Do you know where he is?'

'No,' said Katelina.

The doctor remained, looking at her. He had resumed his professional hat. He said, 'It was an extremely severe injury. On occasion . . .'

'He was drunk but not helpless,' Katelina said. 'I don't know where he went.'

He left. After a while she went out herself and, avoiding the torches, sought the cool air where, on the horizon, an indigo band met a paler one, and the scent of the roses was paired with the salt of the sea.

Between herself and the sea stood tall pillars, an arch and a cornice, underlit by a herbaceous glow, pink as peonies. She sensed warmth, and an odour newly familiar. But she was not in the sugar yards. She stood on the pictured pagan terrazzo of the Sanctuary of Venus, where sweet oils were fetched by the Graces to cauldrons like the ones she now saw, wreathed in silvery vapour, glowing apple-gold from the fires of their hearths.

The coals were real. The fires throbbed, like the fires of Hephaistos. In their light she saw the white broken steps and the avenues and the pale half-hidden plinths, with their curious statues bending, kneeling, formally upright. Venus in the arms of the crippled god. Venus couched with her lover Adonis. She could

hear the island speaking under her feet, and trembled, listening to
it.

Without a plinth, a god with a pure, Attic body stood, his
curling head bent. Sweet in the night, a man's voice murmured in
Greek. 'Who dare pasture his cattle in the lord's fold?' The fires
flickered. The sea breathed in the distance. The same voice said,
'Whose then is the sacrifice? Male blood is all the altar will drink.'
Then softly: 'Don't speak.'

Katelina knew by then whose the voice was; but could only
guess who reclined at his feet. Then a woman said, 'You are
foolish. First, my dear, you must learn. Marco and Luigi Martini
are in dispute. The Knights and Martini have diverted the
Kouris.'

'How sad,' Nicholas said, still in Greek. The glow from the fire
lit his skin, and the linen draped over his shoulder and the still,
classical line of his body. He said, 'You should have rope in your
hair. Aphrodite will not accept it.'

'It is not, I hope, being offered to Aphrodite,' said Fiorenza of
Naxos.

Chapter 29

NEXT MORNING, Nicholas received the rough awakening that no doubt he deserved. The second time, Loppe made quite sure that he couldn't remain on his mattress so he got up, and made with his eyes shut for the privy, and was sick; which presumably made everyone happy. Then he went back and slid himself into linen breeches and a loose tunic with a scarf round his waist, and a sleeveless robe over that, which was all his skin could bear without buckling. There was some blood about, where his newly-healed wound had come apart, not surprisingly under the circumstances. He said nothing about it and neither did Loppe. Tobie made no appearance. A little later, John le Grant arrived, an event he had forgotten to prepare for and about which no one had reminded him. By then he was sitting with Loppe in his office, going over essential figures for the day's work. John came in like a red-headed sparrow and said, 'Well? How did it go?' He looked again and said, 'Christ. It turned into an orgy?'

'You might say that,' said Nicholas carefully. He began to pull himself together, in order to forestall anyone doing it for him. Some time ago, he had finally realised that he was irredeemably alone. Up till then, the others had deferred to his special skills and allowed him therefore to lead them, but the old companionship had remained, and the hare-brained exploits; and the times of ease, when he was teased and indulged and insulted as a boy among men.

But since then, others had joined him. John le Grant had never known the apprentice in Flanders; neither had Crackbene. The Venetians among whom he was working; the Mamelukes; the Lusignan court all took him for what he was now, and he couldn't revert, if he was to carry the company forward. Zacco had seen that, before he did. Zacco, conducting his own subtle enquiry for his own ends, had said to him, in one of those curious sickbed visits in Nicosia: 'Why do you not take your own advice? If I have erred, you have erred also. You have brought your company to follow the happy meteor that is Niccolò, instead of a cause, or a target, or a purpose. They come for money, of course; for adventure perhaps; but for you most of all. And thus you demean them, you make of them nurses. What is your doctor, but a man who acts as your mother? What is your negro, but a man whom you will one day have to turn off, or else make your lover? Is it that you do not have a true purpose, Niccolò? Is it that all this is just a means to surround yourself with a family?'

He was clever, Zacco. At the time, Nicholas had laughed and then said, 'My lord, you mean well; but you haven't met all my company. I doubt if my lawyer or my priest think of themselves as my nurses. But I understand what you say. It is something to be avoided.'

To which Zacco had merely said, 'If you can avoid it. If you can do without it. There are many men, otherwise strong, who cannot face bitter winds without lovebands. Consider those you have bound. Consider what they lose if you fall, or you stumble.'

He had made some answer and, having time, had considered it for several nights until Tobie, in his motherly role, had shown anxiety. Despite Zacco's personal bias, there was truth in what he said. For ten months Nicholas had been alone, owing responsibility to no one. Then he had rejoined his community, and found it comfortable. Months ago, he had realised what was happening. He had just been slow to stop it. Perhaps because, in the long run, he did have a purpose.

Now, outfacing le Grant's mild freckled leer, Nicholas said, 'The visit was a brilliant success. We showed Little Venice all over Stavros. I couldn't stop Loppe exaggerating. Corner, Loredano and Zorzi came, and they'll tell the other Venetians about it. They took away the impression that we are efficient, well-equipped and liable to be extremely productive.'

'The Martini?' said le Grant.

'Weren't there. I gather,' Nicholas said, 'that they and Episkopi are having some difference of opinion over water rights.'

'Fancy,' said John le Grant. He rubbed his nose, leaving it shining. He said, 'Well, they got the right impression then; but for God's sake, let's keep friendly with Zacco. What did you decide about the new pounding mill?'

'To do it,' Nicholas said. 'Or with a crop yield like this, we'll be burning our surplus, unless the Martini burn it first.'

Loppe said, in his velvet voice, 'We know we'll get a bottleneck at the refinery stage, but expansion there will have to come later.'

'Running out of money?' said John.

'No,' said Nicholas. 'But fuel, vats, skilled sugar boilers and, of course, time. We'll have to farm out some of the refining or start throwing out juice. It can be done. We've found two places that will process the next lot. Next year, it'll all be in tune. Are you coming to Stavros? In an hour I'm going to look at the madder crop for the dyeyards, and then see a man about wine for the army. How is the army?'

'I'm glad you asked,' said John le Grant. 'You'd better go and look at your madder and leave Loppe to look after the wine. King James wants you back.'

'And when he decreeth a matter, he doth but say unto it "Be!" and it is. Why?' said Nicholas. 'I sent Crackbene up. The siege ought to be biting.'

'Well, they've run out of cod roe and pork titbits and the best sorts of sausage,' le Grant said, 'but they're not eating the cats yet, despite what one hears. The castle's well stocked. I've cast the gun, thanks to Crackbene and your timber. Zacco wants to use it.'

'I can imagine. He's bored, he wants a quick end, and he wants to get on to Famagusta. What did you tell him?'

'The truth,' said John le Grant. 'It's a nice big gun. If you rolled it up under the walls, it'd blow a hole through, and you could send Astorre through yelling murder. But the castle isn't St Hilarion. It's got a lot of food, and hundreds of highly trained soldiers, a lot of them Knights of the Order. There's no way he can get that gun near enough to shoot through a wall. It has to be out of reach and constantly battering while the rations get low. Nothing dramatic. Just misery. Then they surrender. You hope.'

Nicholas said, 'How did he take it?'

'Zacco? He has to hear it from you. He won't believe the blockade was so bad through the winter, and he won't believe it is absolute now. But it is. You haven't seen a town being starved?' John le Grant said.

'For Carlotta? I'll be most impressed if they do,' Nicholas said. 'That's what your gun is for. Saving the face. Kyrenia'll give in. The nasty one is going to be Famagusta. The Genoese won't die for Carlotta, but they'll let themselves be blown to bits before they'll give up their port and their property. I reckon we'll be investing Famagusta just about the time the next cane harvest comes in, so the sugar plans had better be perfect. And the dyeworks. Did you call at Nicosia? How is jasmine-breasted Diniz?'

'I've brought you a report from Bartolomeo,' said le Grant. 'And another from Venice. Why don't you let that little fool go? Zorzi says you've bought and paid for him.'

'I'm waiting until I get over my temper,' Nicholas said. 'A report from *Venice*? How?'

'From Gregorio. I've opened it. It was coming by galley, and one of Crackbene's boats intercepted it. You know Crackbene's been hired by Zacco? He's running two royal galleys as well as our round ship.'

Unfolding the paper, Nicholas nodded and ran his eye down. It was addressed to the company, so contained nothing personal, naturally. News of the Bank, which looked promising, and which he would read in detail later. News of movements of loans dictated by national happenings. Venice was at war with the Ottomans: a short analysis warning him what that meant. Scotland was sheltering the English Lancastrian King and Queen; the Flemish Queen Mother was less powerful; the Bishop Kennedy more so. In Brussels, Duke Philip was better though aged, and Michael Alighieri of Trebizond, miraculously, was there as his chamberlain.

In Bruges, Tommaso Portinari was bent on making a name for himself and the Medici in the handling of alum. Anselm Adorne, discreet and wealthy as ever, was receiving few public offices under Duke Philip, for reasons unknown. He was, however, still on the friendliest terms with the Charetty company and the demoiselles Tilde and Catherine, about which notes from Julius were appended. Catherine, who had no stake in the company, was insisting stubbornly on attempting to supervise its every move. Tilde, older and swayed by other matters, vacillated between extreme interference and spending money on social pursuits. There were several young men –

'It's a pity about the Medici,' John le Grant said.

There were several young men whom she favoured, and Julius – 'Yes?' said Nicholas.

'It says there. The company's credit is over-extended. If Cosimo dies, his heirs will call on his debtors. That includes the Strozzi.'

And Julius was finding some trouble in fending them off. Godscalc was helping. They would be sorry to hear of the illness of Cosimo de' Medici ... 'I don't know why I bother to read it,' Nicholas said, 'if you're going to tell me all of it. So the Strozzi will be short of capital. So we put through an order for barillo at a good favourable price when the time comes. Loppe, can you do that?'

Loppe said, 'There's a boat in from Alexandria today, someone said. They'll have news from Florence. I'll ask at Salines. Where do you want the barillo delivered?'

'Venice,' said Nicholas. John le Grant was glaring at him.

John le Grant said, 'You madman, are you going ahead with that? Did Gregorio lease the island?'

'I hope so,' Nicholas said. 'Didn't you come across that in the letter? Or no, it was in code. Here it is. Gregorio has leased the island. He thinks I'm mad too. He says all anybody is thinking of is the war with the Turks, and I ought to be thinking of that too. If they take Cyprus, they've got all our sugar.'

'But then, you have another business in Venice. It makes sense to me,' said Loppe blandly.

Nicholas looked up smiling from what else the letter had said in code which was hardly personal either, but something for his eye, and not that of anyone else. Gregorio, his perfect lawyer, had written: *The Republic has received excellent news of your sugar prospects and those of the Corner estates, previously much disrupted by war. The market for Portuguese sugar is now as a result much depressed, the companies worst affected being those recently established and under-financed, such as St Pol & Vasquez. There is much distress over the death of Tristão Vasquez, and the lord Simon his wife's brother publicly blames you for this, and for the detention of his wife and Tristão's young son. Whether there is any truth in the accusation, you will know. But it is likely that, if he can find a ship and raise the money, Simon will either come to Cyprus or send there to make formal complaint. I do not need to tell you either that he regards your involvement with sugar as a direct attack on his livelihood.*

'Oh, dear,' said Nicholas aloud. He turned the paper over. There were another three lines. *Certain indications have come to my notice of abnormal business activity, not attributable to St Pol & Vasquez, which seems to be directed against the Bank, or against you in person. I shall watch; so should you.*

'Oh dear what?' John le Grant said.

'Gregorio. He thinks the House of Niccolò has attracted subversive attention, but has no positive evidence. Is your skin crawling? He probably dreamed about Diniz and his axe.'

'Did you tell him about Diniz and his axe?' said Loppe with extreme smoothness.

Nicholas said, 'No, I didn't. Simon's going to be annoyed if he turns up and finds he's got a little blue nephew. Perhaps I'll tell him then.'

'Simon's going to turn up?' Loppe said, missing out all the courtesies.

John le Grant said, 'Aye, wait a bit. There's something contradictory there. I can see this lord Simon blaming you for the death of the Portuguese. But what's this about your stopping the woman and the boy getting home? The story we got was that the grandfather wouldn't ransom them, and Simon wasn't interested.'

'The story we got,' Nicholas said, 'was that Jordan de Ribérac temporarily couldn't afford it, and Simon was abroad and didn't know about it. Presumably he's come home and found out.'

'Well, like enough. But he can still hardly blame you if it was his father's fault. Unless –'

'Unless Jordan de Ribérac put the blame on me, as of course he has done. One day,' Nicholas said, 'I must introduce you to Jordan de Ribérac. No problem of tunnelling, sapping or metal-casting will ever seem difficult to you again. Meanwhile, we have his son thinking of coming here. I think I really must find a way of getting rid of Katelina van Borselen soon. I can manage a war, a dyeworks and a sugar business, but with Simon as well, I'd have to work to a sand-glass.' He stopped. His voice, it seemed to him, had grown a little shrill. He lowered it. 'Right. I'd better tell Tobie I'm leaving, if I can find him. Whose piss is he drinking this morning?'

'You put him on to it,' John le Grant said. 'Anyway, I've seen him already. Why didn't you tell us about the Emperor David? We were in Trebizond too.'

'I forgot,' Nicholas said. He kept his voice resolutely down. 'I thought you would be upset. I got confused after my wound. Zorzi begged me never to remind him of it.'

'He remembered to bring out your camel,' John le Grant said. 'The Emperor might as well have stuck to his palace and fought on to the end. Or at the very least let Uzum Hasan and the White Sheep have Trebizond. That way, we could have stayed and gone on with the business.'

'So we could,' Nicholas said. 'But that way, we should have missed Tzani-bey and Zacco and Cropnose and Valenza and Fiorenza and Katelina and Simon and Zorzi and laughter-loving Aphrodite herself. That black bloody cone out there, splitting its sides.'

They gazed at him like nurses. His head throbbing, Nicholas swore, and got to his feet, and went off to look at madder.

Four days later, he was at the opposite end of the island in the camp surrounding Kyrenia, engaged in long conciliatory sessions with Zacco inside his tent, and boisterous ones outside it, followed by other carefully orchestrated exchanges with Astorre and Thomas, Crackbene and Umfrid, and all his opposite numbers in the different sections of the army now investing Kyrenia.

The interviews with Zacco were not difficult: the King had quite enough intelligence to know that what John le Grant had told him was true. He merely wished to hear it from Nicholas, and to dispute with him, and perhaps frighten him, and then please him. Encounters with Zacco now took a certain pattern, with an occasional wild foray into the dangerous and the unexpected. Nicholas always enjoyed them.

Since the last occasion, however, he had had a taste of something he had almost forgotten. The day – the evening, the one rather full evening with the princesses of Naxos – had brought back, in its earlier part, the light, the swift, the allusive conversation of Trebizond where, among other luxuries, the Emperor had surrounded himself always with the best minds. Setting the black cone apart, Nicholas had long understood Urbino, who fought in order to buy for his library. On the other hand, there was wisdom to be acquired outside books, as Zacco had shown him. By Urbino's age, perhaps, he himself might have discovered a balance that satisfied him. He wondered if such an idea might pass for another purpose, and decided that it would not, and he had better go and do something practical, such as reminding his men that they were supposed to be colleagues of the emir Tzani-bey.

It was, when you came to think of it, a tribute to Zacco's skill that after eight months, Tzani-bey and he were in the same encampment, on the same campaign together. Of course the emir remembered, as he did, what had happened at the monastery of the cats, and afterwards. Those (including Primaflora) who knew of it would be entitled, he supposed, to regard the present armistice with astonished contempt. Then, four months ago, boarding the Hospitallers' ship, Tzani-bey had been given orders to convince the Genoese that Zacco was no friend of Nicholas; and had treated those orders with licence. That had been witnessed by his own men. So, too, had the emir's brutal success of two months ago, when, without consultation or compunction, Tzani-bey had used Greek fire to force the fall of St Hilarion.

In all their commerce, then and since, the emir's public behaviour had been otherwise wholly correct; his attitude one of smiling formality. Away from Zacco's eyes, matters were slightly different. Food went astray; powder destined for Astorre was diverted; the requirements for ablutions, for prayer oddly occurred when least safe and least convenient to Astorre and his men. To deal with it, as to deal with everything, one had to put oneself in the other man's place. Until he had defeated Carlotta, until the Ottoman danger was past, Zacco could not do without Mameluke help; could not risk offending Cairo.

In his turn, Tzani-bey knew that Cairo sent to Cyprus only her dissidents. If they fought well, they might return to acclaim. If they slipped, Cairo would cut them off without compunction. He had to keep the goodwill of Zacco until Zacco was King of Cyprus. Equally, he would be well advised to prevent Zacco replacing Egyptian with Western help which might – just might – end in sweeping Egypt from Cyprus. So Nicholas had given four months to educating Astorre to deal with the Mamelukes; to presenting to Tzani-bey the portrait of a young Flemish mercenary of modest ability with whom Tzani-bey could work without losing face or the slightest doubt of his own personal ascendancy. All this he continued to consolidate in the week or two it took to set up the cannon and begin, in a stolid way, to discharge it at the walls of Kyrenia. There would be time enough to deal with Tzani-bey. Time enough for the final protest that he had had planned, in loving detail, for a very long time. Cyprus, Island of Love. He thought of Katelina van Borselen at Kouklia, and wondered if the spirits of vengeance were on good or bad terms with the spirits of spring and fertility. He suspected they teamed up with one another. It didn't stop him, any more than he knew it had stopped Katelina.

April had moved into May, and soon May would turn into June and high summer. The flowers, once so aromatic and fresh, were retiring, leaving thorn and dry earth and trickles of mud where the rivers had been. The wine he planned for began to come, and the fodder for animals. He initiated games, at which each section of the army in turn had a chance to shine. He had learned his lesson from the Genoese; from all those he could find who remembered other sieges that had failed through boredom, and bad provisioning. He continued to fraternise with everybody, extending his endeavours even to the Arab physician whose murderous potions had so mortified Tobie. In that instance, as it happened, the first approach had not come from Nicholas but from Abul Ismail himself, when Zacco had made one of his regular visits to the field hospital, Nicholas following.

During any siege, there was little need for senior medical staff. The cases were mostly fever, or dysentery, or the occasional wound from an arrow. Zacco's tour was soon done. He left, with his retinue. The physician had said, detaining Nicholas, 'My lord. Your late injury does not trouble you?'

In the light clothes they all wore, Nicholas supposed its state was obvious enough. 'No. I thank you,' he said.

The lined, bearded face considered his. Abul Ismail said, 'But you would not condescend to let me examine it? I feel responsible. Because of me, your own doctor prefers not to be present.'

'Because of me, I rather think,' Nicholas said. 'Although you went to extremes which he would never contemplate, nor indeed should I. But that is past. No. He has experiments in the south which keep him occupied.'

'The bodies drowning in sugar. We spoke of this once. We have had the same in Damascus. The question is, is it caused by the eating of sugar, or does sugar alleviate the disease? – You would not care to sit there, while we talk of it? It is my chamber, and private. The examination will take no more than a moment.'

It was, indeed, quick and deft. As he covered his shoulder, Abul Ismail said, 'Such excellent suturing deserves better care than you have given it. You have been told, I am sure, how lucky you were. Also, you have escaped your marsh fever so far? This is an island that breeds these sad fits of palsy.'

'I seem to bear a charmed life,' Nicholas said. Now the King had gone, there was silence beyond the curtain, save for the steamy breathing of seething water, and the whisper of a brazier, heating irons. He said, 'And now I must go.'

'Without discussing what lies between us?' said Abul Ismail. He turned from washing his hands and picked up a towel. His box stood beyond with trays of instruments in it: probes and tweezers, needles, syringes and scalpels. Beyond that stood a table like a refiner's, pierced to hold slotted bowls. Except that the bowls contained blood and not sugar. Abul Ismail gathered his robes and sat down. He said, 'I observe you. You owe your success to many things, but mostly to your gift for examining the thoughts of your fellow men. I spoke just now of books, and you were familiar with them. Master Tobie, before our estrangement, told of the manuscripts you brought from Trebizond, enshrining Arab science in the words of the Greeks. Here, I cure Muslim and Christian. At St Hilarion, I performed an action for the sake of the greater good of my nation, and this island and, indeed, the particular salvation of Master Tobie and yourself. I am not afraid to discuss these things. We are civilised. An interchange of views need not lead to abuse, mental or bodily.'

'You could conceive that I might persuade you that your viewpoint is wrong?' Nicholas said.

The Arab smiled. 'You know well that we shall not change our stance by an iota. But I shall understand you, and you me. Will this not serve well for the future? We must live side by side for so long as the war lasts: perhaps longer, if you have your way. You have told no one, for example, that your sugar-master came from that great Turcoman prince, the lord Uzum Hasan?'

Nicholas heard the silence develop and let it; for this needed thought. He said eventually, 'You have friends in Damascus?'

Equally without haste, the Arab took his time to reply. 'And Cairo. And Kharput.' He waited again.

'But you have not yet told Tzani-bey,' Nicholas said thoughtfully. He sat very still, crosslegged on the mattress with his hands between his knees as he had learned to do in the camp of the Ottoman Sultan to which he had come, in the dying days of the Empire of Trebizond, to assist at the fate of its Emperor.

'No,' said Abul Ismail. 'Or your King James, who equally would have to kill you if he knew. Or Venice would abandon him.'

'Perhaps not,' Nicholas said.

The brown-smudged eyes were heavy and still as a Persian painting. The Arab said, 'Because you think the princesses stronger than their husbands? Or . . .' He inhaled and said, 'I see.'

'Perhaps you do,' Nicholas said. 'So why have you told me?'

The man raised his thick brows and tilted his head. 'Is it not self-evident? Sooner or later, you would hear that I knew. You have established a strange web of communications, my lord Niccolò, with your humble travelling friars. Then I might have suffered some accident before I could say, as I say now, that this matter does not concern me. I do not propose, now or at any time, to reveal it. In pledge of which, I have placed my life in your hands, as you have proof of my good intentions. I could have poisoned you many times over.' He did not glance at the knives, or the irons, or the bowls of thick liquid.

Nicholas again let silence fall. Presently he said, 'It was unlikely I should discover such a thing. You have told me for some other purpose?'

'Indeed,' said Abul Ismail. 'A purpose divined by an accident of the soul. In medicine one learns, one talks, one teaches. In life, too, this is necessary. I would have your company, now and then, as, I think, you need some such as mine. Unless you believe your King would be jealous?'

Nicholas smiled. Abul Ismail smiled even more widely, showing spaced yellow teeth. He added, 'Jealous of me, as who would not be? But I speak, of course, of a different congress.'

Even so, the character of the King was such that his anger could not always be avoided. At the beginning of June, Nicholas set in motion an action against Kyrenia designed to accelerate the pressure on the fortress and to help exhaust its ammunition. The King was absent, as sometimes happened, now that the days of great heat had arrived, and cooler sport could be found in the mountains. The short, hard-hitting attack on the castle took place, and Nicholas, returning from it tired and triumphant was struck, on entering the compound of his camp, by a change in the quality of the sound which told him, before ever he saw the activity, that the King had come back. He had barely reached his own tent before a messenger stopped him. The King was breaking in a new horse, and required his assistance.

The signs were ominous. James de Lusignan well knew the magnificent figure he cut, alone with his whip and a rope and an unbroken stallion. In temper, and especially out of it, he would choose this perilous means of exerting himself. Now, half-naked in a fog of white dust, he hurled a rope at his mercenary and spoke through his white teeth. 'You come filthy into my presence?'

'I have fought for you,' Nicholas said. It emerged as a gasp. He took the strain of the rope and his sinews, settling, took up the burden. The horse was broad-built and powerful and angry.

'Why?' said Zacco. 'Did I ask it of you? Did we not agree to wait? Why should the garrison trouble to respond to a pinprick? They must know that we know that they still have some food?'

'They didn't,' said Nicholas, panting. 'They thought we thought they were starving. They thought we were going to throw the whole army against them. Behind those walls, they were terrified.' His shoulder, where the axe sank, was burning violently.

Zacco turned round, got pulled half off his feet, and turned back, twisting the rope round his wrist and cracking his whip. He yelled, 'If the blockade's as good as you say, how did they know we thought that?'

It was getting to be like a piece of jester-dwarves' dialogue. Nicholas began to laugh and let go his rope; Zacco looked angry and then, beginning to smile, jerked his head to bring over a groom. He transferred the plunging horse and flung a sticky arm round the shoulders of Nicholas. He smelt of perfume and sweat and his limbs were heavy with dangerous muscle. 'It was a ruse?'

'Ask Astorre,' Nicholas said. 'Andrea Corner, Marco's brother, works for Queen Carlotta. We know Marco is loyal, but no one in there would be surprised if a letter came over the wall on an arrow, warning Andrea that we were about to storm the castle because we thought they were starving.'

'And they believed this?' Zacco said. 'They wasted ammunition, replying?' He withdrew his arm, bestowing playfully on Nicholas a vicious, upward blow with the side of his palm in passing. He placed his fists on his hips and breathed deeply several times, lips tight, expanding his chest with firm regularity. Then he jerked up his chin and walked on to the cisterns. 'This is nonsense. You've invented it to avoid some hard work with that horse. You hardly thought the castle was going to surrender?'

'My lord King,' Nicholas said, 'the last thing we planned to do was sacrifice the royal troops to some vain expectation. There was a mounted charge, immediately following cannon-fire. Half were Egyptians; half were our men disguised as Egyptians with armour under their robes. And hackbuts, of course. Not expecting Christians, the men on the walls were not ready for firearms. We picked off their archers; sent fire-bolts into their palisades and viewed the state of the walls from much closer. A quick foray, soon over, and not expensive of men.'

At the sluice, he was made to take the slave's role with the buckets and, throwing water, went on being persuasive against all the odds. Immediately afterwards, he was compelled to go back to the horse-ring, but he had Zacco's ear. He had, in the end, Zacco's reluctant commendation. Just after the end, when despite all his energy, Nicholas felt that a rest was something God ought to vouchsafe him, Zacco let him know his real feelings. He said, 'You are slow. You are getting old and slow, and I think I will stop paying you soon. You let your taste for adventure lead you into an unsanctioned battle, and might have wasted your men and mine. You might have been killed.'

'So might you,' Nicholas said. 'In the mountains. You didn't invite me.'

'You are not in season,' said Zacco. The broken horse, sweating and shivering, stood at his side, its head drooping. Zacco stood, his eyes steady and cold, and his smell and that of the horse were the same.

Nicholas said, 'There is a season for fighting, and I am in that.'

'With me, they are the same,' Zacco said. He moved, his muscles oiled over with sweat, and slipping the bridle over the exhausted horse, laid the reins over his shoulder and led it slowly out of the ring. He said, 'Well, Niccolò. Playing at soldiers without sense, without leave, you know you missed a messenger from Nicosia? It seems your silly child in the dyeworks has gone. Now perhaps we can get on with this war.'

Nicholas stood still, hesitated, and walked on again. 'My lord?'

'Yes?' said Zacco, waving to someone.

Nicholas said, 'Diniz Vasquez? My lord, where has he gone, and when?'

'How should I know?' Zacco said. 'Four or five days ago, I presume. They sent to tell the woman at Episkopi, and found she had heard of it, and hearing, had disappeared. But you will not be distressed about that. You wanted nothing to do, as I remember, with Katelina van Borselen. Go and get clean. When I want you, I shall send for you. Tomorrow, perhaps, or the next day.'

They parted. Nicholas stripped, deep in thought, as he walked to his tent, and let his servants sluice him outside, as he had just sluiced the King. Somewhere over the bustling heads he glimpsed the plumed helm of Tzani-bey, and beneath it his face, attentive and still as if watching him, or his scars. If so, he was welcome. In Astorre's quarters, a violent celebration seemed to be taking place without requiring his presence. As the sun's heat began to make itself felt on his bare head, and through his light robe, Nicholas retired to his tent and then, presently, crossed to his little field desk and took up his pen. A shadow fell, and John le Grant said, 'If anyone lost, I suppose it was the horse. Not you, at any rate. That's the King confused, the war advanced, and Katelina and her nephew shamed and neatly got rid of. Who or what next?'

Nicholas finished writing. He said, 'You need to move that bombard, and place another one, much lighter, on the other hill nearer town. Now they've had a shock and lost all those arrows, the garrison won't hold out very much longer. I'm suggesting to Zacco that he slackens the sea blockade in Kyrenia and makes it complete, from now on, at Famagusta. Once the mastic crops are in, the Bank of St George will put all their money and ships into saving the Genoese colony. Genoa won't have any to spare for Queen Carlotta. Kyrenia should fall in two months: Famagusta by winter. I'm going south.'

John le Grant came and sat beside him, his red-fluffed arms folded and smelling of metal and gunpowder. He said, 'The boy and the lady have gone, and not by your orders?'

Nicholas said, 'I could have released the boy any time that I wanted. I gave Bartolomeo no new instructions. The lady was being held against my wishes by the King's mother, and I haven't spoken to her yet. Once I have, I shall go down to Episkopi. If Katelina and her nephew are both conveniently on their way west to Simon in Portugal, I shall come back.'

John le Grant said, 'Where else could they be?'

Nicholas powdered his writing and sat back, thinking a little. He found his teeth had locked like those of a ferret and he was abrading them hard with his thumb knuckle. He changed to a negligent pose. 'Who can guess what has happened? Here was a sad lady. She resented me; she resented Cropnose; she resented captivity. She may have tried to spy for Carlotta. Whatever she may have done, her hands were tied because of the hold I had over Diniz. The moment Diniz escaped, she was free to do as she wished.'

'To hide and kill you?' said John le Grant. As sometimes happened, the mask of his freckles seemed to obliterate his features. He said, 'You're all thumbs with that woman. You were both in Kouklia.'

It was neither a question nor quite a comment. When nothing more came, Nicholas said, 'I didn't touch her in Kouklia.'

'Then you're a fool,' said John le Grant. 'Or you wanted to frighten her. Did you? Whom did you touch, that could have sickened her of the whole vendetta?'

'I don't remember. It was dark,' Nicholas said. He made a great effort, and kept his voice civilised. He said, 'I hope she has left the island. It wouldn't be difficult. She knew ships called from time to time, and the Order would be friendly and, of course, the Martini. If she was really determined, the Martini would help her leave Cyprus.'

John le Grant uncrossed his arms and stretching a finger, hooked up the medallion of the Sword on its ribbon. It hung, revolving one way and then the other. He said, 'And would they send her to Portugal?'

'If there was a ship,' Nicholas said. 'If there was, she and Diniz would be on it. If there wasn't, they would both end up very likely in Rhodes. Katelina would go where she thought the boy was. Rhodes is friendly, and near, and they could wait for a ship of the Order.'

'Then that would be all right, wouldn't it?' said the engineer. In some ways, Nicholas was glad it was John le Grant he was having this conversation with: in other ways it was awkward. Nicholas said, 'It depends. I don't think Carlotta or the Genoese or the Order would harm her.'

'Even if she took cuttings?' le Grant said. 'That was what it was all about, wasn't it? The Vasquez family were taking cane and vine cuttings to Madeira. Fine for the Genoese and the Portugese, but not so good for the people whose crops here were their livelihood. But could she get cuttings away from Episkopi?'

'Probably,' Nicholas said. 'Especially if the Martini were to help her.'

'But –' said John le Grant and stopped. Then he said, 'The Martini are Venetians as well. You mean they'd take her to Rhodes, and see the cuttings never got there? Or see that she never got there?'

'They'd see she got there,' said Nicholas. 'If that's how it happened, she'll be there, safe and well.'

They looked at one another. John le Grant said, 'Until you follow her, and get rid of the cuttings? As you did with the Vasquez? It'll spoil your sugar business as well if Madeira becomes the new source of supply for the Western world.'

Nicholas said nothing.

The engineer said, 'If she's in Rhodes, you will follow her. And that's what the Venetians want. They want you out of Cyprus, away from Kouklia, away from the dyeworks, away from Zacco. You said it yourself. Kyrenia's going to fall; the starving of Famagusta is planned for. Cyprus is saved for the Venetians, but the Venetians don't want the royal franchises to stay with a mercenary. Especially the Martini, who had it before. If she's in Rhodes, and you follow her there, then you're done for.'

'So I don't follow her,' Nicholas said. 'She stays, being expensively quartered in Rhodes, and the gallant Simon finally comes to collect her. I think it's a perfect solution.'

There was another busy silence. 'But,' said John le Grant at length, 'you're going to Nicosia, and possibly south?'

'To make sure she is in Rhodes or in Portugal. Yes. You have it,' Nicholas said. 'Now can I get out? There's a hell of a party going on over there, and I've not had so much as a pistachio nut.' He didn't feel like another staring match, so he lowered his lids and got up and stalked out of the tent, leaving John le Grant, if he wanted, to follow. And before John, of the devious mind, could detect how much he was lying; or could introduce the name he wanted forgotten which was, of course, that of his partner in love, Primaflora.

In Nicosia, Bartolomeo Zorzi strode into the villa with three impeccable ledgers under his arms and a string of justifiable complaints. 'Are we to dye everything crimson? I know we have madder, but look at what your blockade is doing to imports! And all the shore workers down south are servicing war galleys, who bring in nothing but metal and powder and arms. What about the boy? He tried to kill you!'

'Well, his uncle's going to kill me if I don't produce him,' Nicholas said. 'The lord Simon is coming from Portugal, and I want to lay my hands on that boy. Where did he go?'

'Portugal, if you believe the note that he left,' said Bartolomeo. 'And that's what he wrote to his aunt: but I don't see what ship could have taken him. At any rate, someone helped him get out of Nicosia.' The slight pallor he had brought from Constantinople had left Bartolomeo Zorzi: above the rim of black glossy beard his skin was roseate brown. 'He couldn't get clear so fast to the coast without something to carry him. Someone got him a mule, and money, and clothes, and food, and helped him over the wall. One of his father's Genoese friends, it might be? No one saw him. Why worry? If Zacco had found out what that boy tried to do to you, he'd be dead. You should go back to Zacco. Keep your employer happy. The boy is of no consequence. What is an uncle?'

'Ill-intentioned,' said Nicholas. 'Where is Jacopo? I thought he was coming north.'

'You think Jacopo had something to do with this?' said Bartolomeo. His teeth glistened. 'No, my friend. You will find he has stayed in the south with his vineyards. We are simply three brothers, Nicholai, Jacopo and myself, earning a living as best we might – and putting an alum fortune in your way, as I remember. Over this matter of uncles and nephews, we cannot help you.'

It was what he had expected. What he had not expected, but could, on reflection, understand, was his complete inability to attain an audience with the lady Marietta, mother of Zacco. He stayed in Nicosia for three days in case he was mistaken; then took himself south.

The family Corner at Episkopi proved as unhelpful as Marietta. Correction: the family Corner were three-quarters absent, in that – the season now being hot – the princesses Valenza and Fiorenza and their children had returned to Venice under the supervision of Vanni Loredano, and Marco Corner could tell him nothing about his late guest except that she had ungraciously disappeared overnight while he and his staff happened to be somewhat preoccupied with a temporary difficulty.

The nature of the difficulty was apparent to anyone traversing the Episkopi cane fields. Nicholas made four dispositions. The first proved, as he suspected, that no ship bound for Portugal had recently called at Cyprus. The second took him (in Tobie's absence) to the experimental benches Tobie had set up in Kouklia. The third instructed Loppe (in Loppe's absence) that, as a service to Messer Corner, water from the royal viaduct should be provided, in reasonable measure, to assist in the irrigation of the Episkopi estate. The fourth and last ensured that there would be found, in a public place, messages from himself to Tobie, to Astorre, and to

King James of Lusignan, to whose sole service he was irrevocably contracted.

Then Nicholas vander Poele, only deviser of the great game of Cyprus, left Cyprus.

Chapter 30

THIS TIME, the windmills of the jetty at Rhodes stood motionless in the heat, and no spume concealed the green and ochre pile of the City, with the Castello of the Knights on its crest. In the harbour, the fortress of Ayios Nikolaos was nearly finished without the help of an Aberdonian engineer, or of Nicholas the less saintly, now returning.

Last year, velvet-clad, Nicholas had arrived here by galley, and in the company of Tristão Vasquez and his lovesick young son. Here he had seen the winter weeks pass, and had kept his army alive, and got them off safely. And from here he had sailed for Cyprus in tatters, a prisoner of the Genoese and the Order, and without Tristão Vasquez.

His vessel now was a fishing-boat; and he made no attempt to leave when it tied up among the screeching gulls and screeching Rhodians in the fish-harbour. He worked with the rest, barefoot among the bream and mullet and octopus, his cotton drawers dripping with scales, his woollen hat pushed from his brow. Even when the baskets were full and the others had gone off to the tavern he was kept behind, swearing, to put the owner's soup on the stove and light the lamp in the rigging.

It was the arrangement, when he bought the boat from its owner. The owner told no one, and the owner treated him as one of his crew. Nicholas whistled as he worked, and the sky and sea turned madder red, and he thought up new ways of answering the quips and invitations that fell his way now and then from the other boats or the jetty, using all the languages he knew and a lot of words he had lately learned. His skin was an even mid-brown from his face to his toes, and he felt as uncomfortable in his breeches as he supposed all the others were feeling. But he didn't envy the others. He had food and freedom: he felt drunk with good cheer and well-being and, as soon as the skipper came back, he had food and a jar of tarry red wine in a basket to indulge in as well.

And news. As they sat back getting peacefully fuddled in the
fish-stinking poop of the boat, and the moon came out of the sea,
and far-off voices and laughter tickled the quiet between wave-
falls, the skipper said, 'And I asked after the woman. She's on the
island.'

Nicholas grunted. His lack of enthusiasm was not only prudent; it was genuine. It had, of course, been essential to pay this
little visit to Rhodes, and not too difficult, with the game three-
quarters finished behind him. Perhaps he had enjoyed the respite
too much. Liberation without responsibility: he had had it before,
for ten months. Had had it, in a way, all his childhood. Eventually
clearing his mouth, he said, 'The Flemish woman from St Pol &
Vasquez? Where is she staying?'

The fisherman, who came from Apolakia, didn't know him by
sight and – in the absence of other advice – seemed to think he was
being paid to play Cupid to some decadent Knight of the Order.
Until set discreetly to rights on the voyage, he had seized with
gusto the role of taskmaster. He still enjoyed giving orders, which
Nicholas did not mind within limits; and used towards him the
name of Nikko, which Nicholas had suggested himself and which,
in the past, others had called him by, too. Now the man said, 'A
Flemish woman called Borselen? She's not in the City. Was. They
had her up to Carlotta. The word goes that she's waiting to sail but
her firm doesn't have credit; so she was told to take the charity of
the Order so long as it was outside the City. Not much of a catch
there, eh Nikko? Is that why she's leaving her husband? Thinks
you'll get a good job in the fish-market and keep her?'

'Where d'you think she's gone?' Nicholas asked, when he could
speak without laughing.

'They said the Genoese Langue took her over. They've got a
castle at Salakhos, but I doubt if it's in a state for a lady. The
Knights at Monolithos could take her, or the fortress at Pharaclos.
Each of them has a commander from Genoa. If you want to know
any more, you'll have to ask in the City,' said the man. 'Or down
the coast. They know all the gossip down the coast. Depends how
much of a hurry you're in.'

'Not all that much,' said Nicholas. 'Who would know down the
coast?'

'My mother,' said the fisherman, whose name was Boulaki. 'She
does the laundry for Monolithos. My aunt Persefoni. She has the
best roasting-ovens in Pharaclos. I was thinking of going to see
both of them. But it's your boat.'

The wine-vat was empty. Nicholas shook out the last drop over
the side and thumped it down. 'I'd like,' he said, 'to meet your
lady mother. But what do we do for a crew?'

A smile appeared, dispensing a mist of dental decay and pure alcohol. 'Trust Boulaki,' said the man. 'So long as you've got the coins, there's nothing you can't buy in Rhodes. Can you walk?'

'No,' said Nicholas. It was practically true.

'Neither can I. Pity,' said the man called Boulaki. 'I once had three here together. Never could afford more. But I expect you're saving yourself.'

Nicholas began to laugh again, this time unintentionally, and a little later they found they had between them quite a repertoire of good tavern songs. They kept it up until someone climbed across five different boats and tipped a pail of seawater over them.

Boulaki's mother, when Nicholas met her, was cleaning a platter of fish in her yard, under a rickety trellis of vine. The sheets and small-clothes of the Knights of Monolithos were spread on the bushes all the way from her house to the shore, most of it needing darning. Monolithos Castle itself stood to the north on its abrupt rocky headland, hazy in the afternoon heat. Boulaki's mother was very like Boulaki: big-featured and sweaty with a black moustache and a twisted scarf bundling her hair. She handled her knife like an embalmer and her tongue like her knife. Nicholas lingered outside, where the goat was tied up, until Boulaki's voice began to drop out of the contest. The woman's Greek rattled on like a wagon-train. Then she screamed, 'The man!'

Nicholas left the goat and advanced. 'The man?' she said. She had planted a fist on each knee. The knife glinted upright in one of them.

'This is Nikko,' said the fishing-boat's former owner. He was nearly sober.

Her eyes were round, and fringed with stubby black lashes. 'You fornicate with some woman?' she said. 'Some poor Greek woman?' She sounded like Cropnose.

Nicholas said, 'Do I look such a wretch? What would my wife and five children say? Lady, my mistress wants news of her cousin. A Flemish lady called Katelina van Borselen. And maybe also, of a young boy her nephew. It is to help them.'

The black eyes ran him up and down. The woman said, 'My son has a brain like a fish. You bought his boat. What did you pay him?'

He could see, lying beside her, the bag of silver Boulaki had brought from the boat. He named, with humility, the sum it contained. He did not mention the other bag, equally heavy, about which Boulaki had sworn him to silence. The woman said 'Huh!' in a tone of disgust which might have concealed gratification. She said, 'And for that, do I have to feed and conceal you until I get news of this woman? And will you want it when it arrives? If the Knights have not raped her, the Turks will.'

He said, 'No. She is worth money.'

'And your mistress has money? Well, I am glad. Boulaki, your cousins have come. They will show this old married man where to go. The cabin next to the stackyard. It's been out of use since the mule died. Unless, of course, you want to sail on and seek elsewhere?'

It had been a long, sunny day and, like Boulaki, he was not entirely sober. Nicholas said, 'Do you think you could get news?'

'By tomorrow,' said the woman, turning away. She picked up a grey, leathery fish and slit it so that its entrails began to emerge. They were Turkey-red and vermilion.

'He'll stay,' Boulaki said. 'And I'll find him somewhere better to sleep than the stable.' He gripped Nicholas by the shoulder and drew him, ducking, towards the low house and its doorway, and through the house, and out the other side where other houses had settled at intervals into the dust, each with a cistern, an oven, a rectangle of edible greens, a smother of nets, floats and creeper, a heap of baskets, a stack of paddles, a scatter of washing and a smell of fish and goat, lard and badly-dug privies. Further along, a group of men in straw hats were sitting crosslegged in a huddle, drinking and betting on dice. 'This,' said Boulaki, 'is Nikko.'

No one looked up, except when his hand came out and placed a coin on the pile. Then, in due course, the dice were tossed in his direction, and shortly after, a wooden cup was lowered over his shoulder, full of greenish raw wine which he was thirsty enough to drink right away. In due course, he found himself in someone's yard eating fried fish and grey bread and melon in between a lot of laughing and talking. Later, there was singing as well, and they showed him how to dance on his hands. A good deal later, he was led to the shed belonging to Boulaki's mother's late mule by Boulaki's cousins, who were much bigger than Boulaki, and much younger, and who had played no part in the singing or laughing.

The last thing Nicholas saw as he rolled into the straw and the lantern was withdrawn was the gleam in Boulaki's eyes. He had seen them gleam with cupidity, amusement and tears. Tonight, it seemed to him that he detected anxiety. Then the fleas started to bite, and Nicholas sighed and, dismissing it all, tried to settle to sleep, but not so thoroughly that he couldn't be roused if Carlotta, the Knights or the Genoese turned up to kill him. He remembered distinctly, afterwards, settling to sleep with that intention.

The next thing he remembered was Boulaki's spread hand digging into his shoulder. Next, Boulaki kicked him. Nicholas sighed again and, rolling over, lifted his sword. Boulaki flinched back, and the light went out. 'No!' said the fisherman. 'Christ, I wish I'd never brought you. Listen. The boys are telling the Knights. They'll be down for you first thing in the morning. You've got to go.'

'Your cousins?' said Nicholas in the dark. He had his roll pulled together already.

'Filth,' said his saviour in a hoarse whisper. 'And my old mother'd sell her old mother for silver. I got it out of her later. The Flemish woman's at Lindos. That's on the opposite coast, twenty miles over the mountains. It is not far from Pharaclos, where my aunt lives, who is an angel as my mother is a devil. You lost money to Yiannis last night?'

Nichlolas had been careful to lose money to Yiannis; the spokesman, it was clear, among the dice players. He nodded, and Boulaki continued. 'He says you are a good man. He will sell you his mule, and lend you his grandson for guide, for the right sum of money. You must go now.'

For the right sum of money, Nicholas found himself presently padding barefoot from shadow to shadow until, at a safe distance from the village, a voice hissed, and a shadow resolved itself into a boy leading a mule. 'Lord?' said the boy. 'For much money I run beside you to Lindos?'

Nicholas tied his roll on the saddle and then, mounting, bent and scooped up the boy to perch behind him. He said, 'For much money given to your grandfather Yiannis you ride with me to Lindos, and we get there before dawn, and without being seen except by the goats. Is it understood?'

'And then I have much money?' said the boy.

'And then perhaps I will not beat you,' said Nicholas. 'And if I feel like it, there may be a little money as well. Now, go! Go! Go!'

The mule was slow and steady, like a bored man, and, climbing, followed unseen tracks among rocks whose hot dust rose into the still air about them. Sometimes they came to a level place and broke into a trot between thickets of thorn, or heath or broom; sometimes they skirted a dark forest of pine or cypress or oak, or descended to wind among olive trees and across a dry stream. Goats rustled and the mule shuddered at the squawk of a frightened bird. Moths passed like thistledown and he smelt a fox, once. After the steepest part he stopped to rest the animal, and the boy produced cheese and a flask from a saddlebag, and they sat and shared it, speaking almost not at all. The boy seemed uneasy, or frightened, or perhaps merely apprehensive of what the big stranger might do. After obtaining a few unwilling answers, Nicholas left him alone, although he never let him out of his sight. If the plan had been to run away, the grandson of Yiannis was given no chance. Then they resumed their silent journey.

Soon after that, Nicholas became conscious of the first change. The thick warmth of the night seemed here and there diluted, veined with something like freshness, and ahead, for the first time, he thought he could distinguish hill from hill, earth from sky; sky from something else.

He saw they had crossed the island. A single line, fine as a scribe's, ran across his vision, and sharpened. Above and below it hung something that was not colour at all, except perhaps a deep pigeon-grey; or grey mixed with mother of pearl, or pearl mixed with rose madder, or all of that mixed with shearings of silver and gold. . . . Mixed, thickened, ribboned, oh God, with vermilion. By God, Who could afford all that vermilion, as He could afford ultramarine, and love, and revenge, and never get hurt.

The boy said nothing. Below where they had halted, the hills ran unevenly down to the coast. Against the luminous veil of the sea stood a headland crowned with steep rock, and upon the crown floated a palace made of fine columns, pink as the light on the face of the boy riding behind him; pink as the insubstantial light on his hands, on the path, on the boulders about them. 'That is Lindos!' said the boy, loudly and clearly.

And immediately, it seemed, the rocks about them grew figures, black against the pellucid vapours behind – for, of course, now that he could see clearly, so he could be seen. Three men or four, and another below, holding horses. They threw themselves at him together. He fought in silence, with bitterness, but they said nothing, except to mutter directions among themselves as they flung a blanket over his head and, dragging him from his mount, wrapped him in it. Then, tied at elbow and knee, he was slung over someone's tall horse, and was held there, a broad hand on his back, as the animal jolted its way down the hill. Above and behind, he heard the light scramble of the little mule's feet, and the boy's voice, receding. The boy who, of course, had made no effort to help him.

Before very long, he felt his mount reach level ground, and then move from baked earth to something man-set that gave back discreet echoes. A slight difference in sound and in temperature told him he was among buildings; and then the hand on his back tightened as they began climbing again, steeply this time. When his horse turned abruptly, he was all but shaken off: the hand that shoved him this time came from behind. He realised that he had passed through a gateway, and that the small cavalcade had quietly come to a halt. A cock crew distantly and a dog barked somewhere twice. Nearer at hand, someone dismounted and he heard low voices, indistinguishable through the cloth. Then the hand on his back was replaced by many hands, heaving, rolling and lifting. He was half carried, half dragged across a carpet of pebbles, and then allowed to drop on a floor, which did his bruises no good but which at least felt smooth and appeared clean and might not be full of fleas. Someone cut the rope at his knees and his elbows, and someone else grabbed the blanket and tugged it off him. Their boots retreated, and were replaced by a small, high-arched slipper, and a knee draped with extremely fine taffeta and a hand, which stretched out and touched him. Above was a face that he knew, painted with art, and framed in hair half loosened today, in informal style, and half pleated into its little jewelled caul. 'Well, my dear?' said Primaflora.

He closed his eyes from sheer relief, and then opened them and began to laugh, for the same reason. He raised his own hand, with some trouble, and fingering hers, kissed and held it. She said, keeping the initiative, 'Did you think Carlotta had captured you? Or the Knights?'

The men who brought him had gone. He was lying in the inner hall chamber of a modest if well-to-do house, its plaster walls and timber ceiling painted; its windows open on greenery. He said, 'No. They were too quiet. And they didn't climb high enough. Why didn't you send me a message?'

'Would you have believed it?' she said. He sat up and, rising in turn, she drew him to his feet and stood, both hands in his, her head to one side. She said, 'Goats? Fish, certainly. And perhaps lice as well as fleas. I think, my Niccolò, I shall send you back.'

'Water is all that it needs,' Nicholas said. 'You knew I should come for you.'

She smiled and dropped her hands. 'I knew you would come when your contract was finished. When I heard your Flemish demoiselle had appeared, I thought you might come before that. Did Boulaki charge you a great deal?'

He laughed suddenly, thinking. 'Probably half as much as he charged you. You arranged it?'

'I know those boats plying to Cyprus. He was told, if you hired him, to bring you to Lindos.'

'He would have, eventually,' Nicholas said. 'But his mother wanted a cut from the Knights. I suppose Yiannis was in on it, too. It's as well the sugar crop flourished this year, since we've ended up financing the natives of Apolakia. I'm too stiff to bath myself.'

'I thought of that,' said Primaflora. 'Two of the men who brought you will help you. Afterwards, I shall bring you some oils. Are you hungry?'

'Yes,' said Nicholas.

The smile was in her eyes, not her lips. She had not changed, that he could see. She said, 'Amid the plenty of Cyprus?'

He said, 'If you know the boats plying to Cyprus, you will have that news too.'

The smile had sunk from her eyes. She said, 'Yes. But until I saw your face, I didn't believe it.' She turned. 'There is my servant. Follow him. I shall come when you are clean.' He wondered, obeying, what it was about him that gave that away. It irked him, because unless he knew, he could never simulate it.

Behind the low house was a garden too small for a fountain, but full of dark, watered earth and heavy flowers in strange marble troughs and the scent of fruit from the trees and the vines whose shadows lay on the couch where they brought him. It was still so early that the air felt like milk against his odourless skin, bare above virginal, darnfree white towels. He laid his brow on his pillowing arms and closed his eyes, waiting. Normally sparing of sleep, he knew he had had not quite enough to clear his head from the wine. Since it was not a good idea to think he let himself drift, aware of the small stirring sounds of awakening households; of the twitter of sparrows; of a ground-bass of bees. Somewhere, a good way off, a young child was crying. Primaflora said, 'Stay where you are. Have I done this for you before? The oils come from Alexandria.' Drops fell from her palms, teasing him. The liquid was warm, and contained scents he didn't know. Random trails, slow as raindrops, started to contour his body unattended. Where her shadow had been was blank and dazzling sunlight. She said, 'He did that? And you let him?'

There were five good stories he told in rotation about the wound on his shoulder. He realised she might have heard about an accident in the dyeworks. He saw that, of course, she knew the truth, because Katelina would have no reason, now, to conceal it. He said, 'You heard?' It seemed better to turn round and sit cross-legged, while the oil trickled down to his waist.

Her own palms were glossy and spilling. She leaned forward and smoothed their burden over his chest and his back, her eyes on the wound. She said, 'Yes. It was the first thing the demoiselle told the Queen. How her brave nephew had tried to kill the mercenary leader who had sold himself to Zacco.'

Nicholas made considering shapes with his cheeks and his chin. 'I didn't exactly let him,' he said. 'He was a quick learner.'

'But you didn't tell Zacco. The demoiselle says that you meant to, once you'd humiliated the young man enough. Or perhaps you had another humiliation in mind.'

He followed her thought. He said, 'Now that's really tortuous, and you know what a simple Fleming I am. Anyway, he wouldn't get to kill Tzani-bey. Where is the boy, anyway?'

'In Portugal, I assume,' said Primaflora. 'He certainly told his aunt so, and he's certainly not still in Cyprus, or she would never have left. I wondered, myself, why he abandoned her, but she says Zacco promised to free her at the end of the summer anyway. You know, of course, that she sent us reports on all that Zacco was doing?'

'I thought she might. Then why did she leave?' Nicholas said. She touched his good shoulder and turned him as he was speaking and he pressed his face again on his arms, smelling the oil as she opened the bottle.

'She was frightened,' Primaflora said. 'Perhaps you frightened her. Perhaps she gave up all hope of getting rid of you. Perhaps she thought Simon needed her, or that alone she couldn't break down you or your business. Perhaps she knew that Zacco would force her to leave empty-handed, and the Genoese would be more sympathetic.'

Empty-handed. Her small hands eased and pressed over his skin, and the fumes hung in his brain. His eyes suddenly opened.

Primaflora laughed. 'Are you so tired? The sugarcane cuttings, my dear, that are going to ruin your business and Zacco's. That was why she threw herself on the mercy of the Genoese. They are all up there, in the castle at Lindos, being watered daily by order of Imperiale Doria until a ship comes to take her to Portugal. Why else are you here?'

'For you,' he said. 'If you will come.'

The hands smoothed and smoothed without faltering. She said, 'As your mistress?'

His eyes remained open, lowered on his own hands. 'As my wife,' he said. 'If that did not demean you.'

The hands stopped. She said. 'Niccolò?'

He turned and the sun, catching his body, dazzled into his eyes. She stood in a thumbprint of light and said, 'There is no need.'

He lay, his arms at his sides and said, 'I must go back. Zacco would honour you. Only the plants must be destroyed, and the Flemish woman made free to leave on the first boat that arrives. Otherwise her husband will come, and cause trouble.'

She opened her rouged palms above him, and let the supple fingers drift down, wayward as the trickling oil. She said, 'For this?'

He moved involuntarily; and stilled; and smiled with tightened lids. 'Lady? Of course.'

She said, 'I require no fee of marriage. I shall come back with you to Cyprus.'

'When?' he said, selecting a breath. He opened his eyes.

She withdrew her slow, trailing hands and stood, studying him. 'When you are less indolent, my dear,' said Primaflora. 'When you have done what you came to do. I can guide you into the castle. I can find you a boat to take us to Cyprus, once the demoiselle has sailed for home. But that may take a long time.'

'Guide me to the castle,' Nicholas said. 'And when I am less indolent, find us a boat to take us to Cyprus. Katelina can find her own way home.'

By then, he knew he could expect nothing more, having given her, he thought, what she wanted. He turned on his face when she left him, and in time his body obeyed him; and he lay as still as if he were sick in a pawnshop in Sluys, and had just met Simon of Kilmirren, and had just been introduced to a punishment from which there seemed no release.

Chapter 31

I T WAS TRUE that Katelina van Borselen was frightened. Her fear had followed her here, to the sea crag at Lindos where the Castle of the Knights of St John shared its perch with the stones of Byzantium and the temple blocks of the Sanctuary of Athene, which were more ancient still. Her fear was not for Simon, or Diniz, or the destiny of her child. She was afraid of the black cone in the sanctuary of Paphos, and of what she had felt there.

Now Fate had set before her another altar. There, in the sunlight alone, while the Knights slumbered or prayed and the sounds from the village below hardly rose above the hiss of the cicadas, Katelina gazed down the gnarled rock to the sea, and wondered how either Athene or Aphrodite would have fared with a sharp-tongued mother she hated; and a sullen sister, and a hot-tempered, infertile husband. It would have reduced Aphrodite, for a start.

To her right, past the boat-crowded pool of St Paul, the sea stretched blue to the next misty headland and disappeared south into haze. Below the rock on her left lay the white scimitar of a strand, with beached boats cocked along it, and antlike figures asleep in their shade with the floss of netting around them. The sea, seen from above, was of a blue deep enough to be purple, paling as it was washed to the beach over patches of grape-coloured rock. In other places, it was blue-green as malachite. A dyer's labourer would know how to mix up the colour. A trickle of sweat reminded her why she was here and she turned to go down the glassy, worn steps from the temple. She saw, as she lifted her skirt, that the marble was heaped, thick as needles, with lizards; and when she began to walk quickly she caught sight of another, big as a dragon, on the crumbling roof of the stoa above her, its head stiffly erect, its throat gulping. It fled before she did.

In the shed where the plants were it was stifling, despite the open windows and the awning the Genoese squires had helped her put up. The trays would have been better deep in the palace, but

Imperiale Doria was away, and the other brethren cared more for Kolossi than for saving the vineyards and sugarcane fields of other Knights in the colonial west. Without her, the duty of watering would have been little attended to.

Today, someone for once had forestalled her. The rich smell of soaked earth and warm steaming leaves pressed upon her as she stepped into shade, and when she lifted the casting-bottle, her thumb over the top, she saw it was damp still, but empty. A voice said, 'I've given them all they need. Don't be afraid, Katelina. I want to speak to you, nothing more.'

She didn't need to strain her sun-dazzled eyes to put a name to the speaker. After a moment she saw him, or his fuzzed mess of damp hair, and the peeled-open whites of his eyes, and his broad, accommodating shoulders draped today in anonymous black. He stood against the farthest wall of the shed, beyond the trestles of green, and barred by them from the door. The clay of the bottle cracked between her two hands. He said, 'Watch. You'll break it. How can I harm you? You've only to call, and I'm dead.'

First, the shock of finding Nicholas, here. Then the shock when she saw the truth of his words. She said, 'Then I'll call.' Her heart thudded.

He said, 'Give me five minutes first. I had no need to leave Cyprus. I had no need to come here.'

She said, 'Five minutes, why? Diniz is safe. He's on his way home. I'm going home, too.'

'Is he safe?' Nicholas said. 'Are you sure?'

A wash of fright, anger, nausea, swept over her. She said, 'Do you think I'd leave Cyprus before I was sure? I heard he had gone. The man who helped him sent a message. They found him a ship going west.'

'Who?' said Nicholas.

She said, 'Is that why you came? To find out?'

'To find out if he was safe, that was all. He should have stayed. So should you. I would have seen that you got home, Katelina,' he said. He drew a breath and didn't use it.

She said, 'You were going to say, Wherever home is?'

'No,' he said sharply. After a moment he said, 'I was going to say, Unless you were anxious to wait for Simon. Didn't you know he was planning to come for you?'

She laughed. 'I don't believe it.' Then she said, 'Or no, I do. He found out we were captured because of you. Is that why you want to make sure you've got rid of us?'

He was collected again. 'You've guessed it,' he said. 'And by the time your husband could arrive on Cyprus, the Genoese will be the King's prisoners and it might be difficult to get you both away. Or all of you, if Diniz had stayed.'

The plants dripped: the air was thick as pulped mash. She laid down the bottle and leaned her hands on it. 'You really think the Genoese will surrender? You should talk to Imperiale Doria. He has ships. He has money. The Dominican friars gave the Queen all their plate and Piozasque pledged it to Doria for silver.'

'Did he?' said Nicholas. 'The rumour I heard was that Doria himself was having to borrow.'

'Maybe,' she said. 'But he has security, and he uses reliable bankers. A firm who are ready with money enough, when it suits them.'

The bitterness must have showed. 'But not for St Pol & Vasquez?' said Nicholas slowly. 'Are the bankers called Vatachino?'

Despite the heat, her terror lessened. She said, 'Ah! You, too!'

'I knew that would please you,' said Nicholas. He ran his fingers over the plants, his eyes following them. 'Is Simon in trouble, Katelina? The death of Tristão, how difficult will that be?'

'As difficult as you meant it to be, I suppose,' she said. 'You know Simon. You met Tristão. Lucia is frightened of her own shadow. Which would you choose to kill, if you wanted to weaken a business?'

His eyes lifted. He said, 'I'm in Rhodes, among other things, to find out who did kill Tristão. If someone tries to spoil my business, I don't mind retaliating. But not in that way. And if I'd known it would happen, there are some things I would have done differently. As it is, the best asset Simon could have is yourself. You're free. Go home quickly. Go home and take Tristão's place.'

She gazed at him. He spoke as if nothing lay between them; with the earnestness of a brother giving advice. He had left Zacco in Cyprus to come where he would be killed in a moment if recognised. And he had come here, where she was, as if he had nothing to fear. As if he thought she believed all those protestations made on his sickbed in Nicosia just before Zacco came and bent over him. Zacco, who had sent her to Episkopi from which it had proved so simple to escape. Zacco, who had disliked, perhaps, the fact that Nicholas had paid Diniz's ransom. Zacco, who had got rid of Primaflora . . .

Katelina said, 'Why did you come to Rhodes?'

And he said, as if in direct response to her thoughts, 'Primaflora is here.'

It was too pat. She recognised, now, that all Primaflora had told her in the merchants' basilica had been false. Primaflora had abandoned the Queen to escape to Cyprus with Nicholas, and but for Zacco's jealousy they would be together in Cyprus now. But Katelina knew, if anyone did, that Nicholas was not the slave of a courtesan. She heard again the murmur of the cauldrons, and saw the steam, and saw the wife of Marco Corner move into his arms. Katelina said, 'But you have been taught to love men.'

He had been about to say something else, and stopped short. Then he said, 'James of Lusignan?'

'And David of Trebizond,' said Katelina. 'I saw your men's faces, when they heard the news of his capture. You make use of women, that's all. At Kouklia, you wanted to show Marco Corner who was master. You continued to prove yourself master in ways he would never even know. You made him a victim, like Simon. If Fiorenza has a child, I suppose it will pass as Corner's?'

Outside in the courtyard the cicadas hissed in the broken shade of the colonnades, and the olives and date palms stood still in the heat. Nicholas drew a short breath. He said, 'You're not as unworldly as that, Katelina. The princesses of Naxos play games, and the games require partners. And I doubt if it's your concern, but I am not the King's lover.'

He was angry. She looked at him bemused, because he was not only angry, but had failed to conceal it. She said stubbornly, 'But he wishes you to be.'

He had begun to recover. In one cheek a dent appeared, of exasperation, perhaps, or self-mockery. He said, 'Perhaps. But his mother doesn't. You were not sent to Episkopi in the hope that you would escape. Don't you know it yet? I was supposed to take advantage of you, not Fiorenza of Naxos, at Kouklia.'

She gazed at him, feeling sick, her eyes filmed. He moved impulsively and she flinched. He said, standing still, 'You're unwell. It's the heat, I'm sorry. I'll go. I just wanted to be sure you were safe, and the boy. And to tell you to go home as soon as you can. You've nothing to fear from me, Katelina. Nothing. Nothing.' And, perhaps feeling that his words had been too intense, he smiled suddenly and said, 'Anyway, you shouldn't water plants until evening. Didn't they tell you?'

She remembered that comforting smile. Claes. Claikine, Marian his wife used to call him, before she became his wife; when she was just his employer. Around the smile, his face glittered with drops from the screws of his hair. The garment he wore, swung by the movement, offered a glimpse of a scratched and sun-coloured forearm, shaped and rounded by labour, the hairs on it bleached like boar-bristles. The young and powerful arms, and the hands, and the broad shoulders. Her mind emptied, until all that was left was an echo. She shivered, and found the echo still there.

You shouldn't water plants until evening. But he had given them water, from the casting-bottle he had made her lay down, and from which rose a slight acrid odour, barely evident. There was another scent, too. It came from his skin: a tinge of costly sweet oils she had met only once, on a woman.

A black cone, and sweet oil, and sugar. She had nothing to fear from him, it was true. She said, 'I told someone to come for me. Wait. I'll send them away.'

Outside, the white pillars swam in the heat. She had, of course, tried to water the plants in the evening, but only once. Her servant had brought her a lamp, and the Hospitallers had come, black and white, treading two by two from the church of St John, so that incense and myrtle mingled in the acropolis, and taper light touched all its columns. There, where Athene, born of a hatchet-blow, had once received sacrifice, she had been invited to stand with the Knights to observe the birth of the moon from the sea. In their robes, they had watched it in silence, from the appearance of the first unlikely rim until the whole monstrous disc floated up, gold and washed-grey and rust in a night of no colour. When it hung high, a moon-path appeared on the water, with chains of glittering wave-light swirling across it, sensual as Nubian dancers wrapped in gold tissues. Dancers ravishing as a princess of Naxos, or a scion of Trebizond, or James, King of Cyprus, King of Scorpions. And round the lamps, other dancers had fluttered.

But today the sea was blue, and the sun burned as she went on her errand. She thought, when she went back, to find the shed empty, although she had been gone for no more than a moment, but he was still there, his eyes scanning her face. He wore, as she had already guessed, a stolen robe of the Knights of St John. She said, 'Why did you stay?' in both anger and anguish.

And Nicholas, stirring, said, 'In case you had wanted me. But you don't.'

She had betrayed him, and another man perhaps would have struck her. But there was no anger now on his face; only the aspects of thought translating itself into action. There had been, for a moment, a shadow that was more wistful than bitter. She stepped aside to let him pass, running silently, although she knew that by now he would never escape. Already, in the Commander's palace below, men had roused to the alarm she had given. There was only one way out of the citadel, and that was down through the castle, and past the guard at the drawbridge, and down the staircase to the exedra with its ancient carved ship and its notice, vouchsafing to Hagesandros son of Mikion the privilege of a front seat at festivals for services rendered. It seemed likely that Nicholas son of nobody was about to receive a front seat at this rite for nothing.

He had gone only a short way when she saw a sword flash in the sun and a guard leaped out from a doorway in his path. Only one man, but armed. Then she saw that Nicholas, too, had steel in one hand: a knife he must have worn under the robes and which he gripped in his left hand and not his right so that the stab, when it came, took the soldier quite by surprise. The man staggered and fell. As he did so, Nicholas wrenched the sword from his grasp and ran on.

By now, the shouting below drilled through the air: rattling Greek from the garrison; loud, careful Greek from as many of the

twelve Knights as were on their feet, with their swords out of the
scabbard. She had intended to deliver her tormentor to the jurisdiction of the Order. She had intended to shut the door somehow, for
ever, between Nicholas and herself. It struck her, now, that any
excited soldier would be forgiven for executing his own summary
justice. She stood transfixed under the eaves of the church with
their whitened plaster of nests and glimpsed Nicholas vander Poele
as he raced down the steps, and heard the challenge, and then the
clatter of swords, now out of her view. Heard shouting, heard
running footsteps, heard more swordplay and then, for a long time,
nothing but shouting. The sound seemed to weave backwards and
forwards in the lower reaches of the castle, sometimes nearer,
sometimes further away. Katelina stood, staring across the baked
and dazzling ruins and saw that already the lizards were flickering
back to their glassy arena, and the cicadas' buzz had resumed. A
man, living, had stood here. Now he was out of their way. Even
when something moved, it was so far off that the scene hardly
altered. Between the ranked columns a bare-legged servant in
white bounded up the glittering span of the celestial staircase to the
propylaeum. Beyond was the terrace, and the altar, and the temple
enclosing Athene goddess of war, Athene goddess of goldsmiths,
Athene goddess of wisdom, who killed her own father. Beyond that
was the precipice edge, and the sea. Unless he wished to commit
suicide, there was nothing to take a lone labourer there.

She waited, but no one came back and when, much later, she
walked slowly up the same staircase, there was nobody to be seen.
They found her there, to tell her that the spy of the Lusignan had
somehow escaped. She returned to the castle in their company, and
without looking over the wall, then or later.

The Knights' castle at Pharaclos occupied a squat grassy hill to
the north. Its battlements had a remarkably clear view, if distant, of Lindos; and far too clear a view, in the opinion of
Nicholas, of the red clay roofs of the cabins that littered the
landward side of Pharaclos Castle, safely out of view of the shore.
Once he had limped past the cows and the dogs and the goats,
the mules and the poultry, the melon patches, the beans and the
well, it was not hard to find the house of Persefoni, the woman
with the best roasting-ovens in Pharaclos. She was not pleased to
see him.

'Boulaki! Boulaki sent you, you go back to Boulaki. A foul,
fornicating fisherman who starves his own mother.'

'I bought his boat,' Nicholas said. 'He says you are an angel as
his mother is a devil. I need to hide until I can walk. And I need information.'

She didn't ask what was wrong with him, because she could see the bone of his shin. He kept his arms behind his back too, in case she expected him to dance on his hands. She said, 'How much?' And he said, 'Boulaki's boat and as much again as I paid for it, to keep for Yiannis's grandson.'

'Ah!' she said. 'He trusted you with the boy?'

'He got paid for it,' said Nicholas. 'Twice over.'

She shot a look at him. He hoped he looked as he felt, which was resigned, reasonably acquiescent and in some breath-shortening but not life-endangering pain. He knew, as well as she knew, that if he carried that amount on him, he could be killed and robbed in five minutes. He said, 'I can give you half. The rest will be paid by a lady in Lindos. I have to meet her in two weeks on the west coast. Boulaki will speak for us both.'

'Limboulaki,' she said. 'Little boatman. His true name is George. Well, come in. How did you come by all this? You climbed out of her window?'

'It was a very high window,' he said. The fires were all lit under the roasting-ovens, and the shacks, the yard, the cabin shimmered and reeked with the heat. He saw, without protest, that she was opening the door to a hay shed.

She said, 'As you see, no neighbours want to build close to this house. You can stay. There is a bucket. The boy will bring you some food. Show me your hands.'

He brought them forward. She had a weathered brown face, and strong black hair plaited under a rag. She said, 'For half the money in advance, I will bring hot water and linen and ointment. But maybe you're a good healer, and don't need them.'

There was not much he could do. He let himself down and pulled the bag from his satchel and gave it to her. He said, 'But the rest is for the boy.'

'Oh, oh. The boy,' she said, counting it. 'Well, I suppose God tells us to take pity on beggars. I will bind this leg of yours as well. And what clothes are these, for a Christian man to be wearing?'

'You have a son?' he said.

Her eyes moved to him. She said, 'Maybe. But he is a Greek, not a foreigner. The woman in Lindos is foreign?'

'Yes,' he said.

'Your lover? Your wife, it may be?'

'She would like to be,' Nicholas said.

Her mouth opened wide as a fish-scoop. She said, 'Oho! We climb out of a lady's window to escape her? She has no dowry? There is another?'

'There is another. But,' Nicholas said, 'I think we must know one another better before I can tell you.'

He had had a lot of experience with middle-aged women. Within a day, he had a bed inside the house. Within three, she knew about

Katelina, and had promised to help him. He thought it very likely she would then sell him to someone else, but there was little he could do until he could walk again. And Primaflora would wait at the rendezvous they had arranged, since for her sake he would not go back to the villa at Lindos. And from that rendezvous, of course, they would make their way back to Cyprus, as husband and wife.

His injuries were healthily mending; his abrasions and fingertips healing when Boulaki's aunt brought him the news he was waiting for. 'The Flemish lady who waits for a ship. She is going.'

He was sitting at table, whittling out a new puzzle with cautious fingers. He looked up and laid down the knife. 'Good news! When and how?'

The woman sat down and lifted an edge of the puzzle. 'Toys! Child's play! You who should do the work of a man! She rides north at dawn tomorrow from Lindos to the City. She has a good escort. She will sleep on the way at Kalopetra.'

In all their exchanges, usually, she glared at him. When she was being kindest, she glared at him. Now, her head bent, she fingered the puzzle. Nicholas said, his voice gentle, 'It is a strange route, for the City.'

'So,' said the woman. 'You know the route. Before she arrives at the monastery, she will be abandoned. Her escort will be attacked, and will run.'

'And the attackers will kill her?' said Nicholas.

'Not as before. No. No. They will leave her unharmed, but with no protection, no guide and no horse. There are many dangers,' said Boulaki's aunt, 'and that spot, as you know, is deserted. It is natural that she would wish to walk there, where the Portuguese lord met his death. What happens to her, too, must be natural.'

'I see,' said Nicholas. He took the puzzle back and slowly cleared it of sawdust and shavings. He said, 'But how can they be sure she will die?'

The woman said, 'You mistake me. She may die. Death is simple. But for some, there are fates –'

'– worse than death,' Nicholas finished. He looked up. 'So, rape?'

Her black eyes glared. She said, 'Do you not know her? Do you not know what she fears to the point of madness?'

He looked through her, thinking, recalling. A fan. A veil. A napkin at Kouklia. Precious plants, which nevertheless could not be watered by lamplight. And, long ago, an event in the valley of Kalopetra itself. He said, 'How do you know what she fears?'

'It is known,' the woman said. 'Her servant talks. She is watched. They have weaknesses, these rich women with husbands.'

Nicholas said, 'They are cruel, who prey on them.'

She glared at him still. 'Not my nephews,' she said. 'This time they have been told to do nothing. You promised no harm would come to my nephews. You may kill their hirelings again if you wish. I hold you to that.'

'I meant it,' said Nicholas. 'I spoke the truth, too. I can afford to tell no one. Only I shall be there when it happens, if you will get me a mule. Can you do that?'

'You are a good worker,' she said, 'although foreign. I can do that. Save her, marry her, and give her sons. Sons are worth all the gold in the world.'

'They are worth what their mothers are worth,' Nicholas said.

Dressed as Guinevere, Nicholas had of course been before to the ravine he was going to, although riding through a winter's dusk then from the opposite end, and not by himself. Astorre and Tobie had been with him, and an unknown soldier and Loppe, and Katelina. And, of course, Primaflora, riding pillion behind him with her moveable warmth and her golden hair and the gleam, white and gold, of her limbs. It was here they had found dead Tristão, and the youth Diniz, hurt and weeping in hiding. Diniz six months ago, when he was young, and before he came to sink an axe in anyone's shoulder.

Katelina had set out to ride there with four soldiers and no servant that could be detected. Waiting just outside Pharaclos, Nicholas let the small cavalcade pass and then followed, trotting easily on the horse which, after all, Boulaki's aunt had managed to find for him. He suspected that, whatever the outcome, Boulaki's aunt was sure of getting it back.

Not that Katelina's escort made any secret, either, of their passage. They took the usual road north by the coast, passing through Malona and stopping at Arkhangelos. Only at Afandou, thirteen miles short of the City, did they turn west and begin the climb that would cross the ridge and lead down to Kalopetra. Nicholas wondered why Katelina had agreed to spend the night there. Perhaps her woman had been sent on ahead. Perhaps she had been told of a ship she must join. Perhaps, indeed, she had been induced to consider a pilgrimage. Going home to Tristão's widow she could take a flower, a stone from his death-place. Well protected, in clear brilliant sunlight, the spot would hold no present terrors, and only a small debt of mourning.

It was a leisurely journey. Nicholas took his pace from the party he followed, and stopped when they did as the sun rose in the sky. Like them, he chose shade wherever possible, riding between olives and carobs, under massed and opulent lemons and the glossy leaves and choking perfume of oranges. He ate in a resinous pine grove, deep as fleece under his feet, and drowsed among cones, below an animal sheen of green needles. He put off time in a village, throwing dice in the shadow of yellow-green grapes, and bought a melon, and a plaited straw basket to hang from his saddle. He sat his horse talking to haymakers, and swished through dry grass in a rhythmical uproar of grasshoppers. He put up birds, and glimpsed sugarcane once, and identified the oil and incense of churches and finally came, as the sun stood past its zenith, to high places of silence, where he heard only the bray of an ass, and the remote, plodding clink of a bell and the soft, ruffled thud of his riding.

He knew by then that he was only one stage from his destination. He made his last stop, peeling off his soaked peasant's shirt but not the knee-high leather boots that irked his ripped legs and feet. Then he withdrew his mind from its rest, and began to think again.

The ravine was half a mile long. He had seen it only in darkness, but he remembered where the ambush that had killed Tristão had been. They had shot him, and then had come down to look at the body. There could not be so many places in that particular gorge where mounted men could climb down at speed, and escape again. And Katelina would go there. They could depend on it.

He had no wish to come across the ambushers, or to disturb them. He believed what he had been told. They would not risk an attack on the girl. In case she survived, her guard would take care to act out the fiction. They would try to defend her, and fail, and be beaten off. Whatever danger she fell into then was not of their doing. He wondered how long it would be before they turned up at the gates of Kalopetra, nursing some spurious injuries. Not, he guessed, until nightfall. All the harder, by then, to find her or her body. In time, he resumed his dry shirt, and a sleeveless skin jacket given him by Boulaki's aunt which might, she said sourly, just keep out a spent arrow. He had had to abandon the sword he had won at the castle, but he had a good skinning knife in his belt which would do very well, unless he was unlucky. He had also cut himself a stout switch. He didn't expect to have trouble with men. His object was to arrive when the men had departed.

Ahead, the tracks of his quarry led downhill over slopes that in winter must have been slick with marsh-water and mud. Now they were patched with strong colour, shaded by trees and fed by the springs that combed down to unite in the ravine, scouring it into ladders and pools, cutting into the overhang of soft earth and rocks, nourishing the flowering bushes that grew along its sides, and the forest trees that stood with their roots streaming in water, their vaulted barks Gothic-high, their luminous leaves overhead, green as if painted on glass.

It was what Nicholas saw as swinging out from the start of the gorge, he approached its edge further down, where the thunder of water told him the waterfall was. His horse tied out of sight, he moved circumspectly to the side and looked over.

Chapter 32

HE HAD FORGOTTEN how vast the trees were, growing close
in the long, winding chasm where the stream ran. Some
had fallen, their gnarled boles swollen with scaly protube-
rances, their hollows hummocked with webs. Rafts of
pebbles divided the stream: brilliant ferns grew at its edges; moss
gloved everything like double-cut velvet, sheeting the walls of the
ravine and weeping harp-music under the organ-voice of the fall.
To his right, the ladder of water blocked his view. To the left, so
far as the stream ran before turning into the trees, the valley
seemed to be empty.

When Katelina's party came, they would approach from the
opposite side, where there was room for four men and a girl to lead
their horses down to the small grassy strand where Diniz's father
had died. As for himself, the best hiding-place was down there, at
the foot of the fall. Beyond the pool, it would be easy to cross.

That, of course, meant he had to climb down. Nicholas, sighing,
turned and started to hand himself watchfully from rock to rock,
the mist from the cascade acceptably beading his skin and the noise
unacceptably deadening his hearing, so that he spent half the
descent with his chin turned on his shoulder. No one came. He
dug his fingers without pleasure into the caked earth by a clump of
pale cyclamen, and a chaffinch rattled up, calling. Sunlight jumped
in and out of his eyes, and tattooed his arms with a bright, fickle
yellow. He persevered doggedly, swearing each time he dug in his
toes and swearing again as he felt the pull on his shoulder and
neck. After what seemed far too long he landed on the rocks by the
edge of the fall, where the foam dashed and winked and, beyond,
the pool lay still and green. Beyond that, the stream raced ahead on
its business, winding into the green dappled gloom among boulders
and bushes, creepers and the dark trunks of trees. Among the trees,
someone was standing.

Katelina, alone. Which was impossible.

Katelina standing in silence, staring at him. Since he had just been performing in full public glare like a lizard, this was not surprising. Katelina staring at him and about to be joined, he assumed, by her four escorts, all prepared to be ambushed and chased off. This was disastrous.

She had betrayed him before, and there was every reason why she should betray him again. He gave a fast, despairing look at the cliff down which he had just climbed, and decided he was damned if he would climb it again. He thought, letting the waterfall rinse off his hands, that if he could wade over the pool, he might be able to escape round the fall on that side. He moved, and she put both hands up in terrified warning to stop him.

She put them up gradually, like a swimmer. Her face was pallid in the humid green dusk. She didn't look venomous, she looked stricken. He cast a glance over her head. No sound; no movement. Well, no movement. Sound he could scarcely hear, where he was. He stared sightlessly at her, considering. No sight of her escort: but there should be, by now. No sign of their attackers, as he'd expected. But on the steep slope behind her, the slithering track where one person had escaped down from the brink, a track that ended where Katelina stood. And above on the skyline, a mess of broken boughs and tumbled clods as if a struggle had occurred beyond there between more than a few horsemen. And then, as he sought to decipher it all, he became aware of a vibration that was not a sound under his feet. The pounding of many hooves, making off from beyond the ravine.

The sound, he had to assume, of Katelina's absconding escort. It had all happened as Persefoni foretold. Their sham fight had taken place while his ears had been closed by the waterfall. Katelina had been persuaded to run downhill to safety while her guards had met their expected attackers, and after some loud, harmless fighting they'd left. So she found herself alone, she thought, with the one man in the world who had good reason to hurt her.

He might be wrong, in which case he could hardly risk yelling a question. He might be right, and every step she took away from him would place her in danger. Nicholas turned his back on the roar of the waterfall and began, as calmly as possible, to walk down his side of the ravine towards her. All the time he was moving she repeated, with a sort of despair, the slow, urgent motion to halt him, and followed it with a finger to her lips.

Her fear was not connected with him; or not directly. She wanted silence. He halted, baffled. Mime seemed to be the only solution. He pointed uphill behind her, and unsheathing a non-existent sword, conducted a fight with it. He ended with his outspread hand frozen over his head, like a bad acrobat inviting applause, and raised his brows in wordless enquiry.

Across the stream, Katelina was not so far away. He could see now that her face was hollow with strain. She wore a scarlet silk cord round her head, binding a linen veil striped with embroidery, of the kind that Fiorenza and Valenza used as a cloak when they had the fancy to be taken for Greeks. Her grass-stained skirt, tied up at one side for riding, revealed pale woven hose and embroidered kid slippers, sunk among shadowy reeds. She herself seemed oblivious to the wet, uneven ground at her feet. She put her hands fearfully to the cloth at her ears, and again to her lips and finally, with another gradual gesture, turned towards the top of the cliff and pushed the air away from herself, shaking her head with dreamlike urgency.

So her escort and her assailants had gone – or else she wanted him to think that they had.

No, they had gone. No one could imitate the way she looked now. And if they were going when he first heard their hooves, they must be well out of earshot by now. Before he called to her, he thought it as well to listen. Away from the rush of the cataract the green tunnel they occupied seemed filled by a thunderous quiet. The stream produced glottal sounds in a hollow voice. Far out of sight, larksong trembled. Invisible grasshoppers buzzed. In the distance, water eased unctuously over the fall, dark as snail-oil, and dropped in grey and white streaks to the pool. Near at hand, a boulder lay in the water, split, misshapen, ochre-grey dappled with lichenous pebbles.

The atmosphere steamed as the plant-house at Lindos had done, releasing a fungoid smell of earth and leaves, of hidden flowers, of animal life; of decay. Among it all was a scent that he couldn't identify, pungent yet sweet as molasses. For a brief, livid moment, he wondered what on earth he was doing here, and what was happening in Cyprus without him. He saw Katelina's face, and thought she might faint, and then, concentrating at last, realised what she was staring at; what she was trying to tell him.

It had nothing to do with human danger, or soldiers. It had to do with this valley. The boulder he had thought scaled with growth was quilted with something other than lichen. The moss at his back was a speckled, smothering dun instead of emerald green. The bulbous trunk of the tree at his shoulder was dressed in a deep, ruffled garment of brown seamed with yellow, cut with layer on layer of dagging, fine as pastry, fine as shells made of organdie. The stuff clothed the tree to the top and, when he lifted his head, he saw that its leaves, too, were lined with clustering petals of brown heart-shaped silk, veined with chrome. Then he looked again, and saw that, as if heaped with lice, the soft speckled stuff on the tree and the rock and the boulder was full of small movements. There was a prickling mass on the bush at his side, on the stones in the stream, on the flowers, on the grass at her feet and his, bending under the weight of it. He moved, and a petal detached itself from the thick appliqué, fluttering upwards. It had two brown and cream wings, revealing underwings of spotted burnt orange, and a furred body, and fine, whiskered feelers. It spread itself over his arm, twitching, tickling, and then took the air over its shadow. Flying, the thing was nearly two inches long. An insect. A butterfly. A moth, not a butterfly. A moth from a colony of moths numbering millions and millions: covering every growing thing in the valley.

He looked at Katelina then, in absolute silence, for he knew why his presence meant nothing, except as a disturbance, and why the absence of her protectors meant less. He realised, too, something she didn't know. If this valley bred moths, then it would attract and breed all the reptiles that fed on them. This was why men died; why Tristão, felled by a bite, became victim of a murderer's arrow. Whoever planned this knew that Katelina was unlikely to survive. And as the thought came to him, he saw what already writhed about her slender kid slippers, the flowing shadows he had taken for reeds.

It was either one snake or two. He didn't wait to find out. He plunged shouting towards her in a blizzard of spray, his knife out, his arm outflung in warning. He saw her jump back, her mouth open. Even then, she didn't scream. She didn't scream as he floundered out of the stream, and kicked one coiling green back while he stabbed the knife into a second reptile and killed it. Then he made a swift turn on his booted feet, to find the wounded snake upreared and facing him. The hairlike tongue quivered and threatened and the snake hissed and hissed.

He didn't know, intent on his duel, that in inducing that hiss, he had released a signal of danger that would travel echoing through the whole valley. The gleaming, leathery head brushed his hand, darted up to his calves, coiled and uncoiled like a medal of rope. Even when he caught it again with his knife it lurched away, and he had to follow, cutting and stabbing until at length it lay at his feet. It was the only one left: if there were others, they had gone. As he looked down, a deep frilling sound filled the air; a sound of ghostly applause; a sound of ghostly alarm. He looked up. From every tree, leaf and bush the moths rose like goosefeathers sacked by the wind. They lifted, darkening and thickening until the green tunnel was roofed with brown, living insects, obscuring the green. Katelina began to scream, then.

The dark, trembling cloud overhead dyed the stream sullen and tawny: the twilight shadows about Katelina swung and darkened as the ceiling of insects responded, its instinct fine-tuned to her screams. Nicholas turned, sheathing his knife, disregarding the still, scaly bodies that, a moment ago, had seemed the real menace. As he did so, fragile outriders from above were descending, thickening, crowding, fanning his hair; alighting and clustering on his skin. Dry, fluttering wings entered his mouth and stuffed stifling into his nostrils. Katelina's face, like his own, became a shell-mask of moths.

Her screams became spasmodic and clotted: he thought she was dying. He scoured her face clear with a single rough hand, his palm a mess of half-wings and hair feelers and bodies, while with the other he whipped closed the linen stuff of her veil, covering all of her, eyes, mouth and body so that her screams became stifled, then stopped. He ripped off his shirt and added that to her armoury, trapping her hands safely inside it. In a vibrating storm of brown taffeta, the whole body of moths now descended, first to the high trees, then the trunks, then lower, clasping and crowding each surface, mounded deep as fine shavings of tortoiseshell.

They settled on Katelina and on Nicholas, as he held her. They rustled into his lips and his hair, clustered into his eyes and the folds of his ears, heaped themselves, as if magnetised, on the fine banded linen that shrouded the girl from head to foot. In mounds, they flickered under his palms as he grasped her. They clouded round him as he picked her up and started to run in the dizzying heat. And only then did he realise what the scent was in the valley: the clinging odour, sweet as vanilla pods, he had failed to identify. It was still there, all around. But strongest of all, it rose from the girl in his arms. From her clothes. No. From the veil he had wrapped so firmly about her. He lifted a corner of linen and moths buffeted over his fingers, wriggling, avid. On the underside of the cloth he saw a faint, greyish-brown smear which was instantly coated with wings.

Storax. That was what the trees were: the great Hygrambaris on whose resin gods and butterflies fed. And whose oils had been pressed on Katelina, soaked into the reverse of her linen. He had no hands to clear his own face but she was safe, cocooned, her face on his shoulder. Safe, although she was rigid as death and he had, somehow, to get her into the sunlight; away from the trees where every step that he took plastered them both, thicker and thicker with a whiskered, fluttering mass of brown and yellow and orange.

There was no time to ask any of the polite questions one asked a woman, before doing what he was going to do to her. In any case, his lips were smothered shut. As best he could, he stumbled with her as far as the dappled, sunlit dell of the fall, and set her down, clearing his clogged, streaming face. Then he put hands to her scarf and tore it cord and all from her hair, dragging it free of her shoulders and flinging it with his shirt as far off as he could. A carpet of moths rose as he did it, and hesitated, and then flew to fasten upon it again where it lay. The rest dropped and lingered like leaves upon the hot, perfumed skin the veil had laid bare.

Nicholas gave the things no time to cover her face or her hair or her shoulders. He took her by both arms and jumped with her into the pool, pulling her down, ducking her under the surface. He brought her up, commanded 'Breathe!' and thrust her down again. Drowning moths dimpled all the green surface: others swung overhead, waiting to alight once again. He could see the glutinous patches still in her hair, on her neck; and found wet wings alighting on his own bare shoulders, where her scent had stuck.

She seemed almost lifeless, and certainly beyond words. He took her arm and, half swimming, half wading, drove her under the waterfall. There, in a place where she could breathe, surrounded by spray, he rubbed her face and twisted and fretted her hair in the falling, cool water and then, with both hands, tore apart her sticky dress and the chemise below it and pulled them down from her shoulders. He paused at her waist and, stirring for the first time, she laid her trembling hands over his and dragged her skirts down until they jumped and tugged at her ankles. Then she moved, and they were gone in the foam. *And loosed from her bosom the broidered zone, curiously wrought, wherein are fashioned all manner of allurements; therein is love; therein desire; therein dalliance – beguilement that steals the wits even of the wise.*

Aphrodite.

He remembered, in Bruges, how she looked. The black Borselen brows, that she was too strong-minded to pluck and to pencil. The full-blooded mouth; the long hair, thick enough, even wet, to lead his eye down to what it didn't conceal. The pretty breasts, round as fruit with their wet, swollen tips. The rib-cage strong, the waist narrow, the thighs shapely and generous. And the glittering, dark place between them where, with such consequences, she had admitted him.

He saw she was no longer rigid. Her body was quiescent in the quiet, running water. No. Not quiescent. He could feel her burning warmth, and his own. The waterfall thundered about them. His throat tight, he sought to look at her face but was stopped by her hands at his waist. Then she said something he had never expected to hear; and, lifting his eyes from her fingers, he saw her lips were open, and near. He closed them with his own, with her fingers still jammed between them. After a while he untied what she wanted got rid of, and then planted his hands round her and kissed her again, with her fingers no longer between them but behind him.

It seemed likely, in the extreme urgency that began to overwhelm the matter, that they would not really get out of the water. She began moving against him long before they surged to the edge of the pool and afterwards he didn't remember whether or not they arrived separately on the hot, sunny bank. Everything else seemed blotted out by this extraordinary event, dwarfing the terror behind them in its avidity. Its summary nature, or the tension, and the release from tension hurled them both, immediately it was over, into fathomless sleep. After an uncounted passage of time Nicholas woke, leaf-shadow and sun on his back, and moved gently away from his sleeping mistress.

The glade was as it had been when they arrived there. Well, not quite the same, maybe. Beyond the dell where they lay, the trees, the boulders, the mosses slept with their moving moth-burdens, syrup-fed, drowsy in silence. Those who had pursued them and died floated transparent brown in the pool, or lay drying like leaves on the pebbles with ant trails already consuming them. Some idly moving from harvest to harvest, passed transparently over his head, or settled below, heart-shaped, brown seamed with yellow. Some, bigger and brighter, were not moths but stray and beautiful butterflies. Far away, a sleeping cinnamon carpet, lay Katelina's veil and his shirt, where he had thrown them together.

She was going to need something to wear. So was he, apart from his boots. He began to laugh to himself, hoping they had not been an inconvenience. The moths rose when he handled the garments, but beyond brushing his skin, made no effort to settle on him. He scoured both, then hung them to dry on a twig. Though he watched, no moths rushed to alight on them. He did the same for her chemise, when he found it. Her gown was torn to shreds, by her hands or his. Much further down, to his relief, he found his own peasant-breeches, cast up on the bank and half dry. He put them on, and came back, silently, in case he frightened her.

She was sitting up, motionless, her back to him. Her hair, half dried, fell down her back like fine brown hemp of different textures. He continued to walk without sound, allowing himself the modest delight of looking at the silky knobbed tail of her spine, ending in the double whorl of white buttocks whose contours he could not remember exploring. He saw blue veins, like the veins he had glimpsed on the ripe, unfamiliar breasts pressed below him such a short time ago. Such a long time ago. Such an unspeakably long time ago. He realised with a quarter of his mind that whatever had happened was going to happen again, and he couldn't halt it. Then he stopped still.

There was a moth near her, passing through shafted sunlight, and she was watching it. Her face was invisible. But he saw her raise her wrist slowly, and hold it. Like a courtier, the clouded thing landed on it, its orange skirts vanished, and lay, a frail umber shield veined with yellow. She remained without moving until his shadow fell at her side. Even then, she didn't speak until, of its own accord, the moth palpitated, and went on its way.

Then she said, 'It was a test. If I could do it, you were going to come back.'

'You can trust me without that,' he said. 'They are helpless, and don't mean any harm. And they know only one mating.'

He saw from the line of her cheek that she smiled. She looked round at him, and up and, leaning back on one elbow, let him see all he wanted to be reminded of. Then she said, as he had hoped, 'And am I to be the same?'

Part-way through, she saw his hands and caught them saying, 'The rocks at Lindos?' He answered that without words, and didn't use words, either, when later she said, 'I adore you. I will adore you for ever.'

It was necessary afterwards not to sleep; but hard to separate limb from limb so that he could collect their clothes, and dress her, and prevent her from dressing him, or more time would be lost. She said, 'The snakes! Do they respect Franks?'

And he laughed and said, 'We frightened them. No. They live in the dark, where the trees and the butterflies are.' Until then, she had asked him no questions except the small ones of intimacy; and he had mindlessly found himself courting her with Hesiod and Homer and Horace, as befitted the foam-born: *and with her went Eros, and comely Desire followed her at her birth.*

Later, when he had pulled her up from the gorge, and found his saddlebags, and unpacked wine and cheese, bread and melon, he could feel the silence behind him, and knew that the staved-off world had come back, and with it anxiety, if not doubt; and hesitation over the immensity of the gap which now must be bridged by words. He said, 'Rich-crowned Cytherea, you are spent. Eat and drink, and then we shall see what has to be done. Don't let anything worry you.'

Her hands round the wine-cup were trembling. 'I didn't care,' she said. 'They could have come in their thousands. At that moment, I didn't care.'

He said gently, 'They were up against the most powerful thing in the world. You may be frightened of them again, but perhaps never quite so much. Or perhaps not at all. How did it start? The fear?' He was eating melon to prevent himself from touching her again.

She smiled, but her eyes were unseeing. 'My dearest nurse died. The girl who came next had lovers. She let the moths beat on the lamp by my bed while she pleasured them.'

He threw the melon away and laid his arm round her, caressing. 'It doesn't matter.'

'No. I want to tell you. Then the first time Simon touched me was in a garden. There were moths, gnats and a kiss –' She broke off and said starkly, 'I hated him.'

His fingers stopped. He said, 'Don't. I don't. It is not what will help him.'

Then she said, 'Is he your father?'

He laid her hand down. After a moment he drew up his knees and embraced them. He said, 'I believe so. And so did my mother, his first wife.'

He could hear his voice, cool and quite steady. She said, 'But he has never sired children.'

'Oh, yes.' he said. 'A son, born dead before me. Between his death and my birth, Simon claimed never to have slept with my mother. My mother said she had slept with no other. I believed her.'

Katelina said, 'You knew her?'

'Of course,' he said. 'She lived with her father, after Simon cast her off. She died when I was seven.'

'And?' she said.

'And so I was sent to take service in Geneva. I suppose Simon hoped I would stay there for ever. But my mother's father – his wife – his wife's sister –'

'But Marian de Charetty gave you a home,' Katelina said. 'And reared you. And married you.'

'No,' he said. 'I asked her to marry me.' After a bit he said, 'Who told you? That Simon's wife was my mother?'

'Simon,' she said. 'He boasted that you plotted to destroy all your family, but had failed to harm him. He said you believed he was your father. And so, I thought, you had –'

'Plotted to foist my child incestuously and secretly on him. Do you still think so?' he said.

'I haven't been honest,' she said. 'I haven't been honest with you, have I? You came to me because I wanted it. I told you it was safe. You had no way of knowing a child was coming. I don't know why you married.'

'It doesn't matter,' he said. 'Then, you and I couldn't have married; you couldn't have borne it. It all came from unhappiness. I have always known that.'

'I might have killed you,' she said. 'At Lindos . . .'

He turned and smiled at her, his hands tightly clasped. 'You were within your rights. I came to poison the plants. You must know that by now. But not only that. To find out if you were safe, and Diniz. And to make sure you would stay safe.'

She said, 'But why should I not be?' She frowned. 'The fight at the ravine. My escort were attacked, and then left me.' She looked up. 'Left me to the snakes, but for you. Was that planned? How did you know?'

'Through a cunning lady called Persefoni,' Nicholas said. 'She presented you with your life. She set us both under the Fontana Amorosa, and whosoever drinks from that, they are thirsty for ever.' She moved, and he said, 'No. Please. If I touch you again, I

shall never tell you what you have to know. Listen. Someone
didn't want you to live. They tried to kill you before, but only
murdered Tristão. They lay in wait. They knew you would follow
him.'

She was sitting up now, her brows straight. 'Who?'

'The Queen,' he said. 'And perhaps Primaflora.'

'*The Queen?*' she said.

'And Primaflora,' Nicholas said. 'The Lusignan fight to win, and
the Queen is a Lusignan. She failed to persuade me to join her in
Venice; she thought she had me at Bologna; she sent Primaflora to
trap me in Bruges and later in the Abruzzi. She made me a Knight,
when a refusal meant killing my company, and when she thought
you might harm me, she sent out orders to stop you: to kill you, if
need be. Then, when you found your way to Cyprus, she had no
conscience at all about accepting what information you could send
her.'

He stretched, and smiled at her. 'But by then, I had tricked her
by taking service with Zacco, and she wanted me dead. You were
supposed to arrange that. You or Diniz. When you didn't, she used
you to trap me. And to get rid of the plants. She still thinks to
regain Cyprus: she doesn't want sugar plants sent to Madeira. And
I, to be truthful, didn't want Simon to have them. He has done his
best to spoil my trade. It is legitimate to defend myself. I have
never done more than that.'

'And Primaflora?' she said. 'All along, she has acted for Carlotta?'

'All along, she has acted for Primaflora,' Nicholas said. 'She has
no money, no protector. She lives by her wits and a certain . . . love
of style. She has been waiting to see who will win.' He paused. 'We
have been lovers. You know that. And there have been others. You
probably know of them. This is not the place for explanations, but
if I'm being used for a purpose not my own, it seems only fair to
return the compliment. I'm not presuming to say that the exercise
is distasteful; just that it's only an exercise.'

She turned with a sudden, generous gesture, stretching her hand
to his arm, and smoothing it down to his knuckles. She said, 'Your
palms are hurt already. You think that is how Primaflora feels. I
think she is not with you from duty.'

He loosened his hands. 'She is with me for many reasons,' he
said. He hesitated and said, 'The plants were part of her fee.'

'For what?' she said. She turned fully towards him.

'For your safety,' he said. 'As you see, she has cheated.' He
waited and said, 'She is jealous. She won't try again. She will leave
the island before you do.'

Her eyes had grown dark. 'With you?' said Katelina.

'Yes,' he said. 'I am the rest of her fee.'

Silence stretched. She looked down, holding his hands without seeing them. She said, 'I can't go back to Simon.'

Nicholas said, 'You must; because of his son.'

Her grip loosened, and her gaze came up, agonized. She said, 'You have never seen him.'

He had recovered the cool voice, and kept it. 'You and I made him,' Nicholas said. 'With you, he will have a name, and be happy. With me, he will be the bastard of a bastard. And if you leave Simon and don't come to me, who will care for your son?'

She said, 'I wondered, when I was carrying him . . .' She stopped.

'What?' he said. He rose quietly and stood looking down at her.

'If you would want him. If you were fond of children. If you had others. If you would be a kind father. If you would marry me.'

He said, 'I have no others. Servants know how to protect themselves. Katelina, we can't marry. You will have to be father and mother. But as he grows . . . I should like to know something about him.'

'I don't know him,' she said. 'He has your nature, and beauty. I couldn't give my heart to him, as well.'

'Now you can,' Nicholas said.

Her eyes were filled. 'But is that all? Is that all I am to have? I thought in Bruges it was like this because it was the first time.'

'I could have told you it wasn't,' Nicholas said.

'But you didn't tell me,' she said. 'If you had, none of this would have happened.' He made no reply. She said with sudden violence, 'Simon – he is a weak man who has never grown up. He is like Diniz. He is no older than Diniz.'

Nicholas said, 'What do you think Zacco is like? I had to choose between Carlotta and her brother, and chose Zacco because he appeared a strong ruler. But he's also immature, and he's spoiled, so he has to be led, and tempted and coaxed, or he loses his way. I don't sleep with him. You have that advantage with Simon. I have said to you before: help him. You know a lot about trade. Has he built refineries, or has he fallen into the error I have, of finding myself held to ransom by others who got there before me? I shall make a good profit this year, but not the profit I should have made. Warn him.'

Katelina looked up at him thoughtfully. 'You mean it? But you ruined his plants?'

Nicholas said, 'I'll return an attack. But I won't stop him developing his own, legitimate trade. He needs that. He needs you.'

'And the name, then, of the predator?' said Katelina.

He said, 'There is only one firm. You have named it.'

She was sitting so still that he was afraid he had been wrong to speak of it. But her thoughts, it seemed, were on something different. She said, 'How can I advise him? I should need help. I should need to write to you, or see you. I could come to Bruges. You would have reason to pay visits to Bruges. We could meet.'

'And Simon?' Nicholas said. 'He would find out. We couldn't meet without coming together like this. Or I couldn't.'

She rose and kissed him in the way he had just taught her, which was brutally unfair. 'No?' She left her arms round his shoulders, and all her body fitted into his. She said, 'Then come to me. We would take the child. We would marry, eventually. Or does it frighten you, owning a family?'

He took her hands and held her off, without releasing her. 'You know as well as I do,' Nicholas said, 'that Simon will kill to keep his son; and would kill Arigho himself if he thought he was mine.'

In his vehemence, he had used the Italian form. Katelina said, 'Is that what you call him in your mind?'

He squeezed her hands lightly and dropped them, turning. 'I know, of course, you named him after your uncle. Jordan must have been very displeased.' He knelt to pack his small possessions.

'The Heart as Love's Captive,' she said with dislike. 'He was helping King René to paint it, and mocking Simon with every breath. Why doesn't Simon kill Father Jordan?'

Nicholas stood with the packages. 'Because,' he said, 'Father Jordan is probably waiting for Simon to kill you, and me, and the child. He plays games.'

'Like you,' she said. Now they were ready she had turned very pale.

Nicholas said, 'No. I invent puzzles, and their solutions. The solution to this one says that you go straight to the monastery of Kalopetra — I'll take you there — and describe how you fled after the ambush. You will be amazed when the escort turn up, much dishevelled. You will obtain some respectable clothing — how?'

'My servant,' Katelina said. 'She's already there with my baggage.'

'I wondered,' Nicholas said. 'So then you set off, well protected, for the City where, I am told, you will find a ship for the west already awaiting you. Get on board. Get on board, and delay for nothing.' He had no more instructions to give, but he went on rambling as he laid the stole over her loosened hair and folded it over her chemise. 'For she was clad in a robe out-shining the brightness of fire, enriched with all manner of needlework, which shimmered like the moon over her tender breasts, a marvel to see.' He stopped rambling and said, 'No . . . We mustn't . . .'

The silk cord had gone, so he plaited rushes quickly together and set the band round her brow, over the linen. He stood, admiring what he had done. 'And poor broidered zone; but not much the worse. Was it made for you?'

'It was sent me,' said Katelina. 'A gift from the Queen, sent to Lindos. And after I sail for Portugal?' With his help, she mounted, and he vaulted up behind her and, reaching round her, collected the reins.

'And then? Be happy, Katelina,' he said. 'If you think, now, that you know what happiness is. It can be found without me.'

There were tears on her cheeks. She said, 'I know. I know what you've said. But Simon may die. What if Simon should die? I could marry you then.'

'Perhaps,' he said. 'But I have tied myself too, as I told you. I have to pay the rest of my fee to Primaflora. Here, she has all she wants. To persuade her to leave, I couldn't suggest less than marriage.'

He made to shake the reins, but her hand on his held the horse still. Her face had filled with incredulity, with alarm, with dismay. 'A courtesan!' Katelina said. 'When the Queen suggested it, that was an insult. We can escape, you and I, without your having to wed Primaflora.' She hesitated in a way that once she would never have done. 'Unless you want it. I have no right. I am married, and you are not.'

'I am married,' he said. 'Whether I want it or not is irrelevant. It was the price of my life, as well as yours.'

For a long time, she sat motionless within his embrace. He freed the reins and motioned the horse to a walk, then a trot. After a while he heard her say, 'You are married. When did you marry her?'

'At Lindos, before I came to the castle. Without her, I should never have reached you.'

'So you were in no danger?' she said slowly 'Even though I raised the alarm?'

In his turn, he took a long time to answer. Then he said, 'I shall never know. I hope I shall never know.'

She looked round at him then with pain in her face. She said, 'But one day, you may have a son. Another son.'

He smiled at the fierceness in her voice, and shook his head, and said, 'Primaflora is not my family, only my escort. I have the only son I need, and he is in good hands. Rear him well for me.' After that, there was only a short way to go, and she didn't speak.

He helped Katelina to dismount just out of sight of the monastery, but it took much longer to persuade her to free him.

At the last, they stood, their hands still engaged, and faced one another in silence. It was then, resting his eyes on her face, that he saw how it had altered. The resentful anger had gone, and the desperation; and the beauty that had always been there had come to full flower. Her eyes shone like the pool of the waterfall, and her lips were tender with kissing. He recognised the radiance of love given as well as love received, and felt abashed, and thankful, and anguished. She had made the crossing for him. She had opened her heart, and delight should reward her.

They parted. He watched the gate close behind her and, turning his horse, set it at a slow, steady pace to his rendezvous. The country behind him was darkening, but ahead the sky flared with the lakes of evening and soon, topping a rise, he saw before him the sea, with the red disk of the sun sinking into it.

He had come to Lindos at dawn. It seemed a long time ago. Some way off, a donkey brayed; frogs were croaking, and the bushes around him were ghostly with moths. He picked up the reins, and rode downhill to the bay, and the boat, and the ship with Primaflora his wife waiting in it.

Chapter 33

THUS, FOR THE second time in a far from long life Nicholas, returning to Cyprus, had to devise how to ingratiate himself following an unsuitable marriage. He ought to have been in practice; but the circles he was moving in now – and their relationships to him – were both different from the first time and more dangerous. He dealt with the problem, as usual, by maintaining a vast and docile calm in the face of all provocation.

In the fishing-vessel leased by his wife, he landed at Salines. There, he ensconced Primaflora briefly while he paid a swift visit to Kouklia to check progress, and to face Loppe, the first but by no means the easiest of his forthcoming confrontations. He broke the news of his marriage in private, after a round of sugarfield inspections and meetings which had ended with a convivial company meal in the courtyard where, once, they had entertained the family Corner. After the others had left, Loppe sat on with Nicholas under the stars, his light robe glimmering in the lamplight, and listened to the concise and truncated account which was all that Nicholas was prepared to give anybody. It did not, initially, mention Katelina at all, except to say that she would by now have left the island. It stated the bald fact that the plants were destroyed, but not how or where he had done it. Loppe, a patient audience, made no comment until the end. Then he eased his position and said, 'It's no surprise, after the letters you left. King James was much angered with his. What did you tell him?'

'That he was going to lose all the value of his sugar revenues if cane plants of our quality were established in Madeira. That the woman who had taken them had also been spying, and it was in Zacco's interest to have the plants destroyed and the woman induced to leave Rhodes as quickly as possible.'

'By now, he will know you are back,' Loppe said. He suddenly laughed. 'You realise, the demoiselle Katelina was sent to Episkopi by the King's mother for your sake? If you had managed to alter her feelings for you, she would have ceased spying, or having designs on the plants, and your life would have been safe from her. Instead –' He stopped himself. 'Instead you bring back another woman, just as troublesome.'

It was not what he had been going to say, Nicholas recognised. Instead of making Katelina his mistress, he had performed that office for a princess of Naxos, and driven Katelina from the island. He had always suspected Loppe knew that. Loppe knew everything. Nicholas said, 'You think Primaflora may still be serving the Queen? It hardly matters now, if the Queen is losing Kyrenia. If she is dangerous in any other way, it is for me to deal with.'

He waited. He would not get from Loppe, he knew, the kind of inquisition the others would subject him to. Direct questions, from Tobie. Indirect, from John. What, in due course, his more distant connections would make of it – Gregorio and Julius, Godscalc and Anselm Adorne and, most of all, Tilde and Catherine his step-daughters – was something he had had to forecast from the beginning. He was used to planning.

Loppe said, 'There is no reason to be concerned. The King will appreciate that, having helped you to destroy the plants and see the demoiselle safely out of the island, the lady Primaflora could hardly be left to face the Queen's anger.' He paused again, and said, 'The demoiselle Katelina set great store by the plants.'

It was as direct a question as Loppe would ever ask. Nicholas said, 'I have met her, and she knows of the marriage. She is sailing home to her husband: Diniz will be there already. There will be no more trouble. No more trouble even from Simon, perhaps.'

He could hear Loppe's even breathing. The lamps guttered. A glow from the courtyard of Venus told that the copper cauldrons were simmering, adding their heat to the clinging night air. Loppe said, 'Yet she went?'

'There was nothing else to be done,' Nicholas said. He began methodically to rise from the table, but Loppe was first on his feet. 'No,' said Loppe. 'Stay. In the dark, it is peaceful. I shall leave you.'

The rest of his itinerary brought severe trials to the head of the Bank of Niccolò, but by then his command of himself was un-impeachable. He rode back quickly to Salines where there now awaited an escort to take himself and his bride to Nicosia. Prima-flora, beautiful in the heat as she had been in the snows of Bologna, welcomed him back.

He treated her welcome as the work of art it was. In marriage as in concubinage, she studied what he wanted, and gave him some-thing more. If she denied him, as she had done at Lindos, it was for a purpose. He had had no need to tell her, joining her in the fading sunset at Rhodes, that in denying him she had miscalculated; that what he had taken to Katelina had not been unwelcome. He had assured Primaflora the plants were destroyed. He had said no word to her or to anyone of the ravine at Kalopetra. On the first night on board out of Rhodes, she had salved the injuries from his climb and let him sleep without imposing wifely demands. Those came later, and were demanding in a way he had never experienced before, but were not wifely. He knew that in some way he pleased her beyond her expectations, and that sometimes this confused her. He thought perhaps he surprised her by seeking to serve her desires, which were not entirely bizarre and could be fathomed. He didn't know to whom he might be playing traitor in doing all this. He only knew that there were some things that, meantime, he wanted to forget.

He spent a day establishing her in the villa at Nicosia, and introduced her to Galiot his steward, and to Bartolomeo Zorzi, the superintendent of his dyeworks. Galiot's thoughts he could not quite decipher. Zorzi was insultingly impressed as by nothing else in their acquaintance: his bows had been espalier-supple. 'My lady! Ah, Ser Niccolò: if you could win me such a bride from Rhodes!'

'She has sisters,' said Nicholas. 'I have your report: fulfil the Karamanian order. You have replaced the boy Diniz?'

'There is another already in training,' said the dyemaster. 'But what of the young man's aunt? My brother Jacopo was enquiring. The charming Flemish lady?'

'She is well, and returning to Portugal,' Nicholas said. 'Sadly, her vine and sugar cuttings did not survive. If you see Messer Erizzo, you might tell him.'

'He will sympathise,' said Bartolomeo Zorzi. 'But in war, what can one expect? I only trust the lady will reach home and her dear husband safely.'

'I hope she will,' Nicholas said. 'It is a matter of deep concern to my lady wife and myself. I would go so far as to say we both depend on it.'

Then he was on his own, and riding Chennaa at dawn in company with a short supply-train of camels to join the army and Zacco who, he knew very well, would have the news of his arrival, and the manner of it. In proof, he was welcomed by outposts and guards as soon as he entered the encampment and by Astorre's distant shout, heard at the moment that he saw his own pavilion had been re-erected with his personal staff waiting outside.

Inside, it was full of flowers and the person of Tzani-bey al-Ablak, directing the placing of more. The emir turned, his eyes hazy with drugs above the hooked nose and arrogant black moustache. Outside the battlefield he wore a white turban, pinned with a wisp of jewel-set osprey, and his coat was of saffron damask. He

said, 'Why, Pasha, your amiable presence delights us too soon. We
prepare a welcome for you and the divine lady, your wife. The
beloved comes in her litter?'

Behind him, Astorre had arrived at the tent. 'You're back!
You've married the woman!' he said. He looked round. 'Someone's
dead?'

'I think,' Nicholas said, 'that Allah's sage disciple the emir is
offering congratulations on my nuptials, blessed by God and by
Allah, the Best Knower, the Satisfier of All Needs. My lord Tzani-
bey, it is appreciated. Alas, the lady presently remains in Nicosia
but later, I hope, you will knock at our door there. May I offer you
a refreshment?'

'There's wine in my tent,' Astorre said. 'So what's all this about?'

'I think perhaps,' Nicholas said, 'the lord emir would prefer
something different. What may I send for?'

The Mameluke smiled. 'You are kind. But look, your officers
bid you welcome; you are weary no doubt, and would prefer to
drink wine in their company. In any case, I bear a message.
Monseigneur the King bids you attend him.'

'Where is he?' Nicholas said.

'In his tent. He is impatient. Perhaps your men will forgive you,'
said Tzani-bey, 'if you present yourself first to your lord. He has
not been pleased, I fear, with your absence. Such is the tyranny of
generous friendship. Yet which of us would be without it? Friendship or womanly love?'

'It depends on the friends,' Nicholas said. 'And the love. For
these your good works, may Allah the Beneficent, the Merciful
give you reward.'

He watched him leave and then spoke to Astorre, who was
smirking. 'I'd better go. Can you get everyone together? Perhaps
your tent, not mine. Is there anything I should know?'

'He's angry,' said Astorre. 'Zacco. No worry anywhere else.
They're close to giving up now in Kyrenia. The blockade has done
well: Crackbene's moved his ships to Famagusta. Some illness,
some deaths. Master Tobie and the Arab quack have got together
again. John has spent as much time in Kouklia as he's done here,
but no one's complained. Thomas says if you wanted the girl, why
didn't you keep her at Bruges?'

'I thought I'd give Thomas first chance,' Nicholas said. 'This
needs talking about. That's why I want to see everyone. Meantime
reassure them if you can. Nothing has gone wrong. Nothing is
going to go wrong.'

'And the lady?' Astorre said. 'My lord Simon's wife?'

'On her way back to Portugal,' Nicholas said. 'I must go.'

'Good luck,' said Astorre. 'Not that you deserve it. You've got
more than enough already, for a boy of your age.'

If Nicholas had qualms about that, walking to the royal pavilion, he found it simple enough to disguise them. He had taken time to change to fresh clothes, and brush his hair and pin the badge of his Order to his doublet. He saw, as soon as he met Zacco, that in Zacco's eyes, he had taken too much time.

The King was sober. The tent was wholly in order, with servants at the door and within. Within also were Markios of Patras, the King's uncle, and Abul Ismail, the King's physician. Zacco, pacing between them, wore hose and a thin, belted tunic of flowered material, with his shoulders still swathed with the head-cloth from under his helmet. The large eyes and classical features were rose-brown with the sun, and his hair unevenly bleached in long, waving strands, stuck to his brow with the heat. He spun to face Nicholas the moment he darkened the doorway. 'Well, harlot, thief, ungrateful liar!'

Nicholas knelt, his eyes on a piece of Persian carpeting. 'My lord. What have I stolen?'

An extremely vicious grip closed on his arm and forced him upright. 'Time,' said James of Lusignan, his fingers tight. 'Time I have paid for.' He stood, breathing extremely hard, then let go and drew back the edge of his hand. His eyes took the measure of Nicholas, and of a particular place between his left shoulder and neck. Except for setting his teeth, Nicholas waited unmoving. A moment passed, then the blow came. It was sharp, but it fell on his face, turning it sideways. Nicholas let his breath go. James said, 'You have nothing to say?'

'He is spent with fornicating,' said Markios of Patras. 'Who marries a courtesan except for money, or because he has sold something? Whom or what have you sold?'

Nicholas resumed breathing quietly again. He said, 'My lord King, I have given you full return for your silver. The campaign was planned when I left, and my men have helped execute it. I could have done no more had I been here. As for my wife –'

'Wife!' said James of Lusignan. 'She is a whore.'

Nicholas kept his gaze open and lucid. He said, 'Nevertheless you offered once, my lord King, to bring her to me. A man may love a concubine, and even marry her. It was not by my wish that the lady was sent off from Cyprus. If I have now brought her back it is because no man has jurisdiction over whom I may marry. And because I wished her beside me. And because it is not forbidden in Cyprus, surely, of all kingdoms on earth, to love a woman to whom fortune has denied formal rites in the past, and to wish to please her, being free, and to wish her to bear sons such as the one I now serve, brave and just and courageous.'

The King was silent. Markios looked at him. Out of the edge of his sight, Nicholas thought he saw the physician's beard move, as if he were smiling. The King said, 'Where is she? The concubine?'

'The lady Primaflora is in Nicosia,' said Nicholas.

'Spying?' he said.

Nicholas said, 'Illustrious King, she has given up that allegiance. The lady Carlotta your sister would have her killed. Would Your Magnificence give her audience, and question her? She will answer freely.'

The look passed again between the King and his uncle. Then Zacco said, 'The lady my mother will do that. Your marriage is, of course, your own affair. The introduction of a possible traitor is not. She has spent her life serving my sister.'

'She has served many people,' said Nicholas. 'She has never before bound herself, as she and I are now bound. She wishes only to stay in Cyprus with me.'

The King said, 'In any case, you cannot leave. Kyrenia has not fallen. Famagusta shows no sign of surrender. You have not done what you have been paid for.'

'Rest assured, my lord King,' said Nicholas. 'I shall not leave until you have Cyprus. And perhaps my sons will serve you after me.'

The King sat. He looked at the physician, who bowed to him, and then conveyed to Nicholas an undoubted smile. Abul Ismail said, 'You are plainly in health. The King wished to make sure.'

'Thanks to my physicians,' Nicholas said. He stood, watching the Arab leave. A moment later, Markios walked out without speaking.

The King said, 'Sit. What wine have you been drinking in Rhodes? What elixir? What do you seek that we cannot provide?'

Nicholas sat. He said, 'My lord, you have daughters. Did it not please you, the begetting of them?'

The wine came. The servants retreated, all but the man attending the cups. Zacco said, 'And the sugar plants, and the vines. They are dead?'

'Yes. Other thieves and rivals will come,' Nicholas said. 'Plants will be taken again and your market will shrink, but not yet. And when the time does arrive, there are other harvests to find, perhaps even more bountiful. This is a fertile land. There is room for diversity.'

'Is there?' said Zacco. He cradled the cup in one hand, and with the other drew a finger down the cold, misted surface. He said, 'It seemed to me that you might have found your harvest with Carlotta.'

'No,' Nicholas said. 'She was anxious to kill me. You would then, of course, have been sure of my loyalty. I prefer to prove it as I promised: by giving you the rest of your kingdom.'

'And after that?' Zacco said. 'You are free with your promises in some things. For the rest, you prevaricate like an Arab. I dislike it.'

It was what Katelina had said. It was what everyone said. 'I am sorry,' Nicholas answered slowly. 'Perhaps it is prevarication; perhaps it is uncertainty; perhaps it is an attachment to freedom. To me, it is the essence of what lies between us. Should I give you plain answers, removing all doubts, all possibilities?'

For a long time, the King stared into his wine. Then he drank it quickly, and dragging the cloth from his neck, flung it and his cup to the wine-server standing ladle in hand by the tent-wall. The fine clammy scarf fell; the servant, starting, caught the cup and poured a great measure. As he brought it, Zacco pulled the cup from Nicholas also and tossed it to the man. He said, 'When I want such an answer, I will require it of you, and evasion will not serve you then. Do you understand?'

'Yes, my lord King,' Nicholas said. The cup he had been given was full to the brim.

'Good,' said Zacco. 'Now you will remain here with me, drinking measure by measure until one of us falls. Whoever comes to your bed this night, my amorous Niccolò, will lose the profit of their labours: I promise you that.'

Some considerable time later, Tobie said, 'Well, well. He's coming.' He turned into Astorre's tent, where a collation for four had long since taken place and Thomas, in particular, was comatose. John, stripped to the waist, was sitting on a pallet drawing something with silent concentration. Astorre, who had relished his meal, was cleaning his sword: a task he reserved for himself. Tobie, irritated and restless, had been to the doorway a dozen times since news of the drinking-bout spread.

Astorre said, 'Our young bridegroom, you say? Not the King?'

'Not the King. Nearly not Nicholas, by the look of him. He's not coming here.'

'Well, he should,' said the captain, annoyed. 'I've got to be out half the night. I could have slept. Thomas, go and see what he's doing.'

Thomas disappeared, not unwillingly, and came back looking shaken. He said, 'He's there streaming wet by the water-tub, spewing up with a finger to help him. The King too. The King got tired of drinking, and wants to take the leopards out hunting. The Arab quack's trying to stop them.'

'I should hope he is,' Tobie said. He ran from Astorre's tent the considerable distance to his own, picked up a box and ran out again, pouring sweat in the sun. The leopards passed, in a stink of urine and a flash of spotted chrome fur, running on their thick chains.

Abul Ismail appeared in front of him and said, 'Ah, you too. Be at rest. Your lord had the sense, at least, to accept my advice, and persuaded the King. They are weak as fawns, but half sober at least.' He sighed. 'What it is to minister to young men of high temperament. They are mounted. There they go.'

In fury, Tobie saw the hunt assemble and begin to stream past. By the King's side was Nicholas. He was pallid and glistening and hatless but there was a smile melon-wide on his face; and that of Zacco, turned to him, revealed the same nausea, the same determination, the same perverse, reckless delight. Tobie changed his hold on his box, which was paining him, and tramped back to Astorre with a declaration. 'He's mad. He's not worth bothering over. I'm going to bed. If he wants us, he can get us tomorrow.'

'He can get *you* tomorrow,' said Astorre. 'If they're going hunting, I'm going with them. Man, we'll see some sport.'

'They're all mad,' said John le Grant placidly, looking after him. 'That's what you get, when you follow an army. And the craziest person of all is any woman who lets herself get mixed up with them.'

That night Astorre, as befitted his position, took his turn with his men among the besiegers, having seen the kill distributed, and both Nicholas and the King to their tents. Later, as he walked between the quiet ranks, someone gave him a friendly slap on the arm and he found to his surprise that, drunk or sober, Nicholas had elected to join him. They walked together, at first in silence; then climbing from place to place as Astorre launched into his personal account of the siege. He described gun positions and skirmishes; pointed out damage, detailed the garrison's efforts. He grew rosy expounding; he became vehement answering questions. He had trained this fellow. No one else of his age grasped a situation with that sort of speed, or understood him so well. In an hour, whoever else didn't, Astorre received all his reward for his labours.

Towards the end, they climbed the rise and stood on the spot from which they had started. In the distance the castle lay, black against the sea in a night without moon. There were no lights to be seen; no animated guard on the wall-walks. Astorre nodded over. 'They're near to surrendering now. Every day or two, we get someone trying to give themselves up. We got the women out, although not till last week. Don't you want to sit down?'

'You mean you think I'm tired?' Nicholas said. He dropped with a thud on the spent grass. 'Where did you put them?'

'The women? Where you said, in one of the convents. Are ye staying?' His beard stuck up in the air.

'Astorre?' Nicholas said. 'I know you like lording it everywhere, but I don't. Primaflora doesn't want to be received anywhere and neither do I. Yes, I'm staying. We're all staying until Famagusta goes. What ships have tried to get in?'

'Not many,' Astorre said. 'The whole Venetian fleet's on the rampage – they tried to take Lesbos and failed: the stupid fools think they can get back the Morea. And your damned Order –'

'Not mine,' Nicholas said. 'The Pope's dear children, you mean. I heard in Rhodes. They've got enough trouble guarding themselves; and the Genoese can't afford the ships or the money. You don't see a Crusade coming to rescue Carlotta?'

'Not this year,' Astorre said. 'Mind, the wars over there seem to be slackening. The Pope's free of Malatesta. If he got Burgundy to send more than money, they might collect an armed fleet for next summer.'

'But James will have all Cyprus by then,' Nicholas said. 'Or do you have doubts?'

Astorre shook his head. 'We promised him Cyprus and, by God he'll have it. But Famagusta: that's going to be a bad one. Worse than this. I doubt if we'll take it before winter.'

Nicholas said, 'I was beginning to think that. Supply problems, then. This plain turns to mud. I'll have to divide my time between there and Kouklia. And Zacco'll get bored.'

'Will he?' said Astorre.

Nicholas chuckled. 'So isn't it lucky I'm married? What does Thomas say?'

'I told you,' said Astorre. 'He's soft on her. See his eyes light up. That's the sort of woman he fancies for a – for a –'

'For an employer. Well, he's out of luck: she isn't going to be his employer,' Nicholas said. 'She has no share in the Bank, and she has no share in Catherine's trust, or anything to do with Bruges. So spread that around.'

'Ah!' said Astorre. 'Master Tobie'll be relieved.'

'Master Tobie would be relieved if he believed a word of it,' said Tobie's voice. He sat down and took off his helm and his cap, so that his bald head glimmered faintly. 'You're a damned fool,' he said. 'She wants the money.'

'Maybe,' said Nicholas mildly. 'But she signed it away with the marriage contract. I have it. In Latin. She doesn't get anything but my personal possessions. I got the document drawn up in spring by Gregorio.'

Two pairs of eyes gleamed at him in the dark. 'In case?' Tobie said.

'In case,' agreed Nicholas.

'In case you married which one? It seems to me,' Tobie said, 'that you've had every woman in the Levant just recently. What about Katelina and Queen Carlotta?'

'In the same bed,' Nicholas said. 'I don't know. I had a feeling someone was going to marry me, and I knew what a fuss you'd all make if I didn't make sure of your futures.'

'And Zacco?' said Tobie.

'He's accepted the situation, pending a scanning by Cropnose. Who do you think will win that one?'

'I think,' said Tobie slowly, 'that your new lady wife will be permitted to stay. You bastard.'

'Young devil,' said Astorre heartily. He was grinning.

Tobie was not. Nicholas said, 'Oh come on. We're keeping Astorre awake. I'm going back to bed.'

'You do that,' said Astorre. 'But don't wake me tomorrow. Did you get much of a catch?'

'Depends what you're talking about,' said Tobie sourly.

He walked back with Nicholas, pausing when Nicholas paused, which was often, to speak to someone. At the tent, someone ran to help him undress, but he dismissed them. He said to Tobie. 'Well, since you must, come in and say it.'

'I've said it,' said Tobie. 'You bastard.' He stepped into the gloom, sneezed, and stood uneasily watching Nicholas peel off his clothes. He added, 'You've collected a few scars since I saw you last.' He sneezed again.

'I've been to Rhodes and back since you saw me last. The snake in its dust-hole, the cloud wandering over the sky.' He sat down, stripped to his body linen, and said, 'I didn't harm Katelina, or she me. The boy had gone to Portugal, and she's following him. Now Simon won't trouble us. Nor, without the plants, will he flourish much. I'm sorry I had to leave you, but things had to be done, and they're done.'

'Yes, they are, aren't they?' Tobie said. 'That's what I meant. I can think of three reasons why you might want to marry this Primaflora, and all of them frighten me.' He hesitated. 'Is it the child? She could rear Katelina's son if you got him?'

'No,' Nicholas said. 'I'm not that much of a bastard.'

'Then I don't like the other reasons,' Tobie said.

'Try the simplest. She's been my mistress, on and off, since September. She is, you will agree, rather exceptional. You're pea-green envious; that's all that's wrong with you.'

'I think,' said Tobie, 'that I want you to tell me she's pregnant. Because if she isn't, you're playing some game again. A game I can't understand. A damned, deep, devious game that's going to hurt a lot of people. You are, aren't you?' He sneezed, with terrible emphasis.

'She isn't pregnant,' said Nicholas. 'Tobie, shall I put the flowers out, or will you now shift yourself out of my tent and let me get some damned, deep, devious sleep?'

He was mad, and not worth troubling over. Tobie went off dismayed, in a volley of sneezes.

Chapter 34

TTRITION, BRIBERY and plain common sense brought about the fall of Kyrenia a few weeks after Nicholas returned there, and although Carlotta, kept in ignorance, might have been devastated by the news, it held no surprises for the people of Cyprus. The Savoyard knights and their companions marched out, and Zacco and his army crossed the drawbridge and took possession of the castle. There was a banquet, shared by all his captains, when gold plate, money and villages were freely dispensed and no man, Mameluke or white, was favoured over the other. Having garrisoned the citadel, Zacco left. The town outside was long since ruined and empty, and he preferred St Hilarion in the heat of the day. He would admit, when brought to it, that the bulldog policies of this Niccolò had achieved what he himself, had he cared, could have brought about several years ago, with some small application. At any rate, it had been accomplished. The last private nest of the Lusignan Queen had been raided, and Carlotta had no home to return to. Now, in all Cyprus, there remained only Famagusta to recover.

Nicholas, presented with the problem of capitulated Kyrenia, adopted his best bulldog stance and based himself, perforce, in the north in the weeks after his marriage. It was during that time the lady Primaflora was summoned to the Palace at Nicosia to be scrutinised by the King's mother.

Despite the siege, Nicholas had made the short journey many times to sleep at his villa. While there, he naturally spent time at the dyeworks; and twice, he had made the longer journey to Kouklia. Nevertheless, as Primaflora was immoderately aware, he would not have come for these alone, with no heed for the heat of the day. Since Rhodes she had known (since he told her) how he had met the Flemish woman in Lindos; and had equally known (although he had not told her) that Katelina van Borselen had somehow been persuaded or forced into commerce with him.

Whatever had happened, nevertheless, he had not brought the girl back, but had turned her off to go home to her husband. Whatever had happened, the experience had disturbed him. She knew him well enough now to see through some of the camouflage – perhaps all of it. The effects of this unease she found entirely rewarding.

Then Kyrenia surrendered, and he was away, inescapably, for some time. The prisons filled. Atrocity stories filtered through, of the Mamelukes bursting into the citadel; of the destruction, the rampage; the plundering. It would take time to set that to rights, and make of Carlotta's old home a palace fit for her brother to live in. Meantime, Primaflora amused herself perfecting her household, an art in which she had long experience. She made it her business to get on well with the steward, and her pleasure to keep Bartolomeo Zorzi dancing to an almost inaudible tune. She liked to preserve an edge on her training.

When the summons came from the Palace, she took care to dress neither as a lady of pleasure nor a noblewoman. A courtesan was a woman of gifts who attached herself to a great man, and expected to be displayed as a badge of his wealth. Marietta of Patras had come from the Morea in the train of Helen Paleologa, wife of John, King of Cyprus. Whether she came to Cyprus a virgin was unknown. What was patent was the King's installation of her as his mistress, his delight in Zacco her son, and his habit of avoiding the febrile company of Carlotta, his legitimate daughter by Helen. Marietta of Patras was a woman of birth, honoured as a dead monarch's permanent mistress. In status, she ranked as far above Primaflora as Primaflora above a public prostitute. Otherwise Helen, Carlotta's mother, would never, of course, have felt impelled to bite off her nose.

In the dying heat of the day, Cropnose gave audience to Primaflora on her balcony. Muslin fell between arches which overlooked a garden of palms and fountains and citrus trees. Vines shaded it, and pots of brilliant flowers had been placed on the balustrade. At one end there stood a stand made of gold, upon which slept a red and blue bird, its chain hanging. Above, a smaller bird sang in a cage. A woman fingered a lute, and there were two others seated on cushions, one reading. A page behind the only fully-framed chair moved a long-shafted fan over his mistress's head.

Because of the heat, the King's mother wore none of her noses, but a Syrian half-veil, light as a kerchief. An embroidered cloth concealing her hair was bound with a complex gold fillet, and her robe was of Caspian silk woven in Florence. Clasped on her lap, her fingers were rose-tipped and heavily ringed. The upper part of her face was exquisitely painted, and her perfumes were slight, and varied, and seemly. Primaflora, who wore no scent at all, crossed her unadorned wrists and sank to the ground. After a considerable space, the woman above her said, 'You may sit.' A low stool had appeared. Primaflora rose and bestowed herself naturally, so that her skirts fell with grace. The King's mother said, 'So. You are old for the boy.'

'Niccolò, my lady?' said Primaflora. 'He is old enough to lead armies.'

'He is young enough to inflame my son. It is your practice to come between lovers?'

Too well-informed to pretend shock, Primaflora evinced instead a form of gentle regret tinged with reproach. 'Gracious lady, I knew nothing of that. Before we ever reached Cyprus, Niccolò had demonstrated where his desire lay.'

'A year ago,' said the woman. 'He had not met the King then. On my advice, the King sent you off. What makes you so bold as to come back?'

Primaflora bit her lip without disturbing the paint. She said, 'Knowing nothing of this, how can I answer? The parting was hard. You know that Ser Niccolò, to end it, came to fetch me. Was I to spurn him? My feelings for him were – are – fondly engaged.'

'Are they?' said the asthmatic voice with amusement. 'That is dangerous, lady, for one of your calling. And marriage, I should have thought, is a false step you must have been well warned against. With such as you as his wife, how can a man prosper in public life, and earn the gold that you need? How can you leave, should his fortunes alter?'

Primaflora looked down.

'Well?' said the woman. 'Bashful? Hardly. He has expectations you thought worth the venture? You made marriage the price of your body? He made marriage the price of his body?'

Primaflora shook her head and then spread her hands in a sudden gesture of confusion. 'All I know is that he would not have left Rhodes without marriage. He had prospects, but for his friends' sake, I shall not be endowed with more than enough for my needs. But his passion runs deep; and . . .' She hesitated again.

'What?' said the woman, still entertained.

'I would give him sons,' said Primaflora.

'Ha!' said Marietta of Patras, 'I thought there was something of the brood mare about you. You have some already, no doubt, being discreetly raised by their fathers?'

'Yes,' she said.

'Speak up! And daughters, as well?'

Then she looked up. 'No. Only sons. A man such as Niccolò can find himself lonely. I would give him companions for the years to come. I would stay with him and rear them.'

'It is true,' said the old harridan, whining, 'that presently your looks will leave you, and if you have amassed no property, no wise investments, you must plan for your future. But I have to tell you that a man such as Niccolò needs sons less than he needs marriage, and needs a woman at present not at all. What may suit you would be folly for him. Get back to Rhodes.'

Primaflora stood up. She said, 'I am married.'

'That is soon cured,' the woman said. 'With a hatchet. It is your choice.'

So all she had heard of this woman was true. Primaflora remained standing still, although she knew she had blanched. She said steadily, 'You would lose your commander. The King would lose his friend. I know Niccolò.'

'And I know Zacco,' the King's mother said. 'Do you think your Niccolò would ever know how you died? Make some excuse and go back to Rhodes. Once you are there, have your death proclaimed. It will be more convenient, I promise you, than the alternative.'

The woman's eyes over her veil were black as gun-tubes. Primaflora had confronted jealous women before; angry women; threatening women; but none with the power of this one. She said, 'Parted like that, what good would he be? What good would I be?' Then, under the steady stare of the eyes, she said with sudden despair, 'I would share him.'

'How kind,' said the woman. She laughed, and the veil blew out like a flag. 'And you think the King would accept that?'

'I don't know the King,' said Primaflora in a thin voice. She had stopped her tears with the heel of her hand, and face-paint smeared it.

The King's mother snapped her fingers. 'A kerchief. To see you now, who would want you? Go to Rhodes.'

Primflora took the kerchief and drew it over her cheeks and then held it taut, staring at the damp blotches. She said, 'I see you want me to go, for the King's sake. For Niccolò's sake, would you let the King arbitrate?'

The cloth blew reflectively, and again. The King's mother said, 'You think you can persuade the lion that he is not hungry?'

'No,' said Primaflora. She did not try, this time, to keep her voice steady. 'But the quality of any man's service depends on his wellbeing. My death, my banishment would deprive the King of contentment as well as my husband. And sooner or later, another would come in my place.'

Above their heads, the fan brushed the air; the coloured bird woke and stretched one indolent leg; the caged bird, which had been silent, suddenly launched into a piercing, rattling trill. Marietta of Patras turned her head, her breath whistling, and silent hands bore off the cage. The King's mother said, 'You are singularly mature for this boy, but I would not have him distressed before Famagusta is won. Very well. Stay in Nicosia and hold yourself ready. When he returns, I shall ask the King to receive you. Perhaps you will accept his dismissal. Indeed, my woman, you will have no other choice.'

The northern mountains were cool, and the King protracted his stay, taking up residence in St Hilarion, the summer palace of the Lusignans, in the airy apartments of the absent Carlotta and Luis her consort. Long ago, the broad tactics for the next and final stage of this war had been decided; all that remained were a host of small decisions and, of course, the normal government of his kingdom. During this brief interregnum, it pleased Zacco to call Nicholas to St Hilarion for disputatious council meetings which occasionally ended in concord. Problems were more often solved when, after a day of hard, heated riding, the King repaired with his shrewdest advisers to the cool belvedere suspended over the castle's north precipice, with its stupendous view to the sea, and the mountains of Asia beyond. Then, with men of Naples and Sicily like Rizzo di Marino, or Conella Morabit; or with the excellent Bailie of Karpass, or the Venetian commander Pesaro, Nicholas could share the moulding of the King's mind.

At the end of such evenings he found his own bed alone, walking through blackened courts where once Saracen climbers had run with fire among the poisoned and the dying. He had not forgotten. But now, with the campaign against Famagusta looming over him, and the palace full of the wild exhilaration of a conquering army, Nicholas was too occupied to be haunted by anything of the past.

Every day, he passed between the cliff-top fort and the captured castle at its foot, clearing the way not just for the King's casual occupation, but to repair the defences of Kyrenia against the corsair, or Carlotta, or the Turk. More importantly, and as often as he could, he rode to Pesaro's citadel west of Famagusta. The guns, under John's supervision, were already on their way there, and the sutlers with the siege engines. Soon, the full army would move. Twice, he got to Nicosia and could hardly respond to the ardour he found in Primaflora. It was then, too, that he found that her meeting with the King's mother was over – happily, as she told him, smiling; although her welcome would not be complete until the King himself left St Hilarion and sent for her. It seemed satisfactory. He would like to have had Cropnose's version, but their paths didn't cross, and there was no reason, meantime, why he should seek the King's mother.

In any case, he was busy. If he felt, sometimes, that he had heard too little of that interview of Primaflora's, and that there was something of desperation now in her love-making, he didn't pursue it for once; and even the matter of Katelina remained only as an anxiety held well in check. The Levant was in arms: there was danger in every voyage, and no way of telling how a half-Portuguese youth or a Flemish woman would contrive safely to make their way home. From his days as a courier, Nicholas had many sources of information, and had asked them all to report. Venice and Ancona, Naples and Sicily, Florence and Bruges would watch and listen and notify him in due course of their passage, as well as of other things. His Western network for other news was wider even than that, not to mention the other more extravagant system he had discussed with no one except, of course, Loppe. But, of course, there had not been time yet for anyone to report on Katelina, even had shipping been normal. Venice had placed an embargo on Bosphorus trade and was hesitant even over her Alexandria fleet. The Order would keep its vessels for safety at Rhodes. Florence would also be circumspect. It affected his own supplies, as well as the carriage of news, and forced him to make secondary plans, among other things, for the sale of his new sugar crop. But planning was what he liked, and he had contingency plans, too, for whatever news he had in the end of Katelina, good or bad. He had, now, friends in many places, or people who owed him a favour.

He worked through his programme meticulously yet with the flamboyance that entranced Zacco, and invigorated even the sluggish. He somehow managed to pound down to Kouklia on Chennaa, half by night and half by blazing day, and crossing the island was able to see for himself that it had been a more settled and prosperous year. Smitten by war, the plains of Kyrenia were barren, and the sponge-divers of the Karpass had made barely a living. But cistern-drenched wheat and barley had burst yellow over the plain of the Messaoria, and the sickles twinkled and chimed as, booted and belled, harvesters strode to their work among serpents.

The pods of the carob trees dangled, black and leaking rank gum, ripe for cropping. There were pomegranates in baskets and gourds drying on roof-tops. In every village, it seemed, a donkey circled its trough of crushed olives, and the press thudded down, helped by many brown arms, as the mash yielded its oozings through wicker. Where the scent of orange had deadened the senses in March, the resinous odour of olives weighed down the humid, hot air of this journey. Instead of flower-infused silence, the air was filled with the clamour of autumn: the cries, the chaffing, the folk-songs, the team-songs of the villages; the chinking of blades; the rumble of flint-studded boards driven over the threshing-ground. The objecting bray of working donkeys. The shuddering tramp of the oxen spinning the Persian wheels set over every deep well, so that the jars came up, roped with pomegranate wood withies, and tossed their icy water into the stone channels that fed the fields and the housewife's wood buckets. Vines and almonds, lemons and oranges, pomegranates and sugar. In the fields around Kouklia and Akhelia his second crop of cane was strong and healthy and promising; the men in good heart; Loppe full of plans. For a moment Nicholas, too, saw the future as something splendid and bright; a fertile island, well run and blooming, and owing nothing to all the nations that warred round about it. Then he stopped himself and Loppe and said, 'I am glad. This is what we all wanted. But we are not alone on this island. And of all the lands of the world, this is a place armies covet.'

'This and your land,' Loppe had added, after a silence.

'Bruges?' he had surmised solemnly after a moment.

'I was thinking of Simon's island,' had said Loppe. 'The sugar ships should be due in November. Will Famagusta have fallen by then?'

And Nicholas had said, 'More to the point, will the Turkish fleet have gone back to Gallipoli by then? It doesn't matter. We'll get the sugar out somehow. Then our Syrian friend might like a short visit home. Is that why you asked?'

'You know as well as I do,' said Loppe, 'that when Famagusta surrenders, this island will split into flame like a fireball. Nor will it be between brother and sister.'

'I can stop it,' said Nicholas.

'With a cataract that will flood them?' said Loppe. 'The Venetians have bested you once already at least.'

'Ah,' said Nicholas. 'But it's the last time that counts. I agree, the taking of Famagusta will be the signal for a great deal of treachery. But if all goes well, James might end up King of Jerusalem again. Think of all those Syrian cane fields.'

'You're talking rubbish,' said Loppe. 'That will never happen.'

'Of course it will never happen,' Nicholas said. 'But a lot of other things might. There's no sense in letting things become dull.'

Then he thudded back to Nicosia again.

Primaflora was absent when he arrived at the villa and when she returned, an hour later, she was wearing a girdle and a left sleeve he had never seen before, and a jewelled coif with a curled feather in it. She stood in the portico of his chamber and gravely allowed him to admire her. He cogitated, his head on one side. 'Cropnose has made you one of her ladies? No. A better guess. Zacco is back in the Palace, and has agreed that you stay?'

Then she gave one of her small, pleated smiles and said, 'It pleased him, I think, to rob his sister. Even the sleeve came from her. And he has realised that he had nothing to lose even if I am spying for Carlotta. But these, of course, are not his main reasons. I am to stay for your sake. He is fond of you.'

'And you think I am fond of him?' Nicholas said. 'I would ask you to come in and sit down, but you are wearing so many clothes.'

'I can still come in and sit down,' Primaflora said, doing so.

'Yes, I think you are fond of him. But I believe you would be fond of him if he looked like your camel. It is your nature. I think you have grown fond even of Tzani-bey.'

She had said that once before, surprising him, on the voyage from Rhodes. He said now, 'Tzani-bey, I assure you, has not grown fond of me. As I told you, the present war rules us both. He is only waiting, as I am, until Famagusta is taken.'

'So?' she said. 'And that will be next week? The week after? It's a year since you sailed to Cape Gata. Nine months since you came back from Rhodes, and then deserted Cyprus again. You promised Zacco his kingdom this summer, and he is still waiting. He said so this morning. Also, I had to give him news. After four years, the Queen his half-sister is carrying.'

And Zacco was not married. She didn't have to say so. Her conversation, full of spice and amazements, was always different from other people's. He said, 'Famagusta will fall, and with luck, before the rain comes.'

'With luck? Did you win Kyrenia with luck? Or has Famagusta heard what the Mamelukes did?' asked Primaflora.

'Are those the rumours?' Nicholas said. 'The Mamelukes did nothing to the hurt of Kyrenia, because the King stopped them. The Brethren of the Order were set free to go to Kolossi. The Queen's Marshal and all her associates – Montolif, Pardo, de Bon – were allowed to take ship for Rhodes.'

'But they surrendered because they were starving?' said Primaflora. Her voice, for once, was a trifle sharp. 'Eating dogs, cats and mice? An egg sold, we heard, for a hyperper?'

'They certainly didn't have any pork,' Nicholas said. 'But I think a few rats did survive. Kyrenia surrendered because the commander Sor de Naves had been promised wealth, estates, the office of Constable and the hand, when she is out of napkins, of Charlotte, the elder daughter of Zacco. But it was necessary, of course, for the garrison to experience discomfort first. Unfortunately, the other daughter is a little too young, and I don't think Zacco wants a Genoese good-son.'

He always enjoyed her silences, because he knew she was trying to read him. Sometimes, she succeeded. Now she said, 'Why is Famagusta so difficult?'

'Because it's Genoese,' Nicholas said. 'And they are not going to give it up. Also, it's not simply a garrison, it's a fortified city; with damned great walls and ditches and bastions built on three sides of it, and the sea to defend it on the fourth.'

She said, 'A place of that size must contain thousands; and must have to feed thousands. Or have they all left but the soldiers?'

'No,' said Nicholas. 'The children have gone, and the sick, and the older women and men. The rest are all still there, because the blockade was not very efficient till recently. We found two under-ground passages, one to the sea and one to the landward side. It's how they got supplies in, among other means. We have sealed them.'

'But they will have stockpiled all the food and wine, the grain and livestock and powder that they could? What about water?'

'They have some brackish wells, and some very deep ones. Until recently, they had water,' Nicholas said.

'But you have stopped it? In some way you have stopped it? I see,' she said slowly. 'I see why you hope for surrender before the rain comes to refill their cisterns. Or they may linger on, starving all winter, to the shame of Zacco; inviting Christian rescue? What if there is a crusade, and Cyprus is still divided? Venice, Burgundy, Bohemia, the Pope longing to throw out the Egyptians and reinstate Carlotta?'

Nicholas said, 'There can't be a Crusade before next summer. And by that time, if Cyprus is still divided, then I shall be too. But it won't be. Famagusta will fall, and the Pope will regard Cyprus as a unified, Christian kingdom.'

'So you may even join his Crusade?' said Primaflora, surprising him again.

He laughed. 'The Crusade he'll pay for from papal alum? As it happens, there'd be a certain rough justice if I got a wage from it. But no. Even if my fighting contract has ended I shall still, I hope, have my sugar franchise. Only if I lost that would I have to take my little warband elsewhere. Unless you think I should? Are you tired of Cyprus?'

She rose, and crossed the room and, taking a cushion, knelt at his feet, gathering his hands in hers. She said, 'Sometimes you wonder, I know. Sometimes you believe that, with the first change in fortune, I shall go back to Carlotta. Sometimes I think you suspect me of many things. But don't suspect me of wanting to leave you. I didn't tell you this, for if you loved Zacco it might make you dislike him; or change the dealings you have with his mother. While you were in the north, his mother spoke to me.'

'I remember,' he said. Her hands were cool, in spite of the heat. His hands were cold.

She said, 'I kept to myself what she said. She said, under pain of death, I was to leave you, for I interfered with her son and his lover.'

Her eyes, unshadowed, intelligent, were unmoving on his. He said, 'Did you believe her?'

'I believed she hoped it would happen,' said Primaflora. 'Perhaps I was wrong in what I then did. I said you and I were man and wife, and to lose me would break or damage your bond with the King. I asked her to let me put the matter to Zacco himself, and let the King decide. I said that, if need be, I would share you.'

Her gaze remained direct; her body still, but the fingers between his were rigid. Nicholas withdrew his own hands and placed them lightly on her two shoulders. He said, 'And today, the King himself exacted this promise, and you gave it?'

'I am used to sharing,' she said; and laid her cheek in fondness, or in weariness, or in sorrow, on his knee while he stroked her hair, his head bent, and then kissed it.

Nicholas said, 'He has always had hopes. They are always going to be disappointed. Primaflora, now he will blame you.'

She lifted her wet face, smiling at last. She said, 'What is this? You want me to urge you to submit to him? No. All I am saying, my dear, is that you have another reason to end this war quickly. When he is truly King, he will find other favourites, and no reason to keep you or me at his side. But quickly! Quickly!'

And he didn't tease her, or court her, or divert her, because what she had done was risk death, which was a thing better honoured by abstinence. Only, next day, he rode to Famagusta with less than a light heart, to lead his men to the end of the game.

Chapter 35

THE HOT CYPRUS autumn moved from one week to the next, and Zacco prepared for his forthcoming triumph by installing himself in the moated citadel built by his great-grandfather at Sigouri, ten miles west of the besieged Famagusta.

This was not to say that he didn't spend time with the army, lending vigorous help as the trains of oxen dragged the batteries into position, and the wagonloads of food and fodder, weapons and powder bumped fifty miles south-east from Kyrenia to where Famagusta lay, lodged in its bay, divided by ninety broad sea miles from Syria.

As the cannon arrived, so the masons prepared the stone shot, meeting the carts that arrived every day from the agora and temples of Salamis, tipping fluted cylinders and marble capitals and Egyptian granite into the yards. Camels, horses and oxen ground the dried earth to powder, and the deposits of sheep and cattle and goats, pigs and poultry added their stench to that of human and vegetable waste. The physicians were busy, and Nicholas seldom saw Tobie or Abul, spending two-thirds of his time with Astorre and Thomas and John, and the rest at Sigouri, with Zacco.

Here, there was no ambiguity; no difficulty over marriage or courtship; no women at all but the camp-followers, or the whores who were for sale, with other merchandise, from the second, vagabond camp that stood as a fringe to the first. It was at that time like wine to be in the presence of the Lusignan Bastard, ebullient, assured of success, glowing with pride in himself and his army. 'The Feast of St Nicholas!' he had cried, slapping Nicholas one day on the back. 'We shall give you a celebration on your Feast Day, Niccolino, in the place best fitted for it. A Mass in the Cathedral of St Nicholas in Famagusta itself, and a feast in my Palace to follow!'

The Feast of St Nicholas was in the first week of December; a month away. Until the age of seven, Nicholas had received a treat every year on the Feast Day of his patron; and from the age of ten he grew to know that the day would generally be marked for him in some way or another – in many different ways, although not every year – until, of course, his wife Marian died. Now, as if it had never happened before, Nicholas thanked the King, but not as the King wanted.

Later, John le Grant got Nicholas away from Sigouri, put him in a tent and said, 'Right. We're not going to do this in four weeks.'

'I've heard Astorre say that too. So long as neither of you says it aloud. We're not going to do it at all if the King loses interest too early.'

He kept his voice as reasonable as he always did, since there was no point in anyone becoming heated. They had both hoped for a classic siege manoeuvre: a complete blockade of supplies, followed when the city was weak by an assault over ditches infilled by themselves, and preceded by feints, night attacks and heavy bombardment. To this end, a deep trench had been begun long ago: deep enough to bring a file of men and their weapons in safety close under the walls. But, baked by summer, the earth and rock round Famagusta had resisted digging, and the sappers themselves had been depleted by storms of arrows from longbows and crossbows; by the methodical firing of handguns and serpentines. The trench was only three-quarters finished, and wouldn't progress until the rains came. The rain which would turn their campground to mud, and fill the cisterns of Famagusta.

So there faded their hopes of a final assault before winter. That left deprivation. Nicholas said, 'There's still a very good chance they'll surrender. They haven't used their bows or their guns for four days. We know their food is low. You've drained the water table and their wells are either dry or running salt water. The only drink they have left is wine, diluted with whatever is still in the cisterns. They've used all their timber stores and cut up every bucket and table and door to make all those fighting platforms and towers, so they can hardly have plugs for their cannon, and they won't have any fuel except dung. They haven't made a cavalry sortie for three weeks, even though the cannon weren't in place yet: they must be killing and curing the horses. The only missiles they're using are stones. John: they're going to give up before they actually starve. And they're going to give up before that if they've run out of arrows and powder.'

'No, they're not,' John le Grant said. It was hard, sometimes, to be reasonable with John le Grant.

Nicholas said, 'So, why?'

The engineer pursed his face and scraped the sandy bristles on his chin. He said, 'Someone came over the wall. They do, now and then, and our Egyptian friends usually cut out their tongues and their livers. We got to this one in time. A Jew, who thought their quarrel wasn't his quarrel, and was likely right. He knew more than most: the stores and the munitions are locked, and only the Genoese in the castle know how the supplies really go. But this fellow had helped with the stocktaking.'

'And they're living off fresh-cooked lamb and white bread and sweet Commanderie?' Nicholas said.

'They're living off beans and cheese and horse and ass-meat if they can pay for it, but even the price of dogs and cats is getting on the high side. Their cattle are finished: they made the last batch of bread with oxblood to save what's left of the water, and they drink that mixed with wine, of which there isn't all that much, either. They're reduced to five thousand with short commons and sickness, and the extra irony is that a cargo ship diverted from Chios got in just before the port closed. It had a big crew and a full commercial load – wax and mastic and wormwood seed, six bales of carpets and eighty baskets of sulphur, fifty bundles of silk and five hundred oxhides, two hundred barrels of saltpetre and a hundred bales of Syrian soda. Three cases of our very own sugar. Oh, and sixteen tons of alum that must have been left over from Phocoea.' He stopped, his unwinking blue eyes on Nicholas. He had his own sense of drama, John le Grant, as well as a very good memory.

Nicholas said, 'God's left big toe,' in a sad voice.

John le Grant said, 'Precisely. Nothing to eat, of course, excepting the sugar, which will scour the inside out of their stomachs. The ship wasn't even properly victualled for the crew: they'd been going to take food on at Crete. But enough saltpetre and sulphur to keep those guns firing for ever.'

'And alum and oxhides,' said Nicholas slowly. 'That's why the galleries weren't burning. But charcoal? They'd need charcoal.'

'They have it, he says,' said John le Grant in his sensible voice. 'Or if they didn't, they could always burn the ship, couldn't they? They've no beasts to work the powder mill, but men could do it, if they aren't too weak. Or they could mill it by hand. Lacking the piss of a wine-drinking man, the poor sods will have to do without granules. But these two nice bombards that bastard Sor de Naves presented them with? They've got gunpowder enough to keep the whole battery firing for ever. That's why they pretended to stop. They knew by now we'd think they'd run out. They were hoping against hope we'd attack them.'

Nicholas was silent. The engineer said, 'So they've enough powder, very likely, to baulk that final attack we were all counting on, but on the other hand the food is just about finished. A sensible Genoese colony, however stiff-necked, might therefore meet over its ass-bones and set a date for surrender, you'd hope. But here's a twist. They've heard a relieving fleet's on the way.'

'How?' said Nicholas sharply.

'Someone got in from the sea-wall. It isn't hard to cross from the islands. So long as no food's going in, our soldiers don't mind allowing an extra mouth or two into the city. But a rescue fleet? It isn't true, is it?'

'No, it isn't,' Nicholas said. 'I know that much at least about shipping moves. They expect a *Genoese* ship? The Bank is exhausted.'

'They expect a fleet of Genoese ships. And whether they're coming or not, that city is going to hold out to starvation point and beyond, so long as it believes in a rescue.' After a while he said, 'Nicholas? Astorre and Tobie should know, but I wasn't going to announce this in public. God knows what the King will decide to do. Or Tzani-bey.' After another pause, he said, 'It's only a planning problem. This is war, too. It's just a different sort of war from bashing at someone on horseback.'

Nicholas said, 'I'm not sitting fainting with horror: I'm trying to make God-damned plans. First, what happened to the Jew who told you all this?'

'He's dead,' said the engineer, his face expressionless. He added, 'He spoke Italian. No one interviewed him but me.'

'So,' said Nicholas. 'I'm a stiff-necked Genoese sitting starving inside that city. A note flies over my wall telling me there's no fleet on the way: I'm not going to believe it. A trumpet arrives offering a million ducats and freedom: I'm not going to surrender when I know I'm going to win anyway – or at least get supplies to hang on until something happens to Zacco. I might have a traitor or two who would offer to open the gates for a square meal, but I'd kill one of those before he got very far, and I'd turn my guns on any army approaching. So I would probably hold out to starvation point and possibly inadvertently beyond, because there will be disease in that place very soon. And Zacco will walk into his own very dead city.'

'There are alternatives,' John le Grant said.

'Of course. Zacco doesn't know this. Left to himself, he would pretty soon let the blockade ease off for winter, as he's always done. Minimal food will get in, starvation will be avoided, and Famagusta will hold on until, who knows, next summer a Genoese fleet might set out and rescue it.'

'And not left to himself?' the engineer said.

'If he knew this? He'd wait and starve them. Tzani-bey would do the same, only with decorations. Poisoned wells, putrid carcases slung over the walls. He'll suggest that anyway, as soon as he and the King begin to see the surrender isn't coming by the Feast of St Nicholas.'

'It's a damned pity,' said John, 'that you weren't called Stephen. It would've given us another month to play with at least. So what?'

'So three things,' Nicholas said. 'Empty Kyrenia and Salines and Paphos and double the men on those trenches. Establish as heavy a bombardment as the cannon will stand against the walls and the guns by the walls. And let's get rid of the powder. It's bound to be in the fort, and that overlooks the harbour. Mick Crackbene is there sitting outside that harbour with the *Doria* and at least one galley at his disposal. So why not increase his artillery, and give him all the fire-missiles he can carry. Better still, get him to try and slip a man in through the sea-gate. A single explosion would silence their guns. Then we take by assault when the ditch is done. Or perhaps, if they're starved and weary of waiting, by then the people will force Lomellini to a surrender.' He stopped. 'What else can you think of?'

'Broadly the same,' John le Grant said. 'I've changed my mind, too, about something else. Tell the King. If you leave it till later he won't forgive you, or maybe even believe you, if you have to expend soldiers on something he doesn't think necessary.'

Nicholas grunted.

John le Grant said, 'You don't want to, but you're better at it than most. In this game, every employer's an eccentric. Tobie nurses a dream of spending his life in the field with Urbino, but he'd find he's unpredictable too. He's better off with you. At least you're unpredictable in a more interesting way.'

'And that's a damned lie,' Nicholas said. 'You knew what I was going to say throughout this entire conversation.'

'And that was what was interesting,' John le Grant said. 'You said only what I'd expect you to say. So what else is happening?'

'Nothing yet,' Nicholas said. 'Maybe nothing at all. Come on. You're right. We ought to tell the whole story to Zacco.'

Zacco was told and threw himself, burning with zeal, into the new plans. The extra sappers were in place in a week, and the big hooped bombards and mortars, repositioned, were firing their three-hundred pounders as frequently as bombards were ever able to do, with a hundred balls beside each to do it with. Neither their range nor their alignment being of more than average accuracy, the damage they did was haphazard but promising. The medium bombards and basilisks, made by John in his wisdom with trunnions, now showed the virtues of his new two-wheeled carriages, which made them easy to move and regroup whatever the weather. They had powder enough – sixteen tons of it. In the hinterland, under cover, three new fighting-towers and several new engines were taking shape while Mick Crackbene, from his round ship, perfected his trajectories against the stout keep with its four corner towers that housed, they suspected, the city's great store of powder.

They had all grown used to the sounds of the camp: the low

open-air roar of many voices, the lowing of cattle, the chiming of harness and smith-work, the continual creak of John's water-pumps; the intermittent discharge of either cannon or handguns. Now there was an unremitting and thunderous noise of explosions punctuated by clanging and shouting, and the watchful discharge of small arms in a series of smoky thuds from the city walls. Napoleone Lomellini had discovered the absence of the Jew, and had ceased pretence, at least, of possessing no powder.

Three tiring and deafening weeks passed with no obvious change. Once, the King sent a herald with banner, trumpet and tabard, to invite the captain of Famagusta to surrender. The captain replied that the city was well off, sound, and had no intention of relinquishing its hard-won rights to Monseigneur the Bastard who, as was well known, had usurped the legitimate claims of the true Queen, Carlotta. He added that any further approach would be greeted by gunfire. Ten days after the first herald, the King sent another man in, of slightly less seniority, to repeat the royal offer. The Genoese shot him.

About then, word came from Salines, three hours away, to inform Nicholas that the Venetian sugar ship had reached Alexandria and would be leaving soon for Episkopi to pick up the combined Cypriot cargo. Nicholas went to the King and asked leave to absent himself for four days. Zacco gave it, impatiently. That day, the skies had clouded and, for the first time, the weather was cooler. Soon, it would take the better part of two days to pass between Famagusta and Kouklia. Loppe had made the awkward trip once since the siege began. Otherwise they communicated through their agent at Salines. But for the excellence of Loppe and his sugar-master, it would not have been very satisfactory.

On the way this time it rained, but despite his dragging cloak and the glum faces of the small train he took with him, Nicholas made the journey in a condition of numbness that amounted almost to happiness. The country was silent. That is, there was work going on everywhere, but the noise of it was dispersed in the mild cloudy air, no longer staring blue, with the brassy sun striking down on dry earth. The villages were noisy with smiths and coopers and loom-work, dicing and singing, but the noise was contained, and cheerful, and natural. Nowadays, quite a few recognised him, and seemed to bear him no grudges. He stayed the night at Salines, and arrived at noon next day at Kouklia. Only on the last part of his journey had he put his mind to questions of waxed cloth and canvas, cubic capacity and rates of exchange.

It was Advent again. It struck him then how long a year it had been. How last year the crop had meant nothing to him at all; how, without understanding, he had walked about the harbour and warehouses of Episkopi, and the misuse of the Order's cargo of sugar had been simply a matter noted and used as a playing-counter. Now, arriving at his own manor of Kouklia, he recognised as if he had been bred to it the sound and smell and look of each component; each piece of equipment. At Stavros, the new grinding mill had been built. It was empty now, and so was the echoing hall of the old, its oxen safely stabled. In the yard, newly muddy, planks ran between vats, some empty and scoured, some still steaming. Over each, now, a wooden shelter was in place, already bleached by the sun. In the refining sheds, the last of the cones stood, cooling and whitening, and dripping their slow, golden molasses into their jars.

There were not so many men about now. Some had gone back to their villages; some to the pottery; some to begin the maintenance tasks that would take place, at the yard or by the hearth, all through the winter. The rest were employed at present between Stavros and Episkopi, loading and transporting the casks to the warehouses to await the arrival of the all-important galley which was to take them to Venice. Later, he would have to go there. But first, Nicholas walked uphill back to the manor with Loppe, and in the office there read the ledgers and saw what had been done. Then he said, 'Loppe, it's a miracle. You've doubled it.'

Loppe smiled. Throughout the tour, his bearing had been one of well-mannered gravity. It was not perhaps natural but it had served him well, Nicholas knew, from the beginning. Cyprus society did not readily recognise the management skills of a negro. Loppe knew better, of course, than to expect to enter any nobleman's house as a friend.

He never seemed to let it trouble him. But now, in private with Nicholas, Loppe said, 'What's this, a miracle? This is the result of my experience and your money and a touch of genius that follows me whatever I do. If you'd been quicker over the refining equipment –'

It was an old story, and Nicholas did no more than pull a molasses-type face. Left under-equipped by the Martini, it had taken him too long to realise that copper vats were not now to be had; that all the pottery stores had somehow been requisitioned; that skilled men had been seduced away to serve elsewhere. Someone cleverer or luckier than he was had noticed that the way to make money wasn't this way, risking the mice and the drought and the locusts, managing the men and the beasts and all the complexity of arrangements that ended here, in the yard, with crushed cane and coarse syrup fit for refining. Someone had noticed that the easy, clean way was simply to buy the end product and refine. He said, 'How much do we have to send as unrefined sugar?'

And Loppe said, 'A quarter. We lose the profit of half the increased production. It will be better next year. I have three vats on the way from Damascus.'

'And this one firm are refining?' said Nicholas.

'There are others, but their rates are far higher. These are moderate. It is a question,' Loppe said, 'whether it would not be cheaper to let them do all the refining. You could sell the vats, let the men go; run down the pottery. All that would offset their charges.'

'For one year,' Nicholas said. 'After that, they could charge what they pleased. And what would all these people do? Not praise Zacco, at any rate. The Corner are still refining?'

'They are in the same difficulty,' Loppe said. 'You will see them at Episkopi. What is happening at Famagusta?'

He deserved an answer, and Nicholas gave it. He supposed his reserve was apparent. John le Grant had viewed him, it was obvious, as a child enjoying rough play, and brought up suddenly short by reality. He had meant to point out to John le Grant that they had both engaged in extremely rough play at Trebizond, and if he chose to carry out another war contract, he was not doing it blindfold. But it was true that he had forgotten, in the turmoil of Famagusta and Sigouri and the turbulent wake of the Bastard, that there was another régime which lay entirely under his hand, orderly, productive and satisfying to heart and head. He had felt the same, momentarily, stepping into the dyeyard at Nicosia, but put it down to a foolish nostalgia. Or perhaps he was quite mistaken, and what his nature called for was both. At the moment, he would have given quite a lot to stay here, and never return to the other cities again. Even though his wife Primaflora was there and it was four weeks since he had touched her.

This train of thought led to another. He finished his story and said, 'I can't stay long. I'd better go down to Episkopi. Then I'll come back and we'll talk. When this ship has sailed, can you come to Famagusta? Will it run well enough in your absence?'

'How long an absence?' said Loppe. 'Perhaps the siege is over. Perhaps the magazine has blown up already.'

'But that's why I want you there,' Nicholas said. 'Not for the siege; but what's going to happen after it.'

For the rest of the time, they spoke only of business. At Episkopi, he found one of the Martini brothers down by the warehouses. He had met him before, since his second coming from Rhodes, and on both occasions the Venetian was civil, if not effusive. Nicholas supposed honour was partially satisfied. The Martini had helped free the Flemish lady from Zacco. And Nicholas, as was now known, had prevented the acquisition by Madeira of the best vine and cane cuttings in Europe. That of course had not been his prime reason for going to Rhodes. Indeed, he had no proof, until he reached Rhodes that Katelina had taken cuttings with her. But no one but himself happened to know it.

The Order, when he came across its several agents down by the waterside, was civil for no doubt the same reasons. Zacco, as King of all Cyprus, would have the Venetian fleet on his side. So the Knights would have orders to smile on him; forgetting any small item such as the kidnapping of their ship and their cargo. Nicholas, in the course of these encounters, failed to meet John of Kinloch whose regard for him, he rather feared, would be unaltered.

His last visit was to fulfil an invitation from Marco Corner to take supper with him at his house. It had happened on the last occasion as well, for Venice was delighted with Niccolò vander Poele, who had destroyed the plants and was freeing Cyprus, God be good, of the Genoese. Even his marriage to Primaflora in some way had charmed them although, of course, there had been no opportunity for her to visit either Episkopi or Kouklia.

This time, Loredano was there, the perfect Venetian; but not the perfect Venetian princesses. It was a relief; although again, naturally, the subject of Katelina van Borselen arose, and he had to explain, again, that he had seen her last in good health leaving Rhodes. 'A charming guest,' returned Marco Corner, lifting his bulk from a settle and signing a servant to light the small brazier. 'Although her captivity chafed her and her disappearance, as the lord King has found cause to remind me, has deprived him of her considerable ransom. Nevertheless, one would not have wished her to be miserable. The countryside troubled her. Fiorenza observed it. She had a great fear of insects.'

'The lady Fiorenza is sensitive to the feelings of others,' Nicholas said. 'I trust she and her sisters are well?'

'Of course. Of course,' said Marco Corner. 'You will see them in Venice. Surely, when the King is in possession, you will allow yourself a small trip to Venice? It would be wise, in any case, to supervise this vile matter of refineries. You are suffering too? I am told they have touched pawning as well. The Order and Carlotta have cause to know it. You will have to look to your Bank.'

'My Bank,' Nicholas said, 'is as well protected as I am.'

Slithering north in the rain the next day, he thought he ought to be commended for speaking the truth, for what it was worth, which was little.

He returned to find the Cross of St George still flapping from the walls of Famagusta and nothing obviously changed except the weather, which would, of course, put out the slow-matches and the fire-missiles and make it increasingly unlikely that the tower of Famagusta was going to prove combustible. On his way to his tent, he fell in with a captain who told him gloomily that three men had individually been sent in to find and blow up the magazine, and all had presumably died. Meanwhile, the firing from the walls was

undiminished, and the last stages of trenching had proved extremely costly. The city would now, in addition, possess some
water. He then added the news Nicholas had least wanted to hear.
The King had gone back to Nicosia, taking his whole Council with
him.

In the most artistic way, Nicholas swore. The man grinned.
'What have you to worry about? He sent a message for you. It's in
your tent.'

There proved, when he got there, to be two messages. The first,
from the King, summoned him forthwith to Nicosia. The other,
from Philip Pesaro, asked that no matter what time he arrived, he
should ride on immediately to Sigouri.

The Château Franc at Sigouri was ten miles away. It was dusk,
it was wet, and Nicholas had been riding all day. He sent for
Astorre, and there appeared instead Thomas, who reported smartly
that Captain Astorre had been called to Nicosia, and Master Tobie
and Messer le Grant with him. He answered, when pressed, that
he didn't know why, but it was understood that the young fellow
was mad, that is, Monseigneur the King was in one of his fits of
impatience. The rumour was that they were to give up the siege
and have their contracts revoked before Christmas.

Nicholas said, 'Don't believe it. All we need is a bit of good
action. Wait till I get back from Sigouri.'

'They say,' said Thomas, 'that you're not coming back. That the
King'll keep you beside him at the Palace.'

'And that'll be nice and dry and warm for us both. I can see how
the thinking is going. Well, tell them I'll be back whether the King
wants me or not. We said we'd take this damned city, and we're
going to.'

Thomas didn't look immediately cheered, but might relay some
of that, Nicholas thought, where it would help matters. He felt wet
and cold and touched with foreboding. He sent for one man and
Chennaa, swallowed some cold meat and wine and, wrapping
himself in a dry cloak, went and mounted the camel, crooning
love-talk as she rose to her feet and took up her soft, swaying gait.
She was a racing-camel. Although booted and plastered with mud
and out of temper with herself and with him, she deposited him at
the drawbridge of Sigouri in just over an hour. Pesaro met him in
the yard.

Philip Pesaro was a good fighting man in a post that controlled
all north-east Cyprus from Famagusta to the end of the Karpass.
He took Nicholas into his office, shut the door and spoke as soon as
the servants had gone. 'I've got a report from inside Famagusta.
Their food is virtually finished. There are only two thousand still
alive in the city, and the survivors are dying off daily. But Lomellini
and his men will not give up. They will starve to the end, because

they believe rescue is coming by sea.' He paused and said, 'The King is not here. He has offered honourable surrender, and his envoys have been killed or turned back. The responsibility for what is happening does not lie with us. But I must report it to you.'

'Yes,' said Nicholas. He pushed aside, untasted, the food Pesaro's servant had given him. He said, 'Of course, the King has not heard this latest news.' He looked at the window and said, 'I'll go to Nicosia tonight.'

Pesaro said, 'You might as well have your night's rest. I know what the lord King will say. It is no concern of his if the city is stubborn, and suffers. And until after your Feast, he will do nothing.'

Nicholas stopped in the act of rising. He said, '*What?*'

'The Feast of St Nicholas,' said Philip Pesaro. 'You had forgotten. He offered to hold it in Famagusta. Since you have failed to give him Famagusta, he proposes to celebrate it in his own capital. That is why you have to go.' He paused, and said, 'You won't persuade him to do otherwise, Messer Niccolò. Don't think that you can.'

'No,' said Nicholas. 'I shall go, then. But there are some orders I should like carried out. I shall write them down and sign them. Then when this mad Feast is over, I'll bring the King back.'

He wrote, and Pesaro watched. At the end, the captain said, 'I shall do it, of course. But –'

'But it may make no difference,' Nicholas said. 'It probably won't. And I know what you're thinking. Every gun in Famagusta is trained on the end of that trench, and Genoese archers are among the best in the world. But in the end, we may have to save the honour of Genoa the Superb by attacking her.'

Chapter 36

THE FOLLOWING day was the eve of the Feast of St Nicholas. Consumed with rage and anxiety, Tobias Beventini, physician, prowled through the warm, pretty villa of the loveliest woman in Nicosia, bumping into maids carrying baskets of linen and other maids bearing pressed robes and doublets, concealing himself from the man who wanted to trim the fluff round his scalp, and using long Latin words to the other man who wanted to polish his spurs and his jewellery.

He had no jewellery. The last time he had felt like this was in a house in Florence, when he and Julius had been about to visit Cosimo de' Medici and extract a commission to represent the Medici in Trebizond. That time, Nicholas had arrived late as well. Tobie made to sit in a chair and then desisted, because it was inlaid and foreign and breakable. He noticed that John le Grant avoided the furniture too. There were cushions with long, voluptuous tassels, and in the master bedroom (he had looked) the quilt was of white silk brocade.

They had hardly ever been in this house belonging to Nicholas, and never since it received its new mistress. Tobie had previously met Primaflora on rare occasions only – during the search for Tristão and Diniz Vasquez on Rhodes; on the ambushed ship that brought them from Rhodes, and in the King's hall at Kiti immediately after. In Rhodes he had seen a lot of her, right up to her thigh, and Nicholas was right: he was pea-green with envy.

She was still golden, and silken, and goddess-like, and had welcomed John and Astorre and himself with a kind of free, self-possessed amusement that had seemed to make them at once her long-established friends. The house, their chamber, the food were arranged to perfection, and after the brutish clangour of Famagusta they should have been in a state of bewildered gratitude. But John, he noticed, tended to wander outside as often as he felt tempted to do; while Astorre had set up house quite candidly in the kitchens.

Primaflora appeared wholly unruffled, but every now and then someone in royal livery would appear in the yard and go away again. The King was arranging a feast tomorrow for Nicholas, and Nicholas wasn't here yet.

Late in the afternoon, Loppe arrived, which frankly no one had expected, for Loppe was managing things at Kouklia just as Mick Crackbene was guarding the harbour at Famagusta. The surprise was mutual. Tobie explained about the Feast of St Nicholas with many and explicit adjectives, and Loppe clearly thought his exasperation well-founded while refraining, annoyingly, from any breath of criticism of the absent Nicholas. Loppe was, it appeared, expecting to join up with Nicholas on the battlefield, but on hearing the news, obtained Primaflora's permission to stay. Being Loppe, he solved the problem of protocol by returning silently to his role of major domo, having made a small accommodation with Galiot whom, after all, he had trained. His previous incarnations seemed well known to Primaflora who had last seen him, presumably, crossing from the service of the Grand Commander Louis de Magnac to that of Nicholas with total aplomb. She had not seen Nicholas himself, Tobie learned, for five weeks.

He arrived after supper that evening, having spent the previous night, it transpired, at Sigouri. Why it had taken him all day to travel thirty odd miles was not explained. He came directly to the parlour shared by Astorre, John and Tobie, followed by servants attempting to rid him of his wet cloak. They were immediately replaced by Loppe, whose presence he appeared to accept without question and almost without greeting, as he did theirs. On his face, with its childlike planes and arrogant nostrils and affectingly large eyes, was a distinct absence of the play of simple expressions that usually took place there. He looked tired, which he didn't usually do. He looked — which Tobie in particular didn't care for — uncommonly like the way he had looked more than two years before at a place called Skylolimne; and later at another place called Kerasous. Tobie looked at John, and their eyes met. Astorre, wiping peach juice from his beard, threw down his napkin and said, 'Well, you took your time. We might have got this contract finished, but for your God-damned Feast Day. What were you thinking of?'

'I wanted a good meal,' said Nicholas.

Primaflora appeared in the doorway behind him and by instinct, it seemed, he knew it and turned round. Or perhaps, thought Tobie, her scent had something to do with it. She said, without touching him, 'Talk to them. Then find me when you are ready.' Her face was smiling and apparently calm, unless you looked below the painted line of her brows. What it reflected of her husband's face, Tobie couldn't see.

Then Nicholas said, 'No. Please join us. And Loppe. I suppose I have to go to the King.'

'He can wait,' Primaflora said; and crossing the room, held the great chair by the brazier until Nicholas walked over and dropped into it. Then, restraining Loppe with a light hand, she fetched wine and a platter for Nicholas, and poured for them all before she sat down herself.

Nicholas said, 'The Feast Day wasn't my idea. I want it over as quickly as possible.'

'There is Mass tomorrow,' said Primaflora. 'Then a great feast at the Palace. All the Haute Cour will be there. The King has invited every great nobleman, every high officer of the church and the Knights of the Order from Kolossi. The Venetians, the merchants will be present, and even Sor de Naves and the abbot of Bellapaïs from Kyrenia. Only the Mamelukes will be absent. You couldn't leave in less than two days. It is a mark of the King's personal love and regard.'

Astorre snorted. 'He's bored.'

'I told you,' Nicholas said, 'to entertain him while I was away. Do your tricks. Turn somersaults and climb up the underside of a ladder with your armour on. Well, it's too late now, so let's make the best of it. I have something I want the King to agree to. There might be a better chance now than most times.'

'You want to leave?' said John le Grant. It was the first time he had spoken. Very often John le Grant disconcerted Tobie. With Julius, he had always felt more comfortable.

Nicholas said briefly, 'Something else.'

Captain Astorre had been paying small attention. He said, 'And anyway, what did Pesaro want at Sigouri? He said he'd sent for you.'

'He was concerned,' Nicholas said. 'He says the whole army is unsettled because it's known that Famagusta will never give up while it expects a relieving ship to arrive. He says that if the King persists in staying away, there will be mutiny if not now, then when the weather gets wetter and colder. No army expects to keep the field through the winter.'

John le Grant said, 'And so what's his suggestion?'

'It's mine,' Nicholas said. 'It's what I want to put to Zacco. This is December, when truces are common. I want Zacco to invite four leading citizens from Famagusta to share the Feast of the Nativity with him, and to allow food and wine to be sent into the city between then and Epiphany. And during that time, I want those four Genoese to see for themselves, beyond all possible doubt, that there is no question of rescue arriving. Then, I hope and believe, they will surrender.'

'Amid casks of wine and barrels of cheeses?' said Astorre, scowling.

'The food would stop on the sixth day of January. I don't think,' Nicholas said, 'that anyone in Famagusta will have the strength of purpose left to starve to death after that.'

Tobie said nothing nor, after a glance, did John le Grant. It was Primaflora who said, 'Forgive me. This is not women's business. But will starvation not bring surrender without the King being asked to make such concessions? They must be suffering now.'

And Nicholas looked at her with his childish, bovine-eyed face and said, 'You would think so, but no. They have been judicious in storage and, besides, many have died. They could hold out until spring. The King must agree, and then I will give him Famagusta.'

Soon after that, when the rest had retired, Nicholas went alone to the Palace for his long-deferred interview. He found Zacco lightly intoxicated, and playing dice for high stakes among a circle of friends. He was greeted, berated and kept many hours, drinking very much more than he wanted. At no time did the King mention the progress of the war, and it was hardly the place or time to open the subject. At no time, either, did Zacco either seek to be alone with him, or utter a word of reproach about his failure with Famagusta.

They parted eventually on the same curious, jovial note, and Nicholas returned to his villa. The torchlit streets, as he passed through them, were not given up as usual to the cats and the late-night lovers or revellers but were occupied by knots of busy, muttering men, putting up ladders and hoardings, clearing mud, hanging carpets for tomorrow's Festival which was for St Nicholas and himself, not for the burghers of Bruges.

At home, he simply said to Primaflora, 'It was a waste of time. He had drunk too much. So have I.'

They were alone in their chamber, but she was still fully dressed. She said smiling, 'We shall see. Talk to me.'

He found he was too tired to unbutton his doublet. She came to help him, kissing him lightly and absently on the face, the neck, the hands as she unfastened it, and his belt, and the ties of his shirt. She said, 'I have your dress prepared for tomorrow. You must look splendid.'

'And you?' he said. 'Crimson satin and gold? Pearls and ermine?'

She smiled, her eyes on what she was doing. 'No. A gown you will recognise, but fine enough. It seemed unwise, this time, to wear anything of Carlotta's.'

He stopped her hands. 'But you have money?'

She looked up, still smiling. 'You left me a fortune. I didn't need it. My own robe, and your jewels. Besides, the King has sent mantles. One in velvet for you, with the badge of your Order. One of tissue for me. Master Tobie's robes and the dress of your

engineer and your captain have presented a much greater challenge.'

'We're all invited?' Nicholas said. He sat down and laid hands,
with misplaced confidence, on his boots.

'Even to Bartolomeo from the dyeyard, and his brother. And
Nicholas –'

He heard her voice flatten and left his boots alone. He said,
'What is it?'

'Only some sad news from Bartolomeo,' she said. 'His partner
from Constantinople has come. You know the Sultan has been
imprisoning the Venetians and worse? This Messer Girolamo has
escaped from Constantinople, with terrible news about Trebizond.'

There only remained one kind of news that could be terrible.
Nicholas said, 'The Sultan has broken his word? They have killed
the Emperor-in-exile?'

'Yes,' she said. Her eyes were oval, and pain-filled and perfect.
She had a classical nose with curled pink pads like a kitten's; like
Tobie's. A short, deep channel introduced the fruit of her lips. She
said, 'Despite the surrender, the amnesty, the promises. They've
killed David Comnenos and his children.'

'Long live the lord Sultan' said Nicholas. 'All of them?'

'There were seven sons and one unmarried daughter,' she said.

'I know how many there were. All of them?' he repeated.

'The girl Anna is . . . She stays where she was placed. The
youngest son was kept alive, to be reared as a Muslim.'

'He would be nearly four,' Nicholas said. 'And the six other
sons, then, are dead.'

'Yes,' she said. 'You don't ask me why?'

'I am just about to. Why?' Nicholas said.

'It happened, he says, because of a prince of the Turcomans
called Uzum Hasan whose wife was a princess of Trebizond. This
lady, the Turcoman's wife, sent a private message to Adrianople,
inviting a son of the Emperor to join her. She was the exiled
Emperor's niece: it was possibly harmless. But the letter was
intercepted by Amiroutzes the Emperor's Chancellor, who deduced
that the prince Uzum Hasan wished to rear a child of the blood to
lead armies one day against Trebizond. He told the Sultan. The
Imperial family were thrown into prison . . .'

'We knew that much,' said Nicholas.

'. . . and in the Sultan's present mood, he was evidently thought
them now better dead. I am sorry,' said Primaflora. 'It was not
until I saw how Messer Bartolomeo's news was received by your
friends that I realised its importance for you.' She paused. 'You
were fond of the Emperor?'

Nicholas said, 'I was in Trebizond, as I am here, with an army.

The Turk proved stronger. One can feel responsibility without feeling love, otherwise the world would be uninhabited. My face feels green.'

Primaflora sat back on her heels. She said, 'If your stomach ails you, blame Zacco. Perhaps you should go and deal with it. Shall I help you?'

'No,' Nicholas said. 'I'm good at this. So long as you don't arrange a leopard-hunt afterwards. Will you wait? In the hope that there's something worth waiting for?'

But in the end when he went back she was asleep, and he didn't wake her because there were few enough hours before dawn, and he had to get through a day – a series of days – that would put to the test the most dangerous set of manoeuvres he had ever conducted. Nicholas Thaumaturgas, worker of miracles. In any case the blame, as she had said, was most certainly Zacco's.

Of the company of Niccolò, the only truly happy person next day was Captain Astorre, who relished parades and believed in dressing up for them. The weather, though chillier than in Famagusta, was dry and even intermittently sunny. The captain assembled with his fellows in the Dominican monastery next to the Palace, watching bright-eyed as the notables arrived for the procession that would march eastwards from the Porta Santo Domenico to the Cathedral of Santa Sofia. Nicholas, who had missed the victory Mass for Kyrenia for the sake of an axe in his shoulder was present today, in body if not especially in mind, from the look of him. His face was the same colour as that of the King when the royal cohort arrived from the palace. Astorre chuckled. 'So it was like that!' said the captain. 'Well, the poor lady. She wouldn't get much good of him last night.'

Tobie gritted his teeth. Unlike Astorre, who recovered as quickly from his rages as he fell into them, Tobie had not forgotten what lay behind them suspended at Famagusta. He had not forgotten, either, the story Bartolomeo Zorzi had regaled them with last night, and which he supposed had now been repeated to Nicholas. He had tried once already to talk to Nicholas about it, and had been kicked on the ankle by le Grant. He walked all the way to the Cathedral brooding about that inside his new scarlet robe, with the blue mantle and golden links of the Order of the Sword on the shoulders of Nicholas before him. *C'est pour loïauté maintenir*. Well, Queen Carlotta had given him it, and her bastard brother-usurper had confirmed it, so he either had it twice or not at all.

The procession filled all the space there was between buildings, so there were few people about in the street, except peering over shop-ledges or within doorways. The upper windows and galleries were full enough, however, although the faces were more respectful and curious than ecstatic. Trumpets blew all the time, and drums were beating. A smell of incense grew strong as they approached the immense triple portico of the Cathedral, begun in the French style two hundred years ago. He noticed the King stepping forward with a firming of the step. He ought to feel at home. Without the help of the Pope, his royal father had made Zacco Archbishop of Nicosia when he was thirteen, and he had lived in the Archbishop's Palace with Cropnose for years. The present more orthodox incumbent was a tough man as well as an Augustine; accustomed to risky assignments in Cairo. Tobie spared a thought for Cairo, and Mamelukes, and Tzani-bey, and wondered if Nicholas knew what the emir was doing in the Mameluke camp outside Famagusta. One thing for sure: Tzani-bey hadn't been asked to the Feast of St Nicholas, although the Arab physician was here. He had seen him in the city.

Once inside the nave, Tobie's ankle reminded him that if Nicholas was thinking of anything, it was probably another service not unlike this one. That had taken place two years ago, in Trebizond; and had celebrated the Feast of St Eugenios, not St Nicholas; and instead of James, Dei gratia Jerusalem, Cypri et Armenie rex illustrissimus, the chief celebrant had been the dead Vice-Regent of Christ, David Comnenos, twenty-first Emperor of Trebizond, accompanied by his Grand Chancellor and betrayer, George Amiroutzes.

The liturgy began and Tobie moved, craning uneasily. Behind the fountain of plumes that arose from Captain Astorre's headgear was the shining head of Primaflora, its hair looped and plaited under the horns of a cap, and a cameo on a gold chain round her throat. Admiring her, Tobie didn't feel impelled, for a while, to look further. Then he did, and saw Nicholas.

If painful reveries of any kind had once overwhelmed him, they did so no longer. Nicholas was standing so still that the thick painted glass struck motionless light from his chain, and his face was glazed like a jug with mixed colours. Tobie followed the line of his scrutiny. Beside the King and the Archbishop, the Bishops of Paphos and Limassol, the several abbots, the Knights Hospitaller of the Order and the ecclesiastical officers of the Cathedral, stood a thick, black hairy fellow in a battered conical cap with a veil, below which an assortment of robes vaguely Greek and vaguely Coptic did not quite cover the stained brown habit of a Franciscan friar.

Tobie recognised him. A hundred years ago, this man had stamped into the Medici Palace in Florence and nearly wrecked the whole Trapezuntine expedition. He had interfered in the snow by Bologna, so Nicholas said. He had been in Rhodes, and indeed his ship had transported home the body of the Portuguese whom Nicholas had said he hadn't had murdered. Even without hearing the ineffable pitch of his bellow, it was possible to pick this man out in any circle.

It was Ludovico de Severi da Bologna, the Latin Patriarch of Antioch; and Nicholas, animated once again, was bestowing one of his broad, well-meaning smiles on the fellow. The friar returned a light scowl, after which they paid no more attention to one another. Tobie, who regarded the Patriarch with undiluted horror, felt thankful.

The head of the House of Niccolò, who had considerable reservations himself about Father Ludovico da Bologna, was content enough to remain unmolested through the Mass, and the procession back to the Palace, and even the banquet itself, although that presented different pitfalls.

Knowing the King, as he believed, Nicholas had always assumed that now, through his placing at table, Zacco would take his chance to belittle in public this favoured commander who had failed to give him his kingdom as promised. But instead, in a table filled with knights of his name, Nicholas was placed on the King's right, and Nicholas (Conella) Morabit, on his left. Through the meal, it was the same. The King recounted past adventures, selected meats for him, joked about the abstemious habits of the baby St Nicholas, who refused the breast every Wednesday and Friday. The jokes, if coarse, were quite good.

From the other tables, Nicholas could see John's face, red under its freckles, glancing his way more often than not. The churchmen, because of the feast day, kept their own table next to the King's, sharing it with the Knights Hospitaller of St John. He had had a stiff greeting that morning from the Grand Commander Louis de Magnac, whom he had tricked over Loppe, and again on shipboard coming from Rhodes. With him was Brother William de Combort, who had entertained Primaflora so warmly at Rhodes in the belief that she was in Carlotta's employment. Perhaps they all still believed that she was. At any rate, they could see that Zacco, not Carlotta, was going to hold Cyprus; and that they must treat a commander of Zacco's with care.

At another table sat the Venetians: the brothers Martini as well as Corner and Loredano and Paul Erizzo. They looked well satisfied: another crop safely transformed and delivered; Zacco more firmly enthroned and in their perennial debt; their share in bringing Nicholas and his army to Cyprus fully justified, despite the small delay in completing the contract. And after the contract, who knew? Nicholas had seen, as they came in, both Corner and Martini find occasion to shake John le Grant by the hand. As indeed they should, since John le Grant had solved their water dispute. There was no need for them to know that engineer John le Grant was its author.

His eyes rested on the Zorzi brothers. Jacopo, whom he had invited to Kouklia, and whose vineyards he still had not visited. Bartolomeo who managed his dyeworks, and Bartolomeo's partner Girolamo, whom Nicholas had met also on his way to Trebizond, and who had brought the information he didn't wish, at present, to think about. He didn't want, either, to think of the third Zorzi brother, known to the world as Nicholai Giorgio de' Acciajuoli. The Greek with the wooden leg, whose machinations, he sometimes felt, ran as a dark undercurrent below all his own devices, robbing him of his belief in his will. In that message from Constantinople, sent here, and at this time, he saw the hand of Acciajuoli, not of this self-seeking merchant.

And Primaflora. She was admitted, now, to the feasting-hall of the King, and placed at the long women's table presided over by Marietta of Patras, the King's serene and excellent mother. His wife's beauty, little adorned, seemed to draw the lamplight towards her: it shone on the latticework of her sleeves and the exact and regular folds that defined the slender bones of her body. He saw her glance at Ludovico da Bologna whom, of course, she had met in Rhodes, and further back, in the snow with Carlotta. In the snow between Porretta and Bologna, where Nicholas had been called to the rescue, and Ansaldo her lover had died.

Sor de Naves, here with his brother, had also bowed to Primaflora at her table and had taken the chance, stopping Nicholas, to congratulate him on his marriage. Civility was not his objective. 'What habit of the brake or the burrow do you employ, Ser Niccolò, that you attract to yourself so many beautiful females? The Queen has lost her waiting-woman to you, and you have married her?'

Until bribed to surrender Kyrenia, the Sicilian admiral had been one of Carlotta's closest advisers. 'The Queen?' said Nicholas.

'A slip of the tongue. The lady Carlotta. The pity is that you married this lady, dear sir. But perhaps you have children enough, or see no need for them.'

'I suppose,' Nicholas said, 'that like yourself, I believed the matter could wait.' He turned his shoulder, but not quickly enough.

The Sicilian laughed. 'I make a good target. The King's daughter is six. But she is a virgin, be sure; and will bear to me when she bears. Whereas those who eschew bearing, or have too often found means to abort it may prove, like your wife, to be barren.'

'And you think that concerns me?' said Nicholas. 'I must disappoint you.'

The man smiled. 'You had been told. I might have known. At Carlotta's court, it is common knowledge. Well, Ser Niccolò, let me end as I began, and wish you joy of your marriage.'

He hadn't known. It didn't matter. Now, it didn't matter.

He got through the meal. He displayed gratification through all the entertainments that took place during and after the feast, and took the floor with the rest during the slow, formal dancing, in which he had been well taught by the various females attracted to his brake and his burrow. Towards the end, when the Palace was still filled with people, and wine, and hilarity he and Rizzo di Marino were chosen, as he had hoped, to attend the King when he withdrew from necessity. In the moment before they returned, Nicholas spoke. 'My lord. To give me this day at your side was an unforeseen joy, but it oppresses me that it is undeserved: that Famagusta is not yet yours. Before we go back, my lord, might I put something to you, and to Ser Rizzo?'

The King was sober and affable. The Chancellor, an experienced man, knew an opening of consequence when he heard it. An office was found, and the King sat and said, 'Well, what is this? We keep your lady wife waiting.' And, warm with dancing, he pulled off his jewelled hat, so that the brown hair fell free, and opened the close-pearled band of his doublet so that his throat might be bared to the air. He said to Nicholas, 'Ask. This is your night for receiving.'

Afterwards, Nicholas wondered what he had expected from Zacco. The favour of a hearing, which he had. An appreciation that a truce over Christmas might seem magnanimous to his Christian allies, which Zacco appeared to find appealing. But the idea that the season of leisure should be marred by the presence of men from that vicious republic? The conception that a Lusignan should humour the fools, to persuade them that surrender would not be dishonourable? The suggestion that – 'Christ God in heaven,' said James, King of Cyprus, rising slowly to his feet. 'Are you deaf, blind, witless? Do you expect me to send food and wine to the men whose forefathers took mine to wretched imprisonment in Genoa? Who forced the wife of the first James of my line to earn bread with her needle? Who killed with privation his nephew? James, my great-grandfather, would have known what to say to you, despite the badge and the silver buckle you wear. Suggest that to me again, Messer Niccolò, and you will lose them, and more!' said the King.

His face was livid, and his hand had clapped to his sword. Behind him, di Marino had risen also, ready to soothe. Usually, such an explosion could be anticipated. This time, it was so unheralded as to appear almost artificial. Standing, Nicholas said, in the humble voice known to every Bruges magistrate, 'Lord, I would not displease you. I merely seek to end a war. If you give me leave, I will do it in a way that would not dishonour your fore-bears.'

The young man still stood, his breath short, his hand braced on the hilt of his sword. Their eyes were level. 'How?' he said.

'I shall go back and prepare an assault,' Nicholas said. 'Tomorrow, if you will allow me.'

Zacco drew a long breath through pinched nostrils. 'Yes?' he said. 'And that would be quicker than starving them?'

'It could not fail,' Nicholas said. He avoided the Chancellor's eye. He kept still, and calm, and gentle of voice.

'And who would lead it?' said Zacco. 'You?'

'Monseigneur,' said Rizzo di Marino. 'This is a counsel of courage, and I respect it. But our trench is exposed to artillery. The vanguard of such an assault will die.'

'You?' repeated the King.

'Of course,' Nicholas said. 'I should allow the honour to no one else of the lord King's adherents. Unless he wishes to strip me of his confidence.'

Rizzo di Marino said, 'Of course he will take Famagusta. But need our troops suffer the cost of it?'

No one spoke. Nicholas stood, expressing only what he felt, which was patience, and understanding, and a baseless, inbred, unnatural optimism. And gradually, the King's hand relaxed, and his bearing, and lastly his face, across which flickered indistinct and curious emotions: of relief and annoyance, of affection and something that might have been shame. Zacco raised his hand from his sword and took Nicholas by the face in hard fingers. 'I forbid you,' he said. 'I have bought your life. I forbid you to waste it. Starve them. They deserve it.'

Nicholas dropped to one knee. For a moment they remained apart. Then the King's hand touched his cheek, differently, and the King's voice said, 'Enough. Let us return. They will think the worst of three handsome men who have taken leave together.'

There was nothing more to be done. Nicholas cast a single glance at the Chancellor's considering gaze, and followed the King back to the hall. He had nearly reached it when the hand of Ludovico da Bologna grasped his shoulder, and the voice of the Patriarch pronounced in his ear: 'Well, my son. Does the King pay for all night of you, or can the Church claim an hour of your time?'

The King turned. The Patriarch said, 'I ask a favour of James of Cyprus. May the Church, on this Feast Day, command one of its sons?'

'You wish to shrive him?' said Zacco. He gave his most charming laugh. 'You will be disappointed. A well-constructed artefact possesses no sins.'

'If I believed you,' said Ludovico da Bologna, 'I would be the happiest man in Nicosia. But the sins are there, in small corners, to be hunted out. Come, my little lord Niccolò.'

Chapter 37

'WHERE'S YOUR HOUSE?' said the Patriarch of Antioch. 'I want to talk to you.'

'Too far away,' Nicholas said.

'And that concubine will be there. I thought she had a lover at Bologna? I've got rooms at the Dominicans'; that'll do. There's your doctor. And is that fox-headed fellow one of yours? Tell them to come.'

Nicholas stood stock-still, in a condition of protest, thought or even possibly refusal. The fox-headed fellow, in the interests of a deep intellectual curiosity, strolled up and said, 'I'm John le Grant, my lord Patriarch. Everyone in the Levant has heard of Ludovico da Bologna.'

'They ought to,' said the Patriarch. 'I've travelled about it enough. Leave it to the Greeks, and you'll never get a Crusade. It needs Latin stomach to do it. This fellow's been wrangling with Zacco. Didn't think he had it in him. Not the way to keep your fief and your perpetual pension. Are you coming? What's that blood-letter's name?'

'Tobias Beventini. He met you in Florence.'

'I know he met me in Florence. A testy, petulant sort of fellow, they tell me, who bares his scalp instead of his buttocks. Ah, there you are.'

'I'm going home,' said Tobie briefly to Nicholas.

John le Grant put out a hand and pinched a stiff scarlet sleeve. He said, 'You're easy baited. Come on. You don't want to miss this. And when you've time, take a good look at Nicholas.'

A flicker of angry impatience immediately manifested itself in Tobie's face, and he fell into step with the engineer. There were times when John le Grant wondered how Tobie managed to be such a very good doctor and yet fail to ask himself primary questions about Nicholas. Such as, whether the expression you saw was what he wanted you to see, and was genuine. Or what he wanted you to see and was misleading. Or was what he wanted no

one to see at all, and had failed to disguise. A sporting interest in
pursuing such failures was one of the reasons John le Grant stayed
with Nicholas. There were, of course, several others.

The room they were taken to was bare, panelled and had a stone
floor, but had been hastily equipped with stools and benches and
tables for the Patriarch's visit. Against one wall stood a battered
chest covered with donkey-skin, with several pairs of old slippers
beside it and a patched travelling cloak thrown on top. On a side
table stood a pitcher and beakers and a pile of washed linen, some
darned and some not. In the centre of the room stood an extremely
well-tended brazier before which sat two men in low conversation
with broke off as the door opened.

One was the spare, bearded figure of Abul Ismail, the Arab
physician. The other was a heavily-built, muscular man with a
lobster nose and none of his sister's lost beauty. Markios of Patras,
the brother of Cropnose. 'You all know one another,' said Ludovico
da Bologna, pushing Nicholas in with a hand like a bakery paddle.
Tobie followed, and John le Grant just evaded the powerful thrust.
'Oecumenical conference, except we've no Orthodox cantankerous
Greeks and no clip-arsed, fornicating, drug-chewing bastards of
Mamelukes.' He glanced at Abul. 'I make a distinction for Arabs.'

'We thank you,' said the physician politely. John le Grant sat
with the others, casting a glance at the pitcher as he passed. It was
full of water.

The King's uncle said, 'You mystify our friends from the West.
Mamelukes are not a sect, merely children of any faith bought
young, and reared as Muslims to serve and rule Egypt and Syria.
Have you met the present Sultan in Cairo? The first of Greek
birth. Purchased fifty years since, and began as a page in Damascus.' He fixed the Patriarch with an eye. Le Grant recalled that in
his time Markios had led a company of Egyptian Mamelukes in
some of the hottest fighting for Zacco.

Ludovico da Bologna said, 'Don't be afraid to speak out: Abul
Ismail knows all about Mamelukes. Yes, I know Khushcadam.
Yes, I've been in Cairo. Murder and poison, torture, bribes, sales
of office. Terrorising and plunder, all by Mamelukes, and all
countenanced by the Sultan because he's afraid of 'em. They
depend for business on Copts, but Prester John's poor little
Ethiopes are not even permitted to roll eggs at Easter. You can thank
your Creator that vander Poele here has done something about it.'

There was a momentary vacuum, as all the air in the room was
sucked in. Then Markios said, 'Vander Poele has done what?'

Seen in profile, Nicholas had not so much changed colour as
quietly congealed. He stirred. 'The Patriarch is pleased that my
sugar-master comes from Damascus. I have men, and buy equipment from Syrian moderates.'

'And I don't suppose,' Father Ludovico remarked, 'that you had to pay all that much for them either. The prince Uzum Hasan would be glad to make up their salaries.'

'*Uzum Hasan!*' said the King's uncle.

'Vander Poele was in treaty with him in Trebizond. Uzum Hasan, head of the Turcoman tribe of the White Sheep; the strongest sect in all Persia; the biggest rival to Constantinople. It was touch and go – wasn't it, heh? – whether the White Sheep would beat the Turks into Trebizond. The way it turned out was the way young Niccolò wanted it. I am right?'

Fair play, to John le Grant, was fair play. He said judicially, 'I expect that's what you heard; but no, you've got it wrong, Patriarch. We fought the Turks, and the Turks frightened off Uzum Hasan, and the surrender was the Emperor's choice. Or rather . . .' He stopped, his voice fading out; and on reflection stayed stopped. The damage was done. Everyone could see where that trail was leading.

Except Tobie. Tobie said, 'Well, of course: the responsibility for the surrender lay with that traitorous scoundrel Amiroutzes. If you want the facts about Trebizond, Nicholas here will be happy to tell you. In any case, it wasn't Uzum Hasan that we dealt with, it was his mother. Sara, the prince's Syrian . . .' At that point, his tone faltered as well. With fascination, John watched the thoughts enter his mind. The mother of Uzum Hasan was a Syrian. And the wife of Uzum Hasan was mother's sister to Violante, Fiorenza and Valenza of Naxos.

The circumstance of the surrender of Trebizond was not what was being discussed.

Tobie resumed with sudden asperity. 'We had no call to be in touch with Uzum Hasan after that. Or his mother. I suppose Nicholas needed sugar equipment. That would be common enough. Supplies passing between Kouklia and Damascus in Syria.' He had turned rather pale.

It seemed to John le Grant that having gone so far, this thought, at least, must be completed. He said, 'It would be common enough, but that isn't what the Patriarch was implying. Nicholas, did you inspire the letter from Uzum's wife to the Emperor? The one that Amiroutzes betrayed to the Sultan? I don't think I could blame you, but Tobie would be happy if you could say no.'

'Then of course,' Nicholas said, 'I say no.'

'Quite right,' said Ludovico da Bologna. 'Anyone who knows George Amiroutzes knows who the real devil is. The head of a philosopher on the loins of a tomcat. Fell in love with the Duke of Athens' sweet little widow, and tried to get rid of the Patriarch of Constantinople when he wouldn't let him divorce his first wife. The Greek Patriarch, that is. He should try the Latin Patriarch next: that's Bessarion, godfather to one of his sons. Or perhaps not. The other son's converted to Mohammed and they say George is going the same way. *Et Filioque* with a vengeance. And talking of children, Carlotta's lost the heir to her kingdom. Would you care for some water?'

Nicholas said, 'No, thank you. A son?' There was no chance, now, of reading his face. He had schooled it so well that it received the implications of that entire passage of information with no expression at all.

'A premature son,' the Patriarch confirmed. 'So Zacco can take time to frame his marriage plans. And so what was your quarrel with him all about? The King didn't want Uzum Hasan to march in and help clear out the Sultan's rough Mamelukes?'

'The question didn't arise,' Nicholas said. His eyes, and those of the priest, moved and shifted like sun on two knife-blades.

'And you were a fool to put the question that did arise,' said the King's uncle unexpectedly. Nicholas turned his head. Markios said, 'I know what you asked the King to do. Your lady wife told my sister at table of your desire for a truce with Famagusta, your wish to feed the pigs and convince them of their isolation. Your idea that the King and I would lean back in indolence, allowing Famagusta to fatten and snigger, throwing away all the months of striving so that you could save your thick skin from a fight?'

'She said all that?' said Nicholas mildly.

'No,' said the Patriarch. 'I heard her. For a lady of doubtful morals, she put your case well. The rest is merely what the court will also say when they hear. Calm yourself. If I were a liar, I should prettify the past of your wife, but I am not. But this is what I am here to discuss. You have proposed a truce, and the King has refused it?'

'I have proposed to leave Nicosia immediately,' Nicholas said, 'to prepare and lead an attack on Famagusta. He refused to allow it.'

'You were not very convincing, perhaps,' Markios said.

'And when first proposing your truce,' Father Ludovico said, 'did you put yourself out to press that view in any way either? Did you call the Archbishop? The Knights of the Order? Myself? It is regarded as worthy of Christians to feed the starving; to desist from war during the time of our dear Lord's Nativity.'

'No,' said Nicholas. 'From me, he would take no advice of that sort. But you are welcome to try.'

'He will not,' Markios said. 'Forgive me, Father. You speak as if these thieves in Famagusta had rights. I believe, as Zacco believes, that to yield would be a weakness amounting to sin. I should hold no truce. I should pass no food. I should not let them linger, wasting time, wasting money, until the spring brings them fresh hope. I should persuade the King to change his mind, and let Messer Niccolò lead an assault. Of course, in that I should probably fail. We know why Messer Niccolò made the offer. We know with what confidence it must have been made. We have seen the King and his favourite together. There is nothing more certain than that Zacco will not send his friend into danger. Is that not so? Ser Niccolò, is that not so?'

'Yes,' said Nicholas. He got up, with the smooth, small dovetailing of joint and sinew and muscle that was the hallmark of well-realised design, and surveyed them all five, ending with the blue-jowled, pitted face of the priest. He said, 'Since no one can persuade Zacco I have, of course, made the decision myself. I leave for Sigouri tonight, and Famagusta tomorrow. Whoever wishes may follow me. As soon as the assault can be prepared, it will be made. And I don't really see how Zacco or anything else is going to stop me. You will excuse me, I hope.'

With admiration tinged with dread, John le Grant saw Nicholas bow, turn, and, with decision, walk out on the Patriarch. The door closed. Tobie jumped up. Markios laughed. He said, 'Puppies need kicking. You saw.'

'Yes. I saw,' said the priest. 'Your Mamelukes, at least, will give him a welcome. God works in wonderful ways. Allah too, I dare say. Abul Ismail?'

'I should go,' said the Arab, rising. 'If this attack is to be, I too will be needed at Famagusta. And you, my lord Patriarch?'

'Famagusta?' said Father Ludovico in surprise. 'With Christmas coming? My son, the casals of the Patriarchate have not even submitted their dues. A churchman is busy. A churchman is always busier than other people.'

'Come on,' said John le Grant to Tobie. 'We've got some riding to do.'

To Nicholas, the only immediate benefit of that wholly unpleasant discussion was that it shut up both le Grant and Tobie; and even Astorre, when found and brought to the villa, was unnaturally silent except on matters purely martial. An excellent soldier, Astorre simply accepted the prospect of a night ride to Sigouri, and made no bones about his employer's decision that, against the King's wishes, an assault was to be made. All along, Astorre had been longing to get the campaign over and done with.

Meanwhile, there was a need for discretion. Their departure from the royal precincts had not, Nicholas believed, drawn attention. After that display of high temper, Zacco wouldn't send for him, even if sober. And tomorrow, one hoped, he would merely assume that Nicholas had made a pettish departure and was sulking somewhere, awaiting apology or forgiveness. Markios, for one, would not disillusion him.

Primaflora was not at the villa. But now, attending on the King's mother, she might be expected to stay tonight at the Palace. He could imagine the two clever women, and the delicate fencing. He left her a note and, after hesitation, a small parcel which contained the most personal, the most valuable object he possessed. He would have liked to have said goodbye in another way, but this was probably best. There was no doubt at all, if he led this assault, that he would not return. For as long as she lived, she had been provided for. He wondered, once, if she would weep for him as she had done for Ansaldo.

The other note he left with Loppe who had received him, and listened, and then deftly completed his packing. To Loppe himself he had nothing to give save the task in Cyprus which had seemed most worth doing. Nicholas said, 'The company will have the Kouklia franchise so long as the King has a conscience. Run it well, so long as it pleases you. The dyeworks are different. They are lost, I think to the Venetians, whatever happens.'

After some moments of silence, Loppe spoke without apparent emotion. 'You forbid me to come?'

'You know why,' said Nicholas. 'Or does even a temporary steward open no chests; fold no linen away?' And then, answering the look on Loppe's face, he said, 'Don't be sorry. For what I do, I need larger reasons than that.'

To Sigouri was perhaps thirty miles and, although the rain kept away, it was dark and treacherous underfoot and they hardly spoke, men-at-arms or servants or principals, as they guided fresh horses across the grey soil of the Messaoria, splashing over burgeoning rivers; imperceptible to silent villages, churches and monasteries except by a thud of hooves and the swimming spawn of their brands. It was grey daylight when they crossed the moat of the Château Franc and besides himself only Astorre, Nicholas saw, had tried to keep the iron back and square shoulders of duty. Astorre, because he was content under orders. Himself, because alone of them all, he knew what he was committed to. What he had brought them to. What, without him, they would never have had to face. But that was the risk they had taken in joining him.

Their approach had been seen. With Pesaro, striding to meet them, was Thomas. Thomas said, 'The heathen bastards!'

'Wait,' said Nicholas. In the captain's room, hardly cold from the last time, he said, 'Now. Tzani-bey?'

Philip Pesaro looked gaunt. He said, 'We carried out all your orders. We restored the water. We sent loaves over the wall, with a message. The Genoese sent them back. They thought they were poisoned.'

'They've had no food then?' said Nicholas abruptly. 'They are starving still? But you went on trying?'

'Over and over. Until we collected the bread they kept returning and started to use it. Four men have died.'

'It was poisoned,' said Nicholas. 'I asked you —' He heard his voice hardening and stopped. The others, who knew nothing of this, were turning their heads like three blackbirds.

John le Grant said, 'You stopped the pumps? Put water and food into Famagusta without Zacco knowing?'

'No. He didn't know,' Nicholas said. 'Or he wouldn't have agreed to a truce over Christmas.'

Tobie said, 'He didn't agree.'

'No,' said Nicholas. 'And as it turns out, it doesn't much matter. Even if he'd sent in a flock of prime cattle, they'd have known, after this, after St Hilarion, not to touch it. *Why didn't you protect that damned food?*'

That was addressed to Philip Pesaro. The captain said, 'What do you think I feel about it? I did all you asked. I had the emir watched. I had the bread guarded. Still he managed.'

'And you spoke to Tzani-bey?' Nicholas said.

'Oh, I spoke to him,' said the captain. 'He was extremely polite. He said my words were of pellucid clarity and great wisdom, but he knew nothing of poison, and if I wished to complain, he would be glad to take sherbet with you, or with Zacco. But the King hasn't agreed to the truce?'

'No,' said Nicholas. 'There is only the alternative that we spoke of.'

Pesaro's face altered briefly. Then he said, 'I remember. They starve. Or we save the honour of Genoa the Superb by attacking them.'

'Nicholas,' said John le Grant, making three words of it.

He had forgotten the others. He said, 'I'm sorry. I didn't tell you, because it was all planned to — to have its effect. There is no food in Famagusta. They are dying.'

'And you put food in, against the King's orders, before ever you came to Nicosia? And gave the King a false story? And now Tzani-bey has seized the chance to defy you and poison it? Nicholas, you fool, why don't you tell us?' said le Grant.

What would a truthful man say? You are too honest to be trusted with some secrets. One slip of the tongue would have betrayed all I was working for. There are more threads in this web than you even know yet; more than you could understand; more than you would ever forgive. Nicholas said, 'I thought he might agree to the truce. But now, you see, the only way to save them is to fight.'

'Then we fight,' said Astorre. 'I thought we'd agreed on it. And if they're starving, it'll be all the shorter.'

'They can still fire cannon,' said Nicholas. 'No. Let's sleep, and then get to the siege camp. I want to plan. I want to do this thing as well as it can be done, and with as few deaths as we can manage. And before anything else, I want to have a word with Tzani-bey al-Ablak.'

Chapter 38

T HE FOLLOWING NIGHT, Nicholas presented himself with
Astorre at the gate of the Mameluke camp, with its well-
defended ring of wagons and store-houses. He had chosen
an hour at which the emir would certainly have retired,
and might not have heard of his arrival. There was a chance, of
course, that he would be refused entry, but he didn't think so. He,
like the emir, was a commander answering straight to the King.
While Famagusta stood out, the emir should want no altercations
with Zacco. And the bey's communication with Zacco had been
cut. Philip Pesaro had seen to that. For four days, whatever courier
came to Sigouri, he would never get further. After that, it would be
different.

And, of course, if he was shrewd enough, the emir Tzani-bey
would want to bargain with him.

He received Nicholas and Astorre in his pavilion, and within a
reasonable time, although the quilted cover had barely been flung over
the mattress, and the pile of carpets was ruffled. To one side, dropped
unnoticed, lay a silver cup which had not contained sherbet. Among
the many odours was the one that, until this moment, Nicholas had
thrust forgotten deep in his memory. He bowed correctly, and sat
crosslegged on the cushions as offered, while Astorre, smart as
scissors, did likewise. The emir took his place thoughtfully opposite.

Seen in undress, in the vivid fabrics of winter, he was a smaller
man than he seemed in the field, despite the broad shoulders and
sinewy limbs. The sooty eyes, the olive skin, the coarse black mop
of the moustache gave little clue as to his origins. He spoke Arabic,
and fluent Greek, and had acquired reasonable French; he was well
trained in arms, and perhaps in other skills too: an education in
philosophy, divinity, science was open to Mamelukes, and not
always incompatible with brutish behaviour. But if he had a Christian past, it was not apparent in his dress: the crimson hat with the
kerchief wound lightly about it, or the striped Tartar tunic with its

oblique seam, or the coat he wore open over it, its buttons of gold, and the pious inscription of the tirâz embroidered in gold on its sleeve. He had changed his yellow leggings and boots for pointed slippers in soft Moroccan leather.

A long time ago, Zacco had sent this man, lord of his Mamelukes, to fetch Nicholas from the monastery to which the Venetians had brought him. For a year, an open breach with Tzani-bey had been denied him. But now, James was about to be King of all Cyprus and the final reckoning was close. Nicholas wondered whether, sitting there, the emir felt the same bitter exultation that he did.

Nicholas said, 'I will be brief.'

'Because time is short?' said Tzani-bey. 'I agree. The end of such a partnership as ours cannot be long delayed. It is fitting that words should be spoken.'

'Certainly,' Nicholas said, 'we have served the same master.'

The emir placed his brown fingers together. 'You dislike the word partnership? But what have we been but Frank and Saracen, yoked like camel and ass to the plough? You prefer sugar paste and old women, I'm told. Sugar paste, the smooth skin of young girls. Old women, such as the mother of Uzum Hasan; such as the wife who gave you your fortune; such as Marietta of Patras, the mother of the lord Zacco.' He turned to Astorre, who had growled. 'I do not criticise. A man's appetites are half the man, and must be known if you would understand him.'

He turned back to Nicholas. 'I say merely that I know nothing of your late wife. I know Uzum Hasan; and his mother, though courageous, is only his mouthpiece. That is not so with Zacco.'

'You surprise me,' said Nicholas.

The black moustache moved. 'Ah! He is a man with his own will, and much cleverness. She does not work alone. They work together. He must have successors. She gives him women. He prefers his own kind. She selects what will benefit him most. She is harsh. He succours. I am a counter in this game. You also. And when it is finished; when Famagusta is taken, what do you think will happen to you, and to me?'

'Emir,' Nicholas said, 'I was about to inform you. After Famagusta is taken, I propose that you and I face one another in public combat. In spite of what you have said, I should prefer to obtain satisfaction for past injuries from yourself than from either King James or his mother.'

'Spoken like a stout Latin,' said the emir. 'And you imagine you or I will survive to take part in this chivalrous duel? Or that if we do, the survivor will live?'

Nicholas said, 'After the duel, who can say? But it is my intention to attack Famagusta before the King even suspects it is happening. Do you dare join me?'

'When?' said Tzani-bey al-Ablak.

'Within three days,' said Nicholas.

'And we'll take it,' said Captain Astorre. 'With or without you, my lord. We're asking no favours.'

'That is fortunate,' said the emir, 'for I was of a mind to present you with none. Attack Famagusta, by all means. Indeed you must, for you have transgressed as well as I. The pious accusations of Captain Pesaro! Why do Latins profess outrage against poison? Every Frankish court uses it. In your time, Messer Niccolò, you have maimed and killed men in the flower of their youth: what disgusts you about murder in other forms? The King was glad enough to have Kyrenia delivered to him through fire and through illness: it spared lives, no doubt, in the end. Yet there raged the good captain, demanding satisfaction over a minor matter of bread, when I promise you that the King will pay far less heed to my action than he will when he hears of yours. I could not have poisoned the bread, my lord Niccolò, if you had not introduced it, against explicit orders. And if you take Famagusta, it will be because of these actions. These joint actions of yours and mine that have weakened it. The camel and the ass, Messer Niccolò. Do you not see now how we are being used? And how, by fighting each other, we are placing ourselves in Zacco's hands? Everything you have ever done against the Venetians, against the Genoese, against me, has turned to Zacco's personal benefit. When it is done, he will rid himself of us both. And you do not yet know what else you are losing.'

Nicholas smiled. He said, 'How can you guess what I know? You are wise. If you shared this assault, you might lose control of your Mamelukes' conduct, and for what they did, the King would have an excuse to retaliate. Also, we attack without the King's knowledge. If we fail, my company will take the brunt, during and after.'

'I fear,' said Tzani-bey, 'that whatever quarrel we have, there may be little chance after to settle it.'

Nicholas surveyed him gravely. 'I might survive,' he said. 'But of course, you may not wish to meet another man, except with a whip and when he is manacled. In which case, I may have to seek you out. I felt I should warn you.'

The emir Tzani-bey laughed. He said, 'I am warned. I am solemnly warned. How it rankles, that one small experience; that journey from Cape Gata to Zacco's succouring arms! I expected you to pay me for such attentions, my dear. Zacco does.'

'The slut!' said Astorre, once they were outside the camp. 'You should have let me nick them off him.'

'Fine,' said Nicholas. 'But you were there to protect me, not get us all slaughtered. At any rate, now we know the Mamelukes won't be with us, and I feel a bit safer. Not a lot, but a bit. I wonder if Abul Ismail has got to him yet.'

'Could you believe it?' said Captain Astorre, who preferred dealing with certainties. 'The little heathen thought you might combine against Zacco.'

'That's the point,' Nicholas said. 'It sounded as if Abul hadn't joined him. But maybe that was just how it was meant to sound. He's a tricky devil, our emir. Well, let's see how our private war is progressing. If John doesn't blow himself up, we have three days.'

John le Grant, when designing mines, had never been known to make a mistake, and he made none now, although he worked without sleep, as they all did. Until now, the siege plan had been orthodox. Now it had to be different. Despite the immense firing power of the city, they had to cease relying on simple blockade and long-range cannon. They had to breach the walls at close quarters and then scale them, using ladders and fighting-towers. For that, Nicholas had his own company, and another one hundred men picked for him by Pesaro. He had refused to take more. Whatever happened, the losses were going to be his responsibility. And if there were only two thousand living souls in Famagusta several days ago, there would be fewer now who were both soldiers and active. The men firing those guns, manning the walls, shooting from the high galleries might not amount to much more than half that number. Once they had been overcome, there would be no resistance. From inside, he or his men would open the gates, ready for Zacco.

The plan, therefore, had been made by John and Astorre, Pesaro and himself while the Mamelukes kept to their camp, and the King and his other officers prepared to hold Christmas at Nicosia. The weakest stretch of the walls had been identified. Stone and clods and faggots were brought and by day, under murderous fire, were projected at three different points into the great ditch that surrounded the city. By night they were added to, using the trenches. By day, the defenders shot fire-bolts into the rising piles of brushwood, causing them to burst into flame and reducing their height by half. Only on the south side, where his biggest battery of light cannon stood, did Nicholas build his bridge from the start almost entirely with stone. There, by the end of two days, the pile of rubble had reached two-thirds of the way to the top. Nearly high enough for an army to cross, or a siege-tower. The fourth day dawned, and wore through its hours of abrupt rain and mild, blustering wind. They all worked in scuffed brigandines and thick caps, most often with their helmets on top, and they were chilled with weariness, and grim and lewd by turns in the raw, brittle moods that went before battle.

John le Grant said, 'They're not fools, you know. Some of these fellows will be veterans of Caffa. They know what a feint is.'

'But they don't know what your little bundles can do,' Nicholas said. 'And they haven't the strength for heavy digging. There hasn't been a longbow on those walls for two days. Even if they suspect, they can't cover all three places at once. And there remains double bluff. We can always attack from the south, at a pinch.'

'At a hell of a pinch,' said John le Grant. Tonight, two of the piles, including the highest bridge, would be offered nothing but brushwood. The third, already made half of stone, would be raised through the night to ground level and across that, the attack would be made in the dark just before dawn. But long before that, he and John and two chosen men would have planted the mines with their fuses. When the army attacked, they would attack a collapsed wall, over rubble.

'If you've got your sums right,' Nicholas said. 'You don't look as if you could get anything right. Go off and sleep. It'll be dark soon enough. I've sent Pesaro away, and Astorre will keep the gunners at work.'

He watched John trudge off. On him and on Astorre had rested the burden of maintaining the guns, for the noise of the cannonade was vital to their stratagem. Even so, they might all be shot as they crossed the moat with their explosives, or wounded before they could leave, having planted them. Not a bad way to go, in a blaze of your own gunpowder. Either way, it would damage the walls, and Astorre and Pesaro between them might manage to scale them. John had made quite a serious attempt to stop him joining the mining expedition, and then had dropped it. After all, the work was done, and anyone could take Famagusta now who was willing to pay the price in lives from both sides. They would possibly attack with all the more force, to avenge him. Which was not to say that he intended to be a martyr tonight, if he could help it.

He slept a little, waking in his pavilion at dusk of his own accord. The rain had stopped its vibrating patter above him, although the air was laden with moisture and the planked floor of the tent moved on its bedding of grey sand and mud. It was not really cold. Except on the mountains, it never became cold in this island. It seemed a long way, though, from the summer perfume of myrtle and orange-blossom, the brilliance of white fluted marble, the wreathing steam, the orderly practices of the sugar-yards, the worksongs of the scything and the vintage, the glory of the sun setting, of the sun rising out of the sea. From a valley full of doubt and serpents and mischief, sunlight and another manner of glory.

He was glad that the design of his own life seemed, in the end, to be taking a shape that was not entirely haphazard. If, in the real world, you couldn't always realise the perfection of the model, the miniature, the diagram, at least the pattern had something in it to be pleased about. His friends would never lack: his Bank would see to that. Equally, his young step-daughters in Bruges would be protected. Here, if he didn't return, Primaflora would receive his letter, and his parcel, and would understand why he had done what he had done. And far away, his child would grow, in peace henceforth, with a father who would never know he was not his own, and who, with Nicholas gone, would have no reason for spleen or for bitterness. To be his friend, the boy would have Diniz, who would think him his cousin, and who would grow to gentle manhood in the vineyards of Portugal, and honour Tristão his father. And for a loving mother the child would have Katelina, who would cherish him now, and make what she could of her marriage, for the sake of what she had found in Kalopetra.

For himself, nothing bound him. He was vaguely surprised that what sense of loss he did have seemed to be connected in some way with Cyprus. It was the first place he had come to in his own right, with something to give. He had had no time to acquaint himself with his fief, twice seen, and well enough served by its own. Two-thirds of the land he had never visited. He had done what the Phoenicians had done, and the Byzantines, the Romans, the Crusaders, the Genoese and the Mamelukes. He had come for his own ends to this island, and used it. Of his conscious will he had given it nothing, except a single ruler where there had been two. And a sugar factory.

John le Grant said, 'Nicholas? We would go. They've broken through, and the tunnel is ready.' And very willingly, he got up to prepare.

They wore brigandines and soft boots and dulled metal helms strapped over a coif of thick wool. Each had a heavy satchel, a pick, and a knife sheathed at his belt. In addition, Nicholas carried a short bow at his shoulder, with a quiver. They entered the trench, leaving Astorre and Thomas and Pesaro standing silently at the entrance. Then they made their way crouching along it, their feet splashing through muddy water. The way was lined with long narrow carts, each piled with stone, ready for its last journey. They avoided them by touch, for here there was no glimmer of light. Overhead, the nightly bombardment had started.

The night was so dark that the end of the trench was perceptible only as a lightening of the murk, where the ditch of the town lay ahead. Before that, on their left, was a speck of light that didn't come from ditch or cutting, but from the tunnel so laboriously bored, and whose end John's sappers had now finally opened. The men who had pierced the final aperture were waiting to greet them: identifiable as a body of sweat, and heat and small movements that resolved into a murmur, a clink of spade and a clap on shoulder or back. Then they withdrew, leaving the task force of four at the foot of the ditch of Famagusta.

This was immense, and hewn out of bare rock, although clothed now with dirt and bushes and rubbish. Walking to the right in its shadowy depths, one would come sooner or later to one of the three great heaps of rubble that now patched it. Further south was another, and bigger one. But to reach the third, Nicholas bent low and, crossing the ditch like a lizard, reached the base of the wall and, in its shadow, followed it round to the left, John and the other two following.

No challenge came from above. The wall towered, impossibly high, its profile distorted by the hide-covered galleries. Designed long ago, the defences of Famagusta consisted of towers and wall-walks, battlements and arrow slits, without proper seating for cannon, or for the ventilation that cannon demanded. And on this stretch, in particular, there was no provision for crossfire. So the wall here was stronger and higher, and the manning of its towers stretched thinnest. Especially when the defending force was pain-fully slight. And especially when all its fire was being drawn to the southern stretch. All the time he was running, Nicholas was half deaf from the open-air thud of Astorre's guns, maintaining their pre-arranged and regular sequence. In response, there came the pop of fire from the battlements. Against that noise, their presence would hardly be heard, or the stealthy sounds John would make, sinking his petards. Or, later, the manhandling of the carts and the completion of the bridge that, sooner or later, would conduct the whole army across to a ruined wall.

Before he expected, his feet met blocks of stone, and he realised that he had come to the edge of the great sprawling tip of the infill. He waited, and stopped John and the others. Then, keeping close to the wall, they began the swift, careful climb over the rubble. Then John gripped his arm briefly and left him. One of the sappers went with him. The other went on and up, his hand holding his satchel. Nicholas stood, watching the place where the walls met the sky, and the towers, and the galleries, and unslung his bow and bent it.

They had practised this, through these last days. Pesaro knew Famagusta, and had found others who could describe the walls, and their thickness, and their character. From as close as he dared, John had surveyed them himself, over and over. He knew exactly where he wished to slot his explosive, and how long a fuse he needed to give it. The largest explosion would take place at the base, where he was now working and that, too, would take the longest to plant. The guns continued to fire. There were men, Nicholas saw, on the wall-top above him, although not many.

Twice, he saw the glint of metal and once, when the cannon fell silent, he heard distant voices. Beyond the opposite rim of the ditch lay the stretch of rutted wasteland that lay exposed and empty between Famagusta and the bivouacs of his army. Within it, grey and white in their sockets, lay balls fallen short of their target. They reminded him of his puzzles. He looked up suddenly at a noise.

Someone or something had tumbled. Someone. One of the sappers, from a precarious perch a third of the way up the wall. Nicholas could see where he lay, his limbs cocked and black against the paler stone of the wall. Whoever he was, he had had the guts not to shout. John? John?

No. John was ahead of him, softly running and climbing. Nicholas followed, his eyes searching above. The line of the wall-walk was not suddenly crowded. Of the two galleries he could see, he had already decided that one was unmanned. But the other had somebody in it. Several men, all of them at the end closest above them, and peering.

Nicholas caught John by the arm and they stood, their backs pressed to the wall. Far to one side, Nicholas now saw the remaining sapper, also frozen, his eyes on the gallery. The fallen man lay in the ditch, black upon black, and made no sound. A long moment passed. A gun boomed; then another, blanching the sky to the south. They stood in the shadows, unmoving. Then suddenly the sky above them flashed a stuttering crimson, and iron balls and lead shot rapped into the ditch from above, in a din of sharp hackbut explosions. Chipped rock flew, and the noise of it ricochetted from wall to wall of the ditch and then faded. He could hear John breathing, and in the distance, distinguish the dim shape of the sapper. He hadn't moved. They hadn't been seen. It had been a nervous reaction – a test – an act of meaningless defiance from the worn soldiers watching above. They waited. Voices came from the battlements, and a twinkle of steel. Voices from the gallery. A more authoritative voice from above, and dwindling noise, and an absence of glitter. And finally, only the gallery, silent again, with the men on duty watching unspeaking.

After a long spell, John touched Nicholas on the shoulder and pointed. Nicholas nodded. Then, as John began to climb to where the other had been, Nicholas felt his way to the fallen sapper.

He was dead. Nicholas knelt, then lifted him to the base of the wall and knelt again, to make certain. He felt a touch on his shoulder. The other sapper was looking at his partner. Then he whispered, 'Ser Niccolò? You too?'

After that scything spray of stone he had felt the blood, but whatever had cut him, it was minor. He shook his head. The man said, 'Broke my arm. You've to finish mine off. Master John's going up for the high one.'

A one-armed man was no use. Nicholas sent him off back to the tunnel, and glanced upwards. Master John, a natural chimpanzee, was always going for the high one. If he had been able to shout, Nicholas would have told John to let well alone. But he couldn't, so he climbed to the disabled man's perch, and began a sensitive, confident probe, and discovered quite soon how far the man had progressed, and finished the work, fast and easily. He had wanted to do this job with John alone, but miners were professionals, and didn't like laymen interfering. He cut the correct length of fuse, and set it, and lit it, and looked to see how John was doing.

The last mine was giving him trouble, partly because his position on the wall was so insecure. Once, this had been an expanse of perfect, squared masonry, but three years of siege and three months of heavy bombardment had produced enough gouges and bruising to offer some kind of a foothold. Where there was a real flaw was where the explosive itself was being planted.

Because it was difficult, John was unable, he could see, to keep watch around him. The battlements offered small danger: such was the slope of the wall that a man would have had to lean far out to see him. The penthouse above them was different. For the present, John's position was wholly in shadow and the bombardment, if the single, continuous shots could be called so, was lighting the sky from emplacements which, as they planned, left their stretch of wall in welcome shadow. It was possible that flares might be dropped. The real threat was more substantial, and imminent. Somewhere in that clouded black sky there was a moon due to rise very soon now. The disturbance had slowed them, and so had the loss of two workers. Now he and John were still on the wall and, caught by light, would be fully in view from the gallery.

John was not far away, and the stretch of wall that lay between them was not wholly smooth. Bit by bit, Nicholas began to inch towards him. He had progressed halfway when John raised his head and noticed. Nicholas pointed to the sky, made a gesture, and then clutched the wall, swearing. It was his year for skinned fingers, and climbing. It was the end of his year. He knew anyway what John was doing, which was setting the fuse. He waited, watching John's hands shielding the spark from the tinder, and the moment he finished, he turned to descend at his back.

He had taken two steps when the guns stopped.

It had happened before: a mortar would jam, overheat, miss its turn. If caught climbing you checked and adhered to the wall, until the bombardment resumed to cover the rasp of your movements again.

It was not a good place to have to wait, this time. His handholds were slight, and his footholds were almost non-existent: from the way John was clinging, he was worse off. And to the right and

above them were the black floor and lighter awning and sides of the
gallery, which contained three nervous men who had already let off
their handguns at random. His fingers scraping, Nicholas let his
mind dwell for a moment on fuses. They were lit, but they were
long. They had been deliberately set to defer the explosions. There
was intended to be time to descend, to retire through the covert
and to supervise the fast, careful infill of stone that would give
them their bridge when the walls fell. Of course, if a random ball
hit a mine, the wall would collapse before that, killing them, and
the men in the gallery.

He had cramp in both the hands stretched above him. On his
right, John suddenly changed his grip, grunting. The guns had not
begun again. None of them. Why? His ears sang. It was silent, and
they were marooned in the silence. He turned his head, and saw
John's face, tilted enquiringly. There was no point in waiting. He
jerked his head, and began to move down.

As if he had thrown a torch into oil, light exploded. Radiance
spread from the sky, and every object in the wide landscape stood
revealed by it. The wall, the ditch, the countryside, the camps, the
immobile guns and their gunners appeared painted with light on
stark vellum. Above, the cloud banks had parted: the moon poured
down its drenching blue brilliance. Below, a serpent of flame
wreathed the ground: a burning river of light which wound from
behind a dark knoll and spilled, slow as honey, towards the blind
gates of Famagusta.

He witnessed a great procession, black-edged, bearing hundreds
of flambeaux. The torches blazed upon tall tasselled banners, and
lit robes of white and scarlet and gold, borne by men with innocent
faces. In their hands shone the emblems and harness of sanctity:
gold rood glimmered, and monstrance and thurible; and the Crucifix from St Sophia itself rode the night like a ship on their
shoulders. Behind it, rank upon quiet rank, marched the Knights
of St John of Jerusalem, the white linen cross on their mantles. And
the singing was not in his head, but rose from the cowled, slow-
moving figures who edged the bright file with their tapers. Their
petition reached to the walls, clear and pure, low and rhythmic,
invoking God, and forgiveness, and pity.

Behind that, laden with food, came the wagons.

Nicholas turned his face to his arms, and was silent.

He couldn't tell when the singing came to an end, or the Archbishop's voice was first raised, addressing the city; offering it
God's peace and succour so long as the Feast of Christ lasted. He
didn't move until John's hand smote his weak shoulder, and John's
voice said, with desperate hoarseness, 'You thrawn God-damned
fiend of a Fleming!'

He lifted his head, and they looked at one another. John's face was furrowed with tears. Nicholas said, 'I didn't know if they would do it.' His arms over his head were an agony. He began to bring them down, still in a daze, and then remembered, with terrible clarity, where he was and what he was doing. At the same moment, he saw John's eyes suddenly widen. The fuses. The fuses must be put out, or the miracle that was happening out there would be useless.

They scrambled, this time, as if secrecy didn't matter, although of course it did. If they were seen, they'd be picked off. If they failed to reach the fuses in time, they'd be killed with the rest on the wall, and only a little earlier than the men of both sides who would open fire, without doubt, claiming treachery. They shared the task between them, descending first to the biggest mine, by the base of the wall. Next, the one fixed by the dead man. And lastly, the two higher up.

By then, the fuses were short, and there was no time to be nice about quietness. In any case, the wall-walk above them was empty. Only the hide-covered penthouse was occupied, and the three men in that were jammed at the opposite end, craning to watch the brilliant theatre; the exchange at the gates upon which their survival depended. Breathless and dizzy, Nicholas found and pinched out his fuse, and looked across gasping to John. The task was almost done. In a moment, they could take stock, and be thankful together.

Hampered by his terrible perch, the engineer, as before, was making slow work of it. As before, he had not wasted energy in trying to keep watch about him. Not as before, someone this time was leaning out, watching him from the gallery.

They had been seen. Not as yet by all three of the men, but by one who already had his handgun set up, aimed fully at John, and the flare in his hand to ignite it. Without thinking, Nicholas unslung his bow. Clinging with toes and with knees, he leaned into the wall and drew an arrow, fast, from over his shoulder. He had it nocked, and the hemp half drawn back when an extra flare lit the sky, and he saw how close the man was to firing, and how ill he looked, and how young he was: a hollow-faced boy, defending the walls of Famagusta.

Saw, then, that the hollow-faced boy was Diniz Vasquez.

Chapter 39

THERE WAS A moment when Nicholas could have released his arrow: he let it pass. He spoke John's name, to make him look up. Then he tossed his bow to the foot of the wall, and unslung and threw down his quiver. From the gallery, the feverish gaze of Diniz Vasquez held no recognition; but still he hadn't touched fire to his weapon. His two companions, readying theirs, crowded behind him. The boy said, '*What are you doing?*'

Nicholas said, 'We'd planted four mines, before we knew of the truce. We've just made them harmless. Bring us up: we'll tell where they are; you can check them.' His eyes on Diniz, he spoke in Italian. The boy's sunken face changed.

A man said, 'Treachery! The bugle! Sound the bugle! They're Zacco's soldiers. The bastards! The bastards!' He was weeping. He said, 'You thought these turds with candles were churchmen. D'you imagine those wagons hold food? Wait till we turn the guns on them all. Watch their powder blow up. Pour lead shot into their fat, meat-stuffed bellies. And as for you . . .'

It was his handgun that fired, not the boy's. But although he aimed it at Nicholas, it fired into the air, for the boy knocked it sideways and held it. The boy said, 'No. I've sent for the captain. But the men in that column are churchmen. Look. I know them. And look, too. The sides of the wagons are slatted. You can see baskets, Vito, not soldiers. And where is the ditch filled with troops? I see only two men, and a bridge too low yet to be of much use to anyone. You?' He was speaking to Nicholas. Behind him, distantly, a bugle was sounding, followed by the clank and shuffle of armoured men running. The conference outside the gates had ceased, and the torches wavered as men turned to seek the disturbance.

Nicholas said, 'It is a real truce. There is no army coming. Throw us ropes. You can hold us until you have proved it.' Above, the battlements had become crowded with men, and with the mouths of many handguns, pointing downwards. The voice of authority, heard once before, became louder and recognisable, and ceased at the battlements. It said, 'Bring these men up as far as the penthouse, no further. I will speak with them.' The voice of Napoleone Lomellini, last seen in the Lusignan castle of Kiti where he had lied, without pleasure, to try and prevent Nicholas from joining Zacco. And from which Zacco had freed him, on ransom, to take this post once again as his enemy.

There was no reason for a beleaguered host to be gentle when hauling two spies into their precincts, and in their anger and disappointment and fear, the men who handled the drag-ropes would have made sure, but for Lomellini, that these climbers never climbed again. Rising to his feet on the floor of the penthouse Nicholas staggered for a moment, while his wrists were being wrenched back and lashed; and knew from the way John was standing that he had received the same treatment. Where there had been three men there were now a dozen, although he could not now see Diniz Vasquez. Instead, Napoleone Lomellini stood there, no longer furred and beringed, in a helm and cuirass dented and dull in the moonlight. There was no softening in his stare. He said, 'Niccolò vander Poele. I am told there are bombards. Did you plant them?'

'I am the engineer,' John le Grant said. 'They're safe of themselves, I guarantee it; but of course, a chance shot could do for them. If you give me a torch I'll show your pioneers where they are bedded.'

'It seems fair,' said the Genoese captain. 'And if they blow up, you will know you have forgotten one. Take him away and get him to do as he says. Vander Poele will remain.' His face, grotesque in the torchlight, was little but bone, dirt and gristle. He turned to Nicholas. 'I am in no mood for anything but the truth. You will probably die, but certainly you will speak before you die. You, the head of a company, are here as Zacco's sapper? Explain yourself.'

'The King is in Nicosia,' said Nicholas. 'And all his officers. This attack was my own. He knows nothing of it.'

'But the churchmen did,' Lomellini said. 'They came to keep us in parley, while you assault us.'

'No,' said Nicholas. 'The church has come in good faith, and is innocent of any deception. I planned an attack, and have cancelled it. You will find we have lit and put out all our fuses. If you want better proof, ask the churchmen. You will learn Zacco has sent them. You will discover, I am sure, that he has forbidden me or anyone else to attack you. If you doubt me, ask yourself where is my army? If it were a ruse, they should be here to exploit it.'

'Except,' said the captain, 'that the wall has not fallen. You show us some mines: perhaps there are others still due to explode. Perhaps you have spoken the truth, but, waiting in vain, your friends may well think you dead, and carry out an attack to avenge you. What truce can we accept on this basis?' The skin of his face hung on its framework like the hides of the penthouse, and weariness and anger and pain scored his brow as if done by a hatchet.

Nicholas said, 'You have myself as hostage. Let my engineer go back and tell them so.'

The man called Vito said, 'My lord Napoleone. Let me have them both. They will tell me the truth.'

Through the hubbub of agreement that followed, the captain was gazing at Nicholas. He said, 'You would deserve it. You have given me no reason to trust you.'

'We are your prisoners,' Nicholas said. 'Since our story is true, we cannot change it. I will tell you this also. If you take this step, you will lose the offer of truce.'

The eyes of the captain turned dark, and if there was any emotion left in his voice, it was that of distaste. He said, 'From what I hear, that is not impossible. Very well. We stand to arms. I myself will inform the Archbishop what has happened. You and your engineer will be fettered, and will pass the night here, in the penthouse. If there is a cannonade, an explosion, you will be the first to experience it. If the night passes without incident, I may consider the Archbishop's offer. Meanwhile, the gates remain closed.' He paused. He said, 'In the event of trickery, you will know better than to hope for your life. If your story is true, you will be treated according to rank as my prisoner. Meanwhile, the penthouse must serve. I am afraid you have missed the last serving of supper.'

Nicholas heard the grim humour. From where he stood, he could see the long procession outside the walls, motionless now, and the wagons unshackled behind it. He said, 'At least, let the wagons come in.'

'Are we animals?' said the Genoese bitterly. 'That we forsake prudence, right conduct and dignity for the sake of our stomachs? In the morning, should this truce be agreed, leave will be given to draw in the wagons. Until then, we wait. We are accustomed to it.'

The night wore on. Stretched on the floor of the penthouse, Nicholas could glimpse the outside world between the battered planks. The procession from the Cathedral had not deserted the city but remained, silent now, on the land that lay before its main gate, its banners planted like wings about a central pavilion, its walls gold from the brazier within it. In front the Crucifix stood, warding tired men in sleep and in prayer. All around, torches burned; and in the centre candles guarded an altar. The carts, with their peaches and oranges, their almonds and grain, their meat and herbs and pulses and pies, their hens and walnuts and figs, their pumpkins and mutton and collops, their casks of sweet fortified wine stood unattended.

John le Grant, his face barred with light, said, 'Nicholas?'

'The answer is yes,' Nicholas said. John le Grant was not Tobie.

The engineer said, 'Someone waited three days, and told Zacco what you were doing. Who? The Patriarch?'

'Possibly,' Nicholas said. 'And, of course, Tobias Lomellini is Treasurer of the Knights Hospitaller of Rhodes.'

There was a silence. Then – 'And if they hadn't come?' the engineer said. 'You would have gone through with it?'

'I thought I was going through with it,' Nicholas said. He felt bewildered by the ironies of what had happened. He felt terror, and relief, and perplexity, and a consequent inability to plan anything.

John le Grant said, 'But the boy? You believed him safe in Portugal?'

That was another matter. After a while, Nicholas said, 'He left letters. He thought he was going there.'

'So?' said the engineer.

'So Bartolomeo Zorzi,' Nicholas said. 'Diniz escaped so very easily. He would go to Famagusta, where he thought his Genoese friends would help him. He didn't know, as Zorzi did, that the harbour was sealed. Zorzi, you see, is a Venetian. And he has an older brother who tells him, sometimes, what to do.'

'I'm sorry to hear it,' said John le Grant. 'So the lad has been in Famagusta ever since? Then I expect Diniz owes you his life. You and Zacco.'

'Provided,' Nicholas said, 'that they take in the wagons tomorrow.'

'They will, now they have you,' said the engineer. 'They will use you to taste what they've been given. You may die like those men of Pesaro's.'

'Before Famagusta surrenders? No,' said Nicholas. 'That is why I am here. I'll be kept alive until then. After that, you're going to help Diniz.'

'Your dying request?' said John le Grant.

Nicholas turned on him a look of chilly surprise. He said, 'Are you my employee? Am I the head of a banking house? You help Diniz Vasquez or I dilute the shares and merge with the Strozzi. Until you've worked with Lorenzo, you don't know what discontent is.'

'I don't know about discontent,' said John le Grant, 'but I know what its opposite is. And I hope you do. Because for once, I will admit, you deserve it.'

*

Despite the stiffness and soreness they slept towards dawn, and so missed the colloquy at the portals; the ultimatum; and the exchanges which led, soon after daylight, to the opening of the gates of Famagusta, and the entry, drawn by many weak hands, of the carts with their soft, fresh, redolent burdens. The gates closed. Outside, the pavilion was packed and placed in its wagon, and the file reassembled, creased and pallid in daylight, to make its way back to beds, warmth and comfort.

With them walked four thin men in rich-coloured rags. The Genoese, invited by Zacco, had freed a group of their merchants to pass Christmas with James in his Palace. In exchange, Famagusta was to keep two men of Zacco's as surety. One was the Arab Abul Ismail, who had come to offer his skill as a doctor. The other was Niccolò vander Poele, recently arrested, and at present a prisoner. No special diet (mentioned the captain of Famagusta) would be claimed for these two Lusignan hostages. The lord Bastard had provisioned the city. What had been given, being sound, would amply nourish them.

Nicholas woke to the flash of a knife; and found his bonds being cut, and John le Grant already stretching and groaning beside him. Then Napoleone Lomellini came, and informed them succinctly of what had happened, and left. Sickness and pride, in the grey light of day, were set in his unchanging face like a mask. The soldiers who flanked them in his place looked no better.

John was to be released: Nicholas himself was to be marched to the citadel. It was what he had hoped. He had not been prepared for John to stand on the floor of the penthouse, complaining. John said, 'I'm not leaving. If they keep you, they might as well keep me. Unless, of course, Tzani-bey's poisoned the food again. Don't worry. They don't understand Flemish.'

'Some day,' Nicholas said, 'You'll find yourself somewhere where someone does understand Flemish, and they'll cut your ears off, and then all your red hair, wherever you grow it. You've to go back and get hold of the Patriarch and convince those four Genoese that no rescue is coming. It's hardly three weeks to Epiphany. This truce is going to end then. And unless the city knows that it's hopeless, they might simply pick up the whole war again. And that isn't what I risked my skin and yours for.'

'I don't know,' said John le Grant. 'You wouldn't make a bad pioneer if you had a bit more time for practice. All right. You've persuaded me. What do I say about Diniz?'

'Don't upset the Venetians,' Nicholas said. 'Leave that to me, when I get back.' He watched the engineer go, and then turned and let them take him up to the wall-walk, and down into the beleaguered city where, once, the Genoese had planned to keep him hostage while his company fought for Carlotta. Where now he was to be incarcerated as a hostage, a prisoner, an enemy. As a favourite of James, and therefore the most powerful lever for peace and for charity – did they know how to wield it – that the Genoese had ever been granted.

A hundred years before, richest of all cities, concourse of merchants and pilgrims, haunt of courtesans, sink of unnatural vice, pride and luxury, Famagusta housed a hundred thousand citizens within its two miles of walls, and was a place of fine squares and great houses, of mills and warehouses, shops and monasteries, stables and shambles and forges, barracks and ovens, merchants' villas and loggias. A royal palace. A cathedral. A hospice of St John. And three hundred churches.

With the wars of this century, it had shrunk by a third. That meant that one would expect, close by the walls, dilapidated streets and ruinous houses, robbed out for their stone. A piazza made into a drying-field. A warehouse turned into stables. A mill housing poultry. A marketplace harrowed for beans and melons and cucumbers, and vine-covered shacks and sheep pens and orchards among the stumps of great houses.

One would expect to pass those kind of suburbs while lifting the eyes to what still lay in the centre, busy, well kept, and profitable. What could still be seen, in the splendid roof-tops and towers of magnificent buildings. A Genoese city, run on good, efficient, prosperous Genoese lines.

Flanked by his guards, Nicholas stepped down from the wide, crumbling wall-alley into a dark arena of rubble, of stench and of silence. Of the weeds of dilapidation there were none: they had been eaten. Where they had been was raw earth, smothered with the rubbish and dust of bombardment, and pitted with curious mounds and recesses which Nicholas recognised only slowly as rank upon rank of recent, random, haphazard graves. The houses here were ruined and roofless and unoccupied.

Because he had slowed, the man behind struck him a blow. 'Heartburn, is it?' he said. 'A congestion after yesterday's eating? That was the Armenian church. Them that died of typhoid, that's where they were put. There's St Anna's. The women liked to go there, but the priests were the first to die. These last months, the women have taken it over, giving birth in the annexe and taking and bricking the babe up as soon as it breathed, and before it got found and eaten. Do you think God punishes men who eat their own children, Zacco's pageboy? Do we not only die, but go to hell for what we have suffered?'

'Raffo,' said the other man. 'He is hostage. We have to escort him safely.'

'I will. I will,' said Raffo. 'St Francis' monastery, do you see it?

Beautiful, isn't it? A bridge joins it to the old Lusignan palace. The
Lusignans called it their own royal chapel. There are how many
monks? Four, perhaps. They keep the infirmary for those who die
clean of infection, from a falling gable, perhaps, when your serpentines find the right range. And there is the covered market. Not
covered: the flying stone ripped the awnings. And not a market
unless someone finds a birthed dog, or a bird. The roofs are
covered with lime to bring in the birds, but the birds are intelligent:
they know when there is nothing to feed them. Only the worms
from the graveyard, but we are there before them, aren't we?'

'Raffo,' said the other man.

'And the Cathedral,' said the man. 'Do you like our Cathedral of
St Nicholas? The Lusignan used to crown themselves there. King
Peter – was it King Peter? – who used to stamp his feet weeping if
the cook had no oil for his asparagus. We bury our noblemen there,
except that they have to lie at present without coffins. I would take
you in, but for the smell. And there is the Citadel. You will find
people in the yard of the Citadel. Didn't you wonder why all the
streets were empty? All the hearty citizens of this city who can
walk are at the Citadel, because that is where they have locked
up the food, and are distributing it. Otherwise they are afraid we
will kill one another. As if we would so dishonour our mother
republic!'

Nicholas said, 'You had the choice of surrendering.'

'There is a ship coming,' said Raffo. 'We will never surrender.'

Diniz Vasquez was not visible in the shouting throng of people
with sacks, boxes and baskets that crowded the inner yard of the
fort of Famagusta, although Nicholas scanned them all as he was
led across it. He didn't see where their baskets were filled, but he
observed that soldiers had been appointed to escort each laden man
to his house, and that the man's chin would already be glistening,
from the raw food that he chewed as he hastened.

Some were unable to chew, or to hurry. Some carried enough for
a family. Or for those, he supposed, who were too weak or too sickly
to walk here. There were monks moving slowly in pairs, bearing
great crates of foodstuffs between them, with a soldier on guard at
their shoulders. The soldiers stared at the food, and kept swallowing.
He learned, when he asked, that they had eaten already, from stores
given out in the barracks. It explained, he thought, the absence of
Diniz. Nicholas followed where he was led, and climbed the stairs
to the captain's own quarters. Once there, his escort opened a door,
saluted, and left. After a moment, Lomellini rose and came forward.

He had the look of someone felled by sleep, and just wakened.
Nicholas said, 'You have enough to do. Tell me where to stay, and
I will go there. The food is clean, but I will taste if you want it.'

'Whether it is clean or not, they must eat,' said Lomellini. 'I want to speak to you.' Leaning on the edge of his table, he let his hollow eyes rest on Nicholas. He said, 'It seems that you are more our enemy than your master. You planned to attack, while he was planning his truce.'

Nicholas remained where he was. He said, 'Neither of us knew what the other was doing. I believed he would not agree to a truce. I thought an attack the most merciful answer.'

'Merciful?' said Lomellini.

Nicholas said, 'I knew you were starving.'

'And he did not?' said the captain slowly.

'No,' said Nicholas. 'Or he wouldn't have offered his truce. He will not do it again. He has only to wait.' He paused and said, 'This is not the time to discuss it, but if you will use me, I can help you. What you must do meantime is regain your strength. And I have to ask you a favour. I have a relative here. A youth. A boy called Diniz Vasquez. I would see him.'

The captain stood up. He said, 'A room is being prepared. You will be taken there. And yes, the youth Diniz Vasquez has been to see me. He has asked me to send you to his lodging. It is in a house outside the Citadel. He has this privilege, since his kinswoman is dying.'

'My lord, he has no relatives here. It is Diniz Vasquez, the Portuguese youth, I would see,' Nicholas said.

'I speak of Diniz Vasquez,' said the Genoese wearily. 'The vassal you chained to your dyeyard. He escaped, and was joined by the lady. You didn't know of this? A young woman of good family who has not deserved, I am sure, the privation that she has shared with him. You know her, of course. She was a supporter of Queen Carlotta, and Genoa. She was on Rhodes when the father of Vasquez was killed. She came to Cyprus with us both on the ship that was waylaid by Mamelukes. I am not sure whether, as a hostage, you should be allowed near to these people who – although you claim them as relatives – have no cause that I can see to regard you as a friend. But I have placed the boy on his honour. He will not harm you. And the young lady, alas, has not the strength.'

Nicholas said, 'What is her name?'

'Are there so many?' said the captain, his lip curling. 'Her name is van Borselen. Katelina van Borselen, a married lady of Flanders.'

The young squire who led Nicholas this time through the city was rough and angry, but also sick. At the first sign of dissent or hesitation, he fetched his mailed fist full across his captive's bruised face, splitting his lip and causing all his contusions to bleed again. Immediately after, he turned aside to a doorway and vomited.

Nicholas smelt fresh meat and lemons. Unless Napoleone took care, the food he had given out would bring its own troubles. His mind noted this fact among others, ticking efficiently on like a water-clock. The rest of him was suspended in limbo. Diniz was here. Here and starving. That was catastrophic enough. But Katelina? *Katelina?*

He didn't really believe it, all the time he was being dragged through near-empty streets which were no longer silent, but filled with curious brawls, or outbursts of squealing or, what he had just heard, the sound of terrified retching. He didn't believe it up to the moment that he found himself outside a half-house that had once been graced by a classical loggia. Behind its wreck stood a fine double door with an architrave, and behind that an elegant court-yard, its fountain and pillars and statues smashed to splinters by heavy stone shot.

In one wall was a door, and a womanservant disappearing inside it. She gave them a terrified glance, and then bolted. The young Genoese picked his way over the wreckage and, gripping Nicholas, arrived before the same door as it opened again. The man who opened it was Abul Ismail the physician.

The squire said, 'Zacco's other fornicating fat hostage. I'll leave you. Don't think you can get out. I'll be waiting.'

He retreated. Nicholas stood. The Arab said, 'I am sorry.'

'I am not sure,' Nicholas said, 'what you are sorry about.'

The brown, smoky eyes were not especially compassionate; merely lucid. The doctor said, 'I am here attending a patient, and I have to tell you her story. You left the young lady Katelina van Borselen at Rhodes. She was about to sail home to Portugal. On the eve of her sailing, she learned from a spokeswoman of the Queen's that news had come in from Cyprus: that Diniz Vasquez her husband's young kinsman was trapped in Famagusta. She elected to join him. He survives. But her house was struck by a ball from your cannonades.'

He had been feeling cold for some time. Now he felt not only cold but quite bloodless. He said, 'She is very ill? I would have brought her away. Why did Diniz not send me word when it happened?' His voice, he noticed, remained perfectly steady.

'Death has made an appointment with her,' said the Arab. 'Her heart is great: she might live to your Feast of Epiphany. Meanwhile she cannot be moved. She would find no better fate in Nicosia. She would not have you informed, in case it placed your own freedom in jeopardy. But now God has brought you; you are held here a captive, as she is. She fears for you, but is joyful, for now she will see you.' He waited, and then said, 'She will depend on you. Sit. Come in when you are ready.'

Aphrodite, Aphrodite. He said, 'I must go, if she is waiting.'

Chapter 40

SHE LAY IN a room from which all the wood had been stripped, save for the pallet beneath her. What wouldn't burn still remained: bare walls muffled with incongruous tapestries, flooring tamped over with carpets. There was a stand of bronze inlaid with silver, looted perhaps from a rich merchant's house, and a cut of marble propped on an empty brazier and supporting the physician's jars and boxes and bottles. There was a brazier newly in use, and still smoking a little. The air in the room was not yet warm.

From her throat to her feet she was covered in velvet and gold, furs and silk and jewelled embroidery. From her throat to her feet, the housings of her single, stark pallet were royal. The plain sheets that should have served it were also there, but torn into strips and padding and squares, and laid on a tray on the ground. The door closed behind Abul Ismail, and Nicholas looked at his father's wife.

Her face was ivory. Upon those sturdy, well-defined bones the clear, even tint seemed translucent. The hollows under her cheekbones were sepia, and the skin which sank into the new, heavy arcs of her lids, and the shadows beneath ear and chin. Her brown hair, newly combed, coiled ash-dull among all the rich fabrics. But the eyes on him were shining as at Kalopetra, when he had been constrained to leave, and she, for a while, had stood to stop him; stood as close as the flesh on his body. The Fontana Amorosa. Whosoever drinks from that, they are thirsty for ever.

He said, 'They have just told me.'

When he knelt, his eyes were level with hers; he saw them moated with tears. Her hand wanted to rise: he found and made a tent for it with his own. He said, 'Are you in pain?'

'I don't know,' she said. She smiled, arrogant eyebrows clenching, tears sliding into her pillow. She said, 'I used to be. Not now. Not now.' And her breath, as she smiled, began to catch in weak, involuntary sobs; so that he bent over her, his cheek against hers, his arms embracing hers in spectral and impotent comfort. Then he felt her lashes stir at his cheek, and raised his head and kissed the place where they lay, and then her brow, her throat and her chin, while her lips went on smiling. When he drew apart, she said, 'Your face. Your face is marked. Have they hurt you?'

'No,' he said. 'I would have come before. I didn't know. You should have told me.'

'How could you have come?' she said. 'They would have killed you. When I could walk, I would climb the wall and look across to your camp. Then so many fell sick.' She stopped, and then said, 'There were flies. I remembered what you said. Their lives were short, too.'

Nicholas said, 'This should never have happened.'

Her tears had half closed her eyes. He cupped her cheek in his hand and pressed his kerchief under and over her lashes. She said, her eyes shut, 'I chose to come. They told me Diniz was here.' She opened her lids. 'I would rather be here than in Portugal.'

He shook his head, taking her hands again. She said, 'Yes. When must you go?'

'How could I go?' he said, smiling. 'For the length of the truce, I'm a prisoner. They can't stop me seeing you. Unless you get tired of me.'

She had begun to weep again. She said, 'It's just weakness, I'm sorry. Diniz has been so good, and I am so happy. Is that wrong? Is it wrong, what we've done? Will you be punished?'

He knew what she was asking. He said, 'You talked to someone?'

The weeping had stopped. 'A priest,' she said. 'He is dead, now. He said that this is my reparation, and I need fear no other. But you –'

'Simon will never know,' Nicholas said. 'If we've betrayed him once, he has betrayed you many times. And if some greater authority decides the offence requires atonement, then I can only say that I shall pay the cost of it willingly.'

He couldn't tell whether it was enough to comfort her. She smiled, her eyelids heavy. He studied them, smoothing the fragile skin of her hand, and saw them falter shut, and heard her breathing soften and settle. There was no other sound, outside or inside the room. After a while, he let his head sink on his arms, deep among the chilly, metal-chased velvets.

Perhaps he slept. He roused to a touch on his shoulder and Abul Ismail stood at his side. The Arab said, 'Come. Eat and share some of our wine. Your escort will wrench you away soon enough.'

This had been the house of a banker. There were two servants still: the woman he had glimpsed, and a steward more frail and more sullen. The Arab said, 'They blame me for guarding the food. But if they gorge, they will die. The boy Diniz is wiser, though weak. All his food has gone to nourish the lady, and to placate the woman, so that she would stay here and nurse her.'

'And the lady?' Nicholas said.

Long ago, outside Kyrenia, he and this man had come to know a little of one another. He would never be able to read Abul Ismail, as he found he could decipher so many. It had pleased him, that discovery. He had wondered, also, how much the mediciner had been able to guess about his own mind and nature. Whatever it was, he knew he would receive the truth now, however unpleasant, and was aware of nothing but thankfulness that it should be Abul Ismail here to tell him.

Abul Ismail said, 'She was starving before the beams fell on her body. Her limbs lack feeling: she would never have walked. Now she seems to have little pain, and little hunger, although she takes what the boy gives her, and today, we have improved upon that. You must not blame the lad either. He tells me he implored her to let him beg her release, but she refused. She wished to share his fate. She wished to die under the flag of St George, and not the flag of the Lusignan. She is loyal to the allies of her husband, however weak a provider her husband has been. But she has said nothing of that. I am only guessing.'

Nicholas said, 'For what you are doing, I hope God or Allah will reward you. Tomorrow, I will have her taken to Nicosia.'

'No,' said the physician. 'Forgive me. I have said this to the boy. She will die very soon. Such a move would cause her pain, would shorten her days, would deny the stout heart that has kept her here all these weeks. Now you are here, she has all she wants. Take her to Nicosia, but only if you will not do her the service of remaining here, in this town, at her side.'

In face of that, there was no question, now, of disturbing her. The questions he had to ask now were practical ones, to do with comfort and nursing, and the mediciner answered them. Presently Diniz himself, released from duty, walked into the kitchen. The boy said, 'You came.' He paused. He said, 'Senhor Abul will not permit me to dine quite so lavishly.'

'You know what would happen if you did,' the doctor said equally. 'Here is soup. Sit. How are the pains?'

'Worse,' said Diniz. He looked at Nicholas. He said, 'It is a crude business, starving. Did you not know we were here?'

Nicholas said, 'No. I was told you had escaped. Your note said you had gone home to Portugal. I thought you were at home, and the demoiselle also.'

'Your manager helped me,' said Diniz. 'The Venetian, Zorzi.'

The food he had eaten burned in his throat. 'Not by my orders,' said Nicholas.

'No,' said Diniz. 'She said that would be so. You saved her in
Rhodes.'

Diniz Vasquez was like a drawing of himself, done by Colard in
black ink and white powder. There were sores of malnourishment
at the edge of his mouth, and his skin was crossed with premature
folds and lines, like a map of the face of his father. Upon it were
visible the prints of many different thoughts, and some conflict.
Nicholas said, 'Whatever she has told you, it is true. What you
would do for her, so would I.'

'But,' said the boy, 'you married Primaflora?'

'Do you want her?' said Nicholas.

The silence stretched. The boy said, 'Who would want her now?
She is alive?'

Nicholas said, 'But for Primaflora, the food would not have
come today.' It was the truth, in its own macabre way. Stiff with
disbelief, the boy's dark eyes stood in their hollows. Nicholas went
on talking persuasively. 'So the apportioning of blame, as you see,
is not simple. If you wish to go to Nicosia, I could arrange it. I will
stay with her.'

A smell of hot soup filled the room. Like the mark of a slap, an
arc of pink sprang across each of the boy's whitened cheeks. He
watched the bowl, and seized it, and then, meeting the physician's
eyes, took the spoon and fed himself, slowly. After a very short
time, he stopped, and laid the bowl down. He bent his head, his
arms hugging his body. The Arab shook his head, and then rising,
touched his shoulder. 'Have patience. Let it cool. Eat as if it were
poison.'

'Is it?' said the boy.

'No,' said Abul Ismail. 'I have tasted it. Since I came, I have
tasted all I have been asked to. Messer Niccolò has offered, I'm
sure, to do the same. Your body will grow whole again. Why not
do as he says, and let him send you to Nicosia as an envoy?'

Diniz Vasquez looked up. 'To spend Christmas with Zacco?' he
said. His eyes went to the door and returned. He said, 'I would
stay where she is. You will be under guard, for your own safety.'

'Ser Niccolò will be kept, as I am, in the Citadel,' said Abul
Ismail. 'But I am allowed in the streets, with my escort. Once I am
known, and my work, they are unlikely to harm me.'

'I can pull weights,' said Nicholas. 'And carry loads that men
here are too weak to manage. I can be your assistant, unless my
presence would harm you. Food will strengthen their anger. They
know I planned to attack them.'

'They know that if they harm you, their food will stop,' said the
Arab in his precise, guttural voice. 'Work, and they will not resent
the food you eat. On the other hand, there will always be hotheads.
There is one.'

A handgun had fired in the house. Diniz sprang up, but Nicholas reached the door before him, wrenching it open. Outside, smoke and stench met him together. The body of their steward lay on the floor in a pumping fountain of blood. Beyond it stood the young squire who brought him, the smoking tube in his hand, his face stamped with rage and with loathing. The reek of ordure voided from all his clothing. Then he saw Nicholas, and flung the hackbut away and drew his sword with a wet, shaking hand. 'Poisoners!' he said. He took a cumbered step forward, and Diniz Vasquez strode into his path and stood unarmed before him.

'Well, you too!' the boy said. 'We're the same, even the women. Thank God we have water. Come with me, and we'll see to it. Fresh food on empty stomachs, I'm told. I've made them eat everything I do, so I can tell you the food isn't tampered with. We have a doctor, though. Senhor Abul?'

'An old story,' said the Arab. 'Sweat and blood, a true bath of honour. Should starvation be any less honourable? What did the lady your mother have made for flux in her household? Elder flowers in vinegar? Rue in breadcakes? I have something as useful. Come with me. Messer Diniz, I will need you. Messer Niccolò . . .'

Nicholas knelt by the body. He said, 'I will deal with it. Is the woman his wife?'

'She won't mourn him,' said the Arab. 'She will stay. She has seen worse, I dare say, these many months.'

As he had done on the journey to Rhodes, from that time onwards Nicholas gave up his will, his designs, and his planning, and lived from hour to hour simply to work as he was bidden.

Each day he came twice to the banker's house and sat in the sickroom, warm and better furnished now, and kept his lover company; sometimes talking, sometimes in silence. With the coming of fresh food, and the medicines that Abul had sent for, she seemed to rally her strength. She slept, with something of her old determination, in order to be awake when he came; and often she wanted to talk: about Bruges; about the past; about all the foolish exploits that had made Claes the apprentice notorious – the jokes with the gun and the waterwheel; the chases, the skating; the escapade with the ostrich. The first time they had met, he had fished her headgear out of the canal. She had been nineteen, and affronted. 'You were so kind with the children,' she said. 'And Felix. You have that gift, to be liked. Gregorio, the lawyer who fought Simon for you. Your engineer and your doctor. Diniz is ready to take you as friend, or will be soon.'

Once, she spoke of the day of the bombardment. 'The balls didn't often come quite so far. I expect you aimed at the walls.'

'Wherever we aimed, they always fired in another direction,' Nicholas said.

'It was a marble ball. They showed it to me later. There were inscriptions half buffed from the surface, but you couldn't see what shrine they came from.'

Whichever it was, it had brought death to her. 'Aphrodite or Pallas Athene?' Nicholas said lightly. 'I think I prefer either to the Heart as Love's Captive. Since you spoke of it, I've found out the story. The Knight Coeur is a failure. And the lady Sweet Grace is never liberated.'

'Not entirely a failure,' she said. 'The lady escapes from the Manoir de Rébellion. But of course, the three enemies of Love trap her eventually. Shame, Fear and Denial.' She smiled. 'We have escaped them.'

The rest of his time, he spent with Abul Ismail.

The sick who had no one to tend them were spread through the inner, inhabited core of the city, in the monasteries, in the hospice of the Knights of St John with their double chapels. There they were tended by the Brethren of the Order, and elsewhere by those monks who had survived. Still, their strength and their knowledge were limited, and the physician in daily demand. Among the patients were the injured and sick of the army. Once they had had their own barracks, their own surgeons. Now they stood to the walls, and if they fell, had no more help than the civilians had.

The others in need were those still in the care of their families. The roofs were most often not their own: long since, the community had drawn in from its perimeter, sharing its water, its food and its warmth, and distancing itself so far as might be from the walls and the thud of the cannon.

All these people, Abul Ismail visited. He was given a boy, and two soldiers, and a handcart. In that, he took the box of his instruments, and the pills and plasters and powders which took Nicholas and himself half their sleeping time to boil, to mix and to stamp. Every second day, food and medicine were delivered from Zacco and, strictly watched, the doctor was allowed to speak with the courier who came with the convoy. Nicholas was never given that privilege.

For him were the heavy tasks. Now, with new carts, he could drag both water and food to where they were needed. He took the night soil and the corpses to the south wall, where the north wind would scour them, and ground off the flesh of his hands, digging trenches. He never lacked for both helpers and escort, but men on starvation diet take time to respond to good feeding, and their willingness far outran what was left of their strength. And even good food was not proof against the malignance that hung in the air, in the rotting soil, in the ill-washed vessels from which they ate and drank. Typhoid, dysentery struck every third household, and the marshes from the north sent their evil on the sharp, wintry wind. Once, Abul Ismail said, 'You do not eat. I have been watching. You are subject to marsh fever?'

'I am subject only to grief,' Nicholas said. He would have said it to no one else. It happened to be true.

Christmas came, and High Mass in the Cathedral of St Nicholas. The last carts from King James had contained candles, and they stood in front of the altar: stout towers of wax that once would have been raided and eaten. Even so, their numbers seemed to have dwindled. Abul Ismail now had better stuff for his plasters than cobblers' wax.

Katelina had shared in that Mass, carried there by Diniz and Nicholas on a stretcher of rafters and carpets. Latterly, a greyer tinge had coloured her skin; and the scented rosins Abul threw on her brazier disguised a different turn in her illness. But always, welcoming Nicholas, she was washed, combed and seemly, and had formed out of her obstinacy, it seemed, a frail steely courage that endured where others succumbed.

She returned silent from that communion, but roused to the dinner that Abul, Diniz and Nicholas spread in her chamber. She took, too, the first cup from the flask of good wine that Nicholas had found for her. *'Droit de prémices,'* Nicholas said, clasping his hand over hers to keep the stem steady. 'But then, we had that already.' And she drew his hand closer and laid her cheek on it, so that he knew she, too, was thinking of Bruges, when she had allowed him that right, and of Ghent, and of a place by a waterfall. When he lifted his head, Diniz was looking at him. Then he looked away.

After that, he was commanded to the Citadel, to dine with the captain. With Napoleone Lomellini were other Genoese noblemen he had come to know, and sometimes find ways to baulk, when common justice appeared to be slighted. All were shabby; all had about them the cleanliness of icy well-water, spoiled and fetid with the reek of the city, that nothing but fire could dispel.

The meal was stiffly formal. At the end, the captain said, 'I have had a message which concerns both of our hostages. Since this is a Christian festival, I have not sought, Messer Niccolò, the company of your colleague. I wish, therefore, that you will convey to him all I am about to say.'

Since he became first their prisoner and then their enforced guest, Nicholas had rarely met all his present masters; and had thought it best not to seek their company. Today, he had suspected that something was brewing. It was possible, of course, but not likely that Zacco had grown tired of his Christmas truce. His clemency had earned him the regard of the West and would, surely, last until Twelfth Night. It was likelier that Zacco had grown uneasy over his own unforeseen absence. Nicholas had asked to remain. He had been held, in the first place, because he had been caught carrying out what must now appear an ill-judged and irresponsible foray. An act of defiance, in Zacco's terms. So now, perhaps, Zacco wished to replace and recall him. In which case, Nicholas meant to refuse.

Napoleone Lomellini drew out a paper. The labours of his protesting stomach had corroded his dark skin with pustules; he was still sharp of bone and languid in movement, but something of the family vigour was visible. His voice, as he continued, was brusque. 'You will know that James of Lusignan is passing Christmas at Nicosia with four ambassadors from this city. We have heard from them. Talks have taken place. A document has been drawn up, and has been sent here to me for consideration. My colleagues and I have discussed it, and we propose to recommend that its terms be accepted. It will be signed on the sixth day of January. Since it affects you, I shall read you its contents.'

So suddenly it had come, all they were working for. Talks. A document. And acceptance. Nicholas sat perfectly still, his heart shaking him. 'Yes, my lord?' he said.

'I am glad to tell you,' said Napoleone Lomellini, 'that it is the Bastard's intention to lift the siege of Famagusta. This will be done fourteen days after this treaty is signed, and will be followed by a truce of one year.' He looked round at his companions, and then at Nicholas. He had kept triumph out of his voice but not, perhaps, a shade of justifiable satisfaction. 'That is the gist of this document, and I have instructed our envoys to agree to it.'

Nicholas felt as if turned to stone. In all his plans, he had never let himself contemplate an outcome as vicious as that. Zacco had tired of the siege. Zacco had thrown the Genoese twelve months of a truce. St George and the dragon still flew from the walls of Famagusta. For another year, the Genoese could continue to squat in the wreck of the city, clutching the rights to their ruined, foundering colony; promoting nothing; permitting nothing to flourish, either of theirs or the Bastard's. Another year for the divided island to suffer. For himself, another year of detention, at Zacco's whimsy. And at the end of the year, the siege to start all over again.

He realised that he had not thought of it before as detention. He said, 'The lord Abul and I are therefore expected to return to the King at Epiphany?'

'That is for your employer to say,' the captain said. 'Under the terms in this document, two of the Lusignan's men will stay here, and four of the city's will stay in Nicosia until the rescue fleet comes. We are allowing our four men to remain at the Palace. The Bastard may wish you to stay, or to replace you. I shall now read –'

'Rescue fleet?' Nicholas said.

The captain looked up. 'That is the condition of the truce,' he said.

'*Rescue fleet?*' Nicholas repeated.

The Genoese looked angry. He said, 'Do you interrupt your own lord? Ours is a Republic which cares for its citizens, and will support them against a common enemy. There is a relief expedition on the way; carracks which bring arms and soldiers, as well as provisions. It will arrive here before the testing span of this treaty has ended. And when it has come, the armistice will begin, and the hostages on both sides will be freed. That is all, surely, that concerns you?'

'But –' Nicholas said. He drew a long breath. 'You expect a fleet? What fleet? Genoa has nothing to spend. There is no fleet moving or building elsewhere. Every port, every chance ship confirms it. *What fleet*, Ser Napoleone?'

'What do you know of the Republic?' said Lomellini. 'If one single vessel enters the port of Famagusta in the fourteen nights that follow Epiphany, the siege will be lifted. That is what this document says.'

'And if no ship comes?' Nicholas said. 'Or coming, cannot enter in time?'

'It will not happen,' said Lomellini.

Nicholas waited. 'It will not happen,' said the captain once more, and less fiercely. 'But if no ship enters, then Famagusta surrenders to Zacco.'

He could not, at first, even think of his regular call to Katelina. He walked round and round his small chamber, haranguing the walls. Abul Ismail, who had come for news, retired to a cushion and sat, his hands on his lap. At the end, having exhausted himself, Nicholas looked at him, stopped, and then with a groan, dropped to the opposite corner and put his head in his hands. He gave a laugh. 'I apologise.'

'You received a fright,' said the Arab in his judicial way. 'It is natural. If you now set your mind to do so, it will tell you all the components, reasonable and unreasonable, of your fury. This in turn will render you able to master your body. Tell your hands to be still.'

Around the knot of his stomach, everything seemed to be shaking. He told it to stop, and it didn't. The Arab said, 'Why do they think a fleet is coming?'

'Because they don't know what is happening out there,' Nicholas said. 'Their precious Republic has ruined itself over the Naples war. The Fregoso and the Adorno are tearing Genoa apart with their rivalry. The Bank of St George have already advanced Famagusta all they can spare: they have nothing left. And the seas are blocked anyway with the Turkish fleet. They've signed a treaty of surrender, and they don't even know it.'

'It isn't signed yet,' said Abul Ismail.

'It will be, in eleven days,' Nicholas said.

'You are confident,' the Arab said. 'But what you have told me will now be known to these four Genoese in Nicosia. Indeed, is this not what you advised in the first place? Convince them no fleet is coming, and they will bow to surrender? And if that is so: if they are so convinced, why does this document talk of fleets and of truces?'

'They *are* surrendering,' Nicholas said. 'But they have to obtain the leave of the Commander of Famagusta, who still believes in a fleet. Hence the conditional clause. It will make no difference.'

'Unless a fleet comes,' the Arab said. 'Come. The times have been hard on you, these last weeks. To a mind delighting in tactics and devices, grief is not a familiar factor, but it cannot be excluded from any man's calculations. In the simplest of games, one person at least knows the pain of doubt, or defeat. It can be of high value. Success seldom teaches what is worth knowing.' He waited, but did not seem disappointed that Nicholas made him no answer. The Arab said, 'Visit your lady, and then I will prepare you some easement.'

There was nothing of that Nicholas wished to discuss, so he answered only the question. 'Thank you, no. I have seen Tzanibey so reduced.'

'That remedy I do not offer,' said the Arab. 'Although I should advise you not to scorn it. Unreasonable tasks sometimes need unreasonable tools to perform them. No. I think you deserve other excesses.'

It proved to be some extremely strong wine he had hidden. It allowed Nicholas a long, hard night's sleep, followed by a splitting headache in the morning.

Chapter 41

O N THE DAY after Epiphany, Famagusta heard that the treaty had been sworn before the Haute Cour in the Royal Palace of Nicosia, and that the fourteen days of extra truce had begun. A year of peace with the city would follow, provided that, as the city expected, a relief ship or ships arrived before the end of that period, passed the chain and entered the harbour of Famagusta.

If such a ship or ships failed to enter, the city would capitulate by the time January entered its twentieth night. In that event, the ambassadors stipulated that Famagusta would be governed henceforth by James of Lusignan and his Christian lieutenants, and not by Mamelukes, Moors or other infidels, who were to have no authority over Famagustans. The lord James had undertaken that the Sultan in Cairo should not contravene any article of the pact, and his emir Tzani-bey al-Ablak had been asked to give his word to that effect. The Genoese city of Famagusta did not intend to be at the mercy of Mamelukes.

By then, released from stricter vigilance, Nicholas had been able to move from the Citadel to the house of Katelina, and soon Abul Ismail was permitted to join him. As the life of the city began, haltingly, to achieve some simple routine, Nicholas spent his time more and more on the business of medicine. He was good with patients, as he was good with children. He watched Abul Ismail in silence, and helped without flinching. He learned, among other things, what alum served for, besides dyeing. The rest of the time he spent with Diniz, and Katelina.

Once, it had seemed that the candle of her life would burn only till Christmas, and that it was towards that single point that she was spinning out the last hours of her life. Then it became apparent that she was holding to some other lodestar.

She believed in the ship, and was waiting for it. Abul Ismail had said that she was loyal to Genoa, and it seemed this was true, whatever Carlotta had done to her. She had lived among Genoese merchants in Bruges: Anselm Adorne had her respect and affection. Genoa was the home of Simon's company, and he owed his start in Madeira to Genoese money and skill. And through Genoa, the ally of Portugal, she could repay her debt of indifference to Tristão Vasquez, who had married Simon's sister, and her gratitude to the boy Diniz, on whom her eyes rested, half sleeping, in a strange, touching pride.

In the sickroom or with Diniz, Nicholas never threw doubt on the arrival of Katelina's dream fleet. Nor, in the long hours of her sleeping, when he and Diniz shared the same room, did he say more than he thought might reassure the young Portuguese. Any plan for the future depended on the term of the girl's life now ending, and neither could speak of that. Sometimes, though, the boy would now talk of the past. 'You were in Rhodes. The demoiselle spoke of it. She said my father was killed because of her.'

'Because of me,' Nicholas said. 'We had a misunderstanding, the demoiselle and I, and, for a while, she wanted to punish me. The Queen thought my life was in peril, and she should get rid of my enemies. She thought too, she would recover Cyprus. She didn't want Madeira to rob her of vines and of sugar, and your father had tried to do that once. So she had no compunction, I think, in allowing your father to be lured into danger, so that the demoiselle would leave the City to follow him. The assassins meant to kill her. They didn't care whether or not they killed your father or you.'

Diniz said, 'The demoiselle said my father was killed by the Queen and someone else. She didn't say who it was. She said the Queen and somebody else made sure she knew I was in Famagusta. She said you went to Rhodes to find out who killed my father.'

'They were only hired assassins,' Nicholas said. 'Astorre helped me kill two of them. The Queen was behind most of it. She needed mercenaries.'

'But you were already with Zacco when they tried to kill the demoiselle at Kalopetra,' the youth said. He paused. 'Was that why you married the lady Primaflora? Did she warn you of the new plot, and needed protection?'

'She told me where to find Katelina,' Nicholas said. 'I should have stayed, then, to make sure she left safely for Portugal. But I was being hunted as well.'

'But you didn't love Primaflora?' the boy said. 'You wouldn't have married her otherwise?'

'I shouldn't have married her otherwise,' Nicholas said. After a moment he said, 'What do you think you've been watching, these weeks?'

The boy's eyes were dark and level, dense as the Arab's. 'Compassion?' he said. Leaving, Nicholas crashed the door open and then, remembering, closed it soundlessly in the last inch of its movement. The word followed him into the courtyard. When, calmer, he went to her room, Katelina was awake, and he was able to expend on her all that Diniz thought he was capable of.

The following day, Diniz apologised. Nicholas heard it in silence. She was worse, today; her breathing irregular, her words sometimes confused. Latterly, she had been in pain. Today, Abul Ismail had stayed at her side, and now Nicholas had been banished from the sickroom.

Diniz also had stayed, and had found his way out into the yard, and the broken pillars of the loggia, where he had found somewhere to sit out of the wind. Today it was cloudy but bright, and the thick, accustomed smell of the city was better than the hospital smell in the house. Coming out for the same reasons, Nicholas found him there and heard him make his excuses.

His mind was not especially on Diniz. He said, 'You needn't be sorry. None of this is your fault, and a good degree of it is mine, which is why I lose patience easily. I have nearly insulted you, several times, by promising that you will forget all this when you are home again.'

The boy's eyes fell. Nicholas dropped to sit on a block, and picked up a stone, and took out the knife he had been given back. Diniz said, 'You made carvings in Bruges.'

'It passed the time,' Nicholas said.

A short silence followed. Diniz said, 'Katelina says you think we are cousins.'

Both his hands stopped. 'Katelina?' he said.

'She asked me to call her that. She says your mother was Simon's first wife. I call him Simon,' he added.

'He is your uncle,' Nicholas said. He had resumed carving again. 'Did she say anything else?'

'She said that Simon denied he had fathered you, and this was the cause of the feud, and that it would get worse, unless something stopped it. She said that when she was . . . that Simon would think you had killed her. Would think that you had killed my father. That unless something was done, he would kill you.'

'And?' said Nicholas.

'That was all,' said the boy.

That was all. Nicholas looked at what he had been doing, which was nothing very much, and laid down the stone and the knife and, clasping his knees, looked at Diniz. He said, 'Has it shocked you?'

'About your mother? It happens everywhere. It makes me feel different,' Diniz said.

'In what way?'

'We may be cousins. If Simon is your father. If he is, why didn't he believe . . .?'

'It's a long story,' said Nicholas. 'But I was glad for a lot of reasons that you didn't aim true in the dyeyard.' He smiled, watching the boy's face turn crimson. 'I didn't blame you.'

'So why? Why send me there?' Diniz said. The flush was still there, and in his voice something that might have been an appeal.

'Not from spite. Some day I'll tell you. Diniz, you are not to take part in this feud. Katelina was warning you. All she says is true: Simon will blame me for everything. But you can't protect me, no one can. He is beyond believing the truth, especially when the truth itself is not black and white. I expect she has asked you to tell him everything that has happened, and persuade him to make friends and thank me? But she knows, too, in the depths of her heart, that it isn't possible. He is beyond reason, Diniz. What you must do is help him forget; plunge him in business as your father would have done; save him from ruining the rest of his life hunting for vengeance.'

'He'll kill you,' said Diniz. 'She says he'll try to kill you unless one of us gets to him first.'

'He might,' Nicholas said. 'That isn't my fear. My greatest fear – my greatest fear is that I shall find I have to kill him.'

At that point, Abul Ismail came into the yard and said, 'Messer Niccolò.'

They had turned her pillow so that it was fresh, and the tawdry finery had long since been replaced by a smooth, pale quilt that reached to her breast. Over it, the slender bones of her arms showed under the sleeves of her bedgown, with no roundness of flesh left anywhere. The brown hair, the dark brows and, when he took her hand, the open brown depths of her eyes were like molasses drained from white sugar. Lady Sweet Grace.

He said, 'I have a complaint. I've been kept out.'

Her lips were leaden, but able to smile. 'He is a bully,' she said. 'Nicholas. You must hide. I can't wait.'

But for Diniz, he couldn't have followed the thought. He said, 'Simon? I know. I've thought about it. I shall be careful.'

Her fingers stirred in his. She said, 'I can't wait. Abul has told me. When the siege ends, you can leave Famagusta. Go somewhere safe. The King, Astorre will protect you.'

Peace of mind was all he could give her. 'I shall,' he said. 'And Diniz will get safely home. I shall see to that.' He waited again. He found he couldn't pursue the thought to its proper conclusion. He couldn't distress her with his own, raw, terrible dilemma.

She divined it. She said, 'You are wondering about our child, too. If you think it right, I want you to take him.'

He couldn't stop himself showing what he felt. Then he didn't try to stop it. Katelina said, 'I hadn't forgotten.'

There was so little time. He got back half his control, and then all of it. He said, 'We spoke of this. No. Simon must never doubt who his son is. Katelina, who could care for him? Would Lucia take him, now Tristão has gone? Or Tasse – perhaps I could get Tasse. She looked after –'

He stopped. Tasse, adoring, elderly Tasse, had looked after Marian on the journey that led to her death. Katelina said, 'I wrote a message, to Lucia, in case you thought of that. And to Simon. There is another note, just a record. If the child stayed with Lucia, Diniz would be kind.'

'Diniz doesn't know?' Nicholas said.

'No. I've told him you think I should have called my son – what is it?'

'Arigho. It's only a pet name for Henry. And Arro is the little name.'

'Like Claes,' she said, and fell into still, smiling silence. Then she said, 'And Tasse. She looked after Marian. Marian was afraid for you, too. She said you couldn't protect yourself. She saw you learn how.'

His hand cradled hers on the coverlet and he studied each wasted finger, rather than have his face read. He said, 'She brought me up. I used to dream that, one day, I would come to her with the girl I was going to marry.' He raised his head slowly. The hollow eyes on the pillow were filling with tears. He would never have said that to anyone living. He had said it because she was dying; and she knew it. The greatest balm he could bring, brought on a knife-point.

The door opened on the bearded, calm presence of Abul Ismail. He said, 'She is in pain, Messer Niccolò. Give me a moment.'

Their hands fell apart. He bent and kissed the tears in her eyes, resting his lips in their hollows. Then he straightened and left. Standing waiting, he heard the noise of the city oddly magnified, like the clamour of a classical triumph, with guns and bells, drums and trumpets and piping. And the roar of many voices. The door of the sickroom opened, and the doctor came out. He said, 'I need your permission, and the boy's. She is in pain, but wants to endure it. What she may endure now is, however, nothing to what she will face very soon. I would not inflict on her either this knowledge, or this eventual indignity. I ask your leave to remove her pain when it begins to grow past her bearing. You have seen me do this for others. She will drift into sleep.'

'And never waken,' Nicholas said.

'It may shorten her life by a day,' said Abul Ismail. 'I would allow her this peace, if you can. Is the boy there?'

'I shall fetch him,' Nicholas said.

But Diniz was not in the yard when he sought him, or anywhere to be found in the house. In a rage of despair, Nicholas flung open the doors to the street and he was there, running towards him, and the clamour he had heard was real, and louder than he would have thought possible. And Diniz, arriving, flung his arms around him sobbing and said, 'Oh, tell her! Let us tell her! It is coming!'

Then Nicholas held him off, and said, 'What is coming? Diniz, what is it?'

'A ship!' Diniz said. 'A round ship from Genoa. The fire-signals are burning. The ships in the harbour are letting off rockets. We told you it was coming, and you didn't believe us. Zacco drew off his vessels. It will come in. It will save us. The siege will be lifted. And Famagusta stays Genoese!'

Within Nicholas, all the clamour fell silent. He said, 'What is the name of the Genoese ship? Has anyone signalled?'

'Yes!' said Diniz. 'It's the *Adorno*.'

And that, then, was what she had been waiting for.

He said, 'We shall go and tell her. Diniz, she is dying.'

'Then she will die happy,' said Diniz. He stopped. 'You won't be angry with her? She said you and Abul would be set free. The treaty ensured it.'

'I shall be angry neither with her nor with you,' Nicholas said. 'The doctor has something to tell you. Make your decision. Whatever you want, I shall agree to.'

The door of the sickroom was open when they got there, and inside was quietness, and no movement except Abul Ismail's, withdrawing a slow, smoothing hand from the pillow. No movement at all, not even of breathing. '*No!*' said Nicholas in a whisper.

'No?' said Abul Ismail. 'God is great, God has called her. Is this a man who prates of mercy and would deny it another for his own sake? She has won the Truth; she is in Paradise. In the night does she see the sun, and in the darkness does she see light. When God decreeth a matter, it is not for man to deny him.'

'I would have said farewell,' Nicholas said.

'The loss is yours and not hers,' said the Arab. 'She learned that the vessel had come, and was glad, for she said that the young man would speak for her. And she left you her soul, and her son. To hold such a cure, a man must aspire to the crown of humanity. You know, and only you, if you are worthy.'

'No,' said Nicholas. He did not look up.

Her soul and her son. A boy in Bruges, he had been older in wisdom than Katelina. He had let himself fall in with her will, and had not seen that she had no will, but was calling, alone, for a friend. From that had come all this misery. All he had given her was bodily joy, and a life that had ended in pain, among strangers. He said, 'I have destroyed her.'

And: 'Look at her,' said Abul Ismail. 'When you die, you should wish to die thus.' And Nicholas looked, and saw for the last time the face of Katelina van Borselen, into which Abul Ismail read contentment. And it was true, and in that lay the tragedy.

She lay, her eyes closed and smiling, surrendered to death like the moth, symbol of passionate love, which yields its life to the taper that lures it.

She had died, who was not his beloved, and he had killed her.

Outside the sealed city, the advent of the round ship *Adorno* roused the kingdom. One by one, the north-west balefires blossomed in warning, and St Hilarion, Buffavento and Kantara added their signals. The news came to the capital, where James of Lusignan struck the bearer to the floor. It was his mother, arching her brows, who said, 'Zacco. Desist. I think you will find this has been prepared for.'

Outside a grand villa in the same city, a priest in an assortment of ramshackle clothing stopped his mule in the gateway, descended by lifting a leg and bellowed to the first person he met, which was Tobie. 'Are your ankles too weak for your belly? There's a Genoese ship on the way. Zacco's off to the coast with his officers. If you want to see it, start riding.' He retired, lifted a leg, and was carried bobbingly onwards.

'What?' said Loppe, materialising.

'His lordship the Patriarch of Antioch,' Tobie said, beginning to run. 'There's a rescue ship on its way to the Genoese. If it gets into the harbour, it'll stop the surrender. Tell John. I'll get the horses.'

'I heard,' said John le Grant. 'What are you expecting to do about it?'

'Get across to the bay, and watch what happens,' said Tobie. 'It'll make a change. It isn't really a day for the beach, but I'm tired of my sewing. And it would be nice to know who might be on board. Or hadn't you thought of that?'

'Jesus Christ,' said John le Grant. Then he said, 'How is she coming?'

'Round the Karpass, because of the wind. She'll hold off as long as she can; we won't get much of a view, and they are saying shore batteries couldn't do her much damage. Zacco's men will either catch her at sea, or not at all. And once in the harbour, she can unload all she's got through the sea-gate.'

'That's about it,' said John le Grant. 'She would expect, maybe, to get into Kyrenia, then see the Lusignan flag on the castle. At any rate, our Genoese friend has a chance. Round ships can come fast on the north wind, and our galleys will have the worst of it, facing them.' He paused, and said, 'So it's up to Mick Crackbene then, isn't it?'

'Against the wind?' Tobie said.

'We discussed it with Mick,' le Grant said. 'Of course, plans get changed.' He didn't say what he was thinking. *In Trebizond, Mick Crackbene worked for the Genoese against Nicholas, in the very same ship he's now sailing.*

Loppe said, 'The sea-tower in Famagusta is high. Lomellini will see a relief ship is coming. Master Nicholas will have some sort of warning. And he is a hostage, and sacrosanct.'

'Right enough,' said John le Grant. 'Just let's hope that no one forgets it.'

For a month, he had played a master's game lacking a master. Released from Famagusta, he had retired to Nicosia, as Nicholas wanted. Astorre, denied his attack, had stayed with Thomas in camp, uneasily brooding. Philip Pesaro had remained in Sigouri, stupefied with relief, and only briefly touched, it appeared, by Zacco's displeasure. That had been reserved for Nicholas and even there, le Grant wondered how far it was genuine.

The King had forbidden Nicholas to attack, and when defied, had found a method of saving him. His concern for Nicholas was possibly real. But there were, patently, other advantages. No one, knowing the Patriarch, could doubt that, after a day of his voice, Zacco was sick of him. By allowing the Church to intercede, Zacco had ended by pleasing almost everybody. It would not do, however, to let Nicholas think so. Nicholas, therefore, was stuck in Famagusta over Christmas, and needn't hope that Zacco was going to miss him.

That Diniz Vasquez was also in Famagusta was not common knowledge, although le Grant had told Astorre, Loppe and Tobie. Specifically, neither the King nor the court had been informed. Tobie, back in the villa and cascading with loud, screaming sneezes, had proposed marching at once to the dyeworks and shaking Bartolomeo Zorzi by the hand: le Grant dissuaded him. 'No. The boy did well at Famagusta, and Zorzi had no right to do what he did. Nicholas wants us to let it alone. He'll have it out himself with the Venetians.'

'And when will that be?' Tobie had asked. 'After he's had an axe sunk in the opposite shoulder? What can he do for anyone in that graveyard of a city except catch their rot and pass it on to us in the long run? If he'd talked hard enough, they'd have exchanged him.'

John le Grant had said nothing. He had seen some of the men of Famagusta. He had been appalled, as had the rest of the court, at the emaciation of the four ambassadors sent them by the city, but he had not been surprised. He was not surprised, either, when all of them took to their beds within a day of arriving at the Palace.

He hung about the Palace a good deal himself, as he was entitled to do, being the King's only contact with Astorre's army. He called on the Latin Patriarch of Antioch and had a brief, one-sided exchange. Occasionally he saw Primaflora who, from serving Carlotta, had turned her training to attendance on the King's mother. On their first encounter, she had drawn him abruptly into her chamber and asked him to tell her about Nicholas. He had told her the story, and reassured her as far as he was able.

After that, she didn't seek him out, having no doubt more direct news from Zacco. In Loppe's care, the villa ran smoothly without her. After a week, Loppe handed the task back to Galiot, mentioning that business required him in Kouklia. Tobie had been inclined to object, but le Grant helped him pack and assemble his travelling party.

Loppe had had least to say about the incarceration of Nicholas. His journey, John assumed, was either because of genuine business, or because he found it trying to wait in the capital. It irked John himself, the easy carousing of the long, sprawling festival, the noisy pastimes of the court, the King's sudden tempers. He wondered how Loppe would know if Nicholas was sent back before Epiphany, or if there were news of a worse kind. Then he realised that Kouklia was in daily touch with Salines, and Salines, unobtrusively, with Nicosia. He wondered, again, who or what Loppe was eluding.

Then the ambassadors found their feet, and were to be seen at table, and occasionally with the King's special officers. Returning to the villa one day, John le Grant said, 'Something's happening. The Bailie of the Secrète has been with them twice, and Podocataro, the lawyer.' The next day, he said, 'There's rumour of some sort of pact. If the King lifts the siege, I'll mine his privy.'

'We could go home,' Tobie said. 'He'll have broken the contract.'

'I'll leave you to tell him,' said the engineer.

Then the terms became known, and the day the treaty was sworn, they retired to the villa and drank all night to celebrate. Surrender in fourteen days, unless a ship got in. And Nicholas had been sent for. The King regarded his penance as over.

Next day, as silently as he had gone, Loppe returned. The day after that, Tobie was commanded to the Palace and returning, seized Loppe by the arm and marched him into the workroom John le Grant had devised for himself, where he scowled at them both. 'All right. Did either of you know about this?'

John le Grant laid down what he was working on. 'About Nicholas? What? You know all I do.'

'He's written asking to stay in Famagusta for two weeks. The King knows the boy Vasquez is there. He's livid.'

'I didn't tell him,' said John.

'Nicholas told him. In the letter. He also said he felt responsible

for the Flemish lady who, being royally connected, ought to be
well looked after.'

'What Flemish lady?' said John le Grant. Loppe stirred, then
said nothing.

'You didn't know. Katelina van Borselen. Famagusta is full of
God-damned Flemings. She's been trapped there as well as the boy.
Simon's wife as well as his nephew. He says she's ill. I say it's a
trick to persuade him to stay. I think they're trying to hold him.'

Loppe said, 'He can't be harmed, he's a hostage. What is the
King going to do?'

'Well,' said Tobie. 'It began with striking his spurs off for
disobedience, but ended more on the lines of he could stay and rot
for two weeks for all Zacco cared. I thought the Flemish woman
was sailing for Portugal? That was the point. So that Simon
wouldn't come looking for her.'

Soon after that, the news of the round ship arrived: the round
ship called the *Adorno*.

On the hard, muddy ride to the shore, no one spoke very much.
They joined up with others: Philip Pesaro and a group from
Sigouri and later, a familiar glitter of feathers and armour –
Astorre, pounding across from the camp with Thomas behind him.
Every villager who had a mule seemed to be making his way that
day to the beach north of Famagusta, by Salamis. The King was
already there, with half the court and the Mamelukes; and a tent,
shivering in the wind, had been set up but was not so far in use.
For in view, over the ruffled grey sea, was the round ship from
Genoa.

She was large, and low in the water, and the size of her guns showed
quite clearly, as did the red and white flag of St George, glinting in
occasional sunlight below a cloud ceiling harried by blustering wind.

The wind was strong, and from the north. When Zacco's two
war galleys appeared, they seemed hardly to move. The long shells
of the hulls were wiped from view by the heave of the sea, so that
the prow platforms and tents of the poop could no longer be seen,
and only the pennanted masts told where they were, until they
rode into view once more, in a steam of spume from the bite of the
oars. The round ship raced towards them, her canvas taut. Her
bows plunged, shouldering aside streaming seas upon which the
galleys slid and swooped and plummeted like seal pups caught in
the wash of a bear. The *Adorno* fired, and the watchers saw two
patches of smoke, and heard the flat thuds, and saw the dash of
white water between the galleys. One of them had broken away and
appeared to be attempting to struggle upwind. 'They'll have naphtha,' said John. 'And they've got guns. But with that sea and that
wind, the round ship'll outrun them. She'll be in Famagusta before
they can touch her. So where in God's name is Crackbene?'

'There,' said Loppe's quiet voice. He was looking neither to the right nor the left but out to sea, where a round ship was coming in from the south-east, her sails shuddering, her course designed to intersect with the Genoese just outside the harbour. The *Doria*, their own ship, brought by the Venetians and Zacco from the Abruzzi, and a veteran now of the war for which she had been chartered. On the mast flew the red lion of Lusignan, and at the helm, they knew, was Mick Crackbene.

Tobie said, 'Will he do it?'

'Look at his guns,' John le Grant said. 'We designed them for this. They can even be trained upon galleys.'

The crowded strand where they stood was full of noise. It beat about them on the wind as men shook their fists and shouted, faces shining. Zacco stood on high ground, his hat pulled off, his hair blown free of his sable-lined cloak. Beside him, the face of Rizzo di Marino was as intent. Beyond them was the emir, Tzani-bey. Captain Astorre, surveying them all, turned back and caught what they were talking about. 'Crackbene?' he said. 'Knows his job. Knows his mind. And sticks to the rules. A contract's a contract.'

And John le Grant said, 'But if the *Adorno* gets in, the contract falls to be renegotiated, wouldn't you say?'

The *Doria* fired. She let off a salvo of three guns, spaced so that the first ball fell well in front of the Genoese ship. The last was much closer. The Genoese ship replied, firing wide. She was taking in canvas. One of the galleys had vanished from sight. The other had turned and was waiting for the Genoese, standing off on the landward side with her crossbowmen and hackbutters lining her port rail, fore and aft. The Genoese round ship turned to present her poop guns to Mick Crackbene, and the galley sprang into action. In a sequence of thuds, the galley fired into the round ship, her shot exploding into the broad flush planks of the prow; arching over the tumble-home curve that should have protected the gunners. At the same time, her oars sent her spinning into a turn, so that her iron beak pointed outward, ready to gore the towering sides of the Genoese.

For a moment it looked as if the classic capture was about to take place: the low, lean greyhound was about to sink its teeth into the boar. Then the prow guns of the *Adorno* spoke in unison with those of her poop. To seaward, the ship of Mick Crackbene shuddered within a column of smoke which blossomed into red flame. To landward the Lusignan galley disappeared behind a column of spume and of fire. '*Christ!*' said Tobie.

'Look,' said John. 'Look what they have done.'

The galley now limping to landward had been bait. While she presented herself as a target, the second galley had rowed against the wind north. Now she had turned. Now she swayed on the towering waves to the north, and glittering on her prow were the slim copper tubes that had faced the ship of the Order that had brought them all from Rhodes to Cyprus. She had the wind, and the fire. At a spark from her tinder, a sheet of flame could envelop the Genoese. And advancing steadily from the east, limping a little, but with the lines of his guns unimpaired and intact, was Mick Crackbene on the *Doria*. Tobie said, 'The Genoese. She's slowing. She's not making a run for it?'

'She's coming to rock,' John le Grant said. 'There's a reef parallel to the shore. It joins all those islands. The galley behind her has pushed her in, and she's got to change course and then turn, or she'll overshoot the entrance to the harbour. But Mick is blocking her way. That's why he left it so late. He couldn't have done this while she had all that sea room. Look.'

The *Doria* had fired again. This time the ball made a hit. They heard the crash, and saw smoke rise from the forward quarter of the Genoese round ship. At the same moment, a rush of flame came from the rear, followed by a flock of fire-arrows streaming into the rigging. One of the sails burst into flame. 'The second galley, in place at her rear,' said John le Grant. 'And there goes the first, firing into her flank. You see, because of the rocks, she can't reply to Mick's cannon. All she can do is tack forward and crash into him, which would be suicide for them all. He's got her.'

'Has he?' said Tobie. 'How many men will she carry?'

'The Genoese? Less than fifty, most likely. That ship's full of provisions, not soldiers. Good co-ordinated fire might have wrecked the two galleys, and she could have got on course before Crackbene arrived. But she didn't. Listen. He's hailing her.'

'She won't give way?' Tobie said. 'She can't. She's got to get in, or she throws Cyprus away.'

'What do you think she is?' said John le Grant. 'A ship from Olympus, a martyr? She was sent by the Republic, and she's made an honest effort. But behind her is a galley that can burn her down to the waterline, and beside her is Crackbene with a genius for sailing and guns he has hardly used yet. They can give in, or they can die. They have no hope of succeeding.' He looked at Tobie. 'Have you forgotten? They are the enemy.'

'I think I had forgotten,' Tobie said. Across the water, the loud hailers were blaring and squealing as they had in the winter, when Tzani-bey had caught and herded the Order. From the shore, they couldn't hear what was said. But they saw, clearly enough, the galleys take their place on each side of the Genoese ship, and the big ship of Mick Crackbene approach and cast out its grappling irons, and then its nets. Soon the seascape seemed to be occupied by nothing but the two great ships clamped together, with a web of men and weapons passing glittering from the one to the other.

Then the *Adorno*'s sails rattled down, and the flag of St George on her mast trembled, and drooped, and slipped down its cords. Then, running free as a dart, the lion of Lusignan replaced it.

Zacco shouted. They could hear his great cry, and see the flash of his hat flung in the air, and the brown silk of his hair whipping free as a flag against his glistening eyes, and the bright joy-stained red of his cheeks. He swept his friends into his arms and the shouting multiplied and reverberated on and on, up and down the beach and through the distant war-broken theatre of Salamis. John le Grant's powerful fingers dug themselves into Tobie's arm. He said, 'That's it. That's the only ship that's ever going to arrive here. Come the end of the fourteen days, Famagusta surrenders. Nicholas emerges. We get paid. We can go if we want to.'

Tobie was watching Loppe, who had suddenly disappeared to the shore, and was now coming back rather more slowly. He said, arriving, 'The *Doria*'s put off a skiff with a message. The Genoese ship has surrendered. With the King's leave, Master Crackbene takes the captured ship and his prisoners to Salines. Six are dead. The rest will be dispatched north to Nicosia, to coincide with the official surrender.' He broke off and stepped back, for the King had broken free of his friends, and was running alone down the strand to the messenger. He passed beside them all, seeing no one, his eyes fixed on the sea and the skiff, and the two great ships and the galleys beyond, all of them flying the Lusignan flag.

He had been weeping. He let the tears lie on his cheeks, and men cheered as he passed them, their young golden King who had won his crown at last. Who had seen enacted before him the last skirmish in the war which had now given him his own longed-for kingdom of Cyprus.

Loppe watched him go. Loppe turned his eyes from the victorious, the vibrant, the magnificent figure and looked instead towards the chill, battered walls of Famagusta. He said, 'I would not like to be a man in that city tonight.'

Chapter 42

PRIDE HELD SHUT the gates of Famagusta until the fourteenth day after Epiphany had expired without bringing rescue. That night, they dug away the earth and drew the nails from the planks and removed the great bars that had closed all the formal entrances into the city, and completed the bridging of the ditch that led to the land gate. The next morning, in solemn cavalcade, James, King of Cyprus rode in to receive the keys of his city, and the flag of St George and the Dragon was dropped from the walls.

The company of Nicholas were among those who rode with him. This was not the triumphal procession which one day would beat a noisy and brilliant path to a swept and garnished city, but a military operation, to do with the handing over of power. Riding through the battered gates, unarmed, with nothing but the richness of his furs to identify him, James of Lusignan looked like a King, with the youth gone from his face along with the high-spirited way-wardness.

Prepared as they were, the reality of what had happened to Famagusta struck silence from them all. The tumbled buildings. The abandoned houses. The places blackened with fire. The intact ghosts, deeper into the city, of the splendid Frankish villas and lodgings and trading loggias, the fine-cut bulk of the church of St Peter and St Paul, the towering buttresses of the great convent of St Francis, with its empty gardens and cloisters. The disused markets. The silent streets of the craftsmen. And over all, the smell of sickness and death.

To wait for their enemy, the ordinary people of Famagusta had made their way to the heart of the city, where the Cathedral soared like a vast triangled reliquary, flanked by princely buildings and faced, across the piazza, by the handsome, doorless shell of the Palace. They stood in silence: two living hedges of worn and stinking humanity between which the cavalcade passed with no sound but the tinkle of harness. They were Greeks. The uplifted hand of the Archbishop of Nicosia meant nothing to them.

And then, ahead, were the walls of the Citadel, with its draw-bridge down, and the portcullis updrawn to give entry. In its doorway, awaiting them, was a figure in rich, damaged velvets which must be Napoleone Lomellini. Within the court of the castle no doubt attended the garrison, and the Genoese lords, and their former hostages.

One of whom was Nicholas. For several weeks, Tobias Beventini had found it impossible to speak of the apprentice he had chosen to follow, to dissect, to guide, in a medical way, towards the real, adult world. Long ago, he now realised, Nicholas had slipped from his grasp. Alone of all the men who now surrounded him, Tobie carried the knowledge that the son of Katelina van Borselen belonged to Nicholas. He knew what had already befallen every kinsman with whom Nicholas had come in contact. He now knew, too, what had happened, through the contrivings of that tortuous, ingenious mind, to the last exiled Emperor of the dynasty of By-zantium, and all his grown sons. He knew that Katelina van Borselen was in this city, along with the sister's son of Simon, her husband, while alone in Nicosia was Primaflora, the lovely woman Nicholas had taken in marriage after Marian, the simple widow who had founded his fortune.

Once, in the wake of the St Hilarion assault, Tobie had said to John, 'Would you follow vander Poele? After this?'

And the engineer had raised his sandy eyebrows and said, 'After what? You were in Trebizond with him. He hasn't altered, that I can see, since he came away a rich man.' Little that John le Grant said was ever reassuring, no matter how right he might be. It didn't strike Tobie that John, too, had had no wish to talk about Nicholas.

The Great Court of the Citadel of Famagusta was one hundred and sixty feet long, and built to accommodate the grandest of ceremonials. A third of it was occupied by the surrendering forces. Placed to the rear of the Lusignan retinue, the company of Nicholas barely heard the clipped and formal exchanges demanded by proto-col, or the clink of the keys as they were handed over, or the flourish of trumpets that heralded the raising of the Lusignan banner on every wall. Behind Napoleone Lomellini and his noble-men; behind the Pallaviccino, the Doria, the families of Gentile, Verdure, Archerio, de Pastino and the ranked faces, filled with hate, of the soldiers, there stood the men hitherto guarded as hostages. The Arab Abul Ismail, erect and gaunt and impassive in turban and robes. And beside him, a strong, familiar frame un-familiarly reduced, on which hung the soiled and ill-fitting clothes of a labourer. But the colourless face of Nicholas vander Poele with its rarefied structure had nothing in common with the dimpled joker of Bruges. His hair, untended, curled thick as a dog's at his neck under a shapeless wool cap, and his mind was turned patently inwards; far from seeking, or even thinking of the men from whom he had been parted for six weeks.

Towards the end, he lifted his eyes, and looked directly at Tobie and his companions. The next moment he had turned and, by the King's command, had re-entered the Citadel. His gaze had not been blank: he had seen them. But there was in it neither greeting nor welcome. Astorre said, 'He's under orders. Plenty to do. The King'll want him. I've to get the prisoners ready for Nicosia. Why don't you go into the Citadel? Or the Palace. They're making it habitable.'

A voice said, 'Senhores.' Before them stood the bloodless figure of the boy they had last seen, blotched with indigo, in the dyeyard at Nicosia. Diniz Vasquez said, 'The lord Niccolò has been commanded to attend on the King. He asks if you would care to wait for him in our villa. It is not far from here. He asks if you will forgive the discomfort.'

The discomfort. Everyone in this city, including the boy, including Nicholas, looked as if they had been in purgatory for months. Astorre said, 'There you are. Go. I'll tell you if I have to leave the city. Tell him I've got a cook who'll soon fatten him up. He shouldn't have stayed. There was no need for him to have stayed.'

Tobie had never seen Astorre flushed in that way before, with distress or with guilt. It was John who said to the boy, 'He made us leave him.'

'I know,' said the boy. Frighteningly, his eyes had filled with sudden tears.

John said, in French, with his flattest Aberdonian accent, 'She is dead, then.'

The boy looked at him. John said, 'Go on. Take us to the house. Someone will tell us. It will save Nicholas having to do it.'

The rites attending the handing over of a city are not quickly completed, and Nicholas, who had not been invited to attend them, waited a long time apart before Napoleone Lomellini left the King's presence and the Citadel of Famagusta with the escort of honour which would accompany him on the long ride to the capital. His successor was already in the room: Conella Morabit, fellow countryman of Rizzo di Marino, knight and loyal servant of Zacco's whose service went far back, as did that of Rizzo and Goneme and Markios, the brother of Cropnose. Only when all the orders had been given and all the discussions ended did the King dismiss his companions, and Nicholas was admitted to the inner room of the citadel which James had made his own.

'Ah,' Zacco said. 'Aesculapius, son of Apollo. You didn't think I had so much learning, did you? So you have found you prefer nursing to fighting, my Nikko?'

The use of the private name was either good news or bad. Jorgin the page, kneeling to draw the King's boots, gave the visitor an inclination of the head without pausing. He had already relieved the King of his jacket and his hat lay fallen, where he had flung it.

Nicholas said, 'My lord King means to stay in the Citadel?'

The splendid forehead was scored with lines and there were others which might be interpreted as reproach, or bitterness, or even menace. The King said, 'Answer my question.'

Nicholas said, 'The Knights Hospitaller excel at both, my lord. But there were not enough here at the time.'

'They are here now,' said the King. 'Kolossi is empty. You disobeyed orders twice. Is the boy still here?'

'My lord?' Nicholas said.

'The Portuguese boy. He escaped from your dyeyard, I understand, to join the enemy. You wish me to put him to death?'

'He hardly deserves it,' Nicholas said. 'I had already ransomed him. He was merely impatient to return home to Portugal. Now I hope he can do so.' He paused. 'The lady his kinswoman is dead.'

'In your care, I am told. That was what kept you in Famagusta?' Already, some of the severity had left the King's face.

Nicholas said, 'That among other things. The lord King's clemency in these past weeks not only led to the treaty, but will make his rule more acceptable. So will the work Abul Ismail performed for the sick, with what help I could give him.'

'I have noticed,' said Zacco. He kicked Jorgin absently with his toe. 'That is enough. Later. Yes. Your name commands respect. Lomellini mentioned you. I have appointed Conella Morabit to govern the city. How would it please you to be appointed his deputy?'

His face today was not capable of a great range of expression. Nicholas looked up eventually and said, 'My lord. I am more than sensible of the honour.'

The hazel eyes rested on him thoughtfully. 'You have served me for twelve months. Kyrenia is mine. Yours was the shipmaster, obeying your strategy, who helped to give me Famagusta. You and your company have been well rewarded, but a sugar estate, surely, is hardly enough to occupy you. Then there is the difficulty about the dyeworks.'

So it came. 'It is not run to the King's liking?' Nicholas said.

Zacco rose and, passing Nicholas on stockinged feet, poured wine with his own hands and brought it over. Nicholas had risen. Zacco gave him the cup and said, 'Mother in heaven, you smell. Everyone does. Sit down. The yard is superbly well run, and you know it. No. I owe favours. I cannot leave it with you, much as I'd like to. Nor the villa. I had in mind something else. Have you been to your fief? Does it suit you?'

The returns from the fief had been pouring into his Bank at Venice since Zacco had sent Corner to fetch him. 'I am most grateful, sire,' said Nicholas.

'I have extended it,' Zacco said. 'I have also arranged for you to be given the castle within the new boundaries. You already have the right to live in my manor of Kouklia. You will have two properties now. When you come to Nicosia, which I hope will be often, I shall have rooms prepared for you at the Dominicans'. And if you accept the post I am offering, you will have a residence, naturally, here. What do you say?'

Nicholas was silent. He said, 'The fief. Is that dependent on my appointment to Famagusta?'

'You are going to refuse it?' Zacco said. The lines had returned to his face.

Nicholas said, 'My lord, you show me trust and favour beyond what I deserve, but this is a matter not only for me, but for my officers and my company. I would beg the King's leave to postpone my answer. There is, too, another matter which has a bearing.'

'I hardly know,' said the King, 'if I want to hear of another matter.'

His face showed anger, and something else besides anger. Nicholas said, not all that quickly, 'It concerns the King's safety.'

Silence. Then Zacco said, 'You had better tell me.'

Embarking on his monologue, Nicholas was aware that he was not in the fittest state to lay this particular trail. To begin with, he had hoped to keep Abul Ismail's name from the story; and then had realised that it could not be done, and had gone to the Arab, and asked his permission. He had given it.

Through all the days that Katelina lingered, and after, Abul Ismail had tended her like a daughter. The only rite he had not observed was the ceremony she had asked for herself: her burial in the Cathedral of St Nicholas. After that, the physician had seen to the ordering of the room, and had her clothes boxed, and found and taken to Nicholas the three letters she left, one for Simon, one for Lucia his sister, and one which contained no message for Nicholas, although it was inscribed to him. The physician had also brought to Nicholas an object he did not know how to pack. It was a dried and broken chaplet of reeds, hastily plaited, and it had been stored with a veil. Nicholas had taken the package, saying, 'I will see to it.'

It was that evening, when speech was impossible, that Abul Ismail had waited until Diniz was out of the room and then had said, 'I wish to speak on the subject of Cyprus.'

It was true that Cyprus still existed, and the rest of the world, and one was not a child. Nicholas said, 'Would you have preferred Carlotta's rule?'

'I am not sure if I wish the rule of Uzum Hasan,' said the Arab.

Once, by Kyrenia, they had spoken of this. Uzum Hasan, prince of the Turcomans, sometimes allied with the Sultan of Cairo, sometimes ignored him. But against the great army of Osmanli Turks under the Sultan Mehmet at Constantinople, both were united. Ludovico da Bologna had toured Western Europe with envoys from Uzum Hasan, promising combined Muslim and Christian troops to combat Mehmet's forces. Uzum Hasan, as an ally of Cairo, could rid Cairo of its obstreperous Mamelukes. But the cost would be a Turcoman alliance, perhaps a Turcoman power in Egypt. And instead of a Mameluke-ruled overlord, Zacco would have Uzum Hasan.

Nicholas said, 'I have thought of this. I have studied Uzum, and Sultan Mehmet. I think the Mamelukes are dragging Egypt to destruction, and may overrun Cyprus. And if Venice is occupied with the Turk, Zacco will not be able to stay, even as a puppet king, even if I remain with my army. It is my belief that Uzum would prove a tolerant prince, and an acceptable ruler.'

'That is what Tzani-bey is afraid of,' said the Arab.

'He knows of this?' Nicholas said.

'Not from me,' said the physician. 'I gave my word, and I have kept it. But someone close to the Palace knows that you have been in communion with Uzum Hasan over this matter. You may guess who it is. You remember who was present at that meeting at the Dominicans'. For his own ends, the same person has told Tzani-bey al-Ablak of the threat. If the power of the Mamelukes fails, then he loses his post and his life. He will do all he can to prevent it.'

'By returning to Cairo?' said Nicholas.

The physician smiled. 'Do I appear as simple as that? I have been watching you. You know that Tzani-bey is out of favour in Cairo. He is here because, at home, he is a troublemaker. To advance, he needs a coup, a service that will dazzle his Sultan, reinforce the power of the Mamelukes, make it difficult if not impossible for Uzum Hasan to persuade Cairo it needs an alliance. The coup is the murder of James of Lusignan and all his officers.'

Nicholas stopped breathing, and then smoothly recovered himself. He said, 'The emir has four hundred men.'

Abul Ismail nodded. 'So, not enough for an open rebellion. He will seize control in Famagusta. He will come to Famagusta at night, seeking admission. Once into the castle, he and his men will massacre the King and all within, and then ride to take Nicosia. With no leaders, the island will fall into confusion. Then he will send to Cairo, and the Egyptian fleets will arrive. That is the plan.'

'For when?' Nicholas said.

'Two days after the King enters the city of Famagusta, the attack will take place. They will kill James of Lusignan first. Then Markios, the Archbishop, the Chancellor. But not you.'

'Why?' said Nicholas.

And Abul Ismail had said in his prosaic fashion, 'The emir Tzani-bey wishes to take his amusement with you. Cyprus is his prize. You are to be his entertainment.'

'I see,' said Nicholas. He said, after a while, 'I don't know why you have brought this news to me. There is no recompense worthy of it, except that which you will receive from God. But at least, you will not suffer for it: you must be protected. The person who told Tzani-bey of our meeting will have told him, perhaps, that you were present. You knew about Uzum Hasan, but failed to advise the emir of his danger. If he learns that, he will not be slow with his punishment.'

And at last the Arab had smiled. 'Why do I do this? Because I find I am concerned, as are you, with the land that I occupy. There have been good men in my country. Not all Mamelukes have been decadent. But it is time they were checked; and even the threat of Uzum Hasan's plans may be sufficient. On the other hand, this emir is a man of great power, of limited gifts, and of an evil nature. As for protection, who could save me, if he were to suspect? I am safest where I seem most in danger. I shall return today to his camp, and tend his sick, and tell him all he wishes to know of your defences. After that, it is for you and the Lusignan to keep him out.'

Nicholas said, 'The man who betrayed the plan of Uzum Hasan to the emir may now betray the fact that the King has been warned. A later plot, and a worse, may emerge.'

'No,' said Abul Ismail dryly. 'No. I think you are a better planner than that, my lord Niccolò.'

Now, telling the story to Zacco, Nicholas used the name of Abul Ismail. Without it, he would not be believed. But from that moment, Abul's safety was in the King's hands.

He could not tell, as he spoke, how Zacco was receiving it. The King listened unmoving, his wine forgotten, his eyes fixed on his as if he were courting him. At the end, he said, 'I have been deceived more often than you. I think this is a trick.'

Nicholas said, 'Abul Ismail is an old man, a wise man, and one who has dedicated all his days to the healing of the sick. He has returned himself to Tzani-bey's camp. He has nothing to gain, and his life to lose. The only deception could lie in the form of his warning. The attack might come before he says or after, or might take a different form. The plan was made before he entered Famagusta.'

'More than a month ago,' Zacco said. 'Tzani-bey has been planning this for six weeks. Through the festival.' He stopped, and then gave a laugh. 'At least he was sure that Famagusta would fall. Of course. He tried to poison their food.'

'He knew they were starving,' Nicholas said. 'You saved them. You and the Church.'

Zacco turned from the door. 'Rizzo is coming,' he said. 'You will tell this to him. Nicosia should be warned.'

'And you will leave the city?' said Nicholas.

The King turned his head, his eyes alight once more, the colour returned to his skin: rescued from the oppressions of the day by the promise of action and danger. 'What! And remove the bait from the trap? I shall stay here,' he said.

'An open invitation to four hundred Mamelukes?' Nicholas said. 'A trap means a battle. I suggest we try to scotch this before it erupts into Famagusta itself. Meanwhile, it might be best if you spent your nights at the Palace, but put it about that you stay in the Citadel. If there is an attack, or an attempt at one, then Conella Morabit will deal with it.'

'We shall see,' said the King. 'Here is Rizzo. We should send for Pesaro and Conella. You will repeat your message, and we shall debate. My Nicholas, what am I to do with you? I wrest your dyeworks away, and you present me with my life. Rizzo . . . this is Conella's new deputy. A king among men.'

He had not agreed. It didn't matter, not at the moment. He waited until they were all gathered, and explained it all over again.

They let him go to the villa several hours after that, with orders to return to the castle by dusk. By then he had had wine, and not very much food, and the headache had started again that Abul Ismail had explained very simply, and which meant merely that he should rest, and eat lightly, and sleep. Diniz suffered in the same way. He wondered how in God's name he was going to manage without Abul Ismail, and then remembered that he had nothing to manage: the city was full of monks and Hospitallers and there was no one sick any more in his villa. He actually sat down for a moment in the broken loggia, thinking of that, and collecting energy to get up and go in. Loppe found him there.

Being Loppe, he simply sat down beside him, and waited. After a while, Nicholas said, 'Look. Grass growing there, by my foot. I saw a mouse, yesterday.'

'The flamingoes are back at Salines,' Loppe said. 'And Akrotiri. We are getting ready for all the new cuttings. It's pleasant, down there.'

Presently he said, 'Astorre was called away to the Citadel. Master Tobias and Master John are still here. The young man Diniz left, but is coming back. They will let you stay here?'

He was right; it was getting cold, and waiting didn't make it any better. 'No,' said Nicholas. 'Let's go in. I have something to tell you.'

The third time of telling, the story seemed to lose credibility. Not to his hearers, who received it with fury, but to himself. They looked odd, John and Tobie and Loppe in the stuffy parlour with its assortment of stolen furnishings where for six weeks he had been accustomed to seeing other faces. He said, finally, 'Of course, Tzani-bey may have changed his mind. We need more than this before the army could act. In any case, Abul Ismail's life depends on secrecy. I think therefore that it's better Diniz shouldn't have to know.'

The voice of Diniz, behind him, said, 'We don't trust one another?'

Nicholas stood. He wondered if his face looked like the boy's, and supposed that it did. He said, 'We do. I thought you might find ignorance easier. Abul Ismail tells us that the Mamelukes plan to kill the King in Famagusta and take the island.'

The boy said, 'Where is he?'

'He's gone back to the Mameluke camp,' Nicholas said. 'Otherwise they would suspect him. I have to get back to the Citadel now. Have they told you you're free?'

'Yes,' said Diniz.

'You could sail from Salines,' said Nicholas. 'Or Episkopi. No, not Episkopi. They might think you were smuggling cuttings.'

The boy didn't smile. No one smiled. He felt stupid and alien, like one of Prester John's poor Ethiopes, not allowed to concentrate on rolling his egg. He said, 'Where's the Patriarch?'

'In Nicosia,' John le Grant said. 'Collecting dues and keeping pots boiling. He said to make sure you came back. What did that mean?'

'That he's well informed,' said Nicholas, sitting again. After a moment the boy did, as well. Nicholas said, 'I've been asked to stay in Famagusta and help govern it.'

'And will you?' said John. The boy's eyes on his were deep and extremely bright.

'I haven't said,' Nicholas said. 'It seemed best to see if we were going to keep Famagusta first.'

'If you do,' Diniz said, 'I could help you.'

Everyone looked at him but Loppe. Nicholas said, 'I'm not interested in that kind of authority, Diniz. For a while, until they find somebody else. But probably not even then. Cyprus has nothing for you. Your mother needs you.'

'She has Simon,' said Diniz. 'And we are –'

'We are friends,' Nicholas said. 'And you have to be my ambassador. I would like you to go to Nicosia. Not to the dyeworks: the King, as it happens, intends taking them from us. But to the villa. Then to Portugal by the first ship you have news of.'

'The dyeworks? Why?' said John le Grant.

'He has obligations. We are to lose the villa as well. He plans vast, if remote compensations.' Loppe's eyes were on him, and he refrained from looking at Loppe. He said to Diniz, 'Go home. It would be best.'

'I could sail from here,' Diniz said. 'If I sail. I saw Famagusta surrender to Lusignan. I don't want to see it given over to Mamelukes.'

John le Grant cleared his throat. He said, 'Just in case you were thinking of it, Nicholas, I don't think any of us has plans to leave Famagusta at the moment, no matter who is on his way to Nicosia from Salines.'

'You read my very thoughts,' Nicholas said. 'No one knows who was on the *Adorno*?'

'No,' said Tobie. 'Not yet. But whoever they are, they'll all be in Nicosia by now, and no doubt we'll hear soon enough. The boy's better here. He'd foment trouble.'

'I don't think so,' said Nicholas, and gave a half-smile, gazing at Diniz. He said, 'I expect that, like me, he hasn't the energy. I must go back. Tobie, I have something to give you.'

They all looked at him with suspicion. Anxiety and suspicion, when he came to think of it, had been the keynote of the whole conversation. Then Tobie got up and followed him from the room.

The paper addressed to himself was locked away in his box. It was the only one left, since Diniz now held the other two. Nicholas retrieved it rather slowly, and turned to where Tobie was watching him. Tobie said, 'Why are you ill? Zacco sent wagons of food.'

'It needed to be the right kind,' Nicholas said. 'And everything in the city was tainted. Also, I have been practising your trade. Dame Trotula of Salerno. You've been duping us for years. Medicine's easy.'

'He was a good doctor,' said Tobie. 'Abul Ismail, when he wasn't burning the guts out of people. We thought we might get somewhere. On the sugar sickness, I mean.'

'I don't think we should have survived without him,' Nicholas said. Then, since it seemed the subject ought to be mentioned by somebody, he said, 'He nursed Katelina. She died thinking the relief ship had come. Chance. But God-given chance.'

Tobie's voice was tentative, his face moist. He said, 'You made friends with Diniz. And the lady too?'

'Since the summer,' Nicholas said. 'Tobie? You and Godscalc know her son isn't Simon's. You gave your word to keep quiet so long as Katelina was alive. I have to know what you think now.'

Tobie's face turned a deeper red. He said, 'You want the child back?'

Nicholas sighed and sat down. He said, 'No. We spoke of it. She wished me to have him, but it would have been wrong. I want Simon to continue to think the boy his. If I do, will you and Godscalc be content to keep silence?'

'You don't want him?' said Tobie.

Nicholas could feel himself flush. He wound his hands hard together and said, 'What do you think?'

When concentrating, Tobie's eyes became pinpoints of pupil in two sea-blue pebbles. He said, 'I think that's probably the boy's only chance of surviving. If the good lord Simon suspected, he'd kill him. On the other hand –'

'I knew there'd be another hand,' Nicholas said. 'That's why I brought you here.'

'Why?' said Tobie.

'Because Katelina had the same thought. Somewhere, in case it matters: in case Simon dies and the boy is in trouble, there should be a record of who he actually is. And so she left me one.'

He didn't want, when the moment came, to hand it over; but it was sensible. Tobie took it, and opened the covering sheet, and took out the paper inside. The writing was large, and not very black, because she had been so weak, but it was perfectly distinct. It stated that the child known as Henry de St Pol, son of Katelina van Borselen, was not the offspring, as commonly accepted, of the lord Simon de St Pol of Kilmirren, but had been conceived and born to Nicholas vander Poele, burgess of Bruges and presently of the House of Niccolò, Venice. The date of birth was inscribed, and the date on which the letter was written. She had signed it, and had it properly witnessed.

Tobie read it. He had become rather pale. At the end he said, 'It isn't wise. Simon may find it.'

'He won't find it if you carry it,' Nicholas said. 'Take it. If you like, give it to Godscalc if ever you get back to Bruges. I'd say send it, but it might not be safe.'

'You don't want it?' Tobie said.

And Nicholas said, 'It's better in neutral hands. It's better out of Famagusta as well. I want you to go to Nicosia and take Diniz with you. Whoever gets killed in a Mameluke attack, it shouldn't be you or him.'

'But you don't mind getting killed?' Tobie said. 'You only think you don't mind. You're so low in health that you don't know what you're talking about, never mind being able to fight for anybody. Leave Astorre and get out of it.'

All the time they had been talking, he had been conscious of a racket outside: a banging, followed by voices. The door opened. 'There you are!' said Astorre. 'Will you come back? He said to be back by dusk, and he's murderous.'

Nicholas rose. 'You see?' he said to Tobie. 'Wanted by everyone. I have to go. Take care of it. Go to Nicosia.'

'Go to hell,' said Tobias Beventini morosely.

Chapter 43

THE CITADEL that night was uncomfortable, jammed with jaded and irritable men to whom, in their weariness, it seemed that the surrender of Famagusta had made them masters of a festering graveyard. At the centre of it all, overtired and on edge, was Zacco himself.

His temper, on the late return of Nicholas, quite suited Astorre's description of murderous, and it took an hour of endeavour for the men around him, including Nicholas, to soften his mood. It was an example of the curious alchemy that drew men to Zacco no matter what his behaviour. They suffered his whims out of love for him. Whatever he did, he could count on that. Many times he did so, quite deliberately. The rest of the time it was unconscious. It was what made him fit to rule this particular land, rather than his sister Carlotta, who was probably more energetic, probably more gifted, certainly more intellectual. And because he was part of the charmed circle, and had done what he had with his ship and his army, and had shirked abnormally little of the hard work or hard play or his share of the fighting, Nicholas was aware that he was held in regard by the others. He was aware, too, that when the King's immediate anger had died, Zacco remembered something. So, when Astorre was found tramping about outside the door, the King looked up from the drinking, companionable group that was talking him towards his bed, and said, 'Ah, poor Nikko. We are unkind, when he is heartsick, and bereaved of his sad, Flemish lady. Take him away.'

Plodding up the stairs behind Astorre, Nicholas sat down and said, 'You couldn't do that every night? I'm going to sleep on the floor.'

'No, you're not. I've got good news. Master Tobie's got the boy to agree to leave with him. They're riding to Nicosia in the morning.' The toe of his boot did some prodding.

Nicholas said, 'I wasn't asleep, and I'll put myself into bed when

I feel like it. I'm glad to hear it. Astorre, tell Loppe to go with them. Where's John?'

'Holding your other arm,' said John le Grant. 'The sooner you get into bed, the sooner you'll get big and strong and able to fight Tzani-bey.'

It was something Nicholas had given no thought to just recently. He swore; then, finding himself unexpectedly in a bed, went to sleep.

The next night, Tzani-bey rode up to the land gate. He had a small retinue with him, but made no attempt to bring them in, merely requesting leave to walk alone to the Citadel. He was given an escort and taken there. While he remained at the end of the drawbridge, one guard spoke to another, and a captain appeared and crossed to him. 'My lord emir, the Commander regrets. After nightfall, entry here is prohibited. Since I cannot admit you, is there any message I might pass?'

'It was not the Commander I sought,' said Tzani-bey al-Ablak. 'Although – may he be prosperous – I would wish you to convey to him my felicitations on his well-deserved and excellent appointment. I sought out my brother soul Niccolò, with whom I believed I had some business of consequence. I have waited to hear from him. But perhaps he does not care to come out?'

'He is here, most excellent,' Nicholas said. He crossed the drawbridge, taking his time, until he looked down on the emir. He said, 'We spoke of a meeting. You have in mind a time and a place?'

'In the name of Allah, the Beneficent, the Merciful,' said Tzani-bey. 'Is it for myself, full of dross, to suggest it? For me, one day is as well as another. There lie before us auspicious days only. The evil days of this month – the Egyptian days – these are all now behind us with their curses. Whoso may wed a wife, he shall not long have joy of her. And who that taketh any great journey shall never come back again. And he that beginneth any great work shall never make end of it. And he that letteth him blood shall soon die, or never be whole. Such are the dooms of the Dies Nefastae, of which one, as I recall, is your Saint's Day. But why should the ramblings of doctors disturb you? I would fight you on horseback, with sword and with mace, within two days from now. And for your greater contentment, let us make our sport in Famagusta. There is an exercise ground?'

'There to your left,' Nicholas said. 'But would the emir regard it as fitting? The Commander's orders are strict. The emir's entourage would not be permitted.'

'Allah the Best Knower has endeared his faith to me, and I trust you and him. I shall come alone. I shall agree to whatever you choose. The day after tomorrow? An hour after sunrise? You may wish to hold festival; permit games; arrange other combats. It keeps men from wearying. It is not a sweet city at present, Famagusta.'

'It is agreed,' Nicholas said.

'In token of which,' said Tzani-bey, 'I have brought you a gift. This soldier carries it. Open it when I have gone, and think of me when you wear it.'

He left. In the Commander's room in the Citadel, Conella Morabit was waiting for Nicholas. He said, 'Now we know.'

'You had him watched?' Nicholas said.

'Every moment. It was the soldier. The soldier who carried the parcel. A message passed.'

'You heard the pact?' Nicholas said.

'You meet to resolve your dispute in the training field, and he comes alone. What do you make of it?'

'The same as you. All the garrison will come to watch, whether public games are fixed round it or not. While they are out of the citadel, someone will open the gate to the quays.'

'And four hundred armed men will enter, take the Citadel, and kill the King. It agrees with what we know of him. Except that the emir risks his own life.'

'He'll be in the field with me, when it happens,' Nicholas said. 'He can always use me as buffer. In fact, he's got to keep me alive till it's over, which I find rather cheering. I'm not entirely confident of killing Tzani-bey with a mace at the moment.'

Morabit was silent. He said, 'But when he finds he is trapped, he will turn on you. No. The King may not allow this.'

'Then he must have a poor opinion of my wits. Tzani-bey will be the one who is surprised, no one else. Besides,' Nicholas added, 'it's what you might call a matter of honour, and the fount of honour must be James of Lusignan. I have promised myself this for a long time. In fact, when I came, it was a condition of service.'

'I see,' said Conella Morabit. 'I am sorry to hear it, but I shall not, of course, try to persuade you. What, then, is the gift he has brought you? Something offensive?'

Wrapped in linen, the parcel was modest in dimensions and limp in character and innocent of any obvious threat. Nicholas opened it.

Inside was a beautiful cloak, lined with satin. When he lifted it out, it hung to the ground from his fingers, not ponderous as a fur mantle usually was, but weightlessly supple and silken, made by a master from thin, fine perfect skins pieced together with infinite artistry. Their colours glowed in the lamplight: smoke and silver and black, cream and tortoiseshell, orange and butter.

Nicholas loosed his hands as if holding a plague shroud. It fell and slid from his sight. 'Burn it,' he said. 'Get your servant to burn it.'

Conella Morabit stared at him. 'If you wish,' he remarked. 'But it is a thing of great price.'

Nicholas gave the statement some thought. He said, 'And that is very true. I doubt if you can imagine what it has cost, and what it is still going to cost, before I have finished.'

The following day, Astorre came into his own. The King, torn between anger, and foreboding, and love of glorious danger, had been brought to agree to the piece of theatre which his Nikko demanded, and which might or might not prove the focal point of a Mameluke rebellion. Markios had no objections. Rizzo, departed suddenly for Nicosia, had not been present to give an opinion, and William Goneme, after praying briefly for everyone's welfare, seemed to think that God had made a commitment. Pesaro seemed disapproving, but not Sor de Naves and his brother.

Most seemed unconvinced that the Mameluke attack would take place. All were optimistic, so far as his own prospects went. 'If you're right, your contest will hardly have started before the Mamelukes come, and we snare them. If there's no revolt, all the better. The King has said he'll have the duel stopped.'

'He'll have to work hard at that,' said Nicholas to Captain Astorre, who had volunteered to teach him how to use a mace. 'I've waited a year to get hold of Tzani-bey al-Ablak, and I'm not about to give him up to anyone.' Astorre, who loved a challenge, was the right person to say that to; and John le Grant didn't waste his time trying to stop him. Nicholas spent a day filled with bursts of furious activity in the training field, and crashed on to his truckle bed early that evening aching in every stretched and ill-nourished muscle.

Astorre said, 'Well, you'll need your wits about you. But that's a good horse. Your sword is first-class, and your mace was got off one of the best fighters I ever knew, until I got hold of him. Also, you've fought with Muslims and against them. You know their tricks better than most. So when the Mamelukes come, pin him quickly. He won't know you're expecting it. He'll be watching his men.'

'If they come,' Nicholas said. 'What if Abul Ismail was wrong, or the emir guesses? Then he'll attack hard from the beginning, because he won't be waiting for anyone.'

'So what's wrong with that?' said John le Grant. 'A fair fight, face to face. I thought you asked for it. Gallant Knight to eminent Mameluke?'

Astorre looked indignant. 'Except he's not fit for it. Look at him! Putty!'

'Thank you,' said Nicholas, suddenly tickled. On occasion, Astorre's tactics gave way to his truthfulness.

John was looking less serious, perhaps; but still thoughtful. John said, 'That's true. The man's got you at a disadvantage. You're entitled to some compensation. Make the big chivalrous gesture, but take any concession that's going; that would be my advice. The fellow's a weasel.'

He sounded unsympathetic, even exasperated. All right: Tzani-bey had been rough on the way back from Rhodes; had treated Nicholas badly on his trip to meet Zacco; had used brutal tricks when campaigning. To fight him for it in John's book was childish. But then, John didn't know what had taken place in the monastery set among vipers, and on the road between there and Nicosia. Cropnose and Zacco and Markios did; and Tzani-bey and most of his Mamelukes. When exacting payment in public for that, your mind didn't run on concessions.

In Cyprus that year, the last week of January brought a softening that seemed to herald the spring. Outside Famagusta, the almond trees were already in blossom and soon the air would smell of hyacinth and narcissus, and the piercing scent of the orange trees would drench all the island. The skies cleared. Between sunshine and showers the rivers began to run lower; the mud stiffened; the ground became green. The Mameluke lord Tzani-bey al-Ablak, dismissing his entourage at the gates of Famagusta, rode into the city on a white horse whose silver harness and gold-tasselled hipcloth glittered and twinkled in sunlight, and the velvet coat over his mail was magnificent.

From the Citadel, Astorre watched him come, his hand on the shoulder of Nicholas. 'I was right,' he said. 'Chain mail. Flexible, but it can't stand up to piercing. A coif, a helmet, a round shield, and the mace under his knee. I told you –'

'You told me,' said Nicholas. 'What kind of mace?' He turned to pick up his helmet. The mail shirt he wore, on Astorre's advice, was very close to the pattern of the Mamelukes, although the links were different, and bound with small plates. His thighs and knees and calves were protected with armour, and there were plates of it guarding his elbows. Unlike the emir's, his sword was straight and not curved, and his mace was of iron. The lad who had volunteered as his squire held his long Burgundian shield and his gloves and the Milanese bascinet he would buckle over his cap. It was plain, with no nose or ear guards like the emir's, although his neck was protected by mail. Ring mail deflected a scimitar cut, which was why the Mamelukes wore it.

Astorre pronounced on the subject of maces. 'Fins on the head. A piece of pure frippery. But his shaft's ribbed. I like it.'

'I'm glad you like it,' said Nicholas. 'Is everyone where they should be?'

'That's a stupid question,' Astorre said, 'considering. Of course they are. The castle seems empty. The parade ground looks as if it's got the entire population of Cyprus gathered round it. No great impression of pageant, but the King's there, moderately dressed-up, and your courtiers. Not Rizzo.' He paused. 'Will your wife know? The lady Primaflora? She's been waiting for you in Nicosia?'

By now, presumably, quite a select number of people would be waiting for him in Nicosia, including the most beautiful woman there. Despite the Dies Nefastae, he must seem to rank among the preternaturally blessed of this world. Nicholas said, 'Does she know about the revolt? Not unless Tobie has worried her with it. When it's over, I'll explain it myself. And if I can't, there's a farewell packet I left in December. It probably sounds quite old-fashioned by now. If I survive a second time, I must find and revise it. Let's go. Is it all right, my right side going numb like this?'

'You're an idiot,' said Astorre good-naturedly. 'On you go. Remember all I told you. Kill him if you get the chance, but –'

'But not too soon to spoil everyone's plans. Lord of Mercy,' said Nicholas. 'It's not a fight, it's the script for a passion play in twenty-five scenes; costumes free from the guilds and no drinking. Is Ludovico da Bologna out there?'

'No. I don't think so,' said Astorre, looking surprised.

'Good,' said Nicholas. 'I feel better already.'

Whatever his words to Astorre, they had nothing to do with his underlying mood, which had remained unchanged for days. He rode out now into the sun and the wind with his mind implacably set, and stepped through the crowds deaf to their shouting, to enter the vast oblong of dirt upon which this duel was to be fought.

It was not decked out as for a gala, for this was a military occupation, and these were only games. What he was about to take part in was not a game, arms à plaisance; but neither did it have a noble purpose. He was not here as a Knight, to fulfil the Christian purpose of his Order, although what he did might serve James of Lusignan. Perhaps the emir Tzani-bey was here to defend his religion; but for three years he had accepted the payment of Christians to attack other Christians, and if he was bent on revolt, it was chiefly because he perceived a Turcoman threat to all Mamelukes.

These were issues of power, not religion. And whether they existed or not, the fact was that he and Tzani-bey would have fought one another anyway, over a personal grudge. It only happened to be taking place here because he wished the King to be present. If all the other spectators received joy of it, Nicholas had no objection.

Everything about this ground was familiar, as was the feel of his arms: his sword, the weight of his shield and his helm, the balance of the little horse under him. It was a long time since the Abruzzi, when he had seen Felix fall; and he had fought often on horseback since then. He had been fighting in the Abruzzi when he had been captured, the year before last. And brought here. And thought the love of arms was the new love he had discovered.

Behind him stood the castle. To his right ran the sea-wall, with the ocean behind it upon which the *Adorno* had met her fate. On his left, central among the spectators, was the awning hung with the cross and three lions of Lusignan. Beside Nicholas was the flag he had been given, which had upon it a silver cross-hilted sword on a blue field: emblem of the Order he had been admitted to twice (or not at all). At the other end, on a white horse, sat the emir Tzani-bey, his sword drawn. The emir who had chained him, flayed him, exposed him, and used him for his pleasure.

There was a drumroll and a flourish of trumpets: the overture. Then the tripping signal that warned the contestants to be prepared. Then the trumpets for onslaught.

Here there were no lists and no formalities. One did not ride courteously forward, gathering speed, strike, continue and turn, ready to repeat the process. There was no barrier. The emir simply gathered his horse and flung it into a gallop on a course that must collide with his own. And Nicholas, watching him, spurred his horse likewise.

It was one used for ball games, and wiry. If it had been heavier, he would have allowed the collision to happen. As it was, he waited until the last second, and his opponent did the same. The two horses swerved, brushing one another, and the two blades flashed, and met, and parted in a shower of sparks. As he struck, Nicholas was squeezing and turning his horse bodily beneath him.

He was just in time. Tzani-bey had played tzukanion also although not, Nicholas supposed, on the fields of the Emperor of Trebizond. He reappeared under his elbow and struck upwards. Nicholas ducked, and heard the steel pass with a whine. He turned and slashed; met cloth; met leather, tugged free and flung his horse away in a circle.

Tzani-bey had done the same. They sat, breathing quickly, watching one another. He realised that everyone in the world appeared to be screaming. He remembered what he was supposed to be doing; then forgot it. He saw Tzani-bey begin, very gently, to put his horse into a mild trot towards him and advanced his own mount at the same pace. Above the round shield he could see little of the emir's dark face: two glittering eyes on either side of the nose-guard; a flash of teeth below the spreading moustache. His mail coat was long, covering his calves as he rode, and the high-

backed saddle protected his rear. His horse, with no apparent
instruction, suddenly increased its speed on a parallel course;
arrived, and stopped dead as the emir struck.

Nicholas took on his shield a slash that would have cut off his
neck. He felt the jar in his weaker shoulder as he parried, sliding
sideways and forward. The emir leaned, allowing the blade to pass
his side. His horse passaged; turned; the blade came again, cutting
upwards, sideways, down. The little horse under Nicholas
whinnied, jolting him, as a line of red sprang along its haunch.
Nicholas, angry, slashed twice and then retrieved his temper as he
retreated, wheeling. The emir's horse moved, backwards, forwards,
sideways, and then came forward again. This time they stayed
engaged, the horses dancing beneath them, and some of the blows
missed, some were blocked, and some fell. At the same moment,
they both freed themselves and withdrew.

Around the ground, the noise rose and fell without cease. Towards the sea, there was no sound, and none from the Citadel. So
far, nothing had interrupted the duel. If nothing would, and the
duel was what it seemed to be, you would think that Tzani-bey
would fight even harder. On the other hand, he was both vicious
and fit. He might be teasing Nicholas; testing him; tiring him; so
that, in a sudden real onslaught, he could have him at his mercy at
last.

It might be that. Or it might simply be that his force of Mamelukes was coming late. Or was there, but awaiting a signal.

There was nothing that Nicholas could do for he, too, had to
prevaricate. And that was best done on horseback, for as soon as
one or both were unhorsed, the duel could not last very much
longer. Nicholas renewed his grip on his sword, and felt his animal
falter as he put it towards the emir again. The cut had gone deep,
and there might be others. He might have to fight on foot after all.
He said, as he came up, in Arabic: 'Have you learned from your
dancing-girl, emir? Why not fight like a man? I shall see that your
widows are cared for.'

And that brought the serious fighting. He didn't enjoy it. Twice,
he made a hit with his sword-point, and heard the emir grunt, but
he took a spent cut on the helm that dizzied him despite all the
padding, and a slash in the side that filled his clothing with blood.
Through it all he husbanded, as well as he could, what was left of
his energy. No interruption. No disturbance. No relief. Face to
face till the end, perhaps, as he said he had wanted. It came to him
that soon he would have to decide to try and kill Tzani-bey, no
matter what it did to anyone's programme. Either that, or lose the
fight and his life.

He had not quite made up his mind when the decision was made
for him by Tzani-bey. They had circled, closed, circled, drawn off

and were together again. This time, without warning, the emir changed his sword to the hand that held his buckler. And as he closed upon Nicholas, he snatched something from its place in his saddle and brought it down like an axe.

It was neither an axe nor a mace, but an iron bar. Astorre had warned him. Illegal even among Mamelukes, it could, at a blow, take off an arm. A mace might have been deflected by armour. The bar fell between the protective plate and his neck, on the left, on the wound of ten months ago. It shrieked its protest, although Nicholas did nothing but gasp. His eyes became dark. He managed, just, to disengage and ride and heard, through his nausea, the beating hooves as the emir came after him. He didn't have very long, and he couldn't see very well, but – play or not – he was fighting now for his life, and so was Tzani-bey. Nicholas turned, and used his spurs, and this time drove his blood-smothered horse straight at the Mameluke.

The animals crashed together and staggered. Nicholas, dropping his shield, struck the emir with the weight of his shoulder and, drawing his mace, half dislodged him with a blow from the saddle and leaped free as his horse foundered. Tzani-bey's horse, un-governed, started away; the emir's sword hesitated as he fought to control it, his studded boot out of the stirrup. Nicholas stood in the field and, like a Roman thug, swung his mace to gain mo-mentum and released it. It swept the emir from his horse, which snorted and fled. Tzani-bey rose, sword in hand, and confronted him.

There seemed no doubt, now, that the only battle today in Famagusta was the one taking place now, to the death. If Tzani-bey expected support, it hadn't come. If the plot had never existed, Tzani-bey, having toyed with him, was now in no doubt that he fought for his life. They were alone together, on this field, with their swords. Except that Tzani-bey, in place of his shield, was wielding his mace.

A trumpet blew. The emir's eyes flickered, in his glistening face. Then he returned his attention to Nicholas. Blood soaked the handsome Syrian surcoat, as it blotched and stained his own padded jupa and linen and shirt. He felt the weakness of it, but not yet the pains. The old wound was the worst: his white-hot shoulder beat and rang like a forge. The trumpet blew again, and a herald called something. No shouting; no surge of action; no summons to battle. Just a command from the King to cease fighting.

Nicholas laughed at Tzani-bey and the emir, surprisingly, showed his teeth in return. The emir said, 'You do not scamper when called? I commend you.' Then he leaped, his scimitar in the air. But the mace, in his other hand, was whistling down to the Christian sword.

His eyes had not given him away, but his mind did. To avoid the scimitar completely was not possible. But Nicholas took only half of its slice in his body, and his own arm was positioned for all it had to do. As Tzani-bey brought down the mace, Nicholas cut off the emir's right hand.

Warm, thick blood sprayed in his face. The emir's own features were blank. Then the man dropped to his knees, his left hand crossing to grip his right arm with its core of white bone. The mud flooded with crimson. Around them, silence exploded into a herring-gull screaming. Nicholas raised the point of his sword, and pressed it against Tzani-bey's chest and said, 'You are defeated.'

The blood pumped: the weakened fingers could not quite stem it. But the emir's gaze was steady in a face of pallid olive. He said, 'I acknowledge it. I have said my prayers. Dispatch me.'

'Why?' said Nicholas. 'I was to be your entertainment. May I not reserve you for mine? Allow me to help you.' He pulled off his gloves and, freeing the strap of his helm, bound it crudely about the emir's arm over the artery. The emir closed his eyes. He said, 'Of course. Who could gainsay you? I have brought you, in any case, a token of my submission. In the saddlebag of my horse. I had hoped not to have to present it.'

'Is it of the nature of your other gift?' Nicholas said. He rose, and felt himself swaying.

The emir opened his eyes. 'It follows the pattern,' he said. 'Here is your mistress.'

Zacco hit him with his open hand, first on one cheek, then the other. He said to Nicholas, 'You heard the trumpet. I will do that, the next time you disobey me. What is he saying?' The King had run alone on to the field. The others were only now racing after him. His arms were round Nicholas, his face anguished as in Nicosia, the first time.

Nicholas said, 'There is something in his saddlebag. His horse is there.'

The object was a bag made of finely-sewn leather. Tzani-bey, a soldier at either side, knelt in the mud and smiled up at Nicholas. Zacco released him. Nicholas opened the draw-string and tipped to the ground the single object it contained. It lay in the mud, but not contaminated by it; the beard combed, the eyes closed, the mind, with all its learning, withdrawn from the service of mankind. The head of Abul Ismail, the physician.

The emir said, 'If I have misjudged him, he will be in his pavilion in Paradise. But I think he was a traitor. There is a demon, Ser Niccolò, within that artisan clay that forms your nature. Or perhaps you would call it a siren like Melusine; a serpent; a scorpion. An island of scorpions has invited another. I wish you and your lord of Lusignan well of each other.'

'Abul Ismail. Who told you he was a traitor?' Nicholas said.

The Mameluke was gasping now, but his teeth were still set in a smile. He said, 'The King will tell you.'

'The King does not know,' said Zacco steadily. 'A brave man has died, but disloyalty has met the punishment it deserves. But for Abul Ismail, I should be dead on this field.'

The Mameluke was yellow-white, but he laughed. 'How? Have I tried to assassinate you? I am alone.'

'That was not your plan,' the King said. He looked up. The Sicilian Rizzo di Marino dismounted, mud-covered, and came to stand beside him.

The chamberlain said, 'Why is he living?'

'Only to hear your news,' the King said.

Nicholas thought his voice sounded peculiar. He felt extremely cold and oddly isolated. It came to him that all the voices around him sounded strange, and that his eyes were closed. He opened them. Astorre, behind him, said, 'It wasn't bad, but you were stupid to take that one in your side. Go on. Keep standing. I've got you.'

The kneeling man he had maimed said, 'What news?' in clear French, not Arabic.

Rizzo di Marino said, 'Oh, you can guess. I've just come from your camp. I took with me my whole force from Nicosia. You had learned – I shall not ask how – that the King knew of your plot to overthrow him. You cancelled their march to attack Famagusta, and your men were still complaining because of it. It was dark. They hardly heard us arriving.'

'You've raided my camp? Taken my soldiers?' said Tzani-bey.

'Taken them? In a sense,' said Zacco's chancellor. 'In the sense that none of them got to escape us. Two hundred Mamelukes and two hundred foot. They'd have caused quite a battle if you'd changed your mind, and they'd attacked Famagusta.'

'But they didn't,' the emir said.

'No, they couldn't,' said Rizzo di Marino. 'They really couldn't. Not then, or any other day. We killed them all. Every last man is dead.' He turned and said, 'He's heard the news now.'

'So he has,' said the King. He looked at Nicholas. 'Nikko? It is your privilege. You suffered the insult. Abul Ismail was your friend.'

On the face of the emir Tzani-bey al-Ablak was only contempt. 'No,' he said. 'If there has been a massacre, I should guess your little lord Niccolò must be thanked for it. I should guess none of this would have happened without him. Your Nikko will not strike my head off. You will have to do that. But his is the blood that will pay for it.'

He spoke to the King, but his eyes were on Nicholas still, and remained there before and during and after the slash with which the King cut off his head.

Chapter 44

IT WAS EXTRAORDINARY, after that, how difficult it was to leave Famagusta for Nicosia, which Nicholas had fled, to the risk of his life, nearly two months before.

To begin with, of course, he couldn't ride. Indeed, they took him straight from the field to the Franciscan monastery, where he was received with cries of dismay and admiration by the loving, gaunt, familiar faces. Now, the wards where he had served were half empty, and the store cupboards full, and the gardens outside the cloisters green with grass and weeds growing together, and the first waxen petals of cyclamen opening under the bushes.

Infected Famagusta was not the best place for the healing of wounds, but they had fresh ointments and bandaging, and their sutures were nearly as good as Tobie's or Abul's. It was the friars of St Francis who found for him the sundered body of the Arab physician, and took it into their care until it could be committed to the soil of his own land.

Astorre came to see him, and Thomas, and John. Philip Pesaro was among the first, and there were other captains. They tended to talk boisterously of the fight, but not of its implications. It was as if the breaking of a hundred years of Genoese rule in Famagusta had happened in a way that could not be assimilated. As if, occupying itself with bursts of familiar activity, the army which had striven so long to conquer the island was unable to comprehend what had happened. And to this had been added an event of primaeval ferocity. The Mameluke force supplied them by the Sultan at Cairo had been annihilated, and the repercussions of that, in Cairo, in Venice, in Constantinople, had still to be faced.

James of Lusignan came to the convent of the Franciscans later than most, and brought the Archbishop William Goneme with him. There were no tender attentions, as there had been in the villa in Nicosia. The King's face was marked with indecision and his fingers moved restlessly on his knee. Nicholas said, 'This is nonsense. I shouldn't be here. A good horse and some strong boots, and I'll be in Nicosia tomorrow.'

'No!' Zacco said. 'With such cuts? With such loss of blood? Take your ease. And when your mind seeks occupation, go to Sigouri. Call your men there. Acquaint yourself with the castle, its lands, the sugar fields all about it. Nicosia is merely a depot. But what has to be done here? The harbour cleared, the ships raised, the warehouses rebuilt, the villas cleansed and made habitable. The mills and conduits are damaged. The yards are wrecked that used to produce soap and oil, dyes and wine. The food stores are polluted and empty; the quays weed-covered and useless. The workers, the merchants have to be induced to come back. The city needs horses, camels, oxen, goats and cows to be milked; poultry to lay. Its defences must be restored. Where are the records of its customs? How many of its craftsmen have died – the smiths, the coopers, the workers in textiles and metal; the artisans of the arsenal? Where are the women and children, the elders that were sent from the city and must now be brought back? Have you thought of that, Niccolò?'

'Someone must think of it,' Nicholas said. 'But I accepted a contract to fight, and to bring the sugar reeds into profit, and foster the dyeworks. You have other hands for the rest.'

The King rose. 'That contract is ended. I offer you a better one. Should I not? I owe you my kingdom, my life, my wellbeing. Think of it. Take it.'

'And the Mamelukes?' rejoined Nicholas, quickly.

The King gave a disarming smile. 'You prepared the way, my sweet Nikko. The Sultan Khushcadam in Cairo will appear shocked, but will be quickly appeased. Our Archbishop is no naïve ambassador: he has performed this task before, and successfully. With our abundant regrets, he will take glorious presents.' Zacco shot him a sudden radiant glance. 'Nikko? You could go with him.'

Stumbling, alone, about Egypt. Nicholas quelled a snort of feverish laughter and said, 'You are kind, my lord. But I wish, at present, to go back to Nicosia. In a marriage, such decisions belong to both husband and wife.'

He watched the King go, and the Archbishop, pausing to bless him. He rehearsed in his mind all that he wanted to say next time in private to Zacco, and then found that he had rehearsed in his sleep, and it was the following day. He said to the first friar who came near him, 'Where is the King lodging now?'

And the friar, soothing him, said, 'The King has gone to Nicosia, my lord. The others are about to depart also. They stayed, latterly, in the Palace.'

He got to the Palace, finally, using a stick, and eluding his nurses. Zacco had gone, and the horses were waiting for Rizzo di Marino. Nicholas had himself announced to his room.

The Chancellor said, 'I should have come, but the friars tattle. Sit. The King says he has asked you to stay?'

Nicholas sat, and propped his underlip with the knob of his stick. He said, removing it, 'You led the action, I'm told, against the Mamelukes?'

'That is true,' said Rizzo di Marino. 'The emir's absence was, of course, a prime necessity. The King has told you, I am sure, of our gratitude.'

'He endorsed the killing?' Nicholas said.

'My dear Ser Niccolò, he knew nothing of it. Like yourself, he expected the Egyptians to enter Famagusta. I do not mind shouldering blame. It seemed to me,' said the chamberlain, 'that it was better to prevent such an event than to risk the King's life.'

'I am sure the King's uncle agreed,' Nicholas said. 'It is sad, however, that Tzani-bey discovered not merely that we had been warned, but who had warned us. Just as it was useful, one might say, that Tzani-bey learned of the negotiations with Uzum Hasan that led him to plan the revolt. Very few knew of that.'

The Sicilian gazed at him. 'Let me ask you. Do you regret Tzani-bey's death? No. Does the disposal of a pack of leaderless Mamelukes disturb you? Surely not. Then by whatever means these things were enabled to happen, should one criticise them? I do not, and neither should you, I suggest. Take what you are offered, and enjoy it.'

He was loyal. Regrettably, Rizzo di Marino was loyal, and would betray nobody. There was one more piece of information, however, he might be willing to give. 'And stay away from Nicosia?' Nicholas asked.

Rizzo di Marino gazed at him contemplatively. He said, 'I am like you. I take life by the jaws. I do not look for it to be easy or pleasant. Go to Nicosia if you must. But it is not what the King expects. Do not strain his affection, or count on his temper. Your time will come when he finds that, having disposed of the Sultan, he is threatened by Venice.'

The Franciscans had missed him, and were reproachful. He got hold of Astorre, and sent him out of the city with Thomas, to prepare to strike camp and move out on orders. To questions he said, 'Give me two days, then come to Nicosia. Then we'll talk of the future.' He could see the gleam in Astorre's eye, and could imagine how, with Thomas, he'd pass the night listing wars that he fancied. He felt, quite suddenly, in despair.

To John le Grant he said, 'Nicosia late tomorrow. I have rounds to do first. What's the news? Is Crackbene back from Salines? Is the King celebrating, planning, mourning, whoring or just getting drunk?'

'Rumour says,' said the engineer, 'that he got off his horse and went straight to his mother. Crackbene's in Nicosia with his Genoese prisoners from the *Adorno*. Tobie and Loppe have Diniz with them at the villa. Zorzi is still in the dyeyard, prior, I assume, to receiving the business from you by royal command on a big dirty plate. Our good old Venetian friends are all in Nicosia, since the King won't allow them to come here in case they get dragged into corners and slaughtered. The leaders of Famagusta have been lodged till they see what their Republic will pay for them. Your wife is still in the Palace. What else do you want to know?'

Nicholas said, 'Who are Crackbene's Genoese prisoners?'

'I don't know,' said John le Grant. 'If you'll stay here, I'll go to Mick and find out. You think it's someone connected with that poor lady?'

'She thought so,' Nicholas said. 'So did Gregorio. He thought her husband Simon would come. And the ship was the *Adorno*. There's no need to be my errand boy. I've said. I'm going to Nicosia tomorrow.'

The rounds he had spoken of Nicholas did next day himself, while John le Grant waited for him. They were simple enough: the churches, the hospices, the homes where he had worked with Abul Ismail. The villa. And another call.

None of it was very easy, for he was weak, and could walk very little, although he had the sense to take servants with him. It was trying in other ways also, for he saw how much he was needed. Seven weeks of adequate food had not yet brought life and bloom back to the faces he recognised and some had gone, stricken with illness. But now there were children, one or two; and a new baby who wouldn't know the cold brick of the church of St Anna. In the hospice of the Knights of St John he found the brethren he knew and many others newly come and already busy, scouring, cleaning, replenishing and looking after the sick in their ward-cots with martial and relentless energy. They had brought the silver dishes, the porringers, the drinking-tubes; the sheepskin coats for the trip to the privy. Zacco was right. Kolossi was empty.

Louis de Magnac and de Combort were among the brethren. Now Nicholas was greeted with warmth, his trespasses more than forgiven. He returned the greeting as readily, for he saw the Knights himself through different eyes. They too fought and nursed. They too had studied both faces of war and yet persevered. These men had defied the cannon of Famagusta, had walked unarmed through the night in the quiet procession that had delivered the city. Theirs was a sober act of courage and charity that stood apart from the intrigues that had led to it. He didn't have to be told what the schemes had been, or who had framed them. He had recognised the cold-blooded incitement that sought to provoke his attack on Famagusta. He could imagine the suave indiscretion through which finally Zacco would learn of his Niccolò's danger. And he could guess the source of the pressure which at length persuaded men of good works to petition the King, and to set out to provision the city. Greed and guile, shame and desire had generated that merciful armistice. But from all that, life had come, to offset the deaths he had also caused.

Meanwhile, John le Grant waited at the Franciscans', with the easy horses and the good mounted escort that would carry them both to whatever awaited them in Nicosia. Since men were not children, he had left Nicholas to his own devices. The abbot had been succinct. 'Nasty flesh wounds; loss of blood; a general lack of condition. Watch the thigh, the arm. He'll be aware of his shoulder. Rest before he goes; rest halfway there, and he'll do. Sleep and good food, and no fretting. Advice for angels, eh? Not for a young man with that intelligence.' He had shaken his head. 'What he did for us during the siege? He was sent from heaven. And the other. We have prayed, although he was an infidel, for the other.'

John le Grant had been into a church himself that day. Inside the Cathedral of St Nicholas a Mass had been in progress: he found it difficult to get someone to show him the tomb that he looked for, and he walked slowly towards it, for he did not wish to meet Nicholas there. Although swept, the place kept the odours of all the uses to which it had been put these last years. It brought back to mind the church in the fort of St Hilarion; and all that he and Tobie and Nicholas wanted to forget of that day.

The coffin when he found it was new and cheap; one of those brought in by cart from Nicosia until the carpenters could provide a better. On the top was a little sheaf of white sweet-smelling cyclamen, and a wisp of dry, plaited reeds whose significance, if any, was beyond him. It told him at least that Nicholas had managed to get there. And whatever had happened between them Katelina had been bequeathed, in the end, to the shelter of this noble house of the saint of his name. John le Grant left the Cathedral with measured steps, thinking of something that Thomas had once told him, and experiencing an obscure unease of the spirit that could hardly be called dread.

Soon after he got back, Nicholas came, and they set off in silence. Fifteen painful miles on the road, Nicholas said, 'What is the worst possible thing that could happen to you or to me at this moment?'

The dread was still there. John le Grant found his dourest voice and used it. 'You tell me.'

'Because it's going to happen,' said Nicholas. His eyes were on the road ahead. The engineer's followed them. Waiting for them, his legs stuck out like semaphores on either side of his mule, was Ludovico da Bologna, Patriarch of Antioch.

'Psimoloso,' he shouted as soon as they came within earshot. It was incomprehensible.

'Oh, Lord God,' said Nicholas.

The Patriarch rode up.

Wherever he had been that morning, he had not taken time to shave. Beneath his conical hat with its veil his hair sprang out with its usual ferocious vigour. It merged with his thicketed brows and the cores of his nose and his ears. His face was pitted. He looked like a badly-stuffed, boiled leather cuirass. 'And you smell,' he said to John le Grant, as if he had spoken. 'Even the King smelt, by the time he came away. Come on. That's the estate over there. There's a house of sorts. The villagers won't pay their dues because this fellow keeps diverting the river. You'll show me what to do about that, and Launcelot here will listen while I tell him what to do. Bring the men. There's a barn.'

'Where?' said John le Grant.

Nicholas answered. A spark had appeared among the shadows of his bloodless face. 'You heard. Psimoloso,' he said. 'It's one of the casals of the Patriarchate. Over there, on the Pedhieos. Do you want to go there?'

What a moment ago had seemed appalling appeared suddenly to have a certain value. John said, 'Why not? Who's in a hurry?' They turned off the road and progressed slowly, the mule trotting along at their stirrups.

'You'll get bacon for supper,' said the Patriarch of Antioch. 'They do well with pigs around here. Wheat, when the river behaves. Peas. Lentils. Chickpeas. Olives. Carobs. Onions. We do a big trade in onions. Nice, lush country up by Kythrea, too. If he's giving you Sigouri and Prastio, hold out for Palekythro. Fine sugarcane round about there, and it's upriver from me. You can keep these rascals away from my water rights. Of course, he may change his mind about where he wants you.'

'The King?' Nicholas said.

'He'll find out now how much help he'll need in Nicosia. And William will need to be off, smarming over the Sultan in Cairo. We did a good job over Uzum Hasan,' said the Patriarch.

'We?' said Nicholas.

'Well, Venice worked like rats on a wheel to get Uzum to rise against Constantinople. That was last year. He didn't. You got hold of him through Damascus and Karaman, and I did my bit. He didn't fight for us either, but he might. A combined Turcoman and Ethiopian army would have given them all something to think about. Well, better luck next time. To get the Mamelukes done for was something.'

John said, '*Venice* was in parley with Uzum Hasan? So they might have . . . suggested the Trebizond letter?'

'We're all sobbing over the late pervert the Emperor David?' The Patriarch jerked a soiled thumb at Nicholas. 'Could be his fault. Could be my fault. Maybe Zorzi suggested it, the famous letter that killed him, or Corner, or one of these wives that our Niccolò can't keep his hands off. Legitimate gamble: God allows you to use any tool against Turks. Look at Abul Ismail.'

John's voice clashed with that of Nicholas, speaking softly. Nicholas said, 'Who betrayed Abul Ismail? Was it Markios?'

'Of course. It was time to get rid of the Mamelukes. The Palace knew you could help them to do it. They didn't expect you to deal with Uzum Hasan, but they knew you'd make for the emir as soon as Famagusta was free, and whatever you did might be worked up into some sort of rising. *His head in a pig trough*, rumour has it. Well, you got the doctor's skull off as well, but don't pine over it. He'd already made his preferences clear, and Tzani-bey wouldn't have let him survive. Also, there are worse ways than taking off heads. I'll tell you some of them, when we're not having bacon.'

They arrived shortly after; and had the bacon in the course of a remarkably good meal, during which Nicholas fell asleep. His host, continuing to talk, paid no attention to him. At the end he slammed down his knife and said, 'Bed. I hold prayers at dawn. Then I'll go with you to Nicosia.' His eyes followed John's to the table where Nicholas remained among the darkened candles, his head resting on his crossed arms.

The Patriarch said, 'Leave him. He's warm, he's in shelter, he's got food inside him. Zacco says he's got himself surrounded by grandmothers. You've got better sense.'

'We have a working partnership,' said John le Grant.

'Then keep him stretched,' said Ludovico da Bologna. 'Make him work that busy mind till he sweats. Oppose him. Challenge him. Fill him with acid. Then no one will make a meal of him before we find out what he's good for. Have I wakened you?'

A hazy sound emerged from the table. Without enthusiasm, Nicholas slowly unfolded, set his elbows apart, and propped his head on his hands with his eyes shut. He said, 'I got to where he had to stretch me in acid.'

'Well, I'm glad you're awake,' said the Patriarch of Antioch. 'Prayers at dawn, did you hear? Then we go to Nicosia. Master John can go straight to the villa, but I have to take you to the Palace. After, on second thoughts, you've been to the villa. In those clothes, you'd stink the place out.'

Nicholas had opened his eyes. He said, '*You* have to take *me*? Who arranged that?'

'I could make you guess, but I won't. The lady Marietta, crudely referred to as Cropnose. She wants to talk about the *Adorno*.'

Nicholas took down his hands. 'What about the *Adorno*?'

'That man Crackbene of yours, he's a hero,' said the Patriarch. He seized the one remaining lamp and lit a candle from it. 'You'll need that for your room. Rang all the bells in Nicosia for him when Crackbene came back from Salines, and last night the King gave him a feast and a gold cup. Twelve prisoners he brought back, apart from the crew. The King expects to collect a good ransom.'

John le Grant remembered why he hated Ludovico da Bologna. He said, 'Were all the men on the *Adorno* from Genoa?'

'Most of them were,' the Patriarch said. 'One of them wasn't.' He was looking at Nicholas. Nicholas said absolutely nothing.

The Patriarch said, 'But then, you were expecting that. So was the Portuguese boy. Vasquez. Diniz Vasquez. The boy thought you should go into hiding. But the lady Marietta said of course not; she'd send for you.' He grinned at Nicholas. 'Do you want to go into hiding? I could tell her.'

'No,' said Nicholas. 'But tell me his name. The name of the man from the *Adorno* who wasn't Genoese.'

The priest lifted his immense, black-clad shoulders. The candle flared in its wax and his hatted shadow loomed on the white plaster behind him. He said, 'Should I remember? I saw the man. I got a look at him once in St Omer. I made no note of the name.'

Nicholas said, 'What did he look like?' His voice was what you might expect, from a man just awakened from sleep.

The Patriarch lifted the ridge of his brows and surveyed both of them. 'Had she more than one relative, the poor young Flemish lady? Who would you expect to travel to Cyprus, with the boy's father killed, and now his aunt in her grave? I can only tell you that he is a rich man, or he would never have got so much flesh on him. A powerful man, because he treated the servants like vermin and addressed the King as if he were close to an equal. And a malicious man, because he said he had come to marvel at the King's latest protégé, who had made his son a widower and his daughter a widow and himself groom to a strumpet, and all in the space of a twelvemonth.'

Nicholas looked at him, his face totally blank. John thought cautiously, *his son.* This could not, then, be Simon de St Pol, husband of Katelina. Simon de St Pol had been in Venice, and had tried to kill Nicholas then. Without being present, John had heard all the stories and he knew what Simon looked like, which was an Adonis. Nicholas had expected Simon. He had expected him on Rhodes as well. But Simon hadn't come. He had been prevented, or had sent someone else, or had been forced to give way to someone else. And the someone else must be Simon's father.

Nicholas said, 'You are speaking of Jordan de Ribérac.'

'You have it!' said Ludovico da Bologna. 'Ribérac. Land of troubadours. *I am Arnaut who gathers the wind; And hunts the hare with the fox; And swims against the incoming tide.* The vicomte de Ribérac. Not a troubadour. Friend of René of Anjou. Financial adviser to the French King. Doesn't like you. Perhaps you ought to go back to Famagusta.'

'Or to sleep,' said Nicholas. 'Prayers at dawn?'

'I'd advise it,' said the Patriarch of Antioch.

Chapter 45

AMONG THE MANY who feared and detested the vicomte de Ribérac was his Portuguese grandson Diniz Vasquez. The news of de Ribérac's presence in Cyprus reached Diniz in Nicosia on the same day that Nicholas heard it. Nicholas, immobilised under the Patriach's roof at Psimoloso could, as yet, do nothing about it. Diniz, on the other hand, took immediate action.

Once, a child in Portugal, Diniz had feared this cold, obese man for the sake of his mother, who was de Ribérac's daughter. Now he was afraid for other reasons. *I can't wait*, Katelina van Borselen had said in her anguish; expecting her husband to come hunting vander Poele; fearing that without herself to mediate, murder would follow. But instead of Simon, Simon's father had arrived on the relief ship *Adorno*. This gross man who spoke of her husband his heir with contempt; who had welcomed the proposition that a son of René of Anjou should kill Niccolò, the family bane, in the Abruzzi. Or so Katelina had said.

In those months in Famagusta during which he had been forced into manhood, Diniz Vasquez had learned to understand Katelina, the odd, impatient second wife of his uncle, as he had learned to know Niccolò vander Poele, the unacknowledged son of the first. The bond between the two was now plain, and he could at least guess at some of its history. Also, alone of survivors, Diniz knew why she had come to Famagusta, and why she had stayed there. And he was prepared, as she had been, to protect so far as he was able the man whom he now, in his thoughts, called Niccolò.

He was afraid of his grandfather, but he was not a coward. He had left Famagusta in good faith, persuaded by the doctor Beventini that vander Poele would be better off without both of them. On entering Nicosia and the villa, his first resolution, almost forgotten now, had been to challenge Bartolomeo Zorzi, the Venetian who had made his escape from the dyeyard so simple.

The doctor had restrained him. 'Nicholas wants to interview Zorzi himself. If you'd like to watch an artist at work, go and listen to him when he does it. If he lives to do it. When are you leaving?'

Diniz had flushed. 'I can get a room somewhere else.'

'No,' the doctor had said irritably. 'To go home. You've got a mother, haven't you? If she doesn't know that poor girl is dead, she can't take steps to help with her baby. What will happen to it?'

'I don't know,' said Diniz. 'She left letters for Simon and my mother. I haven't opened them.'

'Well, the longer you languish about here, the longer it'll be till they open them.' The doctor's words might be harsh, but Diniz saw he was worried, not angry. In any case, he himself would never leave before vander Poele came. He had no idea, then, that Niccolò intended to settle his score with the Mameluke. He had been stunned, as had all Nicosia, by the news of the massacre at the Mamelukes' camp. He had been terrified by the news from Famagusta, brought by Beventini, who had bounded into the room in a swirl of medical oaths. 'I knew it! The stupid, vindictive young dummy! While Rizzo di Marino was clearing out Mamelukes, Nicholas was engaging Tzani-bey in a cut-throat fight to the death in Famagusta.'

The big negro called Loppe was in the room. He looked up and waited. 'What happened?' said Diniz.

'He chopped off Tzani-bey's hand. Delightful. The emir's dead, and Nicholas is at the Franciscans' getting patched up.'

'You'd better tell his lady wife?' said Loppe after a moment.

The doctor said, 'She knows. She told me. They're all in a state at the Palace. And Crackbene's back from Salines. They've crowned him with flowers and assigned him a royal apartment. They don't know whether they're ringing the bells for the surrender of Famagusta or the happy demise of the emir. The King is expected to ride in today to give Crackbene his victory medal. I'd better get on the road and see to that damned fool in Famagusta. They killed Abul Ismail.'

'What?' said Diniz.

'The emir did it,' said the doctor. 'Found out somehow the Arab betrayed him. They're a mad race, but he was a good doctor. I suppose they fight it all out in Paradise. I'll be off.'

The negro said, 'Master Tobie. If Master Nicholas is with the Franciscans, they will care for him. And Master John is still there.' He used formal speech, as he always did, but Diniz was surprised by a glance which, quick though it was, was less than formal. Loppe added, 'I don't suppose there is news of the prisoners? The men who arrived on the *Adorno*?'

The doctor stopped and frowned at Diniz. He said, 'Well, I might as well tell you. Yes. Crackbene brought back the *Adorno* prisoners.'

Diniz said, 'And Simon my uncle is with them?' He felt sick. Simon was probably here. By now, Simon would know that his wife Katelina was dead.

'No,' said Tobie. 'Not Simon. It's that shameless great bladder that gave Nicholas the scar on his face. Your grandfather, Jordan de Ribérac. And stay away from him, boy. You had your chance with the axe. You've blabbed enough as it is about Nicholas.'

Diniz felt himself flush. He said, 'No, I think I could help.'

'You can,' said the doctor. 'By staying away.' He touched the man Loppe and, turning, made for the door. The negro glanced back once as he left, although Diniz couldn't read his expression. But later, alone in his room, he heard a tap on the door and found Loppe waiting to speak to him.

He had never considered who or what Loppe was. As major domo of the villa, as manager, so they said, of the sugar estates, he was clearly a person of more consequence than he appeared – a former Guinea slave, a negro, the member of an inferior race. But he was also, he had found, a member of the Bank of Niccolò; a voice, if a quiet one, in its deliberations, and a friend of vander Poele whose personal association with him went back for several years. Now Loppe said, 'Master Tobie has decided to stay. It is better. Sometimes Master Nicholas is offered more help than he needs. If he requires any now, it is in another direction.'

Jordan de Ribérac. Diniz said, 'If I could see my grandfather, I might be able to explain what has happened. Otherwise he will blame Messer Niccolò.'

'It is what I wondered,' said the negro. 'I could have you taken to the Palace. I cannot tell if M. le vicomte would see you. Would you come?'

He went, and met total failure. The name of Niccolò vander Poele was known throughout the Palace. Diniz learned where the prisoners of the *Adorno* were held, and saw the guards, and arranged to be admitted to the locked room where his grandfather was. The guards disappeared to speak to his grandfather and returned. He had braced himself in vain. His grandfather refused to entertain him.

He didn't believe them, and sent them back. They returned, lashed by the Ribérac tongue, and told him to go away. He insisted.

That was a mistake, for it caused a disturbance, and finally some other guards came and he was locked in a room until someone checked who he was. He sat nursing a headache of the kind he now shared with Niccolò, and which Abul Ismail had said would disappear. It got worse. He expected, when the door opened, to see the captain of the palace. It wasn't. It was a beautiful woman. It was Primaflora, the wife of Niccolò whom, under normal conditions, Niccolò said he wouldn't have married.

Long ago, Diniz had thought her the fairest woman on earth. He continued to think so even after he had found out she was a courtesan, and was helping Niccolò, and was prepared to allow him what Diniz himself only dreamed of. After his father died, Diniz had ranged himself against vander Poele on account of Primaflora as much as anything.

And then had come her long absence in Rhodes, and his service in the dyeyard, and the act of his that was meant to kill the man he blamed for all his misery. The treacherous act, for which he had been punished. After that, the reality of Primaflora had faded, and he had escaped to Famagusta without seeing her again, and had met Niccolò vander Poele, and had found that, after all, he could trust him. Even when told of his marriage, he had felt no jealousy, except on Katelina's behalf. And he had no doubts now about the quality of Niccolò's commitment to Katelina, before or during her illness. Or indeed to his fellow men. No one who was merely a trickster could have behaved as he did, week after terrible week, when their lives, their relationships, their souls seemed transparent. After Famagusta, all the strivings of everyday life appeared paltry.

Now, seeing Primaflora, his first thoughts were still with Katelina, and the promise he had made. He said, 'The vicomte de Ribérac is my grandfather. Can you help me to see him?'

'Your *grandfather*?' she said. 'But of course I shall help you. Were you stopped? Diniz, how you have suffered! All those months in Famagusta, you and the sad lady Katelina. You were strong, and survived. That is courage. You made your peace with Niccolò, too. You know he is wounded?'

'I heard. It's about that. In a way, it's about that,' said Diniz. 'If I can't see my grandfather, I think Messer Niccolò should be warned to stay away until the vicomte has gone. My grandfather will blame him, you see.'

'For what? For your father's death? But you know now that Niccolò had nothing to do with it?'

'He will think he had. He will think he killed Katelina. Katelina warned Messer Niccolò. She said one of the family would come looking for vengeance. She said that unless one of us could get to him first and explain, he should go into hiding.'

'Niccolò?' said Primaflora. She smiled. 'I know he will want to do whatever that poor lady wanted, but I don't think he should stay locked up in Famagusta for ever. Suppose I take you to your grandfather now? The guards will let me in.'

'They were prepared to let me in,' Diniz said. 'The vicomte won't see me.'

'Ah,' said Primaflora. 'Then perhaps we should wait, and I shall try. Go back to the villa. If the vicomte consents, I shall send for

you. After all, he is only one fat and elderly man. I don't really
think he could succeed where a Mameluke emir lost his life. Leave
it to me.'

He felt some uncertainty. But she spoke with conviction, and he
thought that, from curiosity, his grandfather might very possibly
see her. And, of course, she could defend her husband better than
he could. He left, and found and told his story to Loppe, who
received it with almost no comment. Then he waited, but Primaflora didn't send for him. He was planning to go back to the Palace
when, the following morning, vander Poele and John le Grant rode
in, on either side of the Patriarch of Antioch.

Hooded and cloaked against rain, their shapes and condition
were hardly discernible. But the doctor stood still, saying nothing,
and after a moment dragged off his cap, presenting his scalp to
the rain. He said, 'Jordan de Ribérac's here. Get down. There's a
bed made up. Has anyone seen you?'

'Nothing,' said vander Poele, 'compared to the numbers who are
about to see me. I have to go to the Palace. I've just to change.'

'Who says?' said the doctor. His face had turned red.

'The King's mother, apparently,' vander Poele said. 'The Patriarch is to take me.'

'Take you both, said the priest. 'You and the boy.' He bent an
undisturbed scowl upon Diniz. 'Are you thanking me? I saw your
father's corpse off from Rhodes.'

'I would thank you,' said Diniz, 'if you took me to see my grandfather.'

'Done!' roared Ludovico da Bologna. 'And I'll take a good
dinner off you in payment. He'll be in Cropnose's chamber by
now, and itching to see you and your battered friend here. It was
Cropnose's idea. A nice family reunion. Be sure to thank her.'

'I suppose,' vander Poele said, 'the Lusignan know all about nice
family reunions. Are you coming to this touching occasion?' His
voice was amused, but he stood as if his bones were welded
together, and his skin was the colour of beeswax.

'Me?' said Ludovico da Bologna. 'I, thank God, am not a St Pol
or a Vasquez or a Lusignan. By the way, you don't need to pay me
for lodging. I got that in advance from the Palace.'

He turned away. Niccolò let fall his cloak and said, 'Diniz. You
tried to see your grandfather? Who else did you talk to?'

His face must have changed, because before he could answer,
vander Poele said, 'Never mind.'

Since the *Adorno* arrived, it had been evident to Nicholas that
some such meeting was about to take place, although he had
thought (as he always tended to think) that he would be confronted
by Simon. He had know that he would be unfit, but not that he

would be strapped in so many places with bandaging. Finding clothes to accommodate it all had been a nuisance, and tiring, but he had faced magistrates before in a shakier state. He had faced Tzani-bey, and defeated him. But Tzani-bey was not related to him, which had made it simpler.

The apartment they were taken to was the one to which he had been brought, fettered, sixteen months ago. As before, the walls were hung with silk and with carpets; the service table laden with silver; the red and blue bird shifted from leg to leg on its perch. The woman called Comomutene, or Cropnose, sat as before in her high chair of state, watching him with black, kohl-painted eyes from above her whistling veil, while her ladies stood, their hands gracefully folded, behind her.

Among them was Primaflora. He had forgotten — how could anyone forget? — the precise oval of her chin, and the short curling lips with their pleats. Her small ears, with the golden ringlets falling before them; the fine arch of her brows, and the pale, clear eyes under. She wore a gown he had never seen, embroidered with pearls he could have afforded, but had never had time to find for her. She wore a necklace he could not have afforded. Her gaze, making nothing of his stiffness or his pallor, was concerned only with his mind. He let her see what she wanted to see, but nothing more. Her lids slowly dropped, as if in submission. He turned to the King's mother and bowed as well as he could, while Diniz did likewise. Then he looked fully to one side of the chair where, this time, the hulking figure of Markios was not present. Instead, in a heavy seat fit for his bulk, Jordan de St Pol, vicomte de Ribérac, stared at him.

Tobie had called him a bladder, but the King of France's financial adviser was not a figure of fun. The vicomte de Ribérac was a broad-shouldered man of great size, which he exploited, as now, to suggest the quality and scale of his riches. He was heavily bejewelled. Beneath the extravagance of his headgear his large-featured face rested upon several chins; in a cloak of innumerable sables he filled a large room with his presence. His eyes, sharp in their pouches, scanned first Nicholas, then every inch of his young grandson's body. He was not smiling.

The King's mother said, 'There is the lord Niccolò vander Poele, whom you accuse. There is your grandson, who has worked as a serf in his dyeyard. Ser Niccolò, you know whom you face. He has laid charges against you. He accuses you of the killing of his daughter's husband Tristão Vasquez on Rhodes. He says he has proof that in Famagusta you and an idolatrous doctor, since murdered, brought about the death of his son's wife, Katelina. He claims that you and your manager contrived that his grandson Diniz Vasquez, bought by you and committed to serfdom, should be encouraged to escape so that he would find himself locked and starving inside Famagusta. He says that his son's wife and the boy were initially captured and brought to Cyprus by your agency, and their ransom ignored so that you might do them harm. He asks for your death. Boy, go to your grandfather.'

Nicholas said, 'Excellent lady?'

The veil turned. Nicholas said, 'They are of one blood. The boy should not have to choose. Let him leave us.'

'To *choose*?' said the King's mother. 'Between whom? Between you and his grandfather?'

Diniz stood without moving. He said, 'It isn't a question of choice, but of justice.'

The King's mother looked at the vicomte. He spoke to her, although his eyes didn't move from the boy. 'It is as I warned you. I require medical endorsement, for which I am willing to pay. You see where the child has taken his stance, at the side of his seducer. He knows how his father died; who killed the wife of my son. But he will not say now. He has chosen.'

Raw to the marrow, Nicholas heard him, and drew a hard breath. He had cause to know Jordan de Ribérac's cruelty. He had not been prepared to see it unsheathed to discredit a worn, bereaved boy. Beside him, Diniz had turned first red, then white. Nicholas said, 'You say that of your grandson in public? In public? Even if you believed it is true, and you don't? Will you do even that to get rid of me?'

And Jordan de Ribérac said, 'Remove yourself, Claes. That will stop me.'

Nicholas turned to the chair. 'My lady: let the boy go. This man is a captive. He has no rights here. He should have justice, but he cannot demand it. By process of law, if he has a complaint he may put it, and the courts in his own country will hear it. But why am I brought here to listen to him?'

De Ribérac looked at the chair of state. He said, 'Forgive me. There speaks the voice of privilege, or one who claims it. Have I been misled as to the position this fellow holds in your country? Is he known for these forms of depravity? Has he perhaps climbed to high position because of them?'

The veil blew, reflectively. The King's mother said, 'He holds high position because he has performed commensurate services. He is right. Whatever wrongs have been done you, it is not a matter for our jurisdiction. I shall mete out no punishments. It is my concern only to safeguard my son the King. We place trust in Ser Niccolò. If he has erred, I should like to be told of the circumstances. You call him Claes?'

'His name in the dyeyard,' said Jordan de Ribérac. 'But he called himself Nicholas when he thrust my grandson among the stinking vats in Nicosia. He paid his ransom himself in order to keep him. Ask where the boy lived. In the villa! Ask whether he knew his master's bedroom – he slept there. And ask how the boy got to Famagusta. Did you choose even that, Diniz, rather than continue to suffer? Or did he tire of you first, and release you, knowing where you would fly?'

Diniz said, 'The manager helped me escape. Bartolomeo Zorzi.'

Above the veil, the woman's eyes were intent. The fat man said, 'He saw what was happening? He was sorry for you?'

'No,' said Diniz. 'He worked me as hard as anyone. He was amused by anything that might embarrass Messer Niccolò. When I hit him –'

Nicholas moved, but too late. Diniz stopped. Behind the veil, the wheezing voice said, 'When you hit whom?' Under the broad, elaborate hat, the brows of Jordan de Ribérac were raised, also, in polite enquiry behind which, one could swear, was a gleam.

Diniz said, 'The supposed accident with the axe. It wasn't. I struck Messer Niccolò with it. You can't precisely claim, can you, that we were lovers!' His black hair, disordered, clung to his hot face.

The King's mother said, 'Lovers have tiffs. Messer Niccolò neither punished you nor reported it. Why was that? And why did you strike in the first place?'

'I was angry,' said Diniz. 'I thought he had put me in the dyeyard to shame me. Afterwards, I saw I was wrong. But it was Zorzi who suggested I should finish what I had started and kill him. He said his elder brother wouldn't like it, but his elder brother needn't know. I think he wanted the dyeyard,' said Diniz. The King's mother stared at him. So did Nicholas.

The vicomte de Ribérac said, 'I had no idea you had inherited the family temper. My congratulations. You tried to kill your tormentor, just because he put you in a dyeyard?'

'No,' said Diniz. He hesitated.

Nicholas said, 'Tell everything.'

Diniz said, 'I thought he had killed my father. I was wrong. Carlotta arranged it. Carlotta and someone else.'

'Wait,' said the King's mother. 'Why should the lady Carlotta have your father killed? Who told you? And who was the other person involved?'

Nicholas said, 'Forgive me. If this is to continue, honoured lady, would you allow me a seat?' It was not Primaflora who brought it, but a page.

Diniz, oblivious, waited fidgeting to make his reply. He said, 'I had it from the demoiselle Katelina van Borselen. She told me the Queen – that Carlotta – wanted Ser Niccolò in her service, and was trying to remove all impediments. She had designs on the demoiselle, and didn't care which of the party was injured. She said she didn't know who had arranged it.'

The King's mother said, 'It was known, M. de Ribérac, that the Flemish lady held some grudge against Messer Niccolò, and was bent on harming him. Forgive me if I speculate, but perhaps your own poor opinion of Messer Niccolò has grounds in the same family quarrel? Perhaps you even hoped the poor girl would act as your agent? Certainly, you made no effort to ransom and remove her.'

'There is no harm, Highness, in speculation,' said the fat man's mellow voice. 'If the gold did not come, it was simply because I was financially pressed. And my son, whose proper task of course it was, was abroad at the time. I would point out, however, that if I did not ransom the demoiselle Katelina, then neither did Claes. He did not wish to buy the young lady who disliked him. He bought the boy.'

Nicholas said, 'The demoiselle would have been free by the autumn. It was arranged with the King. Serenissima, do you wish to hear more? All these matters are finished with.'

'Certainly they are finished with,' said the vicomte de Ribérac, removing a hair from his lapel. He clasped his ringed hands. 'So is Katelina van Borselen, my son's wife. How strange, that she ends in Famagusta as Diniz did. How strange that you find your way there. How inevitable that when Famagusta is freed, she is dead. Of course, your acolyte here will say you didn't kill her.'

The King's mother said, 'Acolyte, M. de Ribérac? We have just heard how he attacked his supposed abductor with an axe and fled to a town under siege to escape him. If Ser Niccolò caused the young lady's death, then surely you can rely on your abused grandson to tell us?'

'Ah,' said the fat man. 'But they are not enemies now. They are now seducer and victim. Does it not tell you something, how their eyes meet? How they stand together, bonded against opposition? Against the boy's own family? Our friend Claes suggested a moment ago that the boy should not be forced to choose. But he has chosen. It is apparent. Let us ask him. Diniz, have you taken any steps to get away from this island since receiving your freedom?'

'No,' said Diniz.

'And are you coming home?' said Jordan de Ribérac.

Diniz said, 'Ser Niccolò has urged me to go back to Portugal. I should prefer to stay here.'

There was a short silence, during which the fat man sank a little back in his chair. The woman said, 'You have made your peace with each other?'

Nicholas said, 'In Famagusta, madame, there is no room today for petty matters. He is my good friend and I am his. No more, but that certainly.'

'You said,' said the woman, 'that you did not kill or cause to be killed Tristão Diniz?'

'No, honoured lady,' said Nicholas.

'But you have no proof. You maintain that you did nothing to hasten the death of Katelina van Borselen?'

'No, lady,' said Nicholas.

It was not true. Because of him, Diniz had gone to Famagusta and Katelina had joined him. Aphrodite. He heard, after a moment, the voice of Diniz in passionate affirmation. A wave of dizziness swept over him, leaving him cold but collected again. Diniz spoke still. He saw the fat man's eyes on his grandson, hooded and motionless in the overfed face. The last time he saw Diniz, his grandson must have been lithe and brown and burnished with vigour, as when Nicholas had met him first at Kolossi. Yet for the hollow-faced youth now before him, with the deep-set eyes and the thin arms and the low and passionate voice the vicomte showed no feeling of pride, or of pity or of shame. No, not shame. He could not believe, no man could believe what he had said of Diniz.

Something of the same thought must have struck Diniz, but not for himself. He looked across at his grandfather and said, 'You knew Katelina. You knew her in Bruges, surely, and in Anjou. You saw her in Brittany. My father said she helped you escape the old King. Don't you even want to know where she is buried?'

And the fat man stirred and said, 'A moody child of no great intellect but with a certain aptness of build. No. Her place of committal doesn't interest me. I should judge that she made sure it was as remote as was practicable from any haunt of her reviled servant Claes.'

Diniz opened his mouth, and there was no way Nicholas could think of to stop him. Then he closed it again, without speaking. For a moment, thinking about that, Nicholas lost the thread of what was happening again. Then he saw that the King's mother was also looking at Jordan de Ribérac. She said, 'Well? Are these all the complaints you wished to make? I have heard them. It seems to me that they have little bearing on the conduct of this kingdom, and that in the absence of proof, it is unlikely that you will quickly satisfy yourself before the time, I hope soon, when your ransom will be paid and you will be permitted to leave for home. The boy, of course, may leave or stay as he wishes.'

'The ransom,' said Jordan de Ribérac, 'has been assessed by a clerk with no knowledge of the world or hold on simple reality. Your royal son will, I hope, be brought to realise this in the interview I plan to hold with him. I shall tell him what has happened. I shall tell him how I have been treated. I shall suggest to him ways in which he may avert what will undoubtedly be the displeasure of France when I return and when I make these facts known. As for the boy, he will wait until I am ready to go, and then will leave with me, whether he wishes it or not. The future of this family rests in the hands of two weaklings: a child of three years, and Master Diniz Vasquez, unmarried at seventeen, and with a history that will fetch him no well-dowered heiress. His duty is at home, with his family company.'

The indulgent gaze, removed from the King's mother, turned on Nicholas. The fat man said, 'Which, of course, he is no more competent to run than that unfortunate mediocrity, my son Simon. Although he is learning. He almost made a success of his Portuguese venture, he was so determined to purloin your market. You are a remarkable stimulant, Claes, in your beef-brained fashion. And you can pay for trained intelligence, whereas Simon believes he has enough under his beautiful hair. Tell me, Claes. Are these clever minions of yours behind this firm of meddlers called Vatachino?'

Proportion came back to the world. Nicholas said, 'Is that why you sailed? To find that out?'

'You are afraid to tell me?' said the vicomte. 'Or no. I speak of a common disease?'

'Consult the Knights Hospitaller, the Corner, Carlotta. We are all suffering, my hired brains included. If you find out who they are, we should all be obliged to you.'

'Should you? Do I gather that you propose to continue your sugar concern? How very unwise,' said the fat man. 'But the magnificent lady is not interested in business.'

'I sell eggs from time to time,' said the King's mother. 'I follow reports. I assumed you both knew that an envoy for the house of Vatachino was in Nicosia at present? To find out who employs him is, I presume, merely a question of asking him.'

Diniz was smiling, and Nicholas felt like doing the same, if his face would obey him. He said, 'Lady, the walls tell you secrets. Where can he be found?'

'At this moment? He is with the King, I believe,' said Marietta of Patras. 'But I do not suggest that you disturb either of them. M. le vicomte, you may leave.'

The fat man rose, and the lights in the room seemed to dim. He said, 'I have been honoured. I am told, gracious lady, that you have given a home to the wife of my friend here. Might I know which she is?'

Cropnose signed. Primaflora moved into the light, like a thing of pale gilt and fine porcelain. She stood gravely collected, while the vicomte surveyed her. At length, he spoke. 'Whatever trade you have, my lovely lady, be sure not to discard it. You have married a husband whose life will be short, and who will keep you in bare feet and darned clothing.' He smiled, his eyes vanishing, his chins widening. 'Next time, seek a rich man. A rich man who husbands his wealth, no matter what his appearance. I have no difficulty in keeping my bed warm.'

'I shall remember,' said Primaflora. She spoke automatically, her face rather pale. The fat man bowed, and walked with ponderous dignity to the door which hastily opened, as no doubt all doors had always opened, before he reached it.

The King's mother said, 'I have a matter to put to Messer Niccolò here. None of you need remain except Primaflora. Boy, you can hope for no favours now the truth about your axe-blow is known. Go to Portugal now, if it irks you to wait for your grandfather.'

Diniz said, 'You have heard him and seen him.'

'Then perhaps your mother needs your help,' Cropnose said. 'Am I speaking in a language you cannot understand?'

Diniz flushed. Nicholas spoke to him directly. 'If the lady permits, I think you should return to the villa.' And as the boy hesitated he said, 'They will find an escort for me.'

The door closed upon silence. Primaflora stood behind the high chair, her eyes avoiding his. The parrot rasped a foot on its perch, and the brazier spat. He sat, sealed in a posture from which he could not readily move, and waited. The King's mother said, 'You have been told, I suppose, that the King's sister has given her lord a dead son. The marriage has not produced heirs and her husband Luis is to be away for some time, settling his considerable debts in the West. It seems fitting, therefore, that James of Cyprus, my son, should renew his search for a bride who will bring him both heirs, and the support of a well-disposed power. These matters take time, and meantime he has begotten many daughters, but few male children that live. I would see him provided in this interim with many strong natural sons, and handsome women to bear them. His eye has fallen on one.'

The parrot ruffled its feathers. 'She is fortunate,' Nicholas said.

'You think so?' said Marietta of Patras. 'Her husband is less so.'

'And what of the lady herself?' Nicholas said. 'Does she have both fortune and happiness?'

Primaflora lifted her head. She said, 'You know I must be the woman. I have found Apollo in the island of Apollo. Forgive me, Niccolò. I would have followed him had he been all that the vicomte threatened me with. Barefoot and in rags, I should follow him. Do I need to tell you? You love Zacco also.'

He did not even glance at Primaflora, although he addressed her. He said, 'So I have lost you? Or do we share, for appearances' sake? Once you proposed we should share in another way.'

And the King's mother, at whom he was looking, replied. 'She

should be married, but not to you or the King. Your vows were
hurriedly taken; they can be dissolved, and the papers returned to
you. Her husband requires to be a man of no prominence, with
whom she will form no attachment. You would not wish to share
her with the King?'

'No,' he said. His head moved, at least. He said, 'The King did
not feel able to tell me?'

The veiled woman said, 'He plans to inform you tomorrow, and,
if you are wise, you will receive it as news. I have told you now, to
help you prepare for it. For the same reason I shall allow you now
to meet this lady for the last time alone. You will say what has to
be said, but you will not touch her. She belongs to the King.'

'I understand,' Nicholas said. He got himself to his feet, wondering how he would walk without touching her. But after he bowed,
Primaflora slipped her hand under his elbow and walked with him
through the door, and along to her chamber for the last time.

Chapter 46

HAD HE DISCOVERED it anywhere in the world, Nicholas would have known that the room he was taken to was Primaflora's. The mirrors, the cushions. The lute and the manuscripts. The table heaped with the objects she loved to gather around her, as well as the precious vials and flasks she used for her art. The scents, mild and sensuous. And the bed. He wondered how much of it ever held Zacco's fierce, erratic attention, apart from the bed.

Perhaps she had followed his gaze; perhaps not. Pressing shut the door at his back, Primaflora turned to face him. She lifted her hands and examined him; touching his bandaged arms, his shoulders; tracing the place beneath the silk where his side was strapped. He made no effort to stop her. She used her smoothing hands to draw herself closer; to gather him into a deepening embrace until no further movement was possible. Her scent and her weight settled against him; he felt as if sunk against wax. His breath caught in his throat, despite everything. Below him was the warmth of her hair, near enough to touch with his lips. Her eyes were two closed shutters of lashes; the lips below were painfully smiling. She said, 'Seven weeks. Seven weeks, and you come to me a cripple?'

Except for the way they were standing, one shouldn't compare this in one's mind – or elsewhere – with another embrace, outside Kalopetra. Katelina had possessed none of these arts: only passion, and instinct. In a thousand ways, Primaflora had been trained to bestow pleasure. He had been the instrument on which she played; the tablet on which she placed her bounty. In the cabin of his own purloined ship the *Doria*; at Kolossi; on the ship taking two sweet-natured men, father and son, to their parting on Rhodes. At sea, after Lindos and their marriage. And then Nicosia, and the bed to which he had returned again and again, denying Zacco.

He knew her arts, and knew also, with absolute certainty, when she lost her hold of them. The hands behind him were unsteady, as were his. It had been more than seven weeks, for seven weeks ago Zacco had made sure that he shouldn't come to her as a husband. He knew how long, to a day, he had been celibate. She said, 'Lie down. Let me sit beside you.' Yet she held him fast, as if unable to free herself.

He said, 'I thought it was forbidden to touch.'

She showed no alarm or confusion, but lifted to him the same intent, anxious gaze which had investigated his wounds. Her grasp relaxed, just a little. She said, 'You must understand. You do. You live by the same rules. I have nothing. I have one profession. When a great man demands what I can give, I am afraid to refuse. But I also wish to practise my skills. It is unwise to tell you this. I should say that he threatened me. It's true that I'm afraid, but he didn't. I wanted to see if I could capture a king. Niccolò? Niccolò? Do you understand?'

'So you leave me,' Nicholas said.

She gave a laugh, and rested her head against him again. She said, 'I've just told you. My profession feeds me, so I follow it. But often, despite it, I starve.' There were tears on her cheeks. Below, the rounded haven of her body beat with his heart. She said, 'Could I be near you, and not touch you? Whenever Zacco will leave me, I shall come to you. Do I not deserve something more than an embrace for telling you that?'

Lindos, and sunlight, and perfumed oil spilling over his body. He put her hands down, and his own arms close around her, and kissed her in the long, airless way which had been his contribution to their union, and which, on the rare occasions he used it, gave private notice of a slow sequence of acts also sparingly offered. As he began to draw back from the kiss, a knock fell on the door at his back.

Neither spoke. The rap came again, and was repeated. She put her finger to her lips, and drew him with her palms to the bed. Her face was white. The blood throbbed through his wounds, and his head. He stroked his hands down to her wrists and freed himself. 'That will be Loppe,' he said, and walked to the door and flung it open.

Loppe's face was fixed; showing nothing of surprise or distaste, censure or apprehension. The sober grey-blue of his coat and doublet sat tidily on his great ebony frame, and his close black hair, perfectly groomed, held the tilt of his soft, folded hat. Across his palms, and unparcelled, lay a light object. On top of that was a packet. Nicholas said, 'Come in.' He turned. 'You don't mind? I asked him to help me home – well, to the villa.'

Primaflora stood by the bed. Sunlight, fountains, sweet scented oil. She looked as if her soul had been stolen, which was as it should be. Loppe said, 'I'll wait outside.'

'First,' said Nicholas, 'Give her the veil. No. Put it on her.'

It was unfair to Loppe, but he hesitated only a moment. Then, laying the packet aside, he shook out the fine thing he had carried. A long linen veil, striped with embroidery and crumpled like tissue for, of course, what is soaked in river-water will not dry itself smoothly. He walked to Primaflora and then, glancing at Nicholas, laid the pretty cloth over her hair, and arranged it to fall from her shoulders. As she felt it she winced, but stood silent. For a moment there was a small tableau: the fair, gilded woman; the negro. Then she said, 'A gift? It is beautiful.' She had to breathe twice as she said it.

'It is yours,' Nicholas said. 'You remember. You wore it once, at Kolossi. Open the packet now.' Loppe had moved. He needed only a sign to walk through the door and close it gently. Nicholas watched him go, and then turned.

She had flung up a hand to the veil. Now she turned it into an ordinary gesture, drawing the linen aside and letting it slip to the bed. She said, her voice clearing, 'Where did you find it? I left it with the Queen.'

'Carlotta,' he corrected her. He said kindly, 'Open the packet. It was to be given to you when I was dead.'

If I survive a second time, I must revise it. He had written it in December, on the night of the Feast of St Nicholas. There was nothing he wanted to add. He watched her as she read it, leaving unopened the personal thing he had also left her. He found a seat and descended carefully into it, still watching. At the end she said slowly, 'Small men are suspicious like this, and see treachery everywhere. You made love to me, and to Zacco, and all the time this is what you were thinking?'

'Recently,' Nicholas said, 'I haven't made love to anyone. But Zacco gives freely – and takes – although his mother usually determines the victim. What had happened was obvious, anyway, from the time Zacco came from Kyrenia. I remember the gowns you wear; I have cause to. There were too many others.'

'You have refused nothing he has given you,' Primaflora said. She walked away from him and back, and threw the letter down on the bed, before coming to stand, looking down on him. She said, 'As for the rest, it is nonsense.'

He said, 'When it was written, I didn't know Katelina was ill in Cyprus. Did you contrive that she went to immolate herself in Famagusta? She heard, from Carlotta she thought, that Diniz was trapped there and starving. But Carlotta has had very little, hasn't she, to do with all this?'

'You didn't tell me the city was starving,' said Primaflora. 'You said it could hold out until spring.'

'And you told Zacco,' Nicholas said. 'You were meant to. Otherwise he would have sent no food, and hoped for a quick surrender. You and the King's conscience, because of you, were what brought those relief wagons that night.'

He fell silent under her stare. She said, 'You used me?'

And Nicholas said, 'Give and take: I play games for a living. Zacco doesn't; you will have found that out already, perhaps. He can be ruthless, and so can his sister. Katelina and her family threatened me and the Cypriot sugar trade, at a time when Carlotta wanted both. Would she have gone to such lengths without you as her agent? The attack on the Portuguese that killed one of them, and brought Katelina there and very close to her death – didn't it matter that Diniz was sixteen, and adored you?'

She said, 'I was with you at the time! How could I have arranged it?'

'You hired killers,' said Nicholas. 'Do you want me to tell you what agents you used? I might not have found out if I hadn't followed Katelina to Rhodes to warn her about you, and made friends of Persefoni and her kinsmen. Katelina might be living today if I'd stayed with her until she left Rhodes, but I thought all I had to do was remove you.'

She backed slowly and sat on her coffer. She said, 'You love schemes, don't you? I wasn't an agent of Carlotta's. She asked me to spy on you, after the death of Ansaldo. When he died, I hated you and I hated her for expecting me to forget him. I didn't know Zacco's Venetian friends were going to trap both of us, or that you would refuse Zacco until you had overtaken your army. Carlotta was powerful. How could I have told her on Rhodes that I would never spy for her, or admitted that I had given myself to you, and not just my body? Do you think I do for any man what you have experienced? Do you, Niccolò? And when she sent you to Kyrenia, I followed. She forbade me, Niccolò, but I followed. You seemed glad.'

She was weeping, her face held immobile. Nicholas said, 'I didn't know, then, that Katelina was on board. I thought I had separated you. But of course, it was all right in the end. Zacco sent you back to Rhodes.' He felt his face crack in what was supposed to be a smile. He said, 'At that time, he wanted no rivals.'

It dried her tears, that reminder. She said, with a spurt of anger, 'And after? What designs could I or the Queen have had after Zacco employed you? She was more likely to encourage Katelina to kill you.'

'I expect she did,' Nicholas said. 'But she had to reckon with Cropnose, who had other plans. And, like Cropnose, you wanted me safe, for a short term, which gave you several good reasons for disposing of Katelina. Carlotta, you saw, was now never going to recover her throne. To get back to Cyprus, you needed me. Until, at least, James of Lusignan had noticed you. The King was always your goal, failing Carlotta. You knew he was young. You thought he was vulnerable. And if he wasn't at least you had a patron for life in your husband.'

With an uncharacteristic gesture, she put her hand to her body. She gathered herself. 'And that, too, was inside your mind while we lay together? That I could kill you, if it happened to suit me?'

'You wouldn't shirk murder,' said Nicholas. 'One other person at least recognized that: you've just seen him. Perhaps I might have been safe. With Zacco, you have influence, but he shares the pleasures of his bed among many, and the starving, as we know, are not his first concern. It would please you very much to be served by us both.'

'One for power, and one for love,' she said. 'You do understand. He is like one of his leopards. He waits for nothing, learns nothing. You learned too much. How to rule your heart with your head.'

'I was trained by a baccalaureate,' he said. 'And, of course, you used the same skills, the same subtlety to take away life, Primaflora. I was at Kalopetra. I heard of the ambush. I saw Katelina wearing that veil and I saw what happened. Who told you that insects drove her mad?'

'I don't remember,' she said; and turned and picked up his package, smoothing it.

'So someone told you,' he said. 'And you know what I am speaking about. What a death you sent her to. A valley of serpents, and a shawl impregnated to drive her crazy with horror.'

'It was the Queen's,' she said. 'I left it with the Queen.' The packet had fallen open in her twisting fingers. It was, of course, the blue and silver emblem of his Order, with its legend. *To remain loyal.* If he had died, that is what she would have received.

She said, 'Which of them gave this to you? The Queen or her worst enemy, Zacco?'

It had come from both sides, and he had accepted it. He said, 'It was a counter. A counter in the same game.'

She studied the badge, moving her thumbs over its surface. Tonight, she had dressed her hair formally. He noticed the pearls in her bent, pleated head, and the golden wisps shadowed her cheeks. She said, 'With your mind so made up, I shan't plead.'

He said nothing. On the nape of her neck was a mole. She had another. If you inhaled carefully, you could name each of the scents she used, and tell from where it was breathing. She sat like a child, with her knees together. She said, 'You will tell Zacco this?' She looked up.

Nicholas rose. She flinched as if she thought he would strike her, and he halted. Then he said, 'No. The King's pride would prevent him from believing me, and he would hate us both. In any case, there has been talking enough. They are all dead or gone, whom you hurt most.'

'But you will find a way to punish me,' said Primaflora. She stood.

'Oh, yes,' Nicholas said. 'I have done so already.'

'How?' she said.

'By depriving you of what you want most,' he said. 'A king's house, a king's bed, a secure future, a patron, a husband. After Zacco, you can hope for no help from Carlotta. And if you ever wanted me as I still want you, that, too, is lost to you. One word in the right place can do more harm than an axe, as you have shown. You will know when it has been spoken.'

He didn't know whether she realised what he was going to do. She didn't speak. There was nothing more he wanted to say, even if speech had not just become difficult. He walked to the door, leaving her where she stood. Loppe was outside. He heard her voice as he left. It said, 'You have forgotten Jordan de Ribérac.'

Because he was full of grim anger, and a very private variety of anguish, Nicholas talked to Loppe in brief outbursts on the way back to the villa and was still talking when Tobie met him in rage on the threshold. He had no memory afterwards of going to bed.

The next morning, he woke to find Astorre at his bedside. The captain, fully dressed and freshly returned, no doubt, from a practice bout in the courtyard, said, 'I thought I'd have a word before the rest finished at table. You're not married any more?'

With extreme clarity, Nicholas remembered that he was not married any more. He said, 'Dispositions are being made, I hear, to end the arrangement. Why?' He moved cautiously and found his limbs, although stiff, seemed to answer him. He contemplated what appeared to be a permanent condition of nausea.

Astorre said, 'Thomas told us it wouldn't work. I can't say I'm sorry. But what about the fat Frenchman?'

The fat Frenchman. Nicholas said, 'Oh. The vicomte de Ribérac. He's here to cause trouble. I don't think he'll manage it. Anyway, he's going to be paid for and sent home. Waves of hate coming from Portugal, but I suppose we can deal with that. Astorre friend, I did promise a conference. Can this wait?'

Astorre twitched back the bedclothes, inspected the bandages and flung them over his charge's body again. 'I said you should've dodged that one,' he said. 'But you weren't bad. No. If I wait, they'll make up your mind for you. You've seen two nasty sieges, and you're recoiling against the whole thing.'

He was awake now. Nicholas battened down the entire seething entity of what was actually happening and put himself in Astorre's place. He said, 'You're wondering about the future of the army. It seems possible that I'll be offered the citadel of Sigouri and its estates, which would give work for a garrison, unless Cairo has other ideas. If the Turks begin to prevail over Venice, Cyprus may well be in danger, and Zacco will need all the help he can get. On the other hand, we've done what we've contracted to do. Would you go for a war somewhere else?'

Astorre sat back. 'You'd think of it?'

'I might not go with you, but I'd think of it. Unless you'd rather be on your own?'

'I could. It comes expensive,' said the captain.

'The Bank would back you. It amounts to the same thing. You know the best wars, in any case. What is there?'

He got up in cautious stages and limped to the privy, and thought afterwards that Astorre had hardly noticed, in his enthusiasm, that he was barely within earshot. He dressed. '... Skanderbeg?' Astorre was saying. 'Doing fine. Paid by Venice to create diversions against Constantinople. Limited, of course. Asked the Pope to give him land in Italy in case he has to retreat. God-awful discipline and terrible sheepskins. I wouldn't think of Skanderbeg, not at the moment.'

'No,' said Nicholas.

'The Naples war's finished. Ferrante holds all the kingdom except Ischia, where John of Calabria's been stuck hoping, they say, for a fleet. He might get one ship, like the *Adorno*. I don't think he'll get even one ship. Naples is safe. Dripping roast. Hell of a pity. They don't need an army.'

'No,' said Nicholas.

'England and France have made peace, God damn them both. Scotland wasn't included, although that Flemish Queen of theirs was supposed to back the Lancastrian Queen, the daughter of René of Anjou. But they say the Flemish Queen's dying. D'you want to support the daughter of René of Anjou?'

'Emphatically not,' Nicholas said.

'Oh? Well, there isn't much else. The Malatesta war's finished. He got beaten. You wouldn't believe it, after all those years. Piccinino's dropped John of Calabria and gone over to the Duke of Milan. The French King's causing plenty of trouble – you knew him?'

'Louis of France. Yes, I knew him.'

'He's trying to lord it over Savoy, and he's persuaded that old fool of Burgundy to sell him back all his frontier towns. He's going to cause trouble.'

'Is that all?' said Nicholas.

'It's not very good, is it?' said Astorre in a depressed way. 'There's only the Crusade.'

'The what?' said Nicholas. He was dressed, and hunting a hairbrush. His bandages stuck, and someone had sutured his stomach.

'Well, the what,' said Astorre. 'I know it's not likely to happen. Louis keeps saying he'll pour in money for warships, but he's really milking the clergy to pay for the Somme towns, not a war. The Pope's made a pact with the Duke of Burgundy and Venice, so they say, but the Duke of Burgundy's old and ailing, and needs all his wits to watch France. Of course the Pope's got all this money.'

'From the alum mines,' Nicholas said. 'You reckon you ought to join the Pope?'

Astorre's beard assumed several angles, and his sewn eye adopted a frown. He said, 'I won't say it's not tempting. Direct war, and no sieges. You'd quite like it.'

Nicholas sat. He said, 'We're looking for something that suits you, not me.'

Astorre went red. He said, 'It's your money. But out of a poor lot, I'd take the Crusade.'

'All right,' said Nicholas, standing up. 'Let's go and put it to the others. But don't let's take too long. De Ribérac will be busy. And Zacco's expecting me, I am told, at the Palace.'

He said that in self-defence but, when he and Astorre joined Tobie, Loppe and John le Grant at table, the next exchange was not as trying as he'd feared. From Loppe, by his wish, they already knew the truth about Primaflora as well as the course of the confrontation with Jordan de Ribérac. As a result, they greeted him with unnatural silence. Loppe rose when he entered and busied himself finding something bland he could swallow. John le Grant looked up, scrutinised him, and then went back to eating. Only Tobie spoke in a growl. 'You need those bandages changed, or they'll pull. I thought you knew all about medicine?' His withering glare at Astorre was more in his usual manner.

Nicholas sat and said, 'I have to see the King. I don't know what mischief de Ribérac may be preparing, but perhaps we ought to clear our minds about what we want to do first. Should Diniz be here?'

John le Grant said, 'He didn't sleep in the villa. I hope he hasn't gone to slaughter the Zorzi. Bartolomeo didn't come to the yard as usual this morning.'

Remembering yesterday, Nicholas thought it unlikely that Diniz had gone off to quarrel with anyone, and could perfectly understand why the last person Diniz wanted to meet was himself. In his shoes, he would have spent the night drinking, and probably whoring. Whoring, very publicly, with a girl. He withdrew his mind from that particular happening and returned to what mattered to all of them. He said, 'Well, Mick Crackbene? Could someone fetch him with Umfrid this afternoon? Or is he at the Palace?'

'In his own lodgings, so far as I know,' Tobie said. 'You really think we have to give up the villa?'

'I really think I want to give up the villa,' said Nicholas. 'And I think I can dispense with the delights of the capital. I don't know what you want to do. So far as I know, we have Kouklia still, or at least the royal licence to run it. There are sugar estates in other places, and these we could run on our own. One is linked with Sigouri, and that might mean keeping the army there. One is Palekythro, about eight miles to the north-east of this place. There are vineyards in the fiefs I've been given. But Astorre's inclination is to look for a war somewhere else. That rather rules out Sigouri, but means we could settle for other estates, and I could run them, or put in a manager, or any or all of you could help me. On the other hand, Astorre will need a proper complement if he's to go off again on his own. Cook, doctor, accountant, company priest.'

'Engineer?' said John le Grant.

'If you want,' said Astorre. He looked pleased. 'You might waste yourself. It earns big money, the kind of work you do.'

John le Grant said, 'Nobody wants to stay and defend Cyprus? Or Nicholas is giving up war for his shop-keeping?'

'Something like that,' Nicholas said. 'Luckily, Astorre isn't giving up war. The Bank will support him. He's hankering at present after a full-scale seaborne attack against the Sultan Mehmet. On the other hand, there's work here for engineers and for shipmasters. Famagusta has to be repaired, ships raised, the harbour made fit for business. What about anyone else? Tobie? Your experiments?'

Tobie still had his cap on. It made him look like a normal physician. He said, 'Is this a choice? Go with the army or stay with the sugar? Or are you going to do anything new?'

'There's the Bank,' Nicholas said. 'I haven't been in Venice since Gregorio really established it. There's a house. I bought some land in the lagoon. There's a galley at Venice, and some day we'll part the King from our round ship. The sugar can manage quite well with a manager and some supervision. We've missed out on the refineries, but there might be something else we could develop further west. All we have is in the Levant, and it's risky.'

'Because of the Turks?' Tobie said.

'And other reasons,' Nicholas said. 'You remember Henry, the Duchess of Burgundy's brother? He ran a school of navigation in Portugal. The idea was to find a spice route round about Africa. It's a good idea. But whoever does it will ruin everyone who depends on the Eastern route including the merchants in Alexandria and Cyprus and the Venetian and Genoese colonies in the east.

Meanwhile, sugar's beginning in Madeira already. The island is fertile, it can draw on slave labour, it could send scores of ships to Lisbon in season to feed the growing sweet tooth of Western Europe, and the price of sugar will drop. Combine that with a new route for importing spices, and you can see that the African coast is where trade will develop, and Venetian banks will feel the chill from it. I don't want ours to be one of them.'

'Africa? Portugal?' Tobie said. He had flushed. Nicholas knew what, alone of them all, he was thinking of.

Nicholas said, 'Simon's there. I don't want to stir him up. On the other hand, the vicomte seems to think he's set on stopping us. He could, if we stayed in the East and he swamped Europe with sugar and spices.'

'Diniz?' said John le Grant, without looking up.

Nicholas said, 'No, my dear John. I am not using him as a spy.'

'All right,' said Tobie. 'But you've said nothing of Bruges. That's your market. That's where the Charetty company is, even though you're no more than an observer.'

'An interested observer. They're my step-daughters,' Nicholas said. 'Tilde owns the Charetty company. I haven't forgotten her or Catherine. Or Godscalc and Julius. They may have ideas what we should do. But the House of Niccolò isn't in Bruges, it's in Venice. If it's anywhere. You may not want to continue with it. If you don't, you can take what you're owed. That won't be a small amount, either. The rent of the casals and the ship, the fee for the army, the profit from all the sugar, the new land we've been given amounts to a very greal deal.'

'Do you want us?' said John le Grant. He sat back, his arms folded, and regarded Nicolas from his freckled face with its shock of roaring red hair. He said, 'No. I'll say that in a different way. I could stay with the Bank, but do my work independently. Tobie could stay with the army, or at Kouklia, or hire himself out as a doctor, and still remain on your strength. Loppe could stay and manage the sugar, or the fiefs, or join Gregorio in Venice, or partner you in Spain or Portugal or Africa or wherever your lunatic ideas will take you. Crackbene could run a fleet here, or operate a ship for you anywhere there is a cargo you wanted to carry. I think we all want to stay with the Bank, although I can't speak for Julius and Godscalc. But do you want to be alone?'

It was, of course, the question he should have been asking himself, and the question he had avoided. It was linked with Bruges and the Venetians; with the insidious princesses of Trebizond, with Primaflora and Katelina and the Mamelukes and most of all, with the warring Lusignans. No, not most of all. Most of all, with Famagusta.

Nicholas said, 'There's what I want, and there's what is best for the company. I may think I've seen all I want to of war, but I can't walk away from it. Someone said it's no fun any more, now that it's not a sport but a profession. It never was a sport. It happens, and someone has to deal with it. Because Astorre's good, he does what he has to do cleanly and as well as he can. But the decisions are made by his masters: by Urbino or Malatesta or Ferrante or France or Milan. If the masters are at odds with one another, or self-seeking, or ineffective or just young and learning the business, you get a Famagusta. If you have the money and power to control wars, you can put in good management. Men will follow that.'

'You're talking about standing armies,' said John le Grant. 'Tell that to the burghers of Bruges, and see what they say.'

'Not necessarily,' Nicholas said.

'A White Company?' Tobie said. 'A really big mercenary troop that can virtually win wars on its own? Have you thought what that means?'

'He hasn't thought about anything,' said John le Grant. 'Except that after that bitch Primaflora he doesn't want to take orders from a Lusignan any more, and that means he must find his own money if he wants to move in circles of power. Am I right?'.

He was insolent. He was wrong. Whether or not Nicholas wished to work with and under Zacco, the link had been severed, and would never now be restored. Or not in a way that would serve any purpose. Rizzo di Marino, Sor de Naves, William Goneme would guide Zacco into the future and, although his business might well stay and flourish, he would have a passing friendship at best, and not the deep-dyed and constant companionship that was the way to the King's heart and mind. Nicholas said, 'If you keep talking, I'll probably believe you. We're too close to events. We don't know yet what Zacco will do. We don't know what Jordan de Ribérac may threaten him with. We have to set our own ideas in order. We'll meet and talk it over again. But think of this. We should consider Gregorio. When we can, we should gather in Venice.'

'And visit your island. You had barillo sent there. What,' said Tobie with sudden irritation, 'what in God's name do you make with barillo?'

'Ask Alessandra Macinghi negli Strozzi and her sons,' remarked Loppe. 'Master Nicholas? You knew the King wished to see you? He has sent a precise command. You have an audience with him at noon.'

Once, he saw the King whenever he pleased. Once, he was married to Primaflora. 'I shall be there,' Nicholas said.

Chapter 47

NICHOLAS RODE from his villa on Chennaa, who was in love with him again, and walked alone into Zacco's Palace to greet the servants he knew, and be led to the royal apartments, which were full of light and sunshine and noise and eager faces. He remembered most of them from days of celebration rather than days of fighting: some were new to him. It was strange, still, to see clean, well-fed bodies with springing hair and fresh clothes and no smell anywhere but the usual kind, and a good deal of scent.

He was here to receive the intimation that his marriage was to be set aside whether he wished it or not, and his wife Primaflora installed as what she already was: the permanent mistress of James, King of Cyprus. He recognised without joy that of those before him, a number must know why he was here, and he wondered if the boy Diniz had been told, in whatever retreat he had found; and if the news had made him feel better, or worse. The boy was so young and had so little, unless you counted a slow-growing trust in himself, tarnished now by de Ribérac's calumny. Diniz had wanted to stay in his company. Now, Nicholas could not imagine what the boy felt, except that he must somehow need help. As soon as he could, he would find him.

Meanwhile, here was rejoicing. Circumspectly triumphant, of course, the Venetians. Paul Erizzo, the Venetian Bailie. The Martini brothers. The bulky presence of the great Marco Corner and his skilful colleague Giovanni Loredano, whose beautiful wives had returned to their Venetian palaces. The Venetians had brought him to Cyprus to please James of Lusignan and for their own profit, and as a result of it, Carlotta and Genoa had been defeated, the Mamelukes disposed of, and James and the Venetians remained. In return for his services Nicholas had received land and money, both of which he would be permitted, he thought, to retain. He had been allowed to enjoy the favour of Zacco, now tempered. He had received from Zacco, not the Venetians, the valuable franchise of the dyeworks, but there, as he had half expected, the Venetians had annexed back the gift. The royal sugar estates were still his to control, but he had no doubt that both the Corner and the Martini were laying plans to regain them. In which case, they would have to reckon with the other plans he had in mind to prevent that. Nicholas bestowed his wide, dimpled smile on Erizzo, Corner and the rest, and they smiled and bowed in return.

There was the dark face of the Chancellor Rizzo di Marino, who unsurprisingly had grasped the chance so temptingly offered to get rid of the Mameluke army in Cyprus. On Rizzo's head lay the blame, of course, for the massacre, and not on that of James, or of Markios or, indeed on his own. He would accept, however, that the death of Tzani-bey had been contrived by himself. It had suited the King and perhaps had even suited Cairo. The Sultan would complain, and raise the tribute, but was unlikely to replace the emir with another. Cairo, now, would want to keep its forces at home.

There was the admiral Sor de Naves, whom Nicholas did not happen to like, but whom he treasured for the sake of one, small conversation. The lawyer Philip Podocataro, who had failed to recruit him for Zacco in Venice and had no doubt recommended other ways of persuasion. And whose treaty, this month, had brought about the surrender of Famagusta. With him were two faces Nicholas had not expected to see: those of Jacopo and Bartolomeo Zorzi. He was moving towards them when the King called him over.

He was flushed, and had been drinking. Unless you knew him well, it was not obvious, for James of Lusignan was young, and strong, and carried his drink as well as he carried all his other excesses. Below the brim of his hat, his eyes were open and sparkling, with their flecks of green and grey and warm brown, the mingled colours of the Lusignan inheritance. A curl of feather mixed with his hair, and he wore a sideless tunic over his doublet whose high collar was thick-sewn with jewels.

With him was a beauty. Not a woman, although his black hair curled inwards at the nape of his neck over a little collar of goose-down, and the hands smoothing over a drawing were ringed and long-fingered and fine. Then the stranger looked up, and Nicholas saw a pure oval face with a cleft chin and deep-fringed dark eyes. The femininity of the impression was destroyed by the substance and shape of the nose, and by the robust structure of thigh and ankle and calf. Everything about the newcomer's person conformed to the highest requirements of Zacco's known tastes, and was set forth here, of intent, before Nicholas. A Lusignan did not feel shame before a well-liked Flemish friend who possessed a small prize that he coveted. A Lusignan said, 'I am King. I attract what is comely and deserve it. I spread my table with sweets, and it should please you, from friendship, to add to them.' Understanding Zacco, Nicholas waited.

The King said, 'Dear Nikko, see. The plans for the new Palace. We are rebuilding Famagusta. The Bishop, too, will have something worthy of him. And the drawings there, for the Triumphal Entry. You will see them. You will meet my David here, later. Come. They will excuse us. I have a gift for you. We have a little business to settle.'

The chamber he took him to was the familiar one, with the curtained bed, and the window giving over the balcony, the gardens, the moat. Over the bed lay a robe of silk lined with sable. 'For you. For Famagusta, and what you have suffered. It is too heavy. You will wear it when you are fit. Are you in pain? You must be in pain from your wounds, and the sorrow. Your lovely girl died.'

He had indicated where Nicholas should sit, and had taken his own place, as once before, by the window. His swinging foot this time said that he was unhappy, in spite of the wine, and wished this over, and soon would feel and show irritation. Nicholas had not meant to let him off lightly; but he baulked at having Katelina's name invoked to make Zacco feel better. He said, 'My lord, I have no need of gifts. I have been told what you require for your happiness, and I freely give it you.'

The swinging foot stopped. 'You have been told?'

'By Primaflora,' Nicholas said.

The King looked down at his hands. He said, 'Of course, it is not the custom, in a man seeking office, to marry a courtesan. You did not realise, perhaps, how this could harm your future.'

Nicholas heard him without surprise and without rancour. He had no intention of embarking on the real facts about Primaflora. The King was at present besotted. Whoever spoiled this particular idyll would become, on the instant, his enemy. Instead, Nicholas spoke in what he hoped was his usual voice. 'As perhaps she has told you, it was a marriage born of expediency. She wished to leave Rhodes.'

The hazel eyes rose, and the King's hand went to his lip. 'She told me. She was unkind to you. I am sorry. But she has known men of exceptional ardour and one cannot blame her, perhaps, for a little impatience. But you found consolation. Or perhaps didn't require it?' The King smiled and, leaning forward, laid his hand on that of Nicholas. 'Sometimes I envy you that aloof mind and phlegmatic body. You will never burn in the fire of your passions.'

'I am aware of my good fortune,' said Nicholas.

The King slapped his hand and withdrew. He was smiling. He

said, 'But you are not. I have offered you land, position, revenues, houses. I would give you something more. I lease your round ship, and one day she will be restored to you. When that day comes, I shall give you another. For all your company did, you will have the *Adorno*. She is damaged. When repaired, she will enter my service. But the returns for her use will be yours, and when her duty is over, you will have her. Are you pleased?'

'My lord,' Nicholas said. 'I cannot thank you enough.' He was pleased, in the places where he wasn't searingly angry.

The King planted both feet on the ground. 'But there will be other things. What else can I do?'

Nicholas hesitated. He said, 'I have an enemy here.'

The King, it seemed, had talked with Marietta his mother. He said, 'The Frenchman? I heard. I shall do what I can. Of course, it is difficult. The King of France has the wealth that might save Cyprus one day from the Turks, and the Frenchman, I understand, is his adviser. He has asked to see me.'

'He has no complaint against me that cannot be answered,' Nicholas said. 'He will invent if he has to. I am concerned over the boy Diniz Vasquez, his grandson.'

'Are you? They tell me he caused that,' Zacco said. He nodded, indicating where the axe fell. 'They tell me that the man Zorzi urged him to kill you outright, and then got rid of the boy when he didn't. Do you believe that?'

'Yes,' said Nicholas. 'I think Diniz was truthful. The Venetians missed the bountiful hand of the Lusignan, and resented my tenure of the dyeworks. They have it again, I understand. I have no complaint. A land needs money and help, and must go where such offers.'

The young man in the window was smiling. 'To the point, always. But one chooses the source of the money, the help. Tell me now. When the boy injured you, you protected him. You protected him again in Famagusta. Why? I offered to punish him.'

'He was young. He mistook me. Mercy is not a bad thing. And Famagusta punished him more severely than you could,' Nicholas said. He watched the King's face, and saw there for an instant the look he had seen when the Lusignan rode into that destroyed and desolate city. It passed. The King slipped from his seat and said, 'Famagusta. You must see the plans. I will remember the boy, and see that he chooses whether or not to go with his grandfather. We shall talk again when you have made your choice of other things. Leave the robe. I shall have it sent to you. Come. Come and meet David.'

The hall rang with voices and laughter when the King's attendant opened the doors to allow Zacco to enter. It was slow in dying, for they had all drunk a good deal and he had indulged them. Those who were sober were those who had known why Nicholas had been called to the Palace. You could tell them by their air of expectancy.

Poised, absorbed at a lectern, the King's new acquaintance called David was not immediately roused by the King's step but rested in thought, the soft beard of a quill at his lips. He dropped his hand to make a small note and lifted his eyes as the King brought Nicholas to him. He laid down the quill quickly and bowed. His eyes, shining on Nicholas, were as dark as the ink he was using, and his head reached no higher than the King's shoulder. The King said, 'Here is Niccolò. You have heard all about him. Niccolò vander Poele. I should have introduced you before. Nikko: M. David de Salmeton.'

A French name. The man's inflection, when he murmured his greeting, was also as French as his own. That was, French mixed with something else – but in his case, not Flemish. The King said, 'And what have you marked? The Grand Bailie will not agree, but I shall insist. Marble. I shall have nothing but marble.'

The chart for the new Palace of Famagusta lay on the lectern. Beside it, neatly listed, was a first assessment of costs. Nicholas said, 'I think perhaps you should get the Grand Bailie very drunk.' He could feel the court watching; the relief, the amusement seeping through the room. The King had prevailed. The Fleming had surrendered his wife without so much as a struggle. There remained, of course, to be seen what they would all have to pay, in slow advancement, in grovelling, to the deprived husband loaded with honours. He turned aside abruptly. The King stopped him, a hand on his good shoulder. 'A realist, this man of numbers. I know, Nikko. The Grand Bailie has told me. Our coffers will not pay for this. I shall not squeeze it out of the peasantry. I shall not even exact more from your sugar. It will be paid for by M. David.'

No one but himself seemed surprised. How long had this man been at court? A few days? Even weeks, before the King came to Famagusta? It was a long time since Nicholas had been in the capital. Nicholas said, 'By M. David? In what way?'

'In the usual way,' said the dark young man, his lips softening. He didn't smile.

The King did. He said, 'You have been locked up, a hostage. You have missed all the news. M. de Salmeton is a broker, Niccolò, like yourself. Like yourself, his firm's business takes many forms. They deal in pawns, dyes, insurance. They have ships. They raise loans, like the one that will rebuild Famagusta. They build sugar refineries.'

'I see,' Nicholas said. 'The name of your firm is Vatachino?'

'That is correct,' said David de Salmeton. 'Of course, you have heard of us. We were happy to take your surplus sugar. M. de Corner and M. de Loredano the same. I hope we have completed our task to your satisfaction.'

'I am glad to meet you,' said Nicholas.

Again, the fine lips softened but didn't part. The broker said, 'Oh, I am not the head of Vatachino. Only an agent.'

'And who is the head, monseigneur?' Nicholas said.

The King laughed again. 'Try to get him to answer that! He says that it is of no importance, or no interest, or even that he doesn't know. He has full powers to deal and to sign, so we cannot torture it out of him. But you are curious, too. How shall we discover?'

Nicholas said, still speaking into the dark, tranquil face, 'But you must have an office?'

'Many,' said the calm, amused voice. 'One in Venice, for example. I have had dealings with your Messer Gregorio. Perhaps he has not wished to worry you with them. And we are about to set up in Bruges. I am interested in dyeworks.'

'You have operated one?' Nicholas said.

The young man lifted and wiped his pen, closed his inkwell and left the lectern, standing with his hands clasped loosely together before him. He looked like a patient, harp-playing angel stopped on his way to a choir. He said, 'We own a dyeworks, monseigneur. Here in Nicosia.'

'Not unless there are two,' said Bartolomeo Zorzi agreeably. Behind his black beard, his face didn't quite match his voice. He said, 'I have the only dyeyard in Nicosia.'

A feeling of incipient ecstasy overcame Nicholas. He looked at the King, and found the King was looking at him, and enjoying it. Nicholas turned. The exquisite person called David said, 'I am most distressed. I believed the news had been broken. It is M. Zorzi, is it not? Of course, the royal dyeworks appeared to be in the King's gift. But unfortunately –'

'Unfortunately?' said Bartolomeo Zorzi. He looked at Jacopo his brother and back again, like a flag changing face in a wind.

'Unfortunately, the King had incurred a large debt. It could not be paid. We were forced to demand it. The only way he could give satisfaction was by leasing to us all the rights in the dyeworks, and a proper basis for their future expenses. The revenues, that is, of the villages of Pactona and Lectora, and five thousand besants on the customs of Nicosia. I regret,' said the broker quite charmingly. Within their wonderful lashes, the frigid eyes displayed no trace of contrition.

Bartolomeo Zorzi said, *'Who do you work for?'*

'Nemesis, I imagine,' Nicholas said. 'And in future, keep out of my way, as well as his. Tell your older brother.'

Zorzi's eyes remained, frowning, on the face of the stranger. So, too, did the hostile gaze of the other Venetians. Like himself, of course, the Corner had suffered from the footprint of this unknown and ominous company. Perhaps also the Knights of St John.

Nicholas hesitated. He said, 'Forgive me, my lord King. You mentioned borrowing. Have you signed an agreement with M. de Salmeton?'

It was never wise to do this to Zacco. He couldn't think of another quick way to do it. The King said, 'It was necessary. You were in Famagusta.'

'Of course. Perhaps another time, we might be of service. Might I know,' Nicholas said, 'what was put forward as security for this and other loans? Apart from the dyeworks?'

The King said, 'Are you afraid for your sugar? It is safe. It is all safe. You've forgotten. I have ransoms for twelve wealthy prisoners, including the vicomte de Ribérac.'

'The ransoms have come?' Nicholas said. He saw, without looking, that he had received a glance from the dark eyes.

The King said, 'How could they, so quickly? But they will. I have sent for de Ribérac.'

A pang of amusement went through Nicholas. He said, 'He will be delighted. He takes a profound interest in the Vatachino.' He took thought, and added, 'Anyway, he thought the ransom too high.' Again, the quick look. This time he returned it. A door opened.

He turned, and so did the extraordinary black changeling at his side. The towering bulk of de Ribérac failed to enter the room. A clerk from the Secrète stood on the threshold instead, and made his way forward, skirts swishing. Between the flaps of his cap he was pale.

'Well?' said Zacco softly. He had sobered.

'My lord King,' said the clerk. 'M. de Ribérac is not in his room. We have made enquiries. We have asked at the gates. We have met messengers on their way from the south. My lord King, M. de Ribérac has escaped.'

'Without paying his ransom?' said the angel.

'He left nothing,' said the clerk.

'How?' said the King. He lifted his fist and crashed it down on the lectern. The inkwell jumped to the floor, split and emptied. Quietly, the young man called David lifted the plan out of harm's way and held it, folded neatly, at his side.

'He had help. From one of Messer Niccolò's men,' said the clerk.

It was, of course, one of the possibilities. It was the only possibility. Nicholas said, 'I know nothing of this. Tell me who?' But he knew. He should have guessed. He should have prepared for it.

The clerk said, 'Your sailing-master, Messer Crackbene, Ser Niccolò. He contrived to take the vicomte through the gates and found mounts for him. They left last night and were in Salines by morning. They have sailed.'

'By what means?' Nicholas said.

The clerk turned to him. His knuckles were white. 'Messer Crackbene took him on the *Doria*.'

Naturally. The contract was over. Crackbene had been paid. Meticulous to the last, he had waited before switching masters, and the fault was not his that Nicholas had failed to foresee it. Nicholas remembered him on the same round ship sailing from Italy: a solid, fair, high-coloured man, put out because he had been forced by Erizzo to take the *Doria* to Cyprus. It had been easy to mistake his indignation for loyalty, and in its way, that was what it had been; for at that time Crackbene had been employed by the House of Niccolò. But now, that covenant was concluded. The ownership of the *Doria* – of any vessel – was not Crackbene's business. He was invited, for a fee, to become master, and if the fee was large enough, he accepted. You could call him a rascal, or you could call him a master mariner without whom Famagusta would have been a condemned city. It didn't matter to Crackbene that the vicomte had stolen the ship. He might not even have known that the *Doria* was once called the *Ribérac*.

Nicholas said, 'I am sorry. I have lost a ship, and you have lost your ransom.'

'At least,' said the clerk, 'the other ransom was paid.'

It was David who spoke, as was to be expected from the King's creditor. He said, 'One ransom had been paid? Whose was that?'

The clerk said, 'A previous prisoner. Messer Niccolò paid it. It doesn't fall into this calculation.'

'Whose?' said Nicholas. Again, he knew. He simply wanted to hear it, before he could bring himself to the task of believing it.

'A youth called Diniz Vasquez,' said the clerk. 'The vicomte was his grandfather. He was not a prisoner, but the vicomte insisted he be found and compelled to go with him. They have left Cyprus, they tell me, for Portugal.'

'I regret,' said the person called David for the second time. He was smiling now: smiling at Nicholas.

Nicholas, too, regretted. Things nothing to do with the loss of his ship, which was a stroke only de Ribérac could have thought of. He regretted the implications of this news as it affected one stricken family. He regretted the harm done by Primaflora, out of ambition, jealousy, a dread of the future, all mixed and half defeated by the one attribute a courtesan should never permit herself: a passion for love.

She had forced Katelina to suffer. She had killed. Primaflora's loss to himself was something that, as yet, he didn't want to call in to measure. But he had used her as well. He had learned from her. And, as he had said, the King's conscience had worked in his favour. She would not, therefore, endure the ultimate punishment through any action of his, although he had taken exaction. Nothing extreme; nothing overt; nothing crude. The King required sons. He had simply sent the King's mother a message, in which Sor de Naves was mentioned.

Regret did not describe what he felt about the death of a highborn, wilful girl who had borne him a son, and had lived only a twisted half-life afterwards. A girl not unlike Primaflora in natural ardour, but constrained and thwarted by the society that she lived in. He didn't know what happiness Katelina had ever had since her childhood, but for the hours they had given each other. Now she had gone, leaving two sets of wounded people staring at one another over a gulf.

One of them was Diniz Vasquez. If he had set out to find him last night, perhaps he could have stopped what had happened. Instead, the boy was at sea, in the grasp of that brutal, impenetrable man, and facing a vengeful, a bitter, a fatherless home. He did not regret, not at all, that Jordan de Ribérac had gone.

The young man called David was watching him. He said, 'The ship that has been purloined was yours? It is a great loss, on top of all your other disappointments. You were not insured?'

'It was mine,' Nicholas said. 'It was insured, by my lawyer in Venice.'

The dark eyes watched and watched. The young man said, 'I heard of no such large transaction. With whom was the business placed?'

'With the Vatachino,' Nicholas said. 'I employed a pseudonym. Happily, by the terms of your company's bond, I stand to lose nothing.'

They faced one another. The young man called David said, 'I am amazed. Of course, they will pay you in full. I must whisper to you, of course, that such a pretty opportunity will not come your way again.'

He laid the plan back on the lectern and picked from its groove the rings he had laid down when writing. They were expensive and heavy, and he assumed them like beads on an abacus. His nails were curved and worn long, and the skin of his hands was like satin.

He said, 'We have a policy, Messer Niccolò. Small firms encroach on our trade, interfere with our plans, dilute our market. We are swiftly overcoming this problem. When the time comes, we shall offer you a reasonable price for your business. You and your colleagues. A man's business colleagues, Messer Niccolò, quite often enjoy the feel of a coin in their palms. It is better than suffering frequent losses, long disappointments. There is only one Vatachino, and it is irresistible.' He paused, almost smiling. He said, 'We go to Africa next. You stay in Cyprus?'

Nicholas looked into the assured, agreeable face and said, 'I have a home here, M. David. But like you, I have business in several places. I should expect to find myself, now and then, where you are. Or even, perhaps, there before you.'

He left the Palace soon after that, and within a week had moved his household out of Nicosia. The King wanted him gone from the capital, and he had no wish to cause further embarrassment. Kouklia could hold all his company, and once he and they had perfected their plans, he could instruct his agents, and take ship for Venice.

He returned to the King's chambers once, for his formal leave-taking. Unwanted encounters had threatened to fill his last days at the villa: he had escaped all but two. In the first, he had been descended upon, close to suppertime, by the Patriarch Ludovico da Bologna who had lectured him on Prester John and the bee-land of Egypt, and to whom he had listened patiently, because of a procession that had come just in time and for which, he could see, he would be asked to pay many times over. In the second, he found himself summoned by the King's mother who, overturning his formal excuses, sent a guard to his door with instructions not to come back without him. So Nicholas walked into the presence of Marietta of Patras as he was, in everyday pourpoint and boots, and stood to formal attention as a prisoner might.

He owed her nothing. The last time he was here, she had allowed Jordan de Ribérac to vilify his own grandson; she had announced that his marriage was ended. From the moment of his first arrival in chains, she had plotted. She had sent Katelina to Episkopi, hoping that he would win her away from Carlotta. Markios her bullying brother had dropped the hints that provoked the Mameluke rising, and in protecting himself and his sister had caused Abul Ismail to die. The escape of Diniz from Nicosia meant that Katelina, no longer useful, would be likely to follow him: in both departures, one could glimpse the hand of the King and his mother. And above all, because of this woman, Primaflora had been encouraged to come to the King – to appeal to the King, when the King's mother appeared to dismiss her. He hoped she knew now what prize she had brought to her son. So far as he was concerned, that was her punishment.

The King's mother received him unveiled. Above the velvets and jewels her painted eyes glittered. Below, she had left undisguised the raw carmine snout of her nose. She said, 'Well? You have many things to accuse me of. Say them.'

He met her fierce gaze with his own, and said nothing at first, because whatever he might feel, there was no place here for an outburst of violence or spleen. It was why he had not wanted to come. He had always recognised her unshakable purpose. She fought for the King and for Cyprus; as in Persia, the lady Sara served none but her son Uzum Hasan. Sara was Uzum's courageous instrument, but Marietta of Patras was the rudder which kept Zacco's brilliant career on its course. Nicholas said, 'Ruthlessness will empty your hand, sooner or later.'

'So I have been told,' Cropnose said. She was not surprised by his moderation, he saw. She had not, therefore, brought him here to foment a quarrel. She said, 'It is not an argument I should have expected from you. To turn the tables upon Tzani-bey, you sent to Uzum Hasan, and as a consequence, the Emperor of Trebizond and his children died. Because you took no heed of a family feud, the lady Katelina came to these islands, and she and the Portuguese paid the penalty. The cause of all these deaths was neglect and self-interest and pure, petty vengeance. And you criticise me?'

If it was true (and it was), she was the last person to whom he would acknowledge it. 'Who else dare criticise you, magnificent lady?' Nicholas said. 'You are saying that you wish the Mamelukes were alive? You should complain to your brother, not me.'

She was silent for a long time. Finally, she stirred. She said, 'I am saying, look to your own motives. Soon, no one will dare gainsay you either, and you will be the worse for it. I wish I had the training of you.'

He caught the note in her voice before it hardened. She was not thinking of him, but of bright, wilful Zacco, the indulged son of his father, who would not accept training or censure. He was not sure what to say. In the end, he said, 'I expect to return. They say I am teachable.'

'You will keep a foothold here,' she said. 'If you are allowed. But the rest of your equipment for life you will no doubt pick up from parasites. Is your mother alive?'

'No, lady,' he said. He tried not to show that she had startled him.

'No. I would have told her,' said Marietta of Patras, 'that she made a child of the wrong sex. But since you cannot give birth to sons, you are better gone from the Palace.'

Travelling south, the others thought they understood his long silence, and made few attempts to distract him. He was riding to Kouklia, but it was not of Kouklia he was thinking. It was three years since he had gone to Bologna, and had fought among men made of sugar. He had chosen war, and had been oppressed by what he had found. He had not looked for love, but had been offered it in many different guises and had tried to deal with it wisely, but had not always succeeded. He had experienced the bereavement of others and had suffered from it himself. All that had happened since Bologna seemed to be bracketed between two silent coffins: one that named him, and the other on which his name had no right to appear.

He had no regrets that he had turned his back on Carlotta, for of the two Lusignan scorpions, she was the lesser. It was Zacco who ruled Cyprus now – Cyprus, island of love and fertility and divine prostitution. Cyprus, the perpetual colony, the perpetual mistress and battlefield. Now James was her master, and would rule as well as any had, despite all that worked against him: even though pulled this way and that by his court, his mother, his temperament. And now, by his new friends the Vatachino. In his distrust of Venice, Zacco had called in a predator; and it would please Nicholas to find him and challenge him.

So he might indeed keep a foothold in Cyprus. Here was the first earth he had owned. Here, he had learned something of what he wanted, if not all of it. Now he must acknowledge responsibilities from which he couldn't escape, for there was no one else left who could carry them. Chief among them, of course, was accountability for his own crazy actions. He thought it a pity, at the back of his mind, that at twenty-three, he should be fettered. He knew that it was generally held that control of his own ingenuity was beyond him. He preserved an open mind on the subject.

In his last meeting with Zacco, the charming broker David de Salmeton had not been present. Nevertheless, it had been very public. James de Lusignan had taken leave of the one-time friend of his soul in open court with the Archbishop and his Chancellor about him. He had thanked Nicholas royally for his services to the throne, and hoped for his speedy return, to enter into his estates and lend the kingdom his counsel. Primaflora was neither there, nor referred to, for which Nicholas was silently thankful.

He didn't expect to forget her, or their union. Wherever he walked, the echo of it stayed with him. *So may thou love me like a branch full of honey, and only me. Around thee I have girt fields of sugarcane to banish all hate; so that thou may adore me, my darling, and never depart.* The words were hers, and not his. He was departing. He had made her no avowals of love, for she had killed Katelina.

At the end, the King came to his side and walked with him out to the yard, where Chennaa was waiting. Then Zacco had laughed. 'Your fondness for that elegant animal! If you had shown us half such tenderness, what might we not have accomplished together?'

'But,' said Nicholas, 'with a beast there is no communion except the bond between rider and ridden. We are a King and a King's loyal companion, and the regard we have for each other will always be greater than that, and endure longer.'

The King stood still, without answering. Nicholas faced him, and saw again how enchanting he was, and how alone, and how young. He said, 'Most excellent, brave and glorious prince, may God give you happiness. You and your island.'

FOR THE BEST IN PAPERBACKS, LOOK FOR THE 🐧

In every corner of the world, on every subject under the sun, Penguin represents quality and variety – the very best in publishing today.

For complete information about books available from Penguin – including Pelicans, Puffins, Peregrines and Penguin Classics – and how to order them, write to us at the appropriate address below. Please note that for copyright reasons the selection of books varies from country to country.

In the United Kingdom: Please write to *Dept E.P., Penguin Books Ltd, Harmondsworth, Middlesex, UB7 0DA*

If you have any difficulty in obtaining a title, please send your order with the correct money, plus ten per cent for postage and packaging, to *PO Box No 11, West Drayton, Middlesex*

In the United States: Please write to *Dept BA, Penguin, 299 Murray Hill Parkway, East Rutherford, New Jersey 07073*

In Canada: Please write to *Penguin Books Canada Ltd, 2801 John Street, Markham, Ontario L3R 1B4*

In Australia: Please write to the *Marketing Department, Penguin Books Australia Ltd, P.O. Box 257, Ringwood, Victoria 3134*

In New Zealand: Please write to the *Marketing Department, Penguin Books (NZ) Ltd, Private Bag, Takapuna, Auckland 9*

In India: Please write to *Penguin Overseas Ltd, 706 Eros Apartments, 56 Nehru Place, New Delhi, 110019*

In Holland: Please write to *Penguin Books Nederland B.V., Postbus 195, NL–1380AD Weesp, Netherlands*

In Germany: Please write to *Penguin Books Ltd, Friedrichstrasse 10–12, D–6000 Frankfurt Main 1, Federal Republic of Germany*

In Spain: Please write to *Longman Penguin España, Calle San Nicolas 15, E–28013 Madrid, Spain*

In France: Please write to *Penguin Books Ltd, 39 Rue de Montmorency, F-75003, Paris, France*

In Japan: Please write to *Longman Penguin Japan Co Ltd, Yamaguchi Building, 2–12–9 Kanda Jimbocho, Chiyoda-Ku, Tokyo 101, Japan*

A CHOICE OF PENGUIN FICTION

The Dearest and the Best   Leslie Thomas

In the spring of 1940 the spectre of war turned into grim reality – and for all the inhabitants of the historic villages of the New Forest it was the beginning of the most bizarre, funny and tragic episode of their lives. 'Excellent' – *Sunday Times*

Only Children   Alison Lurie

When the Hubbards and the Zimmerns go to visit Anna on her idyllic farm, it becomes increasingly difficult to tell which are the adults, and which the children. 'It demands to be read' – *Financial Times* 'There quite simply is no better living writer' – John Braine

My Family and Other Animals   Gerald Durrell

Gerald Durrell's wonderfully comic account of his childhood years on Corfu and his development as a naturalist and zoologist is a true delight. Soaked in Greek sunshine, it is a 'bewitching book' – *Sunday Times*

Getting it Right   Elizabeth Jane Howard

A hairdresser in the West End, Gavin is sensitive, shy, into the arts, prone to spots and, at thirty-one, a virgin. He's a classic late developer – and maybe it's getting too late to develop at all? 'Crammed with incidental pleasures . . . sometimes sad but more frequently hilarious . . . *Getting it Right* gets it, comically, right' – Paul Bailey in the *London Standard*

The Vivisector   Patrick White

In this prodigious novel about the life and death of a great painter, Patrick White, winner of the Nobel Prize for Literature, illuminates creative experience with unique truthfulness. 'One of the most interesting and absorbing novelists writing English today' – Angus Wilson in the *Observer*

The Echoing Grove   Rosamund Lehmann

'No English writer has told of the pains of women in love more truly or more movingly than Rosamund Lehmann' – Marghanita Laski. 'She uses words with the enjoyment and mastery with which Renoir used paint' – Rebecca West in the *Sunday Times* 'A magnificent achievement' – John Connell in the *Evening News*

FOR THE BEST IN PAPERBACKS, LOOK FOR THE 🐧

PENGUIN BESTSELLERS

Is That It?   Bob Geldof with Paul Vallely

The autobiography of one of today's most controversial figures. 'He has become a folk hero whom politicians cannot afford to ignore. And he has shown that simple moral outrage can be a force for good' – *Daily Telegraph*. 'It's terrific . . . everyone over thirteen should read it' – *Standard*

Niccolò Rising   Dorothy Dunnett

The first of a new series of historical novels by the author of the world-famous *Lymond* series. Adventure, high romance and the dangerous glitter of fifteenth-century Europe abound in this magnificent story of the House of Charetty and the disarming, mysterious genius who exploits all its members.

The World, the Flesh and the Devil   Reay Tannahill

'A bewitching blend of history and passion. A MUST' – *Daily Mail*. A superb novel in a great tradition. 'Excellent' – *The Times*

Perfume: The Story of a Murderer   Patrick Süskind

It was after his first murder that Grenouille knew he was a genius. He was to become the greatest perfumer of all time, for he possessed the power to distil the very essence of love itself. 'Witty, stylish and ferociously absorbing . . . menace conveyed with all the power of the writer's elegant unease' – *Observer*

The Old Devils   Kingsley Amis

Winner of the 1986 Booker Prize
'Vintage Kingsley Amis, 50 per cent pure alcohol with splashes of sad savagery' – *The Times*. The highly comic novel about Alun Weaver and his wife's return to their Celtic roots. 'Crackling with marvellous Taff comedy . . . this is probably Mr Amis's best book since *Lucky Jim*' – *Guardian*

FOR THE BEST IN PAPERBACKS, LOOK FOR THE 🐧

PENGUIN BESTSELLERS

Illusions Charlotte Vale Allen

Leigh and Daniel have been drawn together by their urgent needs, finding
a brief respite from their pain in each other's arms. Then romantic love
turns to savage obsession. 'She is a truly important writer' – Bette Davis

Snakes and Ladders Dirk Bogarde

The second volume of Dirk Bogarde's outstanding biography, *Snakes and
Ladders* is rich in detail, incident and character by an actor whose many
talents include a rare gift for writing. 'Vivid, acute, sensitive, intelligent
and amusing' – *Sunday Express*

Wideacre Philippa Gregory

Beatrice Lacey is one of the most passionate and compelling heroines ever
created. There burns in Beatrice one overwhelming obsession – to possess
Wideacre, her family's ancestral home, and to achieve her aim she will risk
everything: reputation, incest, even murder.

A Dark and Distant Shore Reay Tannahill

'An absorbing saga spanning a century of love affairs, hatred and high
points of Victorian history' – *Daily Express* 'Enthralling . . . a marvellous
blend of *Gone with the Wind* and *The Thorn Birds*. You will enjoy every
page' – *Daily Mirror*

Runaway Lucy Irvine

Not a sequel, but the story of Lucy Irvine's life *before* she became a
castaway. Witty, courageous and sensational, it is a story you won't forget.
'A searing account . . . raw and unflinching honesty' – *Daily Express* 'A
genuine and courageous work of autobiography' – *Today*

Oscar Wilde   Richard Ellmann

'Exquisite critical sense, wide and deep learning, and profound humanity . . . a great subject and a great book' – Anthony Burgess in the *Observer* 'The witty subject has found a witty biographer who is also distinguished for his erudition and humanity' – Clare Tomalin in the *Independent*

Presumed Innocent   Scott Turow
The No I International Bestseller

'One of the most enthralling novels I have read in a long, long time' – Pat Conroy. 'If you start *Presumed Innocent* you will finish it . . . it grips like an octopus' – *Sunday Times*

Spring of the Ram   Dorothy Dunnett
Volume 2 in the *House of Niccolò* series

Niccolò has now travelled as far as the frontier of Islam in order to establish the Silk Route for the Charetty empire. Beset by illness, feuds and the machinations of his rivals, he must use his most Machiavellian schemes to survive . . .

A Time of Gifts   Patrick Leigh Fermor

'More than just a Super-travel book . . . it is a reminder that the English language is still a superb instrument in the hands of a writer who has a virtuoso skill with words' – Philip Toynbee in the *Observer* 'I know of no other account of pre-war Europe which conveys so much so powerfully' – Peter Levi

A Fatal Inversion   Barbara Vine

Ten years after the young people camped at Wyvis Hall, the bodies of a woman and child are found in the animal cemetery. Which woman? Whose child? 'Impossible to put down . . . she is a very remarkable writer' – Anita Brookner. 'I defy anyone to guess the conclusion, but looking back, the clues are seen to be there, unobtrusively but cunningly planted, so that it seems one should have known all along' – *Daily Telegraph*

FOR THE BEST IN PAPERBACKS, LOOK FOR THE 🐧

PENGUIN BESTSELLERS

Cat Chaser Elmore Leonard

'*Cat Chaser* really moves' – *The New York Times Book Review* 'Elmore Leonard gets so much mileage out of his plot that just when you think one is cruising to a stop, it picks up speed for a few more twists and turns' – *Washington Post*

The Mosquito Coast Paul Theroux

Detesting twentieth century America, Allie Fox takes his family to live in the Honduran jungle. 'Imagine the Swiss Family Robinson gone mad, and you will have some idea of what is in store . . . Theroux's best novel yet' – *Sunday Times*

Skallagrigg William Horwood

This new book from the author of *Duncton Wood* unites Arthur, a little boy abandoned many years ago in a grim hospital in northern England, with Esther, a radiantly intelligent young girl who is suffering from cerebral palsy, and with Daniel, an American computer-games genius. 'Some of the passages would wring tears of recognition, not pity' – Yvonne Nolan in the *Observer*

The Second Rumpole Omnibus John Mortimer

'Rumpole is worthy to join the great gallery of English oddballs ranging from Pickwick to Sherlock Holmes, Jeeves and Bertie Wooster' – *Sunday Times* 'Rumpole has been an inspired stroke of good fortune for us all' – Lynda Lee-Potter in the *Daily Mail*

The Lion's Cage John Clive

As the Allies advance across Europe, the likes of Joe Porter are making a killing of another kind. His destiny becomes woven with that of Lissette, whose passionate love for a German officer spells peril for Porter and herself – and the battle for survival begins.

FOR THE BEST IN PAPERBACKS, LOOK FOR THE 🐧

PENGUIN BESTSELLERS

Goodbye Soldier   Spike Milligan

The final volume of his war memoirs in which we find Spike in Italy, in civvies and in love with a beautiful ballerina. 'Desperately funny, vivid, vulgar' – *Sunday Times*

A Dark-Adapted Eye   Barbara Vine

Writing as Barbara Vine, Ruth Rendell has created a labyrinthine journey into the heart of the Hillyard family, living in the respectable middle-class countryside after the Second World War. 'Barbara Vine has the kind of near-Victorian narrative drive that compels a reader to go on turning the pages' – Julian Symons in the *Sunday Times*

Rainbow Drive   Roderick Thorp

If Mike Gallagher (acting head of the Homicide Squad, Los Angeles Police Department) hadn't been enjoying himself in the bed of a married German movie producer, he wouldn't have heard the footsteps and seen the Police Department helicopter . . . 'Quite exceptional . . . powerful, gripping and impressive' – *Time Out*

Memoirs of an Invisible Man   H. F. Saint

'Part thriller, part comedy, part science fiction . . . a compelling, often frightening novel. H. F. Saint makes the bizarre condition of his hero believable' – *Listener*

Pale Kings and Princes   Robert B. Parker

Eric Valdez, a reporter on the *Central Argus* has been killed in Wheaton. His chief, Kingsley, suspects he was involved in the local pastime – cocaine smuggling. But, knowing Valdez's penchant for the ladies, it could be sexual jealousy. Spenser is about to find out. 'The thinking man's private eye' – *The Times*

Pearls   Celia Brayfield

The Bourton sisters were beautiful. They were rich. They were famous. They were powerful. Then one morning they wake up to find a priceless pearl hidden under their pillows. Why? . . . 'Readers will devour it' – *Independent*

FOR THE BEST IN PAPERBACKS, LOOK FOR THE 🐧

PENGUIN BESTSELLERS

Relative Strangers Maureen Rissik

Angie Wyatt has three enviable assets: money, beauty and a tenacious instinct for survival. She is a woman fighting for success in a complex world of ambition and corruption. '*Relative Strangers* is a wonderful, intelligently written novel – a pleasure to read' – Susan Isaacs, author of *Compromising Positions*

O-Zone Paul Theroux

It's New Year in paranoid, computer-rich New York, and a group of Owners has jet-rotored out to party in O-Zone, the radioactive wasteland where the people do not officially exist. 'Extremely exciting . . . as ferocious and as well-written as *The Mosquito Coast*, and that's saying something' – *The Times*

Time/Steps Charlotte Vale Allen

Beatrice Crane was the little girl from Toronto with magic feet and driving talent. She was going to be a star. It was more important to her than her family, than friendship or other people's rules . . . more important, even than love.

Blood Red Rose Maxwell Grant

China 1926. As Communist opposition to the oppressive Nationalist army grows, this vast and ancient country draws nearer to the brink of a devastating civil war. As Kate Richmond is drawn into the struggle, her destiny becomes irrevocably entwined with the passions of a divided China and her ideals and her love are tested to the utmost.

Cry Freedom John Briley

Written by award-winning scriptwriter John Briley, this is the book of Richard Attenborough's powerful new film of the same name. Beginning with Donald Woods's first encounter with Steve Biko, it follows their friendship, their political activism and their determination to fight minority rule to Steve Biko's death and Woods's dramatic escape. It is both a thrilling adventure and a bold political statement.

PENGUIN BESTSELLERS

Gorillas in the Mist Dian Fossey

For thirteen years Dian Fossey lived among the gorillas of the Virunga
Mountains in Africa, defending them from brutal slaughter by poachers.
In 1985 she was herself brutally murdered. *Gorillas in the Mist* is her story.
'Fascinating' – Paul Theroux

Presumed Innocent Scott Turow

The No. 1 International Bestseller. 'One of the most enthralling novels I
have read in a long, long time' – Pat Conroy. 'If you start *Presumed
Innocent* you will finish it … it grips like an octopus' – *Sunday Times*

The Second Rumpole Omnibus John Mortimer

Horace Rumpole turns down yet another invitation to exchange the joys
and sorrows of life as an Old Bailey hack for the delights of the sunshine
state and returns again in *Rumpole for the Defence*, *Rumpole and the
Golden Thread* and *Rumpole's Last Case*.

Pearls Celia Brayfield

The Bourton sisters were beautiful. They were rich. They were famous.
They were powerful. Then one morning they wake up to find a priceless
pearl hidden under their pillows. Why? 'Readers will devour it'
– *Independent*

Spring of the Ram Dorothy Dunnett
Volume 2 in the *House of Niccolò* series

Niccolò has now travelled as far as the frontier of Islam in order to
establish the Silk Route for the Charetty empire. Beset by illness, feuds
and the machinations of his rivals, he must use his most Machiavellian
schemes to survive...